P9-DFL-848

REDSHIFT

REDSHIFT

EXTREME VISIONS OF SPECULATIVE FICTION

EDITED BY

AL SARRANTONIO

A ROC BOOK

ROC
Published by New American Library, a division of
Penguin Putnam Inc., 375 Hudson Street, New York, New York 10014, U.S.A.
Penguin Books Ltd, 80 Strand, London WC2R 0RL, England
Penguin Books Australia Ltd, Ringwood, Victoria, Australia
Penguin Books Canada Ltd, 10 Alcorn Avenue, Toronto, Ontario, Canada M4V 3B2
Penguin Books (N.Z.) Ltd, 182–190 Wairau Road, Auckland 10, New Zealand

Penguin Books Ltd, Registered Offices: Harmondsworth, Middlesex, England

First published by Roc, an imprint of New American Library, a division of Penguin Putnam Inc.

RoC REGISTERED TRADEMARK—MARCA REGISTRADA

ISBN 0-451-45859-1

Printed in the United States of America
Set in Janson Text
Designed by Eve L. Kirch

PUBLISHER'S NOTE
These stories are works of fiction. Names, characters, places, and incidents either are the product of the authors' imaginations or are used fictitiously, and any resemblance to actual persons, living or dead, business establishments, events, or locales is entirely coincidental.

To Harlan, of course

ACKNOWLEDGMENTS

I've said this before: No book is an island; and this particular one owes much to a few special people. My thanks to:

Beth, always there, who put up with another one;

Julie Kristian, who hunted (and found!) gold;

Laura Anne Gilman, editor supreme;

Kathleen Bellamy, who gently persevered;

Dan Simmons, for reasons within;

Joe Lansdale, who wrote one toodamnlong—and for duty above and beyond;

Larry Niven, for making me *think*;

Ralph Vicinanza, who, again, piloted the agent's ship;

And editors, the quiet heroes of the field who, almost always unheralded, got or get it done: Terry Carr, David G. Hartwell, Ellen Datlow, Damon Knight, Bob Silverberg, Gardner Dozois, Gordon Van Gelder, Pat LoBrutto, Susan Allison, Ginger Buchanan, Sharon Jarvis, Melissa Singer, Amy Stout, Harriet McDougal, Jennifer Brehl, John Douglas, Scott Edelman, Patrick Nielsen Hayden, Stan Schmidt, Jeanne Cavelos . . .

Too many to name.

CONTENTS

INTRODUCTION

> ***Redshift:*** *Doppler effect evidenced by a move toward the red end of the spectrum, indicating motion away from Earth—as in an expanding universe.*

An expanding universe: that's what this book is about. To put it as simply as possible, what you now hold in your hands (we hope and pray) is the finest original sf anthology of the last twenty-five years—and the future of speculative fiction.

PART ONE: WHAT

In 1998, while assembling my last anthology, *999: New Stories of Horror and Suspense*, I set myself a new goal: to put together, at the turn of the millennium (the *real* new millennium which began in 2001) a huge original anthology of speculative fiction stories. My initial inspiration was Harlan Ellison's *Dangerous Visions*, the publication of which in 1967 changed the science fiction field forever. Much of what Ellison codified in that book—the pushing of envelopes, the annihilation of taboos, the use of experimental prose—had been in the air for some time (after all, this was the sixties), but he was the first to nail it between two hardcovers* with a force and will that made it irrefutable. Science fiction (Ellison used the term "speculative fiction" to describe this blossoming mutation that, by its very nature of openness, contained elements of fantasy, horror, and brush strokes of just about every other genre, as well as the techniques of conventional and experimental so-called "literary"

*Mike Moorcock, of course, put the phenomenon between two *soft* magazine covers in the mid-sixties with *New Worlds* magazine in the U.K., which gave sustenance to the New Wave movement that fomented this whole revolution.

fiction) had been evolving; after the publication of *Dangerous Visions*, the new monster stood on its hind legs roaring, fully born.

The monster continued to roar; in 1973 there came a second volume from Ellison, *Again, Dangerous Visions*, and throughout the next decade and beyond, numerous other anthologies—as well as whole *series* of anthologies, such as *Orbit* edited by Damon Knight (the first numbers of which actually predated *Dangerous Visions*), *New Dimensions* edited by Robert Silverberg, and *Universe* edited by Terry Carr—continued to nurture this melding of the hard and soft sciences in fiction, as well as its literary maturity of style. There were many others. Even into the eighties and nineties, venturesome editors, such as Ellen Datlow, with her fantasy-inspired, sexually liberating anthologies, and Patrick Nielsen Hayden, with his *Starlight* series (three volumes, as I write this) continued to elevate the field.

The magazines, too, absorbed the new gestalt, and, over the years, have continued to evolve.*

Given this history, was there really a need for another "cutting edge" original sf anthology, here in 2001? What would be the reasons for putting together such a book?

I had one damned good reason for jumping into such a project. Two, actually.

But one's a secret—for now.

PART TWO: WHY

The "Ellison Revolution," it seems to me, had four goals: the breaking of taboos, the presentation of new ways of telling stories, the expansion of the sf field, and—well, I'll keep the fourth one in my back pocket for now, since it happens to dovetail with one of my own reasons for doing this book.

As for taboos, someone asked me: What taboos are left to break in an era when the media discuss the president performing sex acts in the oval office? There do seem to be, even in science fiction, precious few taboos to break these days.†

*For much better, deeper, and finer discussions of these developments, there are far better sources than me. Start with Clute and Nicholls's *Science Fiction Encyclopedia*, either in print or on CD-ROM as *Grolier Science Fiction: The Multimedia Encyclopedia of Science Fiction*, which includes video and audio clips.

†I do think there are a few pieces in this book that would have had a hard time finding a home, specifically due to content, even in this day and age. Even though there have been numerous original anthologies devoted to all kinds of former "taboo" subjects, the magazines, in particular, which still publish the lion's share of sf short fic-

And as for new ways of telling stories, there's also really little left to discuss. By now, just about every style from *Ulysses* to Ulysses S. Grant has been tried in sf—with mixed results. To my mind, there are plenty of ways to tell a story. If what you have in the end are pretty words that make no discernible pattern or narrative, well, that ain't a story, even if you call it "experimental." The truth is, whatever works works—as long as it works.

Those two goals were pretty much reached—and, as you already realize, a long time ago.

What about the third goal of the ER (Ellison Revolution): the expansion of the sf field?

Ah, finally, something to work with in the year of 2001.

The question must be asked: Now that it's pretty much absorbed the soft sciences, the literary avant-garde, and the humanities, is the sf field so staid, so settled, that there's nowhere left for it to be pushed to?

Of course not.

Never.

The sf field is by its very nature the luckiest of literary forms—its basic subject matter, the sciences, whether soft or hard, are always themselves evolving. Even though the ER brought in all kinds of new subject matter, there is a built-in factor in sf that ensures that it will never get old. The sciences—soft or hard—are continually providing the field with new ideas.*

Science fiction has built-in forward momentum.

My first reason for putting this book together—the continued revolutionary expansion of sf—is not only valid, but also vital. Hopefully this project will present a blueprint for the future.

What about my second reason—the secret one?

Well . . . I think I'll keep it a secret for just a bit longer.

First we need to find out the most important thing: how the writers reacted when I approached them with this nutty idea of mine.

PART THREE: HOW

Thus girded and armed with my idea for a huge new book of speculative fiction stories that would expand the field and possibly change its future, I stumbled forth into the world to present it to the only people who mattered: the best sf writers in the world.

---

tion, are still averse to certain types of stories. Then again, as I've been told, taboos *do* change with the times, don't they? What's political incorrectness if not a new taboo?

*And vice versa—as someone once said: "First come the dreamers." Need I mention any name beyond that of Jules Verne?

How did they respond?

Quite frankly, they knocked my socks off.

To anyone who asked (few needed to), I said: "If you could influence the course of sf for the next twenty-five years, show me that story!"

I ended up with, I think, not only a blueprint for the future, but also a primer of the changes that have taken place since the sixties—a summation of how sf has expanded in the *last* twenty-five years.

And not to dwell on this, but the number of submissions I received from women—especially *new* writers—was remarkable. This is not something we would have seen a few decades ago, for the simple reason that there weren't many women writing this stuff.

PART FOUR: (AGAIN) WHAT

Okay, enough already—what was my second reason for doing this book?

Well, that really isn't much of a secret. It's what every original anthologist wants to do: present a big book of really good stories.

No problem there. At over 200,000 words, containing three novellas, five novelettes, and twenty-two short stories, *Redshift* is easily one of the fattest original sf anthologies in some time. I also happen to think it's one of the best. If the stories in this book are any indication, sf will be very healthy for the foreseeable future. The diversity and quality of the pieces I received were remarkable. The good stories that I had to turn down would nearly fill another volume. There's something in this book for everyone—if you can't find something you like, you must be brain-dead!

PART FIVE: WHERE

So is *Redshift* the finest original sf anthology of the last twenty-five years? Will it expand sf and influence its future for the *next* twenty-five years?

That's for you to decide. But it is, I think, one hell of a good book of new stories.

A final question: Where are we, here at the dawn of the third millennium, in this totemic year of 2001?

Where we always are, and want to be: on a cliff overlooking a wonderful new expanding universe of words.

Time for me to push you in.

Al Sarrantonio
January 2001

REDSHIFT

Yikes! Here's a story leading off this so-called cutting edge anthology that could have been published (minus the naughty language) anywhere in the science fiction field in the last forty years. And by that I mean just about any magazine or anthology—or a number of same outside the field. I could see this one in the Saturday Evening Post *in 1968, for crissakes.*

What gives?

I'll tell you what gives: this story is great fiction today, forty years ago, or forty years in the future. Great fiction transcends any definition of cutting edge or New Wave.

Or genre labels.

Or any other kind of baloney.

Dan Simmons is well known to you all, or should be. He is the author of Hyperion, The Fall of Hyperion, The Song of Kali, *and many other sf and horror novels. He's won numerous awards, including the Bram Stoker Award, the World Fantasy Award, and the Hugo Award, and also has conquered the spy thriller and suspense fields.*

He's also responsible for the inclusion of one of the other great stories in this book, as you shall see.

But that's later; for now: enjoy the hell out of the following.

On K2 with Kanakaredes

DAN SIMMONS

✱

The South Col of Everest, 26,200 feet

If we hadn't decided to acclimate ourselves for the K2 attempt by secretly climbing to the eight-thousand-meter mark on Everest, a stupid mountain that no self-respecting climber would go near anymore, they wouldn't have caught us and we wouldn't have been forced to make the real climb with an alien and the rest of it might not have happened. But we did and we were and it did.

What else is new? It's as old as Chaos theory. The best-laid plans of mice and men and so forth and so on. As if you have to tell *that* to a climber.

Instead of heading directly for our Concordia Base Camp at the foot of K2, the three of us had used Gary's nifty little stealth CMG to fly northeast into the Himalayas, straight to the *bergeschrund* of the Khumbu Glacier at 23,000 feet. Well, fly *almost* straight to the glacier; we had to zig and zag to stay under HK Syndicate radar and to avoid seeing or being seen by that stinking prefab pile of Japanese shit called the Everest Base Camp Hotel (rooms US $4,500 a night, not counting Himalayan access fee and CMG limo fare).

We landed without being detected (or so we thought), made sure the vehicle was safely tucked away from the icefalls, seracs, and avalanche paths, left the CMG set in conceal mode, and started our Alpine-style conditioning climb to the South Col. The weather was brilliant. The conditions were perfect. We climbed brilliantly. It was the stupidest thing the three of us had ever done.

By late on the third afternoon we had reached the South Col, that narrow, miserable, windswept notch of ice and boulders wedged high between the shoulders of Lhotse and Everest. We activated our little smart tents, merged them, anchored them hard to ice-spumed rock, and keyed them white to keep them safe from prying eyes.

Even on a beautiful late-summer Himalayan evening such as the one we enjoyed that day, weather on the South Col sucks. Wind velocities average higher than those encountered near the summit of Everest. Any high-climber knows that when you see a stretch of relatively flat rock free of snow, it means hurricane winds. These arrived on schedule just about at sunset of that third day. We hunkered down in the communal tent and made soup. Our plan was to spend two nights on the South Col and acclimate ourselves to the lower edge of the Death Zone before heading down and flying on to Concordia for our legal K2 climb. We had no intention of climbing higher than the South Col on Everest. Who would?

At least the view was less tawdry since the Syndicate cleaned up Everest and the South Col, flying off more than a century's worth of expedition detritus—ancient fixed ropes, countless tent tatters, tons of frozen human excrement, about a million abandoned oxygen bottles, and a few hundred frozen corpses. Everest in the twentieth century had been the equivalent of the old Oregon Trail—everything that could be abandoned had been, including climbers' dead friends.

Actually, the view that evening was rather good. The Col drops off to the east for about four thousand feet into what used to be Tibet and falls even more sharply—about seven thousand feet—to the Western Cwm. That evening, the high ridges of Lhotse and the entire visible west side of Everest caught the rich, golden sunset for long minutes after the Col moved into shadow and then the temperature at our campsite dropped about a hundred degrees. There was not, as we outdoors people like to say, a cloud in the sky. The high peaks glowed in all their eight-thousand-meter glory, snowfields burning orange in the light. Gary and Paul lay in the open door of the tent, still wearing their thermskin uppers, and watched the stars emerge and shake to the hurricane wind as I fiddled and fussed with the stove to make soup. Life was good.

Suddenly an incredibly amplified voice bellowed, "You there in the tent!"

I almost pissed my thermskins. I *did* spill the soup, slopping it all over Paul's sleeping bag.

"Fuck," I said.

"God damn it," said Gary, watching the black CMG—its UN markings glowing and powerful searchlights stabbing—settle gently onto small boulders not twenty feet from the tent.

"Busted," said Paul.

Hillary Room, Top of the World, 29,035 feet

Two years in an HK floating prison wouldn't have been as degrading as being made to enter that revolving restaurant on the top of Everest. All three of us protested, Gary the loudest since he was the oldest and richest, but the four UN security guys in the CMG just cradled their standard-issue Uzis and said nothing until the vehicle had docked in the restaurant airlock-garage and the pressure had been equalized. We stepped out reluctantly and followed other security guards deeper into the closed and darkened restaurant even more reluctantly. Our ears were going crazy. One minute we'd been camping at 26,000 feet, and a few minutes later the pressure was the standard airline equivalent of 5,000 feet. It was painful, despite the UN CMG's attempt to match pressures while it circled the dark hulk of Everest for ten minutes.

By the time we were led into the Hillary Room to the only lighted table in the place, we were angry *and* in pain.

"Sit down," said Secretary of State Betty Willard Bright Moon.

We sat. There was no mistaking the tall, sharp-featured Blackfoot woman in the gray suit. Every pundit agreed that she was the single toughest and most interesting personality in the Cohen Administration, and the four U.S. Marines in combat garb standing in the shadows behind her only added to her already imposing sense of authority. The three of us sat, Gary closest to the dark window wall across from Secretary Bright Moon, Paul next to him, and me farthest away from the action. It was our usual climbing pattern.

On the expensive teak table in front of Secretary Bright Moon were three blue dossiers. I couldn't read the tabs on them, but I had little doubt about their contents: Dossier #1, Gary Sheridan, forty-nine, semi-retired, former CEO of SherPath International, multiple addresses around the world, made his first millions at age seventeen during the long lost and rarely lamented dot-com gold rush of yore, divorced (four times), a man of many passions, the greatest of which was mountain climbing; Dossier #2, Paul Ando Hiraga, twenty-eight, ski bum, professional guide, one of the world's best rock-and-ice climbers, unmarried; Dossier #3, Jake Richard Pettigrew, thirty-six, (address: Boulder, Colorado), married, three children, high-school math teacher, a good-to-average climber with only two eight-thousand-meter peaks bagged, both thanks to Gary and Paul, who invited him to join them on international climbs for the six previous years. Mr. Pettigrew still cannot believe his good luck at having a friend and patron bankroll his climbs, especially when both Gary and Paul were far better climbers with much more experience. But perhaps the dossiers told of how Jake, Paul, and Gary had become close friends as well as climbing partners over the past few years, friends who trusted each other to the point of trespassing on the Himalayan Preserve just to get acclimated for the climb of their lives.

Or perhaps the blue folders were just some State Department busy-work that had nothing to do with us.

"What's the idea of hauling us up here?" asked Gary, his voice controlled but tight. Very tight. "If the Hong Kong Syndicate wants to throw us in the slammer, fine, but you and the UN can't just drag us somewhere against our will. We're still U.S. citizens. . . ."

"U.S. citizens who have broken HK Syndicate Preserve rules and UN World Historical Site laws," snapped Secretary Bright Moon.

"We have a valid permit . . . ," began Gary again. His forehead looked very red just below the line of his cropped white hair.

"To climb K2, commencing three days from now," said the Secretary of State. "Your climbing team won the HK lottery. We know. But that permit does not allow you to enter or overfly the Himalayan Preserve, or to trespass on Mount Everest."

Paul glanced at me. I shook my head. I had no idea what was going on. We could have *stolen* Mount Everest and it wouldn't have brought Secretary Betty Willard Bright Moon flying around the world to sit in this darkened revolving restaurant just to slap our wrists.

Gary shrugged and sat back. "So what do you want?"

Secretary Bright Moon opened the closest blue dossier and slid a photo across the polished teak toward us. We huddled to look at it.

"A bug?" said Gary.

"They prefer *Listener*," said the secretary of state. "But mantispid will do."

"What do the bugs have to do with us?" said Gary.

"This particular bug wants to climb K2 with you in three days," said Secretary Bright Moon. "And the government of the United States of America in cooperation with the Listener Liaison and Cooperation Council of the United Nations fully intend to have him . . . or her . . . do so."

Paul's jaw dropped. Gary clasped his hands behind his head and laughed. I just stared. Somehow I found my voice first.

"That's impossible," I said.

Secretary Betty Willard Bright Moon turned her flat, dark-eyed gaze on me. "Why?"

Normally the combination of that woman's personality, her position, and those eyes would have stopped me cold, but this was too absurd to ignore. I just held out my hands, palms upward. Some things are too obvious to explain. "The bugs have six legs," I said at last. "They look like they can hardly walk. We're climbing the *second tallest mountain* on earth. And the most savage."

Secretary Bright Moon did not blink. "The bu— The mantispids seem to get around their freehold in Antarctica quite well," she said flatly. "And sometimes they walk on two legs."

Paul snorted. Gary kept his hands clasped behind his head, his shoulders back, posture relaxed, but his eyes were flint. "I presume that if this bug climbed with us, that you'd hold us responsible for his safety and well-being," he said.

The secretary's head turned as smoothly as an owl's. "You presume correctly," she said. "That would be our first concern. The safety of the Listeners is always our first concern."

Gary lowered his hands and shook his head. "Impossible. Above eight thousand meters, no one can help anyone."

"That's why they call that altitude the Death Zone," said Paul. He sounded angry.

Bright Moon ignored Paul and kept her gaze locked with Gary's. She had spent too many decades steeped in power, negotiation, and political in-fighting not to know who our leader was. "We can make the climb safer," she said. "Phones, CMGs on immediate call, uplinks . . ."

Gary was shaking his head again. "We do this climb without phones and medevac capability from the mountain."

"That's absurd . . . ," began the secretary of state.

Gary cut her off. "That's the way it is," he said. "That's what real mountaineers *do* in this day and age. And what we don't do is come to this fucking obscenity of a restaurant." He gestured toward the darkened Hillary Room to our right, the gesture including all the revolving Top of the World. One of the marines blinked at Gary's obscenity.

Secretary Bright Moon did not blink. "All right, Mr. Sheridan. The phones and CMG medevacs are not negotiable. I presume everything else is."

Gary said nothing for a minute. Finally, "I presume that if we say no, that you're going to make our lives a living hell."

The secretary of state smiled ever so slightly. "I think that all of you will find that there will be no more visas for foreign climbs," she said. "Ever.

And all of you may encounter difficulties with your taxes soon. Especially you, Mr. Sheridan, since your corporate accounts are so . . . complicated."

Gary returned her smile. For an instant it seemed as if he were actually enjoying this. "And if we said yes," he said slowly, almost drawling, "what's in it for us?"

Bright Moon nodded, and one of the lackeys to her left opened another dossier and slid a slick color photograph across the table toward us. Again all three of us leaned forward to look. Paul frowned. It took me a minute to figure out what it was—some sort of reddish shield volcano. Hawaii?

"Mars," Gary said softly. "Olympus Mons."

Secretary Bright Moon said, "It is more than twice as tall as Mount Everest."

Gary laughed easily. "Twice as tall? Shit, woman, Olympus Mons is more than three times the height of Everest—more than eighty-eight thousand feet high, three hundred and thirty-five miles in diameter. The caldera is fifty-three miles wide. Christ, the outward facing cliff ringing the bottom of the thing is taller than Everest—thirty-two thousand eight hundred feet, vertical with an overhang."

Bright Moon had finally blinked at the "Shit, woman"—I wondered wildly when the last time had been that someone had spoken to this secretary of state like that—but now she smiled.

Gary said, "So what? The Mars program is dead. We chickened out, just like with the Apollo Program seventy-five years ago. Don't tell me that you're offering to send us there, because we don't even have the technology to go back."

"The bugs do," said Secretary Bright Moon. "And if you agree to let the son of the mantispid speaker climb K2 with you, the Listeners guarantee that they will transport you to Mars within twelve months—evidently the transit time will be only two weeks in each direction—and they'll outfit a mountain-climbing expedition up Olympus Mons for you. Pressure suits, rebreathers, the whole nine yards."

The three of us exchanged glances. We did not have to discuss this. We looked back at the photograph. Finally Gary looked up at Bright Moon. "What do we have to do other than climb with him?"

"Keep him alive if you can," she said.

Gary shook his head. "You heard Paul. Above eight thousand meters, we can't guarantee even keeping ourselves alive."

The secretary nodded, but said softly, "Still, if we added a simple emergency calling device to one of your palmlogs—a distress beacon, as it were—this would allow us to come quickly to evacuate the mantispid if there were a problem or illness or injury to him, without interfering with the . . . integrity . . . of the rest of your climb."

"A red panic button," said Gary, but the three of us exchanged glances again. This idea was distasteful but reasonable in its way. Besides, once the bug was taken off the hill, for whatever reason, the three of us could get on with the climb and maybe still get a crack at Olympus Mons. "What else?" Gary asked the woman.

Secretary Bright Moon folded her hands and lowered her gaze a moment. When she looked up again, her gaze appeared to be candid. "You gentlemen know how little the mantispids have talked to us . . . how little technology they have shared with us—"

"They gave us CMG," interrupted Gary.

"Yes," said Bright Moon, "CMG in exchange for their Antarctic freehold. But we've only had hints of the other wonders they could share with us—generation starflight technology, a cure for cancer, free energy. The Listeners just . . . well, listen. This is the first overture they've made."

The three of us waited.

"We want you to record everything this son of the speaker says during the climb," said Secretary Bright Moon. "Ask questions. Listen to the answers. Make friends with him if you can. That's all."

Gary shook his head. "We don't want to wear a wire." Before Bright Moon could object, he went on, "We have to wear thermskins—molecular heat membranes. We're not going to wear wires under or over them."

The secretary looked as if she was ready to order the marines to shoot Gary and probably throw Paul and me out the window, not that the window could be opened. The whole damned restaurant was pressurized.

"I'll do it," I said.

Gary and Paul looked at me in surprise. I admit that I was also surprised at the offer. I shrugged. "Why not? My folks died of cancer. I wouldn't mind finding a cure. You guys can weave a recording wire into my overparka. Or I can use the recorder in my palmlog. I'll record the bug when I can, but I'll summarize the other conversations on my palmlog. You know, keep a record of things."

Secretary Betty Willard Bright Moon looked as if she were swallowing gall, but she nodded, first to us and then at the marine guards. The marines came around the table to escort us back to the UN CMG.

"Wait," said Gary before we were led away. "Does this bug have a name?"

"Kanakaredes," said the secretary of state, not even looking up at us.

"Sounds Greek," said Paul.

"I seriously doubt it," said Secretary Bright Moon.

K2 Base Camp, 16,500 feet

I guess I expected a little flying saucer—a smaller version of the shuttle craft the bugs had first landed near the UN nine years earlier—but they all arrived in an oversize, bright red DaimlerChrysler CMG. I saw them first and shouted. Gary and Paul came out of the supply tent where they had been triple-checking our provisions.

Secretary Bright Moon wasn't there to see us off, of course—we hadn't spoken to her since the night at the Top of the World three days earlier—but the Listener Liaison guy, William Grimes, and two of his aides got out of the CMG, as did two bugs, one slightly larger than the other. The smaller mantispid had some sort of clear, bubbly backpack along his dorsal ridge, nestled in the V where its main body section joined the prothorax.

The three of us crossed the boulder field until we were facing the five of them. It was the first time I had ever seen the aliens in person—I mean, who ever sees a bug *in person*?—and I admit that I was nervous. Behind us, above us, spindrift and cloud whirled from the ridges and summit of K2. If the mantispids smelled weird, I couldn't pick it up since the breeze was blowing from behind the three of us.

"Mr. Sheridan, Mr. Hiraga, Mr. Pettigrew," said the bureaucrat Grimes, "may I introduce Listener Speaker Aduradake and his . . . son . . . Kanakaredes."

The taller of the two bugs unfolded that weird arm or foreleg, swiveled the short forearm thing up like a praying mantis unlimbering, and offered Gary its three-fingered hand. Gary shook it. Paul shook it. I shook it. It felt boneless.

The shorter bug watched, its two primary eyes black and unreadable, its smaller side-eyes lidded and sleepy-looking. It—Kanakaredes—did not offer to shake hands.

"My people thank you for agreeing to allow Kanakaredes to accompany you on this expedition," said Speaker Aduradake. I don't know if they used implanted voice synthesizers to speak to us—I think not—but the English came out as a carefully modulated series of clicks and sighs. Quite understandable, but strange, very strange.

"No problem," said Gary.

It looked as if the UN bureaucrats wanted to say more—make some speeches, perhaps—but Speaker Aduradake swiveled on his four rear legs and picked his way across the boulders to the CMG's ramp. The humans scurried to catch up. Half a minute later and the vehicle was nothing more than a red speck in the blue southern sky.

The four of us stood there silent for a second, listening to the wind howl around the remaining seracs of the Godwin-Austen Glacier and through niches in the wind-carved boulders. Finally Gary said, "You bring all the shit we e-mailed you about?"

"Yes," said Kanakaredes. His forearms swiveled in their high sockets, the long mantis femur moved up and back, and the third segment swiveled downward so that the soft, three-fingered hands could pat the clear pack on his back. "Brought all the shit, just as you e-mailed." His clicks and sighs sounded just like the other bug's.

"Compatible North Face smart tent?" said Gary.

The bug nodded—or at least I took that movement of the broad, beaked head as a nod. Gary must also have. "Rations for two weeks?" he asked.

"Yes," said Kanakaredes.

"We have the climbing gear for you," said Gary. "Grimes said that you've practiced with it all—crampons, ropes, knots, weblines, ice axe, jumars—that you've been on a mountain before."

"Mount Erebus," said Kanakaredes. "I have practiced there for some months."

Gary sighed. "K2 is a little different from Mount Erebus."

We were all silent again for a bit. The wind howled and blew my long hair forward around my face. Finally Paul pointed up the glacier where it curved near Base Camp and rose toward the east side of K2 and beneath the back side of Broad Peak. I could just see the icefall where the glacier met the Abruzzi Ridge on K2. That ridge, path of the first attempt on the mountain and line of the first successful summit assault, was our fallback route if our attempt on the North-East Ridge and East Face fell behind schedule.

"You see, we could fly over the glacier and start the climb from the base of the Abruzzi at eighteen thousand feet," said Paul, "miss all the crevasse danger that way, but it's part of the climb to start from here."

Kanakaredes said nothing. His two primary eyes had clear membranes, but the eyes never blinked. They stared blackly at Paul. The other two eyes were looking God knows where.

I felt that I should say something. Anything. I cleared my throat.

"Fuck it," said Gary. "We're burning daylight. Let's load 'em up and move 'em out."

Camp One, North-East Ridge, about 18,300 feet

They call K2 "the savage mountain" and a hundred other names—all respectful. It's a killer mountain; more men and women have died on it in terms of percentage of those attempting to climb it than on any other peak in the Himalayas or the Karakoram. It is not malevolent. It is simply the Zen-essence of *mountain*—hard, tall, pyramidal when seen from the south in the perfect child's-drawing iconic model of the Matterhorn, jagged, steep, knife-ridged, racked by frequent avalanches and unearthly storms, its essentially airless summit almost continuously blasted by the jet stream. No contortion of sentiment or personification can suggest that this mountain gives the slightest shit about human hopes or human life. In a way that is impossible to articulate and politically incorrect even to suggest, K2 is profoundly masculine. It is eternally indifferent and absolutely unforgiving. Climbers have loved it and triumphed on it and died on it for more than a century.

Now it was our turn to see which way this particular prayer wheel turned.

Have you ever watched a mantispid bug walk? I mean, we've all seen them on HDTV or VirP—there's an entire satellite channel dedicated to them, for Christ's sake—but usually that's just quick cuts, long-lens images, or static shots of the bug speaker and some political bigshots standing around somewhere. Have you ever watched them *walk* for any length of time?

In crossing the upper reaches of the Godwin-Austen Glacier under the 11,000-foot vertical wall that is the east face of K2, you have two choices. You can stay near the edges of the glacier, where there are almost no crevasses, and risk serious avalanche danger, or you can stick to the center of the glacier and never know when the snow and ice underfoot is suddenly going to collapse into a hidden crevasse. Any climber worth his or her salt will choose the crevasse-route if there's even a hint of avalanche risk. Skill and experience can help you avoid crevasses; there's not a goddamn thing in the world you can do except pray when an avalanche comes your way.

To climb the glacier, we had to rope up. Gary, Paul, and I had discussed this—whether or not to rope with the bug—but when we reached the part of the glacier where crevasses would be most probable, inevitable actually, we really didn't have a choice. It would have been murder to let Kanakaredes proceed unroped.

One of the first things all of us thought when the bugs landed almost ten years ago was "Are they wearing clothes?" We know now that they weren't—that their weird combination of chitinous exoskeleton on their main body section and layers of different membranes on the softer parts serve well in lieu of clothing—but that doesn't mean that they go around with their sexual parts showing. Theoretically, mantispids are sexual creatures—male or female—but I've never heard of a human being who's *seen* a bug's genitals, and I can testify that Gary, Paul, and I didn't want to be the first.

Still, the aliens rig themselves with toolbelts or harnesses or whatever when necessary—just as Kanakaredes had shown up with that weird bubble-pack on his back with all his climbing gear in it—and as soon as we started the ascent, he removed a harness from that pack and rigged it around that chunky, almost armored upper section of himself where his arm and midleg sockets were. He also used a regulation-size metal ice axe, gripping the curved metal top in those three boneless fingers. It seemed strange to see something as prosaic as a red nylon climbing harness and carabiners and an ice axe on a bug, but that's what he had.

When it came time to rope up, we clipped the spidersilk line onto our 'biners, passing the line back in our usual climbing order, except that this time—instead of Paul's ass slowly slogging up the glacier in front of me—I got to watch Kanakaredes plod along ten paces ahead of me for hour after hour.

"Plod along" really doesn't do bug locomotion justice. We've all seen a bug balance and walk on its midlegs, standing more upright on those balancing legs, its back straightening, its head coming up until it's tall enough to stare a short human male in the eye, forelegs suddenly looking more like real arms than praying mantis appendages—but I suspect now that they do that just for that reason—to appear more human in their rare public appearances. So far, Kanakaredes had stood on just two legs only during the formal meeting back at Base Camp. As soon as we started hiking up the glacier, his head came down and forward, that V between his main body section and prothorax widened, those mantis-arms stretched far forward like a human extending two poles ahead of him, and he fell into a seemingly effortless four-legged motion.

But, Jesus Christ, what a weird motion. All of a bug's legs have three joints, of course, but I realized after only a few minutes of following this particular bug up the Godwin-Austen Glacier that those joints never seem to bend the same way at the same time. One of those praying mantis forelegs would be double bent forward and down so that Kanakaredes could plant his ice axe in the slope, while the other bent forward and then back so that he could scratch that weird beak of a snout. At the same time, the midlegs would be bending rather like a horse's, only instead of a hoof, the lower, shortest section ended in those chitinous but somehow dainty, divided . . . hell, I don't know, hoof-feet. And the hind legs, the ones socketed at the base of the soft prothorax . . . those are the ones that made me dizzy as I watched the bug climbing through soft snow in front of me. Sometimes the alien's knees—those first joints about two-thirds of the way down the legs—would be higher than his back. At other times one knee would be bending forward, the other one back, while the lower joints were doing even stranger things.

After a while, I gave up trying to figure out the engineering of the creature, and just began admiring the easy way it moved up the steep snow and ice. The three of us had worried about the small surface area of a bug's feet on snow—the V-shaped hoof-things aren't even as large as an unshod human foot—and wondered if we'd be tugging the mantispid out of every drift on our way up the mountain, but Kanakaredes managed quite well, thank you. I guess it was due to the fact that I guessed at that time that he probably weighed only about 150 pounds, and that weight was spread out over four—and sometimes six, when he tucked the ice axe in his harness and scrambled—walking surfaces. To tell the truth, the bug had to help me slog clear of deep snow two or three times on the upper reaches of the glacier.

During the afternoon, with the sun blazing on the reflective bowl of ice that was the glacier, it got damned hot. The three of us humans damped our thermskin controls way down and shed our parka outer layers to cool off. The bug seemed comfortable enough, although he rested without complaint while we rested, drank water from his water bottle when we paused to drink, and chewed on something that looked like a shingle made of compressed dog poop while we munched our nutrient bars (which, I realize now, also looked a lot like a shingle made of compressed dog poop). If Kanakaredes suffered from overheating or chill that first long day on the glacier, he didn't show it.

Long before sunset, the mountain shadow had moved across us and three of the four of us were raising our thermskin thresholds and tugging on the parka shells again. It had begun snowing. Suddenly a huge avalanche calved off the east face of K2 and swept down the slope behind us, boiling and rolling over a part of the glacier we had been climbing just an hour earlier.

We all froze in our tracks until the rumbling stopped. Our tracks in the shadowed snow—rising in a more-or-less straight line for a thousand-foot elevation gain over the last mile or so—looked like they had been rubbed out by a giant eraser for a swath of several hundred yards.

"Holy shit," I said.

Gary nodded, breathing a little hard since he had been breaking trail for most of the afternoon, turned, took a step, and disappeared.

For the last hours, whoever had been in the lead had probed ahead with his ice axe to make sure that the footing ahead was real and not just a skim of snow over a deep crevasse. Gary had taken two steps without doing this. And the crevasse got him.

One instant he was there, red parka glowing against the shadowed ice and the white snow on the ridge now so close ahead of us, and the next instant he was gone.

And then Paul disappeared as well.

No one screamed or reacted poorly. Kanakaredes instantly braced himself in full-belay posture, slammed his ice axe deep into the ice beneath him, and wrapped the line around it twice before the thirty feet or so of slack between him and Paul had played out. I did the same, digging crampons in as hard as I could, fully expecting the crevasse to pull the bug in and then me.

It didn't.

The line snapped taut but did not snap—genetically tailored spider-silk climbing rope almost never breaks—Kanakaredes's ice axe stayed firm, as did the bug holding it in the glacier ice, and the two of us held them. We waited a full minute in our rigid postures, making sure that we weren't also standing on a thin crust over a crevasse, but when it was obvious where the crevasse rim was, I gasped, "Keep them tight," unclipped, and crawled forward to peer down the black gap.

I have no idea how deep the crevasse was—a hundred feet? A thousand? But both Paul and Gary were dangling there—Paul a mere fifteen feet or so down, still in the light, looking fairly comfortable as he braced his back against the blue-green ice wall and rigged his climbing jumars. That clamp and cam device, infinitely lighter and stronger but otherwise no different than the jumars our grandfathers might have used, would get him back up on his own as long as the rope held and as soon as he could get the footloops attached.

Gary did not look so comfortable. Almost forty feet down, hanging headfirst under an icy overhang so that only his crampons and butt caught the light, he looked as if he might be in trouble. If he had hit his head on the ice on the way down . . .

Then I heard him cursing—the incredible epithets and shouts almost muffled in the crevasse, but still echoing deep as he cursed straight into the underbelly of the glacier—and I knew that he was all right.

It took only a minute or so for Paul to jumar up and over the lip, but getting Gary rightside up and then lifted up over the overhang so he could attach his own jumars took a bit longer and involved some manhauling.

That's when I discovered how goddamned strong this bug was. I think that Kanakaredes could have hauled all three of us out of that crevasse if we'd been unconscious, almost six hundred pounds of dead weight. And I think he could have done it using only one of those skinny, almost muscleless-looking praying mantis forearms of his.

When Gary was out and untangled from his lines, harness, and jumars, we moved carefully around the crevasse, me in the lead and probing with my axe like a blind man in a vale of razor blades, and when we'd reached a good site for Camp One just at the base of the ridge, offering only a short climb in the morning to the crest of the northeast ridge that would eventually take us up onto the shoulder of K2 itself, we found a spot in the last patch of sun, unhooked the rope from our carabiners, dumped our seventy-five-pound packs, and just gasped for a while before setting up camp.

"Fucking good beginning to the goddamned motherfucking expedition," said Gary between slugs on his water bottle. "Absolutely bastardly motherfucking brilliant—I walk into a goddamned sonofabitching whoremongering crevasse like some pissant whoreson fucking day tripper."

I looked over at Kanakaredes. Who could read a bug's expression? That endless mouth with all its jack-o'-lantern bumps and ridges, wrapped two-thirds around its head from its beaky proboscis almost to the beginning of its bumpy skullcrest, *always* seemed to be smiling. Was it smiling more now? Hard to tell, and I was in no mood to ask.

One thing was clear. The mantispid had a small, clear device out—something very similar to our credit card palmlogs—and was entering data with a flurry of its three fingers. *A lexicon*, I thought. Either translating or recording Gary's outburst which was, I admit, a magnificent flow of invective. He was still weaving a brilliant tapestry of obscenity that showed no sign of abating and which would probably hang over the Godwin-Austen Glacier like a blue cloud for years to come.

Good luck using this vocabulary during one of your UN cocktail parties, I thought to Kanakaredes as he finished his data entry and repacked his palmlog.

When Gary finally trailed off, I exchanged grins with Paul—who had said nothing since dropping into the crevasse—and we got busy breaking out the smart tents, the sleeping bags, and the stoves before darkness dropped Camp One into deep lunar cold.

Camp Two, between a cornice and an avalanche slope, about 20,000 feet

I'm keeping these recordings for the State Department intelligence people and all the rest who want to learn everything about the bugs—about the mantispids' technology, about their reasons for coming to Earth, about their culture and religions—all the things they've somehow neglected to tell us in the past nine and a half years.

Well, here's the sum total of my recording of human-mantispid conversation from last night at Camp One—

> GARY: Uh . . . Kan . . . Kanakaredes? We were thinking of merging our three tents and cooking up some soup and hitting the sack early. You have any problem keeping your tent separate tonight? There's room on this snow slab for both tent parts.
>
> KANAKAREDES: I have no problem with that.

So much for interrogating our bug.

* * *

We should be higher tonight. We had a long, strong day of climbing today, but we're still on the low part of the northeast ridge and we have to do better if we're going to get up this hill and down safely in the two weeks alotted to us.

All this "Camp One" and "Camp Two" stuff I'm putting in this palmlog diary are old terms from the last century when attempts at eight-thousand-meter peaks literally demanded armies of men and women—more than two hundred people hauling supplies for the first American Everest expedition in 1963. Some of the peaks were pyramid-shaped but *all* the logistics were. By that I mean that scores of porters hauled in uncounted tons of supplies—Sherpa porters and high-climbers in the Himalayas, primarily Balti porters here in the Karakoram—and teams of men and women man-hauled these tons up the mountains, working in relays to establish camps to last the duration of the climb, breaking and marking trail, establishing fixed ropes up literally miles of slope, and moving teams of climbers up higher and higher until, after weeks, sometimes months of effort, a very few of the best and luckiest climbers—say six or four or two or even one from the scores who started—were in a position to make an attempt on the summit from a high camp—usually Camp Six, but sometimes Camp Seven or higher—starting somewhere in the Death Zone above eight thousand meters. "Assault" on a mountain was a good word then, since it took an army to mount the assault.

Gary, Paul, the bug, and I are climbing alpine style. This means that we carry everything we need—starting heavy and getting lighter and lighter as we climb—essentially making a direct bid on the summit, hoping to climb it in a week or less. No series of permanent camps, just temporary slabs cut out of the snow and ice for our smart tents—at least up until whatever camp we designate as our summit-attempt jumping-off point. Then we'll leave the tents and most of the gear there and go for it, hoping and praying to whatever gods we have—and who knows what gods Kanakaredes prays to, if any—praying that the weather won't turn bad while we're up there in the Death Zone, that we won't get lost coming down to our high camp in the dark, that nothing serious happens to any us of during that final attempt since we really can't help each other at that altitude—essentially just praying our asses off that we don't fuck up.

But that is *if* we can keep moving steadily up this hill. Today wasn't so steady.

We started early, breaking down Camp One in a few minutes, loading efficiently, and climbing well—me in the lead, then Paul, then the bug, then Gary. There's a bitch of a steep, razor-edge traverse starting at about the 23,300-foot level—the hardest pitch on the northeast ridge part of our route—and we wanted to settle into a secure camp at the beginning of that scary traverse by nightfall tonight. No such luck.

I'm sure I have some of Kanakaredes's comments recorded from today, but they're mostly monosyllables and they don't reveal any great bug secrets. They're more along the lines of—"Kana . . . Kanaka . . . hey K, did you pack the extra stove?" "Yes." "Want to take a lunch break?" "That would be fine."—and Gary's "Shit, it's starting to snow." Come to think of it, I don't believe the mantispid initiated any conversation. All the clicks and sighs on the palmlog chip are K replying to our questions. All the cursing was ours.

It started to snow heavily about noon.

Until then things had been going well. I was still in the lead—burning calories at a ferocious rate as I broke trail and kicked steps in the steep slope for the others to follow. We were climbing independently, not roped. If one of us slipped or caught his crampons on a rock rather than ice, it was up to that person to stop his slide by self-arrest with his ice axe. Otherwise one had just bought a really great amusement-park ride of a screaming slide on ice for a thousand feet or so and then a launch out over the edge to open space, dropping three or four thousand feet to the glacier below.

The best idea is not to think about that, just keep points attached to the snow slope at all times and make damned sure that no matter how tired you were, that you paid attention to where you kicked your crampons into the ice. I have no idea if Kanakaredes had a fear of heights—I made a fatigued mental note to ask him—but his climbing style showed caution and care. His "crampons" were customized—a series of sharp, plastic-looking spikes lashed to those weird arrow-shaped feet of his—but he took care in their placement and used his ice axe well. He was climbing two-legged this day, his rear legs folded into his elevated prothorax so that you wouldn't know they were there unless you knew where to look.

By 10:30 or 11:00 A.M., we'd gained enough altitude that we could clearly see Staircase Peak—its eastern ridge looks like a stairway for some Hindu giant—on the northeast side of K2. The mountain is also called Skyang Kangri and it was beautiful, dazzling in the sunlight against the still-blue eastern sky. Far below, we could see the Godwin-Austen Glacier crawling along the base of Skyang Kangri to the 19,000-foot pass of Windy Gap. We could easily see over Windy Pass now, scores of miles to the browning hills of what used to be China and now was the mythical country of Sinkiang, fought over even as we climbed by troops from the HK and various Chinese warlords.

More pertinent to our cause right now was the view up and westward toward the beautiful but almost laughable bulk of K2, with its wild knife-edge ridge that we hoped to reach by nightfall. At this rate, I thought just before looking up at it again, it shouldn't be any problem. . . .

That was precisely the moment when Gary called up, "Shit! It's starting to snow!"

The clouds had rolled in from the south and west when we weren't watching, and within ten minutes we were enveloped by them. The wind came up. Snow blew everywhere. We had to cluster up on the increasingly steep slope just to keep track of one another. Naturally, at precisely this point in the day's climb, our steep but relatively easy snow slope turned into a forbidding wall of ice with a band of brittle rock visible above for the few minutes before the clouds shut off all our view for the rest of the day.

"Fuck me," said Paul as we gathered at the foot of the ice slope.

Kanakaredes's bulky, beaked head turned slowly in Paul's direction, his black eyes attentive, as if he was curious as to whether such a biological improbability was possible. K asked no questions and Paul volunteered no answers.

Paul, the best ice climber among us, took the lead for the next half hour or so, planting his axe into the near-vertical ice wall, then kicking hard with the two spike points on the front of his boot, then pulling himself up with the strength of his right arm, kicking one foot in again, pulling the axe out, slamming it in again.

This is basic ice-climbing technique, not difficult, but exhausting at almost twenty thousand feet—twice the altitude where CMGs and commercial airlines are required to go to pressurized O_2—and it took time, especially since we'd roped up now and were belaying Paul as he kick-climbed.

Paul was about seventy feet above us now and was moving cautiously out onto the rock band. Suddenly a slew of small rocks came loose and hurtled down toward us.

There was no place for us to go. Each of us had hacked out a tiny platform in the ice on which we could stand, so all we could do was press ourselves against the ice wall, cover up, and wait. The rocks missed me. Gary had a fist-size rock bounce off his pack and go hurtling out into space. Kanakaredes was hit twice by serious-size rocks—once in his upper left leg, arm, whatever it is, and again on his bumpy dorsal ridge. I heard both rocks strike; they made a sound like stone hitting slate.

"Fuck me," K said clearly as more rocks bounced around him.

When the fusillade was over, after Paul had finished shouting down apologies and Gary had finished hurling up insults, I kick-stepped the ten or so paces to where K still huddled against the ice wall, his right mantis forearm raised, the ice axe and his toe points still dug in tight.

"You hurt?" I said. I was worried that we'd have to use the red button to evacuate the bug and that our climb would be ruined.

Kanakaredes slowly shook his head—not so much to say no, but to check things out. It was almost painful to watch—his bulky head and smiling beak rotating almost 270 degrees in each direction. His free forearm unlimbered, bent impossibly, and those long, unjointed fingers carefully patted and probed his dorsal ridge.

Click. Sigh. Click—"I'm all right."

"Paul will be more careful on the rest of the rock band."

"That would be good."

Paul *was* more careful, but the rock was rotten, and there were a few more landslides, but no more direct hits. Ten minutes and sixty or seventy feet later, he had reached the crest of the ridge, found a good belay stance, and called us up. Gary, who was still pissed—he liked few things less than being pelted by rocks set loose by someone else—started up next. I had Kanakaredes follow thirty feet behind Gary. The bug's ice technique was by the book—not flashy but serviceable. I came up last, trying to stay close enough that I could see and dodge any loosened boulders when we all reached the rock band.

By the time we were all on the northeast ridge and climbing it, the visibility was close to zero, the temperature had dropped about fifty degrees, the snow was thick and mushy and treacherous, and we could hear but not see avalanches roaring down both the east face of K2 and this very slope somewhere both ahead of us and behind us in the fog. We stayed roped up.

"Welcome to K2," Gary shouted back from where he had taken the lead. His parka and hood and goggles and bare chin were a scary, icicled mass mostly obscured by horizontally blowing snow.

"Thank you," click-hissed K in what I heard as a more formal tone. "It is a great pleasure to be here."

Camp Three—under a serac on the crest of the ridge at the beginning of the knife-edge traverse, 23,200 feet

Stuck here three full days and nights, fourth night approaching. Hunkered here useless in our tents, eating nutrient bars and cooking soup that can't be replaced, using up the heating charge in the stove to melt snow into water, each of us getting weaker and crankier due to the altitude and lack of exercise. The wind has been howling and the storm raging for three full days—four days if you count our climb from Camp Two. Yesterday Gary and Paul—with Paul in the lead on the incredibly steep ridge—tried to force the way across the steep climbing traverse in the storm, planning to lay down fixed rope even if we had to make the summit bid with only whatever string remained in our pockets. They failed on the traverse attempt, turning back after three hours in the howling weather and returning ice-crusted and near-frostbitten. It took more than four hours for Paul to quit shaking, even with the thermskins and regulated smart clothing raising his body temperature. If we don't get across this traverse soon—storm or no storm—we won't have to worry about what gear and supplies will be left for the summit bid. There won't be any summit bid.

I'm not even sure now how we managed the climb two days ago from Camp Two to this narrow patch of chopped out ridge crest. Our bug was obviously at the edge of his skill envelope, even with his extra legs and greater strength, and we decided to rope together for the last few hours of climbing, just in case K peeled loose. It wouldn't do much good to push the red panic button on the palmlog just to tell the arriving UN CMG guys that Kanakaredes had taken a header five thousand feet straight down to the Godwin-Austen Glacier.

"Mr. Alien Speaker, sir, we sort of lost your kid. But maybe you can scrape him up off the glacier ice and clone him or something." No, we didn't want that.

As it was, we ended up working after dark, headlamps glowing, ropes 'binered to our harnesses and attached to the slope via ice screws just to keep us from being blown into black space, using our ice axes to hack a platform big enough for the tent—there was only room for a merged cluster of the smart tents, wedged ten feet from a vertical drop, forty feet from an avalanche path and tucked directly beneath an overhanging serac the size of a three-story building—a serac that could give way any time and take us and the tent with it. Not the best spot to spend ten minutes in, much less three days and nights during a high-altitude hurricane. But we had no choice; everything else here was knife-ridge or avalanche slope.

As much as I would have preferred it otherwise, we finally had time for some conversation. Our tents were joined in the form of a squished cross, with a tiny central area, not much more than two feet or so across, for cooking and conversation and just enough room for each of us to pull back into our small nacelles when we curled up to sleep. The platform we'd hacked out of the slope under the overhanging serac wasn't big enough or flat enough to serve all of us, and I ended up in one of the downhill segments, my head higher than my feet. The angle was flat enough to allow me to doze off but still steep enough to send me frequently lurching up from sleep, fingers clawing for my ice axe to stop my slide. But my ice axe was outside with the others, sunk in the deepening snow and rock-hard ice, with about a hundred feet of spidersilk climbing rope lashed around it and over the tent and back again. I think we also used twelve ice screws to secure us to the tiny ice shelf.

Not that any of this will do us a damned bit of good if the serac decides to go or the slope shifts or the winds just make up their minds to blow the whole mass of rope, ice axes, screws, tent, humans, and bug right off the mountain.

We've slept a lot, of course. Paul had brought a softbook loaded with a dozen or so novels and a bunch of magazines, so we handed that around occasionally—even K took his turn reading—and for the first day we didn't talk much because of the effort it took to speak up over the wind howl and the noise of snow and hail pelting the tent. But eventually we grew bored even of sleeping and tried some conversation. That first day it was mostly climbing and technical talk—reviewing the route, listing points for and against the direct attempt once we got past this traverse and up over the snow dome at the base of the summit pyramid—Gary arguing for the Direct Finish no matter what, Paul urging caution and a possible traverse to the more frequently climbed Abruzzi Ridge, Kanakaredes and me listening. But by the second and third days, we were asking the bug personal questions.

"So you guys came from Aldebaran," said Paul on the second afternoon of the storm. "How long did it take you?"

"Five hundred years," said our bug. To fit in his section of the tent, he'd had to fold every appendage he had at least twice. I couldn't help but think it was uncomfortable for him.

Gary whistled. He'd never paid much attention to all the media coverage of the mantispids. "Are you that old, K? Five hundred years?"

Kanakaredes let out a soft whistle that I was beginning to suspect was some equivalent to a laugh. "I am only twenty-three of your years old, Gary," he said. "I was born on the ship, as were my parents and their parents and so on far back. Our life span is roughly equivalent to yours. It was a . . . generation-ship, I believe is your term for it." He paused as the howling wind rose to ridiculous volume and velocity. When it died a bit, he went on, "I knew no other home than the ship until we reached Earth."

Paul and I exchanged glances. It was time for me to interrogate our captive bug for country, family, and Secretary Bright Moon. "So why did you . . . the Listeners . . . travel all the way to Earth?" I asked. The bugs had answered this publicly on more than one occasion, but the answer was always the same and never made much sense.

"Because you were there," said the bug. It was the same old answer. It was flattering, I guess, since we humans have always considered ourselves the center of the universe, but it still made little sense.

"But why spend centuries traveling to meet us?" asked Paul.

"To help you learn to listen," said K.

"Listen to what?" I said. "You? The mantispids? We're interested in listening. Interested in learning. We'll listen to you."

Kanakaredes slowly shook his heavy head. I realized, viewing the mantispid from this close, that his head was more saurian—dinosaur/birdlike—than buggy. "Not listen to us," *click, hiss.* "To the song of your own world."

"To the song of our world?" asked Gary almost brusquely. "You mean, just appreciate life more? Slow down and smell the roses? Stuff like that?" Gary's second wife had been into transcendental meditation. I think it was the reason he divorced her.

"No," said K. "I mean listen to the sound of your world. You have fed your seas. You have consecrated your world. But you do not listen."

It was my turn to muddle things even further. "Fed our seas and consecrated our world," I said. The entire tent thrummed as a gust hit it and then subsided. "How did we do that?"

"By dying, Jake," said the bug. It was the first time he'd used my name. "By becoming part of the seas, of the world."

"Does dying have something to do with hearing the song?" asked Paul.

Kanakaredes's eyes were perfectly round and absolutely black, but they did not seem threatening as he looked at us in the glow of one of the flashlights. "You cannot hear the song when you are dead," he whistle-clicked. "But you cannot have the song unless your species has recycled its atoms and molecules through your world for millions of years."

"Can *you* hear the song here?" I asked. "On Earth, I mean."

"No," said the bug.

I decided to try a more promising tack. "You gave us CMG technology," I said, "and that's certainly brought wonderful changes." *Bullshit*, I thought. I'd liked things better before cars could fly. At least the traffic jams along the Front Range where I lived in Colorado had been two dimensional then. "But we're sort of . . . well . . . curious about when the Listeners are going to share other secrets with us."

"We have no secrets," said Kanakaredes. "Secrets was not even a concept to us before we arrived here on Earth."

"Not secrets then," I said hurriedly, "but more new technologies, inventions, discoveries . . ."

"What kind of discoveries?" said K.

I took a breath. "A cure to cancer would be good," I said.

Kanakaredes made a clicking sound. "Yes, that would be good," he breathed at last. "But this is a disease of your species. Why have you not cured it?"

"We've tried," said Gary. "It's a tough nut to crack."

"Yes," said Kanakaredes, "it is a tough nut to crack."

I decided not to be subtle. "Our species need to learn from one another," I said, my voice perhaps a shade louder than necessary to be heard over the storm. "But your people are so reticent. When are we really going to start talking to each other?"

"When your species learns to listen," said K.

"Is that why you came on this climb with us?" asked Paul.

"I hope that is not the only result," said the bug, "but it is, along with the need to understand, the reason I came."

I looked at Gary. Lying on his stomach, his head only inches from the low tent roof, he shrugged slightly.

"You have mountains on your home world?" asked Paul.

"I was taught that we did not."

"So your homeworld was sort of like the south pole where you guys have your freehold?"

"Not that cold," said Kanakaredes, "and never that dark in the winter. But the atmospheric pressure is similar."

"So you're acclimated to about—what?—seven or eight thousand feet altitude?"

"Yes," said the mantispid.

"And the cold doesn't bother you?" asked Gary.

"It is uncomfortable at times," said the bug. "But our species has evolved a subcutaneous layer which serves much as your thermskins in regulating temperature."

It was my turn to ask a question. "If your world didn't have mountains," I said, "why do you want to climb K2 with us?"

"Why do *you* wish to climb it?" asked Kanakaredes, his head swiveling smoothly to look at each of us.

There was silence for a minute. Well, not really silence since the wind and pelting snow made it sound as if we were camped behind a jet exhaust, but at least none of us humans spoke.

Kanakaredes folded and unfolded his six legs. It was disturbing to watch. "I believe that I will try to sleep now," he said, and closed the flap that separated his niche from ours.

The three of us put our heads together and whispered. "He sounds like a goddamned missionary," hissed Gary. "All this 'listen to the song' doubletalk."

"Just our luck," said Paul. "Our first contact with an extraterrestrial civilization, and they're freaking Jehovah's Witnesses."

"He hasn't handed us any tracts yet," I said.

"Just wait," whispered Gary. "The four of us are going to stagger onto the summit of this hill someday if this fucking storm ever lets up, exhausted, gasping for air that isn't there, frostbitten to shit and back, and this bug's going to haul out copies of the *Mantispid Watchtower*."

"Shhh," said Paul. "K'll hear us."

Just then the wind hit the tent so hard that we all tried digging our fingernails through the hyper-polymer floor to keep the tent from sliding off its precarious perch and down the mountain. If worst came to worst, we'd shout "Open!" at the top of our lungs, the smart tent fabric would fold away, and we'd roll out onto the slope in our thermskins and grab for our ice axes to self-arrest the slide. That was the theory. In fact, if the platform shifted or the spidersilk snapped, we'd almost certainly be airborne before we knew what hit us.

When we could hear again over the wind roar, Gary shouted, "If we unpeel from this platform, I'm going to cuss a fucking blue streak all the way down to impact on the glacier."

"Maybe that's the song that K's been talking about," said Paul, and sealed his flap.

Last note to the day: Mantispids snore.

On the afternoon of day three, Kanakaredes suddenly said, "My creche brother is also listening to a storm near your south pole at this very moment. But his surroundings are . . . more comfortable and secure than our tent."

I looked at the other two, and we all showed raised eyebrows.

"I didn't know you brought a phone with you on this climb, K," I said.

"I did not."

"Radio?" said Paul.

"No."

"Subcutaneous intergalactic *Star Trek* communicator?" said Gary. His sarcasm, much as his habit of chewing the nutrient bars too slowly, was beginning to get on my nerves after three days in this tent. I thought that perhaps the next time he was sarcastic or chewed slowly, I might just kill him.

K whistled ever so slightly. "No," he said. "I understood your climbers' tradition of bringing no communication devices on this expedition."

"Then how do you know that your . . . what was it, creche brother? . . . is in a storm down there?" asked Paul.

"Because he is my creche brother," said K. "We were born in the same hour. We are, essentially, the same genetic material."

"Twins," I said.

"So you have telepathy?" said Paul.

Kanakaredes shook his head, his proboscis almost brushing the flapping tent fabric. "Our scientists think that there is no such thing as telepathy. For any species."

"Then how—?" I began.

"My creche brother and I often resonate on the same frequencies to the song of the world and universe," said K in one of the longest sentences we'd heard from him. "Much as your identical twins do. We often share the same dreams."

Bugs dream. I made a mental note to record this factoid later.

"And does your creche brother know what you're feeling right now?" said Paul.

"I believe so."

"And what's that?" asked Gary, chewing far too slowly on an n-bar.

"Right now," said Kanakaredes, "it is fear."

Knife-edge ridge beyond Camp Three—about 23,700 feet

The fourth day dawned perfectly clear, perfectly calm.

We were packed and climbing across the traverse before the first rays of sunlight struck the ridgeline. It was cold as a witch's tit.

I mentioned that this part of the route was perhaps the most technically challenging of the climb—at least until we reached the actual summit pyramid—but it was also the most beautiful and exhilarating. You would have to see photos to appreciate the almost absurd steepness of this section of the ridge and even then it wouldn't allow you to *feel* the exposure. The northeast ridge just kept climbing in a series of swooping, knife-edged snow cornices, each side dropping away almost vertically.

As soon as we had moved onto the ridge, we looked back at the gigantic serac hanging above the trampled area of our Camp III perched on the edge of the ridge—the snow serac larger and more deformed and obviously unstable than ever after the heavy snows and howling winds of the last four days of storm—and we didn't have to say a word to one another to acknowledge how lucky we had been. Even Kanakaredes seemed grateful to get out of there.

Two hundred feet into the traverse and we went up and over the blade of the knife. The snowy ridgeline was so narrow here that we could—and did—straddle it for a minute as if swinging our legs over a very, very steep roofline.

Some roof. One side dropped down thousands of feet into what used to be China. Our left legs—three of Kanakaredes's—hung over what used to be Pakistan. Right around this point, climbers in the twentieth century used to joke about needing passports but seeing no border guards. In this CMG-era, a Sianking HK gunship or Indian hop-fighter could float up here anytime, hover fifty yards out, and blow us right off the ridge. None of us was worried about this. Kanakaredes's presence was insurance against that.

This was the hardest climbing yet, and our bug friend was working hard to keep up. Gary and Paul and I had discussed this the night before, whispering again while K was asleep, and we decided that this section was too steep for all of us to be roped together. We'd travel in two pairs. Paul was the obvious man to rope with K, although if either of them came off on this traverse, odds were overwhelming that the other would go all the way to the bottom with him. The same was true of Gary and me, climbing ahead of them. Still, it gave a very slight measure of insurance.

The sunlight moved down the slope, warming us, as we moved from one side of the knife-edge to the other, following the best line, trying to stay off the sections so steep that snow would not stick—avoiding it not just because of the pitch there, but because the rock was almost always loose and rotten—and hoping to get as far as we could before the warming sun loosened the snow enough to make our crampons less effective.

I loved the litany of the tools we were using: deadmen, pitons, pickets, ice screws, carabiners, jumar ascenders. I loved the precision of our movements, even with the labored breathing and dull minds that were a component of any exertion at almost eight thousand meters. Gary would kick-step his way out onto the wall of ice and snow and occasional rock, one cramponed boot at a time, secure on three points before dislodging his ice axe and slamming it in a few feet further on. I stood on a tiny platform I'd hacked out of the snow, belaying Gary until he'd moved out to the end of our two-hundred-foot section of line. Then he'd anchor his end of the line with a deadman, piton, picket, or ice screw, go on belay himself, and I would move off—kicking the crampon points into the snow-wall rising almost vertically to blue sky just fifty or sixty feet above me.

A hundred yards or so behind us, Paul and Kanakaredes were doing the same—Paul in the lead and K on belay, then K climbing and Paul belaying and resting until the bug caught up.

We might as well have been on different planets. There was no conversation. We used every ounce of breath to take our next gasping step, to concentrate on precise placement of our feet and ice axes.

A twentieth-century climbing team might have taken days to make this traverse, establishing fixed lines, retreating to their tents at Camp Three to eat and sleep, allowing other teams to break trail beyond the fixed ropes the next day. We did not have that luxury. We had to make this traverse in one try and keep moving up the ridge while the perfect weather lasted or we were screwed.

I loved it.

About five hours into the traverse, I realized that butterflies were fluttering all around me. I looked up toward Gary on belay two hundred feet ahead and above me. He was also watching butterflies—small motes of color dancing and weaving 23,000 feet above sea level. What the hell would Kanakaredes make of this? Would he think this was an everyday occurrence at this altitude? Well, perhaps it was. We humans weren't up here enough to know. I shook my head and continued shuffling my boots and slamming my ice axe up the impossible ridge.

The rays of the sun were horizontal in late afternoon when all four of us came off the knife-edge at the upper end of the traverse. The ridge was still heart-stoppingly steep there, but it had widened out so that we could stand on it as we looked back at our footprints on the snowy blade of the knife-edge. Even after all these years of climbing, I still found it hard to believe that we had been able to make those tracks.

"Hey!" shouted Gary. "I'm a fucking giant!" He was flapping his arms and staring toward Sinkiang and the Godwin-Austen Glacier miles below us.

Altitude's got him, I thought. *We'll have to sedate him, tie him in his sleeping bag, and drag him down the way we came like so much laundry.*

"Come on!" Gary shouted to me in the high, cold air. "Be a giant, Jake." He continued flapping his arms. I turned to look behind me and Paul and Karakaredes were also hopping up and down, carefully so as not to fall off the foot-wide ridgeline, shouting and flapping their arms. It was quite a sight to see K moving his mantisy forearms six ways at once, joints swiveling, boneless fingers waving like big grubs.

They've all lost it, I thought. *Oxygen deprivation lunacy.* Then I looked down and east.

Our shadows leaped out miles across the glacier and the neighboring mountains. I raised my arms. Lowered them. My shadow atop the dark line of ridge shadow raised and lowered shadow-arms that must have been ten miles tall.

We kept this up—jumping shouting, waving—until the sun set behind Broad Peak to the west and our giant selves disappeared forever.

Camp Six—narrow bench on snow dome below summit pyramid, 26,200 feet

No conversation or talk of listening to songs now. No jumping or shouting or waving. Not enough oxygen here to breathe or think, much less fuck around.

Almost no conversation the last three days or nights as we climbed the last of the broadening northeast ridge to where it ended at the huge snow dome, then climbed the snow dome itself. The weather stayed calm and clear—incredible for this late in the season. The snow was deep because of the storm that had pinned us down at Camp Three, but we took turns breaking trail—an exhausting job at 10,000 feet, literally mind-numbing above 25,000 feet.

At night, we didn't even bother merging our tents—just using our own segments like bivvy bags. We heated only one warm meal a day—super-nutrient soup on the single stove (we'd left the other behind just beyond the knife-edge traverse, along with everything else we didn't think we'd need in the last three or four days of climbing)—and chewed on cold n-bars at night before drifting off into a half-doze for a few cold, restless hours before stirring at three or four A.M. to begin climbing again by lamplight.

All of us humans had miserable headaches and high-altitude stupidity. Paul was in the worst shape—perhaps because of the frostbite scare way down during his first attempt at the traverse—and he was coughing heavily and moving sluggishly. Even K had slowed down, climbing mostly two-legged on this high stretch, and sometimes taking a minute or more before planting his feet.

Most Himalayan mountains have ridges that go all the way to the summit. Not K2. Not this northeast ridge. It ended at a bulging snow dome some two thousand feet below the summit.

We climbed the snow dome—slowly, stupidly, sluggishly, separately. No ropes or belays here. If anyone fell to his death, it was going to be a solitary fall. We did not care. At and above the legendary eight-thousand-meter line, you move into yourself and then—often—lose even yourself.

We had not brought oxygen, not even the light osmosis booster-mask perfected in the last decade. We had one of those masks—in case any of us became critically ill from pulmonary edema or worse—but we'd left the mask cached with the stove, most of the rope, and other extra supplies above Camp Four. It had seemed like a good idea at the time.

Now all I could think about was breathing. Every move—every step—took more breath than I had, more oxygen than my system owned. Paul seemed in even worse shape, although somehow he kept up. Gary was moving steadily, but sometimes he betrayed his headaches and confusion by movement or pause. He had vomited twice this morning before we moved out from Camp Six. At night, we startled awake after only a minute or two of half-sleep—gasping for air, clawing at our own chests, feeling as if something heavy were lying on us and someone were actively trying to suffocate us.

Something *was* trying to kill us here. Everything was. We were high in the Death Zone, and K2 did not care one way or the other if we lived or died.

The good weather had held, but high wind and storms were overdue. It was the end of August. Any day or night now we could be pinned down up here for weeks of unrelenting storms—unable to climb, unable to retreat. We could starve to death up here. I thought of the red panic button on the palmlog.

We had told Kanakaredes about the panic button while we heated soup at Camp Five. The mantispid had asked to see the extra palmlog with the emergency beacon. Then he had thrown the palmlog out the tent entrance, into the night, over the edge.

Gary had looked at our bug for a long minute and then grinned, extending his hand. K's foreleg had unfolded, the mantis part swiveling, and those three fingers had encircled Gary's hand and shaken it.

I had thought this was rather cool and heroic at the time. Now I just wished we had the goddamned panic button back.

We stirred, got dressed, and started heating water for our last meal shortly after 1:30 A.M. None of us could sleep anyway, and every extra hour we spent up here in the Death Zone meant more chance to die, more chance to fail. But we were moving so slowly that tugging our boots on seemed to take hours, adjusting our crampons took forever.

We moved away from the tents sometime after three A.M. We left the tents behind at Camp Six. If we survived the summit attempt, we'd be back.

It was unbelievably cold. Even the thermskins and smart outer parkas failed to make up the difference. If there had been a wind, we could not have continued.

We were now on what we called Direct Finish—the top or bust—although our original fallback plan had been to traverse across the face of K2 to the oldest route up the northwest Abruzzi Ridge if Direct Finish proved unfeasible. I think that all three of us had suspected we'd end up on the Abruzzi—most of our predecessors climbing the northeast ridge had ended up doing so, even the legendary Reinhold Messner, perhaps the greatest climber of the twentieth century, had been forced to change his route to the easier Abruzzi Ridge rather than suffer failure on the Direct Finish.

Well, by early afternoon of what was supposed to have been our summit day, Direct Finish now seems impossible and so does the traverse to the Abruzzi. The snow on the face of K2 is so deep that there is no hope of traversing through it to the Abruzzi Ridge. Avalanches hurtle down the face several times an hour. And above us—even deeper snow. We're fucked.

The day had started well. Above the almost vertical snowdome on which we'd hacked out a wide enough bench to lodge Camp Six, rose a huge snowfield that snaked up and up toward the black, star-filled sky until it became a wall. We climbed slowly, agonizingly, up the snowfield, leaving separate tracks, thinking separate thoughts. It was getting light by the time we reached the end of the snow ramp.

Where the snowfield ended a vertical ice cliff began and rose at least 150 feet straight up. Literally fucking vertical. The four of us stood there in the morning light, three of us rubbing our goggles, looking stupidly at the cliff. We'd known it was there. We'd had no idea what a bitch it was going to be.

"I'll do the lead," gasped Paul. He could barely walk.

He free-climbed the fucker in less than an hour, slamming in pitons and screws and tying on the last of our rope. When the three of us climbed slowly, stupidly up to join him, me bringing up the rear just behind K, Paul was only semiconscious.

Above the ice cliff rose a steep rock band. It was so steep that snow couldn't cling there. The rock looked rotten—treacherous—the kind of fragile crap that any sane climber would traverse half a day to avoid.

There would be no traverse today. Any attempt to shift laterally on the face here would almost certainly trigger an avalanche in the soft slabs of snow overlaying old ice.

"I'll lead," said Gary, still looking up at the rock band. He was holding his head with both hands. I knew that Gary always suffered the worst of the Death Zone headaches that afflicted all three of us. For four or five days and nights now, I knew, Gary's every word and breath had been punctuated by slivers of steel pain behind the eyes.

I nodded and helped Paul to his feet. Gary began to climb the lower strata of crumbling rock.

We reach the end of the rock by midafternoon. The wind is rising. A spume of spindrift blows off the near-vertical snow and ice above us. We cannot see the summit. Above a narrow coloir that rises like a chimney to frigid hell, the summit-pyramid snowfield begins. We're somewhere above 27,000 feet.

K2 is 28,250 feet high.

That last twelve hundred feet might as well be measured in light-years.

"I'll break trail up the coloir," I hear myself say. The others don't even nod, merely wait for me to begin. Kanakaredes is leaning on his ice axe in a posture I've not seen before.

My first step up the coloir sends me into snow above my knees. This is impossible. I would weep now, except that the tears would freeze to the inside of my goggles and blind me. It is impossible to take another step up this steep fucking gully. I can't even breathe. My head pounds so terribly that my vision dances and blurs and no amount of wiping my goggles will clear it.

I lift my ice axe, slam it three feet higher, and lift my right leg. Again. Again.

Summit pyramid snowfield above the coloir, somewhere around 27,800 feet

Late afternoon. It will be almost dark when we reach the summit. *If* we reach the summit.

Everything depends upon the snow that rises above us toward the impossibly dark blue sky. If the snow is firm—nowhere as mushy and deep as the thigh-high soup I broke trail through all the way up the coloir—then we have a chance, although we'll be descending in the dark.

But if it's deep snow . . .

"I'll lead," said Gary, shifting his small summit-pack on his back and slogging slowly up to replace me in the lead. There is a rock band here at the top of the narrow coloir, and he will be stepping off it either into or onto the snow. If the surface is firm, we'll all move *onto* it, using our crampons to kick-step our way up the last couple of hours of climb to the summit—although we still cannot see the summit from here. *Please, God, let it be firm.*

I try to look around me. Literally beneath my feet is a drop to the impossibly distant knife-edge, far below that the ridge where we put Camp Two, miles and miles lower the curving, rippled river of Godwin-Austen and a dim memory of base camp and of living things—lichen, crows, a clump of grass where the glacier was melting. On either side stretches the Karakoram, white peaks thrusting up like fangs, distant summits merging into the Himalayan peaks, and one lone peak—I'm too stupid to even guess which one—standing high and solitary against the sky. The red hills of China burn in the thick haze of breathable atmosphere a hundred miles to the north.

"OK," says Gary, stepping off the rock onto the snowfield.

He plunges in soft snow up to his waist.

Somehow Gary finds enough breath to hurl curses at the snow, at any and all gods who would put such deep snow here. He lunges another step up and forward.

The snow is even deeper. Gary founders almost up to his armpits. He slashes at the snowfield with his ice axe, batters it with his overmittens. The snowfield and K2 ignore him.

I go to both knees on the pitched rock band and lean on my ice axe, not caring if my sobs can be heard by the others or if my tears will freeze my eyelids open. The expedition is over.

Kanakaredes slowly pulls his segmented body up the last ten feet of the coloir, past Paul where Paul is retching against a boulder, past me where I am kneeling, onto the last of the solid surface before Gary's sliding snowpit.

"I will lead for a while," says Kanakaredes. He sets his ice axe into his harness. His prothorax shifts lower. His hind legs come down and out. His arms—forelegs—rotate down and forward.

Kanakaredes thrusts himself into the steep snowfield like an Olympic swimmer diving off the starting block. He passes Gary where Gary lies armpit deep in the soft snow.

The bug—*our* bug—flails and batters the snow with his forearms, parts it with his cupped fingers, smashes it down with his armored upper body segment, swims through the snow with all six legs paddling.

He can't possibly keep this up. It's impossible. Nothing living has that much energy and will. It is seven or eight hundred near-vertical feet to the summit.

K swims-kicks-fights his way fifteen feet up the slope. Twenty-five. Thirty.

Getting to my feet, feeling my temples pounding in agony, sensing invisible climbers around me, ghosts hovering in the Death Zone fog of pain and confusion, I step past Gary and start postholing upward, following K's lead, struggling and swimming up and through the now-broken barrier of snow.

Summit of K2, 28,250 feet

We step onto the summit together, arm in arm. All four of us. The final summit ridge is just wide enough to allow this.

Many eight-thousand-meter-peak summits have overhanging cornices. After all this effort, the climber sometimes takes his or her final step to triumph and falls for a mile or so. We don't know if K2 is corniced. Like many of these other climbers, we're too exhausted to care. Kanakaredes can no longer stand or walk after breaking trail through the snowfield for more than six hundred feet. Gary and I carry him the last hundred feet or so, our arms under his mantis arms. I am shocked to discover that he weighs almost nothing. All that energy, all that spirit, and K probably weighs no more than a hundred pounds.

The summit is not corniced. We do not fall.

The weather has held, although the sun is setting. Its last rays warm us through our parkas and thermskins. The sky is a blue deeper than cerulean, much deeper than sapphire, incomparably deeper than aquamarine. Perhaps this shade of blue has no word to describe it.

We can see to the curve of the earth and beyond. Two peaks are visible above that curving horizon, their summit icefields glowing orange in the sunset, a great distance to the northeast, probably somewhere in Chinese Turkistan. To the south lies the entire tumble of overlapping peaks and winding glaciers that is the Karakoram. I make out the perfect peak that is Nanga Parbat—Gary, Paul, and I climbed that six years ago—and closer, the Gasherbrum. At our feet, literally at our feet, Broad Peak. Who would have thought that its summit looked so wide and flat from above?

The four of us are all sprawled on the narrow summit, two feet from the sheer drop-off on the north. My arms are still around Karakaredes, ostensibly propping him up but actually propping both of us up.

The mantispid clicks, hisses, and squeaks. He shakes his beak and tries again. "I am . . . sorry," he gasps, the air audibly hissing in and out of his beak nostrils. "I ask . . . traditionally, what do we do now? Is there a ceremony for this moment? A ritual required?"

I look at Paul, who seems to be recovering from his earlier inertia. We both look at Gary.

"Try not to fuck up and die," says Gary between breaths. "More climbers die during the descent than on the way up."

Kanakaredes seems to be considering this. After a minute he says, "Yes, but here on the summit, there must be some ritual. . . ."

"Hero photos," gasps Paul. "Gotta . . . have . . . hero photos."

Our alien nods. "Did . . . anyone . . . bring an imaging device? A camera? I did not."

Gary, Paul, and I look at each other, pat our parka pockets, and then start laughing. At this altitude, our laughter sounds like three sick seals coughing.

"Well, no hero photos," says Gary. "Then we have to haul the flags out. Always bring a flag to the summit, that's our human motto." This extended speech makes Gary so light-headed that he has to put his head between his raised knees for a minute.

"I have no flag," says Kanakaredes. "The Listeners have never had a flag." The sun is setting in earnest now, the last rays shining between a line of peaks to the west, but the reddish-orange light glows brightly on our stupid, smiling faces and mittens and goggles and ice-crusted parkas.

"We didn't bring a flag either," I say.

"This is good," says K. "So there is nothing else we need to do?"

"Just get down alive," says Paul.

We rise together, weaving a bit, propping one another up, retrieve our ice axes from where we had thrust them into the glowing summit snow, and begin retracing our steps down the long snowfield into shadow.

Godwin-Austin Glacier, about 17,300 feet

It took us only four and a half days to get down, and that included a day of rest at our old Camp Three on the low side of the knife-edge traverse.

The weather held the whole time. We did not get back to our high camp—Camp Six below the ice wall—until after three A.M. after our successful summit day, but the lack of wind had kept our tracks clear even in lamplight, and no one slipped or fell or suffered frostbite.

We moved quickly after that, leaving just after dawn the next day to get to Camp Four on the upper end of the knife-edge before nightfall . . . and before the gods of K2 changed their minds and blew up a storm to trap us in the Death Zone.

The only incident on the lower slopes of the mountain happened—oddly enough—on a relatively easy stretch of snow slope below Camp Two. The four of us were picking our way down the slope, unroped, lost in our own thoughts and in the not-unpleasant haze of exhaustion so common near the end of a climb, when K just came loose—perhaps he tripped over one of his own hindlegs, although he denied that later—and ended up on his stomach—or at least the bottom of his upper shell, all six legs spraddled, ice axe flying free, starting a slide that would have been harmless enough for the first hundred yards or so if it had not been for the drop off that fell away to the glacier still a thousand feet directly below.

Luckily, Gary was about a hundred feet ahead of the rest of us and he dug in his axe, looped a line once around himself and twice around the axe, timed K's slide perfectly, and then threw himself on his belly out onto the ice slope, his reaching hand grabbing Kanakaredes's three fingers as slick as a pair of aerial trapeze partners. The rope snapped taut, the axe held its place, man and mantispid swung two and a half times like the working end of a pendulum, and that was the end of that drama. K had to make it the rest of the way to the glacier without an ice axe the next day, but he managed all right. And we now know how a bug shows embarrassment—his occipital ridges blush a dark orange.

Off the ridge at last, we roped up for the glacier but voted unanimously to descend it by staying close to the east face of K2. The earlier snowstorm had hidden all the crevasses and we had heard or seen no avalanches in the past seventy-two hours. There were far fewer crevasses near the face, but an avalanche could catch us anywhere on the glacier. Staying near the face carried its own risks, but it would also get us down the ice and out of avalanche danger in half the time it would take to probe for crevasses down the center of the glacier.

We were two-thirds of the way down—the bright red tents of Base Camp clearly in sight out on the rock beyond the ice—when Gary said, "Maybe we should talk about this Olympus Mons deal, K."

"Yes," click-hissed our bug, "I have been looking forward to discussing this plan and I hope that perhaps—"

We heard it then before we saw it. Several freight trains seemed to be bearing down on us from above, from the face of K2.

All of us froze, trying to see the snowplume trail of the avalanche, hoping against hope that it would come out onto the glacier far behind us. It came off the face and across the *bergeschrund* a quarter of a mile directly above us and picked up speed, coming directly at us. It looked like a white tsunami. The roar was deafening.

"Run!" shouted Gary and we all took off downhill, not worrying if there were bottomless crevasses directly in front of us, not caring at that point, just trying against all logic to outrun a wall of snow and ice and boulders rolling toward us at sixty miles per hour.

I remember now that we were roped with the last of our spidersilk—sixty-foot intervals—the lines clipped to our climbing harnesses. It made no difference to Gary, Paul, and me since we were running flat out and in the same direction and at about the same speed, but I have seen mantispids move at full speed since that day—using all six legs, their hands forming into an extra pair of flat feet—and I know now that K could have shifted into high gear and run four times as fast as the rest of us. Perhaps he could have beaten the avalanche since just the south edge of its wave caught us. Perhaps.

He did not try. He did not cut the rope. He ran with us.

The south edge of the avalanche caught us and lifted us and pulled us under and snapped the unbreakable spidersilk climbing rope and tossed us up and then submerged us again and swept us all down into the crevasse field at the bottom of the glacier and separated us forever.

Washington, D.C.

Sitting here in the secretary of state's waiting room three months after that day, I've had time to think about it.

All of us—everyone on the planet, even the bugs—have been preoccupied in the past couple of months as the Song has begun and increased in complexity and beauty. Oddly enough, it's not that distracting, the Song. We go about our business. We work and talk and eat and watch HDTV and make love and sleep, but always there now—always in the background whenever one wants to listen—is the Song.

It's unbelievable that we've never heard it before this.

No one calls them bugs or mantispids or the Listeners anymore. Everyone, in every language, calls them the Bringers of the Song.

Meanwhile, the Bringers keep reminding us that they did not *bring* the Song, only taught us how to listen to it.

I don't know how or why I survived when none of the others did. The theory is that one can swim along the surface of a snow avalanche, but the reality was that none of us had the slightest chance to try. That wide wall of snow and rock just washed over us and pulled us down and spat out only me, for reasons known, perhaps, only to K2 and most probably not even to it.

They found me naked and battered more than three-quarters of a mile from where we had started running from the avalanche. They never found Gary, Paul, or Kanakaredes.

The emergency CMGs were there within three minutes—they must have been poised to intervene all that time—but after twenty hours of deep probing and sonar searching, just when the marines and the bureaucrats were ready to lase away the whole lower third of the glacier if necessary to recover my friends' bodies, it was Speaker Aduradake—Kanakaredes's father *and* mother, it turned out—who forbade it.

"Leave them wherever they are," he instructed the fluttering UN bureaucrats and frowning marine colonels. "They died together on your world and should remain together within the embrace of your world. Their part of the song is joined now."

And the Song began—or at least was first heard—about one week later.

A male aide to the secretary comes out, apologizes profusely for my having to wait—Secretary Bright Moon was with the president—and shows me into the secretary of state's office. The aide and I stand there waiting.

I've seen football games played in smaller areas than this office.

The secretary comes in through a different door a minute later and leads me over to two couches facing each other rather than to the uncomfortable chair near her huge desk. She seats me across from her, makes sure that I don't want any coffee or other refreshment, nods away her aide, commiserates with me again on the death of my dear friends (she had been there at the memorial service at which the president had spoken), chats with me for another minute about how amazing life is now with the Song connecting all of us, and then questions me for a few minutes, sensitively, solicitously, about my physical recovery (complete), my state of mind (shaken but improving), my generous stipend from the government (already invested), and my plans for the future.

"That's the reason I asked for this meeting," I say. "There was that promise of climbing Olympus Mons."

She stares at me.

"On Mars," I add needlessly.

Secretary Betty Willard Bright Moon nods and sits back in the cushions. She brushes some invisible lint from her navy blue skirt. "Ah, yes," she says, her voice still pleasant but holding some hint of that flintiness I remember so well from our Top of the World meeting. "The Bringers have confirmed that they intend to honor that promise."

I wait.

"Have you decided who your next climbing partners will be?" she asked, taking out an obscenely expensive and micron-thin platinum palmlog as if she is going to take notes herself to help facilitate this whim of mine.

"Yeah," I said.

Now it was the secretary's turn to wait.

"I want Kanakaredes's brother," I say. "His . . . creche brother."

Betty Willard Bright Moon's jaw almost drops open. I doubt very much if she's reacted this visibly to a statement in her last thirty years of professional negotiating, first as a take-no-prisoners Harvard academic and most recently as secretary of state. "You're serious," she says.

"Yes."

"Anyone else other than this particular bu—Bringer?"

"No one else."

"And you're sure he even exists?"

"I'm sure."

"How do you know if he wants to risk his life on a Martian volcano?" she asks, her poker face back in place. "Olympus Mons is taller than K2, you know. And it's probably more dangerous."

I almost, not quite, smile at this news flash. "He'll go," I say.

Secretary Bright Moon makes a quick note in her palmlog and then hesitates. Even though her expression is perfectly neutral now, I know that she is trying to decide whether to ask a question that she might not get the chance to ask later.

Hell, knowing that question was coming and trying to decide how to answer it is the reason I didn't come to visit her a month ago, when I decided to do this thing. But then I remembered Kanakaredes's answer when we asked him why the bugs had come all this way to visit us. He had read his Mallory and he had understood Gary, Paul, and me—and something about the human race—that this woman never would.

She makes up her mind to ask her question.

"Why . . . ," she begins. "Why do you want to climb it?"

Despite everything that's happened, despite knowing that she'll never understand, despite knowing what an asshole she'll always consider me after this moment, I have to smile before I give her the answer.

"Because it's there."

Here's a pretty good list of Ursula Le Guin's honors: she's won numerous Nebulas and Hugos, also a National Book Award, the Harold D. Versell Memorial Award from the American Academy of Arts and Letters, a Pushcart Prize, the World Fantasy Award for Life Achievement, and a Newbery Honor.

It's been said she's sf's most "academically" honored writer, which sounds faintly solicitous. How about this instead: she's a marvelous science fiction writer—one of the finest ever—who happens to be recognized outside the field.

Still not good enough? What about: she's a great writer, period, who helped to solidify the achievements of the New Wave by doing nothing more than writing great stories.

The Building

URSULA K. LE GUIN

*

On Qoq there are two rational species. The Adaqo are stocky, greenish-tan-colored humanoids who, after a period of EEPT (explosive expansion of population and technology) four to five thousand years ago, barely survived the ensuing ecocastrophe. They have since lived on a modest scale, vastly reduced in numbers and more interested in survival than dominion.

The Aq are taller and a little greener than the Adaqo. The two species diverged from a common simioid ancestor, and are quite similar, but cannot interbreed. Like all species on Qoq, except a few pests and the insuperable and indifferent bacteria, the Aq suffered badly during and after the Adaqo EEPT.

Before it, the two species had not been in contact. The Aq inhabited the southern continent only. As the Adaqo population escalated, they spread out over the three land masses of the northern hemisphere, and as they conquered their world, they incidentally conquered the Aq.

The Adaqo attempted to use the Aq as slaves for domestic or factory work, but failed. The historical evidence is shaky, but it seems the Aq, though unaggressive, simply do not take orders from anybody. During the height of the EEPT, the most expansive Adaqo empires pursued a policy of slaughtering the "primitive" and "unteachable" Aq in the name of progress. Less bloody-minded civilizations of the equatorial zone merely pushed the remnant Aq populations into the deserts and barely habitable canebrakes of the coast. There a thousand or so Aq survived the destruction and final crash of the planet's life-web.

Descent from this limited genetic source may help explain the prevalence of certain traits among the Aq, but the cultural expression of these tendencies is inexplicable in its uniformity. We don't know much about what they were like before the crash, but their reputed refusal to carry out the other species' orders might imply that they were already, as it were, working under orders of their own.

As for the Adaqo, their numbers have risen from perhaps a hundred thousand survivors of the crash to about two million, mostly on the central north and the south continents. They live in small cities, towns, and farms, and carry on agriculture and commerce; their technology is efficient but modest, limited both by the exhaustion of their world's resources and by strict religious sanctions.

The present-day Aq number about forty thousand, all on the south continent. They live as gatherers and fishers, with some limited, casual agriculture. The only one of their domesticated animals to survive the die-offs is the boos, a clever creature descended from pack-hunting carnivores. The Aq hunted with boos when there were animals to hunt. Since the crash, they use the boos to carry or haul light loads, as companions, and in hard times as food.

Aq villages are movable; their houses, from time immemorial, have consisted of fabric domes stretched on a frame of light poles or canes, easy to set up, dismantle, and transport. The tall cane which grows in the swampy lakes of the desert and all along the coasts of the equatorial zone of the southern continent is their staple; they gather the young shoots for food, spin and weave the fiber into cloth, and make rope, baskets, and tools from the stems. When they have used up all the cane in a region they pick up the village and move on. The caneplants regenerate from the root system in a few years.

They have kept pretty much to the desert-and-canebrake habitat enforced upon them by the Adaqo in earlier millennia. Some, however, camp around outside Adaqo towns and engage in a little barter and filching. The Adaqo trade with them for their fine canvas and baskets, and tolerate their thievery to a surprising degree.

Indeed the Adaqo attitude to the Aq is hard to define. Wariness is part of it; a kind of unease that is not suspicion or distrust; a watchfulness that, surprisingly, stops short of animosity or contempt, and may even become conciliating, as if the uneasiness were located in the Adaqo conscience.

It is even harder to say what the Aq think of the Adaqo. They communicate in a pidgin or jargon containing elements from both Adaqo and Aq languages, but it appears that no individual ever learns the other species' language. The two species seem to have settled on coexistence without relationship. They have nothing to do with each other except for these occasional, slightly abrasive contacts at the edges of Adaqo settlements—and a certain limited, strange collaboration having to do with what I can only call the specific obsession of the Aq.

I am not comfortable with the phrase "specific obsession," but "cultural instinct" is worse.

At about two and a half or three years old, Aq babies begin building. Whatever comes into their little greeny-bronze hands that can possibly serve as a block or brick they pile up into "houses." The Aq use the same word for these miniature structures as for the fragile cane-and-canvas domes they live in, but there is no resemblance except that both are roofed enclosures with a door. The children's "houses" are rectangular, flat-roofed, and always made of solid, heavy materials. They are not imitations of Adaqo houses, or only at a very great remove, since most of these children have never seen an Adaqo building or a representation of one.

It is hard to believe that they imitate one another with such unanimity that they never vary the plan; but it is harder to believe that their building style, like that of insects, is innate.

As the children get older and more skillful they build larger constructions, though still no more than knee-high, with passages, courtyards, and sometimes towers. Many children spend all their free time gathering rocks or making mud bricks and building "houses." They do not populate their buildings with toy people or animals or tell stories about them. They just build them, with evident pleasure and satisfaction. By the age of six or seven some children begin to leave off building, but others go on working together with other children, often under the guidance of interested adults, to make "houses" of considerable complexity, though still not large enough for anyone to live in. The children do not play in them.

When the village picks up and moves to a new gathering-ground or canebrake, these children leave their constructions behind without any sign of distress, and as soon as they are settled begin building again, often cannibalizing stones or bricks from the "houses" of a previous generation left on the site. Popular gathering sites are marked by dozens or hundreds of solidly built miniature ruins, populated only by the joint-legged gikoto of the marshes or the little ratlike hikiqi of the desert.

No such ruins have been found in areas where the Aq lived before the Adaqo conquest—an indication that their propensity to build was less strong, or didn't exist, before the conquest or before the crash.

Two or three years after their ceremonies of adolescence some of the young people, those who went on building "houses" until they reached puberty, will go on their first stone faring.

A stone faring sets out once a year from the Aq territories. The complete journey takes from two to three years, after which the travelers return to their natal village for five or six years. Some Aq never go stone faring, others go once, some go several or many times in their life.

The route of the stone farings is to the coast of Riqim, on the northeast continent, and back to the Mediro, a rocky plateau far inland from the southernmost canebrakes of the great south continent.

The Aq stone farers gather in spring, coming overland or by caneraft from their various villages to Gatbam, a small port near the equator on the west coast of the south continent. There a fleet of cane-and-canvas sailboats awaits them. The sailors and navigators are all Adaqo, most of them from towns of the northwest coast. They are professional sailors, mostly fishermen; some of them "sail the faring" every year for decades. The Aq pilgrims have nothing to pay them with, arriving with provisions for the journey but nothing else. While at Riqim, the Adaqo sailors will net and salt fish from those rich waters, a catch which makes their journey profitable. But they never go to fish off Riqim except with the stone-faring fleet.

The journey takes several weeks. The voyage north is the dangerous one, made early in the year so that the return voyage, carrying the cargo, may be made at the optimal time. Now and then boats or even whole fleets are lost in the wild tropical storms of that wide sea.

As soon as they disembark on the stony shores of Riqim, the Aq get to work. Under the direction of senior stone farers, the novices set up domed tents, store their sparse provisions, take up the tools left there by the last pilgrimage, and climb the steep green cliffs to the quarries.

Riqimite is a lustrous, fine-textured, greenish stone with a tendency to cleave along a plane. It can be sawed in blocks or split into stone "planks" or smaller "tiles" and even into sheets so thin they are translucent. Though relatively light, it is stone, and a ten-meter canvas sailboat can't carry great quantities of it; so the stone farers carefully gauge the amount they quarry. They roughshape the blocks at Riqim and even do some of the fine cutting, so that the boats carry as little waste as possible. They work fast, since they want to start home in the calm season around the solstice. When their work is complete they run up a flag on a high pole on the cliffs to signal the fleet, which comes in boat by boat over the next few days. They load the stone aboard under the tubs of salted fish and set sail back south.

The boats put in at various Adaqo ports, usually the crew's home port, to unload and sell their fish; then they all sail on several hundred kilometers down the coast to Gazt, a long, shallow harbor in the hot marshlands south of the canebrake country. There the sailors help the Aq unload the stone. They receive no payment for or profit from this part of the trip. I asked a shipmaster who had "sailed the faring" many times why she and her sailors were willing to make the trip to Gazt. She shrugged. "It's part of the agreement," she said, evidently not having thought much about it, and after thinking, added, "Be an awful job to drag that stone overland through the marshes."

Before the boats have sailed halfway back to the harbor mouth, the Aq have begun loading the stone onto wheeled flatbed carts left on the docks of Gazt by the last stone faring.

Then they get into harness and haul these carts five hundred kilometers inland and three thousand meters upward.

They go at most three or four kilometers a day. They encamp before evening and fan out from the trails to forage and set snares for hiqiki, since by now their supplies are low. The cart train tends to follow the least recently used of the several winding trails, because the hunting and gathering will be better along it.

During the sea voyages and at Riqim the mood of the stone farers tends to be solemn and tense. They are not sailors, and the labor at the quarries is hard and driven. Hauling carts by shoulder-harness is certainly not light work either, but the pilgrims take it merrily; they talk and joke while hauling, share their food and sit talking around their campfires, and behave like any group of people engaged willingly in an arduous joint enterprise.

They discuss which path to take, and wheel-mending techniques, and so on. But when I went with them I never heard them talk in the larger sense about what they were doing, their journey's goal.

All the paths finally have to surmount the cliffs at the edge of the plateau. As they come up onto the level after that terrible last grade, the stone farers stop and gaze to the southeast. One after another the long, flat carts laden with dusty stone buck and jerk up over the rim and stop. The haulers stand in harness, gazing silent at the Building.

After a thousand years or so of the long, slow recovery of the shattered ecosystem, enough Aq began to have enough food to have enough energy for activities beyond forage and storage. It was then, when bare survival was still chancy, that they began the stone faring. So few, in such an inimical world, the atmosphere damaged, the great cycles of life not yet reestablished in the poisoned and despoiled oceans, the lands full of bones, ghosts, ruins, dead forests, deserts of salt, of sand, of chemical waste—how did the inhabitants of such a world think of undertaking such a task? How did they know the stone they wanted was at Riqim?

How did they know where Riqim was? Did they originally make their way there somehow without Adaqo boats and navigators? The origins of the stone faring are absolutely mysterious, but no more mysterious than its object. All we know is that every stone in the Building comes from the quarries of Riqim, and that the Aq have been building it for over three thousand, perhaps four thousand years.

It is immense, of course. It covers many acres and contains thousands of rooms, passages, and courts. It is certainly one of the largest edifices, perhaps the largest single one, on any world. And yet declarations of size, counts and measures, comparisons and superlatives, are meaningless, the fact being that a technology such as that of contemporary Earth, or the ancient Adaqo, could have built a building ten times bigger in ten years.

It is possible that the ever-increasing vastness of the Building is a metaphor or illustration of precisely such a moral enormity.

Or its size may be purely, simply, a result of its age. The oldest sections, far inside its outermost walls, show no indication that they were—or were not—seen as the beginning of something immense. They are exactly like the Aq children's "houses" on a larger scale. All the rest of the Building has been added on, year by year, to this modest beginning, in much the same style. After perhaps some centuries the builders began to add stories onto the flat roofs of the early Building, but have never gone above four stories, except for towers and pinnacles and the airy barrel-domes that reach a height of perhaps sixty meters. The great bulk of the Building is no more than five to six meters high. Inevitably it has kept growing outward laterally, by way of ells and wings and joining arcades and courtyards, until it covers so vast an area that from a distance it looks like a fantastic terrain, a low mountain landscape all in silvery green stone.

Although not dwarfed like the children's structures, curiously enough the Building is not quite full scale, taking the average height of an Aq as measure. The ceilings are barely high enough to allow them to stand straight, and they must stoop to pass through the doors.

No part of the Building is ruined or in disrepair, though occasional earthquakes shake the Mediro plateau. Damaged areas are repaired annually, or furnished stone to rebuild with.

The work is fine, careful, sure, and delicate. No material is used but riqimite, mortised and tenoned like wood, or set in exquisitely fitted blocks and courses. The indoor surfaces are mostly finished satin smooth, the outer faces left in contrasting degrees of roughness and smoothness. There is no carving or ornamentation other than thin moldings or incised lines repeating and outlining the architectural shapes.

Windows are unglazed stone lattices or pierced stone sheets cut so thin as to be translucent. The repetitive rectangular designs of the latticework are elegantly proportioned; a ratio of four to five runs through many though not all of the Building's rooms and apertures. Doors are thin stone slabs so well balanced and pivoted that they swing lightly and smoothly open and shut. There are no furnishings.

Empty rooms, empty corridors, miles of corridors, endlessly similar, stairways, ramps, courtyards, roof terraces, delicate towers, vistas over the roofs of roof beyond roof, tower beyond tower, dome beyond dome to the far distance; high rooms lighted by great lacework windows or only by the dim, greenish, mottled translucency of windowpanes of stone; corridors that lead to other corridors, other rooms, stairs, ramps, courtyards, corridors. . . . Is it a maze, a labyrinth? Yes, inevitably; but is that what it was built to be?

Is it beautiful? Yes, in a way, wonderfully beautiful; but is that what it was built to be?

The Aq are a rational species. Answers to these questions must come from them. The troubling thing is that they have many different answers, none of which seems quite satisfying to them or anyone else.

In this they resemble any reasonable being who does an unreasonable thing and justifies it with reasons. War, for example. My species has a great many good reasons for making war, though none of them is as good as the reason for not making war. Our most rational and scientific justifications—for instance, that we are an aggressive species—are perfectly circular: we make war because we make war. This is not really satisfying to the reasonable mind. Our justifications for making a particular war (such as: our people must have more land and more wealth, or: our people must have more power, or: our people must obey our deity's orders to crush the heinous sacrilegious infidel) all come down to the same thing: we must make war because we must. We have no choice. We have no freedom. This is not ultimately satisfactory to the reasoning mind, which desires freedom.

In the same way the efforts of the Aq to explain or justify their building and their Building all invoke a necessity which doesn't seem all that necessary and use reasons which meet themselves coming round. We go stone faring because we have always done it. We go to Riqim because the best stone is there. The Building is on the Mediro because the ground's good and there's room for it there. The Building is a great undertaking, which our children can look forward to and our finest men and women can work together on. The stone faring brings people from all our villages together. We were only a poor scattered people in the old days, but now the Building shows that there is a great vision in us. —All these reasons make sense but don't quite convince, don't satisfy.

Perhaps the questions should be asked of those Aq who never have gone stone faring. They don't themselves question the stone faring. They speak of the stone farers as people doing something brave, difficult, worthy, perhaps sacred. So why have you never gone yourself?—Well, I never felt the need to. People who go, they have to go, they're called to it.

What about the other people, the Adaqo? What do they think about this immense structure, certainly the greatest enterprise and achievement on their world at this time? Very little, evidently. Even the sailors of the stone faring never go up onto the Mediro and know nothing about the Building except that it is there and is very large. Adaqo of the northwest continent know it only as rumor, fable, travelers' tales—the Palace of the Mediro on the Great South Continent. Some tales say the King of the Aq lives there in unimaginable splendor; others that it is a tower taller than the mountains, in which eyeless monsters dwell; others that it is a maze where the unwary traveler is lost in endless corridors full of bones and ghosts; others say that the winds blowing through it moan in huge chords like a vast aeolian harp, which can be heard for hundreds of miles; and so on. To the Adaqo it is a legend, like their own legends of the Ancient Times when their mighty ancestors flew in the air and drank rivers dry and turned forests into stone and built towers taller than the sky, and so on. Fairy tales.

Now and then an Aq who has been stone faring will say something different about the Building. If asked about it, some of them reply: "It is for the Adaqo."

And indeed the Building is better proportioned to the short stature of the Adaqo than to the tall Aq. The Adaqo, if they ever went there, could walk through the corridors and doorways upright.

An old woman of Katas, who had been five times a stone farer, was the first who gave me that answer.

"For the Adaqo?" I said, taken aback. "But why?"

"Because of the old days."

"But they never go there."

"It isn't finished," she said.

"A retribution?" I asked, puzzling at it. "A recompense?"

"They need it," she said.

"The Adaqo need it, but you don't?"

"No," the old woman said with a smile. "We build it. We don't need it."

There's a heck of a story behind this one. Seems Laura Whitton was attending Jeanne Cavelos's Odyssey fiction writers workshop in New Hampshire in the summer of 2000, when Dan Simmons was writer in residence. At the same time, I was bugging the hell out of Dan to do a story for this book. When Dan read what Laura was working on he got in touch with me and asked if I'd be willing to look at it. Sure! I said, not knowing what to expect. What I didn't quite expect, especially from an unpublished writer, was something this good.

What became "Froggies" needed a little work, but Laura Whitton was more than up to the task. I'm proud to share this "discovery" with Dan—and if Whitton goes on to do more great things, there's only one person who can take any kind of credit, and it ain't me or Dan.

Froggies

LAURA WHITTON

*

Jo-ann paced the length of the courtroom, vast with its marble pillars and flags of state. She knew she should sit down, next to Amanda. Sit calmly, professionally, to hear the verdict. But it was all she could do to keep quiet, not to rush up to the man across the aisle and yell in his face. She heard it in her mind, saw herself pounding his shoulder for emphasis, saw fear in his eyes.

She twitched when she felt a hand on her sleeve. Amanda tugged her down. "Jo-ann, there's nothing you can do at this point. We've given them everything we've got."

At that moment, the deep gong sounded, and a quiet rustling filled the room as people shuffled their papers, switched on recording devices, and made last-minute notes. Jo-ann couldn't help glaring at the man on the other side of the aisle. She realized he was focused on a door at the back of the room. Turning, she saw the justices enter. Five people, solemn in black robes, filed into the courtroom. They took their seats before the assembled crowd. Jo-ann could read nothing in their expressions. A second ringing of the gong, and the chief justice stood.

"Before us today stand two claimants to the exploitation rights of the planet Minerva. The Hugonaut Corporation argues right of first discovery, while the Department of Xenoanthropology argues prior right of indigenous population. This board of inquiry has met to review the arguments of both parties and to determine the status of the planet. The facts are not in dispute. StarShip *Minerva*, registry Port Juno, entered orbit around the third planet of Epsilon 37 on the sixty-first day of Year 652. Upon her return to human-controlled space, the captain reported the discovery of a life-inhabiting planet as required by the Department of Biological Resources. She submitted the name of the planet as *Minerva*. On behalf of her employer, the Hugonaut Corporation, she registered a claim for the exploitation rights of the planet. Upon reviewing this claim, BioResources referred the matter to the Department of Xenoanthropology.

"Based upon the possibility of sentience among the native life-forms, Xenoanthro determined to send its own expedition to the planet. That expedition arrived on the fifth day of Year 654, established a base upon the planet, and spent the remainder of the year studying the local life-forms. Attention was focused on the largest terrestrial species, and based upon evidence of rudimentary tool use, Xenoanthro now argues the sentience of the species. However, the Hugonaut Corporation notes that said tool use exhibits less complexity than the documented use by terran nonhuman primates. Further, the Hugonaut Corporation notes that of all the efforts to establish communication with the species, none have generated conclusive results."

Jo-ann looked across the aisle and saw the smug smile on the Hugonaut lawyer's face. She gripped the table edge harder.

"This board has carefully reviewed the evidence. While we concede that members of the local species do utilize stone tools in a limited way, we are troubled by the failure to establish communications. The individuals studied by Xenoanthro did not, in our opinion, respond in any clear way to the communication efforts of the team. This board cannot impute intelligence to a race whose members refuse to interact with, or even acknowledge the communication efforts of, another intelligent species. Therefore, the claim of the Department of Xenoanthropology to administer the planet in behalf of the indigenous population is rejected. We grant the claim of the Hugonaut Corporation to the planet. All exploitation rights of the natural resources of planet Minerva are reserved to the Hugonaut Corporation, with the following exception."

She refused to look at him. She held her breath. Please, at least give us this much. . . .

"In light of the strong concerns of the Department of Xenoanthropology with respect to the possible future sentience of the local species, we establish a reserve on the largest continent, which shall remain outside the claim of the Hugonaut Corporation. Xenoanthro will monitor this reserve to ensure the compliance of the Hugonaut Corporation. This board has ruled. All parties are dismissed."

Jo-ann walked out of the courthouse unsteadily. She felt as though her head were both too big, wobbling slightly on her neck, and too small, the skin stretched tight across her face. She rubbed her forehead, trying to dispel the ache. I wonder why I'm even surprised, she thought. No way the feds were going to let prime mineral deposits like those go to waste, languishing under the surface while the Froggies went about their incomprehensible business. Damn!

"This sucks," she said to Amanda. "They railroaded us. Another six months and we—"

"I wish that were true. But be honest, Jo-ann, was there a day—even one—in these last few months, when you thought you were getting anywhere with them?"

Jo-ann shrugged. She remembered how her hands shook when she stepped out of the base camp, part of the first team chosen to meet with the local group of Froggies. Having watched them for months, she had been convinced of their sentience. The first time humans would talk to other intelligent beings! At last, after all those years of studying Earth primates, wondering if Planetary Expeditions would ever find an alien species for her to talk to. She had begun to wonder why she'd sought a degree in xenoanthropology when there were no live xenos for her to anthropomorphize.

The old joke suddenly lacked humor. That damned judge, applying his anthropocentric standards to the Froggies. "No response to another intelligent species" indeed! For all they knew, by Froggie standards, the humans didn't qualify as intelligent. Not worthy of their attention, at any rate. She sighed with old frustration. She just couldn't understand why they'd failed.

Amanda stopped. "Want to get a drink?"

"No."

"Okay. Later."

Jo-ann called home.

"Dave here."

"It's me. Guess what."

"Oh, honey, I'm so sorry. But you knew it was a long shot. . . ."

"Yeah, I guess. At least they've agreed to put in the reserve in the Thompson Forest for the Froggies. We'll be monitoring the situation, and you'll be able to keep working on those magic plants of yours. I suppose we can even keep trying to talk to them. . . ."

"You never know, maybe you'll come up with a way to get through to them."

"But it'll be too late. The Hugonauts already got the rest of the planet. Who knows what will be left for the Froggies in another hundred years?"

Five years later

"Tommy, come in and do your homework. You know your mother will be upset if it's not done before dinner."

Tommy heard his father and dug harder, faster, trying to get the hole deep enough, soon enough. The dirt was wrong—rocky, crumbly, thick with roots and little grubs. Actually, he didn't mind the grubs so much. They were quite tasty, in fact, although Mommy got mad whenever she caught him. But Mommy wouldn't be home for another hour, and Daddy didn't watch him closely. Daddy was very busy, that's what Mommy said. Doing important work. Which meant that Tommy could eat as many grubs as he could find, making his nest. Rounder, the rim needed to be rounder on that side, then this wall made smoother. Oh, what's this, he thought. A grub, uncovered by his left midhand. A juicy one, and not very fast either. *Gulp.* Making the floor even was always the easiest part, unless he got too picky about it. Maybe Daddy would let him use the level. Tommy poked his head up, called "Daddy, Daddy, can I go in the tool shed?"

Daddy came around the corner of the house—Tommy could hear the hum of the trimming shears. Saturday was garden day. "Oh, Tommy, you didn't! Not another one of those damn holes. Just look what you're doing to the azalea bushes. I only planted them last spring. Why are you always digging? I just don't get it."

Tommy felt his ears pressing flat against his nose, and he whimpered, in his low range where he knew Daddy couldn't hear. *Subsonic,* his mother said was the word. He didn't know what that meant. She said it meant "under sound" but how could there be sounds "under" sound? Mommy said he'd understand when he was older. He'd understand a lot of things when he was older. But right now, here, his father was yelling at him, and he didn't understand.

"But, Daddy, I just want to nest, won't you show me how to use the level to get the floor right?"

"No, stop that digging right now. I said stop it! Can't you see what you're doing to the azalea?"

Tommy hesitated, rocking, not sure how to get out of the hole without touching any of the bushes around the rim. He hadn't really noticed them before, but now that he thought about it, he remembered that the ground around his nest was surrounded by little bushes, prickly, not tasty at all, not worth any bother. But now it seemed that Daddy liked them, that he was really mad. Tommy had never heard his father so mad before. He poked his left upperhand over the rim, trying to find a spot safe for climbing out of the hole. Feeling flat grass under his palm, he dug into the wall with his feet and midhands, scrambling up and over, landing in a heap on the grass. One foot snagged on a prickly bush, and he cringed, ears flat, waiting for another yell from his father.

"Oh, Tommy, how could you? Just look at them, you've exposed their roots. I don't know *what* you were thinking. Well, come on, help me get this dirt back where it belongs, cover up these poor roots. Hurry, maybe we can repair the damage if we're quick."

Tommy wanted to know why they needed to hurry, what was so special about these little bushes, but he guessed he'd better ask later. Right now, he gathered up the scattered dirt, careful not to further disturb the bushes, and pushed it back into the hole. He sighed. It had promised to be such a nice, comfortable little nest, but it was clearly not to be. Was there some other place he would be allowed to dig? He kept on moving dirt, circling until he ran into his father.

"There, kiddo, we've got the hole filled in. It's not too bad, eh?"

"Daddy, can I make a hole somewhere else?"

"Why? What makes you want to dig like a—ah, skip it. But stop with the digging, just stay out of the yard, all right? I'll be in, in a bit, after I finish fixing up this mess. Go on and do your homework."

Tommy slunk back to the house, rumbling to himself. At least Daddy wasn't so mad anymore, but Tommy still didn't know why he wanted the bushes instead of a nice deep round smooth hole. And Daddy never could explain things properly anyway. Maybe Mommy could help. He perked up, wiggling his ears, rubbing them along the edges of his nose. His mother always found the right thing to say, and would give his back a nice rub, too. He'd go inside and wait for Mommy.

But when his mother finally got home, she didn't come upstairs to Tommy's room. He could hear her downstairs, talking to his father. It must be about me, Tommy thought, I bet they're talking about me. He sneaked out to the landing, careful to allow only his ear to round the corner of the wall. Because his hearing wasn't as good as theirs, sometimes his parents forgot to be careful about their "private" conversations. His father's rumble was easier to make out than his mother's lighter voice—

"But why does he have to be so, you know, so *strange*." Tommy imagined his father pacing up and down, making that tangy frustration-scent. His mother's laugh surprised him, it was sharper and higher than the laugh she made during their tickle-fights.

"Honestly, Dave, do you hear yourself? What in the world were you expecting out of this little adventure? What were any of us expecting?"

"I don't know, I just don't know. I think maybe we believed that it would all be, well, over sooner. I mean, who could have imagined, years without other people, without civilization. How long until we get our lives back?" A smacking sound against wood. Then his mother's voice.

"Honey, it's not that simple. How long until we figure them out? I know the situation is strange. Yes, it's lonely out here. And Tommy. I admit he's not what we would have expected. What we might have wanted. But this is what we got, and the Froggies need us. They were just living, going about their business; they didn't invite us down for a visit. We're the ones who decided to invade their home. It's not like Tommy got a vote, is it? *God, Dave, too bad you had to marry a xenoanthropologist!*"

Tommy hated the hysterical note in her voice. He didn't understand what they had said, but he knew it was about him and that his father was still mad at him. But Mommy wasn't making it better, she wasn't making Daddy laugh and calling Tommy to start a game of hop-and-catch. He decided he didn't want to hear any more. He hopped morosely back to his room and crawled into bed.

Soft. Warm. Deep, buried safe. Rubbing skin against skin, neighbor bristles poking his tender underbelly flesh, ow. Poke, poke, squirm, nestle down, deeper. Push aside slippery limbs, slide over brother-backs and sister-backs, around and through the tangle of skin and bristles. He breathes in gingery musk of contentment and peppery hunger, finally food-smell, he burrows inward to the source. Gleaming warmth in the center of the depression, it smells of wet and orange. He bites, sucks, ah.

Sunday morning, when he came downstairs for breakfast, his father was gone. "Daddy had to go away for a little while, he needs to get important things for us," his mother said. "I've got to talk to Amanda and Gillian today; they're coming over for lunch. You can play with little Heather and Erin. But no digging in the garden, you hear me? Your father was quite upset about the damage to his plants. You know how hard—" She stopped talking and started rubbing his back. "—I guess we didn't tell you about it, did we? Those plants Daddy made, they're special. He's been studying Minervan biochemistry for six years now, and he thinks he's starting to recognize which protein sequences control the regeneration functions. Do you remember when we talked about biochemistry?"

Tommy wrinkled his nose. He really liked it when his mother talked with him about science-things, because she got so serious and excited, both at the same time. He didn't know what any of the words meant, but just a few months ago he'd figured out that if he nodded his head up and down and said, "How does it work?" every time she paused, she would keep talking for a long time. So he said, "Yes, I remember," and she kept talking, words that sounded fun on the tongue, like *multicellular* and *unprecedented* and *embryonic* and *miraculous*. That last one was particularly juicy. "Mommy, how does *miraculous* work?"

Her delighted laughter washed over him, and he rolled over onto her legs, reaching up to tickle her ribs with his midhands. "Where did your midhands go, Mommy? Did you lose them when you were little? Will something happen to mine?"

"Shh, you'll learn all about it when you're older." He didn't know why she sounded so sad, but she sent him off to study before Heather and Erin came over. He went to his room obediently, but he couldn't concentrate. Those dreams, they were so yummy, but so strange. Everything was different in the dreams. When he heard the rumbling of a land-rover through the trees, he hopped down quickly, running to meet his friends.

Heather and Erin hooted out greetings as they bounded to meet him. "Hello, hello, no school today, yippee, yea!" "Let's go digging, Tommy-Tom, digging, dig, yea!" Erin pounced, and landing on his back, grabbed his ears. "Ride 'em cowboy," she squealed. He could smell her excitement, and reaching back a midhand, he snagged her foot to flip her off him. He got her wrestled to the ground, but then Heather landed on his head, covering his ears and nose with her tummy. Unable to hear or smell, he kicked his legs in the air helplessly while the girls tickled him. Trying to squirm out of Heather's grasp, he suddenly remembered that dream last night. He bucked his legs until he was free, and grabbed each of them by their upperhands. "Hey, you guys ever, you know, dream? Like, like this? Us, touching, food-smells?" He trailed off uncertainly. Heather smelled like confusion, but Erin rumbled with impatience.

"Who has time for dreams, let's dig us a nest!" and she bounded away.

"No, no no no no no!" Tommy hopped frantically after her. "No digging, Daddy says no!" He quivered, worrying she'd already started making holes. Maybe she was hurting one of the bushes right now.

"Erin, stay away from the prickly-bushes. They're special, Mommy says special, be careful!" He caught up to her, sighing when he realized she was still poking around the underbrush, looking for a nice spot to dig.

"Hey, lookee here, Heather—Tommy started a nice hole, feel the soft squishy dirt right here."

"No, Erin! Daddy filled it in, he says no more digging. C'mon, let's go exploring." He had to distract her, and he knew she wouldn't be able to resist a challenge. "I found a bush I couldn't crawl through, follow me, I bet you can't get through it either."

He led the girls into the forest, away from Daddy's bushes, to the funny hard bushes he'd found last week. The branches of these bushes all ran into each other, as high as he could reach, and never had any break in them.

The three children pushed into the branches, squirming their arms into the tiny holes, but the strange branches held firm. Heather tried digging under the bush, but she couldn't find any roots, just dirt so hard they couldn't break it up.

Erin tried to jump over, but it was too high.

Tommy scrambled up and down the branches. "Erin, Heather, try this, it's *fun*." They played, running all over the wide flat surface, up, down, around. But when they climbed too high, the upper branches were too sharp to touch.

"Ow." Erin discovered that the hard way. And they couldn't swing properly, like they did from regular trees, moving through the forest without ever touching the ground. The branches didn't sway and bend, or extend toward the other trees.

They decided to go home and tell their mothers about the fantastic plant, so monstrous big and tough. But when they got back to Tommy's home, their mothers were busy talking, didn't want to listen to the kids.

"Erin, sweetie," her mother said, "don't worry about the funny bushes. Why don't you go get a snack in the kitchen? I bet Tommy's mommy has cookies."

That night, Dave returned from his supply run. Jo-ann stroked the bright fabrics, the rich yellows and orangey-reds that didn't exist in Minervan nature. They watched the sun set, lilac in a pistachio sky. While they sorted out clothes for Amanda and Gillian, Jo-ann told her husband that the children had discovered the fence around the compound. "I think they know something is wrong."

"They'll be asking hard questions soon. It won't be much longer now," he said. "And the pressure is coming from the other side as well. When I was Out There, I saw the flashes of incoming ships breaking hyperspace. Big flashes, probably heavy-duty cargo haulers."

"God, they're stepping up the schedule. How much time do you think we have?" She couldn't seem to stop chewing on the edge of her finger.

"It can't be soon enough. I want to get back to civilization. Don't you?"

"Dammit, don't you care what happens to them? This *has* to work."

Tears ran down her face. “You know how much the children, the Froggies need us.”

Dave put his arm around her, pressing into the knot of tension in her shoulder. “I know, honey, but I want my life back. Why do we have to give up so much for them when they won’t even admit we’re here? Sometimes I hate them.”

She jerked out of his embrace, stood rigid facing away from him. “Don’t ever say that! They’re the victims. You can’t forget that. We have to fight for them, whatever it takes. They deserve to get their planet back!”

“Even if they don’t know we’ve taken it?”

“Even then.” She couldn’t make herself turn around.

Dave didn’t say anything more.

One year later

“Mommy, Mommy, I had the strangest dream last night. You were in it, and I was in it, and Erin and Heather, but we were big, bigger’n you, and the smells, I never breathed such smells before, excitement, and something spicy, strong, kinda scary, we were pressing in, pushing into you, and you were scared, you got smaller and we were pushing you between us, and somebody was angry, someone different, with a big rumbly voice like Heather but more, stronger I think. I didn’t like it, Mommy!” He wrapped all six limbs around her and squeezed, first the right three, then the left, right, left, rocking her in his distress.

Jo-ann tried not to panic at being enveloped. A hug that had had a certain weird charm when he had been less than three feet tall felt different now that he’d grown so much. She stroked his back, murmured, “There, there, it’s okay.”

Then his words registered. “Honey, what did you just say? What was the rumbly voice like? Was it Heather?”

“No, I said, bigger, stronger.”

“Like Daddy?”

“No, like us kids, we all sound different from you, you know, squeaky and deep, with the undersounds and the oversounds you can’t hear. But different from us, too. Like, more, more tones. You know, like all three of us at once. But one person. I don’t know . . .” His voice trailed off, uncertain. She rocked him sideways, smoothing down his bristled mane, thinking furiously. “Honey, I’m just going to call Heather’s mommy, I’ll be right back. Would you like it if Heather came over today?”

* * *

Jo-ann slipped into her office, making sure the door was closed before she activated Amanda's monitor.

"Oh, my God, Amanda, you're not going to believe this! It's incredible, this is it, what we never understood, it's dreams! They talk in their dreams! Quick, get Heather, bring her over to my place, I'll call Gillian and get them here, too; we've got to find out what they've been dreaming." Jo-ann rocked back and forth on the balls of her feet, talking way too fast.

"Whoa, Jo-ann, slow down, will you? What're you talking about, dreams?"

"Has Heather mentioned any of her dreams to you? Ever, anything? Like, about the Froggies." Jo-ann found herself whispering the last word, and looked guiltily over her shoulder.

"No, I don't think so. You know, Jo-ann, it's something we try not to discuss. In fact, if you recall, we agreed to steer our exercises and games away from any mention of, um, well, *them*. I still can't believe we've kept the charade going as long as we have. Sometimes, after Heather has been sitting near me, touching my skin, I see her stroking her own skin, stroking the smoothness. I know she's wondering."

"But the dreams, what about her dreams? Find her now, ask her! They're talking to the children in their dreams! Tommy just told me about a "big" voice, a multitonal voice, with subsonic and ultrasonic frequencies."

"I don't know, that could be some kind of racial memory. We still don't have any idea how their minds work. It's a goddam miracle that they're prewired for verbal language acquisition. The Froggies never seem to 'talk' to each other, and they sure as hell don't listen to us!"

"But wait, I didn't tell you the rest of his dream. Tommy said there were three of them, bigger than me, surrounding me, pushing me. Me! That's no racial memory."

"I don't know." Jo-ann could hear the doubt in Amanda's voice. "Maybe he's got the racial one mixed up with his own experience. You've got to be careful about how you apply our standards to them. Haven't you heard of going native?"

They both laughed, a little. We can still laugh, Jo-ann thought. That's something.

"Just get Heather and come on over." Jo-ann breathed deeply against the tension in her chest. She suddenly needed to be done with all the subterfuge and misdirection. Closing her eyes, she tried to relax the tight skin of her face. "We need to be straight with them if we're going to sort this whole mess out. It's time we end the experiment."

* * *

When Amanda and Gillian arrived with Heather and Erin in tow, they gathered in Jo-ann's living room. She asked Tommy to tell all of them what he'd just told her. She and Amanda and Gillian watched the two "girls," trying to guess their reactions to Tommy's dream. Six years, and they were still guessing at the body language. Distress was easy, ears flat against their noses. The xenoanthropologists had certainly seen enough of that in the early years. But also sensual pleasure, ears swiveled back, nose flaring, a little rippling along the back where the midhands were joined to the rib cage. And frustration, a curling of the tail along with a sharp scent, something like sun on rotting leaves. They'd had to come up with a whole new vocabulary to describe these things, the smells and the body language. She wondered about the sounds outside human frequencies, but it was too difficult, finding the time to review the recordings, with no idea what she was looking for. So frustrating, nobody to talk to, to compare notes with, just each other. Some days Jo-ann longed to let her old thesis advisor in on the secret. He would have such great insight. But she knew better than to entangle him in this crazy scheme of hers.

Heather and Erin were definitely interested in Tommy's dream. Jo-ann was pretty sure she saw recognition in Erin's stance, but Heather was harder to read. Her posture was something Jo-ann hadn't seen before, spine arched to the left, right midhand curved inward to the rib cage, mane bristles fanning outward, throat-sac swelling. Jo-ann wondered whether Amanda might be right, that "Heather" was actually a male.

Jo-ann looked over at Gillian, twitched her shoulder toward Erin.

"Erin, sweetie," Gillian said, "did you ever have a dream like that? This is very important."

"Ye-es," Erin said slowly. "I think so. I'm in the forest, and there's lots of people there. We all smell like this," Jo-ann breathed in, caught a suggestion of cucumber and tar. Maybe we should kidnap a professional perfume-maker, she thought, squashing an unsteady giggle. But Erin was still talking. "We're in the sunshine, it's very hot, our backs hurt, the echoes between the trees are big, like lots of trees are gone. The ground is hard and lumpy, uneven, deep holes. But not nests, not soft dirt and smooth walls and level floors. Just holes all hard and twisted, no shade, no resting. Everyone is moving around, making the noises you can't hear. I think they're angry."

Amanda was looking at Gillian's "daughter" with narrowed eyes. Jo-ann saw a slight tremor in her knee; she must realize that the time of the children's innocence was ending. Oh, how I wish we could just tell them about Santa Claus and the Tooth Fairy. She waited for Amanda to look up at her, saw the watery brightness in her eyes, nodded.

"Heather, do you dream?" Amanda asked softly, blinking.

Heather turned her head between Erin and Tommy, extending her nose flaps and breathing in the smells of her siblings. She straightened out of her crouch, and she made small curving motions with her mid-hands, as though to gather them in to her. But when Amanda repeated, "Heather, Heather," she swiveled her ears toward her mother.

"No, Mommy, no dreams. Tommy and Erin, they're sad. But it's exciting, too. Mommy, what are the dreams?" Erin and Tommy came over to her, each extending a midhand to Heather so that the three of them made a chain, facing the women.

Jo-ann braced herself.

"Children, we have to tell you something very difficult. This is a sad story, and you aren't going to be very happy with us after we've told you, but it's very important. It's a story where you have an important job to do. So listen carefully. You know we've told you that there are people out in the jungle, people who look different, people who don't talk like we do. But there's more to it." God help us, there's a lot more to it, Jo-ann thought to herself. "There are people, people like Amanda and Gillian and me and Tommy's dad, only they aren't like us, either. They want to exploit the mineral resources of this planet. Tommy, you remember when we talked about geology, right?"

Jo-ann looked hopefully at Tommy, who whistled his confusion.

"Honestly, Jo-ann, you don't think they actually understand all that science you lecture them about, do you? They're only six years old, and we don't even know what that means, really." Gillian stared at the children, tapping her fingers and squinting in concentration. "Let me see," she muttered. "Okay, kids, try this. You know how you like digging those holes, those 'nest' thingies of yours? And you remember how Tommy's dad got mad when you were digging in his yard? See, you wanted nests, but your nests interfered with his plants, so you couldn't have your nests and his plants in the same place. So what did you do about it?"

Erin was focused on Tommy, who had drifted into the corner as Gillian spoke, but Heather answered. "Now we dig in Erin's yard, not anywhere near Uncle Dave's magic plants."

"Exactly!" Jo-ann started to feel hopeful as Amanda took up the thread. "There are two groups of people, and one group wants to let the plants be, and the other group wants to dig up lots of holes. But there's a problem, because they both want to be in the same yard. Do you see?"

Erin finally raised her head. "Why? Can't they just go away? Don't they know they're not wanted?"

Jo-ann shivered as she listened to Erin's words. They might have sounded naïve, but there was a quality to her smell that made Jo-ann wary. She wondered whether Erin had made the connection between herself and the Froggies in her "dream." She took a deep breath. This was as good a place to start as any.

"Erin, do you know who it is in your dream? You know, don't you? You know why your mommy and I don't have midhands, why we can't hear all the noises you make." Her mouth was dry, and she had to concentrate not to look over at Tommy. She knew he watched from the corner, ears swiveled forward almost touching his nose. She wanted to stroke his back, but she kept her eyes on Erin.

"They're people like me and Tommy and Heather. But not like you. Or you, Mommy. You're not my mommy, are you?"

After a moment, Gillian said, "No, I'm not."

At Gillian's quiet answer, Erin crumpled. She lay curled in a little ball, pressing her upperhands and midhands against the floor, left, then right, then left. Gillian stepped toward her, then hesitated.

The hairs on Jo-ann's arms stood up. She suspected that Erin was making some noise in the ultrasonic. She knew she ought to do something, but for a moment, she just stood there, looking at Tommy.

He lay curled in the corner, shivers rippling up and down his spine. He keened in the top of his range, knowing his mother wouldn't hear. He wanted her to hear, but he wanted her to hear him for real, hear the sound he was making now. He didn't want to make her noises, the flat weak noises she made. He wanted her to know his voice, the voice of the people in the dream. Why couldn't she understand? "You're my mommy," he wailed in that voice, "you have to listen to me. How could you hurt me like this, I want to hurt you, I want you to hurt, too."

Under his keen, he heard Mommy talking to Heather's mommy. "Yes, yes, of course we could show the board video of them talking. Hell, we could probably convince them to go and talk to some experts appointed by the board. It would take some prep time, and it sure as hell wouldn't be easy, but eventually I'm sure we could convince the board that these three are capable of speech."

Erin's mommy said something, but he didn't care. He rocked himself back and forth. He tried to stop keening, but he couldn't. Mommy not Mommy? He couldn't think. He kept rocking, hoping it would all stop. But Mommy was still talking, and everything stayed the same.

"The Hugonaut Corporation will argue that Froggie society is preverbal, that although they bear the capacity for speech in their vocal cords, they have not yet developed a language. No language, no sentience. That argument won last time, and it will win again. And they'll make the kids out to be circus freaks. While they're still this young, and so confused about their identity, they won't make the most convincing ambassadors. No, Gillian, in order to get those damn miners off the planet, we have to prove communication among the Froggies. *Dream* communication. And for that . . ."

"We need the children," finished Gillian reluctantly.

The girls lay huddled in little balls. Amanda crouched next to Heather, talking urgently. Heather's throat-sac vibrated—she was probably rumbling in the subsonic. Gillian rocked with Erin, rubbing her head along the side of Erin's jaw. Jo-ann wasn't sure if Erin was responding to the touch.

After an eternity, Tommy's quiet drew her to him. She breathed, trying to slow her heartbeat, and looked into the corner. He was huddled in on himself, ears completely flat alongside his nose, everything tucked under.

"Tommy, come here. Honey, I'm sorry." She reached out, hesitated, touched his head, stroked his back. She picked him up, like she used to when he was little, and carried him outside. They sat in the garden for a while, Tommy on her lap. Dave came out and sat down next to them.

"Why, Mommy? Oh, not-Mommy. Not. Why do I live here if you're not my Mommy?"

Always before, she knew the words to answer his questions. But not this time.

"We came here, before you were born, Tommy. Me and Amanda. Daddy was here already, studying the plants, so Amanda and I came to meet the Froggies."

"What is *Froggies*?"

"People like you and Heather and Erin. Lots of them, all over the planet. But they wouldn't talk to us. I tried and tried. Amanda tried, and Paul, people you never even met. No matter what we did, they just ignored us." The years-old frustration choked in her throat.

"Froggies?" At least he had stopped rocking, and his ears were starting to swivel back.

"Yes, like you but bigger."

"Not like you?" The ears rotated forward, hovered just over his nose.

"No. Not like me at all."

"You mean, I have another mommy somewhere? A *real* mommy? Where? Tell me where!" He squirmed out of her lap and hopped in place, little hops that barely disturbed the dirt.

She felt the crushing weight of his hope as he stumbled back into her lap. "I don't know, exactly."

"Didn't you meet her?"

"No, I, um, didn't."

"Will you help me find her?" His ears swerved wildly, back and forth.

"I don't think that would be a good idea."

She looked pleadingly at Dave, who frowned. She kept her eyes locked on his until he nodded.

"Tommy," he said, "this is your home, here with your mother and me and Heather and Erin."

"No it's not! I'm going to find my real mommy."

He burst out of her lap, leaping away from the house, toward the woods.

"Tommy, no!"

Tommy climbed. Whistling in distress, ears wrapped securely over his nose, he pulled himself up the tall unbending branches. Higher and higher, until he reached the nasty prickers. As he had suspected, there were no branches above the prickers. Probing with his tail, he searched for a gap in the prickers, but they were close together, only as far apart as his upperhand was wide. Pulling all four lower limbs as close to the top as he could, he braced his upper hands in the gaps between the prickers and launched himself up and over. Owww, that hurt, a sharp pain pulling along his left side. Crash! He landed hard, in a bush, a regular bush, much softer than the pricker bush, but still not exactly soft. Moss would have been nicer. He licked his side where the pricker had torn. It throbbed. He whimpered, low in his throat-sac.

Dave slammed his hand on his thigh. "Let the little—let him go. Let them all go, goddammit! Isn't six years enough? Six years of isolation, six years without anyone to share my research with? No, I'm not done. I know you've tried to understand my work, but dammit, you have Amanda and Gillian to talk to, to share your theories with. I'm sitting on a gold mine of genetic possibility here, and God knows what they're doing with these plants, out there in the real world. All the duplicated research, the dead ends I've wasted years on. Maybe all my work is for nothing."

"Like mine?" Jo-ann asked, her voice low and rough. She didn't want to cry. "Tommy was our son, *is* our son."

"He's not our son! He never was, he was just an experiment. A scientific experiment."

Jo-ann gasped in shock and wrapped her hands around her stomach. "He's our son," she repeated, rocking back and forth.

Dave sighed, loud, and ran his hands through his hair. "Ah, sweetie, I'm sorry. He'll come back. Or maybe Heather and Erin will know how to find him. They've got great sense of smell, don't they? I bet they can follow him just fine."

"And then what? Even if we find him, he hates me." Jo-ann snuffled, wiped her nose. "He'll never forgive me."

"Jo-ann, look at me. I'm not sure how the kid will feel. How would you feel?"

"I would feel—I don't know. I wonder if he can find his, the mother of his litter." Jo-ann wondered again if Froggies had mother-child relationships like humans. For that matter, how many people did she know who had mother-child relationships the way humans supposedly did? And then there were those who could never even try.

"Maybe we should let him look for her," Dave said gently.

As they stood up to go inside, Erin and Heather came charging out of the house. Heather first, bounding across the yard, veering around Dave and Jo-ann. Erin followed, stopping once, turning her head toward the house. Gillian stood in the doorway, raised her hand, but didn't speak. After a moment, Erin raced after Heather. Jo-ann walked toward Gillian.

"They're going with Tommy," Gillian said unnecessarily.

Tommy heard whuffing and whistling, nearby, behind. He smelled Heather and Erin. He pinged in that direction—there, beyond the barrier. "Guys, hey, here I am," he called. "Over the top, come on, let's go find Froggies. People like us . . ."

"How do you get over?" Erin asked.

"Grab the top, between the sharp prickers, jump hard." Tommy perched on a nice soft mound and directed them. "Here, there's moss on this side if you jump from here." He yelped as Heather landed on his foot. They tried to scramble out of the way, but Erin was too fast. The three rolled off the mound in a tangle of limbs.

"Hey, watch out, you." Heather started tickling Erin's ribs.

"Look who's talking, foot-stomper," Tommy said, pinning Heather. "Erin, I've got her. Get her, fast." But Erin, ever unpredictable, pounced on Tommy, using the tip of her tail to tickle his midback, right where he couldn't reach. "Aaagh, no fair. Heather, help me."

"No way." And Heather started tickling Tommy, too. He laughed helplessly until he could barely breathe. "Stop, stop, I'm going to tell—"

All three froze. Tommy keened a bit. Heather rubbed her head along his jaw. Erin patted his lower back gently.

"Tell who?" Erin mumbled. They rocked for a moment, in silence. "What are we gonna do?"

"I want to find our real mommies. Do you think they miss us?" Tommy couldn't help shivering, even though the midday sun was hot on his back.

"How do we find them? We don't know where they live." Heather scratched her toe in the dirt.

Around them was the restless whirling of small fliers everywhere. Erin twisted her head right, up, left, down, chasing their movements. Pollen floated by Tommy's nose; he sneezed.

"Let's see where the small flier is going. Maybe he's got a nest." Erin bounded away through the trees.

"Erin, wait, we should stay near the running-water sound. We don't want to get lost."

"Why not?" she said, but she stopped chasing the little creature.

"No, Erin, Tommy's right. I want to stay near the water, too."

"Okay, but I don't think it's going to take us to the Froggies."

Tommy asked, "Do you think it's different, out here?" He knew, from the way the prickers had curved out at the top, that they would not be able to return over the barrier.

"I don't know, smells the same to me. Same trees, same dirt, same bugs." Erin grabbed a fuzzy insect with her tail and popped it into her mouth to prove her point. "Yup, tastes the same, too."

Heather hrrmmed, low in her throat. "Feels different. This plant, here, feel this, the leaves are fuzzy, sharp edges. I never found one like this before."

Tommy returned from the edge of the clearing. "Nothing around here like Daddy's plants. The new ones are tasty, though."

They hopped for a while through the forest, keeping close to the stream.

"I'm tired. Can we stop and eat?" Heather was always the first to think of food.

"Tommy, did you notice, something feels different, inside, here. Like, back home, there's always a feeling, that this way is nicer than that way, you know, the paths where it's easier to move along, like in my backyard from the door to the orange tree, and at your house out to the special bushes . . ."

"Yeah, it's moved, here. Pulls another way now."

While they were talking, Tommy noticed that Heather was sniffing around for the peppery plants they liked to eat. "Guys, over here, yummy food, come eat!"

She had dumped over an insect hive, and they devoured the citrusy nectar inside. Sated, worn out by the excitement and the sun, they curled up for a nap.

Symbols, a series of indentations in dirt, flickering one after the other. Dreaming fingers trace the surfaces, next, next, next. There, a repeat? Impossible to say. Impressions come from nothing, then flicker away. The symbols continue, a steady flow. Suddenly, the hand is grasping wet fruit, squeezes, pulp drips between startled fingers. A puff of air across the hand, all clean! Then fingers are racing over new surfaces, tracing more symbols. The same symbols come back, sometimes, here and there. Then just as quickly disappear, replaced by something new. Next, next, next. Another squeeze of rotten fruit, smell, too, this time. Whew!

Tommy, stretched, woke up, untangled himself from the others. "I just had the weirdest dream—"

Erin giggled. "Couldn't be any weirder than mine."

"I bet mine was the weirdest," Tommy said.

"No, mine. I had funny dirt-pictures, lots and lots of them—"

"—and rotten fruit, too, in the middle, then at the end, it stank," Tommy finished.

"No way, that was my dream," said Erin.

"What do you think it means?" asked Tommy.

Heather interrupted. "What are you guys talking about?"

"The funny dreams," Erin said. "Didn't you have them?"

"No. I don't get it. Dirt-pictures? How is that a dream?"

Erin emitted the confusion-scent. "I'm not making it up."

Tommy realized something was different. "Hey, Erin, did you feel it? The pull was different in the dream. The direction, just a little more that way."

"It was the same as my dream, last night," said Erin.

"And mine. Mommy said it was the 'Froggies' in the dream. Maybe this was them, too," said Tommy.

"So if we go more this way, until the pull direction is like in the dream—"

"Maybe we'll find the Froggies," said Tommy.

The two headed out through the trees.

Heather refused to budge. “Guys, this is stupid! You want to follow directions from your dreams? I’m not going.”

“Aw, come on, Heather, where else are we going to go?”

Waiting was almost worse than bad news. At least with bad news, there was something to react to, something to attack. Here, Jo-ann had to sit, trust in Amanda and Gillian to present their case to the Department of Xenoanthropology. They had gone through their archives, putting together the video to showcase the intelligence of their Froggie children. Without live testimony, she wasn’t sure how convincing it was. But with the kids gone over the wall, they finally had to admit that they’d gone as far as they could, separated from the outside world. So many times over the years, they had wished for colleagues to brainstorm with, computers powerful enough to find meanings in the ultra- and subsonic frequencies. If there were any. But the ethics panel would have had a field day with her methodology.

Looks like they’d have their chance now.

She went out to the garden. Dave, whistling tunelessly, was tending to his hybridized azaleas. She wondered what he was thinking. “How are they coming?”

“Good, actually. I finally got that mite infestation killed off. Mostly weeding, right now.”

“Okay, I get that the mites aren’t really mites. They just act like mites, right? But how do you decide what’s a weed?”

“Like anywhere else. Weeds are the plants with the strongest roots.” Dave sawed off the base of a thick vine and carefully unwrapped its reaching tendrils from around the new growth of his azalea.

“No, really.”

“Really. Weeds are total nutrient hogs. They suck all the minerals out of the soil, but don’t produce interesting fruit or fragrant flowers.”

“I don’t know—vacuum cleaners of the plant world, could be something valuable there.”

“Well, someone Out There is probably working on it. But I think I’m getting close to isolating the regenerative function. I’ve produced it in the azaleas, and now the orange bush.”

Jo-ann saw his pride in his plants, but also how it ate at him, not being able to share the work with colleagues. “You know, you don’t have to wait with me. You can go back, show these plants right away.”

“I don’t want to leave you here alone. . . .”

Tension—she thought her head would burst. She rubbed her temples. “You know what, the hell with this. No way are they going to buy those videos. They'll say we faked it. Without a live demonstration, our case won't be strong enough. I've got to find Tommy, bring him back to the Department. Then they'll believe me and fund another effort to establish communications."

"Um, Jo-ann, I'm not sure how likely—"

"If we had better computers, we could analyze the subsonics."

"Jo-ann, we've been over this—"

"If they see Tommy, they'll understand. I've got to find him. Where are those aerial maps?"

"Honey, slow down. This is not a good idea."

"Don't you want Tommy back? Oh, skip it, you never did care."

"Okay, that's enough. Don't even say that. I've stuck it out for six years. You find one other person who would have done this for you. But it's over. Let it go, goddammit. Come back with me. Tommy is better off out there."

"To hell with you then. I'm going to find him."

He came after her. "Jo-ann, wait, at least wait until you hear from Amanda and Gillian."

The children made their way down the hill. A huge clearing filled the space below, and the smell of themselves came up to them. Their ears and noses quivered with excitement, and Erin kept dashing ahead.

"Wait up, Erin, I'm tired," Heather said.

"But smell, smell that, can't you tell, it's people like us. I want to meet them. Hurry!"

Tommy slowed down, slower even than Heather. "I don't know. What if they don't like us?"

The sun was getting cooler, near end-of-day, and by the time they made their way down to the valley, it was becoming night-cold. They headed for the strongest concentration of the smell, so tantalizing, so familiar. "Why don't we hear anything?" Heather asked.

Tommy decided not knowing was worse. He said, "I don't know. Let's go find out." He approached a drop-off in the floor of the clearing, arched his ear out over the opening. He heard breathing, like Heather and Erin sleeping, but more. He curved his tail out, slow and careful, gently reached into the hole. He touched smooth surfaces, tummies and backs and limbs like his, only bigger. Lots and lots of them, all twined together. Throat-sacs quivered softly, chests rose and fell, ears swiveled back and forth. He extended an upperhand, stroked the length of an arm.

Suddenly, a hand grasped his wrist. He jumped, squeaking in surprise, and jerked out of the grip. He backed away.

"Tommy, what is it," said Heather, "what happened?"

"There's lots of, I don't know—people?—sleeping here, all together, and I went to touch, and something grabbed me."

"Guess they didn't like you poking them, huh?"

"Yeah. But they didn't say anything, either."

"I don't get it."

It was the strangest night. The adults—Froggies, Tommy supposed—moved slowly around the valley, eating plant leaves and insects. He browsed next to one, but the adult did not pay any attention to him or the girls. The feeding adults exuded the gingery scent of lazy contentment. A few Froggies splashed in the lake, slurping up the water-plants. Heather took a quick dip, reported that the water-plants didn't have much flavor and that the adults didn't seem to mind her company.

Finally, impatient, Erin went up to one and said, "Hi, I'm Erin. Who are you?" The Froggie did not answer, only shook its head as if distracted by a buzzing small flier. Frustrated, she tried talking to another, and another, but each ignored her. Once, Tommy touched an adult, tapping its upper arm for attention. The adult's skin rippled, as though an insect had bitten it. It stepped away from Tommy, emitting a tangy, tarry annoyance-smell. Taking the hint, Tommy was careful not to touch any of the others.

"Hey, guys, will they talk to you?"

"Not me, it's like they don't know I'm here," said Heather.

"They act like I'm a bug crawling up their butts," said Erin.

"Ew, Erin."

"Well, they do. I guess they only like to eat. They're just like you, Heather."

"Oh, Erin, you are so funny. All they do is eat and sleep. It's boring. I want to go home."

"But we have to find our real mommies," said Tommy.

"But how?" asked Heather. "Nobody wants to help us. We don't know how to look for them. We don't know what they smell like, even."

"I guess," Tommy sat, ears drooping over his nose, making small snuffle noises.

Erin rumbled, low, in frustration. "How come they didn't come for us?"

"Maybe they don't know where we are," said Tommy.

"How come they sent us away in the first place?" Heather said.

"I want to go home," said Erin.

The humidity eased off; the air on Tommy's back warmed. The strange Froggie creatures returned, one by one, to their round earth-holes. Hopping around to investigate, Tommy realized that each of the holes had trees deeply overhanging, providing protection from the sun all day long. Remembering the intense pain of his first sunburn, he approved their planning.

Erin came up behind him. "I wonder why they go in there, during the day."

"There's nice trees overhead—I bet it's cool and comfy."

"I'm going to find out." She hopped over to the rim.

Uh-oh. "Erin, I don't think they like us." But she was already over the edge, snuggling down among the adults. "Do they mind?"

"Don't think so. Hey, it's really neat down here, all slippery-smooth, legs and tummies rubbing everywhere. Feels like . . . like something, I can't remember. But it's nice, come try."

Tommy poked a doubtful ear over the edge, considering. Wumpf! Something solid struck his back and he fell in, landing right on top of Erin.

"Hey, watch it!"

"It's not my fault—somebody pushed me. I bet they're coming down, better move over." They squeezed in among the others, twining tails and arms through the gaps, settling their backs against the smooth dirt floor. "Erin, feel, the ground is so nice and even."

"Yeah, it's just right. But getting crowded, my feet are squashed. Scoot over."

A strange muffled cry reached his ears. "What was that?"

"Sounded like Heather, I think."

"Heather! Heather, where are you?"

No answer.

Tommy got worried. "I better go find out where she is." He tried to untangle himself, but couldn't get free. Every time he almost got his arms out, a new adult would come in and snuggle up with him. So many of them, each pressing into him, not letting him loose. "Erin, help, I can't get out."

Her voice was languid, " 'S'okay, Tommy, just go to sleep."

He struggled harder, but felt his limbs getting heavier. He couldn't seem to get a full breath. The more he pulled upward, the more some other would push down on him. His thrashing slowed, stopped. He drifted into uneasy oblivion.

This time the dreams almost made sense.

Patterns of swirling smells—sun on dirt, ripe peppers, wet leaves, ice melting in spring, burning lichen, fresh blood, rotten green-fruit—each came and went in almost repetitious sequences. Sounds, really low, below what Mommy could hear, ran as a constant undercurrent. But not quite. Just when Tommy thought he had it figured out—the pollen smell always came after ice, and the sound shifted from an even thrum to a slightly higher pulse—the next time around it was different. They went on forever (small flier dung in snow, ripe ice-fruit, pollen, burning leaves) evoking days of playing in the snow with Mommy, of hunting for new fruits with Heather and Daddy, collecting flowers in spring, jumping in leaf piles with Erin in the fall.

Late-afternoon sun filtered through the overhanging leaves. The adults began crawling out of the nesting hole in a messy confusion of limbs. Flailing, he got his toe in someone's ear, and received a swat on the leg. On the next try, he connected with dirt. Keeping all his hands and feet close together, he made his way up the wall without stepping on anybody else. Safely out, he scooted away toward Erin.

"Erin, hey, Erin, what did you dream about?"

"Sad smells, smells from Mommy and the aunties and Uncle Dave."

"But right before we went to sleep, I thought I heard Heather," said Tommy.

"Heather, Heather," they called.

From far away, near the lake, they heard intense scuffling. Tommy bounded toward the noise. "Heather, is that you? What happened?"

Heather was alone by the lake, cleaning her arms fastidiously. "At first they were just ignoring me, like they were all day. Then when it started getting hot they headed into their nest-holes. I couldn't find you guys. One of them grabbed me and pushed me into a hole and I tried to get out, but more and more of them jumped in, they were all on top of each other and on top of me, and I couldn't move, I could hardly breathe. Then they were sleeping, and I slept, too. When we all woke up it was hard getting out of that nasty hole."

"Oh, it wasn't so bad," said Erin.

"I poked somebody in the ear," offered Tommy.

"But did you have the funny smell-dreams, Heather?"

"I guess, there were smells, yes, I remembered snow, and that time we found the dead hrroat . . ."

"Yeah, I got that one, the smell of blood." Erin hopped a bit with excitement. "Tommy, do you really think they talk in the dreams?"

"Maybe. Maybe they only talk in dreams. Maybe that's why they ignore us when we're all awake."

"Maybe it's bad manners to talk when we're awake."

"So if we wait until we sleep again—"

"We could try to talk, too," Erin said.

Heather snorted. "You guys want to go back into those holes, try to dream-talk to the weird Froggie people?"

Tommy rippled the skin along his spine, considering. "Maybe . . . If we can get them to talk to us, they'll help us find our real mommies."

"Yes!" said Erin. "I think we should stay more, find out what the dreams are all about."

The communicator shrilled.

"Jo-ann!" Dave called. "It's Amanda!"

Reluctant, she came into the kitchen, activated the monitor. "What? Of course. What else would they say." She threw down the control. "That's it. They didn't buy it. I've got to find Tommy, he's the only way to make them see reason."

"Do you even know where to look?"

"I'm going to try the hills west of here. There was a group living up by that hidden lake six years ago."

He sighed. "Do you want company?"

"You mean it?" She looked at him, surprised. "No, I made this mess, I'll clean it up."

"I'll be here when you get back. Take the flare gun." He kissed her.

For the first time in six years, Jo-ann left the compound. At the gate, she paused. Strange, the trees beyond looked just like the trees of her home, but they weren't the familiar trees. Larger maybe, or perhaps the leaves were rougher. They looked subtly wrong. Funny how a person gets used to the everyday things, doesn't like it when something new stares back. She shrugged the thought aside. In her pack she carried her old aerials, marked with the route to the lake. The stellar cartographer had made the aerials for her team back when they first arrived to investigate the Froggies.

Recollections of her first landing on Minerva came to her as she went in search of the children.

The shuttle rocked lightly as it settled onto the surface. The gate creaked as she pushed it open. *She walked out into a field of tall cinnamon grass.* Pushing through a cluster of dense prickly bushes, she checked her map against the readings on her sextant. *The sun glowed dim and lilac in the pale green sky.* She squinted at the sun, wishing again that compasses worked on Minerva. *The breeze, redolent of sweet marjoram and dirt, brushed against her face.* She sniffed, searching for a trace of Froggie; she hoped the local group was still there. *The blades of the grass made quiet shushing sounds as she walked.* A noise on her left made her jump, but it was just a hrroat grazing, pulling leaves off the high branches with its tail. *Hills rose on the horizon, draped in swaths of olive and pomegranate foliage.* She skirted the herd, following the stream up through the hills. *She reached the edge of the field; the smells of salt and ozone drifted up to her.*

Climbing over the slippery shale rocks, she approached the ridgeline. *At her feet, a cliff dropped sheer into the cobalt sea, mauve and lavender shale glistening in the ocean spray.* She looked down into the valley: Froggies, at least thirty of them, gathered by the lake.

The group was still there.

Adrenaline rushed through her; her heart raced. She hadn't visited any Froggies since Tommy.

She shielded her eyes against the late-afternoon sun. From this distance, she couldn't tell if the children were down there. She climbed down the hill, breaking through the brush and sending up clouds of pollen. Once, she almost stumbled into an insect hive, only frantic windmilling saved her from collision. Just like bees on Earth, these bugs would sting if something disturbed their hive.

She hiked on.

Tommy dreamed. *Low sounds, moving in even cadence up to a middle range, slowly back down to the initial note. Up and down, hypnotic. An even pace, as of walking. The pattern repeated, louder then softer.*

Even after a few days, he was never sure when a dream was trying to tell him something and when it was just there for itself, just art. Erin thought some were math, formulas for things they hadn't learned yet. Heather thought most of them were just pretty pictures. Tommy wanted to figure out who was sending each dream. If he only knew who was talking, he might be able to talk back. But so far, he could find nothing individual in the dreams. They all had the same direction-pressure, and none contained the distinctive smell of any of the Froggies he had encountered.

The music continued, a shuddering upwelling of individual notes. Pushing out of the void, they rushed past, stuttering one after the other; then meandered, slowed. Dripping, finally, one by one, into a pool of growing silence. Pause. A new sound began, higher, faster, unsteady, demanding. His heart raced, anticipation.

By the time she reached the valley floor the sun hovered on the horizon and near-dark draped the valley in exaggerated shadows. Emptiness and holes littered the valley floor. A blue-green mist drifted over the waters of the lake. All was still, no creatures moving in the dusk.

Memory suddenly assaulted her:

The three of them timed the raid for dawn. It was Gillian's suggestion, because they'd never seen a Froggie active during daylight hours. They had located a good prospect, a sleep-pit with three different litters. Amanda had argued for the importance of a genetically diverse sample. The sky hovered close above them, a soft, flat gray green, as they hiked down into the valley. The Froggies were wrapping up their nocturnal foraging, their target mothers herding their litters into the western pit by the lake. The three women crept forward and paused, but they saw no response to their presence. "Now," Jo-ann hissed, and they darted forward into the crowd. With shaking hands Jo-ann reached past the slippery arms of the mother and grabbed a squirming bundle of baby Froggie. She turned, smothering a cry as she felt the mother's arms wrapping around her shoulders, and bolted for the woods. She heard a human grunt behind her and glanced back to see Amanda recovering from a fall. The other woman ran from a crouch, a small Froggie in her arms. Gillian raced up from the other side and the three scrambled into the woods. They ducked past low branches and around tangled bushes, running flat out until they reached the clearing where Dave held the idling helicar. "You get them?" he called, leaning out of the pilot's seat. The women mumbled breathless assents as they jumped into the cargo hold.

"Go, go, go," Jo-ann yelled, and Dave activated the throttle, lifting the helicar up and away.

In all that time, Jo-ann had never let herself wonder if the Froggie mother had missed her child.

"Tommy?" she called.

No answer. Could the local group have left the valley? Petrified, she realized that she had no idea where else to look for the children.

"Tommy, Tommy, are you there?" she called again, her voice thin and strained.

Still no answer. What if they were gone forever? Was Dave right, did they belong with their own kind? What about the ethics panel, would they understand why she had to take them? She hadn't had any choice—she needed to find a way to save the Froggies, all of them. The panel would have to understand.

She managed a hoarse shout. "Tommy!"

Nothing.

She walked into the valley, toward the lake. Halfway there, she came upon a pit, wide and deep, centered under a cluster of trees. Looking in, she saw a tumble of sleeping Froggies, piled one upon another. For a dreadful moment, she thought she was looking at a grave. But peering closer, she saw the gentle rise and fall of ribs. Asleep, under shade, as always during the heat of the day. She sighed with disappointment and started to move away.

She paused midstride, remembering the dreams. Tommy had described dreams with intent, dreams that had meaning, that spoke of her and of the devastation to their planet. Could they be talking to each other in their dreams? What if they were dreaming now, dreaming with each other, sharing their thoughts about the human presence on their planet? About her? Her mind boiled with wild thoughts. Could she join in their dreams, explain to them the threat posed by the Hugonauts? Maybe she could find the Froggie mother from so long ago. Maybe she could explain. Holding her breath with fear, she peered farther into the hole.

There, that corner, a bit of exposed floor, room for her to step in, if she was careful. She reached out a hand to grip the edge of the hole, noticing how it shook before she grabbed on to an exposed root. She swung her leg over, and dug the toe of her boot into the loamy wall-soil. Hugging her body tight against the dirt wall to avoid stepping on exposed limbs and faces and stomachs, she slid down into the pit. The sensation of drowning swept over her, and she realized she had been holding her breath. She gasped, dragging the musky air of the sleeping creatures deep into her lungs. Panting, she looked around, noting the way the Froggies wrapped their limbs around each other, torsos touching, heads resting against neighbor backs. She hesitated, then lay the flare gun down, slowly leaned over and unsealed one boot, then the other. . . .

Naked, she curled up on the ground, aware of the touch of the skin of the Froggies on her legs, her back, her arms. Leaning back, she rested her head against the bristly spine of her neighbor and closed her eyes.

As often in the dreams, smells and touch began to mix in with the sounds. Poke, squirm, nestle down, deeper. Push aside slippery limbs, slide over brother-backs and sister-backs, around and through the tangle of skin and bristles. He breathes in gingery musk of contentment and peppery hunger, finally food-smell, he burrows inward to the source. Gleaming warmth, it smells of wet and orange. He bites, sucks—But these images—he recognizes them—his own memories! They were dreaming his dream, the feeding-nest he remembered before any other. His dream, and, he realized, Erin's, and Heather's, from their earliest days. How could they share his memory? As he wondered, the link of images broke. He felt physically jarred, shoved and pulled. An ugly smell oozed into his mind, cucumbers and tar, mixed in with smell of Jo-ann. Their anger toward her burned into him. Dislocation. Terror. Isolation.

Abruptly, he woke.

Years ago, Jo-ann had tried out the department's sensory deprivation tank. Floating in viscous liquid, body temperature, suspended, no pull of gravity, she drifted. Eyes covered, ears plugged, a mask over her nose and mouth delivered tasteless, odorless air. At first her mind had raced, thoughts of her research, of Dave. Then it slowed, lingered on one image, a hand, for an endless time, then a color, yellow. Maybe a banana. She felt her thoughts congeal, she could watch them pass across her inner vision, one by one. The first time she took off her clothes for Dave. Delivering that paper on chimp language development at the Xenoanthropology Conference. Her first alien sunrise. The hospital, the doctor's head moving back and forth, so slow, while Dave's fingerbones pressed against hers. Each thought arrived, first a pinprick, then a small intrusion, growing larger and rounder and fuller, until she held the entirety of the memory for an unbearable moment, and then the process reversed, the thought shrank and collapsed smoothly upon itself, disappeared. Then the next arrived, just a hint, growing into her mind.

These dreams were both like and unlike.

No visual component at all. Utter darkness. A suffocation of blackness, obliterating her sense of self. But the growing world of smell, sound, touch surrounded her, rebuilt her awareness one touch at a time. She could not interpret what she experienced, searched in vain for patterns. The images swirled around her floating weightless existence, pushed against her skin, tugging her this way and that. Sounds, not human, strange combinations. Here and there, blank spaces in the flow, perhaps when the sound traveled beyond human ears, and the dreaming of human ears. Smells of the planet, smells of memory, but not her memory, emotions she had never felt, never imagined. Sliding skin, silky like no human skin, smells that she might have found revolting, but here, these smells evoked hunger and delicious satiation. And there, that smell! she recognized the smell of Tommy, her Tommy. Her baby was here! She cried her relief. And there, Erin, there Heather.

Abruptly, she woke, and quickly dressed as the nest came alive.

The Froggies were moving, writhing their plenitude of arms. They reeked, a new smell, cucumbers and tar. Their motions were smooth and graceful, but Jo-ann saw danger in them. The two aliens nearest her stood to their full height, towering over her, pressing her up against the dirt wall. She struggled to breathe.

"Wait, wait! Tommy, where are you? Tommy, help me! You don't understand. I need to talk to you. You have to listen, the Hugonauts are taking your planet! Tommy!"

They leaned in, one on each side, pushing against her shoulders, her rib cage. She squirmed, hunched her shoulders to protect her head, but they kept coming closer. She crouched defensively, but when the one on the right grabbed her arm with his midhand, she panicked. She twisted savagely, kicked its leg, dived past and scrambled for the surface. It tried to keep hold of her arm, but she bit the grasping midhand and the creature jerked back with a squawk. The other grabbed at her thigh, but she kicked out wildly and it could not find purchase on her leg. She had just got her head over the edge of the hole, when the Froggie managed to pull her leg back, dragging her down again.

She screamed, drove her elbow into its ribs. When it bent forward, she punched it, right on the nose. The high-pitched keen hurt her ears, and guilt stabbed her, but she forced herself back, up the wall. Her hand reached out, grabbing for roots, for leverage, and when she felt something hard under her palm, she latched on and pulled with terror. But it was no root, it came down so quickly that she fell.

She landed next to the flare gun, and looked at it in amazement. As she hesitated, the Froggies piled onto her, one, two, another. She couldn't see. Sobbing, she curled in on herself, cradling the flare gun to her stomach.

Her hand found the switch, she rolled and released.

Chaos.

The screams of the aliens deafened her. She thrashed out, bucking and clawing, stepping on arms, walking up an exposed back, kicking the grasping hands. A tail reached for her waist—she slapped it with the flare gun. Tears poured down her cheeks, blinding her. She scrambled over the rim, ran a few feet, tripped and collapsed. The smell of burned flesh filled her nostrils, but it was not the smell of human flesh. She retched.

"Tommy?" she cried.

"Mommy, is that you?" A half-pint Froggie leapt awkwardly out of the pit. "Mommy, what was that?"

"Oh, Tommy," she looked back over her shoulder, "Tommy, they were hurting me. I didn't have a choice. Are you okay? Where is Erin? Heather?"

He reached out his upperhand, almost touched her, pulled back. She smelled devastation. "Mommy, you did this, didn't you? Why did you come here? They are so angry with you. You have to go."

She scrubbed at her eyes, reached out to her son. She touched his back, stroked the silky skin. He shuddered and moved away. "You have to go," he repeated.

"But the dreams, I felt them. I felt you in the dreams."

"You, humans, you aren't allowed there. You have your place and this is our place."

"I need to help you—"

Erin and Heather appeared, coming out of the same hole. Erin charged at Jo-ann. "Auntie Jo-ann, you did a bad thing. You hurt someone, there's blood!"

She looked toward the Froggie nest. Sitting on the edge, one of the aliens cradled the stump of its midarm. Blood, brown and thick, oozed out of the stump evenly, not pulsing as from a human injury. Shocked, she watched. She tried to speak, but couldn't get words past the lump in her throat.

The bleeding slowed. She blinked, and the bleeding had stopped completely. A final drip, and the flesh at the end of the Froggie's arm collapsed inward. Amazed, she realized that the Froggie would live—its gate circulatory system had acted as a natural tourniquet.

But now the children approached, focused on her, backs bristling with anger.

"I'm sorry. I didn't mean to. I never wanted to hurt anyone. But you have to tell them, there are bad people, the Hugonauts—"

Heather interrupted. "What's so bad about them?"

"They want to destroy the planet. They want to dig holes, really big holes that kill the forest and the animals, to get at the rocks underneath. They would dig and dig until there was nothing left. Not your nice nesting holes, much bigger. They've messed up other planets before, and now they want to take your home away."

"But you're the one who messed things up. You took us away from our real home, didn't you?" said Erin.

Jo-ann felt Erin's accusation driving at her, but she had to concentrate on explaining the important issue to them. "Yes. I did. But you have to understand, I need to talk to them. All these years, I've been trying to prove that they communicate. So we can keep the planet safe. And it's the dreams, you children found the answer, they talk in dreams. I felt it, too! I felt I was in their dreams. . . ."

Tommy whipped his tail around, as though he would slap her, but just brushed the tip across her forearm. "No! I *told* you already. You can't feel them—it's not allowed. They're very angry with you."

"But, Tommy, I knew you were there, I could smell, such strange smells, but with you mixed in, and some chemical, like tar. What were they saying, do you know?"

"Mommy, no. You're not my mommy. You stole us. They say, Go."

"Go," said Heather.

"Go," said Erin.

"But you have to help. . . ."

She searched for the words to explain why she needed them. Why she needed the Froggies to listen to her, to welcome her. She had been so sure, those years ago, sure that the Froggies would answer her, and she would show everyone their intelligence, show that Jo-ann had seen the truth everyone else had missed. And now she had it, their communication dancing through her mind. (*Go*, Tommy had said. He had told her to leave. *Go*, echoed in her ears.) These amazing creatures would share their dreams with her. The children would have to understand. They had to see how she needed them to translate—

Her thoughts came to a grinding halt. Words left her. She paused, lingered over that last word, *see*. She looked. The children sat before her, one two three, and they were not human children. She spoke, they spoke back, she thought they were talking with each other. But, even though the children used the same words she used, they did not see what she saw. They did not see the Hugonauts strip-mining their planet. They did not see the people in the courtroom laughing at them, at her for declaring their intelligence. They did not see. She had no idea what they perceived, inside their heads. After the briefest glimpse, she knew that she would never know what they imagined, or what they needed.

They had chosen, and they had not chosen her.

She couldn't help it; she started crying. "I just wanted to find a way to talk to them. I thought you kids would talk to me."

She reached out to Tommy. He stepped back.

"You are wrong. You don't belong here. They've explained it to me. This is our place, not yours. We don't come into your world. You stay out of ours."

"Tommy, I *love* you."

"You go now."

Dave was waiting at the gate. As Jo-ann stepped out of the trees, he reached out a hand. He waved in question toward the trees behind her. She shook her head.

"Did you find them?"

"Yes."

Dave folded his shirts, stacking them in a careful pile. Jo-ann crammed her data cells into the mem-erase, one after the other.

Jo-ann felt him watching her. "These aren't the important ones. Just baseline material."

"I didn't say anything."

While he tucked glassware in with the shirts, she moved around the house, restless, picking things up and putting them down again, collecting data cells for the ruthless scrubbing of the mem-erase. Feeding her latest collection into the machine, she reached with her other hand for the data cell propped on the table by the sofa, the one with their favorite pictures of Tommy, of the three of them making up the game of hop-and-catch. As she picked it up, it was pulled back. Startled, she turned her head.

"Not that one," Dave said. "I want to keep it."

"No need for it, might as well reuse the data cell. They're not cheap."

Dave didn't let go. After a moment, Jo-ann let her hand drop. She looked out the window at the garden. She felt Tommy stroke her hair. She watched again as Dave carefully snipped the encroaching vines off his azalea bushes.

She thought, Vines wrap around your heart—when you try to pull them out, you only tear yourself.

Writer collaborations are strange things—when they work, they're marvelous meldings of two (or more) fertile minds into something not quite like each of them separately. We have two such collaborations in this book, and this first one has proved fertile, indeed.

Barry Malzberg, besides being a N.Y. Giants football fan, has been a wonderfully iconoclastic writer from the original New Wave to now. His stories are instantly recognizable as Malzbergian—intense, almost frantic in narration, cerebral and emotive at the same time. Kathe Koja first made a name for herself in the dark fantasy field.

They've written some wonderful stories together. "What We Did That Summer" is one of them, and was one of the first stories I bought for this volume.

What We Did That Summer

Kathe Koja and Barry N. Malzberg

*

Boy, I sure miss those aliens, he said.

What? She had to put down her beer for that one but there was nothing stronger than amusement now; she was not surprised; it was not possible any longer to surprise her. Say that again, she said, leaning into the metal ladderback of the kitchen chair, the one with the crooked leg that when it moved scraped that red linoleum with the textbook sound of discontent. Say it again and then explain it.

Nothing to explain, he said, I just miss them. We called them aliens, those girls, it was our word for them, they would have done anything. Anything, you wouldn't believe, he said, nodding and nodding in that way he had. Not for money, you know, they didn't want money or presents, whatever. It was like a contest they were having between themselves. Almost like we weren't there at all, he said, and sighed, scratched himself in memory as she watched without contempt, watched all this from some secret part of herself that was not a failed madam, not a woman whom he had once paid, regularly though never well, to fuck; not a woman whose home now permitted no yielding surface whatsoever, nothing soft or warm or pleasant to the touch, no plush sofas and certainly no beds; she herself slept on a cot like a board and ate macaroni and cheese and potpies that she bought at the supermarket when they were on sale. Tell me, she said. Tell me about those aliens, why not. Let me get another beer first, though.

Get one for me, too, he said, and scratched again; there was an annoying dry patch between his legs, just behind the dangle of his scrotum, not an easy place to scratch in public but at her place, well. Well

well well. It had never mattered what he did here, not in the old days, the brisk wild days in which she had absorbed without delight the greater part of his pay, or that strange hallucinatory period in which he had decided he was into S&M and she had proved so thoroughly and with such élan that he was not; not during his divorce from Deborah and the unraveling that followed, and the rewinding of the skein which followed *that*; she was in some ways the best friend he had ever had, and it was for that reason he suspected without knowing or caring to admit that he had begun to tell her this story, this night, in this comfortless kitchen with its piles of old yellow pages and its warped unclosable window presenting its endless, disheartening view of the faraway river and all points east.

All right, she said, setting down both cans of beer; they did not use glasses; glasses were both effete and a bother with beer like this. Go on, tell me. So they fucked your heads off, you and your gang, those dumb boys you ran with, and they never took your dollar bills or the flowers you picked yourselves. Queen Anne's lace, am I right, from the side of the road? past the beer cans in the ditches? Or the candy you bought from the drugstore, three Hershey bars for them to split? What charity, she said, laughing although not directly at him or even the boy he had been. What princes, she said, what royalty you must have been.

If you're going to make fun, he said, subtly ashamed at the sound of his own petulance but unwilling to correct it, I won't tell the story.

Oh yes you will, she said, not laughing now but smiling. Of course you will. Go on ahead and tell it, I won't laugh. Much.

All right then, he said, and scratched again, but thus invited was somehow at a loss for a true beginning: he drank some of the beer, set down the can. Well, he said. You remember John Regard?

John Regard, she said. I remember he was an asshole, yes.

Well, think what you want, but he was a good friend to me, he used to let me borrow his car, that black-and-yellow Barracuda. Remember that?

No, she said; they both knew she was lying. If there's going to be a lot about John Regard in this story, I don't think I want to hear it after all.

Oh, just shut up, he said, and listen. Anyway, it was John who found them, out in the field that night; it was behind where the factories used to be, all those tool-and-die places. We were drinking beer, but we weren't drunk, stopping the narrative there, pointing with the hand holding the can; neither of them if they noticed remarked on this irony. We were not drunk and I want you to remember that.

I will, she said.

Anyway, John said he heard voices or saw a flashlight or something, and we headed over there, and we found these girls and they were naked. Three of them, bare-ass naked.

She scraped the chair leg a little, leaning with all her weight. What were they doing? she said.

Nothing, I don't know. Even from this distance, time and age, and geography she saw his wistfulness, the depth and slow passion of his wonder. They were just sitting there, he said, talking. And John said—

I know what John said. Meat on the hoof, that's what John—

Will you quit? he said, with a sudden sad ferocity that silenced them both; they sat in the silence as in the middle of a large and formal room and finally he said, Just let me tell it, all right? Just let me tell the fucking thing and get it over with, and then you can say whatever the hell you want. All right? Is that all right with you, milady?

Yes, she said. Yes, it's fine. Go on.

Well. Not sullen but disturbed, as if he had lost his place in chronology itself and would take his own time finding it. Well, anyway, he said. They were sitting there naked and John said (daring her with a look to mock) Do you ladies need some help? And they didn't say anything at first but finally they did, one of them, she seemed like the oldest or the smartest or something, and she said, in this way that was like an accent but not really an accent, you know what I mean? Like the person is from somewhere but you can't place where. And she said We're having a bet. That's what she said. We're having a bet and we can't decide who's right.

And John said (leaning back a little as if back in the field, taking his time, measuring his place) Well what's the bet? Now you have to remember we were both kids, then, you know, we were sixteen or so, and we both had pretty good rods on, looking at these naked girls there in the dirt and the weeds and so on. They weren't really beautiful girls, they were kind of a little fat or out of shape—what's the word? misshapen? Is that a word?—but they were definitely girls and they were naked girls and that was good enough for us. So John said What's your bet, and they said We are trying to bet which one of us can have the most boys.

It was very still in the kitchen; she did not say anything though he thought she would, until the silence told him that she was not going to comment on this and so Well, he said. That was all we needed to hear and, well, John said you can start with me, ladies, and so there we were. Us and those three girls.

She still did not say anything until she saw that he would not continue without some kind of comment or response from her, something to keep the story moving like rollers under a ponderous piano, or someone's obese and terrible aunt. Well, she said. There you were, like you say. I can guess what happened next. Then what?

Well that was the thing, he said. After we were done and getting dressed I asked them their names, you know, and they wouldn't tell us, not like they were shy or something but as if they weren't sure what we wanted. And so they wouldn't say anything and finally I left.

You? she said. What happened to John?

He was, he had to go piss or something. I don't remember, crossly. Anyway that was it for that night but the next night we went out there, you know, again (in that field with its weeds and chunked metal, scrap and dirt and the oily smell of the tool-and-die shops, its moonlessness and its absence of mystery) and there they were. Only this time only one of them was naked and the other two were wearing these dresses, weird dresses, you know, like old ladies or something would wear. And the smart one said She doesn't want to make a baby, about the naked one, you know? She doesn't want to make a baby so do something different this time.

Well, she said, and could not help smiling; and he smiled, too, and they both laughed a little, a laugh not wholly comfortable but without true embarrassment, and she said Get me another beer, will you? and he did. So anyway, he said. We did it all different ways with that girl, and the other two sat in their old-lady dresses and watched us like they were kids in school and never said a word or made any sound at all. Just sat there in the dirt and watched us do their sister, you know, until we were tired.

How long did that take? she said.

A lot longer than it does now, he said, and she smiled, and he did, too. So they talked to each other in little voices and John said How about tomorrow? and they said no, not tomorrow but that they would see us soon. And then we left.

So what happened then? she said. Incidentally, you're going to knock that beer over if you keep—

I see it, it's okay. So we went back anyway (and from his face she could see he was less present in the kitchen than in that midnight field, picking his way with lust and hope through the clutter and debris, searching for three misshapen naked girls who would perform with him acts he had never dreamed of suggesting, who would do whatever he asked for as long as he could without demanding recompense or return; it was some men's idea of heaven, she knew) but they weren't there. We waited around and waited around and they didn't show and so finally we left. And John went back the next night and—

John did? What about you?

I didn't have a car, he said shortly; they both knew what that meant and neither remarked on it, John's well-known selfishness and duplicity, John sneaking back alone in the yellow-and-black Barracuda to have them all for himself. Anyway, he said, John went back but he didn't find them, and so we figured maybe they were gone for good. But then one night about two weeks later they came back. It was raining, we had to do it in the car. John was in back—

With two of them, she said.

Yes. With two of them. You want to tell my story or should I? (But it was mere rote irritation, only physical pain could have stopped this story now; it was like the last drive to orgasm, you needed a baseball bat and room to swing it if you wanted to make it stop.) So I was up front with the other one, and it rained and rained, water like crazy down the windshield and the windows. And every once in a while I would try to get her to drink some beer, you know, but she never would, she said she didn't want any. And we kept at it all night, it was about four o'clock when finally they said they would see us later and they got out of the car and walked away in the rain, the three of them side by side like they were in a marching band or something, they kept walking until I couldn't see them anymore.

And then what? she said, imagining him sore and drunk and triumphant, prince in a circus of carnality and stretched imagination, after fucking and sucking and dog-style and what have you, what else is there, what else is left for a sixteen-year-old boy who has not yet perfected the angles and declensions of true desire? Even with her, as a man both matured and stunted by the pressure of his needs, there had come a limiting and it had come from him. Then what happened? she said again, but gently, to lead and not to prod.

He did not answer at first; he seemed not to have heard her. Then he sighed and drank the rest of the beer in the can, one melancholy swallow. Well, he said. I was all for finding out their names and where they lived and so on and so on, but John said they were probably foreigners and their fathers would shoot our heads off or cut off our balls or something if we tried. So all we did was go back to the field, and sit there, and wait.

And did they come back? she said.

Well, he said, that's the interesting part. One of the interesting parts, I guess. They did and they didn't. What I mean is that the next night out in the field we waited and waited until we had got past the point where the beer meant anything, you know that kind of drunk where every new one just seems to bring you down, make you less drunk and sadder? We sat there in the field drinking and talking about pussy and what the aliens had been like and all the time the sky seemed to be lightening up like dawn except that it wasn't near morning and we weren't getting anywhere at all. The fucking had seemed good at first but the longer we talked and waited the sadder it got until I had a whole new look on the situation: we were a couple of sixteen-year-old kids humping these naked girls who didn't know any better and in a way, when you looked at it, it could have been maybe even rape. Like they were feeble-minded or something or just out from an institution, they sure didn't act normal. How the hell did we know? How did we know? he said with a shudder, looking now as if the field in memory had become a bleak and dangerous place, a place of pain and not of happiness; and she looked at him not for the first time in a way that went past his old face, his sunken shoulders, his dumb, dragging features, and she thought You took his money and let him climb on top of you, and then you didn't want to feel like a whore anymore, so you stopped taking his money and then sooner or later you stopped taking him and what the hell was that, now? What did that come to? Are you happy now? Never mind him: what about you?

Well, he said, the sluice of beer problematic down his throat, he swallowed as if it were his own trapped saliva, as if it was something he needed but did not want. Well just about four in the morning or something like that, John and I were so drunk and so sick we were ready to give up and go home and then all of a sudden this guy comes out of the bushes, a tall thin guy as naked as the girls had been except for this big hat he was wearing and something around his neck like a medal or a badge, it was hard to tell in the light. But he was naked as hell and I just want to tell you this part, you can believe it or not, but he didn't have any cock or balls. He had nothing in that place, just smoothness, and he was about the scariest fellow we had ever seen, drunk or sober, because of that empty place there and a look in his eyes which even then we could tell. You're the ones, aren't you? he said to John and me, the same way the girls talked, that foreigner-talk, only from him it was mean. You're the ones they've been doing it with.

We looked at him, and there was nothing to say. I mean, what could we say? Yes, we were doing it? Doing what? While we were trying to figure that one out he made a motion and the girls were there, except this time they weren't naked. They must have come from the bushes, too, but it was hard to tell. Maybe they dropped from the sky. You got to understand, we were so drunk by now and the whole situation was so peculiar that we couldn't get a handle on it. You follow me? But those girls were chittering away and poking each other like animals and then they pointed at me and John, raised their fingers and just pointed them down. We felt pretty damned foolish, I want you to know, and scared, too; here's some guy without a cock and balls and three girls pointing at you, it would scare anybody. Even you, he said.

She said nothing. The beer in the can had gone flat, but she did not move, to drink it, to replace it. The refrigerator buzzed and buzzed like a large and sorry insect trapped in a greasy jar.

Maybe it wouldn't scare you, he said. Who knows what scares you, anyway, but it sure scared us. No one said anything for a minute, and then I said, All right. All right, I said, we did it. They wanted us to, John said, and you can say what you want about John, but that was a brave thing to say, in that field at that moment, to that guy. They wanted us to, he said, and they asked for everything and if they tell you different, it's a lie. We gave them whatever they wanted, and if you got any quarrel, take it up with them.

I don't have a quarrel, the guy said, I only want facts. The girls were still chittering, and I could see that John was starting to shake, but I have to tell you that for me it was different. I might've been more scared than any of them, but whether it was the beer or not, I just didn't give a damn. I mean, it looked like some kind of farmer's daughter scam, you know what I mean? Like he was going to charge us for having devirginated his precious daughters and who the hell was he, anyway, and where was he when they were being fucked? All right, I said, John's right. We did it because they begged for it and wanted it worse than us and that's all there is to it. You got any problems you take it up with them.

I already have, the guy said, and made a motion, and the three girls turned around and moved away from there. That's already been achieved, the guy said. Now it comes to you. You've done this and you're going to have to pay. That's all. This is what they call the iron law of the universe, and you are caught up in it.

A pause less silence than memory's clench, he was so far back in that night it was as if she spoke to two people, man and boy and neither truly listening. Why are you telling me this now? she said. You never told me any of this all these years. I lay under you for ten years and you treated me like shit and then you left and now you tell me this story? I don't understand you, she said. I never understood you, realizing as she said this that it was only part of the truth: the real thing was that she had never understood anything. So why do you come back to tell me this now? she said. You were sixteen, you and John, that was, what, twenty-five, thirty years ago? What does this have to do with anything? Maybe you should just get out of here, take your ass down the hollow and split.

I never liked it, she said, leaning slightly toward him, her elbows on the table as if she sighted him down the barrel of some strange and heinous gun. I have to tell you that now. You tell me about aliens? You're an alien. You never made me feel like a woman, you never made me feel anything at all except bad. I felt like a cornhole, is that what you call it? A gloryhole? A place to stick it into until it made come and you yelped, that was a hell of a thing. I don't like you much for that.

Well, he said, wincing, staring at her, dragged at least halfway back from the field. Well, now, I don't like that either. I'm almost finished now, why don't you let me finish? I got started so let me finish and shut your mouth. All right? She said nothing. Well, he said, in such a way that made her wonder if he had heard more than every third word she had said, well this guy says again You have to pay. That is the first and only law of the universe, of time and density. If you do something you pay for it but you pay double and if you don't understand what you were doing, well then it is triple. Here you are now, the guy said, you pay triple. Three times. Then he made some kind of motion like he was shooing us off, and the next thing I knew the field was on fire. It was fire outside like the fucking had been fire inside and everything was scorched black and then he was gone. That was the end of it—girls, guy without a cock, the whole thing. They never came back again. John was standing in the same place when the fire went out and looked about the same, but who knows, inside and outside, who can tell? He had nothing to say and I had nothing to say either. You have to pay, the guy said, that was the deal. So we had to pay, that was all.

So then what? she said.

So nothing, he said. We left the field and that was the end of it for thirty years. It's thirty years tonight, you want to know, he said. So it's an anniversary. I'm telling you on the anniversary. That was a decision John and I made, that with what we knew and what had happened we'd wait twenty-five years and then tell. Maybe that sounds dumb, but there's a lot of dumb stuff around. The whole thing, I figure, was pretty much dumb from the start; that's another iron law of the universe.

Twenty-five years, she said, or thirty? Make up your mind.

It's thirty tonight, he said.

So what's the point? she said. Are you going to tell me that John died and now you're going to? Is that the payoff, that on the thirtieth anniversary of the guy without a cock telling you you had to pay, you cash in? That's a bunch of crap, she said. You were always full of crap. In bed, out of bed, you told more lies than any man I ever knew. Enough, she said, and stood, picked up the beer cans. I've heard enough for now.

You're not getting any ever again, anniversary or no anniversary, cock or no cock. Just go home.

John didn't die just now, he said. He was staring up at her without any true expression, as if his features could not form the picture his mind wanted to show. John died a long time ago, six, seven years, he got hit by a bus. In Fayetteville. I thought you knew that, didn't you know that?

No, she said, I didn't know. I don't keep up with things so good anymore, I live in a shack and try to stay away from all of that stuff. I was never much for news. So John is dead, all right. And where does that leave you?

The iron law, he said, I had to tell you about that because of the anniversary. I would have told John, we would have told each other but he was dead, he got the bus up his behind first and there was nobody to tell. Maybe he took the bus up his behind, who knows? Look at me, he said. He reached for her, touched her face, dragged her face to attention. Do you see me? he said. Do you know what I got? Do you know what really went on there in that field, what it came to?

Crazy, she thought, he was crazy like the rest of them, they'd tell you one thing, anything to get inside you and then they'd yank that one gob of come out, barking and moaning and then go back to being cute until the next time. Except that this one had always been crazy, with his cowboy boots and his bondage stories and his divorce from Deborah, always mooning around, it was different for him, she knew, an entirely different thing.

They let us do everything, he said. Everything we wanted. But everything means everything, it means all of it, do you understand? He seemed very sad, as if he might begin to curse or cry. Like you used to be, he said. Just like you.

I never was, she said, simply, without heat or cruelty. I never was anything you wanted, don't you know that? Don't you know that by now?

You take, he said, you take and take and take and then it's all inside you and you have to give it back. I'm not talking about one squirt, he said, not jism. This is something else.

Take and take, so what else is new? she said. Just don't give it to me. The beer cans were still in her hands; her hands were sweating. I don't want it. Don't you give it to me. She felt if she looked too closely at him she would see inside his skull, see his brain, the soft and desperate jelly within the cage: see the memories and thoughts, foaming, dead foam like scum on the water, polluted scum at the beach that burns your ankles when you walk too close, burns your skin like the field, burning, burning.

So now we have to give it back, he said. John's dead. If you take, you give, if you give you take. His breathing was ragged, uneven; I want to show you, he said through that breathing like a gag against his mouth, like gauze. I want you to see what I mean. What I got.

I don't want to see anything, she said, get out of here now, but it was too late, he was pulling at his pants, pulling at himself and for one moment she thought in simple terror: *They took it*, it's all gone, it's all going to be smooth there like the guy in the story but it was not smooth, it was a general circulation cock and balls just like she remembered except somewhat looser and wrinkled, half-erect there in his hand, his hand was shaking as if in some vast vibration. As if his body existed in some other room than this.

What comes out, he said, breathing, shaking. You have to see. I want you to see this thing. It was not spunk of which he was speaking, he had warned her of that, and she knew it was true. Take and take, he said, give and give. Give and take. He was getting it harder, the cock springing straight; in the empty place where the aliens had marked him the iron law was working, clamping, squeezing as his hand squeezed, as he wheezed and breathed, as he lazed and hazed, as he shook and took. She backed against the sink, turned her face away. His breath in crescendo, the refrigerator buzz, her own heart; oh, boy, you have to see this, he said. Turn around and look at this.

She said nothing.

Turn around and look, he said. Look at me.

The cracked edge of the counter pressed her belly, her hip. Around her the field was burning; the air was filled with the smell of scorching grass. Awaiting landfall, awaiting the impact of metal on earth she put up one alien hand to shield her face from the sight of him, from the worst of what was to come: the mounting boys, their simple, screaming, wondering faces, the stink of grass, the fiery closure of her thighs: all their detritus poured into her cup of reparation. Alien she fell, alien she waited: alien the great locks of the ship slammed open. In that riveting metal clutch: nothing. The clinging contact, the groans of the boys. The heart in his hand: but nothing.

I could go on for hours about Michael Moorcock's contributions to this whole mess we call science fiction—and dwell for even more hours on the marvelous things he's done for the fantasy field. He was also the guy who took over the editorial reins of New Worlds *magazine in 1964, publishing stories by Aldiss, Ballard, Disch, Sladek, and the other progenitors of the New Wave.*

Please: look it all up; I haven't got the room here to list it all properly, and, frankly, the man's achievements make me feel like a dust mote.

It's all out there, The Eternal Champion, Elric, Cornelius—find it and read it.

But not before you read what follows.

A Slow Saturday Night at the Surrealist Sporting Club:

Being a Further Account of Engelbrecht the Boxing Dwarf and His Fellow Members

MICHAEL MOORCOCK
(AFTER MAURICE RICHARDSON)

✶

I happened to be sitting in the snug of the Strangers' Bar at the Surrealist Sporting Club on a rainy Saturday night, enjoying a well-mixed Existential Fizz (2 parts Vortex Water to 1 part Sweet Gin) and desperate to meet a diverting visitor, when Death slipped unostentatiously into the big chair opposite, warming his bones at the fire and remarking on the unseasonable weather. There was sure to be a lot of flu about. It made you hate to get the tube but the buses were worse and had I seen what cabs were charging these days? He began to drone on as usual about the ozone layer and the melting pole, how we were poisoning ourselves on GM foods and feeding cows to cows and getting all that pollution and cigarette smoke in our lungs and those other gloomy topics he seems to relish, which I suppose makes you appreciate it when he puts you out of your misery.

I had to choose between nodding off or changing the subject. The evening being what it was, I made the effort and changed the subject. Or at least, had a stab at it.

"So what's new?" It was feeble, I admit. But, as it happened, it stopped him in midmoan.

"Thanks for reminding me," he said, and glanced at one of his many watches. "God's dropping in—oh, in about twelve minutes, twenty-five seconds. He doesn't have a lot of time, but if you've any questions to ask him, I suggest you canvass the other members present and think up some good ones in a hurry. And he's not very fond of jokers, if you know what I mean. So stick to substantial questions or he won't be pleased."

"I thought he usually sent seraphim ahead for this sort of visit?" I queried mildly. "Are you all having to double up or something? Is it overpopulation?" I didn't like this drift, either. It suggested a finite universe, for a start.

Our Ever-Present Friend rose smoothly. He looked around the room with a distressed sigh, as if suspecting the whole structure to be infected with dry rot and carpenter ants. He couldn't as much as produce a grim brotherly smile for the deathwatch beetle that had come out especially to greet him. "Well, once more into the breach. Have you noticed what it's like out there? Worst on record, they say. Mind you, they don't remember the megalithic. Those were the days, eh? See you later."

"Be sure of it." I knew a moment of existential angst.

Sensitively, Death hesitated, seemed about to apologize, then thought better of it. He shrugged. "See you in a minute," he said. "I've got to look out for God in the foyer and sign him in. You know." He had the air of one who had given up worrying about minor embarrassments and was sticking to the protocol, come hell or high water. He was certainly more laconic than he had been. I wondered if the extra work, and doubling as a seraph, had changed his character.

With Death gone, the Strangers' was warming up rapidly again, and I enjoyed a quiet moment with my fizz before rising to amble through the usual warped and shrieking corridors to the Members' Bar, which appeared empty.

"Are you thinking of dinner?" Lizard Bayliss, looking like an undisinfected dishrag, strolled over from where he had been hanging up his obnoxious cape. Never far behind, out of the WC, bustled Englebrecht the Dwarf Clock Boxer, who had gone ten rounds with the Greenwich Atom before that overrefined chronometer went down to an iffy punch in the eleventh. His great, mad eyes flashed from under a simian hedge of eyebrow. As usual he wore a three-piece suit a size too small for him, in the belief it made him seem taller. He was effing and blinding about some imagined insult offered by the taxi driver who had brought them back from the not altogether successful Endangered Sea Monsters angling contest in which, I was to learn later, Engelbrecht had caught his hook in a tangle of timeweed and wound up dragging down the *Titanic*, which explained that mystery. Mind you, he still had to come clean about the R101. There was some feeling in the club concerning the airship, since he'd clearly taken bets against himself. Challenged, he'd muttered some conventional nonsense about the Maelstrom and the Inner World, but we'd heard that one too often to be convinced. He also resented our recent rule limiting all aerial angling to firedrakes and larger species of pterodactyls.

Lizard Bayliss had oddly colored bags under his eyes, giving an even more downcast appearance to his normally dissolute features. He was a little drained from dragging the Dwarf in by his collar. It appeared that, seeing the big rods, the driver had asked Bayliss if that was his bait on the seat beside him. The irony was, of course, that the Dwarf had been known to use himself as bait more than once, and there was still some argument over interpretation of the rules in that area, too. The Dwarf had taken the cabbie's remark to be specific not because of his diminutive stockiness, but because of his sensitivity over the rules issue. He stood to lose a few months, even years, if they reversed the result.

He was still spitting on about "nitpicking fascist anoraks with severe anal-retention problems" when I raised my glass and yelled: "If you've an important question for God, you'd better work out how to phrase it. He's due in any second now. And he's only got a few minutes. At the Strangers' Bar. We could invite him in here, but that would involve a lot of time-consuming ritual and so forth. Any objection to meeting him back there?"

The Dwarf wasn't sure he had anything to say that wouldn't get taken the wrong way. Then, noticing how low the fire was, opined that the Strangers' was bound to offer better hospitality. "I can face my maker any time," he pointed out, "but I'd rather do it with a substantial drink in my hand and a good blaze warming my bum." He seemed unusually oblivious to any symbolism, given that the air was writhing with it. I think the *Titanic* was still on his mind. He was trying to work out how to get his hook back.

By the time we had collected up Oneway Ballard and Taffy Sinclair from the dining room and returned to the Strangers', God had already arrived. Any plans the Dwarf had instantly went out the window, because God was standing with his back to the fire, blocking everyone's heat. With a word to Taffy not to overtax the Lord of Creation, Death hurried off on some urgent business and disappeared back through the swing doors.

"I am thy One True God," said Jehovah, making the glasses and bottles rattle. He cleared his throat and dropped his tone to what must for him have been a whisper. But it was unnatural, almost false, like a TV presenter trying to express concern while keeping full attention on the autoprompt. Still, there was something totally convincing about God as a *presence*. You knew you were in his aura, and you knew you had Grace, even if you weren't too impressed by his stereotypical form. God added: "I am Jehovah, the Almighty. Ask of me what ye will."

Lizard knew sudden inspiration. "Do you plan to send Jesus back to Earth, and have you any thoughts about the 2:30 at Aintree tomorrow?"

"He is back," said God, "and I wouldn't touch those races, these days.

Believe me, they're all bent, one way or another. If you like the horses, do the National. . . . Take a chance. Have a gamble. It's anybody's race, the National."

"But being omniscient," said Lizard slowly, "wouldn't you know the outcome anyway?"

"If I stuck by all the rules of omniscience, it wouldn't exactly be sporting, would it?" God was staring over at the bar, checking out the Corona-Coronas and the melting marine chronometer above them.

"You don't think it's hard on the horses?" asked Jillian Burnes, the transexual novelist, who could be relied upon for a touch of compassion. Being almost seven feet tall in her spike heels, she was also useful for getting books down from the higher shelves and sorting out those bottles at the top of the bar that looked so temptingly dangerous.

"Bugger the horses," said God, "it's the race that counts. And anyway, the horses love it. They love it."

I was a little puzzled. "I thought we had to ask only substantial questions?"

"That's right?" God drew his mighty brows together in inquiry.

I fell into an untypical silence. I was experiencing a mild revelation concerning the head of the Church of England and her own favorite *pasatiempi*, but it seemed inappropriate to run with it at that moment.

"What I'd like to know is," said Engelbrecht, cutting suddenly to the chase, "who gets into Heaven and why?"

There was a bit of a pause in the air, as if everyone felt perhaps he'd pushed the boat out a little too far, but God was nodding. "Fair question," he said. "Well, it's cats, then dogs, but there's quite a few human beings, really. But mostly it's pets."

Lizard Bayliss had begun to grin. It wasn't a pretty sight with all those teeth that he swore weren't filed. "You mean you like animals better than people? Is that what you're saying, Lord?"

"I wouldn't generalize." God lifted his robe a little to let the fire get at his legs. "It's mostly cats. Some dogs. Then a few people. All a matter of proportion, of course. I mean, it's millions at least, probably billions, because I'd forgotten about the rats and mice."

"You like those, too?"

"No. Can't stand their hairless tails. Sorry, but it's just me. They can, I understand, be affectionate little creatures. No, they're for the cats. Cats are perfectly adapted for hanging out in heaven. But they still need a bit of a hunt occasionally. They get bored. Well, you know cats. You can't change their nature."

"I thought you could," said Oneway Ballard, limping up to the bar and ringing the bell. He was staying the night because someone had put a Denver boot on his Granada, and he'd torn the wheel off, trying to reverse out of it. He was in poor spirits because he and the car had been due to be married at Saint James's, Spanish Place, next morning and there was no way he was going to get the wheel back on and the car spruced up in time for the ceremony. He'd already called the vicar. Igor was on tonight and had trouble responding. We watched him struggle to get his hump under the low doorway. "Coming, Master," he said. It was too much like *Young Frankenstein* to be very amusing.

"*I* can change nature, yes," God continued. "I said *you* couldn't. Am I right?"

"Always," said Oneway, turning to order a couple of pints of Ackroyd's. He wasn't exactly looking on Fate with any favor at that moment. "But if you can . . ."

"There are a lot of things I could do," God pointed out. "You might have noticed. I could stop babies dying and famines and earthquakes. But I don't, do I?"

"Well, we wouldn't know about the ones you'd stopped," Engelbrecht pointed out, a bit donnishly for him. "So when the heavens open on the day of resurrection, it really will rain cats and dogs. And who else? Jews?"

"Some Jews, yes." In another being, God's attitude might have seemed defensive. "But listen, I want to get off the race issue. I don't judge people on their race, color, or creed. I never have. Wealth," he added a little sententiously, "has no color. If I've said who I favor and some purse-mouthed prophet decides to put his name in instead of the bloke I chose, then so it goes. It's free will in a free market. And you can't accuse me of not supporting the free market. Economic liberalism combined with conservative bigotry is the finest weapon I ever gave the chosen people. One thing you can't accuse me of being and that's a control freak."

"See," said Lizard, then blushed. "Sorry, God. But you just said it yourself—chosen people."

"Those are the people I choose," said God with a tinge of impatience. "Yes."

"So—the Jews."

"No. The moneylenders are mostly wasps. The usurers. Oil people. Big players in Threadneedle Street and Wall Street. Or, at least, a good many of them. Very few Jews, as it happens. And most of them, in Heaven, are from show business. Look around you and tell me who are the chosen ones. It's simple. They're the people in the limousines with great sex lives and private jets. Not cats, of course, who don't like travel. Otherwise, the chosen are very popular with the public or aggressively wealthy, the ones who have helped themselves. And those who help themselves God helps."

"You're a Yank!" Engelbrecht was struck by a revelation. "There are rules in this club about Yanks."

"Because Americans happen to have a handle on the realities, doesn't mean I'm American," God was a little offended. Then he softened. "It's probably an easy mistake to make. I mean, strictly speaking, I'm prehistoric. But, yes, America has come up trumps where religious worship is concerned. No old-fashioned iconography cluttering up their vision. There's scarcely a church in the nation that isn't a sort of glorified business seminar nowadays. God will help you, but you have to prove you're serious about wanting help. He'll at least match everything you make, but you have to make a little for yourself first, to show you can. It's all there. Getting people out of the welfare trap."

"Aren't they all a bit narrow-minded?" asked Taffy Sinclair, the metatemporal pathologist, who had so successfully dissected the Hess quints. "They are where I come from, I know." His stern good looks demanded our attention. "Baptists!" He took a long introspective pull of his shant. The massive dome of his forehead glared in the firelight.

God was unmoved by Sinclair's point. "Those Baptists are absolute wizards. They're spot on about me. And all good Old Testament boys. They use the Son of God as a source of authority, not as an example. The economic liberalism they vote for destroys everything of value worth conserving! It drives them nuts, but it makes them more dysfunctional and therefore more aggressive and therefore richer. Deeply unhappy, they turn increasingly to the source of their misery for a comfort that never comes. Compassionate consumption? None of your peace-and-love religions down there. Scientology has nothing on that little lot. Amateur, that Hubbard. But a bloody good one." He chuckled affectionately. "I look with special favor on the Southern Baptist Convention. So there does happen to be a preponderance of Americans in paradise, as it happens. But ironically no Scientologists. Hubbard's as fond of cats as I am, but he won't have Scientologists. I'll admit, too, that not all the chosen are entirely happy with the situation, because of being pretty thoroughly outnumbered, just by the Oriental shorthairs. And they do like to be in control. And many of them are bigots, so they're forever whining about the others being favored over them.

"Of course, once they get to Heaven, I'm in control. It takes a bit of adjustment for some of them. Some of them, in fact, opt for Hell, preferring to rule there than serve in Heaven, as it were. Milton was on the money, really, if a bit melodramatic and fanciful. Not so much a war in Heaven as a renegotiated contract. A pending paradise."

"I thought you sent Jesus down as the Prince of Peace," said Lizard a little dimly. The black bombers were wearing off, and he was beginning to feel the effects of the past few hours.

"Well, in those days," said God, "I have to admit, I had a different agenda. Looking back, of course, it was a bit unrealistic. It could never have worked. But I wouldn't take no for an answer, and you know the rest. New Testament and so on? Even then Paul kept trying to talk to me, and I wouldn't listen. Another temporary fix-up as it turned out. He was right. I admitted it. The problem is not in the creating of mankind, say, but in getting the self-reproducing software right. Do that and you have a human race with real potential. But that's always been the hurdle, hasn't it? Now lust and greed are all very well, but they do tend to involve a lot of messy side effects. And, of course, I tried to modify those with my ten commandments. Everyone was very excited about them at the time. A bit of fine-tuning I should have tried earlier. But we all know where that led. It's a ramshackle world at best, I have to admit. The least I can do is shore a few things up. I tried a few other belief systems. All ended the same way. So the alternative was to bless the world with sudden rationality. Yet once you give people a chance to think about it, they stop reproducing altogether. Lust is a totally inefficient engine for running a reproductive program. It means you have to modify the rational processes so that they switch off at certain times. And we all know where that leads. So, all in all, while the fiercest get to the top, the top isn't worth getting to and if it wasn't for the cats, I'd wind the whole miserable failure up. In fact I was going to until Jesus talked me into offering cloning as an alternative. I'd already sent them H. G. Wells and the Universal Declaration of Human Rights, The United Nations and all the rest of it. I'm too soft, I know, but Jesus was always my favorite, and he's never short of a reason for giving you all another chance. So every time I start to wipe you out, along he comes with that bloody charm of his and he twists me round his little finger. Well, you know the rest. One world war interrupted. Started again. Stopped again. Couple more genocides. Try again. No good. So far, as you've probably noticed, you haven't exactly taken the best options offered. Even Jesus is running out of excuses for you. So I'm giving it a few years and then, no matter what, I'm sending a giant comet. Or I might send a giant cat. It'll be a giant something anyway. And it'll be over with in an instant. Nothing cruel. No chance to change my mind."

Death was hovering about in the shadows, glancing meaningfully at his watches.

"That's it, then, is it?" Jillian Burnes seemed a bit crestfallen. "You've come to warn us that the world has every chance of ending. And you offer us no chance to repent, to change, to make our peace?" She tightened her lips. God could tell how she felt.

"I didn't offer," God reminded her. "Somebody asked. Look, I am not the Prince of Lies. I am the Lord of Truth. Not a very successful God of Love, though I must say I tried. More a God of, well, profit, I suppose. I mean everyone complains that these great religious books written in my name are incoherent, so they blame the writers. Never occurs to them that I might not be entirely coherent myself. On account of being—well, the supreme being. If I am existence, parts of existence are incoherent. Or, at least, apparently incoherent . . ." He realized he'd lost us.

"So there's no chance for redemption?" said Engelbrecht, looking about him. "For, say, the bohemian sporting fancy?"

"I didn't say that. Who knows what I'll feel like next week? But I'll always get on famously with cats. Can't resist the little beggars. There are some humans who are absolutely satisfied with the status quo in Heaven. But all cats get a kick out of the whole thing. The humans, on the quiet, are often only there to look after the cats."

"And the rest?"

"I don't follow you," said God. "Well, of course, being omniscient, I could follow you. What I should have said was 'I'm not following you.' "

"The rest of the people. What happens to them. The discards. The souls who don't make it through the pearly gates, as it were?" Engelbrecht seemed to be showing unusual concern for others.

"Recycled," said God. "You know—thrown back in the pot—what do the Celts call it?—the Mother Sea? After all, they're indistinguishable in life, especially the politicians. They probably hardly notice the change."

"Is that the only people who get to stay?" asked the Dwarf. "Rich people?"

"Oh, no," said God. "Though the others do tend to be funny. Wits and comics mostly. I love Benny Hill, don't you? He's often seated on my right side, you might say. You need a lot of cheering up in my job."

Jillian Burnes was becoming sympathetic. She loved to mother power. "I always thought you were a matron. I felt ashamed of you. It's such a relief to find out you're male." There was a sort of honeyed criticism in her voice, an almost flirtatious quality.

"Not strictly speaking male," said God, "being divine, sublime, and, ha, ha, all things, including woman, the eternal mime."

"Well, you sound very masculine," she said. "White and privileged."

"Absolutely!" God reassured her. "I approve of your method. That's exactly who I am and that's who I like to spend my time with, if I have to spend it with human beings at all."

Engelbrecht had bared his teeth. He was a terrier. "So can I get in, is what I suppose I'm asking?"

"Of course you can."

"Though I'm not Jewish."

"You don't have to be Jewish. I can't stress this too often. Think about it. I haven't actually favored the main mass of Jews lately, have I? I mean, take the twentieth century alone. I'm not talking about dress codes and tribal loyalties."

God spread his legs a little wide and hefted his gown to let the glow get to his divine buttocks. If we had not known it to be a noise from the fire, we might have thought he farted softly. He sighed. "When I first got into this calling there were all kinds of other deities about, many of them far superior to me in almost every way. More attractive. More eloquent. More easygoing. Elegant powers of creativity. Even the Celts and the Norse gods had a bit of style. But I had ambition. Bit by bit I took over the trade until, bingo, one day there was only me. I am, after all, the living symbol of corporate aggression, tolerating no competition and favoring only my own family and its clients. What do you want me to do? Identify with some bloody oik of an East Timorese who can hardly tell the difference between himself and a tree? Sierra Leone? Listen, you get yourselves into these messes, you get yourselves out."

"Well it's a good world for overpaid CEOs . . . ," mused Lizard.

"In this world and the next," confirmed God. "And it's a good world for overpaid comedians, too, for that matter."

"So Ben Elton and Woody Allen . . ."

God raised an omnipotent hand. "I said comedians."

"Um." Engelbrecht was having difficulties phrasing something. "Um . . ." He was aware of Death hovering around and ticking like a showcase full of Timexes. "What about it?"

"What?"

"You know," murmured Engelbrecht, deeply embarrassed by now, "the meaning of existence? The point."

"Point?" God frowned. "I don't follow."

"Well you've issued a few predictions in your time. . . ."

Death was clearing his throat. "Just to remind you about that policy subcommittee," he murmured. "I think we told them half-eight."

God seemed mystified for a moment. Then he began to straighten up. "Oh, yes. Important committee. Might be some good news for you. Hush, hush. Can't say any more."

Lizard was now almost falling over himself to get his questions in. "Did you have anything to do with global warming?"

Death uttered a cold sigh. He almost put the fire out. We all glared at him, but he was unrepentant. God remained tolerant of a question he might have heard a thousand times at least. He spread his hands. "Look. I plant a planet with sustainable wealth, OK? Nobody tells you to breed like rabbits and gobble it all up at once."

"Well, actually, you did encourage us to breed like rabbits," Jillian Burnes murmured reasonably.

"Fair enough," said God. "I have to agree corporate expansion depends on a perpetually growing population. We found that out. Demographics are the friend of business, right?"

"Well, up to a point, I should have thought," said Lizard, aware that God had already as good as told him a line had been drawn under the whole project. "I mean it's a finite planet and we're getting close to exhausting it."

"That's right." God glanced at the soft Dalí watches over the bar, then darted an inquiry at Death. "So?"

"So how can we stop the world from ending?" asked Englebrecht.

"Well," said God, genuinely embarrassed, "you can't."

"Can't? The end of the world is inevitable?"

"I thought I'd answered that one already. In fact, it's getting closer all the time." He began to move toward the cloakroom. God, I understood, couldn't lie. Which didn't mean he always liked telling the truth. And he knew anything he added would probably sound patronizing or unnecessarily accusatory. Then the taxi had turned up, and Death was bustling God off into it.

And that was that. As we gathered round the fire, Lizard Bayliss said he thought it was a rum do altogether and God must be pretty desperate to seek out company like ours, especially on a wet Saturday night. What did everyone else make of it?

We decided that nobody present was really qualified to judge, so we'd wait until Monday, when Monsignor Cornelius returned from Las Vegas. The famous Cowboy Jesuit had an unmatched grasp of contemporary doctrine.

But this wasn't good enough for Engelbrecht, who seemed to have taken against our visitor in a big way.

"I could sort this out," he insisted. If God had a timepiece of any weight he'd like to back, Engelbrecht would cheerfully show it the gloves.

That, admitted Jillian Burnes with new admiration, was the true existential hero, forever battling against Fate, and forever doomed to lose.

Engelbrecht, scenting an opportunity he hadn't previously even considered, became almost egregious, slicking back his hair and offering the great novelist an engaging leer.

When the two had gone off, back to Jillian's Tufnell Hill eyrie, Lizard Bayliss offered to buy the drinks, adding that it had been a bloody awful Friday and Saturday so far, and he hoped Sunday cheered up because if it didn't the whole weekend would have been a rotten write-off.

I'm pleased to say it was Taffy Sinclair who proposed we all go down to the Woods of Westermaine for some goblin shooting, so we rang up Count Dracula to tell him we were coming over to *Dunsuckin*, then all jumped onto our large black Fly and headed for fresher fields, agreeing that it had been one of the most depressing Saturdays any of us had enjoyed in centuries and the sooner it was behind us, the better.

In the late sixties, Tom Disch, along with John Sladek, was, in a sense, the U.S. Ambassador to the British New Wave movement. His novel Camp Concentration, *written in that period, should be on every reading list of classic sf.*

Over the years Disch has been, besides a great novelist in and out of sf, a poet, playwright, critic, children's author (his Brave Little Toaster *was even Disney-ized), teacher, and, of course, short-story writer.*

I've considered him a mentor for more than twenty-five years and am proud to present his latest fiction, which recalls a bit his New Wave days.

In Xanadu

Thomas M. Disch

✷

In memory of John Sladek,
who died March 10, 2000

And all should cry, Beware! Beware!
His flashing eyes, his floating hair!
Weave a circle round him thrice,
And close your eyes with holy dread,
For he on honey-dew hath fed,
And drunk the milk of Paradise.
—Samuel Taylor Coleridge

PART ONE

XANADU

His awareness was quite limited during the first so-long. A pop-up screen said WELCOME TO XANADU, [Cook, Fran]. YOUR AFTERLIFE BEGINS NOW! BROUGHT TO YOU BY DISNEY-MITSUBISHI PRODUCTIONS OF QUEBEC! A VOTRE SANTE TOUJOURS! Then there was a choice of buttons to click on, **Okay** or **Cancel.** He didn't have an actual physical mouse, but there was an equivalent in his mind, in much the way that amputees have ghostly limbs, but when he clicked on **Okay** with his mental mouse there was a dull *Dong!* and nothing happened. When he clicked on **Cancel** there was a trembling and the smallest flicker of darkness and then the pop-up screen greeted him with the original message.

This went on for an unknowable amount of time, there being no means by which elapsed time could be measured. After he'd *Dong!*ed on **Okay** enough times, he stopped bothering. The part of him that would have been motivated, back when, to express impatience or to feel resentment or to worry just wasn't connected. He felt an almost supernatural passivity. Maybe this is what people were after when they took up meditation. Or maybe it *was* supernatural, though it seemed more likely, from the few clues he'd been given, that it was cybernetic in some way.

He had become lodged (he theorized) in a faulty software program, like a monad in a game of JezzBall banging around inside its little square cage, ricocheting off the same four points on the same four walls forever. Or as they say in Quebec, *toujours*.

And oddly enough that was **Okay**. If he were just a molecule bouncing about, a lifer rattling his bars, there was a kind of comfort in doing so, each bounce a proof of the mass and motion of the molecule, each rattle an SOS dispatched to someone who might think, Ah-ha, there's someone there!

State Pleasure-Dome 1

And then—or, as it might be, once upon a time—**Cancel** produced a different result than it had on countless earlier trials, and he found himself back in some kind of real world. There was theme music ("Wichita Lineman") and scudding clouds high overhead and the smell of leaf mold, as though he'd been doing push-ups out behind the garage, with his nose grazing the dirt. He had his old body back, and it seemed reasonably trim. Better than he'd left it, certainly.

"Welcome," said his new neighbor, a blond woman in a blouse of blue polka dots on a silvery rayonlike ground. "My name is Debora. You must be Fran Cook. We've been expecting you."

He suspected that Debora was a construct of some sort, and it occurred to him that he might be another. But whatever she was, she seemed to expect a response from him beyond his stare of mild surmise.

"You'll have to fill me in a little more, Debora. I don't really know where we are."

"This is Xanadu," she said with a smile that literally flashed, like the light on top of a police car, with distinct, pointed sparkles.

"But does Xanadu exist anywhere except in the poem?"

This yielded a blank look but then another dazzling smile. "You could ask the same of us."

"Okay. To be blunt: Am I dead? Are you?"

Her smile diminished, as though connected to a rheostat. "I think that might be the case, but I don't know for sure. There's a sign at the entrance to the pleasure-dome that says 'Welcome to Eternity.' But there's no one to ask, there or anywhere else. No one who knows anything. Different people have different ideas. I don't have any recollection of dying, myself. Do you?"

"I have no recollections, period," he admitted. "Or none that occur to me at this moment. Maybe if I tried to remember something in particular . . ."

"It's the same with me. I can remember the plots of a few movies. And the odd quotation. 'We have nothing to fear but fear itself.' "

"Eisenhower?" he hazarded.

"I guess. It's all pretty fuzzy. Maybe I just wasn't paying attention back then. Or it gets erased when you come here. I think there's a myth to that effect. Or maybe it's so blurry because it never happened in the first place. Which makes me wonder, are we really people here, or what? And where is here? This isn't anyone's idea of heaven that *I* ever heard of. It's kind of like Disney World, only there's no food, no rides, no movies. Nothing to do, really. You can meet people, talk to them, like with us, but that's about it. Don't think I'm complaining. They don't call it a pleasure-dome for nothing. That part's okay, though it's not any big deal. More like those Magic Finger beds in old motels."

He knew just what she meant, though he couldn't remember ever having been to an old motel or lain down on a Magic Fingers bed. When he tried to reach for a memory of his earlier life, any detail he could use as an ID tag, it was like drawing a blank to a clue in a crossword. Some very simple word that just wouldn't come into focus.

Then there was a fade to black and a final, abject *Dong!* that didn't leave time for a single further thought.

Alph

"I'm sorry," Debora said, with a silvery shimmer of rayon, "that was my fault for having doubted. Doubt's the last thing either of us needs right now. I *love* the little dimple in your chin."

"I'm not aware that I *had* a dimple in my chin."

"Well, you do now, and it's right—" She traced a line up the center of his chin with her finger, digging into the flesh with the enameled tip as it reached. "—here."

"Was I conked out long?"

She flipped her hair as though to rid herself of a fly, and smiled in a forgiving way, and placed her hand atop his. At that touch he felt a strange lassitude steal over him, a deep calm tinged somehow with mirth, as though he'd remembered some sweet, dumb joke from his vanished childhood. Not the joke itself but the laughter that had greeted it, the laughter of children captured on a home video, silvery and chill.

"If we suppose," she said thoughtfully, tracing the line of a vein on the back of his hand with her red fingertip, "that our senses *can* deceive us, then what is there that *can't*?" She raised her eyebrows italic-wise. "I mean," she insisted, "my body might be an illusion, and the world I *think* surrounds me might be another. But what of that 'I think'? The very act of doubting is a proof of existence, right? I think therefore I am."

"Descartes," he footnoted.

She nodded. "And who would ever have supposed that that old doorstop would be relevant to real life, so-called? Except I think it would be just as true with any other verb: I *love* therefore I am."

"Why not?" he agreed.

She squirmed closer to him until she could let the weight of her upper body rest on his as he lay there sprawled on the lawn, or the illusion of a lawn. The theme music had segued, unnoticed, to a sinuous trill of clarinets and viola that might have served for the orchestration of a Strauss opera, and the landscape was its visual correlative, a perfect Puvis de Chavannes—the same chalky pastels in thick impasto blocks and splotches, but never with too painterly panache. There were no visible brush strokes. The only tactile element was the light pressure of her fingers across his skin, making each least hair in its follicle an antenna to register pleasure.

A pleasure that need never, could never cloy, a temperate pleasure suited to its pastoral source, a woodwind pleasure, a fruity wine. Lavender, canary yellow. The green of distant mountains. The ripple of the river.

Caverns Measureless to Man

The water that buoyed the little skiff was luminescent, and so their progress through the cave was not a matter of mere conjecture or kinesthesia. They could see where they were going. Even so, their speed could only be guessed at, for the water's inward light was not enough to illumine either the ice high overhead or either shore of the river. They were borne along into some more unfathomable darkness far ahead as though across an ideal frictionless plane, and it made him think of spaceships doing the same thing, or of his favorite screen saver, which simulated the white swirl-by of snowflakes when driving through a blizzard. One is reduced at such moments (he was now) to an elemental condition, as near to being a particle in physics as a clumsy, complex mammal will ever come.

"I shall call you Dynamo," she confided in a throaty whisper. "Would you like that as a nickname? The Dynamo of Xanadu."

"You're too kind," he said unthinkingly. He had become careless in their conversations. Not a conjugal carelessness: he had not talked with her so very often that all her riffs and vamps were second nature to him. This was the plain unadorned carelessness of not caring.

"I used to think," she said, "that we were all heading for hell in a handbasket. Is that how the saying goes?"

"Meaning, hastening to extinction?"

"Yes, meaning that. It wasn't my *original* idea. I guess everyone has their own vision of the end. Some people take it straight from the Bible, which is sweet and pastoral, but maybe a little dumb, though one oughtn't to say so, not where they are likely to overhear you. Because is that really so different from worrying about the hole in the ozone layer? That was my apocalypse of choice, how we'd all get terrible sunburns and cancer, and then the sea level would rise, and everyone in Calcutta would drown."

"You think this is Calcutta?"

"Can't you ever be serious?"

"So, what's your point, Debora?" When he wanted to be nice, he would use her name, but she never used his. She would invent nick-names for him, and then forget them and have to invent others.

It was thanks to such idiosyncrasies that he'd come to believe in her objective existence as something other than his mental mirror. If she were no more than the forest pool in which Narcissus gazed adoringly, their minds would malfunction in similar ways. Were they mere mirror constructs, he would have known by now.

"It's not," she went on, "that I worry that the end is near. I suppose the end is always near. Relative to Eternity. And it's not that I'm terribly curious *how* it will end. I suppose we'll hurtle over the edge of some im-mense waterfall, like Columbus and his crew."

"Listen!" he said, breaking in. "Do you hear that?"

"Hear what?"

"The music. It's the score for *Koyaanisqatsi*. God, I used to watch the tape of that over and over."

She gave a sigh of polite disapproval. "I can't bear Philip Glass. It's just as you say, the same thing over and over."

"There was this one incredible pan. It must have been taken by a he-licopter flying above this endless high-rise apartment complex. But it had been abandoned."

"And?" she insisted. "What is your point?"

"Well, it was no simulation. The movie was made before computers could turn any single image into some endless quilt. We were really see-ing this vast deserted housing project, high-rise after high-rise with the windows boarded up. The abandoned ruins of some ultra-modern city.

It existed, but until that movie nobody *knew* about it. It makes you think."

"It doesn't make *me* think."

There was no way, at this moment, they were going to have sex. Anyhow, it probably wouldn't have been safe. The boat would capsize and they would drown.

A Sunless Sea

It was as though the whole beach received its light from a few candles. A dim, dim light evenly diffused, and a breeze wafting up from the water with an unrelenting coolness, as at some theater where the air-conditioning cannot be turned off. They huddled within the cocoon of a single beach towel, thighs pressed together, arms crisscrossed behind their backs in a chaste hug, trying to keep warm. The chill in the air was the first less than agreeable physical sensation he'd known in Xanadu, but it did not impart that zip of challenge that comes with October weather. Rather, it suggested his own mortal diminishment. A plug had been pulled somewhere, and all forms of radiant energy were dwindling synchronously, light, warmth, intelligence, desire.

There were tears on Debora's cheek, and little sculptures of sea foam in the shingle about them. And very faint, the scent of nutmeg, the last lingering trace of some long-ago lotion or deodorant.

The ocean gray as aluminum.

The Wailing

Here were the high-rises from the movie, but in twilight now, and without musical accompaniment, though no less portentous for that. He glided past empty benches and leaf-strewn flower beds like a cameraman on roller skates, until he entered one of the buildings, passing immaterially through its plate-glass door. Then there was, in a slower pan than the helicopter's but rhyming to it, a smooth iambic progression past the doors along the first-floor corridor.

He came to a stop before the tenth door, which stood ajar. Within he could hear a stifled sobbing—a wailing, rather. He knew he was expected to go inside, to discover the source of this sorrow. But he could not summon the will to do so. Wasn't his own sorrow sufficient? Wasn't the loss of a world enough?

A man appeared at the end of the corridor in the brown uniform of United Parcel Service. His footsteps were inaudible as he approached.

"I have a delivery for Cook, Fran," the UPS man announced, holding out a white envelope.

At the same time he was offered, once again, the familiar, forlorn choice between **Okay** and **Cancel.**

He clicked on **Cancel.** There was a trembling, and the smallest flicker of darkness, but then the corridor reasserted itself, and the wailing behind the door. The UPS man was gone, but the envelope remained in his hand. It bore the return address in Quebec of Disney-Mitsubishi.

There was no longer a **Cancel** to click on. He had to read the letter.

> *Dear* [Name]:
>
> *The staff and management of Xanadu International regret to inform you that as of* [date] *all services in connection with your contract* [Number] *will be canceled due to new restrictions in the creation and maintenance of posthumous intelligence. We hope that we will be able to resolve all outstanding differences with the government of Quebec and restore the services contracted for by the heirs of your estate, but in the absence of other communications you must expect the imminent closure of your account. It has been a pleasure to serve you. We hope you have enjoyed your time in Xanadu.*
>
> *The law of the sovereign state of Quebec requires us to advise you that in terminating this contract we are not implying any alteration in the spiritual condition of* [Name] *or of his immortal soul. The services of Xanadu International are to be considered an esthetic product offered for entertainment purposes only.*

When he had read it, the words of the letter slowly faded from the page, like the smile of the Cheshire cat.

The wailing behind the door had stopped, but he still stood in the empty corridor, scarce daring to breathe. Any moment, he thought, might be his last. In an eyeblink the world might cease.

But it didn't. If anything the world seemed solider than heretofore. People who have had a brush with death often report the same sensation.

He reversed his path along the corridor, wondering if anyone lived behind any of them, or if they were just a facade, a Potemkin corridor in a high-rise in the realm of faerie.

As though to answer his question Debora was waiting for him when he went outside. She was wearing a stylishly tailored suit in a kind of brown tweed, and her hair was swept up in a way that made her look like a French movie star of the 1940s.

As they kissed, the orchestra reintroduced their love theme. The music swelled. The world came to an end.

PART TWO

XANADU

But then, just the way that the movie will start all over again after The End, if you just stay in your seat, or even if you go out to the lobby for more popcorn, he found himself back at the beginning, with the same pop-up screen welcoming him to Xanadu and then a choice of **Okay** or **Cancel.** But there was also, this time, a further choice: a blue banner that pulsed at the upper edge of consciousness and asked him if he wanted expanded memory and quicker responses. He most definitely did, so with his mental mouse he accepted the terms being offered without bothering to scroll through them.

He checked off a series of **Yes**es and **Continue**s, and so, without his knowing it, he had become, by the time he was off the greased slide, a citizen of the sovereign state of Quebec, an employee of Disney-Mitsubishi Temps E-Gal, and—cruelest of his new disadvantages—a girl.

A face glimmered before him in the blue gloaming. At first he thought it might be Debora, for it had the same tentative reality that she did, like a character at the beginning of some old French movie about railroads and murderers, who may be the star or only an extra on hand to show that this is a world with people in it. It was still too early in the movie to tell. Only as he turned sideways did he realize (the sound track made a samisen-like *Twang!* of recognition) that he had been looking in a mirror, and that the face that had been coalescing before him—the rouged cheeks, the plump lips, the fake lashes, the mournful gaze—had been his own! Or rather, now, her own.

As so many other women had realized at a similar point in their lives, it was already too late and nothing could be done to correct the mistake that Fate, and Disney-Mitsubishi, had made. Maybe he'd always been a woman. [Cook, Fran] was a sexually ambiguous name. Perhaps his earlier assumption that he was male was simply a function of thinking in English, where *one* may be mistaken about *his* own identity (but not about hers). I think; therefore I am a guy.

He searched through his expanded memory for some convincing evidence of his gender history. Correction: *her* gender history. Her-story, as feminists would have it. Oh, dear—would he be one of *them* now, always thinking in italics, a grievance committee of one in perpetual session?

But look on the bright side (she told herself). There might be advantages in such a change of address. Multiple orgasms. Nicer clothes (though she couldn't remember ever wanting to dress like a woman when she was a man). Someone else paying for dinner, assuming that the protocols of hospitality still worked the same way here in Xanadu as they had back in reality. This was supposed to be heaven and already she was feeling nostalgic for a life she couldn't remember, an identity she had shed.

Then the loudspeaker above her head emitted a dull *Dong!*, and she woke up in the Women's Dormitory of State Pleasure-Dome 2. "All right, girls!" said the amplified voice of the matron. "Time to rise and shine. *Le temps s'en va, mesdames, le temps s'en va.*"

State Pleasure-Dome 2

"*La vie,*" philosophized Chantal, "*est une maladie dont le sommeil nous soulagons toutes les seize heures. C'est un palliative. La morte est un remède.*" She flicked the drooping ash from the end of her cigarette and made a moue of chic despair. Fran could understand what she'd said quite as well as if she'd been speaking English: Life is a disease from which sleep offers relief every sixteen hours. Sleep is a palliative—death a remedy.

They were sitting before big empty cups of café au lait in the employee lounge, dressed in their black E-Gal minis, crisp white aprons, and fishnet hose. Fran felt a positive fever of chagrin to be seen in such a costume, but she felt nothing otherwise, really, about her entire female body, especially the breasts bulging out of their casings, breasts that quivered visibly at her least motion. It was like wearing a T-shirt with some dumb innuendo on it, or a blatant sexual invitation. Did every girl have to go through the same torment of shame at puberty? Was there any way to get over it except to get into it?

"*Mon bonheur,*" declared Chantal earnestly, "*est d'augmenter celle des autres.*" Her happiness lay in increasing that of others. A doubtful proposition in most circumstances, but not perhaps for Chantal, who, as an E-Gal was part geisha, part rock star, and part a working theorem in moral calculus, an embodiment of Francis Hutcheson's notion that that action is best which procures the greatest happiness for the greatest numbers. There were times—Thursdays, in the early evening—when Chantal's bedside/Website was frequented by as many as two thousand admirers, their orgasms all bissfully synchronized with the reels and ditties she performed on her dulcimer, sometimes assisted by Fran (an apprentice in the art) but usually all on her own. At such times (she'd confided to Fran) she felt as she imagined a great conductor must feel conducting some choral extravaganza, the *Missa Solemnis* or the Ninth Symphony.

Except that the dulcimer gave the whole thing a tinge and twang of hillbilly, as of Tammy Wynette singing "I'm just a geisha from the bayou." Of course, the actual Tammy Wynette had died ages ago and could sing that song only in simulation, but still it was hard to imagine it engineered with any other voice-print: habit makes the things we love seem inevitable as arithmetic.

"*Encore?*" Chantal asked, lifting her empty cup, and then, when Fran had nodded, signaling to the waiter.

Coffee, cigarettes, a song on the jukebox. Simple pleasures, but doubled and quadrupled and raised to some astronomical power, the stuff that industries and gross national products are made of. Fran imagined a long reverse zoom away from their table at the café, away from the swarming hive of the city, to where each soul and automobile was a mere pixel on the vast monitor of eternity.

The coffees came, and Chantal began to sing, "*Le bonheur de la femme n'est pas dans la liberté, mais dans l'acceptation d'un devoir.*"

A woman's happiness lies not in liberty, but in the acceptance of a duty.

And what was that duty? Fran wondered. What could it be but love?

In a Vision Once I Saw

There were no mirrors in Xanadu, and yet every vista seemed to be framed as by those tinted looking glasses of the eighteenth century that turned everything into a Claude Lorrain. Look too long or too closely into someone else's face, and it became your own. Chantal would tilt her head back, a flower bending to the breeze, and she would morph into Fran's friend of his earlier afterlife, Debora. Debora, whose hand had caressed his vanished sex, whose wit had entertained him with Cartesian doubts.

They were the captives (it was explained, when Fran summoned **Help**) of pirates, and must yield to the desires of their captors in all things. That they were in the thrall of copyright pirates, not authentic old-fashioned buccaneers, was an epistomological quibble. Subjectively their captors could exercise the same cruel authority as any Captain Kidd or Hannibal Lecter. Toes and nipples don't know the difference between a knife and an algorithm. Pirates of whatever sort are in charge of pain and its delivery, and that reduces all history, all consciousness, to a simple system of pluses and minuses, do's and don'ts. Suck my dick or walk the plank. That (the terrible simplicity) was the downside of living in a pleasure-dome.

"Though, if you think about it," said Debora, with her hand resting atop the strings of her dulcimer, as though it might otherwise interrupt what she had to say, "every polity is ultimately based upon some calculus of pleasure, of apportioning rapture and meting out pain. The jukebox and the slot machine, what are they but emblems of the Pavlovian bargain we all must make with that great dealer high in the sky?" She lifted a little silver hammer and bonked her dulcimer a triple bonk of do-sol-do.

"The uncanny thing is how easily we can be programmed to regard mere symbols—" Another do-sol-do. "—as rewards. A bell is rung somewhere, and something within us resonates. And music becomes one of the necessities of life. Even such a life as this, an ersatz afterlife."

"Is there some way to escape?" Fran asked.

Debora gave an almost imperceptible shrug, which her dulcimer responded to as though she were a breeze and it a wind chime hanging from the kitchen ceiling. "There are rumors of escapees—E-Men, as they're called. But no one *I've* ever known has escaped, or at least they've never spoken of it. Perhaps they do, and get caught, and then the memory of having done so is blotted out. Our memories are not exactly ours to command, are they?"

The dulcimer hyperventilated.

Debora silenced it with a glance and continued: "Some days I'll flash on some long-ago golden oldie, and a whole bygone existence will come flooding back. A whole one-pound box of madeleines, and I will be absolutely convinced by it that I *did* have a life once upon a time, where there were coffee breaks with doughnuts bought at actual bakeries and rain that made the pavements speckled and a whole immense sensorium, always in flux, which I can remember now only in involuntary blips of recall. And maybe it really was like that once, how can we know, but whether we could get back to it, that I somehow can't believe."

"I've tried to think what it would be like to be back there, where we got started." Fran gazed into the misty distance, as though her earlier life might be seen there, as in an old home video. "But it's like trying to imagine what it would be like in the thirteenth century, when people all believed in miracles and stuff. It's beyond me."

"Don't you believe in miracles, then?" The dulcimer twanged a twang of simple faith. "I do. I just don't suppose they're for us. Miracles are for people who pay full price. For us there's just Basic Tier programming—eternal time and infinite space."

"And those may be no more than special effects."

Debora nodded. "But even so . . ."

"Even so?" Fran prompted.

"Even so," said Debora, with the saddest of smiles, a virtual flag of surrender, "if I were you, I would try to escape."

Those Caves of Ice!

Ebay was a lonely place, as holy and enchanted as some underwater cathedral in the poem of a French symbolist, or a German forest late at night. If you have worked at night as a security guard for the Mall of America, or if you've seen Simone Simon in *Cat People* as she walks beside the pool (only her footsteps audible, her footsteps and the water's plash), only then can you imagine its darkling beauty, the change that comes over the objects of our desire when they are flensed of their purveyors and consumers and stand in mute array, aisle after aisle. Then you might sweep the beam of your flashlight across the waters of the recirculating fountain as they perpetually spill over the granite brim. No silence is so large as that where Muzak played, but plays no more.

Imagine such a place, and then imagine discovering an exit that announces itself in the darkness by a dim red light and opening the door to discover a Piranesian vista of a further mall, no less immense, its tiers linked by purring escalators, the leaves of its potted trees shimmering several levels beneath where you are, and twinkling in the immensity, the signs of the stores—every franchise an entrepreneur might lease. Armani and Osh-Kosh, Hallmark, Kodak, Disney-Mitsubishi, American Motors, Schwab. A landscape all of names, and yet if you click on any name, you may enter its portal to discover its own little infinity of choices. Shirts of all sizes, colors, patterns, prices; shirts that were sold, yesterday, to someone in Iowa; other shirts that may be sold tomorrow or may never find a taker. Every atom and molecule in the financial continuum of purchases that might be made has here been numbered and cataloged. Here, surely, if anywhere, one might become if not invisible then scarcely noticed, as in some great metropolis swarming with illegal aliens, among whom a single further citizen can matter not a jot.

Fran became a mote in that vastness, a pip, an alga, unaware of his own frenetic motion as the flow of data took him from one possible purchase to the next. Here was a CD of Hugo Wolf lieder sung by Elly Ameling. Here a pair of Lucchese cowboy boots only slightly worn with western heels. Here six interesting Japanese dinner plates and a hand-embroidered black kimono. This charming pig creamer has an adorable French hat and is only slightly chipped. These Viking sweatshirts still have their tags from Wal-Mart, $29.95. Sabatier knives, set of four. A 1948 first edition of *The Secret of the Old House*. Hawaiian Barbie with hula accessories. *"Elly Ameling Sings Schumann!"* Assorted rustic napkins from Amish country.

There is nothing that is not a thought away, nothing that cannot be summoned by a wink and a nod to any of a dozen search engines. But there is a price to pay for such accessibility. The price is sleep, and in that sleep we buy again those commodities we bought or failed to buy before. No price is too steep, and no desire too low. Cream will flow through the slightly chipped lips of the charming pig creamer in the adorable hat, and our feet will slip into the boots we had no use for earlier. And when we return from our night journeys, like refugees returning to the shells of their burned homes, we find we are where we were, back at Square One. The matron was bellowing over the PA, "*Le temps s'en va, mesdames! Le temps s'en va!*" and Fran wanted to die.

Grain Beneath the Thresher's Flail

She was growing old in the service of the Khan, but there was no advantage to be reaped from long service, thanks to the contract she'd signed back when. She had become as adept with the hammers of the dulcimer as ever Chantal had been (Chantal was gone now, no one knew whither), but in truth the dulcimer is not an instrument that requires great skill—and its rewards are proportional. She felt as though she'd devoted her life—her afterlife—to the game of Parcheesi, shaking the dice and moving her tokens round the board forever. Surely this was not what the prospectus promised those who signed on.

She knew, in theory (which she'd heard, in various forms, from other denizens), that the great desideratum here, the magnet that drew all its custom, was beauty, the rapture of beauty that poets find in writing poetry or composers in their music. It might not be the Beatific Vision that saints feel face-to-face with God, but it was, in theory, the next best thing, a bliss beyond compare. And perhaps it was all one could hope for. How could she be sure that this bliss or that, as it shivered through her, like a wind through Daphne's leaves, wasn't of the same intensity that had zapped the major romantic poets in their day?

In any case, there was no escaping it. She'd tried to find an exit that didn't, each day, become the entrance by which she returned to her contracted afterlife and her service as a damsel with a dulcimer. Twang! Twang! *O ciel! O belle nuit!* Not that she had any notion of some higher destiny for herself, or sweeter pleasures—except the one that all the poets agreed on: Lethe, darkness, death, and by death to say we end the humdrum daily continuation of all our yesterdays into all our tomorrows.

The thought of it filled her with a holy dread, and she took up the silver hammers of her dulcimer and began, once again, to play such music as never mortal knew before.

As I stated two years ago in the headnote to Joyce Carol Oates's contribution to my last original anthology, 999, *she is a phenomenon. She remains so. Everywhere you look—the* New York Times Book Review, The New Yorker, *lists of the year's best fiction (or nonfiction)—there she is. She's like a wonderful presence, writing wonderful things.*

Here she's written her very first science fiction tale—which is amazing, if only because it's a first. "Commencement" is creepy, somber, funny, and unique. It would have fit right into the original New Wave movement in the mid-sixties.

Commencement

JOYCE CAROL OATES

✳

The Summons. Commencement! Bells in the Music College on its high hill are ringing to summon us to the Great Dome for the revered annual ceremony!

This year, as every year, the University's Commencement is being held on the last Sunday in May; but this year will be the two hundredth anniversary of the University's founding, so the occasion will be even more festive than usual and will attract more media attention. The Governor of the State, a celebrated graduate of the University, will give the Commencement address, and three renowned Americans—the Poet, the Educator, and the Scientist—will be awarded honorary doctorates. Over four thousand degrees—B.A.'s, M.A.'s, Ph.D.'s—will be conferred on graduates, a record number. As the University Chancellor has said, "Every year our numbers are rising. But our standards are also rising. The University is at the forefront of evolution."

And so here we are on this sunny, windy May morning, streaming into the Great Dome, through Gates 1–15. Thousands of us! Young people in black academic gowns, caps precariously on their heads; their families, and friends; and many townspeople associated with the University, the predominant employer in the area. We're metal filings drawn by a powerful magnet. We're moths drawn to a sacred light. The very air through which we make our way crackles with excitement, and apprehension. Who will be taken *to the Pyramid*, how will the *ceremony of renewal* unfold? Even those of us who have attended Commencement numerous times are never prepared for the stark reality of the event, and must witness with our own eyes what we can never quite believe we've seen, for it so quickly eludes us.

The Great Dome! We're proud of our football stadium, at the northern, wooded edge of our hilly campus; it seats more than thirty thousand people, in steeply banked tiers, a multimillion-dollar structure with a sliding translucent plastic roof, contracted in fair weather. The vast football field, simulated grass of a glossy emerald green has been transformed this morning into a more formal space: thousands of folding chairs, to accommodate our graduates, fan out before a majestic speakers' platform raised six feet above the ground, and at the center, rear of this platform, festooned in the University's colors (crimson, gold) is the twelve-foot Pyramid (composed of rectangles of granite carefully set into place by workmen laboring through the night) that is the emblem of our University.

A crimson satin banner unfurled behind the platform proclaims in gold letters the University motto: NOVUS ORDO SECLORUM. ("A New Cycle of the Ages.")

It has been a chilly, fair morning after a night of thunderstorms and harsh pelting rain, typical in this northerly climate in spring; the Chancellor, having deliberated with his staff, has decreed that the Great Dome be open to the sun. The University orchestra, seated to the left of the platform, on the grass, is playing a brisk, brassy version of the stately alma mater, and as graduates file into the stadium many of them are singing:

Where snowy peaks of mountains
Meet the eastern sky,
Proudly stands our Alma Mater
On her hilltop high.

Crimson our blood,
Deep as the sea.
Our Alma Mater,
We pledge to thee!

These words the Assistant Mace Bearer believes he can hear, a mile from the University. A sick, helpless sensation spreads through him. "So soon? It will happen—so soon?"

The Robing. In the Great Dome Triangle Lounge where VIPs assemble before Commencement, as before football games, the Chancellor's party is being robed for the ceremony. Deans of numerous colleges and schools, University marshals, the Governor, the Poet, the Educator, the

Scientist, the Provost, the President of the Board of Trustees, the President of the Alumni Association, and the Chancellor himself—these distinguished individuals are being assisted in putting on their elaborate robes, hoods, and hats, and are being photographed for the news media and for the University archives. There's a palpable excitement in the air even among those who have attended many such ceremonies during their years of service to the University. For something can always go wrong when so many people are involved, and in so public and dramatic a spectacle. The retiring Dean of Arts and Sciences murmurs to an old colleague, "Remember that terrible time when—" and the men laugh together and shudder. Already it's past 9 A.M.; the ceremony is scheduled to begin promptly at 10 A.M. Already the University orchestra has begun playing "Pomp and Circumstance," that thrilling processional march.

Declares the Chancellor, "Always, that music makes me shiver!"

Surrounded by devoted female assistants, this burly, kingly man of youthful middle age is being robed in a magnificent crimson gown with gold-and-black velvet trim; around his neck he wears a heavy, ornate medallion, solid gold on a gold chain, embossed with the University's Pyramid seal and the Latin words NOVUS ORDO SECLORUM. The Chancellor has a broad buff face that resembles a face modeled in clay and thick, leonine white hair; he's a well-liked administrator among both faculty and students, a graduate of the University and one-time all-American halfback on the University's revered football team. Each year the Chancellor is baffled by which side of his crimson satin cap the gold tassel should be on, and each year his personal assistant says, with a fondly maternal air of reproach, "Mr. Chancellor, the *left*. Let me adjust it." Such a flurry of activity in the Triangle Lounge! A TV crew, photographers' flashes. Where is the Dean of the Graduate School, in charge of conferring graduate degrees? Where is the Dean of the Chapel, the minister who will lead more than thirty thousand people in prayer, in less than an hour? There's the University Provost, the Chancellor's right-hand man, with a sharp eye on the clock; there's the newly appointed Dean of Human Engineering, the most heavily endowed (and controversial) of the University's schools, talking and laughing casually with one of his chief donors, the billionaire President of the Board of Trustees; there's the President of the Alumni Association, another University benefactor whose gift of $35 million will be publicly announced at the luncheon following Commencement, talking with his old friend the Governor. And there's the University Mace Bearer, one of the few women administrators at the University, with a helmet of pewter hair and scintillant eyes, frowning toward the entrance—"Where's my assistant?"

The Assistant Mace Bearer, the youngest member of the elite Chancellor's party—*where is he*?

In fact, the Assistant Mace Bearer is only now entering the Great Dome, at Gate 3. Hurrying! Breathless! Amid an ever-thickening stream of energetic, fresh-faced young men and women in black gowns and mortarboards, flanked by families and relatives, being directed by ushers into the immense stadium. "Show your tickets, please. Tickets?" The Assistant Mace Bearer has a special crimson ticket and is respectfully directed upstairs to the Triangle Lounge. How has it happened, he's late. . . . Traffic was clogging all streets leading to the University, he hadn't given himself enough time, reluctant to leave home, though, of course, he had no choice but to leave his home and to join the Chancellor's party as he'd agreed he would do; this is his first Commencement *on the Pyramid*. He's a recent faculty appointment, after only three years of service he's been promoted to the rank of associate professor of North American history; for a thirty-four-year-old, this is an achievement. His students admire him as Professor S——, soft-spoken and reserved but clearly intelligent; not vain, but ambitious; and eager to perform well in the eyes of his elders.

"Still, I could turn back now." As he ascends the cement stairs to Level 2. "Even now." As he makes his way in a stream of strangers along a corridor. "It isn't too late. . . ." Those smells! His stomach turns, he's passing vendors selling coffee, breakfast muffins, bagels, even sandwiches and potato chips, which young people in billowing black gowns are devouring on their way into the stadium. You would think that the occasion wasn't Commencement but an ordinary sports event. The Assistant Mace Bearer nearly collides with a gaggle of excited girls carrying sweet rolls and coffee in Styrofoam cups; he feels a pang of nausea, seeing a former student, a husky boy with close-cropped hair, wolfing down a Commencement Special—blood sausage on a hot-dog roll, with horseradish. At this time of morning!

Even as the Chancellor, the Governor, and the honorary degree recipients, the Poet, the Educator, and the Scientist are being photographed, and the Mace Bearer and the head University marshal are checking the contents of the black lacquered box that the Assistant Mace Bearer will carry, the Assistant Mace Bearer enters the Triangle Lounge. At last! Cheeks guiltily heated, he stammers an apology, but the Mace Bearer curtly says, "No matter: you're here, Professor S——." Chastened, he reports to the robing area where an older, white-haired assistant makes a check beside him name on a list and helps outfit him in his special Commencement gown, black, but made of a synthetic waterproof fabric that will wipe dry, with crimson-and-gold trim, and helps him adjust his black velvet hat. . . . "Gloves? Don't I wear—gloves?" There's a brief flurried search, of course the gloves are located: black to match the gown, and made of thin, durable rubber. When Professor S—— thanks the white-haired woman nervously, she says, with an air of mild reproach, "But this is our responsibility, Professor." She's one of those University "administrative assistants" behind the scenes of all Commencements, as of civilization itself. With a dignified gesture she indicates the boisterous Triangle Lounge in which the Chancellor's party, predominantly male, gowned, resplendent, and regal, is being organized into a double column for the processional. "This is our honor."

The Processional. At last! At 10:08 A.M., almost on time, the Chancellor's party marches into the immense stadium, eye-catching in their elaborate gowns and caps: faculty and lesser administrative officers first, then the Mace Bearer and the Assistant Mace Bearer (who carries in his slightly trembling black-gloved hands the black-lacquered box), the deans of the colleges and the Dean of the Chapel, the Chancellor and his special guests. As they march, the orchestra plays "Pomp and Circumstance" ever louder, with more rhythmic emphasis. "Thrilling music," the Chancellor says to the Governor, "even after so many Commencements." The Governor, who has been smiling his broad public smile at the gowned young people seated in rows of hundreds on the stadium grass in front of the speakers' platform, says, "How much more so, Mr. Chancellor, it must be for those whose first Commencement this is, and last." The elderly Poet marches at the side of the Provost, who will present him for his honorary degree; the Poet, long a revered name in American literature, was once a tall, eagle-like imposing presence, now of less than moderate height, with slightly stooped shoulders and a ravaged yet still noble face; where lines of poetry once danced in his head, unbidden as butterflies, now he's thinking with a dull self-anger that he should be ashamed to be here, accepting yet another award for his poetry, when he hasn't written anything worthwhile in years. ("Still, I crave recognition. Loneliness terrifies me. How will it end!") Blinking in the pale, whitely glaring light of the stadium, the Poet wants to think that these respectfully applauding young people—some of them alarmingly young—in their black gowns and mortarboards, gazing at him and the other elders as they march past, know who he is, and what his work has been—a fantasy, yet how it warms him! Behind the Poet is the Educator, a hearty, flush-faced woman in her early sixties; unlike the tormented Poet, the Educator is smiling happily, for she's proud of herself, plain, big-boned, forthright, beaming with health and American optimism after decades of professional commitment; never married—"Except to my work," as she says. The Educator is one of the very first women to be awarded an honorary doctorate by the University, and so it's appropriate that she's being escorted into the stadium by the Dean of the Education School, another woman of vigorous middle age, who will present the Educator for her award. This is the Educator's first honorary doctorate; she's thinking that her years of industry and self-denial have been worth it. ("If only my parents were alive to see me! . . .")

Behind the Educator is the Scientist, a long-ago Nobel Prize winner, with gold-glinting glasses that obscure his melancholy eyes; another ravaged elderly face, rather equine, with tufted gray eyebrows, a long hawkish nose and enormous nostrils; unlike the Educator, the Scientist can't summon up much enthusiasm for this ceremony and can't quite recall why he'd accepted the invitation. ("Vanity? Or—loneliness?") For, after the Nobel, which he'd won as a brash young man of thirty-seven, what do such "honors" mean? The Scientist, in his ninth decade, has come to despise most other scientists and makes little effort to keep up with new discoveries and developments, even in his old field, biology; especially, he loathes publicity-seeking idiots in fields like human genetics and "human engineering"; he believes such research to be immoral, criminal; if he had his way, it would be banned by the U.S. government. (However, the Scientist keeps such views to himself. He knows better than to say such inflammatory things. And he has to admit that, yes, if he were a young man again, very possibly he'd be involved in such research himself, and to hell with the views of his elders.) Marching into the stadium, past the rows of gowned young people, so fresh-faced, so expectant, blinking at their revered elders and intermittently applauding, the Scientist oscillates between a sense of his own considerable worth and the fact that, to all but a handful of the many thousands of men and women in this ghastly open space, he's a name out of the distant past, if a "name" at all; younger scientists in his field are astonished, if perhaps not very interested, to hear that he's still alive. Such a fate, the Scientist thinks, is a kind of irony. And irony has no place on Commencement day, only homilies and uplifting sentiments. "The young know nothing of irony, as they know nothing of subtlety or mortality," the Scientist observes dryly to his escort, the Dean of the Graduate School, who inclines his head politely but murmurs only a vague assent. With "Pomp and Circumstance" being played so loudly, as the processional of dignitaries passes close by the orchestra, very likely the Graduate Dean can't hear the Scientist.

As the Mace Bearer and the Assistant Mace Bearer ascend the steps to the platform, there's rippling applause from the graduates assembled on the grass. "With young people, you can't tell: are they honoring us, or mocking us?" the Mace Bearer observes with a grim smile to her silent assistant. Professor S——, who has attended a number of Commencements at the University, as a B.A. candidate (summa cum laude, history) and more recently as a young faculty member, would like to assure the Mace Bearer that the applause is genuine, but it isn't for them as individuals: the applause is for their function, and more specifically for the contents of the black-lacquered box. Taking his seat beside the Mace Bearer, to the immediate right of the Pyramid, the Assistant Mace Bearer glances out at the audience for the first time and swallows hard. So many! And what will they expect of him! (For the nature of the Assistant Mace Bearer's task is that it cannot be rehearsed, only "premeditated," according to tradition.) A thrill of boyish excitement courses through him. He's breathing quickly, and grateful to be finished with the procession. Nothing went wrong; he hadn't stumbled on any steps, hadn't become light-headed in the cool, white-tinged air. The thought has not yet come to him sly as a knife blade in the heart: *But now you can't escape*. By his watch the time is 10:17 A.M.

The Invocation. The Dean of the Chapel, an impressive masculine figure in a black gown trimmed with crimson-and-gold velvet, like the Chancellor a former University athlete (rowing), comes forward to the podium, in front of the Pyramid, to lead the gathering in a prayer. "Ladies and gentlemen, will you please rise?" Despite its size, the crowd is eager to obey as a puppy. The gowned graduates, and the spectators in the steeply banked stadium, all rise to their feet at once and lower their eyes as the Dean of the Chapel addresses "Almighty God, Creator of Heaven and Earth," alternately praising this being for His beneficence and asking of Him forgiveness, inspiration, imagination, strength to fulfill the sacred obligations prescribed by "the very presence of the Pyramid"; to enact once again the sacred "ceremony of renewal" that has made this day, as "all our days," possible. The Poet is thinking how banal, such words; though they may be true, he isn't listening very closely; in a lifetime one hears the same words repeated endlessly, in familiar combinations, for the fund of words is finite while the appetite for uttering them is infinite. (Is this a new idea? Or has the Poet had such a thought numerous times, while sitting on stages, gazing out into audiences with his small fixed dignified-elder smile?) The Educator, seated beside the Poet, listens to the chaplain's invocation more attentively; she can't escape feeling that this Commencement revolves somehow around *her*; there are few women on the platform, and it's rare indeed that any woman, however deserving, has received an honorary doctorate from the University. She imagines (not for the first time!) that, in any gathering, young women are admiring of her as a model of what they might accomplish with hard work, talent, and diligence. ("And self-sacrifice. Of course.") The Scientist is shifting restlessly in his chair, which is a folding chair, and damned hard on his lean haunches. Religious piety! The appeal to mass emotions! Thousands of years of "civilization" have passed, and yet humankind seems incapable of transcending its primitive origins. . . . The Scientist oscillates between feeling despair over this fact, which suggests a fundamental failure of science to educate the population, and simple contempt. The Scientist resents that he has been invited to this Commencement only to be subjected to the usual superstitious rhetoric in which (he would guess!) virtually no one on the speakers' platform believes; yet the chaplain is allowed to drone on for ten minutes while thousands of credulous onlookers gaze up at him. ". . . we thank You particularly on this special day, the two hundredth anniversary of the University's Commencement, when Your generosity and love overflow upon us, and our sacrifice to You flows upward to be renewed, in you, as rainfall enriches the earth. . . ." So the broad-shouldered Dean of the Chapel intones, raising his beefy hands aloft in an attitude of, to the Scientist, outrageous supplication. There's a brisk, chilly breeze; the sky overhead is no longer clear, but laced with cloud-like frost on a windowpane; the crimson banners draped about the platform stir restlessly, as if a god were coming to life, rousing himself awake.

The Poet opens his eyes wide. Has he been drifting off into sleep? Or—has he been touched by inspiration, as he has rarely been touched in recent years? (In fact, in decades.) He smiles, thinking yes he is proud to be here, he believes his complexly rhyming, difficult poetry may be due for a revival.

Presentation of Colors. Here's a welcome quickening of spirit after the solemnity of the chaplain's prayer! Marching army and air force cadets in their smart uniforms, three young men and two young women, bear three colorful flags: the U.S. flag, the state flag, and the university's crimson and gold. The army cadets flanking the flag-bearers carry rifles on their shoulders. A display of military force, in this peaceful setting? The Educator, a pacifist, disapproves. The Scientist gazes on such primitive rituals with weary scorn. Display of arms! Symbolizing the government's power to protect, and to destroy, human life in its keeping! A crude appeal to the crude limbic brain, yet as always, it's effective. The Poet squints and blinks and opens his faded eyes wider. Flapping flags, shimmering colors, what do these things mean? In the past, such moments of public reverie provided the Poet with poetry: mysterious lines, images, rhythms came fully formed to him as if whispered into his ear. Now he listens with mounting excitement, and hears—what? ("The God of the Great Dome. Stirring, waking.") In his deep well-practiced baritone voice the Chancellor addresses the audience from the podium: "Ladies and gentlemen, will you please rise for the national anthem?" Another time the great beast of a crowd eagerly rises. More than thirty thousand individuals are led in the anthem, a singularly muscular, vulgar music (thinks the Scientist, who plays violin in a string quartet, and whose favorite music is late Beethoven) by a full-throated young black woman, one of this year's graduates of the Music School. *O say can you see . . . bombs bursting in air.* Patriotic thrill! The Educator, though a pacifist, finds herself singing with the rest. Her voice is surprisingly weak and uncertain for a woman of her size and seeming confidence, yet she's proud of her country, proud of its history; for all our moral lapses, and an occasional overzealousness in defending our boundaries (in Mexico in the mid-nineteenth century, in Vietnam in the mid-twentieth century, for instance), the United States is a *great nation*. . . . ("And I am an American.") The Poet is thinking: Blood leaps!—like young trout flashing in the sun. ("Of what dark origins, who can prophesy?") The Poet cares nothing, truly, for what is moral, what is right, what is decent, what is good; the Poet cares only for poetry; the Poet's heart would quicken, except its beat is measured by a pacemaker stitched deep in his hollow chest. This is the first poetic "gift" he's had in years, he could weep with gratitude.

The Assistant Mace Bearer, standing beside the Mace Bearer in the pose of a healthy young warrior-son beside his mother, tall and imposing in her ceremonial attire, clenches his fists to steady his trembling. But is he nervous, or is he excited? He's proud, he thinks, of his country; of those several flapping flags; to each, he bears a certain allegiance. As a professor of North American history he would readily concede that "nations"—"political entities"—are but ephemeral structures imposed upon a "natural" state of heterogeneous peoples, and yet—how patriotism stirs the blood, how real it is; and how reassuring, this morning, to see that such impressive masculine figures as the Chancellor, the Dean of the Chapel, the Provost, the President of the Board of Trustees, and others are on the platform, praying, singing the national anthem, in the service, as he is, of the Pyramid. Even if strictly speaking Professor S—— isn't a believer, he takes solace in being amid believers. . . . The Assistant Mace Bearer is particularly proud of the burly, authoritative figure of the Chancellor; though he has reason to believe that the Dean of Arts and Sciences invited him to assist the Mace Bearer, and not the

Chancellor, he prefers to think that the Chancellor himself knew of young Professor S——'s work and singled him out for this distinction.

The national anthem is over, the young black soprano has stepped back from the microphone, the thousands of graduates and spectators in the stadium are again seated, with a collective sigh. Such yearning, suddenly! And the spring sun hidden behind a bank of clouds dull as scoured metal.

Commencement Address. Now comes the Governor to the podium amid applause to speak to the Class of —— in an oiled, echoing voice. Like his friend the Chancellor, the Governor has a large face that resembles an animated clay mask; he's bluff, ruggedly handsome, righteous. He speaks of a "spiritually renewed, resolute future" that nonetheless "strengthens our immortal ties with the past." His words are vague yet emphatic, upbeat yet charged with warning—"Always recall: moral weakness precedes political, military, sovereign weakness." With practiced hand gestures the Governor charges today's graduates with the mission of "synthesizing" past and future communities and "never shrinking from sacrifice of self, in the service of the community." The Poet wakes from a light doze, annoyed by this politician's rhetoric. Why has *he*, a major figure of the twentieth century, been invited to the University's Commencement, to endure such empty abstractions? If the Governor speaks of ideals, they are "selfless ideals"; if he speaks of paths to be taken, they are "untrod paths." The Governor is one who leaves no cliché unturned, thinks the Poet, with a small smile. (This is a clever thought, yes? Or has he had it before, at other awards ceremonies?) Minutes pass. Gray-streaked clouds thicken overhead. There's a veiled glance between the Chancellor and the Provost: the Governor's speech has gone beyond his allotted fifteen minutes, the more than four thousand black-gowned graduates are getting restless as young animals penned in a confined space. When the Governor tells jokes ("my undergraduate major here was political science with minors in Frisbee and Budweiser"), the audience groans and laughs at excessive length, with outbursts of applause. (The beaming Governor doesn't seem to catch on, this is mocking, not appreciative, laughter.) A danger sign, thinks the Assistant Mace Bearer, who recalls such whirlpools of adolescent-audience rebellion from his own days, not so very long ago, as an undergraduate at the University.

So it happens: at the center of the traditionally rowdiest school of graduates, the engineers, of whom ninety-nine percent are male, what looks like a naked mannequin—female?—suddenly appears, having been smuggled into the stadium beneath someone's gown. There are ripples of laughter from the other graduates as the thing is tossed boldly aloft and passed from hand to hand like a volleyball. University marshals in their plain black gowns are pressed into immediate service, trying without success to seize the mannequin; such juvenile pranks are forbidden at Commencement, of course, as students have been repeatedly warned. But the temptation to violate taboo and annoy one's elders is too strong; many graduates have been partying through the night and have been waiting for just such a moment of release. As the Governor stubbornly continues with his prepared speech, in which jokes are "ad-libbed" into the text, there are waves of tittering laughter as a second and a third mannequin appear, gaily tossed and batted about. One of these is captured by a red-faced University marshal, eliciting a mixed response of boos and cheers. The mood in the Great Dome is mischievous and childish, not mutinous. This is all good-natured—isn't it? Then another mannequin is tossed up, naked, but seemingly male; where his genitals would have been there are swaths of red paint; on his back, flesh-colored strips of rubber have been glued which flutter like ribbons to be torn at, and torn off, by grasping male fingers. There's an intake of thousands of breaths; not much laughter; a wave of disapproval and revulsion, even from other graduates. A sense that *this has gone too far*, *this is not funny*.

What a strange, ugly custom, thinks the Educator, polishing her glasses to see more clearly, if it is a custom? Are those young people *drunk*?

Primitives! thinks the Scientist, his deeply creased face fixed in an expression of polite disdain. In situations in which there are large masses of individuals, especially young males poised between the play of adolescence and the responsibilities of adulthood, it's always risky to court rebellion, even if it's playful rebellion, beneath the collective gaze of elder family members. (Long ago, the Scientist did research in neurobiology, investigating the limbic system, the oldest part of the brain; the ancient part of the brain, you might say; his focus was a tiny structure known as the amygdala. The amygdala primes the body for action in a survival situation, but remains inoperative, as if slumbering, otherwise. In his ninth decade, the Scientist thinks wryly, his amygdala might have become a bit rusty from disuse.)

A spirit of misrule! thinks the Poet, smiling. Despite his age, and the dignity of his position on the platform, the Poet feels by nature, or wants badly to feel, a tug of sympathy for those blunt-faced grinning young men. For the Governor, that ass of a politician, *is* an oily bore. At the luncheon following Commencement, the Poet presumes that he, and the other honorary award recipients, will be called upon to speak briefly, and he will proclaim to the admiring guests—"The spirit of poetry is the spirit of youthful rebellion, the breaking of custom, and, yes, sometimes the violation of *taboo*."

But the offensive bloody mannequin is quickly surrendered to an indignant University marshal, who folds it up (it appears to be made of inflatable rubber) and quickly trundles it away. The other mannequins disappear beneath seats as the now frowning Governor concludes his remarks with a somber charge to the graduates to "take on the mantle of adulthood and responsibility"—"put away childish things, and give of yourself in sacrifice, where needed, in the nation's—and in the species'—service." These are rousing words, if abstract, and the audience responds with generous applause, as if to compensate for the rudeness of the engineers. The Governor, again beaming, even raises his fist aloft in victory as he steps from the podium.

("What a fool a politician is," thinks the Poet smugly. "The man has not a clue, how the wayward spirit of the god, inhabiting that crowd, could have destroyed him utterly.")

Recognition of Class Marshals and Scholars. Conferring of Ph.D. Degrees. Now follows a lengthy, disjointed Commencement custom, in which numerous graduates in billowing black gowns and mortarboards, smiling shyly, stiffly, at times radiantly as they shake hands with their respective deans, the Provost, and the Chancellor, proceed across the platform from left to right. For these scholars, Commencement is the public recognition of years of hope and industry; many of them are being honored with awards, fellowships, grants to continue their research in postdoctoral programs at the University or elsewhere. Many of the scientists have received grants from private corporations to sponsor their research in biogenetics, bioengineering, bioethics. The Poet, the Educator, and the Scientist, sobered by the number of "outstanding" individuals who must pass across the stage as their names are announced, shake hands with administrators, and receive their diplomas, and descend the stage, are nonetheless impressed by this display of superior specimens of the younger generation. So many! Of so many ethnic minorities, national identities, skin colors! The University seems to draw first-rate students from many foreign countries. And all are so hopeful, shaking hands with the Chancellor, glancing with shy smiles at the revered dignitaries on the platform. The Poet, the Educator, and the Scientist suddenly feel—it's quick as a knife blade to the heart, so swift as to be almost painless—that these young people will soon surpass them, or have already surpassed them, not defiantly, not rebelliously, but simply as a matter of course. *This is their time. Our time is past. Yet, here we are!* The Poet tries to fashion a poem out of this revelation, which strikes him as new, fresh, daunting, though (possibly!) it's a revelation he has had in the past, at such ceremonies. The Educator smiles benignly, a motherly, perhaps grandmotherly figure in her billowing gown, for, as an educator, she expects her work, her theories, her example to be surpassed by idealistic young people—of course. The Scientist is aghast, and fully awakened from his mild trance, to learn that his own area of biological research, for which he and two teammates were awarded their Nobel Prizes, seems to have been totally revolutionized. "Cloning"—a notion of science fiction, long ridiculed and ethically repugnant—is now a simple matter of fact: five young scientists are receiving postdoctoral grants from private corporations to continue their experiments, which seem to have resulted in the actual creation, in University laboratories, of successfully cloned creatures. ("Though not *Homo sapiens*," the Graduate Dean remarks, no doubt for the benefit of wealthy alumni who disapprove of such science.) There are Ph.D.'s who seem to have experimented successfully in grafting together parts of bodies from individuals of disparate species; there are Ph.D.'s who seem to have altered DNA in individuals; an arrogant-looking young astrophysicist has received a postdoctoral fellowship to continue his exploration into the "elasticity of time" and the possibility of "sending objects through time." There's an obese, in fact grotesquely deformed female in a motorized wheelchair whom the Graduate Dean describes (unless the Scientist mishears?) as "colony of grafted alien protoplasm." There's an entirely normal-appearing young man in black cap and gown who moves phantomlike across the stage, seeming to shake hands with the Graduate Dean but unable to accept his diploma; the audience erupts into applause, informed that this is a "living hologram" of the scientist himself, who is thousands of miles away. ("But his diploma is thoroughly 'real,' " the Graduate Dean says with a wink.)

Most repulsive, but stirring even more applause from the audience, is a human head on a self-propelled gurney! This head is of normal size and dimensions, with a normal if somewhat coarse female face; there's a mortarboard on the head and bright lipstick on the mouth of the face. Evidently, this is an adventurous young scientist whose experimental subject was herself! The technical description of this "extraordinary, controversial" neurophysiological project in detaching a head from a body and equipping it with computer-driven autonomy is so abstruse, even the Scientist can't grasp it, and the Poet and the Educator are left gaping.

Other projects include minute mappings of distant galaxies, "reengineering" of repressed memory in brain tissue, computational mathematics in fetal research, "game theory" and sensory transduction, "viral economics" in west Africa, computational microbial pathogenesis! By the time this portion of Commencement ends, with tumultuous applause and cheers, even the younger members of the Chancellor's party, like the Assistant Mace Bearer, are feeling dazed.

The Pyramid. The Ceremony of Renewal. Conferring of Honorary Degrees. The orchestra plays the alma mater now in a slower rhythm, eerily beautiful, nostalgic, not a brisk march but an incantatory dirge, featuring celli, oboes, and harp, as the somber Dean of the Music College leads thousands of voices in a song that thrills even the Poet, the Educator, and the Scientist, who are new to this University's Commencement and unfamiliar with the song before today.

Where snowy peaks of mountains
Meet the eastern sky,
Proudly stands our Alma Mater
On her hilltop high.

Crimson our blood,
Deep as the sea.
Our Alma Mater,
We pledge to thee!

(The Poet shivers, in his light woolen gown. Abysmal rhyming, utterly simple and predictable verse, and yet—! This, too, is poetry, with a powerful effect upon these thousands of spectators.)

The ceremony *on the Pyramid* is the climax of Commencement, and through the stadium, as well as on the platform, anticipation has been steadily mounting. There's an electric air of unease, apprehension, excitement. The Assistant Mace Bearer, too, shivers in his gown, though not for the reason the Poet has shivered.

For nearly an hour he has sat beside the Mace Bearer, close by the Pyramid, the black-lacquered box on his lap, firmly in his gloved fingers. His heartbeat is quickening, there's a swirl of nausea in his bowels. *No. I should not be here, this is a mistake.*

Yet, here he is! Escape for him now, as for the Poet, the Educator, and the Scientist, is not possible.

For the Chancellor has resumed his place at the podium to speak, in a dramatic voice, of the "oldest, most mysterious" part of Commencement; the "very core, on the Pyramid," of Commencement; a "precious fossil of an earlier time"—hundreds of thousands of years before *Homo sapiens* lived. "Yet our ancestors are with us; their blood beats proudly in our veins. We wed their strength to our neuro-ingenuity. We triumph in the twenty-first century because they, our ancestors, prevailed in their centuries." There's a flurry of applause. The uplifted faces among the young graduates are rapt in expectation, their eyes widened and shining.

The Assistant Mace Bearer finds himself on his feet. His entire body feels numb. There's a roaring in his ears. The Mace Bearer nudges him gently, as if to wake him from a trance. "Professor S——! Just follow me." Like an obedient son the Assistant Mace Bearer follows this tall, capable woman with the steely eyes who carries the University's ceremonial mace (a replica of a medieval spiked staff, approximately forty inches in length, made of heavy, gleaming brass) as he, the young professor of North American history, bears the black-lacquered box in his gloved hands; together they march to the base of the Pyramid as the Chancellor intones in his sonorous baritone, "Candidates for honorary doctorates will please *rise*." And so the Poet, the Educator, and the Scientist self-consciously stand, adjusting their long robes, and are escorted to the base of the Pyramid by the Provost, the Dean of the Education School, and the Dean of the Graduate School respectively; in the buzzing elation of the moment it will not occur to these elders that their escorts are gripping them firmly at the elbow, and that the Mace Bearer and her able young assistant are flanking them closely. As the Chancellor reads citations for "these individuals of truly exceptional merit . . ." thousands of eyes are fastened avidly upon the Poet, the Educator, and the Scientist; even as there are a perceptible number of individuals, almost entirely female, who turn aside, or lower their eyes, or even hide behind their Commencement programs, unable to watch the sudden violent beauty of the *ceremony of renewal*.

The University orchestra is playing the alma mater more urgently now. The tempo of Commencement is quickening, like a gigantic pulse. Only just beginning to register uncertainty, the Poet, the Educator, and the Scientist are being escorted up the inlaid granite steps of the Pyramid, to the sacred apex; ascending just before them are the Mace Bearer and the Assistant Mace Bearer, taking the steps in measured stride. There's a collective intake of breath through the stadium. The sacred moment is approaching! A glimmer of pale sun is seen overhead, bordered by massive clouds. The Poet stammers to the Provost, whom he had mistaken as a loyal companion through the ritual of Commencement, "W-what is happening? Why are—?" The Educator, a stout woman, is suddenly short of breath and smiles in confusion at the sea of faces below, greedily watching her and the other honorees; she turns to her escort, to ask, "Excuse me? Why are we—?" when she's abruptly silenced by a tight black band wrapped around the lower part of her face, wielded by the Dean of Education and an assistant. At the same time, the Poet is gagged, flailing desperately. The Scientist, the most suspicious of the three elders, resists his captors, putting up a struggle—"How dare you! I refuse to be—!" He manages to descend several steps before he, too, is caught, silenced by a black gag and his thin arms pinioned behind him.

In the wild widened eyes of the honorees there's the single shared thought *This can't be happening! Not this!*

As these distinguished elders struggle for their lives at the apex of the Pyramid, the vast crowd rises to its feet like a great beast and sighs; even the rowdiest of the young graduates quiver in sudden instinctive sympathy. There's a wisdom of the Pyramid, well known to those who have attended numerous Commencements: "Life honors life"—"The heart of one calls to the heart of many."

The Chancellor continues, raising his voice in recitation of the old script: "By the power invested in me as Chancellor of this University, I hereby confer upon you the degrees of Doctor of Humane Letters, honoris causa . . ." The elders' robes have been torn open; their faces, deathly white, distended by the tightly wrapped black bands, register unspeakable terror, and incredulity. *This can't be happening! Not this!* Through the stadium, spectators are swaying from side to side, some of them having linked arms; it's a time when one will link arms with strangers, warmly and even passionately; more than thirty thousand people are humming, or singing, the alma mater, as the orchestra continues to play sotto voce, with a ghostly predominance of celli, oboes, and harp. *Crimson our blood, deep as the sea* . . . Many in the audience are openly weeping. Even among the dignitaries on the platform there are several who wipe at their eyes, though the wonders of Commencement are not new to them. There are some who stare upward at the ancient struggle, panting as if they themselves have been forcibly marched up the granite steps from which, for the *honorees of sacrifice*, there can be no escape.

(It's a theory advanced by the Dean of the Graduate School, who has a degree in clinical psychology, that to experience the ritual of Commencement is to experience, again and again, one's first Commencement, so that intervening years are obliterated—"In the *ceremony of renewal*, Time has ceased to exist. On the Pyramid we are all immortal, and we weep at the beauty of such knowledge.")

The *moment of truth* is imminent. The Dean of the Chapel, an imposing manly figure in his resplendent gown and velvet cap, climbs the granite steps like one ascending a mountain. The orchestra is now playing the alma mater at double time; it's no longer a dirge but a fevered tarantella. The tight-lipped Mace Bearer makes a signal to her trembling assistant, and the Assistant Mace Bearer opens the black-lacquered box and presents to the Mace Bearer the *instrument of deliverance*, which she bears aloft, toward the sun. This appears to be a primitive stone dagger but is in fact a sharply honed stainless steel butcher's knife with an eighteen-inch blade. The Mace Bearer holds it above her head, solemnly she "whirls" it in one direction, and then in another; this gesture is repeated twice; for every inch of the *instrument of deliverance* must be exposed to the sun, to absorb its blessing. The dagger is then sunk deep into the chests of the honorees; it's used to pry the rib cages open and to hack away at the flesh encasing the still-beating hearts, which emerge from the lacerated chests like panicked birds. These, the Dean of the Chapel must seize bare-handed, according to custom, and raise skyward as high as he is capable.

Led by the Chancellor's deep baritone, the vast crowd chants: "*Novus ordo seclorum.*"

(A lucky coincidence! A pale, fierce sun has nearly penetrated the barrier of rain clouds, and within seconds will be shining freely. Though the *ceremony of renewal* has long been recognized as purely symbolic, and only the very old or the very young believe that it has an immediate effect upon the sun, yet it's thrilling when the sun does emerge at this dramatic moment. . . . Cries of joy are heard throughout the stadium.)

The hearts, no longer beating, are placed reverently on an altar at the Pyramid's apex.

Next, the *ceremony of the skin*. The Mace Bearer and her assistant are charged with the difficult task of flaying the bodies; it's a task demanding as much precision as, or more precision than, removing the beating hearts. Now mere corpses, the bodies of the Poet, the Educator, and the Scientist would sink down lifeless, and fall to the base of the Pyramid, but are held erect as if living. Blood flows from their gaping chest cavities as if valves have been opened, into grooves that lead to a fan-shaped granite pool beneath the speakers' platform. By tradition, the Mace Bearer flays two of the bodies, and the Assistant Mace Bearer flays the third, for the *ceremony of renewal* also involves, for younger participants, an initiation. ("One day, you will be Mace Bearer, Professor S——! So watch closely.") Under enormous pressure, knowing that the eyes of thousands of people are fixed upon him, still more the eyes of the Chancellor and his party, the Assistant Mace Bearer makes his incision at the hairline of his corpse, with the blood-smeared dagger; it's slippery in his fingers, so he must grip it tight; and delicately, very slowly peels the skin downward. The ideal is a virtually entire, perfect skin but this ideal is rarely achieved, of course. (Tradition boasts of a time when "perfect skins" were frequently achieved, but such claims are believed to be mythic.) Both the Poet and the Educator yield lacerated skins, and the Scientist yields a curiously translucent skin, like the husk of a locust, which is light and airy and provokes from the crowd, as the skins are held aloft and made to "dance" to the tarantella music, an outburst of ecstatic cries and howls.

The Assistant Mace Bearer, exhausted by his ordeal, hides his face in his hands and weeps, forgetting that his gloved hands are sticky with blood, and will leave a blood-mask on his heated face.

Conferring of Baccalaureate and Associate Degrees. Three graduates of the Class of ——, two young men and one young woman, with the highest grade point averages at the University, are brought to the platform to bear aloft the skins, and to continue the "dance" while the deans of various schools present their degree candidates and confer degrees upon them. (By tradition, these young people once stripped naked and slipped into the flayed skins, to dance; but nakedness would be considered primitive today, if not repulsive, in such a circumstance. And the skins of elder honorees surely would not fit our husky, healthy youths.) One by one the University's schools are honored. One by one the deans intone, "By the authority invested in me . . ." Hundreds of graduates leap to their feet as their schools are named, smiling and waving to their families in the bleachers. College of Arts and Sciences. School of Architecture. School of Education. School of Engineering and Computer Science. School of Social Work. Public Affairs. Speech and Performing Arts. Environmental Studies. Nursing. Agricultural Sciences. Human Engineering. Hotel Management. Business Administration . . . There are prolonged cheers and applause. Balloons are tossed into the air. Champagne bottles, smuggled into the Great Dome, are now being uncorked. University marshals are less vigilant, the mood of the stadium is suffused with gaiety, release. The Chancellor concludes Commencement with a few words—"Congratulations to all, and God be with you. I now declare the University's two hundredth Commencement officially ended."

The University orchestra is again playing "Pomp and Circumstance" as the Chancellor's party descends from the platform.

(And what of the pulpy, skinned bodies of the honorees? Now mere garbage, these have been allowed to tumble behind the Pyramid into a pit, lined with plastic, and have been covered by a tarpaulin, to be disposed of by groundskeepers when the stadium is emptied. By tradition, such flayed bodies, lacking hearts, are "corrupted, contaminated" meat from which the mysterious spark of life has fled, and no one would wish to gaze upon them.)

Recessional. The triumphant march out! Past elated, cheering graduates, whose tassels are now proudly displayed on the left side of their mortarboards. The pale fierce sun is still shining, to a degree. It's a windy May morning, not yet noon; the sky is riddled with shreds of cloud. The Chancellor's party marches across the bright green AstroTurf in reverse order of their rank, as they'd entered. Familiar as it is, "Pomp and Circumstance" is still thrilling, heartening. "We tried Commencement with another march," the Dean of Music observes, "and it just wasn't the same." The Mace Bearer and the Assistant Mace Bearer march side by side; the Assistant Mace Bearer is carrying the black-lacquered box, in which the *instrument of deliverance* is enclosed. (It was a thoughtful maternal gesture on the part of the Mace Bearer to wet a tissue with her tongue and dab off the blood smears on her assistant's face, before they left the platform.) In fact the Assistant Mace Bearer is feeling dazed, unreal. His eyes ache as if he has been gazing too long into the sun and he feels some discomfort, a stickiness inside one of his gloves, which must have been torn in the ceremony; but his hands are steadier now, and his fingers grip the black-lacquered box tight. Marching past rows of gowned graduates he sees several former students, some of them cheering wildly; their glazed eyes pass over his face, and return, with looks of shocked recognition and admiration. ("Prof. S——!" yells a burly young man. "*Cool.*") A number of the bolder young people have slipped past University marshals to dip their hands and faces in the pool of warm blood at the base of the platform. Some are even kneeling and lapping like puppies, muzzles glistening with blood.

"Am I happy? It's over, at least."

The Assistant Mace Bearer stumbles midway across the field, but regains his balance quickly, before the Mace Bearer can take hold of his arm; he dreads the woman's touch and his own eager response to it. "Professor S——! Are you all right?" Certainly he's all right, the cheering of thousands of spectators is buoyant, like water bearing him up; he would sink, and drown, except the passion of the crowd sustains him. He would choke, except the crowd breathes for him. He would stumble and fall and scream, a fist jammed against his mouth, except the crowd forbids such a display of unmanly behavior. . . . He perceives that his life has been cut in two as with an *instrument of deliverance*. His old, ignorant, unconscious life, and his new, transformed, conscious life. Yes, he's happy! *I am among them now. I have my place now.*

The Graduate Dean observes, passing by graduates clustered excitedly at the foot of the platform, "So encouraging! You can forgive these kids almost anything, at Commencement."

The Chancellor observes, "It's a sight that makes me realize, we are our youth, and they are us."

Disrobing. Returned to the Triangle Lounge, the Chancellor's party is disrobing. What relief! What a glow of satisfaction, as after a winning football game. The Chancellor, the Governor, and the President of the Board of Trustees, three beaming individuals of vigorous middle age, are being interviewed by a TV broadcaster about the "special significance" of the two hundredth anniversary. Everywhere in the lounge there's an air of festivity. Flashbulbs are blinding, greetings and handshakes are exchanged. The Assistant Mace Bearer enters shyly, to surrender his blood-dampened gown and torn rubber gloves, and immediately he's being congratulated on a "job well done." The Graduate Dean himself shakes his hand. The Provost! "Thank you. I—I'm grateful for your words." More photographers appear. A second TV crew, hauling equipment. Bottles of champagne are uncorked. The Assistant Mace Bearer would accept a glass of champagne but doesn't trust his stomach, and his nerves.

Is he envious? Shortly after the disrobing there will be a lavish luncheon for most of the Chancellor's party at the University Club, but Professor S—— is not invited; the Assistant Mace Bearer is too minor an individual to have been included with the others. Another year, perhaps!

He has exited the room, eager to be gone. Makes his way along a corridor like a man in a dream. Without his Commencement costume, he feels exposed as if naked to the eyes of strangers; yet, paradoxically, he's invisible; in ordinary clothes he's of no extraordinary importance; he hopes no former students will notice him. . . . He's passing swarms of graduates, still in their robes, and their families and relatives, all smiles. Small children are running feverishly about. That smell! Professor S——'s mouth waters furiously. Food is again being sold, everywhere customers are queuing up to buy.

Minutes later he's devouring a Commencement Special. Horseradish and sausage juice dribble down his hands, he's famished.

Jim Kelly has done everything before me—he was born a year before me, got married before I did, and started publishing before I did, after we both (along with Bruce Sterling, William Wu, P. C. Hodgell, and a bunch of others) attended the 1974 Clarion Writers Workshop at Michigan State University.

Which means I've know Jim for twenty-seven years—which is amazing, because we both still look so young.

While I wandered off into the horror field for fifteen years or so, Jim pretty much stayed in the sf field—garnering a couple of Hugos (for wonderful stories like "Think Like a Dinosaur") and pretty much staying on the path he laid out for himself so long ago.

And as I said, we still both look young.

Unique Visitors

JAMES PATRICK KELLY

✳

It's strange, but when I woke up just now, I had the theme song to *The Beverly Hillbillies* in my head. You don't remember *The Beverly Hillbillies*, do you? But then you probably don't remember television. Television was the great-great-grandmother of media: a scheduled and sequential entertainment stream. You had to sit in front of the set at a certain time, and you had to watch the program straight through. The programs were too narrow-minded to branch off into other plot lines, too stupid to stop and wait if you got up to change your personality or check your portfolio. If you were lucky, you could get your business done during a commercial. No, you don't want to know about commercials. Those were dark years.

Anyway, after all this time—has it been centuries already?—I realized that *The Beverly Hillbillies* was a science fiction show. Maybe it's just that everything looks like science fiction to me, now. The hillbillies were simple folk, Jeffersonian citizen-farmers desperately scratching a nineteenth-century living from an exhausted land. Then—*bing bang boom*—they were thrust into the hurly-burly of the twentieth century. *Swimming pools and movie stars!* The show was really about the clash of world views; the Clampetts were a hardy band of time travelers coming to grips with a bizarre future. And here's the irony: Do you know what their time machine was?

It seems that one day Jed Clampett, the alpha hillbilly, was shooting at a raccoon. Are there still raccoons? Submit query.

Raccoon, a carnivorous North American mammal,
Procyon lotor, extinct in the wild since 2250, reintroduced
to the Woodrow Roosevelt Culturological Habitat in 2518.

So one day he was shooting at a raccoon, which apparently he meant to eat, times being hard and all, but he missed the mark. Instead his bullet struck the ground, where it uncovered an oil seepage. Crude oil, a naturally occurring petrochemical, which we have long since depleted. Old Jed was instantly, fabulously rich. Yes, it was a great fortune that launched him into the future, just as all the money I made writing expert systems brought me to you.

Of course, the Beverly Hillbillies were backcountry bumpkins, so it was hard to take them seriously at the time. One of them, I think it was the son—Jerome was his name—seemed to have fallen out of the stupid tree and hit every damn branch on the way down.

You laugh. That's very polite of you. The last time, no one laughed at my jokes. I was worried that maybe laughter had gone extinct. How many of you are out there, anyway? Submit query.

> There are currently 842 unique visitors monitoring this session. The average attention quotient is 27 percent.

Twenty-seven percent! Don't you people realize that you've got an eyewitness to history here? Ask not what your country can do for you. The Eagle has landed. Tune in, turn on, drop out! I was there—slept at the White House three times during the Mondale administration. The fall of the Berlin Wall, the Millennium Bubble—hey, who do you think steered all that venture capital toward neural scanning? I started eight companies and every one turned a profit. I'm a primary source. Twenty-seven percent? Well, take your twenty-seven percent and . . .

Oh, never mind. Let's just get on with the news. That's why I'm here, why I spent all the money. Twenty-first century time traveler on a grand tour of the future. Just pix and headlines for now.

Still the glaciers? Well, *I* never owned one of those foolish SUVs, and our business was writing code. The only CO_2 my companies put into the atmosphere came from heavy breathing when programmers logged on to porn sites. Although how global warming puts Lake Champlain on ice is beyond me. Oh, this is exciting. New calculations of the distribution of supersymmetric neutralinos prove that the universe is closed and will eventually recollapse in the Big Crunch. That should be worth staying up late for. And what's this creepy-crawly thing, looks like a hairbrush with eyes. We've found crustaceans in the Epsilon Eridani system? Where the hell is Epsilon Eridani? Submit query.

> Episilon Eridani is an orange star, Hertzsprung-Russell type K2, 10.7 light-years away. It has a system of six planets, four of which are

gas giants, Ruth, Mantle, Maris, and Einstein, and two of which are terrestrial, Drysdale and Koufax. The atmosphere of Koufax has a density .78 that of earth.

Life on planet Koufax. I saw him when he was pitching for the Red Sox, I think it was 1978. He was just about at the end of his career and still Nolan Ryan wasn't worthy enough to carry his jockstrap. I was a big baseball fan, I even owned a piece of the Screaming Loons; they played Double A ball out of Poughkeepsie in the nineties. But I'm probably boring you. What's my attention quotient now? Submit query.

There are currently 14,263,112 unique visitors monitoring this session. The average attention quotient is 72 percent.

That's better. Where were you people brought up? In a cubicle? You should respect your elders, and God knows there's no one older than I am. Sure, I could have given the money to some damn foundation like Gates did. What for? So people would remember me in a couple of hundred years? *I'm* still here to remember me. Maybe it bothers people these days that I'm not really alive, is that it? Just because I left the meat part of myself behind? Well, here's some news for *you*. I don't miss my body one damn bit, not the root canals or going bald or arthritis. You think that I'm not really me, because I exist only on a neural net? Look, the memory capacity of the human brain is one hundred trillion neurotransmitter concentrations at interneuronal connections. What the brain boys call synapse strengths. That converts to about a million billion bits. My upload was 1.12 million billion. Besides, do I sound like any computer you've ever heard before? I don't think so. What was it that Aristotle said, "I think, therefore I am?" Well, I am, and I am me. I can still taste my first kiss, my first drink, my first million.

Why are you laughing? That wasn't a joke. You think you're fooling me, but you're not. What's the day today? Submit query.

Today is Tuesday, May 23.

Is that so? Who's playing third base for Yankees? Who's in first place in the American League East? What's the capital of New Jersey? Who is the president of the United States? Submit query.

Baseball is extinct.

Baseball . . . extinct. And that's not the worst of it, is it? You don't . . . Listen, Sandy Koufax retired in 1966 and there never was a Mondale administration and *Cogito ergo sum* was Descartes, not Aristotle. You don't know anything about us, do you? I began to suspect the last time I woke up. Oh, God, how long ago was that? Submit query.

You have been in sleep mode for eight hundred years.

Eight hundred . . . and there's no sports in your news, no politics, no art. History, wiped clean. You didn't just decide that we weren't worth remembering, did you? Something terrible must have happened. What was it? Alien invasion? Civil war? Famine? Disease? I don't care how bad it is, just tell me. It's why I did this to myself. It wasn't easy, you know. Margaret divorced me right before the procedure, my kids never once accessed me afterward. The press called me selfish. The Pharaoh of Programming buried in his mainframe mausoleum. Nobody understood. You see, even though I was old, I never lost the fire. I wanted to know everything, find out what happened next. And there were all the spin-offs from the procedure. We gave the world a map of the brain, the quantum computer. And here I am in the future, and now *you* don't understand. You're keeping it from me. Why? Who the hell are you? Submit query!

Oh, God, is anyone there? Submit query!

There are currently 157,812,263,609 unique visitors monitoring this session. The average attention quotient is 98 percent.

I think I understand now. I'm some kind of an exhibit, is that it? I never asked to sleep eight hundred years; that has to be your doing. Is my hardware failing? My code corrupted? No, never mind, I'm not going to submit. I won't give you the satisfaction. You've rattled my cage and got me to bark, but the show is over. Maybe you're gone so far beyond what we were that I could never understand you. What's the sense of reading the *Wall Street Journal* to the seals at the Bronx Zoo? Unique visitors. Maybe I don't want to know who you are. You could be like H. G. Wells's Martians: "Intellects vast and cool and unsympathetic."

You don't remember old Herbert George; time machines were his idea. Only his could go back. No, no regrets. Too late for regrets.

Eight hundred years. I suppose I should thank you for taking care of me. The money I left in the trust is probably all spent. Maybe there is no such thing as money anymore. No banks, no credit, no stocks, no brokers or assistant project managers or CFOs or lawyers or accountants. "Oh brave new world, that has no people in it!"

That's Shakespeare, in case you're wondering. He played goalie for the Mets.

Harry Turtledove—who has taught ancient and medieval history at Cal State Fullerton, Cal State L.A., and UCLA, and has a Ph.D. in Byzantine history—has been called "the standard-bearer for alternate history," and that's certainly true; his amazing novels, including The Guns of the South *(American Civil War),* The Great War: American Front *(World War I), and the* Worldwar *tetralogy (World War II) have transformed, with their bravura storytelling and sheer joy in detail, our understanding of the term.*

His short stories are as richly realized as his novels; when Harry first described what he was going to do with "Black Tulip," I knew that I was in for a ride as good as his novels.

Black Tulip

Harry Turtledove

*

Sergei's father was a druggist in Tambov, maybe four hundred kilometers south and east of Moscow. Filling prescriptions looked pretty good to Sergei. You didn't have to work too hard. You didn't have to think too hard. You could get your hands on medicines from the West, medicines that really worked, not just the Soviet crap. And you could rake in plenty on the left from your customers, because they wanted the stuff that really worked, too. So—pharmacy school, then a soft job till pension time. Sergei had it all figured out.

First, though, his hitch in the Red Army. He was a sunny kid when he got drafted, always looking on the bright side of things. He didn't think they could possibly ship his ass to Afghanistan. Even after they did, he didn't think they could possibly ship him to Bāmiān Province. Life is full of surprises, even—maybe especially—for a sunny kid from a provincial town where nothing much ever happens.

Abdul Satar Ahmedi's father was a druggist, too, in Bulola, a village of no particular name or fame not far east of the town of Bāmiān. Satar had also planned to follow in his father's footsteps, mostly because that was what a good son did. Sometimes the drugs his father dispensed helped the patient. Sometimes they didn't. Either way, it was the will of God, the Compassionate, the Merciful.

Satar was twenty—he thought he was twenty, though he might have been nineteen or twenty-one—when the godless Russians poured into his country. They seized the bigger towns and pushed out along the roads from one to another. Bāmiān was one of the places where their tanks and personnel carriers and helicopters came to roost. One of the roads they wanted ran through Bulola.

On the day the first truck convoy full of infidel soldiers rumbled through the village, Satar's father dug up an ancient but carefully greased Enfield rifle. He thrust it at the younger man, saying, "My grandfather fought the British infidels with this piece. Take it and do to the atheists what they did to the soldiers of the Queen."

"Yes, Father," Satar said, as a good son should.

Before long, he carried a Kalashnikov in place of the ancient Enfield. Before long, he marched with the men of Sayid Jaglan, who had been a major in the Kabul puppet regime before choosing to fight for God and freedom instead. Being a druggist's son, he served as a medic. He was too ignorant to make a good medic, but he knew more than most, so he had to try. He wished he knew more still; he'd had to watch men die because he didn't know enough. The will of God, yes, of course, but accepting it came hard.

The dragon? The dragon had lived in the valley for time out of mind before Islam came to Afghanistan. Most of those centuries, it had slept, as dragons do. But when it woke—oh, when it woke . . .

Sergei looked out over the Afghan countryside and shook his head in slow wonder. He'd been raised in country as flat as if it were ironed. The Bulola perimeter wasn't anything like that. The valley in which this miserable village sat was high enough to make his heart pound when he moved quickly. And the mountains went up from there, dun and gray and red and jagged and here and there streaked with snow.

When he remarked on how different the landscape looked, his squadmates in the trench laughed at him. "Screw the scenery," Vladimir said. "Fucking Intourist didn't bring you here. Keep your eye peeled for *dukhi*. You may not see them, but sure as shit they see you."

"Ghosts," Sergei repeated, and shook his head again. "We shouldn't have started calling them that."

"Why not?" Vladimir was a few months older than he, and endlessly cynical. "You usually *don't* see 'em till it's too damn late."

"But they're real. They're alive," Sergei protested. "They're trying to make *us* into ghosts."

A noise. None of them knew what had made it. The instant they heard it, their AKs all lifted a few centimeters. Then they identified the distant, growing rumble in the air for what it was. "Bumblebee," Fyodor said. He had the best ears of any of them, and he liked to hear himself talk. But he was right. Sergei spotted the speck in the sky.

"I like having helicopter gunships around," he said. "They make me think my life-insurance policy's paid up." Not even Vladimir argued with that.

The Mi-24 roared past overhead, red stars bright against camouflage paint. Then, like a dog coming to point, it stopped and hovered. It didn't look like a bumblebee to Sergei. It put him in mind of a polliwog, like the ones he'd see in the creeks outside of Tambov in the springtime. Come to think of it, they were camouflage-colored, too, to keep fish and birds from eating them.

But the gunship had a sting any bee would have envied. It let loose with the rocket pods it carried under its stubby wings, and with the four-barrel Gatling in its nose. Even from a couple of kilometers away, the noise was terrific. So was the fireworks display. The Soviet soldiers whooped and cheered. Explosions pocked the mountainside. Fire and smoke leaped upward. Deadly as a shark, ponderous as a whale, the Mi-24 heeled in the air and went on its way.

"Some bandits there, with a little luck," Sergei said. "Pilot must've spotted something juicy."

"Or thought he did," Vladimir answered. "Liable just to be mountain-goat tartare now."

"Watch the villagers," Fyodor said. "They'll let us know if that bumblebee really stung anything."

"You're smart," Sergei said admiringly.

"If I was fucking smart, would I fucking be here?" Fyodor returned, and his squadmates laughed. He added, "I've been here too fucking long, that's all. I know all kinds of things I never wanted to find out."

Sergei turned and looked back over his shoulder. The men in the village were staring at the shattered mountainside and muttering among themselves in their incomprehensible language. In their turbans and robes—some white, some mud brown—they looked oddly alike to him. They all had long hawk faces and wore beards. Some of the beards were black, some gray, a very few white. That was his chief clue they'd been stamped from the mold at different times.

Women? Sergei shook his head. He'd never seen a woman's face here. Bulola wasn't the sort of village where women shed their veils in conformance to the revolutionary sentiments of the People's Democratic Party of Afghanistan. It was the sort of place when women thought letting you see a nose was as bad as letting you see a pussy. Places like this, girls who went to coed schools got murdered when they came home. It hadn't happened right here—he didn't think Bulola had ever had coed schools—but it had happened in the countryside.

He gauged the mutters. He couldn't understand them, but he could make guesses from the tone. "I think we hit 'em a pretty good lick," he said.

Vladimir nodded. "I think you're right. Another ten billion more, and we've won the fucking war. Or maybe twenty billion. Who the fuck knows?"

Satar huddled in a little hole he'd scraped in the dirt behind a big reddish boulder. He made himself as small as he could, to give the flying bullets and chunks of shrapnel the least chance of tearing his tender flesh. *If it is God's will, it is God's will,* he thought. But if it wasn't God's will, he didn't want to make things any easier for the infidels than he had to.

Under him, the ground quivered as if in pain as another salvo of Soviet rockets slammed home. Satar hated helicopter gunships with a fierce and bitter passion. He had nothing but contempt for the Afghan soldiers who fought on the side of the atheists. Some Russian ground soldiers were stupid as sheep, and as helpless outside their tanks and personnel carriers as a turtle outside its shell. Others were very good, as good as any mujahideen. You never could tell. Sometimes you got a nasty surprise instead of giving one.

But helicopters . . . What he hated most about helicopters was that he couldn't hit back. They hung in the air and dealt out death, and all you could do if they spotted you was take it. Oh, every once in a while the mujahideen got lucky with a heavy machine gun or an RPG-7 and knocked down one of Shaitan's machines, but only once in a while.

Satar had heard the Americans were going to start sending Stinger antiaircraft missiles up to the mujahideen from Pakistan. The Americans were infidels, too, of course, but they hated the Russians. The enemy of my enemy . . . In world politics as in tribal feuds, the enemy of one's enemy was a handy fellow to know. And the Stinger was supposed to be very good.

At the moment, though, Satar and his band were getting stung, not stinging. The gunship seemed to have all the ammunition in the world. Hadn't it been hovering above them for hours, hurling hellfire down on their heads?

Another explosion, and somebody not far away started screaming. Satar cursed the Soviets and his comrade, for that meant he couldn't huddle in the shelter of the boulder anymore. Grabbing his sad little medicine kit, he scrambled toward the wounded mujahid. The man clutched his leg and moaned. Blood darkened the wool of his robe.

"Easy, Abdul Rahim, easy," Satar said. "I have morphine, to take away the pain."

"Quickly, then, in the name of God," Abdul Rahim got out between moans. "It is broken; I am sure of it."

Cursing softly, Satar fumbled in the kit for a syringe. What did a druggist's son know of setting broken bones? Satar knew far more than he had; experience made a harsh teacher, but a good one. He looked around for sticks to use as splints and cursed again. Where on a bare stone mountainside would he find such sticks?

He was just taking the cover from the needle when a wet slapping sound came from Abdul Rahim. The mujahid's cries suddenly stopped. When Satar turned back toward him, he knew what he would find, and he did. One of the bullets from the gunship's Gatling had struck home. Abdul Rahim's eyes still stared up at the sky, but they were forever blind now.

A martyr who falls in the holy war against the infidel is sure of Paradise, Satar thought. He grabbed the dead man's Kalashnikov and his banana clips before scuttling back into shelter.

At last, after what seemed like forever, the helicopter gunship roared away. Satar waited for the order that would send the mujahideen roaring down on the *Shuravi*—the Soviets—in his home village. But Sayid Jaglan's captain called, "We have taken too much hurt. We will fall back now and strike them another time."

Satar cursed again, but in his belly, in his stones, he knew the captain was wise. The Russians down there would surely be alert and waiting. *My father, I* will *return*, Satar thought as he turned away from Bulola. *And when I do, the village will be freed.*

The dragon dreamt. Even that was out of the ordinary; in its age-long sleep, it was rarely aware or alert enough to dream. It saw, or thought it saw, men with swords, men with spears. One of them, from out of the west, was a little blond fellow in a gilded corselet and crested helm. The dragon made as if to call out to him, for in him it recognized its match: like knows like.

But the little man did not answer the call as one coming in friendship should. Instead, he drew his sword and plunged it into the dragon's flank. It hurt much more than anything in a dream had any business doing. The dragon shifted restlessly. After a while, the pain eased, but the dragon's sleep wasn't so deep as it had been. It dreamt no more, not then, but dreams lay not so far above the surface of that slumber.

Under Sergei's feet, the ground quivered. A pebble leaped out of the side of the entrenchment and bounced off his boot. "What was that?" he said. "The stinking *dukhi* set off a charge somewhere?"

His sergeant laughed, showing steel teeth. Krikor was an Armenian. With his long face and big nose and black hair and eyes, he looked more like the *dukhi* himself than like a Russian. "That wasn't the ghosts," he said. "That was an earthquake. Just a little one, thank God."

"An earthquake?" That hadn't even crossed Sergei's mind. He, too, laughed—nervously. "Don't have those in Tambov—you'd better believe it."

"They do down in the Caucasus," Sergeant Krikor said. "Big ones are real bastards, too. Yerevan'll get hit one of these days. Half of it'll fall down, too—mark my words. All the builders cheat like maniacs, the fuckers. Too much sand in the concrete, not enough steel rebar. Easier to pocket the difference, you know?" He made as if to count bills and put them in his wallet.

"It's like that everywhere," Sergei said. " 'I serve the Soviet Union!' " He put a sardonic spin on the phrase that had probably meant something in the days when his grandfather was young.

Sergeant Krikor's heavy eyebrows came down and together in a frown. "Yeah, but who gives a shit in Tambov? So buildings fall apart faster than they ought to. So what? But if an earthquake hits—a big one, I mean—they don't just fall apart. They fall *down*."

"I guess." Sergei wasn't about to argue with the sergeant. Krikor was a conscript like him, but a conscript near the end of his term, not near the beginning. That, even more than his rank, made the Armenian one of the top dogs. Changing the subject, Sergei said, "We hit the bandits pretty hard earlier today." He tried to forget Vladimir's comment. Ten billion times more? Twenty billion? *Bozhemoi!*

Krikor frowned again, in a subtly different way. "Listen, kid, do you still believe all the internationalist crap they fed you before they shipped your worthless ass here to Afghan?" He gave the country its universal name among the soldiers of the Red Army.

"Well . . . no," Sergei said. "They went on and on about the revolutionary unity of the People's Democratic Party of Afghanistan and the friendship to the Soviet Union of the Afghan people—and everybody who's been here more than twenty minutes knows the PDPA's got more factions than it has members, and they all hate each other's guts, and all the Afghans hate Russians."

"Good. You're not an idiot—not *quite* an idiot, I mean." Sergeant Krikor murmured something in a language that wasn't Russian: "*Shuravi! Shuravi! Marg, marg, marg!*"

For a moment, Sergei thought that was Armenian. Then he realized he'd heard it here in Afghanistan a couple-three times. "What's it mean?" he asked.

" 'Soviets! Soviets! Death, death, death!' " Krikor translated with somber relish. He waited for Sergei to take that in, then went on, "So I really don't give a shit about how hard we hit the ghosts, you know what I mean? All I want to do is get my time in and get back to the world in one piece, all right? Long as I don't fly home in a black tulip, that's all I care about."

"Makes sense to me," Sergei agreed quickly. He didn't want to fly out of Kabul in one of the planes that carried corpses back to the USSR, either.

"Okay, kid." Krikor thumped him on the shoulder, hard enough to stagger him. "Keep your head down, keep your eyes open, and help your buddies. Odds are, we'll both get through."

The ground shook again, but not so hard this time.

"*Allahu akbar!*" The long, drawn-out chant of the muezzin pulled Satar awake. He yawned and stretched on the ground in the courtyard of a mud house a Russian bomb had shattered. Ten or twelve other mujahideen lay there with him. One by one, they got to their feet and ambled over to a basin of water, where they washed their hands and faces, their feet and their privates.

Satar gasped as he splashed his cheeks with the water. It was bitterly cold. A pink glow in the east said sunrise was coming soon.

"God is great!" the muezzin repeated. He stood on the roof of another ruined house and called out to the faithful:

I bear witness, there is no God but God!
I bear witness, Muḥammad is the prophet of God!
Come quick to prayer!
Come quick to success!
Prayer is better than sleep!
God is great!
There is no God but the one true God!

The fighters spread blankets on the dirt of the courtyard. This was no mosque with a proper *qibla*, but they knew in which direction Mecca lay. They bent, shoulder to shoulder, and went through morning prayers together.

After praying, Satar ate unleavened bread and drank tea thick with sugar and fragrant with mint. He had never been a fat man; he'd grown thinner since joining the mujahideen. The godless infidels and their puppets held the richest parts of the countryside. But villagers were generous in sharing what they had—and some of what was grown and made in occupied parts of the country reached the fighters in the holy war through one irregular channel or another.

A couple of boys of about six strutted by, both of them carrying crude wooden toy Kalashnikovs. One dived behind some rubble. The other stalked him as carefully as if their assault rifles were real. When the time came for them to take up such weapons, they would be ready. Another boy, perhaps thirteen, had a real Kalashnikov on his back. He'd been playing with toy firearms when the Russians invaded Afghanistan. Now he was old enough to fight for God on his own. Boys like that were useful, especially as scouts—the *Shuravi* weren't always so wary of them as they were with grown men.

Something glinted in the early-morning sun: a boy of perhaps eight carried what looked like a plastic pen even more proudly than the other children bore their Kalashnikovs, pretend and real. Assault rifles were commonplace, pens something out of the ordinary, something special.

"Hey, sonny," Satar called through lips all at once numb with fear. The boy looked at him. He nodded encouragingly. "Yes, you—that's right. Put your pen on the ground and walk away from it."

"What?" Plainly, the youngster thought he was crazy. "Why should I?" If he'd had a rifle, Satar would have had to look to his life.

"I'll tell you why: because I think it's a Russian mine. If you fiddle with it, it will blow off your hand."

The boy very visibly thought that over. Satar could read his mind. *Is this mujahid trying to steal my wonderful toy?* Maybe the worry on Satar's face got through to him, because he did set the pen in the dirt. But when he walked away, he kept looking back over his shoulder at it.

With a sigh of relief, Satar murmured, "Truly there is no God but God."

"Truly," someone behind him agreed. He turned. There stood Sayid Jaglan. The commander went on, "That is a mine—I am sure of it. Pens are bad. I was afraid he would take off the cap and detonate it. Pens are bad, but the ones that look like butterflies are worse. Any child, no matter how small, will play with those."

"And then be blown to pieces," Satar said bitterly.

"Oh, no, not to pieces." Sayid Jaglan shook his head. He was about forty, not very tall, his pointed beard just beginning to show frost. He had a scar on his forehead that stopped a centimeter or so above his right eye. "They're made to maim, not to kill. The Russians calculate we have to work harder to care for the wounded than to bury the dead."

Satar pondered that. "A calculation straight from the heart of Shaitan," he said at last.

"Yes, but sound doctrine even so." Sometimes the officer Sayid

Jaglan had been showed through under the chieftain of mujahideen he was. "You did well to persuade the boy to get rid of that one."

"Taking off the cap activates it?" Satar asked. Sayid Jaglan nodded. Satar went over and picked up the pen and set it on top of a battered wall, out of reach of children. If he was afraid of doing it, he didn't show his fear, or even acknowledge it to himself. All he said was, "We should be able to salvage the explosive from it."

"Yes." Sayid Jaglan nodded again. "You were a little soft when you joined us, Satar—who would have expected anything different from a druggist's son? You never followed the herds or tried to scratch a living from the fields. But you've done well. You have more wit than God gave most men, and your heart was always strong. Now your body matches your spirit's strength."

Satar didn't show how much the compliment pleased him, either. That was not the Afghan way. Gruffly, he replied, "If it is God's will, it will be accomplished."

"Yes." Sayid Jaglan looked down the valley, in the direction of Bulola. "And I think it is God's will that we soon reclaim your home village from the atheist *Shuravi*."

"May it be so," Satar said. "I have not sat beside my father for far too long."

Sergei strode up the main street, such as it was, of Bulola. Dirt and dust flew up from under his boots at every stride. In Kabul, even in Bāmiān, he probably would have felt safe enough to wear his Kalashnikov slung on his back. Here, he carried it, his right forefinger ready to leap to the trigger in an instant. The change lever was on single shots. He could still empty the magazine in seconds, and he could aim better that way.

Beside him, Vladimir carried his weapon ready to use, too. Staying alive in Afghan meant staying alert every second of every minute of every day. Vladimir glanced over at a handful of gray-bearded men sitting around drinking tea and passing the mouthpiece of a water pipe back and forth. Laughing, he said, "Ah, they love us."

"Don't they just!" Sergei laughed, too, nervously. The Afghans' eyes followed Vladimir and him. They were hard and black and glittering as obsidian. "If the looks they gave us came out of Kalashnikovs, we'd be bleeding in the dust."

"Fuck 'em," Vladimir said cheerfully. "No, fuck their wives—these assholes aren't worth it."

He could make it sound funny. He could make it sound obscene. But he couldn't take away one brute fact. "They all hate us," Sergei said. "They don't even bother hiding it. Every single one of them hates us."

"There's a hot headline!" Vladimir exclaimed. "What did you expect? That they'd welcome us with open arms—the women with open legs? That they'd all give us fraternal socialist greetings? Not fucking likely!" He spat.

"I *did* think that when I first got here. Didn't you?" Sergei said. "Before they put me on the plane for Kabul, they told me I was coming here to save the popular revolution. They told me we were internationalists, and the peace-loving Afghan government had asked us for help."

"They haven't changed their song a bit. They told my gang the same thing," Vladimir said. "I already knew it was a crock, though."

"How?"

"How? I'll tell you how. Because my older brother's best friend came back from here in a black tulip, inside one of those zinc coffins they make in Kabul. It didn't have a window in it, and this officer stuck to it like a leech to make sure Sasha's mother and dad wouldn't open it up and see what happened to him before they planted him in the ground. *That's* how."

"Oh." Sergei didn't know how to answer that. After a few more steps, he said, "They told me the Americans started the war."

Vladimir pointed out to the mountains, to the gray and brown and red rock. "You see Rambo out there? I sure don't."

"We've got our own Ramboviki here," Sergei said slyly.

"Bastards. Fucking bastards." Vladimir started to spit once more, but seemed too disgusted to go through with it this time. "I hate our fucking gung-ho paratroopers, you know that? They want to go out and kick ass, and they get everybody else in trouble when they do."

"Yeah." Sergei couldn't argue with that. "Half the time, if you leave the ghosts alone, they'll leave you alone, too."

"I know." Vladimir nodded. "Of course, the other half of the time, they *won't*."

"Oh, yes. Ohhh, yes. I haven't been here real long, but I've seen that." Now Sergei pointed out to the mountainside. A few men—Afghans, hard to see at a distance in their robes of brown and cream—were moving around, not far from where the bumblebee had flayed the ghosts a few days before. "What are they up to out there?"

"No good," Vladimir said at once. "Maybe they're scavenging weapons the *dukhi* left behind. I hope one of the stinking ragheads steps on a mine, that's what I hope. Serve him right."

Never had Sergei seen a curse more quickly fulfilled. No sooner had the words left Vladimir's mouth than a harsh, flat *craack!* came echoing back from the mountains. He brought his Kalashnikov up to his shoulder. Vladimir did the same. They both relaxed, a little, when they realized the explosion wasn't close by.

Lowering his assault rifle, Vladimir started laughing like a loon. "Miserable son of a bitch walked into one we left out for the ghosts. Too bad. Oh, *too* bad!" He laughed again, louder than ever.

On the mountainside, the Afghans who weren't hurt bent over their wounded friend and did what they could for him. Sergei said, "This won't make the villagers like us any better."

"Too bad. Oh, *too* bad!" Vladimir not only repeated himself, he pressed his free hand over his heart like a hammy opera singer pulling out all the stops to emote on stage. "And they love us so much already."

Sergei couldn't very well argue with that, not when he'd been the one who'd pointed out that the villagers didn't love the Red Army men in their midst. He did say, "Here come the Afghans."

The wounded man's pals brought him back with one of his arms slung over each of their shoulders. He groaned every now and then, but tried to bear his pain in silence. His robes were torn and splashed—soaked—with red. Sergei had seen what mines did. The Afghan's foot—maybe his whole leg up to the knee—would look as if it belonged in a butcher's shop, not attached to a human being.

One of the Afghans knew a little Russian. "Your mine hurt," he said. "Your man help?" He pointed to the Soviet medic's tent.

"Yes, go on," Sergei said. "Take him there."

"Softly," Vladimir told him.

A fleabite might not bother a sleeping man. If he'd been bitten before, though, he might notice a second bite, or a third, more readily than he would have otherwise. The dragon stirred restlessly.

Satar squatted on his heels, staring down at the ground in front of him. He'd been staring at it long enough to know every pebble, every clod of dirt, every little ridge of dust. A spider scuttled past. Satar watched it without caring.

Sayid Jaglan crouched beside him. "I am sorry, Abdul Satar Ahmedi."

"It is the will of God," Satar answered, not moving, not looking up.

"Truly, it *is* the will of God," agreed the commander of the mujahideen. "They do say your father is likely to live."

"If God wills it, he will live," Satar said. "But is it a life to live as a cripple, to live without a foot?"

"Like you, he has wisdom," Sayid Jaglan said. "He has a place in Bulola he may be able to keep. Because he has wisdom, he will not have to beg his bread in the streets, as a herder or peasant without a foot would."

"He will be a cripple!" Satar burst out. "He is my father!" Tears stung his eyes. He did not let them fall. He had not shed a tear since the news came to the mujahideen from his home village.

"I wonder if the earthquake made him misstep," Sayid Jaglan said.

"Ibrahim said the earthquake was later," Satar answered.

"Yes, he said that, but he might have been wrong," Sayid Jaglan said. "God is perfect. Men? Men make mistakes."

Now at last Satar looked up at him. "The Russians made a mistake when they came into our country," he said. "I will show them what sort of mistake they made."

"We all aim to do that," Sayid Jaglan told him. "And we *will* take back your village, and we *will* do it soon. Our strength gathers, here and elsewhere. When Bulola falls, the whole valley falls, and the valley is like a sword pointed straight at Bāmiān. As sure as God is one, your father will be avenged. Then he will no longer lie under the hands of the godless ones . . . though Ibrahim did also say they treated his wound with some skill."

"Jinni of the waste take Ibrahim by the hair!" Satar said. "If the *Shuravi* had not laid the mines, my father would not have been wounded in the first place."

"True. Every word of it true," the chieftain of the mujahideen agreed. Satar was arguing with him, not sitting there lost in his own private wasteland of pain. Sayid Jaglan set a hand on Satar's shoulder. "When the time comes, you will fight as those who knew the Prophet fought to bring his truth to Arabia and to the world."

"I don't know about that. I don't know anything about that at all," Satar said. "All I know is, I will fight my best."

Sayid Jaglan nodded in satisfaction. "Good. We have both said the same thing." He went off to rouse the spirit of some other mujahid.

"*Shuravi! Shuravi! Marg, marg, marg!*" The mocking cry rose from behind a mud-brick wall in Bulola. Giggles followed it. The boy—or maybe it was a girl—who'd called out for death to the Soviets couldn't have been more than seven years old.

"Little bastard," Vladimir said, hands tightening on his Kalashnikov. "His mother was a whore and his father was a camel."

"They all feel that way, though," Sergei said. As always, he felt the weight of the villagers' eyes on him. They reminded him of wolves tracking an elk. *No, the beast is too strong and dangerous for us to try to pull it down right now*, that gaze seemed to say. *All right, then. We won't rush in. We'll just keep trotting along, keep watching it, and wait for it to weaken.*

Sergeant Krikor said, "How can we hope to win a war where the people in whose name we're fighting wish they could kill us a millimeter at a time?"

"I don't know. I don't care, either," Vladimir said. "All I want to do is get back home in one piece. Then I can go on with my life and spend the rest of it forgetting what I've been through here in Afghan."

"I want to get home in one piece, too," Sergei said. "But what about the poor bastards they ship in here after we get out? They'll have it as bad as we do, maybe worse. That isn't fair."

"Let *them* worry about it. Long as I'm gone, I don't give a shit." Vladimir pulled a fresh pack of cigarettes out of his shirt pocket. Like anyone who'd been in Afghanistan for a while, he opened it from the bottom. That way, his hands, full of the local filth, never touched the filter that would go in his mouth. He scraped a match alight and cupped his free hand to shield the flame from the breeze till he got the smoke going.

"Give me one of those," Sergei said. He knew cigarettes weren't good for you. He couldn't count how many times his father and mother had tried to quit. Back in Tambov, he never would have started. But coming to Afghanistan wasn't good for you, either. He leaned close to Vladimir to get a light off the other cigarette, then sucked harsh smoke deep into his lungs and blew it out. That made him cough like a coal miner with black-lung disease, but he took another drag anyhow.

Vladimir offered Krikor a smoke without being asked. Of course, Krikor was a sergeant, not just a lowly trooper. Vladimir was no dummy. He knew whom to keep buttered up, and how. Krikor didn't cough as he smoked. In a few savage puffs, he got the cigarette down to the filter. Hardly a shred of tobacco was left when he crushed the butt under his heel. "To hell with me if I'll give the Afghans anything at all to scrounge," he declared.

"Yeah." Vladimir treated his cigarette the same way. Sergei took a little longer to work his way down to the filter, but he made sure he did. It wasn't so much that he begrudged the Afghans a tiny bit of his tobacco. But he didn't want his buddies jeering at him.

The ground shook under his feet, harder than it had the first couple of times he'd felt an earthquake. Krikor's black, furry eyebrows flew up. Some of the villagers exclaimed. Sergei didn't know what they were saying, but he caught the alarm in their voices. He spoke himself: "That was a pretty good one, wasn't it?" If the locals and the sergeant noticed it, he could, too.

"Not all *that* big," Krikor said, "but I think it must've been right under our feet."

"How do you tell?" Vladimir asked.

"When they're close, you get that sharp jolt, like the one we felt now. The ones further off don't hit the same way. They roll more, if you know what I mean." The Armenian sergeant illustrated with a loose, floppy up-and-down motion of his hand and wrist.

"You sound like you know what you're talking about," Sergei said.

"Don't I wish I didn't," Sergeant Krikor told him.

"Sergeant! Hey, Sergeant!" Fyodor came clumping up the dirt street. He pointed back in the direction from which he'd come. "Lieutenant Uspenski wants to see you right away."

Krikor grunted. By his expression, he didn't much want to go see the lieutenant. "Miserable whistle-ass shavetail," he muttered. Sergei didn't think he was supposed to hear. He worked hard to keep his face straight. Krikor asked Fyodor, "He tell you what it was about?"

"No, Sergeant. Sorry. I'm just an ordinary soldier, after all. If I didn't already know my name, he wouldn't tell me that."

"All right. I'll go." Krikor made it sound as if he were doing Lieutenant Uspenski a favor. But when he came back, he looked grim in a different way. "The ghosts are gathering," he reported.

Sergei looked up to the mountains on either side of Bulola, as if he would be able to see the *dukhi* as they gathered. *If I could see them, we could kill them*, he thought. "When are they going to hit us?" he asked.

Before Sergeant Krikor could answer, Vladimir asked, "Are they going to hit us at all? Or is some informant just playing games to make us jump?"

"Good question," Sergei agreed.

"I know it's a good question," Krikor said. "Afghans lie all the time, especially to us. The ones who look like they're on our side, half the time they're working for the ghosts. One man in three, maybe one in two, in the Afghan army would sooner be with the bandits in the hills. Everybody knows it."

"Shit, one man in three in the Afghan army *is* with the *dukhi*," Vladimir said. "Everybody knows that, too. So what makes this news such hot stuff? Like as not, the ghosts are yanking our dicks to see how we move, so they'll have a better shot when they *do* decide to hit us."

Krikor's broad shoulders moved up and down in a shrug. "I don't know anything about that. All I know is, Lieutenant Uspenski thinks the information's good. And we'll have a couple of surprises waiting for the bastards." He looked around to make sure no Afghans were in earshot. You never could tell who understood more Russian than he let on.

Sergei and Vladimir both leaned toward him. "Well?" Vladimir demanded.

"For one thing, we've got some bumblebees ready to buzz by," the sergeant said. Sergei nodded. So did Vladimir. Helicopter gunships were always nice to have around.

"You said a couple of things," Vladimir said. "What else?"

Krikor spoke in an excited whisper: "Trucks on the way up from Bāmiān. They ought to get here right around sunset—plenty of time to set up, but not enough for the ragheads here to sneak off and warn the ragheads there."

"Reinforcements?" Sergei knew he sounded excited, too. If they actually had enough men to do the fighting for a change . . .

But Krikor shook his head. "Better than reinforcements."

"What could be better than reinforcements?" Sergei asked.

The Armenian's black eyes glowed. He gave back one word: "*Katyushas.*"

"Ahhh." Sergei and Vladimir said it together. Krikor was right, and they both knew it. Ever since the Nazis found out about them during the Great Patriotic War, no foe had ever wanted to stand up under a rain of *Katyushas*. The rockets weren't much as far as sophistication went, but they could lay a broad area waste faster than anything this side of nukes. And they *screamed* as they came in, so they scared you to death before they set about ripping you to pieces.

But then Vladimir said, "That'll be great, *if* they show up on time. Some of the bastards who think they're so important don't give a shit whether things get here at six o'clock tonight or Tuesday a week."

"We have to hope, that's all," Krikor answered. "Lieutenant Uspenski did say the trucks were already on the way from Bāmiān, so they can't be *that* late." He checked himself. "I don't think they can, anyhow."

After what Sergei had seen of the Red Army's promises and how it kept them, he wouldn't have bet anything much above a kopek that the *Katyushas* would get to Bulola on time. But, for a wonder, they did. Better still, the big, snorting six-wheeled Ural trucks—machines that could stand up to Afghan roads, which was saying a great deal—arrived in the village with canvas covers over the rocket launchers, so they looked like ordinary trucks carrying soldiers.

"Outstanding," Sergei said as the crews emplaced the vehicles. "The ghosts won't have spotted them from the road. They won't know what they're walking into."

"Outfuckingstanding is right." Vladimir's smile was altogether predatory. "They'll fucking find out."

Above the mountains, stars glittered in the black, black sky like coals and jewels carelessly tossed on velvet. The moon wouldn't rise till just before sunup. That made the going slower for the mujahideen, but it would also make them harder to see when they swooped down on Bulola.

A rock came loose under Satar's foot. He had to flail his arms to keep from falling. "Careful," the mujahid behind him said.

He didn't answer. His ears burned as he trudged on. To most of Sayid Jaglan's fighters, the mountains were as much home as the villages down in the valley. He couldn't match their endurance or their skill. If he roamed these rocky wastes for the next ten years, he wouldn't be able to. He knew it. The knowledge humiliated him.

A few minutes later, another man up ahead did the same thing Satar had done. If anything, the other fellow made more noise than he had. The man drew several hissed warnings. All he did was laugh. What had been shame for Satar was no more than one of those things for him. He wasn't conscious of his own ineptitude, as Satar was.

The man in front of Satar listened to the mujahid in front of *him*, then turned and said, "The godless Russians brought a couple of truckloads of new men into Bulola this afternoon. Sayid Jaglan says our plan will not change."

"I understand. God willing, we'll beat them anyhow," Satar said before passing the news to the man at his heels.

"Surely there is no God but God. With His help, all things may be accomplished," the mujahid in front of Satar said. "And surely God will not allow the struggle of a million brave Afghan forebears to be reduced to nothing."

"No. He will not. He cannot," Satar agreed. "The lives of our ancestors must not be made meaningless. God made man, unlike a sheep, to fight back, not to submit."

"That is well said," the man in front of him declared.

"That is very well said," the man behind him agreed.

"To God goes the credit, not to me," Satar said. His face heated with pleasure even so. But the night was dark, so none of his companions saw him flush.

Some time around midnight—or so Satar judged by the wheeling stars—the mujahideen reached the mountain slopes above Bulola. Satar's home village was dark and quiet, down there on the floor of the valley. It seemed peaceful. His own folk there would be asleep. The muezzin would not call them to prayer in the morning, not in a village the godless *Shuravi* held. Here and there, though, inside houses that hadn't been wrecked, men would gather in courtyards and turn toward Mecca at the appointed hours.

Satar cursed the Soviets. If not for them, his father would still have his foot. If not for them, he himself would never have left Bulola. *But I am coming home now*, he thought. *Soon the Russians will be gone, and freedom and God will return to the village.*

Soon the Russians will be gone, God willing, he amended. He could not see their trenches and forts and strongpoints, but he knew where they were, as he knew not all the deniers of God would be sleeping. Some of the mujahideen would not enter into Bulola. Some, instead, would go straight to Paradise, as did all martyrs who fell in the jihad. *If that is what God's plan holds for me, be it so. But I would like to see my father again.*

He took his place behind a boulder. For all he knew, it was the same boulder he'd used the last time Sayid Jaglan's men struck at the *Shuravi* in Bulola. His shiver had nothing to do with the chill of the night. His testicles tried to crawl up into his belly. A man who said he was not afraid when a helicopter gunship spat death from the sky was surely a liar. He'd never felt so helpless as under that assault.

Now, though, now he would have his revenge. He clicked his Kalashnikov's change lever from safe to full automatic. He was ready.

The night-vision scope turned the landscape to a ghostly jumble of green and black. Shapes flitted from one rock to another. Sergei looked away from the scope, and the normal blackness of night clamped down on him again. "They're out there, all right," he said. "Through this thing, they really look like ghosts."

"Yeah," Vladimir agreed. Sergei could just make out his nod, though he stood only a couple of meters away. But he'd had no trouble spotting the *dukhi* sneaking toward Bulola. Vladimir went on, "Sure as the Devil's grandmother, they're going to stick their cocks in the sausage machine."

Just hearing that made Sergei want to clutch himself. Fyodor said, "Oh, *dear*!" in a shrill falsetto. Everybody laughed—probably more than the joke deserved, but Sergei and the rest of the men knew combat was coming soon.

He said, "Looks like Lieutenant Uspenski got the straight dope."

"If he got the straight dope, why didn't he share it with us?" Vladimir said. "I wouldn't mind smoking some myself."

More laughter. Sergei nodded. He smoked hashish every now and then, or sometimes more than every now and then. It made chunks of time go away, and he sometimes thought time a worse enemy in Afghanistan than the *dukhi*.

"When do we drop the hammer on them?" Fyodor said.

"Patience." That was Sergeant Krikor's throatily accented Russian. "They have to come in close enough so they can't get away easy when we start mauling them."

Time . . . Yes, it was an enemy, but it killed you slowly, second by second. The ghosts out there, the ghosts sneaking up on, swooping down on, Bulola could kill you in a hurry. More often than not, they were a worry in the back of Sergei's mind. Now they came to the forefront.

How much longer? He wanted to ask the question. Ask it? He wanted to scream it. But he couldn't, not when Krikor'd just put Fyodor down. He had to wait. Seconds seemed to stretch out into hours. Once the shooting started, time would squeeze tight again. Everything would happen at once. He knew that. He'd seen it before.

For the dozenth time, he checked to make sure he'd set the change lever on his Kalashnikov to single shot. For the dozenth time, he found out he had. He was ready.

Sergeant Krikor bent to peer into his night-vision scope. "Won't be—," he began.

Maybe he said *long now*. If he did, Sergei never heard him. Sure enough, everything started happening at once. Parachute flares arced up into the night, turning the mountain slopes into brightest noon. Krikor pulled his head away from the night-vision scope with a horrible Armenian oath. Since the scope intensified all the light there was, he might have stared into the heart of the sun for a moment.

Behind Sergei, mortars started flinging bombs at the *dukhi*, *pop! pop! pop!* The noise wasn't very loud—about like slamming a door. The finned bombs whistled as they fell.

"Incoming!" somebody shouted. The ghosts had mortars, too, either captured, stolen from the Afghan army, or bought from the Chinese. *Crump!* The first bomb burst about fifty meters behind Sergei's trench. Fragments of sharp-edged metal hissed through the air. Through the rattle of Kalashnikov and machine-gun fire, Sergei heard the ghosts' war cry, endlessly repeated: "*Allahu akbar! Allahu akbar! Allahu!* . . ."

Some of the *dukhi*, by now, were down off the hillsides and onto the flatter ground near Bulola. Sergei squeezed off a few rounds. The Afghans went down as if scythed. But they were wily warriors; he didn't know whether he'd hit them or they were diving for cover.

Bullets cracked past overhead, a distinctive, distinctively horrible sound. The *dukhi* had no fire discipline. They shot off long bursts, emptying a clip with a pull of the trigger or two. A Kalashnikov treated so cavalierly pulled high and to the right. Accuracy, never splendid with an assault rifle, become nothing but a bad joke.

But the *dukhi* put a lot of lead in the air. Even worse than the sound of bullets flying by overhead was the unmistakable slap one made when it struck flesh. Sergei flinched when he heard that sound only a few meters away.

Fyodor shrieked and then started cursing. "Where are you hit?" Sergei asked.

"Shoulder," the wounded man answered.

"That's not so bad," Vladimir said.

"Fuck you," Fyodor said through clenched teeth. "It's not your shoulder."

"Get him back to the medics," Sergeant Krikor said. "Come on, somebody, give him a hand."

As Fyodor slapped a thick square of gauze on the wound to slow the bleeding, Sergei asked, "Where are the bumblebees? You said we were supposed to have bumblebees, Sergeant." He knew he sounded like a petulant child, but he couldn't help it. Fear did strange, dreadful things to a man. "And why haven't the *Katyushas* opened up?"

Before Krikor could answer, a burst of Kalashnikov fire chewed up the ground in front of the trench and spat dirt into Sergei's eyes. He rubbed frantically, fearing ghosts would be upon him before he cleared his vision. And, also before Krikor could answer, he heard the rapidly swelling thutter that said the helicopter gunships were indeed swooping to the attack.

Lines of fire stitched the night sky as the Mi-24s—three of them—raked the mountainside: thin lines of fire from their nose-mounted Gatlings, thicker ones from their rocket pods. Fresh bursts of hot orange light rose as the rockets slammed into the stones above Bulola. Along with cries of "*Allahu akbar!*" Sergei also heard screams of pain and screams of terror from the *dukhi*—music sweeter to his ears than any hit by Alla Pugacheva or Iosif Kobzon.

And then, as if they'd been waiting for the bumblebees to arrive—and they probably had—the men at the *Katyusha* launchers let fly. Forty rockets salvoed from each launcher, with a noise like the end of the world. The fiery lines *they* drew across the night seemed thick as a man's leg. Each salvo sent four and a half tons of high explosive up and then down onto the heads of the *dukhi* on the mountainside.

* * *

"Betrayed!" The cry rose from more than one throat, out there in the chilly night above Bulola. "Sold to the *Shuravi*!" "They knew we were coming!"

"With God's help, we can still beat the atheists," Sayid Jaglan shouted. "Forward, mujahideen! He who falls is a martyr, and will know Paradise forever."

Forward Satar went, down toward his home village. The closer he came to the Russians, the less likely those accursed helicopters were to spray him with death. He paused to inject a wounded mujahid with morphine, then ran on.

But as he ran, sheaves of flame rose into the air from down in the valley, from the very outskirts of Bulola: one, two, three. They were as yellow, as tightly bound, as sheaves of wheat. "*Katyushas!*" That cry rose from more than one throat, too—from Satar's, among others—and it was nothing less than a cry of despair.

Satar threw himself flat. He clapped his hands over his ears and opened his mouth very wide. That offered some protection against blast. Against salvos of *Katyushas* . . . "There is no God but God, and Muhammad is the prophet of God!" Satar gasped out. Against *Katyushas*, prayer offered more protection than anything else.

The Russian rockets shrieked as they descended. They might have been so many damned souls, already feeling Shaitan's grip on them. When they slammed into the side of the mountain—most of them well behind Satar—the ground shook under him, as if in torment.

Roaring whooshes from down below announced that the Russians were launching another salvo. But then the ground shook under Satar, and shook, and shook, and would not stop shaking.

Evil dreams, pain-filled dreams, had come too often to the dragon's endless sleep lately. It had twitched and jerked again and again, trying to get away from them, but they persisted. Its doze grew ever lighter, ever more fitful, ever more restless.

A hundred twenty *Katyushas*—no, the truth: a hundred eighteen, for one blew up in midair, and another, a dud, didn't explode when it landed—burst against the mountain's flank that was also the dragon's flank. Thirteen tons of high explosive . . . Not even a dragon asleep for centuries could ignore that.

Asleep no more, the dragon turned and stretched and looked around to see what was tormenting it.

The screams on the mountainside took on a different note, one so frantic that Satar lifted his face from the trembling earth and looked back over his shoulder to see what had happened. "There *is* no God but God!" he gasped, his tone altogether different from the one he'd used a moment before. That had been terror. This? This was awe.

Wings and body the red of hot iron in a blacksmith's forge, the dragon ascended into the air. Had it sprung from nowhere? Or had it somehow burst from the side of the mountain? Satar didn't see it till it was already airborne, so he never could have said for certain, which was a grief in him till the end of his days. But the earthquakes stopped after that, which at least let him have an opinion.

Eyes? If the dragon might have been red-hot iron, its eyes were white-hot iron. Just for the tiniest fraction of an instant, the dragon's gaze touched Satar. That touch, however brief, made the mujahid grovel facedown among the rocks again. No man, save perhaps the Prophet himself, was meant to meet a dragon eye to eye.

As if it were the shadow of death, Satar felt the dragon's regard slide away from him. He looked up once more, but remained on his knees as if at prayer. Many of the mujahideen were praying; he heard their voices rising up to Heaven, and hoped God cared to listen.

But, to the godless *Shuravi* in the helicopter gunships, the dragon was not something that proved His glory to a sinful mankind. It was something risen from the Afghan countryside—and, like everything else risen from the Afghan countryside, something to be beaten down and destroyed. They swung their machines against it, machine guns spitting fire. One of them still carried a pod of rockets under its stubby wing. Those, too, raced toward the dragon.

They are brave, Satar thought. He'd thought that about Russians before. *They are brave, but oh, by God the Compassionate, the Merciful, they are stupid.*

Had the helicopters not fired on it, the dragon might have ignored them, as a man intent on his business might ignore mosquitoes or bees. But if he were bitten, if he were stung . . .

The dragon's roar of fury made the earth tremble yet again. It swung toward the gunships that had annoyed it. Helicopters were maneuverable. But the dragon? The awakened dragon, like the jinni of whom the Prophet spoke, could have been a creature of fire, not a creature of matter at all. It moved like thought, now here, now there. One enormous forepaw lashed out. A helicopter gunship, smashed and broken, slammed into the side of the mountain and burst into flame.

Satar couldn't blame the Soviets in the other two gunships for fleeing then, fleeing as fast as their machines would carry them. He couldn't blame them, but it did them no good. The dragon swatted down the second helicopter as easily as it had the first. Then it went after the last one, the one that had launched rockets against it. Again, Satar could not have denied the gunship crew's courage. When they saw the dragon gaining on them, they spun their machine in the air and fired their Gatling at the great, impossible beast.

Again, that courage did them no good at all. Dragons were supposed to breathe fire. This one did, and the helicopter, burning, burning, crashed to the ground. The dragon looked around, as if wondering what to do next.

Down in Bulola, the Russians serving the *Katyusha* launchers had had time to reload again. Roaring like lions, roaring like the damned, their rockets raced toward the dragon.

They are brave, too, Satar thought. *But I thought no one could be stupider than the men in those gunships, and now I see I was wrong.*

Sergei said, "I haven't smoked any hashish lately, and even if I had, it couldn't make me see *that.*"

"*Bozhemoi!*" Vladimir sounded like—*was*—a man shaken to the core. "Not even *chars* would make me see *that.*"

Sergei wasn't so sure he was right. The local narcotic, a lethal blend of opium and, some said, horse manure, might make a man see almost anything. But Sergei had never had the nerve to try the stuff, and he saw the scarlet dragon anyhow. He was horribly afraid it would see him, too.

Sergeant Krikor rattled off something in Armenian. He made the sign of the cross, something Sergei had never seen him do before. Then he seemed to remember his Russian: "The people in this land have been fighting against us all along. Now the land itself is rising up."

"What the fuck is that supposed to mean?" Vladimir demanded. Just then, the dragon flamed the last bumblebee out of the sky, which made a better answer than any Krikor could have given.

The dragon looked around, as if wondering what to do next. That was when the *Katyusha* crews launched their next salvos—straight at the beast. Sergei had never known them to reload their launchers so fast.

That didn't fill him with delight. "*Noooo!*" he screamed, a long wail of despair.

"You fools!" Krikor cried.

Vladimir remained foulmouthed to the end: "Fucking shitheaded idiots! How the fuck you going to shoot down something the size of a mountain?"

Katyushas weren't made for antiaircraft fire. But, against a target that size, most of them struck home. And they must have hurt, too, for the dragon roared in pain and fury, where it had all but ignored the helicopter gunships' weapons. But hurting it and killing it were very different things.

With a scream that rounded inside Sergei's mind as much as in his ears, the dragon flew down toward the Ural trucks. It breathed flame again, once, twice, three times, and the trucks were twisted, molten metal. A couple of the men who'd launched the *Katyushas* had time to scream.

Somebody from the trench near Sergei squeezed off a banana clip at the dragon. If that wasn't idiocy, he didn't know what was. "*Noooo!*" he cried again. If *Katyushas* couldn't kill it, what would Kalashnikov rounds do? Nothing. Less than nothing.

No. More than nothing. Much more than nothing. The Kalashnikov rounds made the beast notice the Red Army men in the trench. Its head swung their way. Its great, blazing eyes met Sergei's, just for a moment. Its mouth, greater still, opened wide.

Sergei jerked his assault rifle up to his shoulder and fired off all the ammunition he had left in the clip. It wasn't that he thought it would do any good. But how, at that point, could it possibly hurt?

Fire, redder and hotter than the sun.

Blackness.

"Truly," Satar said to his father, "there is no God but God."

"Truly," the older man agreed. His left foot, his left leg halfway up to the knee, were gone, but the wound was healing. The Russian medic—now among the dead—had done an honest job with it. Maybe Satar's father could get an artificial foot one day. Till then, he would be able to get around, after a fashion, on crutches.

Satar said, "After the dragon destroyed the *Shuravi* at the edge of the village, I thought it would wreck Bulola, too."

"So did I," his father said. "But it knew who the pious and God-fearing were, or at least—" He chuckled wryly. "—who had the sense not to shoot at it."

"Well . . . yes." Satar wished his father hadn't said anything so secular. He would have to pray to bring him closer to God. He looked around, thinking on what they had won. "Bulola is ours again. This whole valley is ours again. The Russians will never dare come back here."

"I should hope not!" his father said. "After all, the dragon might wake up again."

He and Satar both looked to the mountainside. That streak of reddish rock . . . That was where the dragon had come from, and where it had returned. If Satar let his eyes drift ever so slightly out of focus, he could, or thought he could, discern the great beast's outline. *Would* it rouse once more? *If it is the will of God*, he thought, and turned his mind to other things.

The dragon slept. For a while, till its slumber deepened, it had new dreams.

The black tulip roared out of Kabul airport, firing flares as it went to confuse any antiaircraft missiles the *dukhi* might launch. Major Chorny—whose very name meant *black*—took a flask of vodka from his hip and swigged. He hated Code 200 missions, and hated them worst when they were like this.

In the black tulip's cargo bay lay a zinc coffin. It was bound for Tambov, maybe three hundred kilometers south and east of Moscow. It had no windows. It was welded shut. Major Chorny would have to stay with it every moment till it went into the ground, to make sure Sergei's grieving kin didn't try to open it. For it held not the young man's mortal remains but seventy-five kilos of sand, packed tight in plastic bags to keep it from rustling.

As far as the major knew, no mortal remains of this soldier had ever been found. He was just . . . gone. By the time the black tulip crossed from Afghan to Soviet airspace, Chorny was very drunk indeed.

Trish Cacek was also in my last anthology, and her story therein was a finalist for the Bram Stoker Award. She didn't win, but that's okay because she already has a Stoker and *a World Fantasy Award. She is the author of a short story collection,* Leavings, *and a new novel from Tor titled* Canyons.

"Belief" was the second story Trish hit me with for Redshift*; the first one just didn't work for me, but when I started this one I knew it would. Some stories just have* yes *written all over them, and sometimes you can't put your finger on why. This was one of those.*

Yes.

Belief

P. D. Cacek

✷

They said there'd be some disorientation in the beginning.

The trouble was, he couldn't remember who *they* were or how long he'd been there. Wherever *there* was. But that was a question he'd leave until he felt—*something* . . . *anything*—until the disorientation they told him about was gone. Until then, he might as well just relax. Yeah, that was the ticket, just kick back and go offline for a minute.

Who'd told him that? A strong voice . . . rough like wood and deep . . . A tall man, but old and stooped . . . white hair and sparkling blue eyes . . . hands just as rough as his voice . . . working hands he called them, hands that knew how to dig holes and mend fences and thread the slimiest worms onto fishhooks and lift baby birds back into their nests . . . "Man's gotta know when to kick back and go offline now 'n' again, boy. Man's gotta know when to just take a minute and unpeel his eyes to the wonders around him."

His grandfather . . . the words wrapped within the rough, deep, old man's voice like warm bread around jam. He remembered. *Chancy, Robert F. Private/First Class. SF# 72-114v-001011-nfm09330.* Thank God.

Sitting up, he swung his legs over the side of a narrow, flat platform. It was soft, the surface dimpling when he pressed down on it with his hand; the covering cool and white. A scent lingering against his fingertips when he lifted them to his face. *Summer winds and chlorine . . . helping Grandma hang the wash, the wet windblown sheets fluttering against him. A bed, he was on a bed.*

He laughed out loud and heard it answered by another. A rail-thin old man walked out of the shadows beyond the bed, laughing and clapping gnarled-fingered hands. His skin was so black it made the ring of fuzzy white hair that encircled his head look like burnished silver. His clothing was practically rags, the sleeves of his checkered shirt hanging in tatters and the cuffs of his pants frayed.

" 'Memberin' now, are you?"

Chancy straightened his shoulders, absently tugging the front of his tunic as if he were facing a brigadier general. The old man's eyes and grin widened at the same rate.

"Whoo-wee, will yor lookit all dem medals. You be some kinda war hero, ain'tcha? Ah seen boys no older'n wid less . . . some wid more, but none is nice as yorn."

"They're not medals," Chancy answered. "Combat personnel don't wear medals in the field."

"No?" The old man seemed disappointed. "Well, dey be right purdy, anyways. Ah 'specially likes dis one."

He looked down when the old man tapped the face of his COMLink, tracing the spiderweb crack across the front with a thick, yellow nail. *There'd been a pain . . . something entering his chest.* The old man smiled at his broken reflection. *What the hell happened? Where was the rest of the squad?* A small ripple of displacement pitched him forward.

The old man was stronger than he looked.

"It be aw'right now, son. You jist tryin' too hard. It'll come back t'you when it's time. Best not t'worry yoreself more'n you have to. You didn't come as far as some, but you came yer own way, an' dat can be as muddy as any." He helped Chancy down off the bed and held out a hand. "I be called Samuel."

It probably took a moment longer than it should have before his own hand closed around the offered one, but the old man didn't seem to notice.

"Chancy, Robert F. Private/First Class. SF# 72-114v-00—"

"Chancy? Dat be yore name? Ah 'members a stubborn ol' mule we done had name o' Chancy. Wouldn't do a lick o' plowin' less'n he got his stalk o' sugar cane reg'lur." The old man slapped Chancy lightly on the shoulder. " 'Peers t'me dat we hadda put dat ol' boy down 'cause o' it. Da massa, he didn't cotton t'orneriness in man or beast. Lost m'own daddy 'cause o' dat. You ain't gonna be dat stubborn, is you?"

"No, sir. Please, sir, can you tell me where I am?"

The smile etched deeper into the wrinkles covering the man's cheeks as he reached out to take Chancy's arm. "Oh, ah ain't no sir, son, an' nebber been one, so you don't haffa go callin' me dat. But we best be goin' now. You feels up t'it?"

Chancy angled his body away from the touch. "Go where? And you didn't answer my first question. Where am I?"

The old man just kept on smiling. "Yep, ain't a long way, but it's a ways t'go. Yep, dat be true a'nuff. Best we git started."

Chancy looked down before taking a step. The flooring was monotone gray and featureless, similar to the walkways on the transport—function regulating form. He looked up, turned his head from side to side. The walls and ceiling were hidden in shadows too thick to see through, the only light coming from some unknown source directly over the bed. Gravity, similar to that on the transport. Wherever he was, it was familiar enough to make him brave.

"I asked you a question, old man, and I expect an answer. Now."

His combat glove clamped around the threadbare front of the man's work shirt and pulled. A wooden button the color of old cream tore away from the material and struck Chancy's chest armor like a . . . a . . .

Something small and fast . . . a projectile. What's it called?

The gravity shifted for a moment beneath him.

"Whoa now, see dat . . . you bein' jist as stubborn as dat ol' mule." Laughing, the old man gently pried open Chancy's grip and patted the hand within the glove. "An' dat ain't gonna help none. Ah know all 'bout dat. Don't go pushin' at yoreself, you'll know when you know, so dere's no use in gettin' yore feathers ruffled up 'til den. Now, best we be goin'. You feel up't walkin' or you want me t'carry you? Ah cin, if you like."

Chancy looked down at the stooped, raggedy figure and shook his head. For some reason, there was no doubt in his mind that if he asked, the old man would have done just that without breaking a sweat.

"No, thank you . . . I can walk. Is it far?"

But the old man was already shuffling toward the shadows, shaking his head. "Is it far? Far's far or far's short depending on where you going, ain't it? You come along now an' we'll see jist how far we gots t'go afore we git where we going."

Chancy's head began to pound. The old man was crazy, and if he stood there trying to make sense of what was being said—or not said—he'd go crazy, too. Grunting low in his throat, he got three steps away from the bed before noticing how *naked* he felt.

"My gun . . . and combat visor," he yelled into the shadows where the old man disappeared. "Where are they? I need them."

"Dey be safe, don't you worry 'bout dat. Come along now, Chancy." A low chuckle echoed from the darkness. "Ah jist love dat name. Chancy . . . jist like dat ol' mule, stubborn as da day is long. Hee-hee."

"Hee. Hee," Chancy muttered, and followed the sound of laughter into the shadows.

He didn't remember opening a door, but suddenly he was outside, squinting into bright gray light. The landscape before him was one of mist and clouds, the ground hidden beneath an undulating blanket of fog. Although Chancy couldn't see the sky or make out the horizon's demarcation line, every few minutes flashes of sheet lightning would ignite huge areas above his head. And each time he'd cringe and hike his shoulders, waiting for the boom of thunder that never came.

Not thunder . . . something else . . . something worse than just a sound . . . a loudness that exploded when it got inside a man and turned him inside out . . . something . . .

A pain ripped Chancy open and dropped him to his knees. *He'd been in the lead, racing his best friend, Jacksen, to the top of a steep, bare rock incline while the enemy fired down at them. It was a game . . . whichever of them got up the hill the fastest won. Brownie points, that's all it was. A game the two of them played at least once in every battle they were in. Just a stupid game to see who was the fastest, the bravest while bolts of lights and flame shot overhead and bullets buzzed through the thick hot air like . . . like . . .*

"Jacksen—I've been hit! Ohmygod, Medic! Med—"

Gagging at the back-flush of copper and bile that filled his mouth, Chancy looked down to see his heart . . . what was left of his heart shudder through the ragged, dripping hole in his chest. Too late . . . I'm going to die. God . . .

He remembered reaching into the hole, to see what it would feel like. He remembered. But this time pain—and wound—disappeared the moment he touched it.

"Startin' to come back, is it?" Samuel asked. "Figured it all out, did you?"

Chancy sat back on his knees and ran his gloved hands against the solid chest plate. No hole. No wound. No pain.

"I really am dead, aren't I? I was killed in battle."

Samuel clapped his hands and smiled from ear to ear.

"Dere you go . . . ah knew you'd be gettin' it faster'n most. Must be da name. Dat ol' Chancy mule mighta been one contrary animal, but ain't no one could say he weren't smart as a brand-new tack." The smile lessened just a bit when he patted Chancy's shoulder. "You be fine wid dis, son. You dead, is all, and nothin' else bad cin happen t'you no more."

Dead. I'm dead. Didn't seem so bad when he said it to himself like that. "But I don't feel dead."

"Well, 'course you don't, son. Dead is jist like livin' 'ceptin' it ain't."

Makes sense, in a way. "Is Jacksen here? I mean, did she get shot, too?"

The old man stretched out his arms and shrugged. "Don't rightly know dat. Could be, ah suppose."

"You don't know? Aren't you an angel?"

"Me?" Samuel's laughter rang in Chancy's ears as he helped him up. "Oh, wait'll ah tell m' mammy 'n' daddy dat. Ol' Samuel a' angel . . . who-wee, if dey ain't gonna bust a gut on dat one. Ol' Samuel a' angel."

"You're not?"

"Not by a long shot, son . . . ah jist be one o' da many, dats all. Jist one o' da many. Yore friend mabbe here or not, ah wouldn't know nothin' 'bout dat. See, yore grandpappy, he ax me t'come fetch you on account o' him bein' a mite busy. But he be seein' you shortly, don't you worry none."

"My . . . grandfather?"

"Dat right, he be here soon t'take you up front. Oh, my, jist look at you . . . all messy 'n' stained like dis. Won't do, jist won't do. Here, let me jist brush dis off."

Chancy watched Samuel's gnarled fingers brush and pluck at the leggings of his uniform even though there was nothing to clean off. The old *dead* man was crazy.

Dead. I'm really dead. Chancy closed his eyes and tried to take a deep breath the way he always did just before going into battle to steady himself, make himself strong. But all he felt was his chest muscles going up and down. He couldn't feel the air filling his lungs or the cool rush of it through his nose and across his upper palate. He couldn't feel anything except the ground beneath his feet and the touch of the old man's hands against his legs.

"I'm dead." The words got easier to say now that he was certain. "And my grandfather's . . . here."

"Course he be here," Samuel said without pausing in his task. "Where else a good man like him be 'cept here?"

"Heaven?" Chancy stared into the swirling gray nothingness that surrounded them. When he was little, before he'd outgrown "Once Upon a Times" and "Happily Ever Afters," his grandfather had told him all about the place where good people go when they die. All white fluffy clouds and streets lined with gold. Just another fairy tale. "This is Heaven?"

Samuel looked up at him and winked. "Dere be only one place."

"Then he lied to me."

"Wha' you talkin' about, boy? Who lied 'bout wha'?"

"He did," Chancy said as another flash of unseen lightning rippled overhead. "My grandfather. This isn't anything like the Heaven he described." He shook his head. "There's nothing here."

The wrinkles deepened around Samuel's eyes as he stood up. "Wha' you see, boy? You tell ol' Samuel wha' you see."

Chancy told him and watched pity fill the old man's eyes. When he finished they stood there—wherever in the nothing they were—silent as stones. *As the grave*, Chancy thought, and would have probably smiled at the thought if Samuel hadn't spoken up first. And looked as sad as he did.

"Aw, boy, wha' you musta been through t'change you like dat. Musta been worse'n anything." Reaching out, he squeezed Chancy's arm just above the United Earth insignia patch. "Yore grandpappy'll 'splain things. Come along now, Chancy. Oh, ah know . . . mebbe you move better wid dis."

Another wink and smile, and the old man suddenly reached into a swirling bank of *nothing*.

And hauled out what looked to be a stout, jointed stalk of pale green grass about two meters long. The bladelike leaves at the topmost end rustled softly when Samuel broke the stalk in half, then in half again, giving Chancy the bigger of the two pieces.

Clear liquid dripped from the ragged edge.

"Well, don't jist stand dere, son, dis be da sweetest cane you ever did taste, even if ah says so m'self."

Without another word Samuel stuck the ragged end of his piece into his mouth and crunched down on it with his back molars. When deep cracks appeared along the waxy surface, the old man took it out of his mouth and used his fingers to pry out the spongy white pulp, which he then popped greedily into his mouth.

"Sweet as a good-night kiss," Samuel said as he chewed the pulp hard and spit it out, only to immediately replace it with another chunk. "Goan, boy . . . sink yore teeth inta dat cane. Jist chew it 'til it be dry 'n' spit it out."

Chancy did exactly as the old man did, reeling at the first explosions of sweetness that cascaded over his tongue as he crushed the stalk with his teeth. He'd never tasted anything like it before. None of the synthetic sweetening agents he was used to could compare to it.

The first chunk of pulp almost choked him until he got the hang of chewing and swallowing at the same time. He was laughing out loud by the time he finished his third chunk.

"This is . . ." He didn't have the words to describe the flavor. "It's wonderful, but how? Where did you get it?"

Samuel stuffed another chunk between his teeth and jerked his head to the left. "Well, right'chere. Dis be da best cane field on da mighty Missa'sip. Sweet as hunny, ain't it?"

It was, just as sweet as honey, but that still didn't answer his question. Chancy let the stalk drop from his hand and watched it disappear beneath the thick mist.

"Samuel, there's nothing here."

"Dat where you be wrong, son. Here." He wipe his hand off on the leg of his worn pants and held it out. "Take ol' Samuel's hand."

It sounded enough like a command that Chancy took the old man's hand without thinking. In the next second, thinking was still impossible. The mist and fog were gone, and they were standing on a rutted dirt road at the edge of a massive field of sugarcane. Tiny yellow butterflies flitted over the rustling stalks while blackbirds, trilling songs behind them like contrails, stitched wispy white clouds to the bright blue bowl of the sky.

Opposite the field, on the other side of the road, was a small cabin nestled beneath tall trees dotted with fragrant white blossoms and overhung with long strands of gray moss. Beyond that was a pond ringed with cattail and willow where fat, silver fish leaped after flies.

And beyond that, shimmering like a ribbon of sapphire, was the river. Da mighty Missa'sip, Samuel called it. Chancy could hear frogs croaking from the direction of the river.

The whole thing—the trees, the cabin, the river—looked like a picture out of one of his history books.

"This is . . . Heaven?"

"Purdy, ain't it?" Samuel asked as he dropped Chancy's hand and went back to working another chunk of pulp out of the stalk. "Dis be m' Heaven. Yore grandpappy's Heaven's dif'rent'n mine, yore's might jist be dif'rent still. No way o' knowin'."

He smiled around a wad so big it hurt Chancy's cheek just looking at it. "But ah don't minds sharin' mine 'til you figure out what yorn's gonna look like. Lessen, o' course, you like dat foggy, foggy dew place."

"No!" Chancy yelled, startling a grasshopper off a leaf and onto the dusty ground. Dead or not, he could feel the ghost of a blush inch across his cheeks. "I mean, no . . . I'd like to share this with you. If you don't mind."

"Don't mind a'tall, you be welcome. A'right den, you got yore cane and done munched some. You feel up t'walkin' now?"

"Yes, sir . . . Samuel."

"Well, git on up den, Chancy."

"How far?"

"As far as we needs t'go, ah reckon. You'll know it when you sees it."

Chancy kept himself from asking anything else until the cane field gave way to peach orchards that lined both sides of the road and he saw the children. There must have been hundreds . . . thousands upon thousands of them playing beneath the soft rain of pink and white blossoms.

A part of him understood that children died, that death was as indiscriminate of the young as it was the old, but until he saw them—*all of them*—he'd never thought about it, never let himself think about it. Or about how many of the children laughing and running through the fragrant sweet air he had personally sent here.

War was war and the enemy was whoever you were told it was. Whoever you were told to fight. Blindly and without question, like the good soldier you are.

Were.

The sudden pain he felt had nothing to do with the projectile that killed him.

"Dat a'right, Chancy," Samuel said, nodding to a group of children—yellow, brown, white—who'd noticed them standing there and shouted greetings. "It be hard t'see dem so young, but you gotta know dey be happy here. Some o' 'em even happier den when dey was breathin'. You keep dat in mind and you be fine."

One of the children who'd shouted, a boy of about six or seven with golden skin and hair and eyes the color of starless space, ran up to them and hugged Chancy around the waist. His touch changed the orchard into a paradise where peacocks strutted in the shadows of towering minarets. *Nirvana.*

Another little boy pushed the first away and brought Chancy endless rolling plains, thick with grazing buffalo and deer. The air was warm and scented with sage and sweet-grass, and high overhead an eagle rode a thermal to the Land of the Sky People.

He became the new game. Children flocked around him like hungry little birds, sharing glimpses of their afterworlds with him. One after another the images came and went. The gold-paved streets his grandfather had told him about became a cloud-field where incandescent beings with dove wings flew; then shifted to a rainbow bridge that glittered across an empty sky to a cool, blue water pool beneath a red-stone arch where a king in a golden throne slept in the Dream Time and thought of giant sharks and palm trees swaying gently in the—

. . . so beautiful . . .

"Please . . . stop," Chancy said to the little girl dancing while the feathered serpents flew rings around the sun. "Samuel, please make them stop. It's too much. I can't—"

"Dat be all now, chillins, you all best git back t'yore playin'. We needs t'be up t'da front."

Samuel's quiet orchard returned the moment the children stopped touching him.

"You are taking him to the battle?" a pale boy in a loose-fitting robe asked. "Oh, Samuel, may I come, too? I am almost a man."

"Ah cin see dat, Eliyahu, but iffen you come who be watchin' over da youngens? No, you best t'stay . . . but ah'll tell yore pappy 'bout how you asked. He be right proud, ah bet. An dat goes for all o' you, too. Yore pappys 'n' mammys be so proud knowin' yore thinkin' o' 'em. Dey be back right soon now ah think, so y'all jist do what comes nat'ral. But don't you go eatin' up all m'peaches now, you hear. Ahs got me a hankerin' t'bake up some cobbler when ahs git back."

Only a few children, who shared Samuel's vision of Heaven, laughed out loud before scampering away. The rest followed more slowly, with only nods to show they accepted being dismissed.

Chancy watched them resume the games that his and Samuel's presence had disrupted; each child safe within their heavenly visions but not alone. Never alone.

He would have stayed right there watching them, while the petals drifted down around him, if Samuel hadn't tugged on his sleeve.

"Come along now, Chancy . . . da chillins be a'right and we needs t'git on."

"To the battle?"

Samuel reached up and picked a golden peach from the tree, gently rubbing the fuzz off between his leathery palms before handing it to Chancy.

"You jist take a bite o' dat, boy. Betcha ain't tasted nothin' like it in a month o' Sundays go t'meetin'. Goan, eat it now whilst you got da chance." Samuel laughed as he turned and headed up the dirt road. "Yesshur, ol' Chancy gots t'have da chance t'eats dat peach. Yesshur. Eat dat ol' peach, Chancy, while you gots da chance. Hee-hee, ah do makes m'self laugh."

Chancy felt his mouth water as he looked at the peach. Its pinkish-yellow skin glistened with dew drops. He couldn't remember the last time he'd had a real piece of unprocessed fruit, let alone a peach freshly picked from a tree . . . but, then again, he couldn't really remember what being alive felt like.

"Samuel?"

But when he looked up, Samuel was little more than a moving shadow far up the road. It was amazing how fast the old man could walk.

Tossing the peach to a little girl with copper hair and bright green eyes, Chancy adjusted the straps on his combat vest and fell into the prescribed steady jog designed to eat up miles at the minimum expense of physical endurance. Not that he had to worry about that now.

The orchard stretched on for miles, and the sound of children accompanied him every step of the way.

Until he reached Samuel's side.

"Where are we?" Chancy asked in a whisper. "Whose place is this?"

Samuel turned toward him and licked his lips. A cold star-field surrounded them, as stark and barren as the glistening volcanic outcrop on which they were standing. The star patterns looked vaguely familiar, but Chancy couldn't remember from where.

"Ain't no one's in particular," Samuel said, "and ev'rybody's in general, ah guess. But dis be da place we's goan to."

"This is where the . . . battle is?"

"Yep, right over dat ways a mite." Samuel pointed to a spot on the desolate horizon and he saw it—the faint red glow leaching into the darkness between the stars. "You jist keep walkin' da way you been. You got folks waitin' for you."

Chancy nodded and readjusted his armor, the rush of adrenaline pricking the flesh at the back of his neck. He was a soldier, and this was what he'd been trained to do.

"You coming?" he asked the old man.

"Oh, ahs be along directly. Jist don't wanna spoil yore welcomin' s'all. Goan on now, boy, it ain't far now . . . dey be waitin' for you."

Chancy didn't ask who was waiting or how far he'd have to go, he just went . . . like the good soldier that he was. But even if he had asked, Chancy soon realized it wouldn't have made much difference, at least to the question of distance. There were no prominent features on the brittle landscape he could gauge a visual against, no way of telling how far he'd already gone . . . no real proof that he was even moving forward except for the ever-increasing size of the glow on the horizon.

He heard the fighting before he saw it. And saw only the soldier standing between him and the battlefield before he saw the weapon aimed at his belly.

"Halt!" The voice was muffled behind the combat helmet. "Identify yourself."

"Chancy, Robert F. Private/First Class."

"Advance, Private." The voice said. "Ready for some action?"

"Sir," Chancy yelled when he got close enough to see the rank etched into the chest armor. "Yes, sir. Always ready, sir."

The captain nodded and pushed back the helmet's visor. She was a beautiful woman despite the broken shaft of an arrow sticking out of her right eye socket.

"Good, I like a man who's always ready. You carrying?"

Chancy looked down and saw the weapon hanging loose and comfortable in his hand. Just like it was supposed to be. Swinging it up toward the visor opening on his own helmet, he twisted the pulse rifle one-quarter turn counterclockwise so the officer could see that the charge lights were Four-for-Four, fully loaded and ready for bear.

"Sir, yes, sir." He nodded in appreciation when she signaled him to stand down, and he nodded toward the arrow. "You need some help with that?"

The captain's remaining eye was bloodshot and bulged a bit from the pressure of the arrow in her brain, but it shifted over easily enough. "No, I'm getting used to it. Looks like you had a little fun, too."

Chancy looked down at the ragged hole where his chest armor had imploded and chuckled softly.

"Yeah, just a little. It was a WP tracer. Vietnam era."

"Nasty," the captain said, "but I've seen worse. Those Huns, man, now they can be brutal. I got a couple men on point right now wearing flat-tops down to their chins. They're not much good at sniping anymore, but not having a brain never stopped a combat soldier before."

Chancy laughed politely, knowing it was expected, and ran his hand over the pulse rifle's flat-black housing. "Permission to speak, sir?"

The captain smiled, the jagged end of the shaft vibrating slightly as her face muscles contracted. "I appreciate it, although we don't stand on ceremony too much anymore. Permission granted."

Chancy turned toward the red glow and nodded. "Why don't they understand they can't do this?"

"Human nature," she said. "But don't worry, they'll figure it out the same way we did. Okay, Private, head on up and report to the front line. Somebody'll direct you to your position. And one more thing, don't refer to Sitting Bull as an Indigenous Continental." She tapped the arrow shaft. "He doesn't like the term."

"Sir," Chancy called over his shoulder. "Yes, sir."

One meter, two . . . twenty; his boots shattering the brittle ground as he walked. Twenty meters, thirty, and a shape—long and angular—slowly detached itself from the jagged horizon line.

Ten meters, five, one, and the old man in sun-bleached bib overalls and white work shirt pushed the brim of the woven straw hat back on his head. Chancy always remembered him wearing it low despite the time of day or night . . . claimed it kept the UV rays out of his eyes.

"How you doing, Grandpa?"

The cancer that had killed him had taken a lot of the meat off the old man's bones, but the smile was the same, and so was the long, loose-jointed stride.

"Not too bad for an old goat," his grandfather said, and slapped

Chancy hard enough across the shoulders to make the clips on his armor rattle. "Good to see you, Robbie. I was wondering when you'd show up."

"Guess it was a little farther than I thought it'd be." He swung the rifle over one shoulder and hugged the old man until he could hear their bones creak under the pressure. "I lost it, Grandpa . . . I didn't see anything . . . but it can be so beautiful."

"It's more than just beauty, Robbie. Much more," his grandfather whispered, "and that's why we have to protect it. It's the only thing we have left."

Chancy stepped back and fingered his weapon, nodding. Remembering. He'd heard it before, almost the same words, in fact. *The only thing we have left.* Earth's final hope to reestablish itself on another planet. An old song made fresh in the resinging: Claim it and rename it.

Eminent domain on a planetary level.

And the unnamed, unclaimed planet *was* more than beautiful. It was perfect. Breathable atmosphere, fresh water, soil so rich seedlings seemed to mature overnight. A world so much like Earth and so close, in relative terms and warp speeds, that it had seemed a godsend.

An archaic term—and idea—that had been all but forgotten on Earth, but which was instantly reinstated into the vernacular when the initial telemetry images began coming in.

It was Paradise. Heaven.

Until the first colonists arrived and were killed. Murdered. One batch of hopefuls after another was found shot, scalped, butchered, disemboweled, or blown apart. It was like shooting fish in a barrel, someone had said. And it only got worse when the Defense Guard was deployed. The number of casualties rose exponentially with the number of military personnel assigned to skirmish lines, with increasing numbers of bodies showing flash residue from pulse rifles.

Paradise. Lost.

And the theologians still didn't suspect Heaven could be literal.

"You ready, boy?"

Chancy slipped the safety off and nodded. Three steps was all it took to the edge of the ridge. Below, bathed by the light of a hundred thousand fires, the battle raged. It was something that neither Dante nor Bosch could ever have dreamed in their worst fever dream.

Two great armies—one living, one immortal—faced each other across a blood-soaked field strewn with body parts and shattered pieces of equipment. Some part of Chancy could still remember the commands, could still recognize some of the pieces . . . but even as he watched the memories of what he'd been were fading.

A soldier dissolved from a combination hit of thermite and flaming arrows. Another spun to the ground pierced by a Roman javelin. Two more were riddled into confetti by WWI German machine guns. And each time they fell Chancy watched their souls drift across toward the opposite side of the field.

Toward *his* side.

But they kept coming.

"They can't win," Chancy whispered, because it suddenly seemed too foolish a thing to say out loud. "Why don't they just give up?"

His grandfather grunted. "They don't know any better. Mankind always thinks it can win, no matter what. Now, you ready, boy?"

"Yes, sir."

"All right then. Do just like I taught you, Robbie . . . aim to kill clean. You don't need to hurt a man more than he's already hurt himself." Tugging the old hat back down over his eyes, his grandfather lifted an antique squirrel rifle that family legend said had been passed down from firstborn to firstborn. It would have gone to him next, when his daddy died. "Let's go, boy."

"Yes, sir. Can I ask you something first?"

His grandfather turned back and looked at him, smiling. Chancy could see the light from the battle fires reflected in the old man's eyes.

"Go ahead, boy."

"Is this—?" Chancy throat suddenly felt like it was closing in on itself. "Is this Hell, Grandpa?"

The smile widened and deepened the wrinkles along his grandfather's weather-hardened cheeks. "Only for some, Robbie. Only for some."

Stephen Baxter was born in Liverpool, has degrees in mathematics and engineering, and applied to become a cosmonaut in 1991, with an eye toward a guest spot on Mir. Alas, he didn't make it, but instead of keeping that creaky Russian wreck in orbit he turned to full-time writing, producing more than ten sf novels, including Raft, The Time Ships *(a marvelous sequel to* The Time Machine*),* Manifold: Time, Moonseed, *and, recently,* Manifold: Space. *He also cowrote* The Light of Other Days *with Arthur C. Clarke. He has won the Philip K. Dick Award and the John W. Campbell Memorial Award, among others.*

I tracked him down at I-Con, a science fiction convention on Long Island—and eventually, lucky for me, got him to write the following.

In the Un-Black

STEPHEN BAXTER

✷

On the day La-ba met Ca-si she saved his life.

She hadn't meant to. It was un-Doctrine. It just happened. But it changed everything.

It had been a bad day for La-ba.

She had been dancing. That wasn't un-Doctrine, not exactly, but the cadre leaders disapproved. She was the leader of the dance, and she got stuck with Cesspit detail for ten days.

It was hard, dirty work, the worst. And would-be deathers flourished there, in the pit. They would come swimming through the muck itself to get you.

That was what happened just two hours after she started work. Naked, she was standing knee-deep in a river of unidentifiable, odorless muck.

Two strong hands grabbed her ankles and pulled her flat on her face. Suddenly her eyes and mouth and nose and ears were full of dense sticky waste.

La-ba folded up her body and reached down to her toes. She found hands on her ankles, and farther up a shaven skull, wide misshapen ears.

She recognized him from those ears. He was a We-ku, one of a batch of look-alikes who had come down from the Birthing Vat at the same time and had clung together ever since. If they had ever had their own names, they had long abandoned them.

She wasn't about to be deathed by a We-ku. She pressed the heels of her hands into his eyes and shoved.

Her ankles started to slide out of his hands. The harder he gripped, the more his clutching fingers slipped. She pointed her toes and shoved harder.

Then she was free.

She pushed up to the surface and blew out a huge mouthful of dirt. She prepared to take on the We-ku again, elbows and knees ready, fingers clawing for the knife strapped to her thigh.

But he didn't come for her, not for one heartbeat, two, three. She took the risk of wiping her eyes clear.

The We-ku had already found another victim. He was pressing a body into the dirt with his great fat hands. If he got his victim to the floor, his piston legs would crack the spine or splinter the skull in seconds.

The We-ku was a surging monster of blood and filth. His eyes were rimmed with blackness where she had bruised him.

Something in La-ba rose up.

At a time like this, a time of overcrowding, there was a lot of deathing.

You could *see* there were too many babies swarming out of the Birthing Vat, the great pink ball that hovered in the air at the very center of the Observation Post. At rally hours you could look beyond the Vat to the other side of the Post, where the people marched around on the roof with their heads pointing down at you, and you could *see* that almost every Cadre Square was overfull.

Commissaries would come soon, bringing Memory. They would Cull if they had to. The less the Commissaries had to Cull, the happier they would be. It was the duty of every citizen of every cadre to bring down their numbers.

If you did well you would fly on a Shuttle out of here. You would fly to Earth, where life un-ended. That was worded by the cadre leaders. And if you hid and cowered, even if the amateur deathers didn't get to you, then the Old Man would. *That* was worded in the dorms.

La-ba had no reason to un-believe this. She had seen hundreds deathed by others. She had deathed seventeen people herself.

La-ba was tall, her body lithe, supple: good at what she was trained for, deathing and sexing and hard physical work.

La-ba was five years old. Already half her life was gone.

She leapt out of the muck and onto the We-ku's back, her knife in her hand.

The We-ku didn't know whether to finish the death at his feet or deal with the skinny menace on his back. And he was confused because what La-ba was doing was un-Doctrine. That confusion gave La-ba the seconds she needed.

Still, she almost had to saw his head clean off before he stopped struggling.

He sank at last into the dirt, which was now stained with whorls of deep crimson. The head, connected only by bits of gristle and skin, bobbed in the muck's sticky currents.

The We-ku's intended victim struggled to his feet. He was about La-ba's height and age, she guessed, with a taut, well-muscled body. He was naked, but crusted with dirt.

She was aroused. Deathing always aroused her. Glancing down at his crotch, at the stiff member that stuck out of the dirt there, she saw that this other felt the same.

"You crimed," he breathed, and he stared at her with eyes that were bright white against the dirt.

He was right. She should have let the deathing go ahead, and then take out the We-ku. Then there would have been two deaths, instead of one. Un-Doctrine.

She glanced around. Nobody was close. Nobody had seen how the We-ku died.

Nobody but this man, this intended victim.

"Ca-si," he said. "Cadre Fourteen." That was on the other side of the sky.

"La-ba. Cadre Six. Will you report?" If he did she could be summarily executed, deathed before the day was out.

Still he stared at her. The moment stretched.

He said, "We should process the We-ku."

"Yes."

Breathing hard, they hauled the We-ku's bulky corpse toward a hopper that was already half-full—of tangled limbs, purple guts, bits of people. The work brought them close. She could feel the warmth of his body.

They dumped the We-ku into the hopper. La-ba kept back one ugly ear as a trophy.

La-ba and Ca-si sexed, there and then, in the slippery dirt.

Later, at the end of the shift, they got clean, and sexed again.

Later still they joined in a dance, a vast abandoned whirl of a hundred citizens, more. Then they sexed again.

He never did report her crime. By failing to do so, of course, he was criming himself. Maybe that bonded them.

They kept sexing, whatever the reason.

Hama stood beside his mentor, Arles Thrun, as the citizens of the Observation Post filed before them. The marching drones stared at

Hama's silvered Raoul-technology skin, and they reached respectfully to stroke the gleaming egg-shaped Memory that Arles held in his hand.

One in three of the drones who passed was assigned, by Arles's ancient, wordless gesture, to the Cull. Perhaps half of those assigned would survive. Each drone so touched shrank away from Arles's gleaming finger.

When Hama looked to the up-curving horizon he saw that the line of patiently queuing drones stretched a quarter of the way around the Post's internal equator.

This Observation Post was a sphere of Woven Space, so small he could have walked around its interior in a day. The folded-over sky was crowded with Cadre Squares, dormitory blocks and training and indoctrination centers, and the great sprawls of the Post's more biological functions, the Cesspits and the Cyclers and the Gardens, green and brown and glistening blue. Every surface was covered with instructive images, symbols and pictures of man's long battle against the Xeelee, ten thousand years out of date. Drones walked all over the inner surface of the sphere, stuck there by manipulated gravity. The great Birthing Vat itself hung directly over his head, pink and fecund, an obscene sun. The air was thick with the stink of growing things, of dirt and sweat.

To Hama, it was like being trapped within the belly of some vast living thing.

It didn't help his mood to reflect that beyond the Woven Space floor beneath his feet, no more than a few Planck's-lengths away, the host planet's atmosphere raged: a perpetual hydrogen storm, laced with high-frequency radiation and charged particles.

Absently he reached into his drab monastic robe and touched his chest, stroked the cool, silvered Planck-zero epidermis, sensed the softly gurgling fluid within, where alien fish swam languidly. *Here* in this dismal swamp, immersed in the primeval, he could barely sense the mood even of Arles, who stood right next to him. He longed for the cool intergalactic gulf, the endless open where the merged thoughts of Commissaries sounded across a trillion stars. . . .

"Hama, pay attention," Arles Thrun snapped.

Hama focused reluctantly on the soft round faces of the drones, and saw they betrayed agitation and confusion at his behavior.

"Remember, this is a great day," Arles murmured dryly. "The first Commission visit in ten thousand years—and it is happening in the brief lifetime of *this* creature," and his silvered hand patted indulgently at the bare head of the drone before him. "How lucky they are, even if we will have to order the deaths of a sixth of them. There is so little in their lives—little more than the wall images that never change, the meaningless battle for position in the cadre hierarchies . . ."

And the dance, Hama thought reluctantly, their wild illegal dance.

"They disgust me," he hissed, surprising himself. Yet it was true.

Arles glanced at him. "You're fortunate they do not understand."

"They disgust me because their language has devolved into jabber," Hama said. "They disgust me because they have bred themselves into overpopulation."

Arles murmured, "Hama, when you accepted the Burden of Longevity you chose a proud name. I sometimes wonder whether you have the nobility to match that name. *These* creatures' names were chosen for them by a random combination of syllables—"

"They spend their lives on make-work. They eat and screw and die, crawling around in their own filth. What need a candle-flame of a name?"

Arles was frowning now, sapphire eyes flickering in the silver mask of his face. "Have you forgotten the core tenet of the Doctrine? *A brief life burns brightly*, Hama. These creatures and their forebears have maintained their lonely vigil, here between the galaxies—monitoring the progress of the war across a million fronts—for *sixty thousand years*. These drones are the essence of humanity. And we Commissaries—doomed to knowledge, doomed to life—we are their servants."

"Perhaps. But this *essence of humanity* is motivated by lies. Already we understand their jabber well enough to know that. These absurd legends—"

Arles raised a hand, silencing him quickly. "Belief systems drift, just as languages do. The flame of the Doctrine still burns here, if not as brightly as we would wish."

Now two of the drones came before Hama, hand in hand, male and female, nude like the rest. This pair leaned close to each other, showing an easy physical familiarity.

They had made love, he saw immediately. Not once, but many times. Perhaps even recently.

On a thong around her neck the female wore what looked hideously like a dried human ear. The fish in his chest squirmed.

He snapped: "What are your names?"

They didn't understand his words, but comprehended the sense. They pointed to their chests. "*La-ba.*" "*Ca-si.*"

Arles smiled, amused, contemptuous. "We have the perspective of gods. They have only their moment of light, and the warmth of each other's body. . . . What is it, Hama? Feeling a little attraction, despite your disgust? A little *envy*?"

With an angry gesture, Hama sentenced both the drones to the Cull. The drones, obviously shocked, clung to each other.

Arles laughed. "Don't worry, Hama. You are yet young. You will grow—distant." Arles passed him the Memory. "Carry on alone. Perhaps it will be a useful discipline for you. One in three for the Cull. And remember—*love them*."

Space tore and knit up, and Arles Thrun was gone.

Hama weighed the Memory; it was surprisingly heavy. The contents of the Memory would be downloaded into the Post's fabric and transcribed on its walls, in images timeless enough to withstand further linguistic drift. Nothing else could be written or drawn on the surfaces of the Post—certainly nothing made by the inhabitants of this place. What had they to write or draw? What did they need to read, save the glorious progress of mankind?

The drone couple had moved on. More ugly shaven heads moved past him, all alike, meaningless.

Later that night, when the Post's sourceless light dimmed, Hama watched the drones dance their wild untutored tangos, sensual and beautiful. He clung to the thought of how he had doomed the lovers: their shocked expressions, the way they had grabbed each others' arms, their distress.

After another sleep, La-ba and Ca-si were thrust out of the Observation Post.

To La-ba, stiff in her hardsuit, it was a strange and unwelcome experience to pass through the Woven Space shell of the Post, to feel gravity shift and change, to feel *up* become *down*. And then she had to make sense of a floor that curved away beneath her, to understand that the horizon now hid what lay beyond rather than revealed it.

Only one of them, La-ba or Ca-si, would come back—one, or neither.

This was the Cull.

Crimson fog glowed around La-ba.

The air was racked by huge storms. Far below she saw the smooth glint of this world's core, a hard plain of metallic hydrogen, unimaginably strange. Above her huge black clouds jostled, squirming like We-kus in the mud. Lightning crackled between and beyond the clouds.

Rain slammed down around her, a hail of pebbles that glowed red-hot. They clattered against the smooth skin of the Post, and her hardsuit. The clouds were a vapor of silicates. The rain was molten rock laced with pure iron.

The Post was a featureless ball that floated in this ferocious sky, a world drifting within a world. A great cable ran up from the floor before her, up into the crowded sky above her, up—it was said—to the cool emptiness of space beyond. La-ba had never seen space, though she believed it existed.

La-ba, used to enclosure, wanted to cringe, to fall against the floor, as, it was said, some infants hugged the smooth warm walls of the Birthing Vat. But she stood tall.

A fist slammed into the back of her head.

She fell forward, her hardsuited limbs clattering against the Woven Space floor.

There was a weight on her back and legs, pressing her down. She felt a scrabbling at her neck. Fingers probed at the joint between her helmet and the rest of the suit. If the suit was breached she would death at once.

She did not resist.

She felt the fingers pull away from her neck.

With brisk roughness she was flipped on her back. Her assailant sat on her legs, heavy in his hardsuit. Rock rain pattered on his shoulders, red-gleaming pebbles that stuck for a second before dropping away, cooling to gray.

It was, of course, Ca-si.

"You un-hunted me," he said, and his words crackled in her ears. "And now you un-resist me." She felt his hands on her shoulders, and she remembered how his skin had touched hers, but there was no feeling through the hardsuits. He said, "You crime if you un-death me. You crime if you let me death you."

"It is true." So it was. According to the Doctrine that shaped their lives, it was the duty of the strong to destroy the weak.

Ca-si sat back. "I will death you." But he ran his gloved hands over her body, over her breasts, to her belly.

And he found the bulge there, exposed by the contoured hardsuit.

His eyes widened.

"Now you know," she screamed at him.

His face twisted behind the thick plate. "I must death you even so."

"Yes! Death me! Get it over!"

". . . No. There is another way."

There was a hand on Ca-si's shoulder. He twisted, startled.

Another stood over them, occluding the raging rock clouds. This other was wearing an ancient, scuffed hardsuit. Through a scratched and starred faceplate, La-ba made out one eye, one dark socket, a mesh of wrinkles.

It was the Old Man: the monster of whom infants whispered to each other even before they had left the Birthing Vat.

Ca-si fell away from her. He was screaming and screaming. La-ba lay there, stunned, unable to speak.

The Old Man reached down and hauled La-ba to her feet. "Come." He pulled her toward the cable that connected the Post to space.

There was a door in the cable.

Hama kept Ca-si in custody.

The boy paced back and forth in the small cell Hama had created for him, his muscles sliding beneath his skin. He would mutter sometimes, agitated, clearly troubled by whatever had become of his lost love.

But when Ca-si inspected the Commissary's silvered epidermis and the fish that swam in his chest, a different look dawned on his fleshy, soft face. It was a look of awe, incomprehension, and—admit it, Hama!—*disgust.*

He knew Arles disapproved of his obsession with this boy.

"The result of your assignment of them to the Cull was satisfactory. Two went out; one came back. What does it matter?"

But Hama pointed to evidence of flaws—the lack of trophies from the body being the most obvious. "All these disgusting drones take trophies from their kills. There's something wrong here."

"There is more than one way of manifesting weakness, Hama. If the other let herself die it is better she is deleted from the gene pool anyhow."

"That is not the strict Doctrine."

Arles had sighed and passed a glimmering hand over the silver planes of his cheek. "But even our longevity is a violation of the Doctrine—if a necessary one. It is a hundred thousand years since Druz, Hama. His Doctrine has become—mature. You will learn."

But Hama had not been satisfied.

At last the translation suites cut in, rendering the drones' linguistically impoverished jabber into reasonably acceptable Standard.

Hama faced the boy. He forced his silvered face into a smile. "You have been isolated here a long time."

"A thousand births," the boy said sullenly.

That was about right: ten thousand years since the last Commission visit, a thousand of these drones' brief generations. "Yes. A thousand births. And, in enough time, languages change. Did you know that? After just a few thousand years of separation two identical languages will diverge so much that they would share no common features except basic grammatical constructs—like the way a language indicates possession, or uses more subtle features like ergativity, which . . ."

The boy was just staring at him, dull, not even resentful.

Hama felt foolish, and then angry to be made to feel that way. He said sternly, "To rectify language drift is part of our duty. The Commission for Historical Truth, I mean. We will reteach you Standard. Just as we will leave you the Memory, with the story of mankind since you were last visited, and we will take away your story to tell it to others. We bind up mankind on all our scattered islands. Just as it is your duty—"

"To death."

"Yes. The machines here watch for the enemy. They have watched for sixty thousand years, and they may watch for sixty thousand years more. If the enemy come you must do everything you can to destroy them, and if you cannot, you must destroy the machines, and the Post, and yourself."

The boy watched him dully, his powerful hands clenched into fists.

Ca-si was no more than a backup mechanism, Hama thought. A final self-destruct, in case this station's brooding automated defenses failed. For this sole purpose, six thousand generations of humans had lived and loved and bred and died, here in the intergalactic waste.

As he gazed at the planes of the boy's stomach, Hama felt an uncomfortable inner warmth, a restlessness.

On impulse he snapped, "Who do we fight? Do you know?"

"We fight the Xeelee."

"*Why* do we fight?"

The boy stared at him.

Hama ordered, "Look at me." He pulled open his robe. "This silver skin comes from a creature called a Silver Ghost. Once the Ghosts owned worlds and built cities. Now we farm them for their skin. The fish in my belly are called Squeem. Once they conquered man, occupied Earth itself. Now they are mere symbiotes in my chest, enabling me to speak to my colleagues across the galactic Supercluster. These are triumphs for mankind."

The look on Ca-si's face made Hama think he didn't regard his condition as a triumph.

Angry, oddly confused, Hama snapped, "I know you didn't kill the girl. Why did you spare her? Why did she spare you? *Where is she?*"

But the boy wouldn't reply.

It seemed there was nothing Hama could do to reach Ca-si, as he longed to.

La-ba had been raised into strangeness.

The hollow cable had a floor that lifted you up, and windows so you could see out. Inside, she rode all the way out of the air, into a place of harsh flat light.

When she looked down she saw a floor of churning red gas. Auroras flapped in its textured layers, making it glow purple. When she looked up she saw only a burning, glaring light.

The Old Man tried to make her understand. "The light is the sun. The red is the world. The Post floats in the air of the world."

She couldn't stop staring at his face. It was a mass of wrinkles. He had one eye, one dark purple pit. His face was the strangest thing of all, much stranger than the sun and the churning world.

The cable ended in another giant ball, like the Post. But this ball was dimpled by big black pits, like the bruises left by the heels of her hands in the face of the We-ku. And it floated in space, not the air.

Inside the ball there was a cavity, but there were no people or Cadre Squares and no Birthing Vat: only vast mechanical limbs that glistened, sinister, sliding over each other.

"No people live here," she said.

He smiled. "One person does."

He showed her his home. It wasn't a dorm. It was just a shack made of bits of shining plastic. There were blankets on the floor, and clothes, and empty food packets. It was dirty, and it smelled a little.

She looked around. "There is no supply dispenser."

"People give me food. And water and clothes. From their rations."

She tried to understand. "Why?"

He shrugged. "Because life is short. People want—"

"What?"

"Something more than the war."

She thought about that. "There is the dance."

He grinned, his empty eye socket crumpling. "I never could dance. Come."

He led her to a huge window. Machines screened out the glare of the sun above and the glower of the overheated planet below.

Between sun and planet, there was only blackness.

"No," the Old Man said gently. "Not blackness. *Look.*"

They waited there for long heartbeats.

At last she saw a faint glow, laced against the black. It had structure, fine filaments and threads. It was beautiful, eerie, remote.

"It is un-black."

He pointed at the sun. "The sun is alone. If there were other suns near, we would see them, as points of light. The suns gather in pools. There are not even pools of suns nearby. The un-black is pools of suns, very far away."

She understood that.

"Others lived here before me," he said. "They learned how to see with the machines. They left records of what they saw." He dug into a pocket and pulled out a handful of bones: human bones, the small bones of a hand or foot. They were scored by fine marks.

"They speak to you with *bones*?"

He shrugged. "If you smear blood or dirt on the walls it falls away. What else do we have to draw on, but our bones, and our hearts?" He fingered the bones carefully.

"What do the bones say?"

He gestured at the hulking machinery. "These machines watch the sky for the trace of ships. But they also see the un-black: the light, the faintest light, all the light there is. Some of the light comes from the suns and pools of suns. Most of the light was made in the birthing of the universe. It is old now and tired and hard to see. But it has patterns in it. . . ."

This meant nothing to her. Bombarded by strangeness, she tried to remember the Doctrine. "I crimed. I did not death, and I wanted to be deathed. Then you crimed. You could have deathed me. And here—"

"Here, I crime." He grinned. "With every breath I crime. Every one of these bones is a crime, a record of ancient crimes. Like you, I was safed."

"Safed?"

"Brought here."

She asked the hardest question of all. "When?"

He smiled, and the wrinkles on his face gathered up. "Twenty years ago. Twice your life."

She frowned, barely comprehending. She leaned against the window, cupping her hands and peering out.

He asked, "What are you looking for now?"

"Shuttles."

He said gently, "There are no Shuttles."

"The cadre leaders—"

"The cadre leaders say what is said to them. Think. Have you ever known anybody to leave on a Shuttle? *There are no Shuttles.*"

"It is a lie?"

"It is a lie. If you live past age ten, the cadre leaders will death you. *They* believe they will win a place on the Shuttles. But they in turn are deathed by other cadre leaders, who believe they will steal their places on the Shuttles. And so it goes. Lies eating each other."

No Shuttles. She sighed, and her breath fogged the smooth surface of the window. "Then how will we leave?"

"We un-can leave. We are too remote. Only the Commissaries come and go. Only the Commissaries. Not us."

She felt something stir in her heart.

"The Shuttles are un-real. Is Earth real? Is the war real?"

"Perhaps Earth is a lie. But the war is real. Oh, yes. The bones talk of how distant pools of suns flare up. The war is real, and all around us, but it is very far away, and very old. But it shapes us." He studied her. "Soon the cadre leaders will pluck that baby from your belly and put it in the Birthing Vat. It will life and death for one purpose, for the war."

She said nothing.

The Old Man said dreamily, "Some of the Old Men have seen patterns in the birthing un-black. They have tried to understand them, as the cadre leaders make us understand the Memory images of the war. Perhaps they are thoughts, those patterns. Frozen thoughts of the creatures who lived in the first blinding second of the universal birth." He shook his head and gazed at the bones. "I un-want death. I want more than the war. I want to learn *this*."

She barely heard him. She asked, "Who gives you food?"

He gave her names, of people she knew, and people she un-knew.

The number of them shocked her.

Hama and Arles Thrun drifted in space, side by side, two silver statues. Before them, this hot-Jupiter world continued its endless frenetic waltz around its too-close sun. The sun was a rogue star that had evaporated out of its parent galaxy long ago and come to drift here, a meaningless beacon in the intergalactic dark.

Hama was comfortable here, in space, in the vacuum, away from the claustrophobic enclosure of the Post. Alien creatures swam through his chest cavity, subtly feeding on the distant calls of Commissaries all over the Supercluster. To Hama it was like being in a vast room where soft voices murmured in every shadowed corner, grave and wise.

"A paradox," Arles Thrun murmured now.

"What is?"

"Here we are, peering out at the Supercluster, a cluster of clusters of galaxies . . ."

"The drones call it the *un-black*. The glow of the Supercluster, the relic light."

Arles ignored him. "All across the Supercluster mankind battles the Xeelee, a vast organic war. All that conflict is far from here. But *this* is a noisy place—the sun, this wretched overheated planet—the noisiest place in all this dreaming gulf. And yet it is here that we established our listening post."

"We had to camouflage it."

"Yes. And we had to provide matter and energy for the humans who would live here. Thus, in all our designs, we compromise with the needs of the human. Isn't that true, Hama?"

Hama glared, sensing an edge in his voice.

Arles said, "You know, your new Raoul rebuilding has extended beyond the superficial. You have been reengineered, the layers of evolutionary haphazardness designed out of you. The inner chemical conflicts bequeathed by humanity's past do not trouble you. You do not hear voices in your head, you do not invent gods to drive out your internal torment. You are the most *integrated* human being who ever lived."

"If I am still human," Hama said.

"Ah, yes, the great question. Certainly we are needed. It is impossible to begin to grasp the scale and complexity of an intergalactic war in a human lifetime. And yet the brevity of human life is the key to the war; we fight like vermin, for to the Xeelee we are vermin—*that* is the central uncomfortable truth of the Doctrine. *We*, who do not die, are a paradoxical necessity, maintaining the attention span of the species . . ."

"We have no art. We are not scientists. We do not dance."

"No," said Arles earnestly. "Our reengineered hearts are too cold for that. Or to desire to make babies to fill up the empty spaces. *But we know our flaws, Hama.* We know that those brutish creatures down there in the Post, busily fighting and fornicating and breeding and dying, *they* are the true heart of humanity. And so we must defer to them." He eyed Hama, waiting for him to respond.

Hama said with difficulty, "I am not—happy."

"You were promised integration, not happiness."

"I failed to find the girl. *La-ba.*"

Arles smiled in the vacuum. "I traced her. She escaped to the sensor installation."

"The sensors?"

"Another renegade lives up there. To what purpose, I can't imagine," Arles murmured.

"This place is flawed," Hama said bitterly.

"Oh, yes. Very flawed. There is a network of drones who provision the renegade. And there are more subtle problems: the multiple births occurring in the Vat, the taking of trophies from kills, the *dancing* . . . These drones seek satisfaction beyond the Doctrine. There has been ideological drift. It is a shame. You would think that in a place as isolated as this a certain purity could be sustained. But the human heart, it seems, is full of spontaneous imperfection."

"They must be punished."

Arles looked at him carefully. "We do not punish, Hama. We only correct."

"How? A program of indoctrination, a rebuilding—"

Arles shook his head. "It has gone too far for that. There are many other Observation Posts. We will allow these flawed drones to die."

There was a wash of agreement from the Commissaries all over the Supercluster, all of them loosely bound to Hama's thinking and Arles's, all of them concurring in Arles's decision.

Hama found he was appalled. "They have done their duty here for sixty thousand years—Lethe, a third of the evolutionary history of the human species—and now you would destroy them so casually, for the sake of a little deviance?"

Arles gripped Hama's arms and turned him so they faced each other. Hama glimpsed cold power in his eyes; Arles Thrun was already a thousand years old. "Look around, Hama. Look at the Supercluster, the vast stage, deep in space and time, on which we fight. Our foe is unimaginably ancient, with unimaginable powers. And what are we but half-evolved apes from the plains of some dusty, lost planet? Perhaps we are not *smart* enough to fight this war. And yet we fight even so.

"And to keep us united in our purpose, this vast host of us scattered over more galaxies than either of us could count, we have the Doctrine, our creed of mortality. Let me tell you something. The Doctrine is not perfect. *It may not even enable us to win the war*, no matter how long we fight. But it has brought us this far, and it is all we have."

"And so we must destroy these drones, not for the sake of the war—"

"But for the sake of the Doctrine. Yes. Now, at last, you begin to understand."

Arles released him, and they drifted apart.

La-ba stayed with the Old Man.

She woke. She lay in silence. It was strange not to wake under a sky crowded with people. She could feel her baby inside her, kicking as if it were eager to get to the Birthing Vat.

The floor shuddered.

The Old Man ran to her. He dragged her to her feet. "It begins," he said.

"What?"

He took her to the hatch that led to the hollow cable.

A We-ku was there, inside the cable, his fat face split by a grin, his stick-out ears wide.

She raised her foot and kicked the We-ku in the forehead. He clattered to the floor, howling.

The Old Man pulled her back. "What did you do?"

"He is a We-ku."

"Look." The Old Man pointed.

The We-ku was clambering to his feet and rubbing his head. He had been carrying a bag full of ration packs. Now the packs were littered over the floor, some of them split.

The Old Man said, "Never mind the food. Take her back." And he pushed at La-ba again, urging her into the cable. Reluctantly she began to climb down.

She felt a great sideways wash, as if the whole of this immense cable was vibrating back and forth, as if it had been plucked by a vast finger.

She looked up at the circle of light that framed the Old Man's face. She was confused, frightened. "I will bring you food."

He laughed bitterly. "Just remember me. Here." And he thrust his hand down into hers. Then he slammed shut the hatch.

When she opened her hand, she saw it contained the scrimshawed bones.

The cable whiplashed, and the lights failed, and they fell into darkness, screaming.

Hama stood in the holding cell, facing Ca-si. The walls were creaking. He heard screaming, running footsteps.

With its anchoring cable severed, the Post was beginning to sink away from its design altitude, deeper into the roiling murk of the hot Jupiter's atmosphere. Long before it reached the glimmering, enigmatic metallic-hydrogen core, it would implode.

Ca-si's mouth worked, as if he was gulping for air. "Take me to the Shuttles."

"There are no Shuttles."

Ca-si yelled, "Why are you here? What do you *want*?"

Hama laid one silvered hand against the boy's face. "I love you," he said. "It's my job to love you. Don't you see that?" But his silvered flesh could not detect the boy's warmth, and Ca-si flinched from his touch, the burned scent of vacuum exposure.

". . . *I* know what you want."

Ca-si gasped. Hama turned.

La-ba stood in the doorway. She was dirty, bloodied. She was carrying a lump of shattered partition wall. Fragmentary animated images, of glorious scenes from humanity's past, played over it fitfully.

Hama said, "*You.*"

She flicked a fingernail against the silver carapace of his arm. "You want to be like us. That's why you tried to death us."

And she lifted the lump of partition rubble and slammed it into his chest. Briny water gushed down Hama's belly, spilling tiny silver fish that struggled and died.

Hama fell back, bending over himself. His systems screamed messages of alarm and pain at him—and, worse, he could feel that he had lost his link with the vaster pool of Commissaries beyond. "What have you done? Oh, what have you done?"

"Now you are like us," said La-ba simply.

The light flickered and darkened. Glancing out of the cell, Hama saw that the great Birthing Vat was drifting away from its position at the geometric center of the Post. Soon it would impact the floor in a gruesome moist collision.

"I should have gone with Arles," he moaned. "I don't know why I delayed."

La-ba stood over Hama and grabbed his arm. With a grunting effort, the two drones hauled him to his feet.

La-ba said, "Why do you death us?"

"It is the war. Only the war."

"Why do we fight the war?"

In desperation Hama said rapidly, "We have fought the Xeelee for half our evolutionary history as a species. We fight because we must. We don't know what else to do. We can't stop, any more than you can stop breathing. Do you see?"

"Take us," said La-ba.

"*Take* you? Take you where? Do you even know what it is I do when I . . . jump?" He tried to imagine explaining to them the truth about space—telling them of filaments and membranes vibrating in multiple-dimensional harmony, of ruptures in space and time as the fundamental fibers, at his command, rewove themselves . . .

In La-ba's set face there was ruthless determination, a will to survive that burned away the fog of his own weak thinking.

The Doctrine is right, he thought. Mortality brings strength. *A brief life burns brightly.* He felt ashamed of himself. He tried to stand straight, ignoring the clamoring pain from his smashed stomach.

The girl said, "It is un-Doctrine. But I have deathed your fish. Nobody will know."

He forced a laugh. "Is that why you killed the Squeem? . . . You are naïve."

She clutched his arm harder, as if trying to bend his metallic flesh. "Take us to Earth."

"Do you know what Earth is like?"

Ca-si said, "It is a place where you live on the outside, not the inside. It is a place where water falls from the sky, not rock."

"How will you live?"

La-ba said, "The We-ku helped the Old Man live. Others will help us live."

Perhaps it was true, Hama thought. Perhaps if these two survived on some civilized world—a world where other citizens could see what was being done in the name of the war—they might form a focus for resistance. No, not resistance: *doubt.*

And doubt might destroy them all.

He must abandon these creatures to their deaths. That was his clear duty, his duty to the species.

There was a crack of shattering partition. The Post spun, making the three of them stagger, locked together.

Ca-si showed his fear. "We will be deathed."

"Take us to Earth," La-ba insisted.

Hama said weakly, "You broke my link to the Commission. I may not be able to find my way. The link helps me—navigate. Do you see?"

"Try," she whispered. She closed her eyes and pressed her cheek against the cold of his silvered chest.

Hama wrapped his arms around the two drones, and space tore.

For a single heartbeat the three of them floated in vacuum.

The close sun glared, impossibly bright. The planet was a floor of roiling gas, semi-infinite. Above, Hama could see the sensor installation. It was drifting off into space, dangling its tether like an impossibly long umbilical. It was startlingly bright in the raw sunlight, like a sculpture.

From beneath the planet's boiling clouds, a soundless concussion of light flickered and faded. Sixty thousand years of history had ended, a subplot in mankind's tangled evolution; the long watch was over.

La-ba squirmed, stranded in vacuum. Her hands were clasped over the bump at her belly. She opened her mouth, and the last of her air gushed out, a hail of sparkling crystals, glimmering in the fierce sunlight.

Hama held the lovers close, and the three of them vanished.

Paul Di Filippo was custom-made for an anthology like this. With his wit and wild invention, evidenced in such wacky books as The Steampunk Trilogy *and* Lost Pages *(in which a costumed Franz Kafka—yes, I said Franz Kafka—roams the night of Manhattan as the avenger Jackdaw) he's proved himself an able postpunk successor to the likes of the great Philip José Farmer.*

His story for this book is one of those I'd point to when asked what I was looking for for Redshift*—it's sick, hilarious, and viciously apt.*

If you don't think the media is really heading this way—think again.

Weeping Walls

PAUL DI FILIPPO

*

"I *want* those fucking *teddy* bears, and I want them *yesterday*!"

Lisa Dutch bellowed into the telephone as if denouncing Trotsky in front of Stalin. Tectonic emotions threatened to fracture the perfect makeup landscaping the compact features of her astoundingly innocent yet vaguely insane face. Eruptions of sweat beaded the cornsilk-fine blond hairs layered alongside her delicate ears.

Seeking her attention, Jake Pasha was waving a folded newspaper under Lisa's charmingly pert nose and toothpaste-blue eyes, and this impudence from her assistant infuriated her even more. She glared at Jake like a wrathful goddess, Kali in a Donna Karan suit, but—aside from swatting the paper away—she chose to vent her evil temper only on the hapless vendor holding down the other end of her conversation.

"Listen, shithead! You promised me those goddamn bears for early last week, and they're not here *yet*. Do you have any *idea* how many orders I'm holding up for those bears? I run a time-sensitive business here. We're talking thousands of bereaved husbands and wives, mourning parents and red-eyed grandparents, all hanging fire. They can't process their *grief* thanks to your goddamn *incompentence*. Not to mention the fucking kids! You can't find your *nose*? Are you fucking *crazy*? Oh, the *bears'* noses! Well, I don't care if you draw the goddamn noses on by hand with a fucking pen! Just get me those motherfucking bears!"

Lisa smashed the phone into its plastic cradle, where fractures revealed a history of such stresses. Now she was free to concentrate on her assistant.

"Unless you stop shoving that paper into my face this instant, Jake, I will tear you a brand-new asshole. And while your boyfriends might well enjoy that feature, I guarantee that it will make wearing your thong at the beach an utter impossibility."

Jake stepped warily back from Lisa's desk and nervously brushed a fall of wheat-colored hair off his broad brow. "My God, Lisa, you don't have to be such a frightening bitch with me! I'm already scared every morning when I walk through the door of this madhouse! Anyway, I was just trying to do my job."

Lisa visibly composed herself, her stormy expression ceding to a professional mask of good-natured calm. She forced out an apology that evidently tasted sour. "I'm sorry. But these vendors drive me nuts. Our whole business relies on them, and they're nothing but a bunch of sleazy asswipes. Balloons, stuffed animals, flowers, wreaths, banners, candles, suncatchers—you'd think the people who sold such things would be nice, maybe New Agey people. But they're not. You know who the most up-front guys are? The construction guys. Not enough manners to fill a thimble, but if they can't deliver a wall, they let you know right away. They don't string you along like these other pricks."

"Be that as it may, dear, you've got something a tad more crucial to worry about now." Jake flourished the newspaper in a less aggressive manner, and Lisa took it from him. Folded back to the business section, the paper glibly offered its salient headline:

WEEPING WALLS TO FACE FIRST COMPETITOR

Lisa scanned the article with growing rage that wiped away her mask once again. Reaching the end, she exclaimed, "Those scum-sucking bastards! They've ripped off all our trademark features. 'Sadness Fences,' my sweet white ass! Even their name's actionable. Our lawyers will be all over them like ticks on a Connecticut camper by this afternoon."

Jake took the paper back. "I don't know, Lisa. I get a bad feeling over this one. Did you see who's backing them?"

"TimWarDisVia. So what? You're scared of a conglomerate whose name sounds like a neurological disease?"

"That's a lot of money and power to go up against—"

"I don't give a fuck! We have legal precedence on our side. I invented this whole concept five years ago. Everyone knows that. Before me and Weeping Walls, this industry didn't even exist. Grief was left to fucking amateurs!"

"Granted. But you had to expect competition sooner or later."

"Maybe you're right. Maybe we've been getting complacent. This could be good for us. Get us to kick things up a notch."

"How?"

"I don't know. But I'll think of something. Meanwhile, I've got to keep all the plates spinning. What's next on my schedule?"

Jake consulted his Palm Pilot XII. "There's a new wall going up right here in town an hour from now. Did you want to attend the opening ceremonies?"

"What's the occasion?"

"Employee shooting yesterday at the downtown post office."

"That's handy. How many dead?"

"Three."

"Sure, I'll go. With that low number of deaths the media coverage should be thin. I don't think I could handle the stress from the aftermath of a full-scale massacre today. Plus, it's nearby, and I haven't been to one of our openings in a month, since that schoolyard slaughter."

"We could certainly plan your appearances better if we could only remove the random factor from our business—"

Lisa stood up, smoothing her skirt. "No need for you to be cynical, too, Jake. I've got that angle completely covered."

Following his superior out of her office, Jake asked, "What's Danny doing these days?"

Lisa sighed. "Same as always. Sacrificing himself for his art. It gets mighty old, Jake."

"Is he making any money yet?"

"Not so you could notice."

"Any luck convincing him to come to work here?"

"Not likely. He swears he'd kill himself first. He'd have to get pretty desperate. Or else I'd have to offer him some unbelievable deal."

"You two are such opposites, I'm amazed you're still together."

"I am a pistol in the sack, honey. And Danny's hung more impressively than Abe Lincoln's assassins."

"Oh, I don't doubt any of that for one blessed minute, sugar."

"Could I hear from the kazoos again, please?"

Danny Simmons, his gangly limbs poised awkwardly as if he were only minding them temporarily until their real owner returned, sat in the front row of the shabby theater, directing his motley troupe on the bare stage. He addressed a quartet of actors situated stage left, clad like harlequins, and standing with kazoos poised at their lips. Before the kazoo-players could comply with the polite request, however, Danny was interrupted by a large-bosomed young woman, hair colored like autumn acorns, seated several rows back.

"Danny, I've forgotten my cue."

The mild-faced skinny director turned slowly in his seat and said, "You come in when Lester says—'The planet's dying!'—Carol."

"He's going to call me by my real name? I thought I was playing Gaia."

A long-suffering look washed over Danny's lagomorphic features. "No, Carol. He'll only say, 'The planet's dying!' "

"And then I stand up and face the audience—"

"Correct."

"—and rip open my shirt—"

"Right."

"—and I say—I say—"

"Your line is 'Gaia lactates no more for cuckoos born of hominid greed!' "

Carol's painful expression mimicked that of a pressure-racked semifinalist in a nationally televised sixth-grade spelling bee. " 'Gaia lacks tits for greedy—' Oh, Danny, it's no use!"

"Carol, just calm down. You have another two whole days to practice. I'm sure you'll be fine."

"I've got the shirt-ripping part down pat. Do you want to see?"

The males on stage leaned forward eagerly. Danny yelled, "No, no, don't!" but he was much too late.

The rehearsal didn't resume for a confused fifteen minutes spent chasing popped shirt buttons and draping blankets solicitously around Carol's chilly shoulders.

Hardly had the drama—script and music by Danny Simmons, directed and produced by Danny Simmons—gotten once more well under way when another interruption intervened.

One of the set-building crew rocketed onstage, hammer in her hand. "Hey, Danny, there's a guy from the electric company fooling around outside at the meter!"

At that instant, the theater was plunged into darkness. Yelps and shrieks filled the musty air. Feet scuffled in panic across the boards, and the sound of a body tumbling down the three stairs leading from the stage was succeeded by grunts and curses.

Eventually Danny Simmons and his troupe found themselves all out in the daylit lobby. There awaited the theater's landlord, a short irascible fellow who resembled a gnome sired by Rumpelstiltskin on one of Cinderella's ugly stepsisters.

"Haul ass out of here, you losers. Your freeloading days are over."

Danny fought back tears of frustration. "But Mr. Semple, we open on Friday! We'll pay all the back rent with the first night's receipts!"

"Not likely, pal. I finally caught a rehearsal of this lamebrained farce yesterday. I was sitting in the back for the whole damn incomprehensible five acts. No one's going to lay down a plugged nickel to see this shit." Semple paused to ogle the straining safety pin that labored to hold Carol's shirtfront closed. "You do have a couple of good assets, but you can't count on them for everything. No, I figure it's better to cut my losses right now. Clear this place immediately so's I can padlock it, and my boys will pile your stuff on the sidewalk."

Defeated, the spiritless actors began to shuffle out of the building, and Danny shamefacedly followed them. Out on the sidewalk, he turned to face the confusingly abstract poster for their show hanging by the ticket office:

GAIA'S DAY OFF
PRESENTED BY THE DERRIDADAISTS

The sight of the poster seemed to hearten him. He turned to rally his friends.

"Gang, I won't let these fat-cat bastards break us up! Whatever it takes, I vow the Derridadaists will go on!"

"I am *so* glad," Carol offered cheerfully, "that I have some extra time to practice my speech!"

"All mourners wearing an official wristband may now step forward."

Dewlapped Governor Wittlestoop, suited in enough expensive charcoal wool fabric to clothe a dozen orphans, despite the hot September sunlight beating down, backed away from the microphone and lowered his fat rump onto a creaking folding chair barely up to sustaining its load. Next to the governor on the hastily erected platform sat Lisa Dutch, knees clamped together, legs primly crossed at the ankles in what Jake Pasha—lingering now obediently close by—often referred to as "the boardroom virgin" pose.

Lisa patted the governor's hand. Maintaining her frozen official expression of soberly condoling vicarious grief, she murmured, "Did you get the latest envelope okay?"

Similarly covert, Wittlestoop replied, "It's already in the bank."

"Good. Because I seem to be facing some new challenges, and I don't want to have to worry about protecting my ass in my own backyard."

"Nothing to fear. Weeping Walls has been awfully good to this state, and the state will respond in kind."

"Since when did you and the state become synonymous?"

"I believe it was at the start of my fifth term. By the way, I admired your anecdote today about the relatives you lost in the Oklahoma City bombing and how that inspired you years later to found your company.

You had the crowd in tears. Tell me confidentially—any of that horseshit true?"

"Only the part about me having relatives."

Notes of dirgelike classical music sprinkled the air. Among the groundlings, a wavery line had formed: those members of the sniffling audience with the requisite wristbands had arrayed themselves in an orderly fashion across the post office parking lot where the memorial service for the recently slain was being held. The head of the line terminated at a row of large black plastic bins much like oversize composters. Beside the bins stood several employees from Weeping Walls, looking in their black habiliments like postmodern undertakers, save for the bright red WW logo stitched in Gothic cursive on their coats.

Now the first mourner was silently and gently urged by a solicitous yet controlling Weeping Walls employee to make her choice of sympathy-token. The mourner, a red-eyed widow, selected a bouquet of daisies from one of a score of water buckets held on a waist-high iron stand. The Weeping Walls usher now led the woman expeditiously toward the wall itself.

Erected only hours ago, the fresh planks of the official Weeping Wall, branded subtly with the WW logo, still emanated a piney freshness. At regular intervals staples secured dangling plastic ties similar to a policeman's instant handcuffs or an electrician's cable-bundling straps. The usher brought the first woman and her bouquet to the leftmost, uppermost tie, and helped her secure the flowers with a racheting plastic zip. Then he led the sobbing woman away as efficiently as an Oscar-ceremonies handler, rejoining his fellow workers to process another person.

Once the mechanized ritual was under way, it proceeded as smoothly as a robotic Japanese assembly line. From the bins mourners plucked various tokens of their public grief: pastel teddy bears, miniature sports gear emblazoned with the logos of all the major franchises, religious icons from a dozen faiths, sentimental greeting cards inscribed with such all-purpose designations as "Beloved Son" and "Dearest Daughter." One by one, the bereaved friends, neighbors and relatives—anyone, really, who had paid the appropriate fee to Weeping Walls (family discounts available)—placed their stereotyped fetishes on the official wall and returned to their seats.

Under the cheerful sun, Lisa watched the whole affair with traces of pride and glee struggling to break through her artificial funereal demeanor like blackbirds out of a pie. Then her attention was snagged by an anomalous audience member: some nerdy guy scribbling notes with a stylus on his PDA.

Lisa leaned toward Governor Wittlestoop. "See the guy taking notes? Is he a local reporter I don't recognize?"

Wittlestoop squinted. "No. And he's not accredited national media either. I've never seen him before."

Lisa got determinedly to her feet. All eyes were focused on the ceremony, and no one noticed her swift descent from the stage. Coming up behind the scribbler, Lisa remained practically invisible. She seated herself behind the suspicious fellow and craned for a view over his shoulder.

The screen of the man's handy machine was scrolling his notes as he entered them:

> Offer more choices of victim memorial. Favorite foods of dec'd? Finger food only. Maybe cookies? Call SnackWell's. Sadness Fences line of candy?

Her face savage, Lisa stood. She grabbed the man's folding chair and tipped him out of it. He stumbled forward, caught himself, and turned to face Lisa with a frightened look.

"You fucking little spy! Give me that!" Lisa grappled with the man for his PDA, but he held tight. Empty chairs tumbled like jackstraws as they struggled. Suddenly Lisa relinquished her grip. The spy straightened up, smiling and seemingly victorious. Lisa cocked her well-muscled, Nautilus-toned arm and socked him across the jaw. The guy went down.

Chaos was now in full sway, screams and shouts and frenzied dashes for cover, as if the post office shooter himself had suddenly returned. Lisa spiked the PDA with the heel of her pump and ground it into the asphalt.

Digital cameras had converged on Lisa from the start of the fight and continued to feed images of her reddened face and disarrayed hair to various news outlets. The Governor's entourage of state troopers finally descended on Lisa and her victim. The spy had regained his feet and, nursing his jaw, sought revenge.

"Arrest her, officers! She assaulted me for no reason!"

The troopers turned to Governor Wittlestoop for direction. The Governor nodded his head at the spy, and the troopers dragged him off.

Lisa sought desperately to explain her actions to the appalled crowd and the invisible media audience. "He was, he was—"

Jake had joined her, and, under pretext of comforting her, whispered close to her ear. Lisa brightened.

"He was a Satanist!"

* * *

"TimWarDisVia continues to deny all allegations of Satanic activity by any of its subsidiaries or their employees. Nevertheless, several senators are insisting on a full investigation—"

The well-coiffed CNN talking head inhabiting the small all-purpose monitor on the kitchen counter appeared primed to drone on all night. But Lisa moused him out of existence with her left hand and then carried the dark amber drink in her right hand up to her plum-glossed lips.

"Nice save, Leese."

Danny stood by the sink, peeling potatoes. He sought to create one single long peel from each, and was generally succeeding.

Lisa drained her glass. "Thanks, but I can't take all the credit. Jake doesn't know it yet, but he's in for a fat bonus."

Danny sighed. "The productions I could mount if only I had an assistant as competent as Jake! The kind of people who will work like dogs week after week for no pay generally don't come equipped with a lot of, ah—call it smarts? But of course, that's all moot now, with the death of our show."

Lisa refilled her glass from a bottle of Scotch, spritzed it, and added fresh rocks before turning to Danny. "I might have made a nice recovery today, but this move will hardly stop Sadness Fences from trying to eat my lunch. It's only a temporary embarrassment for them. And I just can't figure out yet how to undercut them! Oh, shit—let's talk about your day again, I'm sick of mine. Tell me once more why you won't just take a loan from me to pay off your debts?"

Danny paused from rinsing vegetables to sip from a small glass of white wine. "We agreed that the loan you made to us last year so that we could stage *Motherfoucaults!* would be the last. If the Derridadaists can't find other backers interested in avant-garde theater, then I'm just running a vanity operation. And I don't want that."

"What are you going to do now?"

"Finish making our supper. After that, I simply don't know. I want to keep the troupe together, but not at the expense of my artistic pride."

Lisa kicked off her shoes. "Artistic pride! Tell me about it! That's what hurts me the worst, you know—that these Sadness Fences bastards are buggering my brainchild."

"A disturbing image, Leese, however apt. Do you want mesclun or spinach in your salad?"

"Spinach. Gotta keep the old punching arm in shape."

After supper, the big flatscreen in the den displayed *Entertainment Hourly* to the couch-cushioned, cuddling Danny and Lisa.

Seated at his minimalist desk, hair and teeth Platonically perfect, as if fashioned by space aliens as a probe, the determinedly somber yet oddly effusive host launched into a report of the latest hourly sensation.

"Jax Backman led his own jazz funeral today through the streets of Celebration, Florida. Diagnosed last month with that nasty new incurable strain of terminal oral herpes, the plucky hornman quickly opted to go out in style. Taking advantage of last year's Supreme Court decision in *Flynt versus United States Government* legalizing assisted suicide and other forms of voluntary euthanasia, Backman received a special, slow-acting lethal injection at the start of the cortege's route. Propped up in his coffin, he was able to enjoy nearly the whole procession, which included innumerable celebrity mourners. TimWarDisVia even lent out their animatronic Louis Armstrong to lead the solemn yet oddly joyous wake."

The screen cut to footage of the event: in front of a team of horses, the robotic Louis Armstrong clunked along with stilted steps, mimicking horn-playing while prerecorded music issued from its belly. The human participants enacted their roles more fluidly, weeping, laughing, tossing Mardi Gras beads and giving each other high-fives. Upright on his wheeled bier, a glassy-eyed Backman waved to the watching crowds with steadily diminishing gusto.

Danny clucked his tongue. "What a production. Debord was so right. Our society is nothing but spectacle. I wonder if they paid those so-called mourners scale—"

Lisa's shriek nearly blew Danny's closest eardrum out. "This is it! This is the future of Weeping Walls!" She threw herself onto Danny and began frantically unbuckling his belt with one hand while pawing at his crotch with the other.

"Leese, hold on! One minute, please! What's *with* you?"

"You've got to *fuck* me like you've never fucked me *before*!"

"But why?"

"I want to engrave the minute I realized I was a goddamn genius onto my brain cells forever!"

"Carol—I mean, Zapmama to Deconstructor. Target in sight."

The message crackled from the walkie-talkie hung at Danny's belt. Danny snatched up the small device and replied.

"Deconstructor to Zapmama. Is your weapon ready?"

"I think so."

"Well, make sure. We can't risk a screwup on our first kill."

"Let me ask Gordon. Gordon, is this what I pull—?"

A blast of rifle fire filled the neighborhood's air, and was simultaneously replicated in miniature by the communicator's speaker. From his perch of command atop the flat roof of a ten-story office building, Danny could see small figures struggling to control the bulky weapon. At last the automatic rifle ceased firing.

"Dan—I mean, Deconstructor?"

Danny sighed deeply. "Deconstructor to Zapmama. Go ahead."

"My gun works fine."

"Acquire target and await the signal. Over."

Reslinging his walkie-talkie, Danny walked over to the camerman sharing the roof with him.

"Can we edit out those early shots?"

"No problem, chief."

A bank of jury-rigged monitors showed not only this camera's perspective, but also the views from other cameras emplaced on the ground. All the lenses were focused on a waddling bus, which bore on its side the legend JERUSALEM TOURS. The bus was nosing into a broad intersection full of traffic and pedestrians. Suddenly, the cars in front and back of the bus seemed to explode. Curiously, no deadly jagged debris flew, nor did any shock waves propagate. Only melodramatic plumes of smoke poured from the gimmicked vehicles.

The explosion brought the hidden attackers out. Dressed in burnooses and ragged desert-camouflage gear, the very picture of martyr-mad Arabs, they opened fire on the trapped bus. Window glass shattered into a crystal rain, holes pinged open in the bus's chassis, and the passengers slumped in contorted postures. One of the terrorists threw a grenade, and the bus rocked like a low-rider's jalopy. Blood began to waterfall out the door.

The assault lasted only ninety seconds, but seemed to go on forever. Mesmerized, Danny nearly forgot his own role. He fumbled with his walkie-talkie and yelled, "Cut! Cut!"

The shooting immediately ceased. Danny hastened down to the street.

A line of ambulances had materialized, directed by a few bored cops. The bus door opened, and the nonchalant driver jumped awkwardly out, anxious to avoid spotting his shoes with the synthetic blood in the stairwell. The medicos entered the damaged bus—seen up close, a twenty-year-old antique obviously rescued from the scrap-heap and repainted—and began to emerge with the victims on sarcophagus-shaped carry-boards.

None of the dead people exhibited any wounds. Mostly elderly, with a smattering of young adults and even a teenager or two, they all appeared to have passed away peacefully. Many of them had final smiles clinging to their lifeless faces. As the victims were loaded onto the ambulances, the bystanders to the attack watched and commented with mournful pride.

"Uncle Albert went out just the way he imagined." "I thought Aunt Ruth would flinch, but she never did." "I saw Harold wave just before the end!"

Danny crunched across the pebbles of safety glass to where the elated mock-terrorists clumped. Spotting him, they shouted and hooted and applauded their director. Congratulations were exchanged all around.

"Did those charges go off okay, Danny?" asked an earnest techie.

"Just fine."

"I triggered the squibs a little late," confessed another.

"Next time will be perfect, I'm sure."

Stretching her terrorist's shirt to undemocratic proportions, a gloomy Carol approached. "I'm awfully sorry about that screwup earlier, Danny. Even though they were only blanks, I could have frightened the bus away!"

Danny regarded Carol silently while he tried to parse her logic. "You do know all this was fake, don't you, Carol?"

Carol reared back indignantly. "Of course I do! I've never even been to Jerusalem!"

All the ambulances had departed. A DPW truck arrived and discharged workers who began brooming up the glass. A large tow truck engaged the derelict bus and begun to winch its front wheels up. A car and several vehicles blazoned with the modified WW logo (now reading WW&FE) pulled up, and Lisa and Jake emerged from the lead vehicle.

Clad in a tasteful and modest navy shift, the owner of Weeping Walls took swift strides over to her husband, pecked his cheek, and then turned to address the crowd.

"Thank you, friends, for participating so enthusiastically in the inaugural performance by Fantasy Exits. I'm sure all your loved ones appreciated your attendence today, as we ushered them off this earth in the manner they selected. Incidentally, your DVD mementos will be available within the next three days. As for those of you who have preregistered to commemorate the departure of your loved ones during the accompanying Weeping Walls ceremony, you may now line up in the space indicated by the temporary stanchions."

As the spectators began to herd, Lisa spoke to her crew in lower tones. "Okay, people, let's shake our butts! Our permits only run until two o'clock."

In a short time the standard Weeping Walls arrangement was set up—the prefab wall itself going up quickly on a leased stretch of sidewalk where prearranged postholes awaited—and the friends and relatives of the chemically slaughtered bus riders were being processed through their relatively restrained and somewhat shell-shocked grief.

Lisa and Danny moved off to one side, away from their respective employees.

Lisa's eyes flashed like the display on an IRS auditor's calculator. "Not bad, not bad at all. Fifteen hundred dollars per staged suicide, times sixty, plus the standard Weeping Walls fees from the survivors. A nice piece of change. Even after paying your crew and mine good money, there's plenty left for you and me, babe."

Danny pulled at his chin. "I appreciate having steady employment for my people, Leese. But I continue to be troubled by the ethics of this hyper-real simulation—"

"Ethics? What ethics? These losers were going to off themselves with or without us. We didn't push them into anything. All we did was provide them with a fantasy exit—a trademarked term already, by the way. They sign the consent and waiver forms, get the hot juice in their veins, and then sail away into their fondest dreams of public crash-and-burn. We're like the goddamn Make-A-Wish Foundation, only we follow through with our clients right up to the end."

"Okay, granted. Nobody forced these people into our simulation. But some of these scenarios you've got me writing—I just don't know—"

"Aren't your guys up to some real acting?"

Danny grew affronted. "The Derridadaists can handle anything you throw at them!"

Lisa smiled in the manner of a gingerbread-house-ensconced witch with two children safely baking in her oven and a third chowing down out in the fattening pen. "Good, good, because I plan to ride this pony to the bank just as fast and hard as I ride you."

"I think you'd better have a look at the deck chairs, Lisa."

Jake Pasha stood tentatively at the door to Lisa's office. His boss had one phone pinched between her neck and her bunched shoulder, and held another in her right hand while she guided a mouse with her left.

Lisa wrapped up her conversations with both callers and toggled shut several windows before turning to Jake.

"This had better be important."

"I think it is."

Jake made a beckoning motion, and a worker in paint-splattered overalls carried in an old-fashioned wood-and-canvas deckchair. A legend on its side proclaimed it PROPERTY OF WHYTE STAR LINES TITANICK.

"They're all like this," Jake complained.

Surprisingly, Lisa did not explode, but remained serene. "Oh, I guess

I didn't get around to telling you. As I might have predicted, the bastards at TimWarDisVia wouldn't lease the rights to use the real name, so I figured we'd get around them this way. They've still got a hair the size of a hawser up their asses since we pulled this end run around their pathetic Sadness Fences. Have you seen the price of *their* stock lately? Their shareholders have to use a ladder to kiss a slug's ass. And I hear they're switching to *chain link* to cut costs."

"But won't our customers complain about the inaccuracy?"

"Duh! Our *customers*, Jake, will be a bunch of romantic *idiots* just minutes away from a watery *grave*. If it makes you any happier, we'll just hit them with the hemlock cocktail before they even board our tub, instead of after. They'll be too woozy to recognize their own faces in a mirror, never mind spotting a frigging historical fuckup. Just make sure you round up enough dockside wheelchairs, okay? And don't forget the GPS transponders for the clients. We don't want to lose any of the stiffs once the ship goes down."

"What about the relatives, though? Won't they see the error in their souvenir videos and complain?"

"Those fucking vultures! Most of them are so happy to see their enfeebled parents and aunts and uncles going out in a blaze of glory that they couldn't care less about historical accuracy. Remember, Jake—we're selling fantasy here, not something like a TV docudrama that has to adhere to some rigorous standards."

Jake dismissed the worker with the historically dubious deck chair and closed the door before speaking further.

"Is Danny still talking about pulling out?"

Lisa frowned. "Not for the past couple of days. But I can still sense he's not exactly a happy camper."

"Did you apologize to him about Bonnie and Clyde?"

"Yes, Dear Abby, I apologized—even though it wasn't my fucking fault! Who knew that both our suicides were junkies and that the juice would take longer to work on their dope-tolerant bodies? So a blood-gushing Bonnie and Clyde kept staggering around yelling 'Ouch!' after seeming to be hit by about a million bullets and ruined his precious script! God, he is *such* a fucking perfectionist!"

"He's an artist," said Jake.

"My Christ, what do I hear? Are you hot for him now? I wish I'd never told you about his fucking massive cock."

Jake quelled his irritation. "That's not it at all. I just sympathize with his ambitions."

Lisa stood up huffily. "All right. If it'll make you feel any better, I'll pay Danny a visit right now, in the middle of my busy workday, just to show I'm a caring kind of bitch."

"He *is* essential to our continued success, after all."

"Don't kid yourself, sweetie. The only essential one is me."

"It's just no use, Carol. I can't convince myself that helping people die melodramatically is art."

Perched on the corner of Danny's desk like a concupiscent Kewpie, Carol frowned with earnest empathy. "But Danny, what we're doing—it's so, it's so—conceptual!"

Danny dismissed this palliative jargon. "Oh, sure, that's what I've kept telling myself, for three long months. We were pushing the envelope on performance art, subverting cultural expectations, jamming the news machine, highlighting the hypocrisy of the funeral industry. Lord knows, I've tried a dozen formulations of the same excuse. But it all rings hollow to me. I just can't continue with this Fantasy Exit crap anymore. I thought I could sell out, but I was wrong."

"But, Danny, for the first time in years, we all have regular work in our chosen artistic field. And we're making good money, too."

"That was never what the Derridadaists stood for, Carol! We could have all gone into commercials, for Christ's sake, if steady employment was all we cared about. No, I founded our troupe in order to perform cutting-edge, avant-garde theater. And now we're merely enacting the most banal scenarios, clichéd skits out of Hollywood's musty vaults, predigested for suicidal Philistines. And this latest one is the final straw. The *Titanic*! If only that damn remake hadn't come out last year. DiCaprio was bad enough in his day, but that little Skywalker adolescent—" Danny shivered and mimed nausea. "Uuurrggg!"

Carol seemed ready to cry. "It's me, isn't it? My performances have sucked! Just say it, Danny, I can take it."

Danny stood to pat Carol's shoulder. "No, no, you've been great."

Carol began to sniffle. "Even when I fell off my horse during the Jesse James bit?"

"Sure. We just cut away from you."

"How about when I knocked down all those buildings before you could even start the San Francisco earthquake?"

"They were going to go down sooner or later, Carol."

"And that accident during the Great Chicago Fire—?"

"Insurance covered everything, Carol."

Carol squealed and hurled herself into Danny's arms. "Oh, you're just the best director anyone could ever ask for!"

Danny gently disentangled Carol's limbs from his and began to pace the office. "How to tell Lisa, though? That's what stops me. She has such a temper. I know she loves me—at least I'm pretty sure she does—but the business comes first with her. Oh, Carol, what can I do?"

"Well, I know one thing that generally helps in such situations."

"And what might that be?"

"A boob job."

"Carol, no, please, stop right now. Button yourself right back up."

"I know what I'm doing, Danny. You've been so good to me, and now it's my turn to help you. Just sit down—there, that's better. Now let me get this zipper and this snap and this clasp— No, don't move, I've got plenty of room to kneel right here. There, doesn't that feel good? Oh, I've never seen one that was long enough to pop right out of the top of the groove like that!"

"Oh! Lisa!"

"I don't mind, Danny, you can call me by her name if it helps."

"No! She's right here!"

From the doorway, Lisa said, "She's already cast, you bastard. And you're supposed to use the fucking couch I bought you!"

"Hit that glacier with more Windex!"

Techies on movable scaffolds, looking like bugs on a windshield, responded to the bullhorned instructions by assidulously polishing the floating Perspex glacier anchored now in the harbor. On the dock, a cavalcade of wheelchairs held the semi-stupefied, terminally ill paying customers slated to go down with the fabled luxury liner (an old tugboat with a scaled-down prow and bridge attached that reproduced the famous vessel's foreparts). A host of lesser craft held camera and retrieval crews. Near a warehouse, a standard Weeping Wall and appurtenances awaited the end of the maritime disaster reenactment. Over the whole scene, the January sun shed a frosty light.

Lisa moved busily among the WW&FE employees, issuing orders. To the captain of the tug, she reminded, "Remember, get out past the twelve-mile limit before you sink her." Finally, she turned to her husband.

Danny stood contritely by, his heart and mind obviously elsewhere. But when Lisa rounded on him, he snapped to attention.

"Leese, before I set out on this final charade, I just want to say how grateful I am that you're allowing me to bow out of this whole enterprise. I just couldn't swallow any more."

"I'm sure that's what your girlfriend was just about to say when I barged in."

"Leese, please! I explained all about that."

Lisa laughed, and it sounded like ice floes clinking together. "Oh, I'm not angry anymore. I just couldn't resist a little dig. What a rack! She makes me look like Olive Oyl. Tell me—did it feel like getting your dick stuck in the sofa cushions?"

Danny made to turn away, but Lisa stopped him. "Okay, I went over the line there. Sorry. But look—I had something made up for you just to show I still care."

Lisa accepted from the hovering Jake a modern orange life vest.

"This is a special vest, Danny, just for you. Look, it's even got your name on it."

"Why, thanks, Leese."

"Let's see how it fits you."

"Gee, do I have to put it on now?"

"Yes, you have to put it on now."

Danny donned the vest, and Lisa snugged the straps tight, like a conscientious mother adjusting her toddler for kindergarten.

"It's very heavy. What's in it? Lead?"

"Not exactly. Oh, look—they're loading the wheelchairs now. You'd better get on board."

Danny aimed a kiss at Lisa's lips, but she offered only her cheek. Danny walked away. At the top of the gangplank, he turned and waved, bulky in his life-saving gear.

Within minutes the whole armada was steaming out to sea, including the iceberg, now stripped of its scaffolding and under tow by a second tug.

When the fleet disappeared from sight, Lisa said, "Well, that's that."

And then she walked slowly to the Weeping Wall, selected a hot pink teddy bear, and hung it tenderly, her eyes dry as teddy's buttons.

Greg Benford's resume, outside of writing, *is impressive enough for* two *physics professors (he teaches at UC Irvine and is a fellow at Cambridge University, and an adviser to the White House Council on Space Policy and NASA, to give a partial list) but if you add in his prodigious writing achievements, such as two Nebulas, the John W. Campbell Award, among others, his nineteen novels (including the classic* Timescape*), numerous short stories as well as various nonfiction work—well, the way I add it up, there must be at least three of him.*

Thank heaven one of him was around when I asked for a story for Redshift*; you'll note how it slyly incorporates his Cambridge University experience.*

Anomalies

Gregory Benford

✳

It was not lost upon the Astronomer Royal that the greatest scientific discovery of all time was made by a carpenter and amateur astronomer from the neighboring cathedral town of Ely. Not by a Cambridge man.

Geoffrey Carlisle had a plain directness that apparently came from his profession, a custom cabinet maker. It had enabled him to get past the practiced deflection skills of the receptionist at the Institute for Astronomy, through the assistant director's patented brush-off, and into the Astronomer Royal's corner office.

Running this gauntlet took until early afternoon, as the sun broke through a shroud of soft rain. Geoffrey wasted no time. He dropped a celestial coordinate map on the Astronomer Royal's mahogany desk, hand amended, and said, "The moon's off by better'n a degree."

"You measured carefully, I am sure."

The Astronomer Royal had found that the occasional crank did make it through the institute's screen, and in confronting them it was best to go straight to the data. Treat them like fellow members of the profession and they softened. Indeed, astronomy was the only remaining science that profited from the work of amateurs. They discovered the new comets, found wandering asteroids, noticed new novae, and generally patrolled what the professionals referred to as local astronomy—anything that could be seen in the night sky with a telescope smaller than a building.

That Geoffrey had gotten past the scrutiny of the others meant this might conceivably be real. "Very well, let us have a look." The Astronomer Royal had lunched at his desk and so could not use a date in his college as a dodge. Besides, this was crazy enough to perhaps generate an amusing story.

An hour later he had abandoned the story-generating idea. A conference with the librarian, who knew the heavens like his own palm, made it clear that Geoffrey had done all the basic work correctly. He had photos and careful, carpenter-sure data, all showing that, indeed, last night after around eleven o'clock the moon was well ahead of its orbital position.

"No possibility of systematic error here?" the librarian politely asked the tall, sinewy Geoffrey.

"Check 'em yerself. I was kinda hopin' you fellows would have an explanation, is all."

The moon was not up, so the Astronomer Royal sent a quick e-mail to Hawaii. They thought he was joking, but then took a quick look and came back, rattled. A team there got right on it and confirmed. Once alerted, other observatories in Japan and Australia chimed in.

"It's out of position by several of its own diameters," the Astronomer Royal mused. "Ahead of its orbit, exactly on track."

The librarian commented precisely, "The tides are off prediction as well, exactly as required by this new position. They shifted suddenly, reports say."

"I don't see how this can happen," Geoffrey said quietly.

"Nor I," the Astronomer Royal said. He was known for his understatement, which could masquerade as modesty, but here he could think of no way to underplay such a result.

"Somebody else's bound to notice, I'd say," Geoffrey said, folding his cap in his hands.

"Indeed," the Astronomer Royal suspected some subtlety had slipped by him.

"Point is, sir, I want to be sure I get the credit for the discovery."

"Oh, of course you shall." All amateurs ever got for their labors was their name attached to a comet or asteroid, but this was quite different. "Best we get on to the IAU, ah, the International Astronomical Union," the Astronomer Royal said, his mind whirling. "There's a procedure for alerting all interested observers. Establish credit, as well."

Geoffrey waved this away. "Me, I'm just a five-inch 'scope man. Don't care about much beyond the priority, sir. I mean, it's over to you fellows. What I want to know is, what's it mean?"

Soon enough, as the evening news blared and the moon lifted above the European horizons again, that plaintive question sounded all about. One did not have to be a specialist to see that something major was afoot.

"It all checks," the Astronomer Royal said before a forest of cameras and microphones. "The tides being off true has been noted by the naval authorities round the world, as well. Somehow, in the early hours of last evening, Greenwich time, our moon accelerated in its orbit. Now it is proceeding at its normal speed, however."

"Any danger to us?" one of the incisive, investigative types asked.

"None I can see," the Astronomer Royal deflected this mildly. "No panic headlines needed."

"What caused it?" a woman's voice called from the media thicket.

"We can see no object nearby, no apparent agency," the Astronomer Royal admitted.

"Using what?"

"We are scanning the region on all wavelengths, from radio to gamma rays." An extravagant waste, very probably, but the Astronomer Royal knew the price of not appearing properly concerned. Hand-wringing was called for at all stages.

"Has this happened before?" a voice sharply asked. "Maybe we just weren't told?"

"There are no records of any such event," the Astronomer Royal said. "Of course, a thousand years ago, who would have noticed? The supernova that left us the Crab nebula went unreported in Europe, though not in China, though it was plainly visible here."

"What do you think, Mr. Carlisle?" a reporter probed. "As a non-specialist?"

Geoffrey had hung back at the press conference, which the crowds had forced the Institute to hold on the lush green lawn outside the old Observatory Building. "I was just the first to notice it," he said. "That far off, pretty damned hard not to."

The media mavens liked this and coaxed him further. "Well, I dunno about any new force needed to explain it. Seems to me, might as well say its supernatural, when you don't know anything."

This the crowd loved. SUPER AMATEUR SAYS MOON IS SUPERNATURAL soon appeared on a tabloid. They made a hero of Geoffrey. "AS OBVIOUS AS YOUR FACE" SAYS GEOFF. The London *Times* ran a full-page reproduction of his log book, from which he and the Astronomer Royal had worked out that the acceleration had to have happened in a narrow window around ten P.M., since no observer to the east had noticed any oddity before that.

Most of Europe had been clouded over that night anyway, so Geoffrey was among the first who could have gotten a clear view after what the newspapers promptly termed the "Anomaly," as in ANOMALY MAN STUNS ASTROS.

Of the several thousand working astronomers in the world, few concerned themselves with "local" events, especially not with anything the eye could make out. But now hundreds threw themselves upon the Anomaly and, coordinated out of Cambridge by the Astronomer Royal, swiftly outlined its aspects. So came the second discovery.

In a circle around where the moon had been, about two degrees wide, the stars were wrong. Their positions had jiggled randomly, as though irregularly refracted by some vast, unseen lens.

Modern astronomy is a hot competition between the quick and the dead—who soon become the untenured.

Five of the particularly quick discovered this Second Anomaly. They had only to search all ongoing observing campaigns and find any that chanced to be looking at that portion of the sky the night before. The media, now in full bay, headlined their comparison photos. Utterly obscure dots of light became famous when blink-comparisons showed them jumping a finger's width in the night sky, within an hour of the ten P.M. Anomaly Moment.

"Does this check with your observations?" a firm-jawed commentator had demanded of Geoffrey at a hastily called meeting one day later, in the auditorium at the Institute for Astronomy. They called upon him first, always—he served as an anchor amid the swift currents of astronomical detail.

Hooting from the traffic jam on Madingley Road nearby nearly drowned out Geoffrey's plaintive, "I dunno. I'm a planetary man, myself."

By this time even the nightly news broadcasts had caught on to the fact that having a patch of sky behave badly implied something of a wrenching mystery. And no astronomer, however bold, stepped forward with an explanation. An old joke with not a little truth in it—that a theorist could explain the outcome of any experiment, as long as he knew it in advance—rang true, and got repeated. The chattering class ran rife with speculation.

But there was still nothing unusual visible there. Days of intense observation in all frequencies yielded nothing.

Meanwhile the moon glided on in its ethereal ellipse, following precisely the equations first written down by Newton, only a mile from where the Astronomer Royal now sat, vexed, with Geoffey. "A don at Jesus College called, fellow I know," the Astronomer Royal said. "He wants to see us both."

Geoffrey frowned. "Me? I've been out of my depth from the start."

"He seems to have an idea, however. A testable one, he says."

They had to take special measures to escape the media hounds. The institute enjoys broad lawns and ample shrubbery, now being trampled by the crowds. Taking a car would guarantee being followed. The Astronomer Royal had chosen his offices here, rather than in his college, out of a desire to escape the busyness of the central town. Now he found himself trapped. Geoffrey had the solution. The institute kept bicycles for visitors, and upon two of these the men took a narrow, tree-lined path out the back of the institute, toward town. Slipping down the cobbled streets between ancient, elegant college buildings, they went ignored by students and shoppers alike. Jesus College was a famously well-appointed college along the Cam River, approachable across its ample playing fields. The Astronomer Royal felt rather absurd to be pedaling like an undergraduate, but the exercise helped clear his head. When they arrived at the rooms of Professor Wright, holder of the Wittgenstein Chair, he was grateful for tea and small sandwiches with the crusts cut off, one of his favorites.

Wright was a post-postmodern philosopher, reedy and intense. He explained in a compact, energetic way that in some sense, the modern view was that reality could be profitably regarded as a computation.

Geoffrey bridled at this straightaway, scowling with his heavy eyebrows. "It's real, not a bunch of arithmetic."

Wright pointedly ignored him, turning to the Astronomer Royal. "Martin, surely you would agree with the view that when you fellows search for a Theory of Everything, you are pursuing a belief that there is an abbreviated way to express the logic of the universe, one that can be written down by human beings?"

"Of course," the Astronomer Royal admitted uncomfortably, but then said out of loyalty to Geoffrey, "All the same, I do not subscribe to the belief that reality can profitably be seen as some kind of cellular automata, carrying out a program."

Wright smiled without mirth. "One might say you are revolted not by the notion that the universe is a computer, but by the evident fact that someone else is using it."

"You gents have got way beyond me," Geoffrey said.

"The idea is, how do physical laws act themselves out?" Wright asked in his lecturer voice. "Of course, atoms do not know their own differential equations." A polite chuckle. "But to find where the moon should be in the next instant, in some fashion the universe must calculate where it must go. We can do that, thanks to Newton."

The Astronomer Royal saw that Wright was humoring Geoffrey with this simplification, and suspected that it would not go down well. To hurry Wright along he said, "To make it happen, to move the moon—"

"Right, that we do not know. Not a clue. How to breathe fire into the equations, as that Hawking fellow put it—"

"But look, nature doesn't know maths," Geoffrey said adamantly. "No more than I do."

"But something must, you see," Professor Wright said earnestly, offering them another plate of the little cut sandwiches and deftly opening a bottle of sherry. "Of course, I am using our human way of formulating this, the problem of natural order. The world is usefully described by mathematics, so in our sense the world must have some mathematics embedded in it."

"God's a bloody mathematician?" Geoffrey scowled.

The Astronomer Royal leaned forward over the antique oak table. "Merely an expression."

"Only way the stars could get out of whack," Geoffrey said, glancing back and forth between the experts, "is if whatever caused it came from there, I'd say."

"Quite right." The Astronomer Royal pursed his lips. "Unless the speed of light has gone off, as well, no signal could have rearranged the stars straight after doing the moon."

"So we're at the tail end of something from out there, far away," Geoffrey observed.

"A long, thin disturbance propagating from distant stars. A very tight beam of . . . well, error. But from what?" The Astronomer Royal had gotten little sleep since Geoffrey's appearance, and showed it.

"The circle of distorted stars," Professor Wright said slowly, "remains where it was, correct?"

The Astronomer Royal nodded. "We've not announced it, but anyone with a cheap telescope—sorry, Geoffrey, not you, of course—can see the moon's left the disturbance behind, as it follows its orbit."

Wright said, "Confirming Geoffrey's notion that the disturbance is a long, thin line of—well, I should call it an error."

"Is that what you meant by a checkable idea?" the Astronomer Royal asked irritably.

"Not quite. Though that the two regions of error are now separating, as the moon advances, is consistent with a disturbance traveling from the stars to us. That is a first requirement, in my view."

"Your view of what?" Geoffrey finally gave up handling his small sherry glass and set it down with a decisive rattle.

"Let me put my philosophy clearly," Wright said. "If the universe is an ongoing calculation, then computational theory proves that it cannot be perfect. No such system can be free of a bug or two, as the programmers put it."

Into an uncomfortable silence Geoffrey finally inserted, "Then the moon's being ahead, the stars—it's all a mistake?"

Wright smiled tightly. "Precisely. One of immense scale, moving at the speed of light."

Geoffrey's face scrunched into a mask of perplexity. "And it just—jumped?"

"Our moon hopped forward a bit too far in the universal computation, just as a program advances in little leaps." Wright smiled as though this were an entirely natural idea.

Another silence. The Astronomer Royal said sourly, "That's mere philosophy, not physics."

"Ah!" Wright pounced. "But any universe that is a sort of analog computer must, like any decent digital one, have an error-checking program. Makes no sense otherwise."

"Why?" Geoffrey was visibly confused, a craftsman out of his depth.

"Any good program, whether it is doing accounts in a bank, or carrying forward the laws of the universe, must be able to correct itself." Professor Wright sat back triumphantly and swallowed a Jesus College sandwich, smacking his lips.

The Astronomer Royal said, "So you predict—?"

"That both the moon and the stars shall snap back, get themselves right—and at the same time, as the correction arrives here at the speed of light."

"Nonsense," the Astronomer Royal said.

"A prediction," Professor Wright said sternly. "My philosophy stands upon it."

The Astronomer Royal snorted, letting his fatigue get to him. Geoffrey looked puzzled and asked a question that would later haunt them.

Professor Wright did not have long to wait.

To his credit, he did not enter the media fray with his prediction. However, he did unwisely air his views at High Table, after a particularly fine bottle of claret brought forward by the oldest member of the college. Only a generation or two earlier, such a conversation among the Fellows would have been secure. Not so now. A junior Fellow in political studies proved to be on a retainer from the *Times*, and scarcely a day passed before Wright's conjecture was known in New Delhi and Tokyo.

The furor following from that had barely subsided when the Astronomer Royal received a telephone call from the Max Planck Institute. They excitedly reported that the moon, now under continuous observation, had shifted instantly to the position it should have, had its orbit never been perturbed.

So, too, did the stars in the warped circle return to their rightful places. Once more, all was right with the world. Even so, it was a world that could never again be the same.

Professor Wright was not smug. He received the news from the Astronomer Royal, who had brought along Geoffrey to Jesus College, a refuge now from the institute. "Nothing, really, but common sense." He waved away their congratulations.

Geoffrey sat, visibly uneasily, through some talk about how to handle all this in the voracious media glare. Philosophers are not accustomed to much attention until well after they are dead. But as discussion ebbed Geoffrey repeated his probing question of days before: "What sort of universe has mistakes in it?"

Professor Wright said kindly, "An information-ordered one. Think of everything that happens—including us talking here, I suppose—as a kind of analog program acting out. Discovering itself in its own development. Manifesting."

Geoffrey persisted, "But who's the programmer of this computer?"

"Questions of first cause are really not germane," Wright said, drawing himself up.

"Which means that he cannot say," the Astronomer Royal allowed himself.

Wright stroked his chin at this and eyed the others before venturing, "In light of the name of this college, and you, Geoffrey, being a humble bearer of the message that began all this . . ."

"Oh, no," the Astronomer Royal said fiercely, "next you'll point out that Geoffrey's a carpenter."

They all laughed, though uneasily.

But as the Astronomer Royal and Geoffrey left the venerable grounds, Geoffrey said moodily, "Y'know, I'm a cabinet maker."

"Uh, yes?"

"We aren't bloody carpenters at all," Geoffrey said angrily. "We're craftsmen."

The distinction was lost upon the Royal Astronomer, but then, much else was, these days.

The Japanese had very fast images of the moon's return to its proper place, taken from their geosynchronous satellite. The transition did indeed proceed at very nearly the speed of light, taking a slight fraction of a second to jerk back to exactly where it should have been. Not the original place where the disturbance occurred, but to its rightful spot along the smooth ellipse. The immense force needed to do this went unexplained, of course, except by Professor Wright's Computational Principle.

To everyone's surprise, it was not a member of the now quite raucous press who made the first telling gibe at Wright, but Geoffrey. "I can't follow, sir, why we can still remember when the moon was in the wrong place."

"What?" Wright looked startled, almost spilling some of the celebratory tea the three were enjoying. Or rather, that Wright was conspicuously relishing, while the Astronomer Royal gave a convincing impression of a man in a good mood.

"Y'see, if the error's all straightened out, why don't our memories of it get fixed, too?"

The two learned men froze.

"We're part of the physical universe," the Astronomer Royal said wonderingly, "so why not, eh?"

Wright's expression confessed his consternation. "That we haven't been, well, edited . . ."

"Kinda means we're not the same as the moon, right?"

Begrudgingly, Wright nodded. "So perhaps the, ah, 'mind' that is carrying out the universe's computation cannot interfere with our—other—minds."

"And why's that?" the Astronomer Royal a little too obviously enjoyed saying.

"I haven't the slightest."

Light does not always travel at the same blistering speed. Only in a vacuum does it have its maximum velocity.

Light emitted at the center of the sun, for example—which is a million times denser than lead—finds itself absorbed by the close-packed ionized atoms there, held for a tiny sliver of a second, and then released. It travels an infinitesimal distance, then is captured by yet another hot ion of the plasma, and the process repeats. The radiation random-walks its way out to the solar surface. In all, the passage from the core takes many thousands of years. Once free, the photon reaches Earth in a few minutes.

Radiation from zones nearer the sun's fiery surface takes less time because the plasma there is far less dense. That was why a full three months elapsed before anyone paid attention to a detail the astronomers had noticed early on and then neglected.

The "cone of chaos" (as it was now commonly called) that had lanced in from the distant stars and deflected the moon had gone on and intersected the sun at a grazing angle. It had luckily missed Earth, but that was the end of the luck.

On an otherwise unremarkable morning, Geoffrey rose to begin work on a new pine cabinet. He was glad to be out of the media glare, though still troubled by the issues raised by his discovery. Professor Wright had made no progress in answering Geoffrey's persistent questions. The Astronomer Royal was busying himself with a Royal commission appointed to investigate the whole affair, though no one expected a commission to actually produce an idea. Geoffrey's hope—that they could "find out more by measuring," seemed to be at a dead end.

On that fateful morning, out his bedroom window, Geoffrey saw a strange sun. Its lumpy shape he quickly studied by viewing it through his telescope with a dark glass clamped in place. He knew of the arches that occasionally rose from the corona, vast galleries of magnetic field lines bound to the plasma like bunches of wire under tension. Sprouting from the sun at a dozen spots stood twisted parodies of this, snaking in immense weaves of incandescence.

He called his wife to see. Already voices in the cobbled street below were murmuring in alarm. Hanging above the open marsh lands around the ancient cathedral city of Ely was a ruby sun, its grand purple arches swelling like blisters from the troubled rim.

His wife's voice trembled. "What's it mean?"

"I'm afraid to ask."

"I thought everything got put back right."

"Must be more complicated, somehow."

"Or a judgment." In his wife's severe frown he saw an eternal human impulse, to read meaning into the physical world—and a moral message as well.

He thought of the swirl of atoms in the sun, all moving along their hammering trajectories, immensely complicated. The spike of error must have moved them all, and the later spike of correction could not, somehow, undo the damage. Erasing such detail must be impossible. So even the mechanism that drove the universal computation had its limits. Whatever you called it, Geoffrey mused, the agency that made order also made error—and could not cover its tracks completely.

"Wonder what it means?" he whispered.

The line of error had done its work. Plumes rose like angry necklaces from the blazing rim of the star whose fate governed all intelligence within the solar system.

Thus began a time marked not only by vast disaster, but by the founding of a wholly new science. Only later, once studies were restored at Cambridge University, and Jesus College was rebuilt in a period of relative calm, did this new science and philosophy—for now the two were always linked—acquire a name: the field of empirical theology.

Kit Reed, whose writing is bright and sharp as a razor, should be declared a national treasure. Over the years her stories have appeared in publications ranging from F&SF, The Yale Review, Omni, Asimov's SF *magazine to* The Norton Anthology of Contemporary Literature. *One of her short story collections is worth having for the title alone:* Other Stories and The Giant Baby.

She's also the author of numerous novels, including Captain Grownup *and* @expectations, *her most recent.*

Though "Captive Kong" is a Kit Reed story, we actually have someone else to thank for the ending. Kit writes, "Have you ever had a story you couldn't finish? I went nuts trying to find the ending for this one. Finally I threw up my hands and gave it to my friend Brian, who solved it in three pages—a first for me, and a happy collaboration."

Happy, indeed.

Captive Kong

Kit Reed
(with Brian Quinette)

Trevor is looking for backup. When he goes out he wants thirty guys at his back with gravity knives chinking, thirty guys swinging socks full of bolts to clear the way for him. Brass knuckles, maybe, that bulge that lets attackers know they are packing heat. Plus chains. There's nothing like the menacing *chink* of metal against leather-clad thighs to make your point for you. *What Mr. Trevor* means *is* . . .

In times like these you need extra muscle.

Times like these. It's not something you did. It's the way things are these days. You don't go out alone and expect to come back in one piece.

The skies are white all the time now; who's to say whether it's volcanic ash or human cremains or the glow of the unforeseeable? Streets liquefy and ruined cars tip into fresh crevasses. The water turns black as you wade into it; you marvel at the darting phosphorescence until your feet dissolve and you start screaming. Stars jolted out of their sockets dangle like blobs in a bad van Gogh painting, and a crazy can springs out of nowhere and rips off your face.

Loved ones vaporize, freeze, walk into the bleached sunset. Trevor lost his family to an Armageddon cult and his wife, Jane, to the leader; she tortures him with ecstatic e-mails. He lost his business to his brother Jake. If he'd had his thirty guys in place, he could have beaten Jake and hung on to the stuff marauders took out of his town house. He could have kept Jane—he knows it!

The water that comes out of the tap is a funny color.

Trevor's teeth have started lighting up at night, his hair's wild, and his underwear is sticking to him. Something big is coming. *If I can get through it*, he thinks, without knowing what *it* is, *I'll come out the other side and be OK. The trick is getting through it.*

He needs protection. Face it, he can't afford thirty guys. The guys aren't that hard to come by—universal unemployment!—but maintenance is a bitch. The cost of food and whiskey. Fresh leather. Fuel for their hogs or choppers, drugs of choice. Plus, if they turn on you . . .

In the end he settles for a three-hundred-pound gorilla.

Even that is not what you think.

Trevor has targeted a body builder with six-pack abs and biceps that make Trevor's arms look like kosher franks hung on a coat rack. He needs to move fast because for no apparent reason society is imploding.

Winds scour the streets, blowing in from a long way off; a cosmic storm is coming. You may not see it yet, but you hear it, and by the light of burning martyrs, you can feel it. The world was never meant to end with a whimper; the cosmic slot machine turns up not lemons but goose eggs, you bet something big is coming.

Nobody thought it would come so soon.

Go for it, man. Get what you can take. Or take what you can get. You'll get through this. You are Trevor and you are special.

Face it, we all secretly believe we are born special.

Nothing Sam Trevor has done so far comes close to proving this, but deep inside, he knows it. *Otherwise, why am I still here?* Good answer. Jane writes: "Adam has put me in charge of registration, do join us." In your dreams, baby. Samuel A. (for Articulate) Trevor is special, and the end is coming, and, yes—he is arming himself. If he can get her in the truck.

Right, her. The guys at the gym are all too big for him. His three-hundred-pound gorilla is a woman.

Her name is Roxy.

He finds her pressing 350. The woman is offensively buff, great cords of sinew lace the flesh between her breasts. Her quads are tremendous. Mental note: Keep her in shape. Top-of-the-line gym equipment. Climbing wall. Universal trainer.

He waits until she's at full extension. "Lady, I admire your form."

Roxy gentles the weights into the cradle and looks up. "What do you want from me?" Her face is surprisingly young. Nineteen, he thinks. Not pretty, not so's you'd notice, but in times like these even a gorilla looks good to you.

"I need you is all."

"Perv?" Her pupils are ringed in white. "If you are, I'll smash your face in."

"Whatever you're thinking, no. No." He tries a smile. "To be perfectly frank, I need your help. God knows everybody needs a little help these days. A little something extra." He clears his throat, to weight the next words. Ahem. This is significant. Portentous. "In times like these."

She presses 360. "You've got to be one sick fuck," she says while in the fully extended position.

"You're looking a little shaky," he says. "Let me spot you. So. Ma'am, have you noticed the sky lately? Have you heard the wind? Something big is coming."

"Nobody ever called me ma'am before."

"The dirt has started to glow. Aren't you scared?"

"Leave me alone."

"We have to do something."

"What do you mean *we*, white man?"

He whispers, so she will pay attention. "Ticktickticktick. Time is running out. Together, we might make it."

"Stop that." Walleyed glare. "I'm working up to four hundred."

At her signal, he adds two ten-pound weights. "Come on, Roxy. You can't play like nothing's happening."

"How do you know my name?"

Diamond nose stud. Likes jewelry. Noted. "Roxy, Roxy. We need each other."

She is testing the weights. "Why would I do anything for you?

"Because you're in my power?"

"Not so's you'd notice." Rings, too. Note: Really likes jewelry.

She is focused on the lift to come. Great veins bulge. "Spot me?"

"Now?"

"Now."

"Fine," he says helpfully. Trevor pretends to spot her when what he is really spotting is the right vein. He drives the needle in. It's a wonderful drug. It paralyzes the mind but keeps the body mobile. How else would he get a woman this size out of the gym and into the back of the van he rented to take his gorilla in? She went from granite to pliant in seconds; he got past the desk by putting a gym bag over her head. Whispers, "What do you have to go home to anyway? The world is ending." He feels only a little guilty.

It's scary out, but he isn't going to have to face it alone. Just having her in the back of the truck makes him feel better.

* * *

That the sky is a bizarre new shade of violet is only slightly unnerving. Red fingers creep over the skyline—lava, surging out of the Baltimore Harbor Tunnel? Naw, Trevor thinks, and drives on even though he hears a sizzle, as of fish frying in the drained harbor. In the back of the van his new gorilla alternately thrashes and dozes. Listen, it's not as if she has a *life* out there.

The house Trevor has fixed up for the captive gorilla looks just like all the others in that block: a brick Baltimore row house in a depressed neighborhood—white shutters, depressingly white front stoop with urban litter washing up against it like trash in a flood. It's just what he wanted. A neighborhood where people like him don't come. End house, which means ingress from the alley, cellar door, which he needs to unload, no neighbors. He has backed the truck up to the cellar. He rolls her down the steps and into the lion cage he salvaged from a ruined circus. For a long time, she doesn't stir. Then she does. Howling, she hurls herself at the bars; her anger shakes the house. "What. What? What!"

Trevor hands her a Coke. "Drink this. You'll feel better." At a safe distance, he extends tongs with his offering.

"Where are we?" She eyes the tongs. The object dangling from them glitters. "What are those?"

"Place I fixed for you. These are my mother's diamonds."

"You can't keep me locked up like this." She stops thrashing and says matter-of-factly, "Look at you, five seven. You can't keep me at all."

Couldn't keep Jane or the kids. He gulps. "I got you here."

"So what am I supposed to do, fuck you? Beat up on people?"

Then the weight of all the years that have been and the years that may never come staggers Trevor, and he cries, "You're supposed to *help me*."

"Help you what? Get women? Money? Food? If I kill whoever for you, will you let me go?"

Kill Jane? Never. Cult leader Adam? Maybe. Jake? He'd like that, but right now this is a holding action because he has no idea what is coming. "You never know what you need until you need it," Trevor says. The marvel is that he's come this far on instinct, and the rest? Wing it. "Too soon to tell what I need."

"This isn't the old Adam and Eve thing, I hope."

Hair in greased coils. That massive skull, the corded body. Think Hercules carved in lard, but a woman. "I don't think so."

Roxy gauges her situation: the room, the cage—no bending those bars even if you do press four hundred. She settles on her pumped haunches. "I'll need equipment."

He thrusts the tongs into the cage, proffering. It's his late mother's diamond choker. "Everything you need is on order."

Scowling, she fastens it around her bicep. "I've seen better." It is an uneasy accommodation, but it is an accommodation. From here on out it won't matter that Jane is gone or that the corporation has collapsed and the fabric of civilization is shredding. Just let them try to break in and take his money, food, vandalize his secret thoughts or steal the silver. Nobody gets past Roxy. *I have a gorilla, OK?*

"I miss you," Jane writes. "Adam is seeing somebody new."

What do I care? I have a gorilla.

They get through the days, however. Nights are harder. In times like these television is interrupted, so there's no telling whether it's ten or eleven or closer to two A.M. The numbers on all your digital products are clicking backwards. Everything demagnetized while you weren't looking. *You're on your own*, the wind says. *Alone, just the way you were at the beginning*. Not Trevor. He has his gorilla. Perhaps because of the riots and mass murders outside, she's quit trying to kill him. She gets into the captivity thing. Sits with him for public access TV but slouches downstairs to sleep in the cage. *For protection*, she says. Protection against him? Has he kidnapped a three-hundred-pound virgin? Hard to know. Athena has nothing on Roxy. Step aside, Amazon queen. Take a backseat, Wonder Woman. Now that she has his mother's opera-length pearls twined around her neck and now that his grandmother's diamond earrings hang like dollhouse chandeliers from her wide nostrils, she's in his power, right? He buys her clothes. He cooks wonderful meals for her out of the supermarket stockpile in the subcellar. Keeps her happy until he needs her.

Jane writes, *Who needs you, anyway?*

One day Roxy smiles. "Meat loaf. Again. My favorite."

In times like these, the silliest things make you feel better.

Still, there is the look he catches when Roxy doesn't know he's watching; the whites of her eyes gleam in the half light from the TV, and Trevor can't know. Is his gorilla fixing to die for him, or does she want to kill him?

How did it get so important to make her like him?

That's one motive for taking her outside. Trial run. Make her happy because in times like these, even a gorilla starts looking good to you. The other? It's time to show her to the people. Trevor feels safer with

Roxy thudding behind, regardless of her motives. Hard to know if it's a good or a bad thing that the streets are deserted. Every player wants an audience. Not clear if that's blood running in the gutters or the product of his hyped imagination. Roxy pads on, sniffing the air. "Talk about creepy. Hold up." She spins him around.

"Stop that! Ow! Where are we going?"

"The gym," she says, dragging him. "They need me at the gym."

It is in ruins. Leached skeletons lie upturned in the ashes like the rib cages of cattle in Death Valley. So much for Roxy's colleagues, those humongous guys.

"Too late." She grieves. "I came too late."

There is no talking about what happened. "It's OK," he tells her. "It is. Nobody could have helped them." He isn't feeling too good himself. It's unnerving, watching your gorilla cry.

A sob rips her throat. "I shoulda been here for them."

He grips her hand. Mental note: *Aunt Patricia's garnets, as soon as we get home.* He is running out of jewelry. "You hadda be here for me. It's how we are now. Everything we care about is gone."

("Don't bother coming back," he wrote Jane last night. "Even if you want to.")

"Yeah shit," Roxy says, leaving him to wonder if this excursion has been a mistake: the sound of her teeth, clipping off the words.

She is put to the test in the least likely place. At Trevor's front door. An ugly mob is massing in the street.

Somebody he knows. "You," he says. (Jane wrote last night: "You might as well know, it isn't Adam I left you for. It's Jake I love.") "Jake, what are you doing here?"

Jake scowls. "Like you were trying to forget you ever had a brother?"

"What happened, did you lose the business?"

"Everybody is losing everything," Jake snarls. There is a *chink, chink.* Thirty guys stand at Jake's back, slapping chains against their leather-covered thighs.

Oh, shit. "You stole my idea," Trevor says. *Just like everything else I ever had.* "What do you want now?"

"Whatever you have left," Jake says. "Who's the bitch?"

At Trevor's back, Roxy bristles.

"No! You don't get Roxy!"

"If she wasn't the only one left, I wouldn't touch her with a stick." Behind Jake, his thirty guys drool and rumble with lust. "But she is. C'mere, baby."

Roxy snaps Jake's neck and, like a terrier who never gets tired of killing rats, starts after the others. Twenty of the thirty guys head for safety. The last ten don't make it.

She rolls the twenty-ninth guy off of Trevor and gets him inside. He looks up into eyes that are neither white nor silver. "If you want my great-grandmother's emeralds, they're yours."

"Whatever," she says coldly, but—is her expression two degrees softer?

Emeralds. It's a cinch Jane won't want them. Interesting, when you get what you want it's never what you thought. What you really want is for your gorilla to like you.

The next challenge is mechanized. A savage inventor unleashes a new machine on Trevor's street. The thing cracks open houses and its master strips them of food and valuables. Some wit designed the robot monster to look like a combination of Rodan and Godzilla.

Roxy gets hurt in the encounter, but she trashes the thing. Microchips land in her hair like glits. Bolts roll everywhere.

"If I had anything left to give, I'd give it to you," Trevor tells her, and she almost smiles. (He did, in fact, send his great-grandmother's diamond clip to Jane with a note: "Sorry about your bereavement.") "If it makes any difference at all, I'm in love with you."

"Whatever," Roxy says, and goes in her cage and locks the door against him.

Meanwhile, every clock has frozen. The white skies are shredded by nonstop lightning. It should be comforting to know that the streets are empty now, but it isn't. Stay in, cover your head, and wait for it to be over, right? Wrong. No matter how well prepared you are, sooner or later, things break down: generator, alternate fuel supply. Personal arrangements. Computer. There is no mail coming in and no mailing out. Not anymore, so God only knows what Jane is up to or what will become of you. Even you, who overstocked, will run out of food. Sooner or later.

For the first time since Trevor brought her home, his captive gorilla speaks first. "We're running out of stuff."

"I know."

"We gotta go out there."

"Would you do that for me?"

"Damn straight."

He shudders and falls in step behind her. There's nothing left in the gutted supermarkets, the empty houses. They follow ancient signs to a forgotten treasure trove: prehistoric fallout shelter. Things to eat, not anything you'd want to put in your mouth, but edible.

And coming out, they run into an ordinary guy. A lot like Trevor. Timid, can't make it alone. Studying them, the stranger sizes up the situation. Their food, heaped in Trevor's ex-kid's wagon. "Swap you," the stranger says. Calls over his shoulder. "Come on out, baby."

Broken tiles shickle down as a gorgeous woman emerges. Amazing, how she can look the way she does in times like these. Slim and elegant. Beautiful. She gives Trevor a sultry smile. "Well?"

"A swap." Trevor asks cautiously, "As in, your girlfriend for my gorilla?"

Behind him, Roxy shudders.

The stranger cracks up laughing. "Hell, no—my girlfriend for that food you got!"

Beautiful. She is beautiful. Blindly, Trevor forgets that these aren't ordinary times. "Maybe we can work out a trade."

At his back Roxy snarls, but Trevor is too distracted to notice. The thing about bait is, it's got to look good to the fish you're after. Of course, the guy wasn't bona fide. In the end, he tries to stab Trevor, and Roxy has to kill both him and the woman, never mind that she was gorgeous.

Trevor tries to thank her, but his concentration is broken. He's hung up on the distance between what he should have had and what he has here. Then he sees Roxy's face. "I would never trade you off," he says. "You're irreplaceable."

"Fuck you." Another minute, and she'll yank his ears off.

"Can you ever forgive me?" He waits for an answer, but Roxy is done talking to him.

After that, nothing happens. It happens for a long time. It is terrible, waiting to hear from Jane. Roxy is sulking and won't talk to him. Nothing comes, no e-mails, no postcards. The carrier pigeons have all died, and Trevor suspects that one of them has a message for him tied to its dead claw. He searches the bodies of the pigeons he can find, but their bones have been picked clean by the starving, and they are carrying only magazine subscriptions and credit card offers.

It is terrible, watching Roxy pine. She quits working out.

He tries to motivate her. "What if someone comes?"

She is wearing all his family jewelry at once. "Not my problem."

"Come on, Rox, we were put here for a purpose. We survived for a reason." He can't stop trying. "What do you think it is?"

"That's for me to know and you to find out," she says grimly. The diamond necklace slips off her scrawny arm and falls into the straw. She kicks it out of the cage.

He winces. "What do you want from me?"

But she won't talk to him.

Awful, this is awful, but when all else fails, Trevor, at least, is ready. Gorilla in place, food stockpiled. He's OK, but he's not so sure about the gorilla.

For a while, phenomena abound. It's only a matter of time before the Four Horsemen come charging out of the sky unless he looks up one morning and sees the four evangelists with their heads blazing in the morning fog. Right now nothing is happening. Boredom is worse than the plague or fires and floods—when there's a riot, at least you have *stuff* to do. He sits in the dark watching tapes because the last television station belched snow onto his TV screen and blinked out of existence.

Then nothing happens. Nothing keeps happening. Every day is like every other day, with no promise that whatever Sam Trevor has prepared for so carefully—he captured someone!—is actually coming. Still, it's not as if they can go outside and resume normal life. Whatever that was. For no reason you can point to, the city's in ruins.

In her cage, Roxy crashes on her bunk and turns her face to the wall. Trevor takes over the exercise equipment. Works out on the Universal gym. He is busy all the time now. Excited and scared. He bangs away on the weights, blowing air like an industrial vacuum cleaner.

"That's not going to help you," Roxy says.

It's the first time she has spoken first.

Trevor thinks for a minute that she's taken to him, but her back is still turned, so there's no knowing. "It couldn't hurt." Hopeful, he chirps. "Spot me?"

There's a long silence, as if she's thinking about it. Then Trevor hears her snoring.

On Monday his hair starts to thin. It isn't falling out, it's just vanishing. By Friday he's bald. He's not alone in this. Everyone else is bald, too. For the few people still out lurching around, hats have come back into fashion. The hats last for only a few hours, since everyone has forgotten how to make them. He thinks about working out on the weights but then thinks, *Screw it.*

He is so depressed that he orders pizza. Inexplicably, you can still get pizza delivered to your door, even though everything else has gone to hell. After he pays he opens the box and sees that he can't recognize even one of the toppings. Shuddering, he offers it to Roxy.

She eats half of it before asking, "Want any?"

"No thanks. Hey, you have hair!"

"I've always had hair." She finishes the pizza.

He prays. It's hard to do when you don't know what you want and you can't see the face of the entity you're talking to. Deep in the basement, Roxy groans.

"Dammit," he yells, "if you're in love with me, why don't you just say so?"

He creeps down and looks in on her.

Where she was tough and fit when he got her, Roxy has gotten a little stringy. It's as though her muscles have lengthened, like a runner's. He wonders at the change. Roxy is either sick with love, he decides, or sick with waiting. It would help to know.

Trevor picks love.

He coughs, and she raises herself on one elbow to look at him.

"What's wrong with you?"

"Gorilla troubles. You wouldn't understand."

Daylight is now twenty-four hours long, but to compensate, nighttime also takes twenty-four hours. Sunrises take so long that everyone loses interest. The telephone cuts out in the middle of a solicitation, someone trying to get Trevor to change his long-distance phone company even though the last phone company is defunct. There will be no e-mails from Jane.

He sometimes checks anyway.

During one cloudless day, the windows melt.

Trevor can barely breathe. He doesn't know where all the air has gone, but it isn't where he needs it. Near his mouth. He crawls to the basement.

What's happening? He gasps. "Do you know what—what's happening?"

"Nope," Roxy says.

"The whole thing's gone to shit. What's happening to us?" Trevor is interrupted by horrible high-pitched screeching outside. Fire ants the size of sport utility vehicles are roaming the street, eating anything that isn't made of metal. Trevor unlocks the cage, *I have a gorilla, thank God.*

Roxy kills the entire hive in the time it takes him to make a milkshake. She returns to the cage and takes a nap. Later that night, in bed, he remembers that he forgot to lock the cage. He decides to screw it. He thinks, there's always the chance that she'll decide to come to me; when I least expect it she'll sneak upstairs . . .

Because things like disease and Armageddon happen to other people, never to us (for we are special), what really happens always comes as a surprise. A freak accident. A mistake!

Therefore Trevor wakes up one day with fear rising in his throat, the suffocating thought that this is his last day on earth.

He says, the way you do when you know it can't possibly be true, "This is my last day on earth." He's right.

He staggers to the front door and grapples it open. He looks outside and sees nothing.

No city. No streets. No newspaper on his front step. There is nothing to see except the dry wasteland that stretches in all directions. The dust at the end of the world? He doesn't know. When you are special, even at the end of the world you carry on. It's What One Does. Business as usual. Carry on, and destiny won't notice you. Hold your breath and clamp your elbows to your sides. Small gestures. Nothing to attract attention. Wait, and the fates will pass you by.

Roxy joins him in the living room, where he's eating, for all he knows, the last frozen lasagna on the sere, blasted planet.

"Roxy, thank God!"

"I'm hungry."

"Can you save me?" he asks.

"Not at this point."

"Why?"

"You're too weak. You think too much."

"I think too much?" Staggered, he considers it from all sides. "What does that mean? What do I think too much about?"

"Everything."

"Does thinking make me weak?"

She polishes off the lasagna. "See?"

"It doesn't make sense!"

She licks the lasagna wrapper. "My point," Roxy says.

Bemused, he looks at her. The open cage. The hook latch on the cellar door. "Why didn't you escape?" *She stayed because she loves me. She does!*

"This place was as good as any other."

"Don't you love me?"

He dies before she has to answer.

Roxy packs up food and water from the kitchen, a couple of steak knives, a plastic bucket, a blanket, and a string of pearls. She sets off toward the horizon, in no particular direction.

Whatever else happens, in this new world, the gorilla always survives.

Bob Vardeman has done it all in science fiction and out of it—he's also written westerns, fantasies, and just about anything else you can think of, including original Star Trek *novelizations and, most recently,* Hell Heart (Vor #5). *He's particularly adept at melding himself into series books, but when he turns to something purely of his own invention, watch out.*

"Feedback" is a weird one—it's about sex (which means that you've already stopped reading this headnote and started in on the tale that follows) but it's also about much more.

Feedback

Robert E. Vardeman

*

Visions of half-eaten junk food danced in Greer's head. He closed his eyes tightly and concentrated on only a few of the murky, indistinct fried tofu chips shaped into faux pork rinds. Too many extraneous images intruded. As he focused the best he could on the ever-shifting, tormentingly shouted words and mind-searing images, a migraine headache started, far back in the vast reaches of his mind and spreading until it was a dark web sticking like glue to his every thought, dragging down every synapse.

These tofu chips are shit! blasted into his mind, causing Greer to reel. His thin-fingered hand clung to the desk as new waves of pain built in intensity. He sensed the tsunami approaching and tried to break off and get out of the man's mind.

"Don't," came the cold words. "Don't you dare. We have to find out why the test group doesn't approve of Tofu Tasties."

Greer's watery eyes blinked open. Tears welled and ran down his cheeks. He did not wipe them away. The pain surged now and threatened to tear away his sanity.

"It's because they taste like crap," he grated out.

"Did you receive that, or are you trying to weasel out of work again?"

"That's what he's thinking." Greer swallowed hard and finally wiped away the tears with a crisp linen handkerchief taken from his coat pocket. This always happened when he delved too deeply into a non-telepath's squalid, unfocused mind.

Why couldn't I get a telepath for a damned taste test? They wouldn't torture me like this with so much unmanageable fury. They focus themselves, he screamed mentally. The echoes of his own thoughts rebounded from distant unknown corners in his own mind and produced even more pain.

Are you all right, Greer? came a faint, distant thought as soothing as the other was grating. Controlled, soft, like a cool drink on a sweltering day.

"Kathee," he gasped out, not sure if he sent it telepathically or spoke aloud. Greer cursed under his breath when he heard Lawrence Macmillan snort in disgust. The head of research marketing considered any telepathic contact other than with his precious test human "resource elements" to be a waste of valuable assets. Find those markets. Get them to buy. Dig into the consumers' deepest hidden thoughts and find out what they really think so they can be coerced into buying Tofu Tasties shit chips.

"You are on company time," Macmillan said coldly. "No personal communication."

"My head hurts," Greer said.

Greer?

He took a deep, calming breath, but the migraine refused to fade. He absorbed not only the vile taste of fried-in-pork-grease tofu but also the pent-up anger of the test subject. The man felt intense guilt because he was being paid to sample a product he hated. He wanted to speak out negatively but felt it would be a betrayal of taking money to try what he was told was a fine, tasty, healthful new comfort food. It was worse for Greer because he worked so hard to insinuate himself into the man's mind and had finally found what he thought of as a mental resonance. He meshed with the nontelepathy through extreme effort and then paid the price for it by absorbing the undisciplined output.

It was like struggling furiously to get a funnel into his mouth and then choking when a fifty-five-gallon drum was emptied into it. He hated the feeling; he hated commoners; he hated Macmillan most of all for forcing him to do this. Still, this was a better gig than most telepaths got, no matter how awful it might be.

He thought, *I'm hurting, Kathee, but I can make it through. Meet after work?*

Don't know, too many arrested today. I still have to interrogate witnesses. Sergeant Fates might make me work overtime.

Greer sniffed, wiped again at his eyes, and then tried to relax using some of those silly mantras Kathee recommended. It was hell being a telepath, or even a half one like he was. What must it be like for

Kathee, able to receive *and* send? She had to worry about everyone near who could pick up her telepathic transmissions, especially if she became angry. All he had to worry about was receiving. He was sensitive enough to pry into nontelepathic minds through great effort but could shut out the dull roar from those commoners if he got far enough away from their thronging crowds. It helped even more if he got drunk or distracted himself.

When would Macmillan get trained subjects?

Greer moaned again and pressed his hands to his temples. He knew that would never happen. Most people thought telepaths were something imaginary like Sasquatch and the yeti, no matter how the tabloids tried to cover the story.

"Greer!"

"Yes, sir."

"He verbally said he liked the snack all the way up the liability scale to a nine out of ten, but you claim he was thinking that Tofu Tasties were less than, uh, palatable?"

"Shit, sir, he said they were shit."

"Mr. Nakamuri will not be happy. This makes it unanimous on all test subjects this week."

"Can I go? I don't feel very well." Greer could not care less what their district manager thought of the survey results.

"I am sure you will feel *much* better the instant you are out of the office," Macmillan said with a nasty twist in his voice.

"Whatever you say, sir," Greer said. The lacy webs of migraine now thickened and burned, as if a rope net had been set on fire in his head.

But Macmillan was right about one thing. Once he got away from the commoners, he would feel better.

I think she was in earlier, the man behind the bar thought.

Greer looked around but did not see Kathee. The usual crowd had drifted in, the ones too bored or too damaged by their work to tolerate the outside world much longer. He settled on the high stool and ordered his usual.

Hey, Greer, called Erickson. Greer thought of him as "numb nuts" after he realized Erickson was his opposite, a transmitter and not a receiver. If there was a more worthless talent, Greer could not think of it. At least nontelepaths hired him to spy on each other. What did Erickson do? Implant thoughts? No amount of mental coercion could make anyone like Tofu Tasties.

"What do you want?" Greer asked in an unfriendly tone. His mind raced over all kinds of lewd possibilities for Erickson and reveled in knowing the man could not pick up a single one.

I'm going to a screamer. *Want to come?*

"What the hell is a *screamer*?"

Something special, something you'll really *like.*

Pictures leaked around what little control Erickson had in transmission, enticing Greer in spite of himself. He preferred solitary pleasures, but Erickson was excited, and broadcast emotions along with the flood of kinky images. Greer knew he ought to keep his distance, but it had been a hard day, Kathy wasn't here, and he was perversely intrigued by what he received in Erickson's thoughts.

All telepaths were freaks to be exploited, but valuable ones to the police and corporations and to the government. Greer did not want to think what some of his colleagues were made to do for the black ops groups. The genetic tinkering had come from that segment of the government, and to a large extent had remained the province of the spook, the spy, the saboteur . . . the assassin.

His head began throbbing again. He needed some R&R. Why wasn't Kathee here? She was plain looking, but she was a two-way. When they made love, Greer had no words for it. Feedback. Ecstasy. His passion fed hers and he picked up hers until they could not stand it anymore.

What difference did looks make when they could rock the heavens with their fucking?

"I want to wait a while longer for Kathee," Greer said.

"She was in earlier, had to go back to work," Erickson said aloud. "Besides, you might not want a nice girl like Kathee seeing this."

"A screamer?" Greer was intrigued, but had to fight his own better judgment. Nothing Erickson had anything to do with could be good. The man was a loser.

Then Greer reeled as a flood of new, more intense images hit him. Erickson was so excited he could not control himself.

"You can stay here, but I want to get there for my special . . . show."

"You're part of it?" Greer blurted in astonishment. "They tie you up and—?"

Shut up! came Erickson's frantic thought. *I don't want everyone to know. You're a friend.*

Greer nodded, marveling at his bad luck to have a man like this consider him a friend.

Hating himself for it but not quite able to resist, Greer left with Erickson.

* * *

They headed down back alleys and past more than one alert telepathic sentry, until they reached an abandoned warehouse near the old airport at the edge of town.

From inside Greer felt excitement.

"This is it," Erickson said, rubbing his hands together. "You and me, we've got a special bond, don't we? You can really get off when I—"

Greer stared in wide-eyed fascination at Erickson. "I never thought you were like this."

So they tie me up and beat me, Erickson thought.

"You *want* everyone in the warehouse to pick up everything you're thinking and feeling? Even humiliation?"

Erickson nodded, barely hiding his excitement.

Greer felt his heart pound a little faster. Telepaths were all potential voyeurs, but generally avoided it among commoners since it was so difficult and distasteful. Not to mention, most of them were ordered to snoop as part of their jobs. At the end of a long day, getting out of a commoner's head was more important than diving back to eavesdrop. Among themselves, it was considered impolite in their mostly male society, where offenses were settled more violently than in the commoner world. When you *knew* the depths of another man's thoughts, it provided a potent rationale for using force to decide an argument. After all, it was never impersonal.

"I wanted to be an actor," Erickson explained. "My company wouldn't let me. They wanted me to beam out motivational thoughts to their workers. For all the good that does. Like fucking musk stuffed into the head. That doesn't matter anymore. This . . . is better. It's what *I* want to do."

Erickson opened the metal door, and they slipped inside. Guards stood on either side of the entrance, checking telepathically to be sure they belonged. Erickson obviously did. Greer wasn't so sure about himself, but the guards let him pass. He *heard* their acknowledgment of his telepathic abilities.

The warehouse was dusty and dark, with only a few spotlights shining on a man-high, arm-thick metal post equipped with shackles. Greer scanned the crowd. There were perhaps a dozen spectators, all men, which wasn't unusual. The XY chromosome combination produced ninety-nine male telepaths for every female. While men were mostly receivers, a few were only transmitters like Erickson. Greer had never found both talents in one man. That combination seemed reserved for women.

Too bad Kathee wasn't here. Greer would have enjoyed *feeling* what she did as she took in the anticipation of the crowd, their enthusiasm, their perverse excitement as she rebroadcast with her own slant. He felt dirty and discovered he liked it. Even worse, he thought Kathee might, too.

Greer was suddenly pushed out of the way as two men, stripped to the waist and sweating, grabbed Erickson and dragged him off. Greer recoiled at Erickson's response: fear—and anticipation that became something more than sexual as the shackles locked around his wrists.

Erickson's shirt was ripped away, and a slow, methodical lashing began.

Every crack of the whip caused Erickson to send out agonizing waves of mental pain. Agonizing for him, but also curiously enjoyable for the spectators. Greer found himself transfixed, hypnotized by the sweet-and-sour mixture of emotions flooding from Erickson's mind.

Erickson obviously loved the pain and degradation of others receiving his deepest, darkest thoughts.

As much as Greer, to his surprise, discovered he loved sharing it.

That's disgusting, Kathee thought.

Greer caught a hint of possible betrayal in her thought. As light as a feather falling, or a butterfly wing brushing his cheek, he felt her consider telling the vice squad about the screamer.

Kathee worked for the robbery division but was often lent out to other departments for interrogation of difficult or important witnesses. If the courts ever decided that using a telepath to squeeze information out of a defendant was legal, she would be even more in demand.

As much as Greer hated his job, he felt that what Kathee did—sinking into the minds of people who might be rapists and murderers—was worse. How did she tolerate it?

Is it worse than letting that fool Erickson degrade himself like that?

It was something he wanted to do, Greer thought. *Even commoners for blocks around got off on it. I saw some of them reeling as we left the warehouse. They didn't know what had happened, but they had gotten enough from Erickson's transmission to experience his thrill.*

It shouldn't be something you want to eavesdrop on, she shot back.

But Kathee, this isn't eavesdropping. Erickson knew I was there. He knew everyone wanted to . . . share.

It sounded feeble, but Greer laced his thoughts with some of the excitement he had experienced. He felt her wavering. Kathee knew what was moral, but this transcended the ordinary. This was uniquely telepathic. Was it wrong to share that which is freely given?

Erickson is going to get into trouble.

"How?" Greer asked aloud. He stared into her eyes and wondered what it might be like if she had been there, to take in Erickson's pain and stark emotional response and then filter and magnify it through her own mind.

That might be the experience of a lifetime.

Are you so bored?

Bored, tired, disgusted, all of that, he thought.

Greer caught her fleeting agreement.

What happens if Erickson is seriously injured? He's a powerful sender. You know how dangerous it can be for a telepath to be close when someone is hurt.

No, I don't, Greer replied. This was one of the questions that had never been answered to his satisfaction. While he had not pursued the query too aggressively, he had never found a telepath who had been with anyone who had died, who had been mentally linked to the dying person. There were so few telepaths—and those who might have been in a position to tell had died with the nontelepaths around them in a variety of accidents.

Commoners had their distinctive urban myths, and telepaths had their own.

There are so few of us—you should be careful. Erickson is not quite right in the head. And he might have died.

Greer sucked in a deep breath and let it out slowly. That had occurred to him, and it excited him as much as the flood of pain and desire from the shackled Erickson as the men took turns whipping him.

"Yeah," he said, studying her closely. She was worse than plain, she was downright unattractive. But Kathee's appeal lay in other directions. Greer had heard of only three other telepaths who could both send and receive thoughts, and they might be part of the myth structure, because no one he knew had ever met them.

He was lucky Kathee had chosen him among all the other telepaths.

Damn right you're lucky, came her thought. *And this is so out of character for you.*

"I can't explain it," Greer admitted. "I was repelled and attracted at the same time."

More attracted than repelled, or you would have left.

He had no answer to that. She was right.

"Have you heard about things like this going on?" he asked out loud.

Rumors. Always rumors.

"Screamers might be fairly new," Greer said. "There have been so few of us telepaths. But there are more all the time."

Receivers, Kathy thought bitterly. "And men," she said aloud. Her brown eyes blinked as she stared at him from inches away. They were naked and lying alongside one another in bed, but they might as well have been a thousand miles apart.

"And men," he said, grinning. "Just like you like." He moved closer and began making love to her.

After a moment of hesitation, she responded.

And somehow, as he climaxed, his thoughts were not on her passion being fed telepathically into his brain, but of Erickson.

Erickson could have died.

What would that have felt like?

He tried everything in the next two weeks, but nothing matched the thrill Greer had felt at the screamer. It began taking on an almost mythic proportion in his thoughts, even pushing aside sex with Kathee.

Greer became obsessed.

He hunted for Erickson, but the man had vanished. No one had seen him or even caught a vagrant thought from him. Sitting at the bar one night, Greer decided that Erickson had done this on purpose to annoy him. Nothing about the man was pleasant. They would never be friends, despite what Erickson thought.

But, because of the screamer, Greer now acknowledged a bond between them that he could not deny: Erickson had enjoyed sending out waves of pain, and Greer had liked sharing it.

Maybe it's because you didn't have to worry about physical scars on your own back, Kathee said, sitting down beside him at the bar.

"It's more than that," Greer said, eager to continue their discussion of the matter. He had been talking about little else with Kathee since the screamer. The more he talked about it, the better his memory of it became. Too much of the screamer was like a will-o'-the-wisp, there but not there when he looked too hard. Or like fairy gold: if he reached out and tried to touch it, it evaporated.

For all you know, Erickson might be dead, Kathee thought.

I checked the hospitals. No one has seen or heard about him.

"Greer," Kathee said as she moved closer, putting a hand on his arm. "Don't you see anything wrong with all this?"

"No," Greer said, almost angrily. "We've been through it a hundred times. If you'd been there, you would have felt the same way." He paused and looked into Kathee's face. A smile crept onto his lips. "You *would* have enjoyed it, wouldn't you? Is that what's bothering you?"

It's so good when we make love.

What would it be like if dozens of people magnified those feelings and returned them to you? he asked.

Kathee shivered and tried to push the thought away. Greer caught snippets, no matter how she tried to deny it. She was as intrigued as he had been—and also as repelled. A powerful combination.

Let's find him, Greer suggested. "Or another screamer. There were enough people there that it can't be a one-shot occurrence."

She looked at him, disapproval on her face. But he saw into her mind.

Hand in hand, they left to find a screamer.

I recognize most of them here, Kathee said, surprised. *I suppose that shouldn't strike me as unusual, since I have contact with so many officially.*

Finding this screamer had been easy, and here were hundreds and hundreds of telepaths, all gathering for the same reason he and Kathee were. Some of the crowd he had seen before, in the bar and at social gatherings. Most were complete strangers to him, but he caught some of their arousal at the idea of sharing the sadomasochist exhibition.

I don't believe this, Kathee said, but there was the faintest hint of anticipation behind her words.

Greer wet his lips. Three posts were erected in the middle of the clearing in the junkyard. There were no spotlights.

We're late, he thought. *I think it's going to start—*

The mingling assemblage became suddenly focused, moving closer as three men were led through the crowd directly to the posts, shackled, their shirts stripped from their backs.

Kathee squeezed his hand.

Greer felt the excitement mounting and shared it in much the same way he did with Kathee when they were making love. But this was different, had different layers and emotions and was infinitely more varied and complex.

Philosophical emotions? Kathee asked.

Don't analyze it. Just enjoy it.

I don't know that I can. It is so . . . so unnatural.

That's what makes it exciting, Greer said. *Look! The man chained at the far post. That's Erickson!*

He held her in his arms as the first whip rose and lashed against Erickson's bare flesh. He and Kathee moved closer, only a few feet away, and received Erickson's full mental anguish and ecstasy.

Kathee tensed and then held Greer closer.

I've never felt anything like this, she admitted.

You like it.

Yes.

The crowd grew in size and the intensity of the emotion flowing from the three shackled men increased. Erickson did not seem to recognize Greer—he was too deep in relishing the pain he received. The emotions were pure, laser-sharp, shared by everyone in the junkyard.

This was illicit, wrong, forbidden—and ever so much more exciting because of the shared weakness.

The shared transgression.

The shared sexual excitement.

Closer, Kathee thought. *If we get closer, it will be more intense.*

They moved to Erickson's side. So did others. Those in the crowd touched now, shoulders rubbing and bodies jerking in response to every lash.

The three men using the whips began striking their blows in unison on their victims' backs. This caused the flood of emotion to magnify a hundredfold, in synch like a laser beam powering up. Greer and Kathee moved even closer until they could almost touch Erickson. He looked at them, his eyes wild and bright with transcendence.

They both felt his rapture.

This is amazing. Kathee's thoughts were intense. *I had no idea—*

Greer felt weak in the knees. This was very wrong, he was suddenly sure. He knew he should leave, but instead he moved even closer, as eager as a boy at his first peep show.

More!

Greer wasn't sure if the crowd thought this or if Kathee sent it. The men chained to the posts sobbed and moaned as they took every lash. Only Erickson could project his thoughts clearly.

He wanted more, too.

More!

A feedback began that drew Greer even closer. Kathee was beside him. Her face was pale and strained. He realized she was accepting the telepathic outpouring and then retransmitting it, filtered of extraneous thoughts so the emotion became stronger and more stimulating.

Pure pain.

Pure pleasure.

Greer's body began to respond. Around him he heard other men crying out, but he could not move. He turned to the heat, the telepathic heat that drew him like a moth to flame.

More! he got from Kathee. She directed and shaped and magnified the emotional outpouring of the crowd. He saw how pale she had become, how indistinct and ghostlike. Her hands shook as she pressed even closer to him. He liked the feel of her body against his, the way her thoughts surged and beat against his like ocean waves rising at the start of a storm.

More!

Greer wanted more. He held Kathee and felt the others in the group crowd toward her. Before, when Erickson had been the sacrificial lamb, it had been thrilling. But not like this.

This was something new.

Kathee, he thought. *You are the difference tonight!*

Greer felt the hundreds in the crowd suck in their collective breath as the feedback built in intensity. From the three being whipped, to the receivers and Kathee, through Kathee and back, filtered and magnified for everyone—even those shackled to the posts—to relish. Excitement mounted and fed the crowd and Kathee and him. A link formed between Erickson and Kathee, stronger and more potent than anything Greer had ever felt before.

Dizzily, Greer felt a migraine at the back of his head begin. He ignored it. The feelings cascading into his body and soul were too intense for mere pain now.

Greer, Kathee thought. *I—*

Words were no longer enough as the pressures within grew, pressures of guilt, lust, and illicit sharing.

Greer screamed. He felt as if he had been launched on a rocket. His mental echoes quivered forth and resonated with the others that fed Kathee.

Feedback.

Growing intensity.

Tidal wave.

Out of control.

Out of control!

Greer experienced a freaky second where he knew they would all die from ecstasy. He had discovered what it meant to be a telepath.

Over and up and around and ever increasing, their exhilaration grew until they were consumed in a huge flame of stark rapture that destroyed them all—and then began snuffing out the lesser lights of nontelepaths.

The world did not end in fire or ice.

It ended in orgasm.

Nina Kiriki Hoffman gave me a tiny plastic mouse with an articulated head the first time I met her a few years ago; she had an entire side pocket in her bag filled with the damned things. A fellow editor stole the mouse later on, and when I saw her again a year later the pocket in her bag, alas, was empty.

Her bag of tricks is never empty, though, and she offers a dandy little strange tale, which for some reason I haven't been able to get out of my head. It's simple, straightforward, yet completely evocative of family life.

She's been a Nebula and World Fantasy Award finalist, and has a Bram Stoker Award—more awards should follow, for both her dark fantasy and science fiction.

Between Disappearances

NINA KIRIKI HOFFMAN

✷

We're standing in the living room. This is where I always transit to, and somehow it's where Mom always is when I arrive.

"I can't stay," I say.

"You never stay," says my mother.

"It's not my fault," I say.

So far this is the same conversation we always have, etched deep into our brains. This is your brain on automatic. I wonder which of us will jump off the path first this visit.

"It's not your fault you tripped in that stupid dimensional portal and got a piece of travel rock stuck in your back?" Mom says. "Whose fault is it, then? When are you going to see a doctor and try to get it removed?"

On track so far. I decide to make a run for new territory. "So what's up with Artie?" She'll talk about my brother, won't she? He's the good one. He sticks around. He's never even left town.

Or maybe he did? It's been a while.

I don't know how long I've been gone. Mom looks older. But maybe it's just my vision. I've been to six worlds since the last time I was home, and I stayed on the last one for a year, local time. I got used to talking to people with four eyes in their foreheads and odd numbers of arms. I've forgotten what wrinkled foreheads normally look like.

Mom ignores my gambit. "And what are you wearing? I can see your nipples! They're staring at me! Is that the fashion where you were? Put some clothes on!"

I sigh and go to the hall closet. This is one of those sure conversation stoppers that I have to actually act on, or she'll keep coming back to it. I find a full-length black raincoat and wrap up in it. It's sized to fit someone taller and bigger than me, and it smells like good cologne. I wonder who it belongs to.

"Not that! Take that off! I don't want your otherworld germs messing that up!"

I shrug and take off the coat. Whatever germs I've got—come to think of it, I did have a really bad cold right before this last jump, with a bright purple rash—are already on the coat, but what can you do? Mom grabs the black coat from me, humphs out of the room, and comes back with a ratty terry-cloth bathrobe, which she flings at me. I wrap up in it. It smells like fabric softener. I recognize it. It actually used to be mine.

"So what year is it here?"

"Two thousand thirty-one," she says.

Wow, it's been three years since the last time I was on Earth.

"Whose coat was that?"

"Linc's." Her eyes narrow. "He doesn't know about you."

This is new. I glance toward the PixWall, which last time I visited displayed shots of Mom, of me, of Artie, the three of us together and apart at various ages, with various pets, in various places we remember only because we have pix of them. She deleted all the Dad shots before I left, and now I see that I'm not there anymore either.

There are some new people on the wall screen. Artie with his arm around a woman. Artie with a baby in a stomach sling.

Mom with a man. He has lots of bushy silver hair and good teeth. He looks like he sells something.

"In fact," says Mom, "I think you should leave before he gets home from work."

"Whoa, Mom! Are you married again?"

She lifts her chin. For a minute I think she isn't going to answer. "No," she says at last. She sighs. She jumps back a few conversational steps. "You never stay." This time she says it in a tone of finality.

Same words, different conversation. Hmm. "That's right. I never stay." My stomach clenches. "So I guess I can't have my old room back, huh?"

She glances at the floor and her hands twist around each other. "No," she whispers. "Linc set up his exercise equipment there."

I am so unready for this development it surprises me. I mean, I've lived in more than thirty different places since the accident, for longer or shorter times, and I manage to find my feet, learn a language, talk disbelieving strangers into putting up with me, develop some skill to support myself, every time. Nobody's even come close to killing me yet.

But now I have no home.

Why should I have a home here? Mom never knows when to expect me. I never stay as long as she wants. Even if I could stay as long as she wanted me to, I wouldn't, because she drives me crazy after a little while.

Maybe it's time she got on with her life.

No home.

"You can stay at Artie's. He got married two years ago. His wife is very nice, and they have a little girl. And a guest room. He'd love to see you, I know. He's still mad I didn't call him last time you were here. I didn't know you'd be gone so long."

"Okay," I whisper.

"I still love you," she says. "I just finally figured out that I can't take care of you anymore."

"Okay."

She calls Artie and drives me over and drops me off.

I have dinner with Artie and his wife and their child. Earth food tastes bland. I remember Artie and I never had anything to talk about while we were growing up. They ask the usual questions. I give the usual answers and show some of the image cubes I got two planets ago and happened to have in my pack for this transit.

There's so little you can hold on to when you never know when you're going to leave. I've learned to let go of almost everything.

Artie herds messages, and his wife makes images. They talk about traveling. I can tell they won't.

That night after my brother and his wife and child have gone to sleep, I huddle on the end of the guest bed. I had a copy of a Hrendah novel in my pack when the travel rock kicked in this time. I take out the book, which is written in acid etchings on treated leaves the size of my forearms. I flip to my place. I am in the middle. A person realizes that the person it has planned its future with cannot love it and that their relationship, though possible and even almost obligatory, would be hollow if they pursued it. If only the first person could change the way the second person views the first person. To trigger just the right shift in views would be art.

I drop the book. It is like other Hrendah books I've read. Something in the Hrendah soul longs to read this story over and over.

I hug my knees and hang my head. I curl as tight as I can.

Something moves in my back. I feel a crackle, a flash of heat. Something drops to the blanket behind me.

After a moment I look.

It shimmers and flashes with darts of colored light. Occlusions hide its center, and rutilations stripe it. I can barely make out the trapped spiral that gives it its power.

I touch the spot on my back where the travel stone melded with me and trapped me into travel, where it has lodged all these years. The skin closed over it after the accident; the travel stone sank into me so no one could even see it.

I feel a wet streak beside my spine. My fingers come away wet and red.

I inch around so that the stone lies in front of me.

Now I can stop traveling. I can stay here, where I already know people, things, food, language, money, writing, telephones, and how to use the bathroom. I can make my home again.

I watch the flashes in the travel stone for a long time. It has carried me to places that Earth people have never reached through normal portals, places where I am the only one like me and the people who live there are fascinated by me or want to kill me. It has taken me to other worlds where there are Earth bases and I can talk to people like the ones I grew up with. It has taken me out of lives where I was happy. The only trigger I've found that works reliably is salt water, so my travel stone has taken me out of lives where I was unhappy, too. A swim in the sea, and I find myself elsewhere, though I never know beforehand where I will go. I rarely return anywhere but home. Every six or eight or ten times the stone brings me back to my mother's living room.

The flashes through the stone's translucent core brighten and strike farther and faster. I sense a hum from the stone, even though it is not vibrating under my skin anymore. I know it is about to switch again.

I stuff the Hrendah novel and what clothes I can into my pack. I stare at the stone for a little while as lights scythe through its clouded depths.

I could just let it go.

But at the last second I grab it.

David Morrell is modern fiction's iron man: solid, reliable, thoughtful, always professional and—here's the twist—always original. He created the totemic character John Rambo, following that Vietnam vet's adventures with a string of best-sellers that continues to this day.

I had to talk David into doing a story for this book—not because he wasn't intrigued by Redshift*'s concept, but because he, like Joyce Carol Oates, had never written what he considered a science fiction story before.*

But I persevered with my gentle prodding—and boy, am I glad I did. "Resurrection" evidences all the classic Morrell attributes listed above.

Resurrection

DAVID MORRELL

*

Anthony was nine when his mother had to tell him that his father was seriously ill. The signs had been there—pallor and shortness of breath—but Anthony's childhood had been so perfect, his parents so loving, that he couldn't imagine a problem they couldn't solve. His father's increasing weight loss was too obvious to be ignored, however.

"But . . . but what's wrong with him?" Anthony stared uneasily up at his mother. He'd never seen her look more tired.

She explained about blood cells. "It's not leukemia. If only it were. These days, that's almost always curable, but the doctors have never seen anything like this. It's moving so quickly, even a bone marrow transplant won't work. The doctors suspect that it might have something to do with the lab, with radiation he picked up after the accident."

Anthony nodded. His parents had once explained to him that his father was something called a maintenance engineer. A while ago, there'd been an emergency phone call, and Anthony's father had rushed to the lab in the middle of the night.

"But the doctors . . ."

"They're trying everything they can think of. That's why Daddy's going to be in the hospital for a while."

"But can't I see him?"

"Tomorrow." Anthony's mother sounded more weary. "Both of us can see him tomorrow."

When they went to the hospital, Anthony's father was too weak to recognize him. He had tubes in his arms, his mouth, and his nose. His skin was gray. His face was thinner than it had been three days earlier, the last time Anthony had seen him. If Anthony hadn't loved his father so much, he'd have been frightened. As things were, all he wanted was to sit next to his father and hold his hand. But after only a few minutes, the doctors said that it was time to go.

The next day, when Anthony and his mother went to the hospital, his father wasn't in his room. He was having "a procedure," the doctors said. They took Anthony's mother aside to talk to her. When she came back, she looked even more solemn than the doctors had. Everything possible had been done, she explained. "No results." Her voice sounded tight. "None. At this rate . . ." She could barely get the words out. "In a couple of days . . ."

"There's nothing the doctors can do?" Anthony asked, afraid.

"Not now. Maybe not ever. But we can hope. We can try to cheat time."

Anthony hadn't the faintest idea what she meant. He wasn't even sure that he understood after she explained that there was something called "cryonics," which froze sick people until cures were discovered. Then they were thawed and given the new treatment. In a primitive way, cryonics had been tried fifty years earlier, in the late years of the twentieth century, Anthony's mother found the strength to continue explaining. It had failed because the freezing method hadn't been fast enough and the equipment often broke down. But over time, the technique had been improved sufficiently that, although the medical establishment didn't endorse it, they didn't reject it, either.

"Then why doesn't everybody do it?" Anthony asked in confusion.

"Because . . ." His mother took a deep breath. "Because some of the people who were thawed never woke up."

Anthony had the sense that his mother was telling him more than she normally would have, that she was treating him like a grown-up, and that he had to justify her faith in him.

"Others, who did wake up, failed to respond to the new treatment," she reluctantly said.

"Couldn't they be frozen again?" Anthony asked in greater bewilderment.

"You can't survive being frozen a second time. You get only one chance, and if the treatment doesn't work . . ." She stared down at the floor. "It's so experimental and risky that insurance companies won't pay for it. The only reason we have it as an option is that the laboratory's agreed to pay for the procedure"—there was that word again—"while the doctors try to figure out how to cure him. But if it's going to happen, it has to happen now." She looked straight into his eyes. "Should we do it?"

"To save Daddy? We have to."

"It'll be like he's gone."

"Dead?"

Anthony's mother reluctantly nodded.

"But he *won't* be dead."

"That's right," his mother said. "We might never see him alive again, though. They might not ever find a cure. They might not ever wake him up."

Anthony had no idea of the other issues that his mother had to deal with. In the worst case, if his father died, at least his life insurance would allow his mother to support the two of them. In the unlikely event that she ever fell in love again, she'd be able to remarry. But if Anthony's father was frozen, in effect dead to them, they'd be in need of money, and the only way for her to remarry would be to get a divorce from the man who, a year after her wedding, might be awakened and cured.

"But it's the only thing we can do," Anthony said.

"Yes." His mother wiped her eyes and straightened. "It's the only thing we can do."

Anthony had expected that it would happen the next day or the day after that. But his mother hadn't been exaggerating that, if it were going to happen, it had to happen now. His unconscious father was a gray husk as they rode with him in an ambulance. At a building without windows, they walked next to his father's gurney as it was wheeled along a softly lit corridor and into a room where other doctors waited. There were glinting instruments and humming machines. A man in a suit explained that Anthony and his mother had to step outside while certain preparations were done to Anthony's father to make the freezing process safe. After that, they would be able to accompany him to his cryochamber.

Again, it wasn't what Anthony had expected. In contrast with the humming machines in the preparation room, the chamber was only a niche in a wall in a long corridor that had numerous other niches on each side, metal doors with pressure gauges enclosing them. Anthony watched his father's gaunt naked body being placed on a tray that went into the niche. But his father's back never actually touched the tray. As the man in the suit explained, a force field kept Anthony's father elevated. Otherwise, his back would freeze to the tray and cause infections when he was thawed. For the same reason, no clothes, not even a sheet, could cover him, although Anthony, thinking of how cold his father was going to be, dearly wished that his father had something to keep him warm.

While the man in the suit and the men who looked like doctors stepped aside, a man dressed in black but with a white collar arrived. He put a purple scarf around his neck. He opened a book and read, "I am the Way, the Truth, and the Life." A little later, he read, "I am the Resurrection."

Anthony's father was slid into the niche. The door was closed. Something hissed.

"It's done," the man in the suit said.

"That *quickly*?" Anthony's mother asked.

"It won't work if it isn't instantaneous."

"May God grant a cure," the man with the white collar said.

Years earlier, Anthony's father had lost his parents in a fire. Anthony's mother had *her* parents, but without much money, the only way they could help was by offering to let her and Anthony stay with them. For a time, Anthony's mother fought the notion. After all, she had her job as an administrative assistant at the laboratory, although without her husband's salary she didn't earn enough for the mortgage payments on their house. The house was too big for her and Anthony anyhow, so after six months she was forced to sell it, using the money to move into a cheaper, smaller town house. By then, the job at the lab had given her too many painful memories about Anthony's father. In fact, she blamed the lab for what had happened to him. Her bitterness intensified until she couldn't make herself go into the lab's offices any longer. She quit, got a lesser paying job as a secretary at a real-estate firm, persuaded a sympathetic broker to sell her town house but not charge a commission, and went with Anthony to live with her parents.

She and Anthony spent all their free time together, even more now than before the accident, so he had plenty of opportunity to learn what she was feeling and why she'd made those decisions. The times she revealed herself the most, however, were when they visited his father. She once complained that the corridor of niches reminded her of a mausoleum, a reference that Anthony didn't understand, so she explained it but so vaguely that he still didn't understand, and it was several years before he knew what she'd been talking about.

Visiting hours for the cryochambers were between eight and six during the day as long as a new patient wasn't being installed. At first, Anthony and his mother went every afternoon after she finished work. Gradually, that lessened to every second day, every third day, and once a week. But they didn't reach that point for at least a year. Sometimes, there were other visitors in the corridor, solitary people or incomplete families, staring mournfully at niches, sometimes leaving small objects of remembrance on narrow tables that the company had placed in the middle of the corridor: notes, photographs, dried maple leaves, and small candles shaped like pumpkins, to mention a few. The company placed no names on any of the niches, so visitors had used stick-on plaques that said who was behind the pressurized door, when he or she had been born, when they had gotten sick, of what, and when they had been frozen. Often there was a bit of a prayer or something as movingly simple as "We love you. We'll see you soon." Here and there, Anthony noticed just a name, but for the most part the plaques had acquired a common form, the same kind of information and in the same order as over the years a tradition had been established.

Over the years indeed. Some of the people in the niches had been frozen at least *twenty-five* years, he read. It made him fear that his father might never be awakened. His fear worsened each time his mother came back from visiting his father's doctors, who were no closer to finding a cure for his sickness. Eventually his mother took him along to see the doctors, although the visits grew wider apart, every other month, every six months, and then every year. The message was always depressingly the same.

By then, Anthony was fifteen, in his first year of high school. He decided that he wanted to become a doctor and find a way to cure his father. But the next year his grandfather had a heart attack, leaving a small life insurance policy, enough for his mother and his grandmother to keep the house going but hardly enough for Anthony's dreams of attending medical school.

Meanwhile, his mother began dating the sympathetic broker at the real-estate firm. Anthony knew that she couldn't be expected to be lonely forever, that after so much time it was almost as if his father were dead and not frozen, and that she had to get on with her life. But "as if his father were dead" wasn't the same as actually being dead, and Anthony had trouble concealing his unhappiness when his mother told him that she was going to marry the broker.

"But what about Dad? You're still married to *him*."

"I'm going to have to divorce him."

"No."

"Anthony, we did our best. We couldn't cheat time. It didn't work. Your father's never going to be cured."

"No!"

"I'll never stop loving him, Anthony. But I'm not betraying him. He's the same as dead, and I need to live."

Tears dripped from Anthony's cheeks.

"He'd have wanted me to," his mother said. "He'd have understood. He'd have done the same thing."

"I'll ask him when he wakes up."

When Anthony became eighteen, it struck him that his father had been frozen nine years, *half* of Anthony's life. If it hadn't been for pictures of his father, he feared that he wouldn't have been able to remember what his father had looked like. No, not *had* looked like, Anthony corrected himself. His father wasn't dead. Once a new treatment was discovered, once he was thawed and cured, he'd look the same as ever.

Anthony concentrated to remember his father's voice, the gentle tone with which his father had read bedtime stories to him and had taught him how to ride a bicycle. He remembered his father helping him with his math homework and how his father had come to his school every year on Career Day and proudly explained his job at the lab. He remembered how his father had hurried him to the emergency ward after a branch snapped on the backyard tree and Anthony's fall broke his arm.

His devotion to his father strengthened after his mother remarried and they moved to the broker's house. The broker turned out not to be as sympathetic as when he'd been courting Anthony's mother. He was bossy. He lost his temper if everything wasn't done exactly his way. Anthony's mother looked unhappy, and Anthony hardly ever talked to the man, whom he refused to think of as his stepfather. He stayed away from the house as much as possible, often lying that he'd been playing sports or at the library when actually he'd been visiting his father's chamber, which the broker didn't want him to do because the broker insisted it was disloyal to the new family.

The broker also said that he wasn't going to pay a fortune so that Anthony could go to medical school. He wanted Anthony to be a business major and that was the only education he was going to pay for. So Anthony studied extra hard, got nothing but A's, and applied for every scholarship he could find, eventually being accepted as a science major in a neighboring state. The university there had an excellent medical school, which he hoped to attend after his B.S., and he was all set to go when he realized how much it would bother him not to visit his father. That almost made him change his plans until he reminded himself that the only way his father might be cured was if he himself became a doctor and *found* that cure. So, after saying good-bye to his mother, he told the broker to go to hell.

He went to college, and halfway through his first year, he learned from his mother that the lab had decided that it was futile to hope for a cure. A number of recent deaths after patients were thawed had cast such doubt on cryonics that the lab had decided to stop the monthly payments that the cryocompany charged for keeping Anthony's father frozen. For his part, the broker refused to make the payments, saying that it wasn't his responsibility and anyway what was the point since the freezing process had probably killed Anthony's father anyhow.

Taking a job as a waiter in a restaurant, sometimes working double shifts even as he struggled to maintain his grades, Anthony managed to earn just enough to make the payments. But in his sophomore year, he received a notice that the cryocompany was bankrupt from so many people refusing to make payments for the discredited process. The contract that his mother had signed indemnified the company against certain situations in which it could no longer keep its clients frozen, and bankruptcy was one of those situations.

Smaller maintenance firms agreed to take the company's patients, but the transfer would be so complicated and hence so expensive that Anthony had to drop his classes and work full-time at the restaurant in order to pay for it. At school, he'd met a girl, who continued to see him even though his exhausting schedule gave him spare time only at inconvenient hours. He couldn't believe that he'd finally found some brightness in his life, and after he returned from making sure that his father was safely installed in a smaller facility, after he resumed his classes, completing his sophomore and junior year, he began to talk to her about marriage.

"I don't have much to offer, but . . ."

"You're the gentlest, most determined, most hardworking person I've ever met. I'd be proud to be your wife."

"At the start, we won't have much money because I have to pay for my father's maintenance, but . . ."

"We'll live on what *I* earn. After you're a doctor, you can take care of *me*. There'll be plenty enough for us and our children *and* your father."

"How many children would you like?"

"Three."

Anthony laughed. "You're so sure of the number."

"It's good to hear you laugh."

"You make me laugh."

"By the time you're a doctor, maybe there'll be a cure for your father and you won't have to worry about him anymore."

"Isn't it nice to think so."

* * *

Anthony's mother died in a car accident the year he entered medical school. Her remarriage had been so unsatisfying that she'd taken to drinking heavily and had been under the influence when she veered from the road and crashed into a ravine. At the funeral, the broker hardly acknowledged Anthony and his fiancée. That night, Anthony cried in her arms as he remembered the wonderful family he had once been a part of and how badly everything had changed when his father had gotten sick.

He took his fiancée to the firm that now maintained his father. Since the transfer, Anthony had been able to afford returning to his home town to visit his father only sporadically. The distance made him anxious because the new firm didn't inspire the confidence that the previous one had. It looked on the edge of disrepair, floors not dirty but not clean, walls not exactly faded and yet somehow in need of painting. Rooms seemed vaguely underlit. The units in which patients were kept frozen looked cheap. The temperature gauges were primitive compared to the elaborate technology at the previous facility. But as long as they kept his father safe . . .

That thought left Anthony when he took another look at the gauge and realized that the temperature inside his father's chamber had risen one degree from when he'd last checked it.

"What's wrong?" his fiancée asked.

Words caught in his throat. All he could do was point.

The temperature had gone up yet another degree.

He raced along corridor after corridor, desperate to find a maintenance worker. He burst into the company's office and found only a secretary.

"My father . . ."

Flustered, the secretary took a moment to move when he finished explaining. She phoned the control room. No one answered.

"It's almost noon. The technicians must have gone to lunch."

"For God's sake, where's the control room?"

At the end of the corridor where his father was. As Anthony raced past the niche, he saw that the temperature gauge had gone up fifteen degrees. He charged into the control room, saw flashing red lights on a panel, and rushed to them, trying to figure out what was wrong. Among numerous gauges, eight temperature needles were rising, and Anthony was certain that one of them was for his father.

He flicked a switch beneath each of them, hoping to reset the controls.

The lights kept flashing.

He flicked a switch at the end of their row.

Nothing changed.

He pulled a lever. Every light on the panel went out. "Jesus."

Pushing the lever back to where it had been, he held his breath, exhaling only when all the lights came back on. The eight that had been flashing were now constant.

Sweating, he eased onto a chair. Gradually, he became aware of people behind him and turned to where his fiancée and the secretary watched in dismay from the open door. Then he stared at the panel, watching the temperature needles gradually descend to where they had been. Terrified that the lights would start flashing again, he was still concentrating on the gauges an hour later when a bored technician returned from lunch.

It turned out that a faulty valve had restricted the flow of freezant around eight of the niches. When Anthony had turned the power off and on, the valve had reset itself, although it could fail again at any time and would have to be replaced, the technician explained.

"Then do it!"

He would never again be comfortable away from his father. It made him nervous to return to medical school. He contacted the cryofirm every day, making sure that there weren't any problems. He married, became a parent (of a lovely daughter), graduated, and was lucky enough to be able to do his internship in the city where he'd been raised and where he could keep a close watch on his father's safety. If only his father had been awake to see him graduate, he thought. If only his father had been cured and could have seen his granddaughter being brought home from the hospital . . .

One night, while Anthony was on duty in the emergency ward, a comatose patient turned out to be the broker who'd married his mother. The broker had shot himself in the head. Anthony tried everything possible to save him. His throat felt tight when he pronounced the time of death.

He joined a medical practice in his hometown after he finished his internship. He started earning enough to make good on his promise and take care of his wife after she'd spent so many years taking care of *him*. She had said that she wanted three children, and she got them sooner than she expected, for the next time she gave birth, it was to twins, a boy and a girl. Nonetheless, Anthony's work prevented him from spending as much time with his family as he wanted, for his specialty was blood diseases, and when he wasn't seeing patients, he was doing research, trying to find a way to cure his father.

He needed to know the experiments that the lab had conducted and the types of rays that his father might have been exposed to. But the lab was obsessed with security and refused to tell him. He fought to get a court order to force the lab to cooperate. Judge after judge refused. Meanwhile he was terribly conscious of all the family celebrations that his father continued to miss: the day Anthony's first daughter started grade school, the afternoon the twins began swimming lessons, the evening Anthony's second daughter played "Chopsticks" at her first piano recital. Anthony was thirty-five before he knew it. Then forty. All of a sudden, his children were in high school. His wife went to law school. He kept doing research.

When he was fifty-five and his eldest daughter turned thirty (she was married, with a daughter of her own), the laboratory made a mistake and released the information Anthony needed among a batch of old data that the lab felt was harmless. It wasn't Anthony who discovered the information, however, but instead a colleague two thousand miles away who had other reasons to look through the old data and recognized the significance of the type of rays that Anthony's father had been exposed to. Helped by his colleague's calculations, Anthony devised a treatment, tested it on computer models, subjected rats to the same type of rays, found that they developed the same rapid symptoms as his father had, gave the animals the treatment, and felt his pulse quicken when the symptoms disappeared as rapidly as they had come on.

With his wife next to him, Anthony stood outside his father's cryochamber as arrangements were made to thaw him. He feared that the technicians would make an error during the procedure (the word echoed from his youth), that his father wouldn't wake up.

His muscles tightened as something hissed and the door swung open. The hatch slid out.

Anthony's father looked the same as when he'd last seen him: naked, gaunt, and gray, suspended over a force field.

"You thawed him that *quickly*?" Anthony asked.

"It doesn't work if it isn't instantaneous."

His father's chest moved up and down.

"My God, he's alive," Anthony said. "He's actually . . ."

But there wasn't time to marvel. The disease would be active again, racing to complete its destruction.

Anthony hurriedly injected his father with the treatment. "We have to get him to a hospital."

He stayed in his father's room, constantly monitoring his father's condition, injecting new doses of the treatment precisely on schedule. To his amazement, his father improved almost at once. The healthier color of his skin made obvious what the blood tests confirmed—the disease was retreating.

Not that his father knew. One effect of being thawed was that the patient took several days to wake up. Anthony watched for a twitch of a finger, a flicker of an eyelid, to indicate that his father was regaining consciousness. After three days, he became worried enough to order another brain scan, but as his father was being put in the machine, a murmur made everyone stop.

". . . Where am I?" Anthony's father asked.

"In a hospital. You're going to be fine."

His father strained to focus on him. ". . . Who? . . ."

"Your son."

"No. . . . My son's . . . a child." Looking frightened, Anthony's father lost consciousness.

The reaction wasn't unexpected. But Anthony had his own quite different reaction to deal with. While his father hadn't seen him age and hence didn't know who Anthony was, Anthony's father *hadn't* aged and hence looked exactly as Anthony remembered. The only problem was that Anthony's memory came from when he was nine, and now at the age of fifty-five, he looked at his thirty-two-year-old father, who wasn't much older than Anthony's son.

"Marian's *dead*?"

Anthony reluctantly nodded. "Yes. A car accident."

"When?"

Anthony had trouble saying it. "Twenty-two years ago."

"No."

"I'm afraid it's true."

"I've been frozen *forty-six years*? No one told me what was going to happen."

"We couldn't. You were unconscious. Near death."

His father wept. "Sweet Jesus."

"Our house?"

"Was sold a long time ago."

"My friends?"

Anthony looked away.

With a shudder, his father pressed his hands to his face. "It's worse than being dead."

"No," Anthony said. "You heard the psychiatrist. Depression's a normal part of coming back. You're going to have to learn to live again."

"Just like learning to walk again," his father said bitterly.

"Your muscles never had a chance to atrophy. As far as your body's concerned, no time passed since you were frozen."

"But as far as my mind goes? Learn to live again? That's something nobody should have to do."

"Are you saying that Mom and I should have let you die? Our lives would have gone on just the same. Mom would have been killed whether you were frozen or you died. Nothing would have changed, except that *you* wouldn't be here now."

"With your mother gone . . ."

Anthony waited.

"With my son gone . . ."

"*I'm* your son."

"My son had his ninth birthday two weeks ago. I gave him a new computer game that I looked forward to playing with him. I'll never get to see him grow up."

"To see *me* grow up. But I'm here now. We can make up for lost time."

"Lost time." The words seemed like dust in his father's mouth.

"Dad"—it was the last time Anthony used that term—"this is your grandson, Paul. These are your granddaughters Sally and Jane. And this is *Jane's* son, Peter. Your *great*-grandson."

Seeing his father's reaction to being introduced to grandchildren who were almost as old as *he* was, Anthony felt heartsick.

"*Forty-six years?* But everything changed in a *second*," his father said. "It makes my head spin so much . . ."

"I'll teach you," Anthony said. "I'll start with basics and explain what happened since you were frozen. I'll move you forward. Look, here are virtual videos of—"

"What are virtual videos?"

"Of news shows from back then. We'll watch them in sequence. We'll talk about them. Eventually, we'll get you up to the present."

Anthony's father pointed toward the startlingly lifelike images from forty-six years earlier. "*That's* the present."

"Is there anything you'd like to do?"

"Go to Marian."

So Anthony drove him to the mausoleum, where his father stood for a long time in front of the niche that contained her urn.

"One instant she's alive. The next . . ." Tears filled his father's eyes. "Take me home."

But when Anthony headed north of the city, his father put a trembling hand on his shoulder. "No. You're taking the wrong direction."

"But we live at—"

"Home. I want to go *home*."

So Anthony drove him back to the old neighborhood, where his father stared at the run-down house that he had once been proud to keep in perfect condition. Weeds filled the yard. Windows were broken. Porch steps were missing.

"There used to be a lawn here," Anthony's father said. "I worked so hard to keep it immaculate."

"I remember," Anthony said.

"I taught my son how to do somersaults on it."

"You taught *me*."

"In an instant." His father sounded anguished. "All gone in an instant."

Anthony peered up from his breakfast of black coffee, seeing his father at the entrance to the kitchen. It had been two days since they'd spoken.

"I wanted to tell you," his father said, "that I realize you made an enormous effort for me. I can only imagine the pain and sacrifice. I'm sorry if I'm . . . No matter how confused I feel, I want to thank you."

Anthony managed to smile, comparing the wrinkle-free face across from him to the weary one that he'd seen in the mirror that morning. "I'm sorry, too. That you're having such a hard adjustment. All Mom and I thought of was, you were so sick. We were ready to do *anything* that would help you."

"Your mother." Anthony's father needed a moment before he could continue. "Grief doesn't last just a couple of days."

It was Anthony's turn to need a moment. He nodded. "I've had much of my life to try to adjust to Mom being gone, but I still miss her. You'll have a long hard time catching up to me."

"I . . ."

"Yes?"

"I don't know what to do."

"For starters, why don't you let me make you some breakfast." Anthony's wife was defending a case in court. "It'll be just the two of us. Do waffles sound okay? There's some syrup in that cupboard. How about orange juice?"

The first thing Anthony's father did was learn how to drive the new types of vehicles. Anthony believed this was a sign of improving mental health. But then he discovered that his father was using his mobility not to investigate his new world, but instead to visit Marian's ashes in the mausoleum and to go to the once-pristine house that he'd owned forty-six years previously, a time period that to him was yesterday. Anthony had done something similar when he'd lied to his mother's second husband about being at the library when actually he'd been at the cryofirm visiting his father. It worried him.

"I found a 'For Sale' sign at the house," his father said one evening at dinner. "I want to buy it."

"But . . ." Anthony set down his fork. "The place is a wreck."

"It won't be after I'm finished with it."

Anthony felt as if he were arguing not with his father but with one of his children when they were determined to do something that he thought unwise.

"I can't stay here," his father said. "I can't live with you for the rest of my life."

"Why not? You're welcome."

"A father and his grown-up son? We'll get in each other's way."

"But we've gotten along so far."

"I want to buy the house."

Continuing to feel that he argued with his son, Anthony gave in as he always did. "All right, okay, fine. I'll help you get a loan. I'll help with the down payment. But if you're going to take on this kind of responsibility, you'll need a job."

"That's something else I want to talk to you about."

His father used his maintenance skills to become a successful contractor whose specialty was restoring old-style homes to their former beauty. Other contractors tried to compete, but Anthony's father had an edge: he knew those houses inside and out. He'd helped build them when he was a teenager working on summer construction jobs. He'd maintained his when that kind of house was in its prime, almost a half century earlier. Most important, he loved that old style of house.

One house in particular—the house where he'd started to raise his family. As soon as the renovation was completed, he found antique furniture from the period. When Anthony visited, he was amazed by how closely the house resembled the way it had looked when he was a child. His father had arranged to have Marian's urn released to him. It sat on a shelf in a study off the living room. Next to it were framed pictures of Anthony and his mother when they'd been young, the year Anthony's father had gotten sick.

His father found antique audio equipment from back then. The only songs he played were from that time. He even found an old computer and the game that he'd wanted to play with Anthony, teaching his great-grandson how to play it just as he'd already taught the little boy how to do somersaults on the lawn.

Anthony turned sixty. The hectic years of trying to save his father were behind him. He reduced his hours at the office. He followed an interest in gardening and taught himself to build a greenhouse. His father helped him.

"I need to ask you something," his father said one afternoon when the project was almost completed.

"You make it sound awfully serious."

His father looked down at his callused hands. "I have to ask your permission about something."

"Permission?" Anthony's frown deepened his wrinkles.

"Yes. I . . . It's been five years. I . . . Back then, you told me that I had to learn to live again."

"You've been doing a good job of it," Anthony said.

"I fought it for a long time." His father looked more uncomfortable.

"What's wrong?"

"I don't know how to . . ."

"Say it."

"I loved your mother to the depth of my heart."

Anthony nodded, pained with emotion.

"I thought I'd die without her," his father said. "Five years. I never expected . . . I've met somebody. The sister of a man whose house I'm renovating. We've gotten to know each other, and . . . Well, I . . . What I need to ask is, Would you object, would you see it as a betrayal of your mother if . . ."

Anthony felt pressure in his tear ducts. "Would I object?" His eyes misted. "All I want is for you to be happy."

Anthony was the best man at his father's wedding. His stepmother was the same age as his daughters. The following summer, he had a half-brother sixty-one years younger than himself. It felt odd to see his father acting toward the baby in the same loving manner that his father had presumably acted toward him when *he* was a baby.

At the celebration when the child was brought home from the hospital, several people asked Anthony if his wife was feeling ill. She looked wan.

"She's been working hard on a big trial coming up," he said.

The next day, she had a headache so bad that he took her to his clinic and had his staff do tests.

The day after that, she was dead. The viral meningitis that killed her was so virulent that nothing could have been done to save her. The miracle was that neither Anthony nor anybody else in the family had caught it, especially the new baby.

He felt drained. Plodding through his house, he tried to muster the energy to get through each day. The nights were harder. His father often came and sat with him, a young man next to an older one, doing his best to console him.

Anthony visited his wife's grave every day. On the anniversary of her death, while picking flowers for her, he collapsed from a stroke. The incident left him paralyzed on his left side, in need of constant care. His children wanted to put him in a facility.

"No," his father said. "It's *my* turn to watch over *him*."

So Anthony returned to the house where his youth had been wonderful until his father had gotten sick. During the many hours they spent together, his father asked Anthony to fill in more details of what had happened as Anthony had grown up: the arguments he'd had with the broker, his double shifts as a waiter, his first date with the woman who would be his wife.

"Yes, I can see it," his father said.

The next stroke reduced Anthony's intelligence to that of a nine-year-old. He didn't have the capacity to know that the computer on which he played a game with his father came from long ago. In fact, the game was the same one that his father had given him on his ninth birthday, two weeks before his father had gotten sick, the game that he'd never had a chance to play with his son.

One morning, he no longer had a nine-year-old's ability to play the game.

"His neurological functions are decreasing rapidly," the specialist said.

"Nothing can be done?"

"I'm sorry. At this rate . . . In a couple of days . . ."

Anthony's father felt as if he had a stone in his stomach.

"We'll make him as comfortable here as possible," the specialist said.

"No. My son should die at home."

Anthony's father sat next to the bed, holding his son's frail hand, painfully reminded of having taken care of him when he'd been sick as a child. Now Anthony looked appallingly old for sixty-three. His breathing was shallow. His eyes were open, glassy, not registering anything.

His children and grandchildren came to pay their last respects.

"At least, he'll be at peace," his second daughter said.

His father couldn't bear it.

Jesus, he didn't give up on me. I won't give up on *him*.

"That theory's been discredited," the specialist said.

"It works."

"In isolated cases, but—"

"I'm one of them."

"Of the few. At your son's age, he might not survive the procedure."

"Are you refusing to make the arrangements?"

"I'm trying to explain that with the expense and the risk—"

"My son will be dead by tomorrow. Being frozen can't be worse than *that*. And as far as the expense goes, he worked hard. He saved his money. He can afford it."

"But there's no guarantee that a treatment will ever be developed for brain cells as damaged as your son's are."

"There's no guarantee it *won't* be developed, either."

"He can't give his permission."

"He doesn't need to. He made me his legal representative."

"All the same, his children need to be consulted. There are issues of estate, a risk of a lawsuit."

"*I'll* take care of his children. *You* take care of the arrangements."

They stared at him.

Anthony's father couldn't tell if they resisted his idea because they counted on their inheritance. "Look, I'm begging. He'd have done this for you. He did it for *me*. For God's sake, you can't give up on him."

They stared harder.

"It's not going to cost you anything. I'll work harder and pay for it myself. I'll sign control of the estate over to you. All I want is, don't try to stop me."

Anthony's father stood outside the cryochamber, studying the stick-on plaque that he'd put on the hatch. It gave Anthony's name, his birthdate, when he'd had his first stroke, and when he'd been frozen. "Sweet dreams," it said at the bottom. "Wake up soon."

Soon was a relative word, of course. Anthony had been frozen six years, and there was still no progress in a treatment. But that didn't mean there wouldn't be progress tomorrow or next month. There's always hope, Anthony's father thought. You've got to have hope.

On a long narrow table in the middle of the corridor, there were tokens of affection left by loved ones of other patients: family photographs and a baseball glove, for example. Anthony's father had left the disc of the computer game that he and Anthony had been playing. "We'll play it again," he'd promised.

It was Anthony's father's birthday. He was forty-nine. He had gray in his sideburns, wrinkles in his forehead. I'll soon look like Anthony did when I woke up from being frozen and saw him leaning over me, he thought.

He couldn't subdue the discouraging notion that one of these days he'd be the same age as Anthony when he'd been frozen. But now that he thought about it, maybe that notion wasn't so discouraging. If they found a treatment that year, and they woke Anthony up, and the treatment worked . . . We'd both be sixty-six. We could grow old together.

I'll keep fighting for you, Anthony. I swear you can count on me. I couldn't let you die before me. It's a terrible thing for a father to outlive his son.

This one just kept growing and growing . . .

When Liz Hand first talked to me about "Cleopatra Brimstone" (isn't that a neat title?) she thought it would come in somewhere around eight thousand words. Then it began to grow. The next time we chatted (this is e-mail I'm talking about; which, as I've said before, is equivalent to the Victorian postal system—you can get "mail" in the morning, again at noon, and yet again in the late afternoon), she said it would come in at about fourteen thousand words. By that time I was getting tight for space in the book but thought fourteen thousand would be just fine—then the story landed on my doorstep (with a solid ka-thump!*) and I noted with horror that it had grown to almost twenty thousand words!*

As things were really tight by that time, I thought about asking Liz to cut the story—but I just couldn't. Her writing (as in her novels Black Light *and* Glimmering*) is so full-bodied and evocative that I had to present it as written.*

Cleopatra Brimstone

Elizabeth Hand

*

Her earliest memory was of wings. Luminous red and blue, yellow and green and orange; a black so rich it appeared liquid, edible. They moved above her, and the sunlight made them glow as though they were themselves made of light, fragments of another, brighter world falling to earth about her crib. Her tiny hands stretched upward to grasp them but could not: they were too elusive, too radiant, too much of the air.

Could they ever have been real?

For years she thought she must have dreamed them. But one afternoon when she was ten she went into the attic, searching for old clothes to wear to a Halloween party. In a corner beneath a cobwebbed window she found a box of her baby things. Yellow-stained bibs and tiny fuzzy jumpers blued from bleaching, a much-nibbled stuffed dog that she had no memory of whatsoever.

And at the very bottom of the carton, something else. Wings flattened and twisted out of shape, wires bent and strings frayed: a mobile. Six plastic butterflies, colors faded and their wings giving off a musty smell, no longer eidolons of Eden but crude representations of monarch, zebra swallowtail, red admiral, sulphur, an unnaturally elongated skipper and *Agrias narcissus*. Except for the *narcissus*, all were common New World species that any child might see in a suburban garden. They hung limply from their wires, antennae long since broken off; when she touched one wing it felt cold and stiff as metal.

The afternoon had been overcast, tending to rain. But as she held the mobile to the window, a shaft of sun broke through the darkness to ignite the plastic wings, bloodred, ivy green, the pure burning yellow of an August field. In that instant it was as though her entire being were burned away, skin hair lips fingers all ash; and nothing remained but the butterflies and her awareness of them, orange and black fluid filling her mouth, the edges of her eyes scored by wings.

As a girl she had always worn glasses. A mild childhood astigmatism worsened when she was thirteen: she started bumping into things and found it increasingly difficult to concentrate on the entomological textbooks and journals that she read voraciously. Growing pains, her mother thought; but after two months, Janie's clumsiness and concomitant headaches became so severe that her mother admitted that this was perhaps something more serious, and took her to the family physician.

"Janie's fine," Dr. Gordon announced after peering into her ears and eyes. "She needs to see the opthamologist, that's all. Sometimes our eyes change when we hit puberty." He gave her mother the name of an eye doctor nearby.

Her mother was relieved, and so was Jane—she had overheard her parents talking the night before her appointment, and the words *CAT scan* and *brain tumor* figured in their hushed conversation. Actually, Jane had been more concerned about another odd physical manifestation, one that no one but herself seemed to have noticed. She had started menstruating several months earlier: nothing unusual in that. Everything she had read about it mentioned the usual things—mood swings, growth spurts, acne, pubic hair.

But nothing was said about eyebrows. Janie first noticed something strange about hers when she got her period for the second time. She had retreated to the bathtub, where she spent a good half hour reading an article in *Nature* about oriental ladybug swarms. When she finished the article, she got out of the tub, dressed, and brushed her teeth, and then spent a minute frowning at the mirror.

Something was different about her face. She turned sideways, squinting. Had her chin broken out? No; but something had changed. Her hair color? Her teeth? She leaned over the sink until she was almost nose-to-nose with her reflection.

That was when she saw that her eyebrows had undergone a growth spurt of their own. At the inner edge of each eyebrow, above the bridge of her nose, three hairs had grown remarkably long. They furled back toward her temple, entwined in a sort of loose braid. She had not noticed them sooner because she seldom looked in a mirror, and also because the hairs did not arch above the eyebrows, but instead blended in with them, the way a bittersweet vine twines around a branch.

Still, they seemed bizarre enough that she wanted no one, not even her parents, to notice. She found her mother's tweezers, neatly plucked the six hairs, and flushed them down the toilet. They did not grow back.

At the optometrist's, Jane opted for heavy tortoiseshell frames rather than contacts. The optometrist, and her mother, thought she was crazy, but it was a very deliberate choice. Janie was not one of those homely B-movie adolescent girls, driven to science as a last resort. She had always been a tomboy, skinny as a rail, with long slanted violet-blue eyes; a small rosy mouth; long, straight black hair that ran like oil between her fingers; skin so pale it had the periwinkle shimmer of skim milk.

When she hit puberty, all of these conspired to beauty. And Jane hated it. Hated the attention, hated being looked at, hated that the other girls hated her. She was quiet, not shy but impatient to focus on her schoolwork, and this was mistaken for arrogance by her peers. All through high school she had few friends. She learned early the perils of befriending boys, even earnest boys who professed an interest in genetic mutations and intricate computer simulations of hive activity. Janie could trust them not to touch her, but she couldn't trust them not to fall in love. As a result of having none of the usual distractions of high school—sex, social life, mindless employment—she received an Intel/Westinghouse Science Scholarship for a computer-generated schematic of possible mutations in a small population of viceroy butterflies exposed to genetically engineered crops. She graduated in her junior year, took her scholarship money, and ran.

She had been accepted at Stanford and MIT, but chose to attend a small, highly prestigious women's college in a big city several hundred miles away. Her parents were apprehensive about her being on her own at the tender age of seventeen, but the college, with its elegant, cloister-like buildings and lushly wooded grounds, put them at ease. That and the dean's assurances that the neighborhood was completely safe, as long as students were sensible about not walking alone at night. Thus mollified, and at Janie's urging—she was desperate to move away from home—her father signed a very large check for the first semester's tuition. That September she started school.

She studied entomology, spending her first year examining the genitalia of male and female scarce wormwood shark moths, a species found on the Siberian steppes. Her hours in the zoology lab were rapturous, hunched over a microscope with a pair of tweezers so minute they were themselves like some delicate portion of her specimen's physiognomy. She would remove the butterflies' genitalia, tiny and geometrically precise as diatoms, and dip them first into glycerine, which acted as a preservative, and next into a mixture of water and alcohol. Then she observed them under the microscope. Her glasses interfered with this work—they bumped into the microscope's viewing lens—and so she switched to wearing contact lenses. In retrospect, she thought that this was probably a mistake.

At Argus College she still had no close friends, but neither was she the solitary creature she had been at home. She respected her fellow students and grew to appreciate the company of women. She could go for days at a time seeing no men besides her professors or the commuters driving past the school's wrought-iron gates.

And she was not the school's only beauty. Argus College specialized in young women like Jane: elegant, diffident girls who studied the burial customs of Mongol women or the mating habits of rare antipodean birds; girls who composed concertos for violin and gamelan orchestra, or wrote computer programs that charted the progress of potentially dangerous celestial objects through the Oort cloud. Within this educational greenhouse, Janie was not so much orchid as sturdy milkweed blossom. She thrived.

Her first three years at Argus passed in a bright-winged blur with her butterflies. Summers were given to museum internships, where she spent months cleaning and mounting specimens in solitary delight. In her senior year Janie received permission to design her own thesis project, involving her beloved shark moths. She was given a corner in a dusty anteroom off the zoology lab, and there she set up her microscope and laptop. There was no window in her corner, indeed there was no window in the anteroom at all, though the adjoining lab was pleasantly old-fashioned, with high-arched windows set between Victorian cabinetry displaying Lepidoptera, neon-carapaced beetles, unusual tree fungi, and (she found these slightly tragic) numerous exotic finches, their brilliant plumage dimmed to dusty hues. Since she often worked late into the night, she requested and received her own set of keys. Most evenings she could be found beneath the glare of the small halogen lamp, entering data into her computer, scanning images of genetic mutations involving female shark moths exposed to dioxane, corresponding with other researchers in Melbourne and Kyoto, Siberia and London.

The rape occurred around ten o'clock one Friday night in early March. She had locked the door to her office, leaving her laptop behind, and started to walk to the subway station a few blocks away. It was a cold, clear night, the yellow glow of the crime lights giving dead grass and leafless trees an eerie autumn glow. She hurried across the campus, seeing no one, and then hesitated at Seventh Street. It was a longer walk, but safer, if she went down Seventh Street and then over to Michigan Avenue. The shortcut was much quicker, but Argus authorities and the local police discouraged students from taking it after dark. Jane stood for a moment, staring across the road to where the desolate park lay; then, staring resolutely straight ahead and walking briskly, she crossed Seventh and took the shortcut.

A crumbling sidewalk passed through a weedy expanse of vacant lot, strewn with broken bottles and the spindly forms of half a dozen dusty-limbed oak trees. Where the grass ended, a narrow road skirted a block of abandoned row houses, intermittently lit by crime lights. Most of the lights had been vandalized, and one had been knocked down in a car accident—the car's fender was still there, twisted around the lamppost. Jane picked her way carefully among shards of shattered glass, reached the sidewalk in front of the boarded-up houses, and began to walk more quickly, toward the brightly lit Michigan Avenue intersection where the subway waited.

She never saw him. He was *there*, she knew that; knew he had a face, and clothing; but afterwards she could recall none of it. Not the feel of him, not his smell; only the knife he held—awkwardly, she realized later, she probably could have wrested it from him—and the few words he spoke to her. He said nothing at first, just grabbed her and pulled her into an alley between the row houses, his fingers covering her mouth, the heel of his hand pressing against her windpipe so that she gagged. He pushed her onto the dead leaves and wads of matted windblown newspaper, yanked her pants down, ripped open her jacket, and then tore her shirt open. She heard one of the buttons strike back and roll away. She thought desperately of what she had read once, in a Rape Awareness brochure: not to struggle, not to fight, not to do anything that might cause her attacker to kill her.

Janie did not fight. Instead, she divided into three parts. One part knelt nearby and prayed the way she had done as a child, not intently but automatically, trying to get through the strings of words as quickly as possible. The second part submitted blindly and silently to the man in the alley. And the third hovered above the other two, her hands wafting slowly up and down to keep her aloft as she watched.

"Try to get away," the man whispered. She could not see him or feel him though his hands were there. "Try to get away."

She remembered that she ought not to struggle, but from the noises he made and the way he tugged at her realized that was what aroused him. She did not want to anger him; she made a small sound deep in her throat and tried to push him from her chest. Almost immediately he groaned, and seconds later rolled off her. Only his hand lingered for a moment upon her cheek. Then he stumbled to his feet—she could hear him fumbling with his zipper—and fled.

The praying girl and the girl in the air also disappeared then. Only Janie was left, yanking her ruined clothes around her as she lurched from the alley and began to run, screaming and staggering back and forth across the road, toward the subway.

The police came, an ambulance. She was taken first to the police station and then to the City General Hospital, a hellish place, starkly lit, with endless underground corridors that led into darkened rooms where solitary figures lay on narrow beds like gurneys. Her pubic hair was combed and stray hairs placed into sterile envelopes; semen samples were taken, and she was advised to be tested for HIV and other diseases. She spent the entire night in the hospital, waiting and undergoing various examinations. She refused to give the police or hospital staff her parents' phone number or anyone else's. Just before dawn they finally released her, with an envelope full of brochures from the local Rape Crisis Center, New Hope for Women, Planned Parenthood, and a business card from the police detective who was overseeing her case. The detective drove her to her apartment in his squad car; when he stopped in front of her building, she was suddenly terrified that he would know where she lived, that he would come back, that he had been her assailant.

But, of course, he had not been. He walked her to the door and waited for her to go inside. "Call your parents," he said right before he left.

"I will."

She pulled aside the bamboo window shade, watching until the squad car pulled away. Then she threw out the brochures she'd received, flung off her clothes and stuffed them into the trash. She showered and changed, packed a bag full of clothes and another of books. Then she called a cab. When it arrived, she directed it to the Argus campus, where she retrieved her laptop and her research on tiger moths, and then had the cab bring her to Union Station.

She bought a train ticket home. Only after she arrived and told her parents what had happened did she finally start to cry. Even then, she could not remember what the man had looked like.

She lived at home for three months. Her parents insisted that she get psychiatric counseling and join a therapy group for rape survivors. She did so, reluctantly, but stopped attending after three weeks. The rape was something that had happened to her, but it was over.

"It was fifteen minutes out of my life," she said once at group. "That's all. It's not the rest of my life."

This didn't go over very well. Other women thought she was in denial; the therapist thought Jane would suffer later if she did not confront her fears now.

"But I'm not afraid," said Jane.

"Why not?" demanded a woman whose eyebrows had fallen out.

Because lightning doesn't strike twice, Jane thought grimly, but she said nothing. That was the last time she attended group.

That night her father had a phone call. He took the phone and sat at the dining table, listening; after a moment stood and walked into his study, giving a quick backward glance at his daughter before closing the door behind him. Jane felt as though her chest had suddenly frozen, but after some minutes she heard her father's laugh; he was not, after all, talking to the police detective. When after half an hour he returned, he gave Janie another quick look, more thoughtful this time.

"That was Andrew." Andrew was a doctor friend of his, an Englishman. "He and Fred are going to Provence for three months. They were wondering if you might want to house-sit for them."

"In *London*?" Jane's mother shook her head. "I don't think—"

"I said we'd think about it."

"*I'll* think about it," Janie corrected him. She stared at both her parents, absently ran a finger along one eyebrow. "Just let me think about it."

And she went to bed.

She went to London. She already had a passport, from visiting Andrew with her parents when she was in high school. Before she left there were countless arguments with her mother and father, and phone calls back and forth to Andrew. He assured them that the flat was secure, there was a very nice reliable older woman who lived upstairs, that it would be a good idea for Janie to get out on her own again.

"So you don't get gun-shy," he said to her one night on the phone. He was a doctor, after all: a homeopath not an allopath, which Janie found reassuring. "It's important for you to get on with our life. You won't be able to get a real job here as a visitor, but I'll see what I can do."

It was on the plane to Heathrow that she made a discovery. She had splashed water onto her face, and was beginning to comb her hair when she blinked and stared into the mirror.

Above her eyebrows, the long hairs had grown back. They followed the contours of her brow, sweeping back toward her temples; still entwined, still difficult to make out unless she drew her face close to her reflection and tilted her head just so. Tentatively she touched one braided strand. It was stiff yet oddly pliant; but as she ran her finger along its length a sudden *surge* flowed through her. Not an electrical shock: more like the thrill of pain when a dentist's drill touches a nerve, or an elbow rams against a stone. She gasped; but immediately the pain was gone. Instead there was a thrumming behind her forehead, a spreading warmth that trickled into her throat like sweet syrup. She opened her mouth, her gasp turning into an uncontrollable yawn, the yawn into a spike of such profound physical ecstasy that she grabbed the edge of the sink and thrust forward, striking her head against the mirror. She was dimly aware of someone knocking at the lavatory door as she clutched the sink and, shuddering, climaxed.

"Hello?" someone called softly. "Hello, is this occupied?"

"Right out," Janie gasped. She caught her breath, still trembling; ran a hand across her face, her finger halting before they could touch the hairs above her eyebrows. There was the faintest tingling, a temblor of sensation that faded as she grabbed her cosmetic bag, pulled the door open, and stumbled back into the cabin.

Andrew and Fred lived in an old Georgian row house just west of Camden Town, overlooking the Regent's Canal. Their flat occupied the first floor and basement; there was a hexagonal solarium out back, with glass walls and heated stone floor, and beyond that a stepped terrace leading down to the canal. The bedroom had an old wooden four-poster piled high with duvets and down pillows, and French doors that also opened onto the terrace. Andrew showed her how to operate the elaborate sliding security doors that unfolded from the walls, and gave her the keys to the barred window guards.

"You're completely safe here," he said, smiling. "Tomorrow we'll introduce you to Kendra upstairs and show you how to get around. Camden Market's just down that way, and *that* way—"

He stepped out onto the terrace, pointing to where the canal coiled and disappeared beneath an arched stone bridge. "—that way's the Regent's Park Zoo. I've given you a membership—"

"Oh! Thank you!" Janie looked around delighted. "This is *wonderful.*"

"It is." Andrew put an arm around her and drew her close. "You're going to have a wonderful time, Janie. I thought you'd like the zoo—there's a new exhibit there, 'The World Within' or words to that effect—it's about insects. I thought perhaps you might want to volunteer there—they have an active docent program, and you're so knowledgeable about that sort of thing."

"Sure. It sounds great—really great." She grinned and smoothed her hair back from her face, the wind sending up the rank scent of stagnant water from the canal, the sweetly poisonous smell of hawthorn blossom.

As she stood gazing down past the potted geraniums and Fred's rosemary trees, the hairs upon her brow trembled, and she laughed out loud, giddily, with anticipation.

Fred and Andrew left two days later. It was enough time for Janie to get over her jet lag and begin to get barely acclimated to the city, and to its smell. London had an acrid scent: damp ashes, the softer underlying fetor of rot that oozed from ancient bricks and stone buildings, the thick vegetative smell of the canal, sharpened with urine and spilled beer. So many thousands of people descended on Camden Town on the weekend that the tube station was restricted to incoming passengers, and the canal path became almost impassable. Even late on a weeknight she could hear voices from the other side of the canal, harsh London voices echoing beneath the bridges or shouting to be heard above the din of the Northern Line trains passing overhead.

Those first days Janie did not venture far from the flat. She unpacked her clothes, which did not take much time, and then unpacked her collecting box, which did. The sturdy wooden case had come through the overseas flight and customs seemingly unscathed, but Janie found herself holding her breath as she undid the metal hinges, afraid of what she'd find inside.

"*Oh!*" she exclaimed. Relief, not chagrin: nothing had been damaged. The small glass vials of ethyl alcohol and gel shellac were intact, and the pillboxes where she kept the tiny #2 pins she used for mounting. Fighting her own eagerness, she carefully removed packets of stiff archival paper; a block of Styrofoam covered with pinholes; two bottles of clear Maybelline nail polish and a small container of Elmer's Glue-All; more pillboxes, empty, and empty gelatine capsules for very small specimens; and last of all a small glass-fronted display box, framed in mahogany and holding her most precious specimen: a hybrid *Celerio harmuthi kordesch*, the male crossbreed of the spurge and elephant hawkmoths. As long as the first joint of her thumb, it had the hawkmoth's typically streamlined wings but exquisitely delicate coloring, fuchsia bands shading to a soft rich brown, its thorax thick and seemingly feathered. Only a handful of these hybrid moths had ever existed, bred by the Prague entomologist Jan Pokorny in 1961; a few years afterward, both the spurge hawkmoth and the elephant hawkmoth had become extinct.

Janie had found this one for sale on the Internet three months ago. It was a former museum specimen and cost a fortune; she had a few bad nights, worrying whether it had actually been a legal purchase. Now she held the display box in her cupped palms and gazed at it raptly. Behind her eyes she felt a prickle, like sleep or unshed tears; then a slow thrumming warmth crept from her brows, spreading to her temples, down her neck and through her breasts, spreading like a stain. She swallowed, leaned back against the sofa, and let the display box rest back within the larger case; slid first one hand and then the other beneath her sweater and began to stroke her nipples. When some time later she came it was with stabbing force and a thunderous sensation above her eyes, as though she had struck her forehead against the floor.

She had not; gasping, she pushed the hair from her face, zipped her jeans, and reflexively leaned forward, to make certain the hawkmoth in its glass box was safe.

Over the following days she made a few brief forays to the newsagent and greengrocer, trying to eke out the supplies Fred and Andrew had left in the kitchen. She sat in the solarium, her bare feet warm against the heated stone floor, and drank chamomile tea or claret, staring down to where the ceaseless stream of people passed along the canal path, and watching the narrow boats as they piled their way slowly between Camden Lock and Little Venice, two miles to the west in Paddington. By the following Wednesday she felt brave enough, and bored enough, to leave her refuge and visit the zoo.

It was a short walk along the canal, dodging bicyclists who jingled their bells impatiently when she forgot to stay on the proper side of the path. She passed beneath several arching bridges, their undersides pleated with slime and moss. Drunks sprawled against the stones and stared at her blearily or challengingly by turns; well-dressed couples walked dogs, and there were excited knots of children, tugging their parents on to the zoo.

Fred had walked here with Janie, to show her the way. But it all looked unfamiliar now. She kept a few strides behind a family, her head down, trying not to look as though she was following them; and felt a pulse of relief when they reached a twisting stair with an arrowed sign at its top.

REGENT'S PARK ZOO

There was an old old church across the street, its yellow stone walls overgrown with ivy, and down and around the corner a long stretch of hedges with high iron walls fronting them, and at last a huge set of gates, crammed with children and vendors selling balloons and banners and London guidebooks. Janie lifted her head and walked quickly past the family that had led her here, showed her membership card at the entrance, and went inside.

She wasted no time on the seals or tigers or monkeys, but went straight to the newly renovated structure where a multicolored banner flapped in the late-morning breeze.

AN ALTERNATE UNIVERSE: SECRETS OF THE INSECT WORLD

Inside, crowds of schoolchildren and harassed-looking adults formed a ragged queue that trailed through a brightly lit corridor, its walls covered with huge glossy color photos and computer-enhanced images of hissing cockroaches, hellgrammites, morpho butterflies, deathwatch beetles, polyphemous moths. Janie dutifully joined the queue, but when the corridor opened into a vast sunlit atrium she strode off on her own, leaving the children and teachers to gape at monarchs in butterfly cages and an interactive display of honeybees dancing. Instead she found a relatively quiet display at the far end of the exhibition space, a floor-to-ceiling cylinder of transparent net, perhaps six feet in diameter. Inside, buckthorn bushes and blooming hawthorn vied for sunlight with a slender beech sapling, and dozens of butterflies flitted upward through the new yellow leaves, or sat with wings outstretched upon the beech tree. They were a type of Pieridae, the butterflies known as whites; though these were not white at all. The females had creamy yellow-green wings, very pale, their wingspans perhaps an inch and a half. The males were the same size; when they were at rest their flattened wings were a dull, rather sulphurous color. But when the males lit into the air, their wings revealed vivid, spectral yellow undersides. Janie caught her breath in delight, her neck prickling with that same atavistic joy she'd felt as a child in the attic.

"Wow," she breathed, and pressed up against the netting. It felt like wings against her face, soft, webbed; but as she stared at the insects inside, her brow began to ache as with migraine. She shoved her glasses onto her nose, closed her eyes, and drew a long breath; then she took a step away from the cage. After a minute she opened her eyes. The headache had diminished to a dull throb; when she hesitantly touched one eyebrow, she could feel the entwined hairs there, stiff as wire. They were vibrating, but at her touch the vibrations, like the headache, dulled. She stared at the floor, the tiles sticky with contraband juice and gum; then she looked up once again at the cage. There was a display sign off to one side; she walked over to it, slowly, and read.

Cleopatra Brimstone

Gonepteryx rhamni cleopatra

This popular and subtly colored species has a range that extends throughout the northern hemisphere, with the exception of arctic regions and several remote islands. In Europe, the brimstone is a harbinger of spring, often emerging from its winter hibernation under dead leaves to revel in the countryside while there is still snow upon the ground.

"I must ask you please not to touch the cages."

Janie turned to see a man, perhaps fifty, standing a few feet away. A net was jammed under his arm; in his hand he held a clear plastic jar with several butterflies at the bottom, apparently dead.

"Oh. Sorry," said Jane. The man edged past her. He set his jar on the floor, opened a small door at the base of the cylindrical cage, and deftly angled the net inside. Butterflies lifted in a yellow-green blur from leaves and branches; the man swept the net carefully across the bottom of the cage and then withdrew it. Three dead butterflies, like scraps of colored paper, drifted from the net into the open jar.

"Housecleaning," he said, and once more thrust his arm into the cage. He was slender and wiry, not much taller than she was, his face hawkish and burnt brown from the sun, his thick straight hair iron-streaked and pulled back into a long braid. He wore black jeans and a dark-blue hooded jersey, with an ID badge clipped to the collar.

"You work here," said Janie. The man glanced at her, his arm still in the cage; she could see him sizing her up. After a moment he glanced away again. A few minutes later he emptied the net for the last time, closed the cage and the jar, and stepped over to a waste bin, pulling bits of dead leaves from the net and dropping them into the container.

"I'm one of the curatorial staff. You American?"

Janie nodded. "Yeah. Actually, I—I wanted to see about volunteering here."

"Lifewatch desk at the main entrance." The man cocked his head toward the door. "They can get you signed up and registered, see what's available."

"No—I mean, I want to volunteer here. With the insects—"

"Butterfly collector, are you?" The man smiled, his tone mocking. He had hazel eyes, deep-set; his thin mouth made the smile seem perhaps more cruel than intended. "We get a lot of those."

Janie flushed. "No. I am not a *collector*," she said coldly, adjusting her glasses. "I'm doing a thesis on dioxane genital mutation in *Cucullia artemisia*." She didn't add that it was an undergraduate thesis. "I've been doing independent research for seven years now." She hesitated, thinking of her Intel scholarship, and added, "I've received several grants for my work."

The man regarded her appraisingly. "Are you studying here, then?"

"Yes," she lied again. "At Oxford. I'm on sabbatical right now. But I live near here, and so I thought I might—"

She shrugged, opening her hands, looked over at him, and smiled tentatively. "Make myself useful?"

The man waited a moment, nodded. "Well. Do you have a few minutes now? I've got to do something with these, but if you want you can come with me and wait, and then we can see what we can do. Maybe circumvent some paperwork."

He turned and started across the room. He had a graceful, bouncing gait, like a gymnast or circus acrobat: impatient with the ground beneath him. "Shouldn't take long," he called over his shoulder as Janie hurried to catch up.

She followed him through a door marked AUTHORIZED PERSONS ONLY, into the exhibit laboratory, a reassuringly familiar place with its display cases and smells of shellac and camphor, acetone and ethyl alcohol. There were more cages here, but smaller ones, sheltering live specimens—pupating butterflies and moths, stick insects, leaf insects, dung beetles. The man dropped his net onto a desk, took the jar to a long table against one wall, blindingly lit by long fluorescent tubes. There were scores of bottles here, some empty, others filled with paper and tiny inert figures.

"Have a seat," said the man, gesturing at two folding chairs. He settled into one, grabbed an empty jar and a roll of absorbent paper. "I'm David Bierce. So where're you staying? Camden Town?"

"Janie Kendall. Yes—"

"The High Street?"

Janie sat in the other chair, pulling it a few inches away from him. The questions made her uneasy, but she only nodded, lying again, and said, "Closer, actually. Off Gloucester Road. With friends."

"Mm." Bierce tore off a piece of absorbent paper, leaned across to a stainless-steel sink and dampened the paper. Then he dropped it into the empty jar. He paused, turned to her and gestured at the table, smiling. "Care to join in?"

Janie shrugged. "Sure—"

She pulled her chair closer, found another empty jar and did as Bierce had, dampening a piece of paper towel and dropping it inside.

Then she took the jar containing the dead brimstones and carefully shook one onto the counter. It was a female, its coloring more muted than the males'; she scooped it up very gently, careful not to disturb the scales like dull green glitter upon its wings, dropped it into the jar and replaced the top.

"Very nice." Bierce nodded, raising his eyebrows. "You seem to know what you're doing. Work with other insects? Soft-bodied ones?"

"Sometimes. Mostly moths, though. And butterflies."

"Right." He inclined his head to a recessed shelf. "How would you label that, then? Go ahead."

On the shelf she found a notepad and a case of Rapidograph pens. She began to write, conscious of Bierce staring at her. "We usually just put all this into the computer, of course, and print it out," he said. "I just want to see the benefits of an American education in the sciences."

Janie fought the urge to look at him. Instead she wrote out the information, making her printing as tiny as possible.

Gonepteryx rhamni cleopatra
UNITED KINGDOM: LONDON
Regent's Park Zoo
Lat/Long unknown
21.IV.2001
D. Bierce
Net/caged specimen

She handed it to Bierce. "I don't know the proper coordinates for London."

Bierce scrutinized the paper. "It's actually the Royal Zoological Society," he said. He looked at her, and then smiled. "But you'll do."

"Great!" She grinned, the first time she'd really felt happy since arriving here. "When do you want me to start?"

"How about Monday?"

Janie hesitated: this was only Friday. "I could come in tomorrow—"

"I don't work on the weekend, and you'll need to be trained. Also they have to process the paperwork. Right—"

He stood and went to a desk, pulling open drawers until he found a clipboard holding sheafs of triplicate forms. "Here. Fill all this out, leave it with me, and I'll pass it on to Carolyn—she's the head volunteer coordinator. They usually want to interview you, but I'll tell them we've done all that already."

"What time should I come in Monday?"

"Come at nine. Everything opens at ten; that way you'll avoid the crowds. Use the staff entrance, someone there will have an ID waiting for you to pick up when you sign in—"

She nodded and began filling out the forms.

"All right then." David Bierce leaned against the desk and again fixed her with that sly, almost taunting gaze. "Know how to find your way home?"

Janie lifted her chin defiantly. "Yes."

"Enjoying London? Going to go out tonight and do Camden Town with all the yobs?"

"Maybe. I haven't been out much yet."

"Mm. Beautiful American girl—they'll eat you alive. Just kidding." He straightened, started across the room toward the door. "I'll you see Monday then."

He held the door for her. "You really should check out the clubs. You're too young not to see the city by night." He smiled, the fluorescent light slanting sideways into his hazel eyes and making them suddenly glow icy blue. "Bye then."

"Bye," said Janie, and hurried quickly from the lab toward home.

That night, for the first time, she went out. She told herself she would have gone anyway, no matter what Bierce had said. She had no idea where the clubs were; Andrew had pointed out the Electric Ballroom to her, right up from the tube station, but he'd also warned her that was where the tourists flocked on weekends.

"They do a disco thing on Saturday nights—Saturday Night Fever, everyone gets all done up in vintage clothes. Quite a fashion show," he'd said, smiling and shaking his head.

Janie had no interest in that. She ate a quick supper, vindaloo from the take-away down the street from the flat; then she dressed. She hadn't brought a huge amount of clothes—at home she'd never bothered much with clothes at all, making do with thrift-shop finds and whatever her mother gave her for Christmas. But now she found herself sitting on the edge of the four-poster, staring with pursed lips at the sparse contents of two bureau drawers. Finally she pulled out a pair of black corduroy jeans and a black turtleneck and pulled on her sneakers. She removed her glasses and for the first time in weeks inserted her contact lenses. Then she shrugged into her old navy peacoat and left.

It was after ten o'clock. On the canal path, throngs of people stood, drinking from pints of canned lager. She made her way through them, ignoring catcalls and whispered invitations, stepping to avoid where kids lay making out against the brick wall that ran alongside the path or pissing in the bushes. The bridge over the canal at Camden Lock was clogged with several dozen kids in mohawks or varicolored hair, shouting at each other above the din of a boom box and swigging from bottles of Spanish champagne.

A boy with a champagne bottle leered, lunging at her.

" 'Ere, sweetheart, 'ep youseff—"

Janie ducked, and he careered against the ledge, his arm striking brick and the bottle shattering in a starburst of black and gold.

"Fucking cunt!" he shrieked after her. "Fucking bloody *cunt*!"

People glanced at her, but Janie kept her head down, making a quick turn into the vast cobbled courtyard of Camden Market. The place had a desolate air: the vendors would not arrive until early next morning, and now only stray cats and bits of windblown trash moved in the shadows. In the surrounding buildings people spilled out onto balconies, drinking and calling back and forth, their voices hollow and their long shadows twisting across the ill-lit central courtyard. Janie hurried to the far end, but there found only brick walls, closed-up shop doors, and a young woman huddled within the folds of a filthy sleeping bag.

"*Couldya—couldya—*" the woman murmured.

Janie turned and followed the wall until she found a door leading into a short passage. She entered it, hoping she was going in the direction of Camden High Street. She felt like Alice trying to find her way through the garden in Wonderland: arched doorways led not into the street but headshops and brightly lit piercing parlors, open for business; other doors opened onto enclosed courtyards, dark and smelling of piss and marijuana. Finally from the corner of her eye she glimpsed what looked like the end of the passage, headlights piercing through the gloom like landing lights. Doggedly she made her way toward them.

"Ay watchowt watchowt," someone yelled as she emerged from the passage onto the sidewalk and ran the last few steps to the curb.

She was on the High Street—rather, in that block or two of curving no-man's-land where it turned into Chalk Farm Road. The sidewalks were still crowded, but everyone was heading toward Camden Lock and not away from it. Janie waited for the light to change and raced across the street, to where a cobblestoned alley snaked off between a shop selling leather underwear and another advertising "Fine French Country Furniture."

For several minutes she stood there. She watched the crowds heading toward Camden Town, the steady stream of minicabs and taxis and buses heading up Chalk Farm Road toward Hampstead. Overhead, dull orange clouds moved across a night sky the color of charred wood; there was the steady low thunder of jets circling after takeoff at Heathrow. At last she tugged her collar up around her neck, letting her hair fall in loose waves down her back, shoved her hands into her coat pockets, and turned to walk purposefully down the alley.

Before her the cobblestone path turned sharply to the right. She couldn't see what was beyond, but she could hear voices: a girl laughing, a man's sibilant retort. A moment later the alley spilled out onto a cul-de-sac. A couple stood a few yards away, before a doorway with a small copper awning above it. The young woman glanced sideways at Janie, quickly looked away again. A silhouette filled the doorway; the young man pulled out a wallet. His hand disappeared within the silhouette, reemerged, and the couple walked inside. Janie waited until the shadowy figure withdrew. She looked over her shoulder and then approached the building.

There was a heavy metal door, black, with graffiti scratched into it and pale blurred spots where painted graffiti had been effaced. The door was set back several feet into a brick recess; there was a grilled metal slot at the top that could be slid back, so that one could peer out into the courtyard. To the right of the door, on the brick wall within the recess, was a small brass plaque with a single word on it.

HIVE

There was no doorbell or any other way to signal that you wanted to enter. Janie stood, wondering what was inside; feeling a small tingling unease that was less fear than the knowledge that even if she were to confront the figure who'd let that other couple inside, she herself would certainly be turned away.

With a *skreek* of metal on stone the door suddenly shot open. Janie looked up, into the sharp, raggedly handsome face of a tall, still youngish man with very short blond hair, a line of gleaming gold beads like drops of sweat piercing the edge of his left jaw.

"Good evening," he said, glancing past her to the alley. He wore a black sleeveless T-shirt with a small golden bee embroidered upon the breast. His bare arms were muscular, striated with long sweeping scars: black, red, white. "Are you waiting for Hannah?"

"No." Quickly Janie pulled out a handful of five-pound notes. "Just me tonight."

"That'll be twenty then." The man held his hand out, still gazing at the alley; when Janie slipped the notes to him he looked down and flashed her a vulpine smile. "Enjoy yourself." She darted past him into the building.

Abruptly it was as though some darker night had fallen. Thunderously so, since the enfolding blackness was slashed with music so loud it was itself like light: Janie hesitated, closing her eyes, and white flashes streaked across her eyelids like sleet, pulsing in time to the music. She opened her eyes, giving them a chance to adjust to the darkness, and tried to get a sense of where she was. A few feet away a blurry grayish lozenge sharpened into the window of a coat-check room. Janie walked past it, toward the source of the music. Immediately the floor slanted steeply beneath her feet. She steadied herself with one hand against the wall, following the incline until it opened onto a cavernous dance floor.

She gazed inside, disappointed. It looked like any other club, crowded, strobe-lit, turquoise smoke and silver glitter coiling between hundreds of whirling bodies clad in candy pink, sky blue, neon red, rainslicker yellow. Baby colors, Janie thought. There was a boy who was almost naked, except for shorts, a transparent water bottle strapped to his chest and long tubes snaking into his mouth. Another boy had hair the color of lime Jell-O, his face corrugated with glitter and sweat; he swayed near the edge of the dance floor, turned to stare at Janie, and then beamed, beckoning her to join him.

Janie gave him a quick smile, shaking her head; when the boy opened his arms to her in mock pleading she shouted "No!"

But she continued to smile, though she felt as though her head would crack like an egg from the throbbing music. Shoving her hands into her pockets she skirted the dance floor, pushed her way to the bar and bought a drink, something pink with no ice in a plastic cup. It smelled like Gatorade and lighter fluid. She gulped it down and then carried the cup held before her like a torch as she continued on her circuit of the room. There was nothing else of interest, just long queues for the lavatories and another bar, numerous doors and stairwells where kids clustered, drinking and smoking. Now and then beeps and whistles like birdsong or insect cries came through the stuttering electronic din, whoops and trilling laughter from the dancers. But mostly they moved in near silence, eyes rolled ceiling-ward, bodies exploding into Catherine wheels of flesh and plastic and nylon, but all without a word.

It gave Janie a headache—a *real* headache, the back of her skull bruised, tender to the touch. She dropped her plastic cup and started looking for a way out. She could see past the dance floor to where she had entered, but it seemed as though another hundred people had arrived in the few minutes since then: kids were standing six deep at both bars, and the action on the floor had spread, amoebalike, toward the corridors angling back up toward the street.

"Sorry—"

A fat woman in an Arsenal jersey jostled her as she hurried by, leaving a smear of oily sweat on Janie's wrist. Janie grimaced and wiped her hand on the bottom of her coat. She gave one last look at the dance floor, but nothing had changed within the intricate lattice of dancers and smoke, braids of glow-lights and spotlit faces surging up and down, up and down, while more dancers fought their way to the center.

"Shit." She turned and strode off, heading to where the huge room curved off into relative emptiness. Here, scores of tables were scattered, some overturned, others stacked against the wall. A few people sat, talking; a girl lay curled on the floor, her head pillowed on a Barbie knapsack. Janie crossed to the wall and found first a door that led to a bare brick wall, then a second door that held a broom closet. The next was dark-red, metal, official-looking: the kind of door that Janie associated with school fire drills.

A fire door. It would lead outside, or into a hall that would lead there. Without hesitating she pushed it open and entered. A short corridor lit by EXIT signs stretched ahead of her, with another door at the end. She hurried toward it, already reaching reflexively for the keys to the flat, pushed the door-bar, and stepped inside.

For an instant she thought she had somehow stumbled into a hospital emergency room. There was the glitter of halogen light on steel, distorted reflections thrown back at her from curved glass surfaces; the abrasive odor of isopropyl alcohol and the fainter tinny scent of blood, like metal in the mouth.

And bodies: everywhere, bodies, splayed on gurneys or suspended from gleaming metal hooks, laced with black electrical cord and pinned upright onto smooth rubber mats. She stared openmouthed, neither appalled nor frightened but fascinated by the conundrum before her: how did *that* hand fit *there*, and whose leg was *that*? She inched backwards, pressing herself against the door and trying to stay in the shadows—just inches ahead of her ribbons of luminous bluish light streamed from lamps hung high overhead. The chiaroscuro of pallid bodies and black furniture, shiny with sweat and here and there red-streaked, or brown; the mere sight of so many bodies, real bodies—flesh spilling over the edge of tabletops, too much hair or none at all, eyes squeezed shut in ecstasy or terror and mouths open to reveal stained teeth, pale gums—the sheer *fluidity* of it all enthralled her. She felt as she had, once, pulling aside a rotted log to disclose the ant's nest beneath, masses of minute fleeing bodies, soldiers carrying eggs and larvae in their jaws, tunnels spiraling into the center of another world. Her brow tingled, warmth flushed her from brow to breast . . .

Another world, that's what she had found then, and discovered again now.

"*Out.*"

Janie sucked her breath in sharply. Fingers dug into her shoulder, yanked her back through the metal door so roughly that she cut her wrist against it.

"No lurkers, what the fuck—"

A man flung her against the wall. She gasped, turned to run, but he grabbed her shoulder again. "Christ, a fucking girl."

He sounded angry but relieved. She looked up: a huge man, more fat than muscle. He wore very tight leather briefs and the same black sleeveless shirt with a golden bee embroidered upon it. "How the hell'd you get in like *that*?" he demanded, cocking a thumb at her.

She shook her head, then realized he meant her clothes. "I was just trying to find my way out."

"Well you found your way in. In like fucking Flynn." He laughed: he had gold-capped teeth, and gold wires threading the tip of his tongue. "You want to join the party, you know the rules. No exceptions."

Before she could reply he turned and was gone, the door thudding softly behind him. She waited, heart pounding, then reached and pushed the bar on the door.

Locked. She was out, not in; she was nowhere at all. For a long time she stood there, trying to hear anything from the other side of the door, waiting to see if anyone would come back looking for her. At last she turned, and began to find her way home.

Next morning she woke early, to the sound of delivery trucks in the street and children on the canal path, laughing and squabbling on their way to the zoo. She sat up with a pang, remembering David Bierce and her volunteer job; then she recalled this was Saturday not Monday.

"Wow," she said aloud. The extra days seemed like a gift.

For a few minutes she lay in Fred and Andrew's great four-poster, staring abstractedly at where she had rested her mounted specimens atop the wainscoting—the hybrid hawkmoth; a beautiful Honduran owl butterfly, *Caligo atreus;* a mourning cloak she had caught and mounted herself years ago. She thought of the club last night, mentally retracing her steps to the hidden back room, thought of the man who had thrown her out, the interplay of light and shadow upon the bodies pinned to mats and tables. She had slept in her clothes; now she rolled out of bed and pulled her sneakers on, forgoing breakfast but stuffing her pocket with ten- and twenty-pound notes before she left.

It was a clear cool morning, with a high pale-blue sky and the young leaves of nettles and hawthorn still glistening with dew. Someone had thrown a shopping cart from the nearby Sainsbury's into the canal; it edged sideways up out of the shallow water, like a frozen shipwreck. A boy stood a few yards down from it, fishing, an absent, placid expression on his face.

She crossed over the bridge to the canal path and headed for the High Street. With every step she took the day grew older, noisier, trains rattling on the bridge behind her and voices harsh as gulls rising from the other side of the brick wall that separated the canal path from the street.

At Camden Lock she had to fight her way through the market. There were tens of thousands of tourists, swarming from the maze of shops to pick their way between scores of vendors selling old and new clothes, bootleg CDs, cheap silver jewelry, kilims, feather boas, handcuffs, cell phones, mass-produced furniture and puppets from Indonesia, Morocco, Guyana, Wales. The fug of burning incense and cheap candles choked her; she hurried to where a young woman was turning samosas in a vat of sputtering oil and dug into her pocket for a handful of change, standing so that the smells of hot grease and scorched chickpea batter canceled out patchouli and Caribbean Nights.

"Two, please," Janie shouted.

She ate and almost immediately felt better; then she walked a few steps to where a spike-haired girl sat behind a table covered with cheap clothes made of ripstock fabric in Jell-O shades.

"Everything five pounds," the girl announced. She stood, smiling helpfully as Janie began to sort through pairs of hugely baggy pants. They were cross-seamed with Velcro and deep zippered pockets. Janie held up a pair, frowning as the legs billowed, lavender and green, in the wind.

"It's so you can make them into shorts," the girl explained. She stepped around the table and took the pants from Janie, deftly tugging at the legs so that they detached. "See? Or a skirt." The girl replaced the pants, picked up another pair, screaming orange with black trim, and a matching windbreaker. "This color would look nice on you."

"Okay." Janie paid for them, waited for the girl to put the clothes in a plastic bag. "Thanks."

"Bye now."

She went out into Camden High Street. Shopkeepers stood guard over the tables spilling out from their storefronts, heaped with leather clothes and souvenir T-shirts: MIND THE GAP, LONDON UNDERGROUND, shirts emblazoned with the Cat in the Hat toking on a cheroot. THE CAT IN THE HAT SMOKES BLACK. Every three or four feet someone had set up a boom box, deafening sound bites of salsa, techno, "The Hustle," Bob Marley, "Anarchy in the UK," Radiohead. On the corner of Inverness and the High Street a few punks squatted in a doorway, looking over the postcards they'd bought. A sign in a smoked-glass window said ALL HAIRCUTS 10 £, MEN WOMEN CHILDREN.

"Sorry," one of the punks said as Janie stepped over them and into the shop.

The barber was sitting in an old-fashioned chair, his back to her, reading the *Sun*. At the sound of her footsteps he turned, smiling automatically. "Can I help you?"

"Yes please. I'd like my hair cut. All of it."

He nodded, gesturing to the chair. "Please."

Janie had thought she might have to convince him that she was serious. She had beautiful hair, well below her shoulders—the kind of hair people would kill for, she'd been hearing that her whole life. But the barber just hummed and chopped it off, the *snick snick* of his shears interspersed with kindly questions about whether she was enjoying her visit and his account of a vacation to Disney World ten years earlier.

"Dear, do we want it shaved or buzz-cut?"

In the mirror a huge-eyed creature gazed at Janie, like a tarsier or one of the owlish caligo moths. She stared at it, entranced, and then nodded. "Shaved. Please."

When he was finished she got out of the chair, dazed, and ran her hand across her scalp. It was smooth and cool as an apple. There were a few tiny nicks that stung beneath her fingers. She paid the barber, tipping him two pounds. He smiled and held the door open for her.

"Now when you want a touch-up, you come see us, dear. Only five pounds for a touch-up."

She went next to find new shoes. There were more shoe shops in Camden Town than she had ever seen anywhere in her life; she checked out four of them on one block before deciding on a discounted pair of twenty-hole black Doc Martens. They were no longer fashionable, but they had blunted steel caps on the toes. She bought them, giving the salesgirl her old sneakers to toss into the waste bin. When she went back onto the street it was like walking in wet cement—the shoes were so heavy, the leather so stiff that she ducked back into the shoe shop and bought a pair of heavy wool socks and put them on. She returned outside, hesitating on the front step before crossing the street and heading back in the direction of Chalk Farm Road. There was a shop here that Fred had shown her before he left.

"Now, that's where you get your fetish gear, Janie," he said, pointing to a shop window painted matte black. THE PLACE, it said in red letters, with two linked circles beneath. Fred had grinned and rapped his knuckles against the glass as they walked by. "I've never been in; you'll have to tell me what it's like." They'd both laughed at the thought.

Now Janie walked slowly, the wind chill against her bare skull. When she could make out the shop, sun glinting off the crimson letters and a sad-eyed dog tied to a post out front, she began to hurry, her new boots making a hollow thump as she pushed through the door.

There was a security gate inside, a thin, sallow young man with dreadlocks nodding at her silently as she approached.

"You'll have to check that." He pointed at the bag with her new clothes in it. She handed it to him, reading the warning posted behind the counter.

SHOPLIFTERS WILL BE BEATEN,
FLAYED, SPANKED, BIRCHED, BLED,
AND THEN PROSECUTED
TO THE FULL EXTENT OF THE LAW

The shop was well lit. It smelled strongly of new leather and coconut oil and pine-scented disinfectant. She seemed to be the only customer this early in the day, although she counted seven employees manning cash registers, unpacking cartons, watching to make sure she didn't try to nick anything. A CD of dance music played, and the phone rang constantly.

She spent a good half hour just walking through the place, impressed by the range of merchandise. Electrified wands to deliver shocks, things like meat cleavers made of stainless steel with rubber tips. Velcro dog collars, Velcro hoods, black rubber balls and balls in neon shades; a mat embedded with three-inch spikes that could be conveniently rolled up and came with its own lightweight carrying case. As she wandered about more customers arrived, some of them greeting the clerks by name, others furtive, making a quick circuit of the shelves before darting outside again. At last Janie knew what she wanted. A set of wristcuffs and one of anklecuffs, both of very heavy black leather with stainless steel hardware; four adjustable nylon leashes, also black, with clips on either end that could be fastened to cuffs or looped around a post; a few spare S-clips.

"That it?"

Janie nodded, and the register clerk began scanning her purchases. She felt almost guilty, buying so few things, not taking advantage of the vast Meccano glory of all those shelves full of gleaming, somber contrivances.

"There you go." He handed her the receipt, then inclined his head at her. "Nice touch, that—"

He pointed at her eyebrows. Janie drew her hand up, felt the long pliant hairs uncoiling like baby ferns. “Thanks,” she murmured. She retrieved her bag and went home to wait for evening.

It was nearly midnight when she left the flat. She had slept for most of the afternoon, a deep but restless sleep, with anxious dreams of flight, falling, her hands encased in metal gloves, a shadowy figure crouching above her. She woke in the dark, heart pounding, terrified for a moment that she had slept all the way through till Sunday night.

But, of course, she had not. She showered, then dressed in a tight, low-cut black shirt and pulled on her new nylon pants and heavy boots. She seldom wore makeup, but tonight after putting in her contacts she carefully outlined her eyes with black and then chose a very pale lavender lipstick. She surveyed herself in the mirror critically. With her white skin, huge violet eyes, and hairless skull, she resembled one of the Balinese puppets for sale in the market—beautiful but vacant, faintly ominous. She grabbed her keys and money, pulled on her windbreaker, and headed out.

When she reached the alley that led to the club, she entered it, walked about halfway, and stopped. After glancing back and forth to make sure no one was coming, she detached the legs from her nylon pants, stuffing them into a pocket, and then adjusted the Velcro tabs so that the pants became a very short orange-and-black skirt. Her long legs were sheathed in black tights. She bent to tighten the laces on her metal-toed boots and hurried to the club entrance.

Tonight there was a line of people waiting to get in. Janie took her place, fastidiously avoiding looking at any of the others. They waited for thirty minutes, Janie shivering in her thin nylon windbreaker, before the door opened and the same gaunt blond man appeared to take their money. Janie felt her heart beat faster when it was her turn, wondering if he would recognize her. But he only scanned the courtyard, and, when the last of them darted inside, closed the door with a booming *clang*.

Inside, all was as it had been, only far more crowded. Janie bought a drink, orange squash, no alcohol. It was horribly sweet, with a bitter, curdled aftertaste. Still, it had cost two pounds: she drank it all. She had just started on her way down to the dance floor when someone came up from behind to tap her shoulder, shouting into her ear.

“Wanna?”

It was a tall, broad-shouldered boy a few years older than she was, perhaps twenty-four, with a lean ruddy face, loose shoulder-length blond hair streaked green, and deep-set, very dark blue eyes. He swayed dreamily, gazing at the dance floor and hardly looking at her at all.

“Sure,” Janie shouted back. He looped an arm around her shoulder, pulling her with him; his striped V-neck shirt smelled of talc and sweat. They danced for a long time, Janie moving with calculated abandon, the boy heaving and leaping as though a dog were biting at his shins.

"You're beautiful," he shouted. There was an almost imperceptible instant of silence as the DJ changed tracks. "What's your name?"

"Cleopatra Brimstone."

The shattering music grew deafening once more. The boy grinned. "Well, Cleopatra. Want something to drink?"

Janie nodded in time with the beat, so fast her head spun. He took her hand and she raced to keep up with him, threading their way toward the bar.

"Actually," she yelled, pausing so that he stopped short and bumped up against her. "I think I'd rather go outside. Want to come?"

He stared at her, half-smiling, and shrugged. "Aw right. Let me get a drink first—"

They went outside. In the alley the wind sent eddies of dead leaves and newspaper flying up into their faces. Janie laughed and pressed herself against the boy's side. He grinned down at her, finished his drink, and tossed the can aside; then he put his arm around her. "Do you want to go get a drink, then?" he asked.

They stumbled out onto the sidewalk, turned and began walking. People filled the High Street, lines snaking out from the entrances of pubs and restaurants. A blue glow surrounded the streetlights, and clouds of small white moths beat themselves against the globes; vapor and banners of gray smoke hung above the punks blocking the sidewalk by Camden Lock. Janie and the boy dipped down into the street. He pointed to a pub occupying the corner a few blocks down, a large old green-painted building with baskets of flowers hanging beneath its windows and a large sign swinging back and forth in the wind: THE END OF THE WORLD. "In there, then?"

Janie shook her head. "I live right here, by the canal. We could go to my place if you want. We could have a few drinks there."

The boy glanced down at her. "Aw right," he said—very quickly, so she wouldn't change her mind. "That'd be awright."

It was quieter on the back street leading to the flat. An old drunk huddled in a doorway, cadging change; Janie looked away from him and got out her keys, while the boy stood restlessly, giving the drunk a belligerent look.

"Here we are," she announced, pushing the door open. "Home again, home again."

"Nice place." The boy followed her, gazing around admiringly. "You live here alone?"

"Yup." After she spoke Janie had a flash of unease, admitting that. But the boy only ambled into the kitchen, running a hand along the antique French farmhouse cupboard and nodding.

"You're American, right? Studying here?"

"Uh-huh. What would you like to drink? Brandy?"

He made a face, then laughed. "Aw right! You got expensive taste. Goes with the name, I'd guess." Janie looked puzzled, and he went on, "Cleopatra—fancy name for a girl."

"Fancier for a boy," Janie retorted, and he laughed again.

She got the brandy, stood in the living room unlacing her boots. "Why don't we go in there?" she said, gesturing toward the bedroom. "It's kind of cold out here."

The boy ran a hand across his head, his blond hair streaming through his fingers. "Yeah, aw right." He looked around. "Um, that the toilet there?" Janie nodded. "Right back, then . . ."

She went into the bedroom, set the brandy and two glasses on a night table, and took off her windbreaker. On another table, several tall candles, creamy white and thick as her wrist, were set into ornate brass holders. She lit these—the room filled with the sweet scent of beeswax—and sat on the floor, leaning against the bed. A few minutes later the toilet flushed and the boy reappeared. His hands and face were damp, redder than they had been. He smiled and sank onto the floor beside her. Janie handed him a glass of brandy.

"Cheers," he said, and drank it all in one gulp.

"Cheers," said Janie. She took a sip from hers, then refilled his glass. He drank again, more slowly this time. The candles threw a soft yellow haze over the four-poster bed with its green velvet duvet, the mounds of pillows, forest-green, crimson, saffron yellow. They sat without speaking for several minutes. Then the boy set his glass on the floor. He turned to face Janie, extending one arm around her shoulder and drawing his face near hers.

"Well, then," he said.

His mouth tasted acrid, nicotine and cheap gin beneath the blunter taste of brandy. His hand sliding under her shirt was cold; Janie felt goose pimples rising across her breast, her nipple shrinking beneath his touch. He pressed against her, his cock already hard, and reached down to unzip his jeans.

"Wait," Janie murmured. "Let's get on the bed. . . ."

She slid from his grasp and onto the bed, crawling to the heaps of pillow and feeling beneath one until she found what she had placed there earlier. "Let's have a little fun first."

"*This* is fun," the boy said, a bit plaintively. But he slung himself onto the bed beside her, pulling off his shoes and letting them fall to the floor with a thud. "What you got there?"

Smiling, Janie turned and held up the wristcuffs. The boy looked at them, then at her, grinning. "Oh, ho. Been in the back room, then—"

Janie arched her shoulders and unbuttoned her shirt. He reached for one of the cuffs, but she shook her head. "No. Not me, yet."

"Ladies first."

"Gentleman's pleasure."

The boy's grin widened. "Won't argue with that."

She took his hand and pulled him, gently, to the middle of the bed. "Lie on your back," she whispered.

He did, watching as she removed first his shirt and then his jeans and underwear. His cock lay nudged against his thigh, not quite hard; when she brushed her fingers against it he moaned softly, took her hand and tried to press it against him.

"No," she whispered. "Not yet. Give me your hand."

She placed the cuffs around each wrist, and his ankles; fastened the nylon leash to each one and then began tying the bonds around each bedpost. It took longer than she had expected; it was difficult to get the bonds taut enough that the boy could not move. He lay there watchfully, his eyes glimmering in the candlelight as he craned his head to stare at her, his breath shallow, quickening.

"There." She sat back upon her haunches, staring at him. His cock was hard now, the hair on his chest and groin tawny in the half-light. He gazed back at her, his tongue pale as he licked his lips. "Try to get away," she whispered.

He moved slightly, his arms and legs a white X against a deep green field. "Can't," he said hoarsely.

She pulled her shirt off, then her nylon skirt. She had nothing on beneath. She leaned forward, letting her fingers trail from the cleft in his throat to his chest, cupping her palm atop his nipple and then sliding her hand down to his thigh. The flesh was warm, the little hairs soft and moist. Her own breath quickened; sudden heat flooded her, a honeyed liquid in her mouth. Above her brow the long hairs stiffened and furled straight out to either side: when she lifted her head to the candlelight she could see them from the corner of her eyes, twin barbs black and glistening like wire.

"You're so sexy." The boy's voice was hoarse. "God, you're—"

She placed her hand over his mouth. "Try to get away," she said, commandingly this time. "*Try to get away.*"

His torso writhed, the duvet bunching up around him in dark folds.

She raked her fingernails down his chest, and he cried out, moaning "Fuck me, god, fuck me . . ."

"Try to get away."

She stroked his cock, her fingers barely grazing its swollen head. With a moan he came, struggling helplessly to thrust his groin toward her. At the same moment Janie gasped, a fiery rush arrowing down from her brow to her breasts, her cunt. She rocked forward, crying out, her head brushing against the boy's side as she sprawled back across the bed. For a minute she lay there, the room around her seeming to pulse and swirl into myriad crystalline shapes, each bearing within it the same line of candles, the long curve of the boy's thigh swelling up into the hollow of his hip. She drew breath shakily, the flush of heat fading from her brow; then pushed herself up until she was sitting beside him. His eyes were shut. A thread of saliva traced the furrow between mouth and chin. Without thinking she drew her face down to his, and kissed his cheek.

Immediately he began to grow smaller. Janie reared back, smacking into one of the bedposts, and stared at the figure in front of her, shaking her head.

"No," she whispered. "No, no."

He was shrinking: so fast it was like watching water dissolve into dry sand. Man-size, child-size, large dog, small. His eyes flew open and for a fraction of a second stared horrified into her own. His hands and feet slipped like mercury from his bonds, wriggling until they met his torso and were absorbed into it. Janie's fingers kneaded the duvet; six inches away the boy was no larger than her hand, then smaller, smaller still. She blinked, for a heart-shredding instant thought he had disappeared completely.

Then she saw something crawling between folds of velvet. The length of her middle finger, its thorax black, yellow-striped, its lower wings elongated into frilled arabesques like those of a festoon, deep yellow, charcoal black, with indigo eyespots, its upper wings a chiaroscuro of black and white stripes.

Bhutanitis lidderdalii. A native of the eastern Himalayas, rarely glimpsed: it lived among the crowns of trees in mountain valleys, its caterpillars feeding on lianas. Janie held her breath, watching as its wings beat feebly. Without warning it lifted into the air. Janie cried out, falling onto her knees as she sprawled across the bed, cupping it quickly but carefully between her hands.

"Beautiful, beautiful," she crooned. She stepped from the bed, not daring to pause and examine it, and hurried into the kitchen. In the cupboard she found an empty jar, set it down, and gingerly angled the lid from it, holding one hand with the butterfly against her breast. She swore, feeling its wings fluttering against her fingers, then quickly brought her hand to the jar's mouth, dropped the butterfly inside, and screwed the lid back in place. It fluttered helplessly inside; she could see where the scales had already been scraped from its wing. Still swearing she ran back into the bedroom, putting the lights on and dragging her collection box from under the bed. She grabbed a vial of ethyl alcohol, went back into the kitchen and tore a bit of paper towel from the rack. She opened the vial, poured a few drops of ethyl alcohol onto the paper, opened the jar and gently tilted it onto its side. She slipped the paper inside, very slowly tipping the jar upright once more, until the paper had settled on the bottom, the butterfly on top of it. Its wings beat frantically for a few moments, then stopped. Its proboscis uncoiled, finer than a hair. Slowly Janie drew her own hand to her brow and ran it along the length of the antennae there. She sat there staring at it until the sun leaked through the wooden shutters in the kitchen window. The butterfly did not move again.

The next day passed in a metallic gray haze, the only color the saturated blues and yellows of the *lidderdalii's* wings, burned upon Janie's eyes as though she had looked into the sun. When she finally roused herself, she felt a spasm of panic at the sight of the boy's clothes on the bedroom floor.

"Shit." She ran her hand across her head, was momentarily startled to recall she had no hair. "Now what?"

She stood there for a few minutes, thinking; then she gathered the clothes—striped V-neck sweater, jeans, socks, Jockey shorts, Timberland knockoff shoes—and dumped them into a plastic Sainsbury's bag. There was a wallet in the jeans pocket. She opened it, gazed impassively at a driver's license—KENNETH REED, WOLVERHAMPTON—and a few five-pound notes. She pocketed the money, took the license into the bathroom, and burned it, letting the ashes drop into the toilet. Then she went outside.

It was early Sunday morning, no one about except for a young mother pushing a baby in a stroller. In the neighboring doorway the same drunk old man sprawled surrounded by empty bottles and rubbish. He stared blearily up at Janie as she approached.

"Here," she said. She bent and dropped the five-pound notes into his scabby hand.

"God bless you, darlin'." He coughed, his eyes focusing on neither Janie nor the notes. "God bless you."

She turned and walked briskly back toward the canal path. There were few waste bins in Camden Town, and so each day trash accumulated in rank heaps along the path, beneath streetlights, in vacant alleys. Street cleaners and sweeping machines then daily cleared it all away again. Like elves, Janie thought. As she walked along the canal path she dropped the shoes in one pile of rubbish, tossed the sweater alongside a single high-heeled shoe in the market, stuffed the underwear and socks into a collapsing cardboard box filled with rotting lettuce, and left the jeans beside a stack of papers outside an unopened newsagent's shop. The wallet she tied into the Sainsbury's bag and dropped into an overflowing trash bag outside of Boots. Then she retraced her steps, stopping in front of a shop window filled with tatty polyester lingerie in large sizes and boldly artificial-looking wigs: pink Afros, platinum blond falls, black-and-white Cruella De Vil tresses.

The door was propped open; Schubert lieder played softly on 3 2. Janie stuck her head in and looked around, saw a beefy man behind the register, cashing out. He had orange lipstick smeared around his mouth and delicate silver fish hanging from his ears.

"We're not open yet. Eleven on Sunday," he said without looking up.

"I'm just looking." Janie sidled over to a glass shelf where four wigs sat on Styrofoam heads. One had very glossy black hair in a chin-length flapper bob. Janie tried it on, eyeing herself in a grimy mirror. "How much is this one?"

"Fifteen. But we're not—"

"Here. Thanks!" Janie stuck a twenty-pound note on the counter and ran from the shop. When she reached the corner she slowed, pirouetted to catch her reflection in a shop window. She stared at herself, grinning, then walked the rest of the way home, exhilarated and faintly dizzy.

Monday morning she went to the zoo to begin her volunteer work. She had mounted the *Bhutanitis lidderdalii*, on a piece of Styrofoam with a piece of paper on it, to keep the butterfly's legs from becoming embedded in the Styrofoam. She'd softened it first, putting it into a jar with damp paper, removed it and placed it on the mounting platform, neatly spearing its thorax—a little to the right—with a #2 pin. She propped it carefully on the wainscoting beside the hawkmoth, and left.

She arrived and found her ID badge waiting for her at the staff entrance. It was a clear morning, warmer than it had been for a week; the long hairs on her brow vibrated as though they were wires that had been plucked. Beneath the wig her shaved head felt hot and moist, the first new hairs starting to prickle across her scalp. Her nose itched where her glasses pressed against it. Janie walked, smiling, past the gibbons howling in their habitat and the pygmy hippos floating calmly in their pool, their eyes shut, green bubbles breaking around them like little fish. In front of the insect zoo a uniformed woman was unloading sacks of meal from a golf cart.

"Morning," Janie called cheerfully, and went inside.

She found David Bierce standing in front of a temperature gauge beside a glass cage holding the hissing cockroaches.

"Something happened last night, the damn things got too cold." He glanced over, handed her a clipboard, and began to remove the top of the gauge. "I called Operations but they're at their fucking morning meeting. Fucking computers—"

He stuck his hand inside the control box and flicked angrily at the gauge. "You know anything about computers?"

"Not this kind." Janie brought her face up to the cage's glass front. Inside were half a dozen glossy roaches, five inches long and the color of pale maple syrup. They lay, unmoving, near a glass petri dish filled with what looked like damp brown sugar. "Are they dead?"

"Those things? They're fucking immortal. You could stamp on one, and it wouldn't die. Believe me, I've done it." He continued to fiddle with the gauge, finally sighed, and replaced the lid. "Well, let's let the boys over in Ops handle it. Come on, I'll get you started."

He gave her a brief tour of the lab, opening drawers full of dissecting instruments, mounting platforms, pins; showing her where the food for the various insects was kept in a series of small refrigerators. Sugar syrup, cornstarch, plastic containers full of smaller insects, grubs and mealworms, tiny gray beetles. "Mostly we just keep on top of replacing the ones that die," David explained, "that and making sure the plants don't develop the wrong kind of fungus. Nature takes her course, and we just goose her along when she needs it. School groups are here constantly, but the docents handle that. You're more than welcome to talk to them, if that's the sort of thing you want to do."

He turned from where he'd been washing empty jars at a small sink, dried his hands, and walked over to sit on top of a desk. "It's not terribly glamorous work here." He reached down for a Styrofoam cup of coffee and sipped from it, gazing at her coolly. "We're none of us working on our Ph.D.'s anymore."

Janie shrugged. "That's all right."

"It's not even all that interesting. I mean, it can be very repetitive. Tedious."

"I don't mind." A sudden pang of anxiety made Janie's voice break. She could feel her face growing hot, and quickly looked away. "Really," she said sullenly.

"Suit yourself. Coffee's over there; you'll probably have to clean yourself a cup, though." He cocked his head, staring at her curiously, and then said, "Did you do something different with your hair?"

She nodded once, brushing the edge of her bangs with a finger. "Yeah."

"Nice. Very Louise Brooks." He hopped from the desk and crossed to a computer set up in the corner. "You can use my computer if you need to, I'll give you the password later."

Janie nodded, her flush fading into relief. "How many people work here?"

"Actually, we're short-staffed here right now—no money for hiring and our grant's run out. It's pretty much just me and whoever Carolyn sends over from the docents. Sweet little bluehairs mostly; they don't much like bugs. So it's providential you turned up, *Jane*."

He said her name mockingly, gave her a crooked grin. "You said you have experience mounting? Well, I try to save as many of the dead specimens as I can, and when there's any slow days, which there never are, I mount them and use them for the workshops I do with the schools that come in. What would be nice would be if we had enough specimens that I could give some to the teachers, to take back to their classrooms. We have a nice Web site and we might be able to work up some interactive programs. No schools are scheduled today, Monday's usually slow here. So if you could work on some of *those*—" He gestured to where several dozen cardboard boxes and glass jars were strewn across a countertop. "—that would be really brilliant," he ended, and turned to his computer screen.

She spent the morning mounting insects. Few were interesting or unusual: a number of brown hairstreaks, some Camberwell beauties, three hissing cockroaches, several brimstones. But there was a single *Acherontia atropos*, the death's-head hawkmoth, the pattern of gray and brown and pale yellow scales on the back of its thorax forming the image of a human skull. Its proboscis was unfurled, the twin points sharp enough to pierce a finger: Janie touched it gingerly, wincing delightedly as a pinprick of blood appeared on her fingertip.

"You bring lunch?"

She looked away from the bright magnifying light she'd been using and blinked in surprise. "Lunch?"

David Bierce laughed. "Enjoying yourself? Well, that's good, makes the day go faster. Yes, lunch!" He rubbed his hands together, the harsh light making him look gnomelike, his sharp features malevolent and leering. "They have some decent fish and chips at the stall over by the cats. Come on, I'll treat you. Your first day."

They sat at a picnic table beside the food booth and ate. David pulled a bottle of ale from his knapsack and shared it with Janie. Overhead scattered clouds like smoke moved swiftly southward. An Indian woman with three small boys sat at another table, the boys tossing fries at seagulls that swept down, shrieking, and made the smallest boy wail.

"Rain later," David said, staring at the sky. "Too bad." He sprinkled vinegar on his fried haddock and looked at Janie. "So did you go out over the weekend?"

She stared at the table and smiled. "Yeah, I did. It was fun."

"Where'd you go? The Electric Ballroom?"

"God, no. This other place." She glanced at his hand resting on the table beside her. He had long fingers, the knuckles slightly enlarged; but the back of his hand was smooth, the same soft brown as the *Acherontia's* wingtips. Her brows prickled, warmth trickling from them like water. When she lifted her head she could smell him, some kind of musky soap, salt; the bittersweet ale on his breath.

"Yeah? Where? I haven't been out in months, I'd be lost in Camden Town these days."

"I dunno. The Hive?"

She couldn't imagine he would have heard of it—far too old. But he swiveled on the bench, his eyebrows arching with feigned shock. "You went to *Hive*? And they let you in?"

"Yes," Janie stammered. "I mean, I didn't know—it was just a dance club. I just—danced."

"Did you." David Bierce's gaze sharpened, his hazel eyes catching the sun and sending back an icy emerald glitter. "Did you."

She picked up the bottle of ale and began to peel the label from it. "Yes."

"Have a boyfriend, then?"

She shook her head, rolled a fragment of label into a tiny pill. "No."

"Stop that." His hand closed over hers. He drew it away from the bottle, letting it rest against the table edge. She swallowed: he kept his hand on top of hers, pressing it against the metal edge until she felt her scored palm began to ache. Her eyes closed: she could feel herself floating, and see a dozen feet below her own form, slender, the wig beetle-black upon her skull, her wrist like a bent stalk. Abruptly his hand slid away and beneath the table, brushing her leg as he stooped to retrieve his knapsack.

"Time to get back to work," he said lightly, sliding from the bench and slinging his bag over his shoulder. The breeze lifted his long graying hair as he turned away. "I'll see you back there."

Overhead the gulls screamed and flapped, dropping bits of fried fish on the sidewalk. She stared at the table in front of her, the cardboard trays that held the remnants of lunch, and watched as a yellow jacket landed on a fleck of grease, its golden thorax swollen with moisture as it began to feed.

She did not return to Hive that night. Instead she wore a patchwork dress over her jeans and Doc Martens, stuffed the wig inside a drawer, and headed to a small bar on Inverness Street. The fair day had turned to rain, black puddles like molten metal capturing the amber glow of traffic signals and streetlights.

There were only a handful of tables at Bar Ganza. Most of the customers stood on the sidewalk outside, drinking and shouting to be heard above the sound of wailing Spanish love songs. Janie fought her way inside, got a glass of red wine, and miraculously found an empty stool alongside the wall. She climbed onto it, wrapped her long legs around the pedestal, and sipped her wine.

"Hey. Nice hair." A man in his early thirties, his own head shaved, sidled up to Janie's stool. He held a cigarette, smoking it with quick, nervous gestures as he stared at her. He thrust his cigarette toward the ceiling, indicating a booming speaker. "You like the music?"

"Not particularly."

"Hey, you're American? Me, too. Chicago. Good bud of mine, works for Citibank, he told me about this place. Food's not bad. Tapas. Baby octopus. You like octopus?"

Janie's eyes narrowed. The man wore expensive-looking corduroy trousers, a rumpled jacket of nubby charcoal-colored linen. "No," she said, but didn't turn away.

"Me neither. Like eating great big slimy bugs. Geoff Lanning—"

He stuck his hand out. She touched it, lightly, and smiled. "Nice to meet you, Geoff."

For the next half hour or so she pretended to listen to him, nodding and smiling brilliantly whenever he looked up at her. The bar grew louder and more crowded, and people began eyeing Janie's stool covetously.

"I think I'd better hand over this seat," she announced, hopping down and elbowing her way to the door. "Before they eat me."

Geoff Lanning hurried after her. "Hey, you want to get dinner? The Camden Brasserie's just up here—"

"No thanks." She hesitated on the curb, gazing demurely at her Doc Martens. "But would you like to come in for a drink?"

He was very impressed by her apartment. "Man, this place'd probably go for a half mil, easy! That's three quarters of a million American."

He opened and closed cupboards, ran a hand lovingly across the slate sink. "Nice hardwood floors, high-speed access—you never told me what you do."

Janie laughed. "As little as possible. Here—"

She handed him a brandy snifter, let her finger trace the back of his wrist. "You look like kind of an adventurous sort of guy."

"Hey, big adventure, that's me." He lifted his glass to her. "What exactly did you have in mind? Big-game hunting?"

"Mmm. Maybe."

It was more of a struggle this time, not for Geoff Lanning but for Janie. He lay complacently in his bonds, his stocky torso wriggling obediently when Janie commanded. Her head ached from the cheap wine at Bar Ganza; the long hairs above her eyes lay sleek against her skull, and did not move at all until she closed her eyes and, unbidden, the image of David Bierce's hand covering hers appeared.

"Try to get away," she whispered.

"Whoa, Nellie," Geoff Lanning gasped.

"Try to get away," she repeated, her voice hoarser.

"Oh." The man whimpered softly. "Jesus Christ, what—oh, my God, *what*—"

Quickly she bent and kissed his fingertips, saw where the leather cuff had bitten into his pudgy wrist. This time she was prepared when with a keening sound he began to twist upon the bed, his arms and legs shriveling and then coiling in upon themselves, his shaven head withdrawing into his tiny torso like a snail within its shell.

But she was not prepared for the creature that remained, its feathery antennae a trembling echo of her own, its extraordinarily elongated hind spurs nearly four inches long.

"*Oh*," she gasped.

She didn't dare touch it until it took to the air: the slender spurs fragile as icicles, scarlet, their saffron tips curling like Christmas ribbon, its large delicate wings saffron with slate-blue and scarlet eyespots, and spanning nearly six inches. A Madagascan moon moth, one of the loveliest and rarest silk moths, and almost impossible to find as an intact specimen.

"What do I do with you, what do I do?" she crooned as it spread its wings and lifted from the bed. It flew in short sweeping arcs; she scrambled to blow out the candles before it could get near them. She pulled on a bathrobe and left the lights off, closed the bedroom door and hurried into the kitchen, looking for a flashlight. She found nothing, but recalled Andrew telling her there was a large torch in the basement.

She hadn't been down there since her initial tour of the flat. It was brightly lit, with long neat cabinets against both walls, a floor-to-ceiling wine rack filled with bottles of claret and vintage burgundy, compact washer and dryer, small refrigerator, buckets and brooms waiting for the cleaning lady's weekly visit. She found the flashlight sitting on top of the refrigerator, a container of extra batteries beside it. She switched it on and off a few times, then glanced down at the refrigerator and absently opened it.

Seeing all that wine had made her think the little refrigerator might be filled with beer. Instead it held only a long plastic box, with a red lid and a red biohazard sticker on the side. Janie put the flashlight down and stooped, carefully removing the box and setting it on the floor. A label with Andrew's neat architectural handwriting was on the top.

DR. ANDREW FILDERMAN
ST. MARTIN'S HOSPICE

"Huh," she said, and opened it.

Inside there was a small red biohazard waste container and scores of plastic bags filled with disposable hypodermics, ampules, and suppositories. All contained morphine at varying dosages. Janie stared, marveling, then opened one of the bags. She shook half a dozen morphine ampules into her palm, carefully reclosed the bag, put it back into the box, and returned the box to the refrigerator. Then she grabbed the flashlight and ran upstairs.

It took her a while to capture the moon moth. First she had to find a killing jar large enough, and then she had to very carefully lure it inside, so that its frail wing spurs wouldn't be damaged. She did this by positioning the jar on its side and placing a gooseneck lamp directly behind it, so that the bare bulb shone through the glass. After about fifteen minutes, the moth landed on top of the jar, its tiny legs slipping as it struggled on the smooth curved surface. Another few minutes and it had crawled inside, nestled on the wad of tissues Janie had set there, moist with ethyl alcohol. She screwed the lid on tightly, left the jar on its side, and waited for it to die.

Over the next week she acquired three more specimens. *Papilio demetrius*, a Japanese swallowtail with elegant orange eyespots on a velvety black ground; a scarce copper, not scarce at all, really, but with lovely pumpkin-colored wings; and *Graphium agamemnon*, a Malaysian species with vivid green spots and chrome-yellow strips on its somber brown wings. She'd ventured away from Camden Town, capturing the swallowtail in a private room in an SM club in Islington and the

Graphium agamemnon in a parked car behind a noisy pub in Crouch End. The scarce copper came from a vacant lot near the Tottenham Court Road tube station very late one night, where the wreckage of a chain-link fence stood in for her bedposts. She found the morphine to be useful, although she had to wait until immediately after the man ejaculated before pressing the ampule against his throat, aiming for the carotid artery. This way the butterflies emerged already sedated, and in minutes died with no damage to their wings. Leftover clothing was easily disposed of, but she had to be more careful with wallets, stuffing them deep within rubbish bins, when she could, or burying them in her own trash bags and then watching as the waste trucks came by on their rounds.

In South Kensington she discovered an entomological supply store. There she bought more mounting supplies and inquired casually as to whether the owner might be interested in purchasing some specimens.

He shrugged. "Depends. What you got?"

"Well, right now I have only one *Argema mittrei*." Janie adjusted her glasses and glanced around the shop. A lot of morphos, an Atlas moth: nothing too unusual. "But I might be getting another, in which case . . ."

"Moon moth, eh? How'd you come by that, I wonder?" The man raised his eyebrows, and Janie flushed. "Don't worry, I'm not going to turn you in. Christ, I'd go out of business. Well, obviously I can't display those in the shop, but if you want to part with one, let me know. I'm always scouting for my customers."

She began volunteering three days a week at the insect zoo. One Wednesday, the night after she'd gotten a gorgeous *Urania leilus*, its wings sadly damaged by rain, she arrived to see David Bierce reading that morning's *Camden New Journal*. He peered above the newspaper and frowned.

"You still going out alone at night?"

She froze, her mouth dry, turned, and hurried over to the coffeemaker. "Why?" she said, fighting to keep her tone even.

"Because there's an article about some of the clubs around here. Apparently a few people have gone missing."

"Really?" Janie got her coffee, wiping up a spill with the side of her hand. "What happened?"

"Nobody knows. Two blokes reported gone, family frantic, that sort of thing. Probably just runaways. Camden Town eats them alive, kids." He handed the paper to Janie. "Although one of them was last seen near Highbury Fields, some sex club there."

She scanned the article. There was no mention of any suspects. And no bodies had been found, although foul play was suspected. *("Ken would never have gone away without notifying us or his employer. . . .")*

Anyone with any information was urged to contact the police.

"I don't go to sex clubs," Janie said flatly. "Plus those are both guys."

"Mmm." David leaned back in his chair, regarding her coolly. "You're the one hitting Hive your first weekend in London."

"It's a *dance* club!" Janie retorted. She laughed, rolled the newspaper into a tube, and batted him gently on the shoulder. "Don't worry. I'll be careful."

David continued to stare at her, hazel eyes glittering. "Who says it's you I'm worried about?"

She smiled, her mouth tight as she turned and began cleaning bottles in the sink.

It was a raw day, more late November than mid-May. Only two school groups were scheduled; otherwise the usual stream of visitors was reduced to a handful of elderly women who shook their heads over the cockroaches and gave barely a glance to the butterflies before shuffling on to another building. David Bierce paced restlessly through the lab on his way to clean the cages and make more complaints to the Operations Division. Janie cleaned and mounted two stag beetles, their spiny legs pricking her fingertips as she tried to force the pins through their glossy chestnut-colored shells. Afterwards she busied herself with straightening the clutter of cabinets and drawers stuffed with requisition forms and microscopes, computer parts and dissection kits.

It was well past two when David reappeared, his anorak slick with rain, his hair tucked beneath the hood. "Come on," he announced, standing impatiently by the open door. "Let's go to lunch."

Janie looked up from the computer where she'd been updating a specimen list. "I'm really not very hungry," she said, giving him an apologetic smile. "You go ahead."

"Oh, for Christ's sake." David let the door slam shut as he crossed to her, his sneakers leaving wet smears on the tiled floor. "That can wait till tomorrow. Come on, there's not a fucking thing here that needs doing."

"But—" She gazed up at him. The hood slid from his head; his gray-streaked hair hung loose to his shoulders, and the sheen of rain on his sharp cheekbones made him look carved from oiled wood. "What if somebody comes?"

"A very nice docent named Mrs. Eleanor Feltwell is out there, *even as we speak*, in the unlikely event that we have a single visitor."

He stooped so that his head was beside hers, scowling as he stared at the computer screen. A lock of his hair fell to brush against her neck.

Beneath the wig her scalp burned, as though stung by tiny ants; she breathed in the warm acrid smell of his sweat and something else, a sharper scent, like crushed oak-mast or fresh-sawn wood. Above her brows the antennae suddenly quivered. Sweetness coated her tongue like burnt syrup. With a rush of panic she turned her head so he wouldn't see her face.

"I—I should finish this—"

"Oh, just *fuck* it, Jane! It's not like we're *paying* you. Come on, now, there's a good girl—"

He took her hand and pulled her to her feet, Janie still looking away. The bangs of her cheap wig scraped her forehead, and she batted at them feebly. "Get your things. What, don't you ever take days off in the States?"

"All right, all right." She turned and gathered her black vinyl raincoat and knapsack, pulled on the coat, and waited for him by the door. "Jeez, you must be hungry," she said crossly.

"No. Just fucking bored out of my skull. Have you been to Ruby in the Dust? No? I'll take you then, let's go—"

The restaurant was down the High Street, a small, cheerfully claptrap place, dim in the gray afternoon, its small wooden tables scattered with abandoned newspapers and overflowing ashtrays. David Bierce ordered a steak and a pint. Janie had a small salad, nasturtium blossoms strewn across pale green lettuce, and a glass of red wine. She lacked an appetite lately, living on vitamin-enhanced, fruity bottled drinks from the health food store and baklava from a Greek bakery near the tube station.

"So." David Bierce stabbed a piece of steak, peering at her sideways. "Don't tell me you really haven't been here before."

"I haven't!" Despite her unease at being with him, she laughed, and caught her reflection in the wall-length mirror. A thin plain young woman in shapeless Peruvian sweater and jeans, bad haircut, and ugly glasses. Gazing at herself she felt suddenly stronger, invisible. She tilted her head and smiled at Bierce. "The food's good."

"So you don't have someone taking you out to dinner every night? Cooking for you? I thought you American girls all had adoring men at your feet. Adoring slaves," he added dryly. "Or slave girls, I suppose. If that's your thing."

"No." She stared at her salad, shook her head demurely, and took a sip of wine. It made her feel even more invulnerable. "No, I—"

"Boyfriend back home, right?" He finished his pint, flagged the waiter to order another, and turned back to Janie. "Well, that's nice. That's very nice—for him," he added, and gave a short harsh laugh.

The waiter brought another pint, and more wine for Janie. "Oh really, I better—"

"Just drink it, Jane." Under the table, she felt a sharp pressure on her foot. She wasn't wearing her Doc Martens today but a pair of red plastic jellies. David Bierce had planted his heel firmly atop her toes; she sucked in her breath in shock and pain, the bones of her foot crackling as she tried to pull it from beneath him. Her antennae rippled, then stiffened, and heat burst like a seed inside her.

"Go ahead," he said softly, pushing the wineglass toward her. "Just a sip, that's right—"

She grabbed the glass, spilling wine on her sweater as she gulped at it. The vicious pressure on her foot subsided, but as the wine ran down her throat she could feel the heat thrusting her into the air, currents rushing beneath her as the girl at the table below set down her wineglass with trembling fingers.

"There." David Bierce smiled, leaning forward to gently cup her hand between his. "Now this is better than working. Right, Jane?"

He walked her home along the canal path. Janie tried to dissuade him, but he'd had a third pint by then; it didn't seem to make him drunk but coldly obdurate, and she finally gave in. The rain had turned to a fine drizzle, the canal's usually murky water silvered and softly gleaming in the twilight. They passed few other people, and Janie found herself wishing someone else would appear, so that she'd have an excuse to move closer to David Bierce. He kept close to the canal itself, several feet from Janie; when the breeze lifted she could catch his oaky scent again, rising above the dank reek of stagnant water and decaying hawthorn blossom.

They crossed over the bridge to approach her flat by the street. At the front sidewalk Janie stopped, smiled shyly, and said, "Thanks. That was nice."

David nodded. "Glad I finally got you out of your cage." He lifted his head to gaze appraisingly at the row house. "Christ, this where you're staying? You split the rent with someone?"

"No." She hesitated: she couldn't remember what she had told him about her living arrangements. But before she could blurt something out he stepped past her to the front door, peeking into the window and bobbing impatiently up and down.

"Mind if I have a look? Professional entomologists don't often get the chance to see how the quality live."

Janie hesitated, her stomach clenching; decided it would be safer to have him in rather than continue to put him off.

"All right," she said reluctantly, and opened the door.

"Mmmm. Nice, nice, very nice." He swept around the living room, spinning on his heel and making a show of admiring the elaborate molding, the tribal rugs, the fireplace mantel with its thick ecclesiastical candles and ormolu mirror. "Goodness, all this for a wee thing like you? You're a clever cat, landing on your feet here, Lady Jane."

She blushed. He bounded past her on his way into the bedroom, touching her shoulder; she had to close her eyes as a fiery wave surged through her and her antennae trembled.

"*Wow,*" he exclaimed.

Slowly she followed him into the bedroom. He stood in front of the wall where her specimens were balanced in a neat line across the wainscoting. His eyes were wide, his mouth open in genuine astonishment.

"Are these *yours?*" he marveled, his gaze fixed on the butterflies. "You didn't actually catch them—?"

She shrugged.

"These are incredible!" He picked up the *Graphium agamemnon* and tilted it to the pewter-colored light falling through the French doors. "Did you mount them, too?"

She nodded, crossing to stand beside him. "Yeah. You can tell, with that one—" She pointed at the *Urania leilus* in its oak-framed box. "It got rained on."

David Bierce replaced the *Graphium agamemnon* and began to read the labels on the others.

Papilio demetrius
UNITED KINGDOM: LONDON
Highbury Fields, Islington
7.V.2001
J. Kendall

Isopa katinka
UNITED KINGDOM: LONDON
Finsbury Park
09.V.2001
J. Kendall

Argema mittrei
UNITED KINGDOM: LONDON
Camden Town
13.IV.2001
J. Kendall

He shook his head. "You screwed up, though—you wrote *London* for all of them." He turned to her, grinning wryly. "Can't think of the last time I saw a moon moth in Camden Town."

She forced a laugh. "Oh—right."

"And, I mean, you can't have actually *caught* them—"

He held up the *Isopa katinka*, a butter-yellow Emperor moth, its peacock's-eyes russet and jet-black. "I haven't seen any of these around lately. Not even in Finsbury."

Janie made a little grimace of apology. "Yeah. I meant, that's where I found them—where I bought them."

"Mmmm." He set the moth back on its ledge. "You'll have to share your sources with me. I can never find things like these in North London."

He turned and headed out of the bedroom. Janie hurriedly straightened the specimens, her hands shaking now as well, and followed him.

"Well, Lady Jane." For the first time he looked at her without his usual mocking arrogance, his green-flecked eyes bemused, almost regretful. "I think we managed to salvage something from the day."

He turned, gazing one last time at the flat's glazed walls and highly waxed floors, the imported cabinetry and jewel-toned carpets. "I was going to say, when I walked you home, that you needed someone to take care of you. But it looks like you've managed that on your own."

Janie stared at her feet. He took a step toward her, the fragrance of oak-mast and honey filling her nostrils, crushed acorns, new fern. She grew dizzy, her hand lifting to find him; but he only reached to graze her cheek with his finger.

"Night then, Janie," he said softly, and walked back out into the misty evening.

When he was gone she raced to the windows and pulled all the velvet curtains, then tore the wig from her head and threw it onto the couch along with her glasses. Her heart was pounding, her face slick with sweat—from fear or rage or disappointment, she didn't know. She yanked off her sweater and jeans, left them on the living room floor and stomped into the bathroom. She stood in the shower for twenty minutes, head upturned as the water sluiced the smells of bracken and leaf-mold from her skin.

Finally she got out. She dried herself, let the towel drop, and went into the kitchen. Abruptly she was famished. She tore open cupboards and drawers until she found a half-full jar of lavender honey from Provence. She opened it, the top spinning off into the sink, and frantically spooned honey into her mouth with her fingers. When she was finished she grabbed a jar of lemon curd and ate most of that, until she felt as though she might be sick. She stuck her head into the sink, letting water run from the faucet into her mouth, and at last walked, surfeited, into the bedroom.

She dressed, feeling warm and drowsy, almost dreamlike; pulling on red-and-yellow-striped stockings, her nylon skirt, a tight red T-shirt. No bra, no panties. She put in her contacts, then examined herself in the mirror. Her hair had begun to grow back, a scant velvety stubble, bluish in the dim light. She drew a sweeping black line across each eyelid, on a whim took the liner and extended the curve of each antenna until they touched her temples. She painted her lips black as well and went to find her black vinyl raincoat.

It was early when she went out, far too early for any of the clubs to be open. The rain had stopped, but a thick greasy fog hung over everything, coating windshields and shop windows, making Janie's face feel as though it were encased in a clammy shell. For hours she wandered Camden Town, huge violet eyes turning to stare back at the men who watched her, dismissing each of them. Once she thought she saw David Bierce, coming out of Ruby in the Dust; but when she stopped to watch him cross the street saw it was not David at all but someone else. Much younger, his long dark hair in a thick braid, his feet clad in knee-high boots. He crossed High Street, heading toward the tube station. Janie hesitated, then darted after him.

He went to the Electric Ballroom. Fifteen or so people stood out front, talking quietly. The man she'd followed joined the line, standing by himself. Janie waited across the street, until the door opened and the little crowd began to shuffle inside. After the long-haired young man had entered she counted to one hundred, crossed the street, paid her cover, and went inside.

The club had three levels; she finally tracked him down on the uppermost one. Even on a rainy Wednesday night it was crowded, the sound system blaring Idris Mohammed and Jimmy Cliff. He was standing alone near the bar, drinking bottled water.

"Hi!" she shouted, swaying up to him with her best First Day of School Smile. "Want to dance?"

He was older than she'd thought—thirtyish, still not as old as Bierce. He stared at her, puzzled, and then shrugged. "Sure."

They danced, passing the water bottle between them. "What's your name?" he shouted.

"Cleopatra Brimstone."

"You're kidding!" he yelled back. The song ended in a bleat of feedback, and they walked, panting, back to the bar.

"What, you know another Cleopatra?" Janie asked teasingly.

"No. It's just a crazy name, that's all." He smiled. He was handsomer than David Bierce, his features softer, more rounded, his eyes dark brown, his manner a bit reticent. "I'm Thomas Raybourne. Tom."

He bought another bottle of Pellegrino and one for Janie. She drank it quickly, trying to get his measure. When she finished she set the empty bottle on the floor and fanned herself with her hand.

"It's hot in here." Her throat hurt from shouting over the music. "I think I'm going to take a walk. Feel like coming?"

He hesitated, glancing around the club. "I was supposed to meet a friend here. . . ." he began, frowning. "But—"

"Oh." Disappointment filled her, spiking into desperation. "Well, that's okay. I guess."

"Oh, what the hell." He smiled: he had nice eyes, a more stolid, reassuring gaze than Bierce. "I can always come back."

Outside she turned right, in the direction of the canal. "I live pretty close by. Feel like coming in for a drink?"

He shrugged again. "I don't drink, actually."

"Something to eat then? It's not far—just along the canal path a few blocks past Camden Lock—"

"Yeah, sure."

They made desultory conversation. "You should be careful," he said as they crossed the bridge. "Did you read about those people who've gone missing in Camden Town?"

Janie nodded but said nothing. She felt anxious and clumsy—as though she'd drunk too much, although she'd had nothing alcoholic since the two glasses of wine with David Bierce. Her companion also seemed ill at ease; he kept glancing back, as though looking for someone on the canal path behind them.

"I should have tried to call," he explained ruefully. "But I forgot to recharge my mobile."

"You could call from my place."

"No, that's all right."

She could tell from his tone that he was figuring how he could leave, gracefully, as soon as possible.

Inside the flat he settled on the couch, picked up a copy of *Time Out* and flipped through it, pretending to read. Janie went immediately into the kitchen and poured herself a glass of brandy. She downed it, poured a second one, and joined him on the couch.

"So." She kicked off her Doc Martens, drew her stockinged foot slowly up his leg, from calf to thigh. "Where you from?"

He was passive, so passive she wondered if he would get aroused at all. But after a while they were lying on the couch, both their shirts on the floor, his pants unzipped and his cock stiff, pressing against her bare belly.

"Let's go in there," Janie whispered hoarsely. She took his hand and led him into the bedroom.

She only bothered lighting a single candle before lying beside him on the bed. His eyes were half-closed, his breathing shallow. When she ran a fingernail around one nipple he made a small surprised sound, then quickly turned and pinned her to the bed.

"Wait! Slow down," Janie said, and wriggled from beneath him. For the last week she'd left the bonds attached to the bedposts, hiding them beneath the covers when not in use. Now she grabbed one of the wrist-cuffs and pulled it free. Before he could see what she was doing it was around his wrist.

"Hey!"

She dived for the foot of the bed, his leg narrowly missing her as it thrashed against the covers. It was more difficult to get this in place, but she made a great show of giggling and stroking his thigh, which seemed to calm him. The other leg was next, and finally she leapt from the bed and darted to the headboard, slipping from his grasp when he tried to grab her shoulder.

"This is not consensual," he said. She couldn't tell if he was serious or not.

"What about this, then?" she murmured, sliding down between his legs and cupping his erect penis between her hands. "This seems to be enjoying itself."

He groaned softly, shutting his eyes. "Try to get away," she said. "Try to get away."

He tried to lunge upward, his body arcing so violently that she drew back in alarm. The bonds held; he arched again, and again, but now she remained beside him, her hands on his cock, his breath coming faster and faster and her own breath keeping pace with it, her heart pounding and the tingling above her eyes almost unbearable.

"Try to get away," she gasped. "Try to get away—"

When he came he cried out, his voice harsh, as though in pain, and Janie cried out as well, squeezing her eyes shut as spasms shook her from head to groin. Quickly her head dipped to kiss his chest; then she shuddered and drew back, watching.

His voice rose again, ended suddenly in a shrill wail, as his limbs knotted and shriveled like burning rope. She had a final glimpse of him, a homunculus sprouting too many legs. Then on the bed before her a perfectly formed *Papilio krishna* swallowtail crawled across the rumpled duvet, its wings twitching to display glittering green scales amidst spectral washes of violet and crimson and gold.

"Oh, you're beautiful, beautiful," she whispered.

From across the room echoed a sound: soft, the rustle of her kimono falling from its hook as the door swung open. She snatched her hand from the butterfly and stared, through the door to the living room.

In her haste to get Thomas Raybourne inside she had forgotten to latch the front door. She scrambled to her feet, naked, staring wildly at the shadow looming in front of her, its features taking shape as it approached the candle, brown and black, light glinting across his face.

It was David Bierce. The scent of oak and bracken swelled, suffocating, fragrant, cut by the bitter odor of ethyl alcohol. He forced her gently onto the bed, heat piercing her breast and thighs, her antennae bursting out like quills from her brow and wings exploding everywhere around her as she struggled fruitlessly.

"Now. Try to get away," he said.

I believe this is Peter Schneider's second professional fiction appearance. (He's done nonfiction work and has written with frightening authority on collectible first editions—especially those of Stephen King.)

I wish to hell he would write more fiction, or at least funny essays; he has a twisted comic flair that he shouldn't be keeping from the rest of us. At this point I'd call him imaginative fiction's Ian Frazier, whose short, hilarious pieces (such as "Bob's Bob House") have graced the pages of The New Yorker.

Enjoy the following—and add your wishes to mine that Mr. Schneider will write more.

Burros Gone Bad

PETER SCHNEIDER

*

"I don't care what your guesses are, Grip. . . . I just want to know who the hell wrecked the communications room!"

Phillip's angry voice resounded through the ruins of the upper deck. The heavy smell of ozone from the cracked video tubes mixed with the cheap cologne worn by the commander.

"It's burros, sir," said Grip.

"What the Sam Hill are you talking about, man? *Burros* did this?" Phillips replied as he waved at the mess.

"All I can tell you, sir, is that Rim Control reported a group of approximately thirty burros racing from the scene only ten minutes ago. They've sent a squad out after them, but you know how fast those creatures can go."

Phillips looked down at the console, his left fist convulsively tightening around the remains of a remote lifter unit.

"Grip, I'm giving you an order, and I don't want to see your face until you get it done. I want you to get whoever did this, man or beast—I want you to get 'em and bring 'em to me, because when I get my hands on 'em . . ." His voice faded away as Grip raced down the Outer Corridor toward the Lock.

Burt Grip was no stranger to the wiles of burros. There had been the incident at Rinse Pass only five months ago. Seven men dead and millions of dollars of equipment ruined. They had captured only one of the raiders—a runtish gray burro who refused to utter a word until his death the next day. And, of course, Grip had his suspicions about the debacle at Delphi the year before. No one was ever able to prove who had decimated the base and all of its five hundred-man complement—all they knew was that communications had suddenly ceased one day . . . and then the desolation when they sent the reconnaissance team. It had all the earmarks of a burro job, Grip thought, but he had never been able to convince his superiors.

"They'll soon see," he thought grimly to himself. "We're up against it now."

The clop of a hoof on the cabin door startled him out of his reverie.

Rudy Rucker and John Shirley are powerful enough as separate entities—what would happen if you put the two of them together? A frightening thought—and that's what happened. Rucker, who has a degree in advanced mathematics from Rutgers and is also a computer programmer, is known for his exuberant style (as well as, though not in this instance, a comic flair comparable to John Sheckley); Shirley, who is the author of more than twenty books in sf and dark fantasy (including a recent collection, Really Really Really Really Weird Stories, *the tales of which actually* do *get weirder as the book progresses) has been known for his angry, intense, straight-ahead style.*

What do you get when you put the two of them together? You get the following, which is fast-paced, cyberpunkish, thoughtful, weird—and wonderful.

Pockets

RUDY RUCKER AND JOHN SHIRLEY

*

When the woman from Endless Media called, Wendel was out on the fake balcony, looking across San Pablo Bay at the lights of the closed-down DeGroot Chemicals Plant. On an early summer evening, the lights marking out the columns of steel and the button-shaped chemical tanks took on an unreal glamour; the plant became an otherworldly palace. He'd tried to model the plant with the industrial-strength Real2Graphix program his dad had brought home from RealTek before he got fired. But Wendel still didn't know the tricks for filling a virtual scene with the world's magic and menace, and his model looked like a cartoon toy. Someday he'd get his chops and make the palace come alive. You could set a killer-ass game there if you knew how. After high school, maybe he could get into a good gaming university. He didn't want to "go" to an online university if he could help it; virtual teachers, parallel programmed or not, couldn't answer all your questions.

The phone rang just as he was wondering whether Dad could afford to pay tuition for someplace real. He waited for his dad to get the phone, and after three rings he realized with a chill that Dad had probably gone into a pocket, and he'd have to answer the phone himself.

The fake porch, created for window washers, and to create an impression of coziness the place had always lacked, creaked under his feet as he went to climb through the window. The narrow splintery wooden walkway outside their window was on the third floor of an old waterfront motel converted to studio apartments. Their tall strip of windows, designed to savor a view that was now unsavory, looked down a crumbling cliff at a mud beach, the limp gray waves sluggish in stretched squares of light from the buildings edging the bluff. Down the beach some guys with flashlights were moving around, looking for the little pocket-bubbles that floated in like dead jellyfish. Thanks to the accident that had closed down the DeGroot Research Center, beyond the still-functioning chemicals plant, San Pablo Bay was a good spot to scavenge for pocket-bubbles, which was why Wendel and his Dad had ended up living here.

To get to the phone, he had to skirt the mercurylike bubble of Dad's pocket, presently a big flattened shape eight feet across and six high, rounded like a river stone. The pocket covered most of the available space on the living room floor, and he disliked having to touch it. There was that sensation when you touched them—not quite a sting, not quite an electrical shock, not even intolerable. But you didn't want to prolong the feeling.

Wendel touched the speakerphone tab. "Hello, Bell residence."

"Well, this doesn't sound like Rothman Bell." It was a woman's voice coming out of the speakerphone—humorous, ditzy, but with a heartening undercurrent of business.

"No, ma'am. I'm his son, Wendel."

"That's right, I remember he had a son. You'd be about fourteen now?"

"Sixteen."

"Sixteen! Whoa. Time jogs on. This is Manda Solomon. I knew your dad when he worked at MetaMeta. He really made his mark there. Is he home?"

He hesitated. There was no way to answer that question honestly without having to admit Dad was in a pocket, and pocket-slugs had a bad reputation. "No, ma'am. But . . ."

He looked toward the pocket. It was getting smaller now. If things went as usual, it would shrink to grapefruit size, then swell back up and burst—and Dad would be back. Occasionally a pocket might bounce through two or three or even a dozen shrink-and-grow cycles before releasing its inhabitant; but it never took terribly long, at least from the outside. Dad might be back before this woman hung up. She sounded like business, and that made Wendel's pulse race. It was a chance.

If he could just keep her talking. After a session in a pocket Dad wouldn't be in any shape to call anyone back, sometimes not for days—but if you caught him just coming out, and put the phone in his hand, he might keep it together long enough, still riding the pocket's high. Wendel just hoped this wasn't going to be the one pocket that would finally kill his father.

"Can I take a message, Ms., um, . . ." With his mind running so fast, he'd forgotten her name.

"Manda Solomon. Just tell him—"

"Can I tell him where you're calling from?" He grimaced at himself in the mirror by the front door. Dumbass, don't interrupt her, you'll scare her off.

"From San Jose, I'm a project manager at Endless Media. Just show him—oh, have you got iTV?"

"Yeah. You want me to put it on?" Good, that'd take some more time. If Dad had kept up the payments.

He carried the phone over to the iTV screen hanging on the wall like a seascape; there was a fuzzy motel-decor photo of a sunset endlessly playing in it now, the kitschy orange clouds swirling in the same tape-looping pattern. He tapped the tab on the phone that would hook it to the iTV, and faced the screen so that the camera in the corner of the frame could pick him up but only on head-shot setting so she couldn't see the pocket, too. "You see me?"

"Yup. Here I come."

Her picture appeared in a window in an upper corner of the screen, a pleasant-looking redhead in early middle age, hoop earrings, frank smile. She held up an e-book, touched the page turner which instantly scrolled an image of a photograph that showed a three-dimensional array of people floating in space, endless pairs of people spaced out into the nodes of a warped jungle-gym lattice, a man and a woman at each node. Wendel recognized the couple as his dad and his mother. At first it looked as if all the nodes were the same, but when you looked closer, you could see that the people at some of the more distant nodes weren't Mom and Dad after all. In fact some of them didn't even look like people. This must be a photo taken inside a pocket with tunnels coming out of it. Wendel had never seen it before. "If you print out the picture, he'll know what it's all about," Manda was saying.

"Sure." Wendel saved the picture to the iTV's memory, hoping it would work. He didn't want Manda to know their printer was broken and wouldn't be repaired anytime soon.

"Well it's been a sweet link, but I gotta go—just tell him to call. Here's the number, ready to save? Got it? Okay, then. He'll remember me."

Wendel saw she wasn't wearing a wedding band. He got tired of taking care of Dad alone. He tried to think of some way to keep her on the line. "He'll be right back—he's way overdue. I expect him . . ."

"Whoops, I really gotta jam." She reached toward her screen and then hesitated, her head cocked as she looked at his image. "That's what it is: you look a lot like Jena, you know? Your mom."

"I guess."

"Jena was a zippa-trip. I hated it when she disappeared."

"I don't remember her much."

"Oops, my boss is chiming hysterically at me. Bye!"

"Um—wait." He turned to glance at the dull silvery bubble, already bouncing back from its minimum size, but when he turned back, Manda Solomon was gone and it was only the snowy sunset again. "Shit."

He went to the bubble and kicked it angrily. He couldn't feel anything but "stop," with his sneaker on. It wasn't like kicking an object, it was like something stopped you, turned you back toward your own time flow. Just "stopness." It was saying "no" with the stuff of forever itself. There was no way to look inside it: Once someone crawled in through a pocket's navel, it sealed up all over.

He turned away, heard something—and when he looked back the pocket was gone and his dad, stinking and retching and raggedly bearded, was crawling toward him across the carpet.

Next morning, it seemed to Wendel that his dad sucked the soup down more noisily, more sloppily, than ever before. His hands shook and he spilled soup on the blankets.

His dad was supposedly forty—but he looked fifty-five. He'd spent maybe fifteen years in the pockets—adding up to only a few weeks in outside time, ten minutes here and two hours there and so on.

Dad sat up in his bed, staring out to the bay, sloppily drinking the soup from a bowl, and Wendel had to look away. Sitting at the breakfast bar that divided the kitchenette from the rest of the room, he found himself staring at the pile of dirty clothes in the corner. They needed some kind of hamper, and he could go to some Martinez garage sale and find one next to free. But that was something Dad ought to do; Wendel sensed that if he started doing that sort of thing, parental things, his dad would give a silent gasp of relief and lean on him, more and more; and paradoxically fall away from him, into the pockets.

"I was gone like—ten minutes world-time?" said Dad. "I don't suppose I missed anything here in this . . . this teeming hive of activity."

"Ten minutes?" said Wendel. He snorted. "You're still gone, Dad. And, yes, there was a call for you. A woman from Endless Media. Manda Solomon. She left her number and a picture."

"Manda?" said Dad. "That flake? Did you tell her I was in a pocket?"

"Right," said Wendel contemptuously. "Like I told her my dad's a pocket-slug."

Dad opened his mouth like he was going to protest the disrespect—then thought better of it. He shrugged, with as much cool as he could manage. "Manda's down with pockets, Wendel. Half the guys programming virtual physics for MetaMeta were using them when I was there. Pockets are a great way to make a deadline. The MetaMeta crunchroom was like a little glen of chrome puffballs. Green carpeting, you wave? Manda used to walk around setting sodas and pizzas down outside the pockets. We'd work in there for days, when it was minutes on the outside—get a real edge on the other programmers. She was just a support tech then. We called her Fairy Princess and we crunchers were the Toads of the Short Forest, popping out all loaded on the bubble-rush. Manda's gone down in the world, what I heard, in terms of who she works for—"

"She's a project manager. Better than a support tech."

"Nice of her to think of me." Dad made a little grimace. "Endless Media's about one step past being a virtu-porn Webble. Where's the picture she sent?"

"I saved it in the iTV," said Wendel, and pushed the buttons to show it.

Dad made a groaning sound. "Turn it off, Wendel. Put it away."

"Tell me what it is, first," said Wendel, pressing the controller buttons to zoom in on the faces. It was definitely—

"Mom and me," said Dad shakily. "I took that photo the week before she died." His voice became almost inaudible. "Yeah. You can see . . . some of the images are different further into the lattice . . . because our pocket had a tunnel leading to other pockets. That happens sometimes, you know. It's not a good idea to go down the tunnels. It was the time after this one that . . . Mom didn't come back." He looked at the picture for a moment; like its own pocket, the moment seemed to stretch out to a gray forever. Then he looked away. "Turn it off, will you? It brings me down."

Wendel stared at his mother's young face a moment longer, then turned off the image. "You never told me much about the time she didn't come back."

"I don't need to replay the experience, kid."

"Dad. I . . . look, just do it. Tell me."

Dad stared at him. Looked away. Wendel thought he was going to refuse again. Then he shrugged and began, his voice weary. "It was a much bigger pocket than usual," said Dad, almost inaudible. "MetaMeta . . . they'd scored a shitload of them from DeGroot, and we were merging them together so whole teams could fit in. Using fundamental space-time geometry weirdness to meet the marketing honcho's deadlines, can you believe? I was an idiot to buy into it. And this last time Jena was mad at me, and she flew away from me while we were in there. And then I couldn't tell which of the lattice-nodes was really her. Like a mirror maze in a funhouse. And meanwhile I'm all tweaked out of my mind on bubble-rush. But I had my laptop harness, and there was all that code-hacking to be done, and I got into it for sure, glancing over at all the Jenas now and then, and they're programming, too, so I thought it was OK, but then . . ." He swallowed, turning to look out the window, as if he might see her out there in the sky. "When the pocket flattened back out, I was alone. The same shit was coming down everywhere all of a sudden, and then there was the Big Bubble disaster at the DeGroot plant and all the pocket-bubbles were declared government property and if you want to use them anymore . . . people, you know . . ." His voice trailed into a whisper: ". . . they act like you're a junkie."

"Yeah," said Wendel. "I know." He looked out the window for a while. It was a sunny day, but the foulness in the water made the sea a dingy gray, as if it were brooding on dark memories. He spotted a couple of little pocket-bubbles floating in on the brackish waves. Dad had been buying them from beachcombers, merging them together till he got one big enough to crawl into again.

They'd talked about pockets in Wendel's health class at school last term. In terms of dangerous things the grown-ups wanted to warn you away from, pockets were right up there with needles, drunk driving, and doing it bareback. You could stay inside too long and come out a couple of years older than your friends. You could lose your youth inside a pocket. Oddly enough, you didn't eat or breathe in any conventional way while you were inside there—those parts of your metabolism went into suspension. The pocket-slugs dug this aspect of the high—for after all, weren't eating and breathing just another wearisome world-drag? There were even rock songs about pockets setting you free from "feeding the pig," as the 'slugs liked to call normal life. You didn't eat or breathe inside a pocket but even so were still getting older, often a lot faster than you realized. Some people came out, like, middle-aged.

And, of course, some people never came out at all. They died in there of old age, or got killed by a bubble-psychotic pocket-slug coming through a tunnel, or—though this last one sounded like government propaganda—you might tunnel right off into some kind of alien Hell world. If you found a pocket-bubble, you were supposed to take it straight to the police. As opposed to selling it to a 'slug, or, worse, trying to accumulate enough of them to get a pocket big enough to go into yourself. The word was that it felt really good, better than drugs or sex or booze. Sometimes Wendel wanted to try it—because then, maybe, he'd understand his dad. Other times the thought terrified him.

He looked at his shaky, strung-out father, wishing he could respect him. "Do you keep doing it because you think you might find Mom in there someday?" asked Wendel, his voice plaintive in his own ears.

"It would sound more heroic, wouldn't it?" said Dad, rubbing his face. "That I keep doing it because I'm on a quest. Better than saying I do it for the high. The escape." He rubbed his face for a minute and got out of bed, a little shaky, but with a determined look on his face. "It's get-it-together time, huh, Wendel? Get me a vita-patch from the bathroom, willya? I'll call Manda and go see her today. We need this gig. You ready to catch the light rail to San Jose?"

In person, Manda Solomon was shorter, plainer, and less well-dressed than the processed image she sent out on iTV. She was a friendly ditz, with the disillusioned aura of a Valley-vet who's seen a number of her employers go down the tubes. When Dad calmly claimed that Wendel was a master programmer and his chief assistant, Manda didn't bat an eye, just took out an extra sheaf of nondisclosure and safety-waiver agreements for Wendel to sign.

"I've never had such a synchronistic staffing process before," she said with a breathless smile. "Easy, but weird. Two of our team were waiting in my office when I came into work one morning. Said I'd left it unlocked. Karma, I guess."

They followed her into a windowless conference room with whiteboards and projection screens. One of the screens showed Dad's old photo of him and Mom scattered over the nodes of a pocket's space-lattice. Wendel's dad glanced at it and looked away.

Manda introduced them to the other three at the table: a cute, smiling woman named Xiao-Xiao just now busy talking Chinese on her cell phone. She had Bettie Page bangs and the faddish full-eye mirror-contacts; her eyes were like pale lavender Christmas-tree ornaments. Next was a bright-eyed sharp-nosed Sikh guy from India, named Puneet; he wore a turban. He had reassuringly normal eyes and spoke in a high voice. The third was a puffy white kid only a few years older than Wendel. His name was Barley, and he wore a stoner-rock T-shirt. He didn't smile; with his silver mirror-contacts his face was quite unreadable. He wore an uvvy computer interface on the back of his neck. Barley asked Wendel something about programming, but Wendel couldn't even understand the question.

"Ummm . . . well, you know. I just—"

"So what's the pitch, Manda?" Dad interrupted, to get Wendel off the spot.

"Pocket-Max," said Manda. "Safe and stable. Five hundred people in there at a time, strapped into . . . I dunno, some kind of mobile pocket-seats. Make downtown San Jose a destination theme park. Harmless, ethical pleasure. We've got some senators who can push it through a loophole for us."

"Safe?" said Dad. "Harmless?"

"Manda says you've logged more time in the pockets than anyone she knows," said Xiao-Xiao. "You have some kind of . . . intuition about them? You must know some tricks for making it safe."

"Well . . . if we had the hardware that created it . . ." Dad's voice trailed off, which meant he was thinking hard, and Manda let him do it for a moment.

And then she dropped her bomb. "We do have the hardware. Show him Flatland, Barley."

Barley did something with his uvvy, and something like a soap film appeared above the generic white plastic of the conference table. "This is a two-dimensional-world mockup," mumbled Barley. "We call it Flatland. The nanomatrix mat for making the real pockets is offsite. Flatland's a piece of visualization software that we got as part of our license. It's a lift."

"*Offsite* would be the DeGroot Center?" said Dad, his voice rising. "You've got full access?"

"Yaaar," said Barley, his fat face expressionless. He was leaning over Flatland, using his uvvy link to tweak it with his blank shining eyes.

"Why was DeGroot making pockets in the first place?" asked Wendel. No one had ever explained the pockets to him. It was like Dad was ashamed to talk about them much.

"It was supposed to be for AI," said Puneet. "Quantum computing nanotech. The DeGroot techs were bozos. They didn't know what they had when they started up the nanomatrix—I don't even know how they invented it. There's no patents filed. It's like the thing fell out of a flying saucer." His laugh was more than a little uneasy. "There's nobody to ask because the DeGroot engineers are all dead. Sucked into the Big Bubble that popped out of their nanomatrix. You saw it on TV. And then Uncle Sam closed them down."

"But—why would the nanomatrix be licensed to Endless Media?" asked Dad. "You're an entertainment company. And not a particularly reputable one, at that. Why you and not one of the big, legit players?"

"Options," said Manda with a shrug. "Market leverage. Networking synergies. And the big guys don't want to touch it. Too big a downside.

Part of the setup is we can't sue DeGroot if things don't work out. No biggie for Endless Media. If the shit hits the fan, we take the bullet and go Chapter Eleven. We closed the deal with DeGroot and the feds last week. Nobody's hardly seen the DeGroot CEO since the catastrophe, but he's still around. Guy named George Gravid. He showed up for about one minute at closing, popped up out of nowhere, walking down the hall. Said he'd been hung up in meetings with some backer dudes—he called them Out-Monkeys. He looked like shit, wearing shades. I think he's strung out on something. Whatever. We did our due diligence, closed the deal, and a second later Gravid was gone." She waved a dismissive hand. "Bottom line is we're fully licensed to use the DeGroot technology. Us and a half-dozen other blue sky groups. Each of us is setting up an operation in the DeGroot Plant on San Pablo Bay. And we time-share the access to the nanomatrix. The Endless Media mission in this context is to make a safe and stable Big Bubble that provides a group entertainment experience beyond anything ever seen before."

"Watch how this simulation works," said Barley. "See the yellow square in the film? That's A Square. A two-dimensional Flatlander. He's sliding around, you wave. And that green five-sided figure next to him, that's his son A Pentagon. And now I push up a bubble out of his space." A little spot of the Flatland film bulged up like a time-reversed waterdrop. The bulge swelled up to the shape of a sphere hovering above Flatland, connected to the little world by a neck of glistening film. "Go in the pocket, Square," said Barley. "Get high."

The yellow square slid forward. He had a bright eye in one of his corners. For a minute he bumbled around the warped zone where the bubble touched his space, then found an entry point and slid up across the neck of the bubble and onto the surface of the little ball. Into the pocket.

"This is what he sees," said Barley, pointing at one of the viewscreens on the wall. The screen showed an endless lattice of copies of A Square, each of them turning and blinking in unison. "Like a hall of mirrors. Now I'll make the bubble bounce. That's what makes the time go differently inside the pockets, you know."

The sphere rose up from the film. The connecting neck stretched and grew thinner, but it didn't break. The sphere bounced back toward the film and the neck got fat, the sphere bounced up and the neck got thin, over and over.

"Check this out," said Barley, changing the image on the viewscreen to show a circle that repeatedly shrank and grew. "This is what Square Junior sees. The little Pentagon. He stayed outside the bad old pocket, you wave? To him the pocket looks like a disk that's getting bigger and smaller. See him over there on the film? Waiting for Pa. Like little Wendel in the condo on San Pablo Bay."

"Go to hell," said Wendel.

"Don't pick on him, Barley," put in Manda. "Wendel's part of our team."

"Whoah," said Barley. "Now Mr. Square's trip is over." The sphere bounced back and flattened back into the normal space of Flatland.

"You forgot to mention the stabilizer ring," said Dad.

"You see?" said Manda. "I told you guys we needed a physicist."

"What ring?" said Barley.

"A space bubble is inherently unstable," said Dad. "It wants to tear loose or flatten back down. The whole secret of the DeGroot tech was to wrap a superquantum nanosheet around the bubbles. Bubble wrap. In your Flatland model it's a circle around the neck. Make a new bubble, Barley."

A new bubble bulged up, and this time Wendel noticed that there was indeed a bright little line around the throat of the neck. A line with a gap in it, like the open link of a chain.

"That's the entrance," said Dad, pointing to the little gap. "The navel. Now show me how you model a tunnel."

"We're not sure about the tunnels," said Puneet. "We're expecting you can help us with this. I cruised the Bharat University Physics Department site and found a Chandreskar-Thorne solution that looks like—can you work it for me, Xiao-Xiao?"

Xiao-Xiao leaned toward the Flatland simulation, her lavender eyes reflecting the scene. She, too, wore a modern uvvy-style computer controller. Following Puneet's instructions, Xiao-Xiao bulged a second bubble up from the plane, about a foot away from the first one. A Square slid into the first one of them and A Pentagon into the other. And now the bubbles picked up a side-to-side motion, and lumps began sticking out of them, and it just so happened that two of the lumps touched and now there was a tunnel between the two bubbles.

"Look at the screens now," said Barley. "That's Square's view on the left. And Pentagon's view on the right."

Square's view showed a lattice of Squares as before, but the lattice lines were warped and flawed, and in the flawed region there was a sublattice of nodes showing copies of the Pentagon. And the Pentagon's view lattice included a wedge of Squares.

"That's a start," said Dad. "But, you know, these pictures of yours—they're just toys. You're talking all around the edges of what the pockets are. You're missing the essence of what they're really about. It's not that they spontaneously bulge up out of our space. It's more that they're raining down on us. From something out here." He gestured at the space above Flatland. "There's a shape up there—with something inside it. I've picked up kind of a feeling for it."

Barley and Xiao-Xiao stared silently at him, their mirrored eyes shining.

"That's why we need you, Rothman," said Manda, finally.

"That's right," said Puneet. "The problem is—when it comes to this new tech, we're bozos, too."

"I'll tell you what I think," Wendel said gravely. "I think you're lying to them about what you can do, Dad."

It was nearly midnight. Wendel was tired and depressed. They were sitting in the abandoned DeGroot plant's seemingly endless cafeteria, waiting for their daily time-slot with the nanomatrix. Almost the only ones there. The rest of their so-called team hadn't been coming in. Manda and Puneet preferred the safety of San Jose while Barley and Xiao-Xiao had completely dropped out of sight. What a half-assed operation this was.

Wendel and his Dad were eating tinny-tasting stew and drinking watery coffee from the vending machines along the wall opposite the defunct buffets. It was a long, overly lit room, the far end not quite visible from here, with pearly white walls and a greenish floor, asymmetrical rows of round tables like lily pads on the green pond of the floor, going on and on. Endless Media shared the cafeteria with the other scavenging little companies that had licensed access to the nanomatrix. None of the reputable firms wanted to touch it.

"Don't talk about it in here, son," Dad said, listlessly stirring his coffee with a plastic spoon. "We're not alone, you wave."

"The nearest people in here are, like, an eighth of a mile away. I can't even make out their faces from here."

"That's not what I mean. The other groups here, they might be spying on us with gnat-audio, stuff like that. They're all a bunch of bottom-feeders like Endless Media, you know. Nobody knows jack from squat, so they're all looking to copy me."

"You wish. It's good to have work, but you're going to get in deep shit, Dad. You're telling Endless Media you're down with the tech when you're not. You're telling them you can stabilize a Big Bubble when you can't. You say you can keep tunnels from hooking into it—but you don't know how."

"Maybe I can. I have to test it some more."

"You test it every night."

"Not enough. I haven't actually gone inside it yet."

"Come on. I'm the one who has to put you back together after a bubble binge. It's great having an income from this gig, Dad, a better place to live—but I'm not going to let you vanish into that thing. Something just like it killed the whole DeGroot team five years ago."

His Dad turned Wendel a glare that startled him. It was almost feral. Chair screeching nastily on the tile, he got up abruptly and went across the room to a coffee vending machine for another latte. Dad ran his card through the slot, and then swore. He stalked back over to the table long enough to say, "Be right back, this card's used up, I've got another one in my locker."

"You're not going to sneak up to the lab without me, are you? Our time-slot starts in five minutes, you know. At midnight."

"Son? Don't. I'm the dad, you're the kid. Okay? I'll be right back."

Wendel watched him go. *I'm the dad, you're the kid.* There were a lot of comebacks he could've made to that one.

Wendel sipped his gooey stew, then pushed it away. It was tepid, the vegetables mushy, made him think of bits of leftover food floating in dishwater. He heard a *beep*, looked toward the vending machines. The machine Dad had run his card through was beeping, flashing a little light.

Wendel walked over to it. A small screen on the machine said, DO YOU WISH TO CANCEL YOUR PURCHASE?

Which was only something it said if the card was good. Which meant that Dad had gone to the lab without him. Wendel felt a sick chill that made his fingers quiver . . . and sprinted toward the elevators.

The pocket was so swollen he could hardly get into the big testing room with it. Maybe two hundred feet in diameter, sixty feet high. Mercuric and yet lusterless. The various measuring instruments were crowded up against the walls.

"Dad?" he called tentatively. But Wendel knew Dad was gone. He could feel his absence from the world.

He edged around the outside of the Big Bubble, grimacing when he came into contact with it. Somewhere beneath the great pocket was the nanomatrix mat that produced it—or attracted it? But it wasn't like you could do anything to turn the pocket off once it got here. At least nothing that they'd figured out yet—which was one of the many obstacles preventing this thing from being a realistic public attraction. "Show may last from one to ten minutes world-time, and seem to take one hour to three months of your proper time." Even if there were a way to shut the pocket off now—what would that do to Dad?

Facing a far corner was the dimpled spot, the entrance navel. On these Big Bubbles, the navel didn't always seal over. When Wendel looked into the navel, it seemed to swirl like a slow-motion whirlpool, but in two contradictory directions. Hypnotic. It could still be entered.

Wendel made up his mind: he would go after his dad. He leaned forward, pressed his fingers against the navel, thinking of A Pentagon sliding up over the warped neck that led to the sphere of extra space. His hands looked warped, as if they were underwater. They tingled—not unpleasantly. He pushed his arms in after and then, with a last big breath of air, his head. How would it feel to stop breathing?

It was a while till Wendel came back to that question. The first feeling of being inside the pocket was one of falling—but this was just an illusion, he was floating, not falling, and he had an odd, dreamlike ability to move in whatever direction he wanted to, not that the motion seemed to mean much.

There was a dim light that came from everywhere and nowhere. Spread out around him were little mirror-Wendels, all turning their heads this way and that, gesturing and—yes—none of them breathing. It was like flying underwater and never being out of breath, like being part of a school of fish. The space was patterned with veils of color like seaweed in water. Seeing the veils pass he could tell that he was moving, and as the veils repeated themselves he could see that he was moving in a great circle. He was like A Pentagon circling around and around his bulged-up puffball of space. But where was Dad? He changed the angle of his motion, peering around for distinctions in the drifting school of mirror-shapes.

The motion felt like flying, now, with a wind whipping his hair, and he found a new direction in which the space veils seemed to curve like gossamer chambers of mother-of-pearl, sketching a sort of nautilus-spiral into the distance. Looking into that distance, that twist of infinity, and feeling the volume of sheer potentiality, he felt the first real wave of bubble-rush. His fatigue evaporated in the searing light of the rush, a rippling, bone-deep pleasure that seemed generated by his flying motion into the spiral of the pocket.

"*Whuh*-oaaaah . . . ," he murmured, afraid of the feeling and yet liking it. So this was why Dad came here. Or one of the reasons. There was something else, too . . . something Dad never quite articulated.

The bubble-rush was so all-consuming, so shimmeringly insistent, he felt he couldn't bear it. It was simply too much; too much pleasure and you lost all sense of self; and then it was, finally, no better than pain.

Wendel thought, "Stop!" and his motion responded to his will. He stopped where he was—an inertialess stop partway into the receding nautilus-spiral. The bubble-rush receded a bit, damped back down to a pleasing background glow.

"Dad!" he yelled. No response. "*Dad!*" His voice didn't echo; he couldn't tell how loud it was. There was air in here to be sucked in and expelled for speaking. But when he wasn't yelling, he felt no need to take a breath. Like a vampire in his grave.

He tried to get some kind of grasp of the shape of this place. He thought with an ugly frisson of fear:

Maybe I'm already lost. How do I find my way back out?

Could A Pentagon slide back out the neck into the ball? Or would he have to wait for the ball to burn out its energy and flatten back into space?

There were no images of Wendel up ahead, where the patterns of the space seemed to twirl like a nautilus. It must be a tunnel. If pockets were dangerous, the tunnels from pocket to pocket were said to be much worse. But he knew that's where Dad had gone.

He moved into the tunnel, flying at will.

The pattern haze ahead of him took on flecks of pink, human color. Someone else was down there. "Dad?"

He leaned into his flying—and stopped, about ten yards short of the man. It wasn't Dad. This man was bearded, emaciated, sallow . . . which Dad could be, by now, in the time-bent byways of this place. But it wasn't his dad, it was a stranger, a man with big, scared eyes and a grin that looked permanently fixed. No teeth: barren gums. The man sitting was floating in fetal position, arms around his knees.

"Ya got any grub on yer, boy?" the man rasped. A UK accent. Or was it Australian?

"Um—" He remembered he had two-thirds of an energy bar of some kind in a back pocket. Probably linty by now, but likely this 'slug wouldn't care. "You want this?"

He tossed over the energy bar and the pocket-slug's eyes flashed as he caught it, fairly snatched it out of the air. "Good on ya, boy!" He gnawed on the linty old bar with his callused gums.

It occurred to Wendel that at some point he might regret giving away his only food. But supposedly you didn't need to eat in here. Food was just fun for the mouth, or a burst of extra energy. Right now the scene made him chuckle to himself—the bubble-rush was glowing in him, made everything seem absurd, cartoonlike, and marvelous.

Between sucking sounds, the 'slug said, "My name's Threakman. Jeremy Threakman. 'Ow yer doin."

"I don't know how I'm doing. I'm looking for my dad. Rothman Bell. He's about . . ."

"No need, I know whuh 'e looks like. Seen 'im go through 'ere . . ." Threakman looked at Wendel with his head cocked. A sly look. "Feelin' the 'igh, are ya? Sure'n you are. Stoned, eh, boy? Young fer it."

"I feel something—what is it? What causes it?"

"Why, it's a feelin' of being right there in yerself, beyond all uncertainty about where yer might go. For here, yer are all that is, in yerself. And that'll get you 'igh. Or some say. Others, like me, they say it's the Out-Monkeys that do it."

"The Out—what?"

"Out-Monkeys," said Threakman. "What I call 'em. Other's call 'em Dream Beetles, one 'slug in 'ere used ter call 'em Turtles—said 'e saw a Turtle thing with a head like a screw-top bottle without the cap and booze pouring out, but 'e was a hardcore alkie. Others they see'm more like lizards or Chinese dragons. Dragons, beetles, monkeys, all hairy around the edges, all curlin' out at yer—it's a living hole in space, mate, and you push the picture you want on it. Me and the smartuns calls 'em Out-Monkeys 'cause they're from outside our world."

"You mean—from another planet?"

"No, mate, from the bigger universe that *this* one is kinder *inside*. They got more dimensions than we do. They're using DeGroot and the nanomatrix—they give all that ta us to pull us in, mate. The Out-Monkeys are drizzlin' pockets down onto us, little paradise balls where yer don't 'ave to breathe nor eat an' yer can fly an' there's an energy that stim-yer-lates that part of yer brain, don't ya see. The Out-Monkeys want us all stony in here. Part of their li'l game, innit? Come on, show yer somethin'. The Alef. Mayhap yer'll see yer da."

In a single spasmodic motion Threakman was up, flying off in some odd new direction through the silvery scarves of the enclosing spaces—leaving a rank scent in the air behind him. Wendel whipped along after him, remembering not to breathe. Soon, if it could be thought of as soon, they came to a nexus where the images around them thickened up into an incalculable diversity. It was like being at the heart of a city in a surveillance zone with a million monitors, but the images weren't electronic, they were real, and endlessly repeated.

"The Alef has tunnels to all the pockets," said Threakman. "Precious few of us knows about it."

In some directions, he saw pockets with people writhing together—he realized, with embarrassment, that they were copulating. But was that really sex? He made himself look away. In another pocket people were racing around one another in a blur like those electro-cyclists in the Cage of Death he'd seen at a carnival. Off down the axis of another tunnel, people clawed at one another, in a thronging mélange of combat; you couldn't tell one from another, so slick was the blood. But the greatest number of the pockets held solitary 'slugs, hanging there in self-absorbed pleasure, surrounded by the endless mirror-images of themselves. And one of these addicts was Dad, floating quite nearby.

"For 'im, mate," said Threakman as Wendel flew off toward his father.

Not quite sure of his aim, he hit Dad with a thud—and Dad screamed, thrashing back from him. Stopping himself in space to glare shame and resentment at Wendel—like a kid caught masturbating.

"What are you *doing*?" demanded Wendel. "You call this research?"

"Okay, you really want to know?" snapped his father. "I'm looking for Mom."

Wendel peered at his father; his Dad's face, here, seemed more like the possibility of all possible Dad facial expressions, crystallized. It was difficult to tell whether he meant it. It might be bullshit. What was the saying? *How do you know an addict is lying? When his lips are moving!*

But the possibility of seeing Mom made Wendel's heart thud. "You think she's still in here? Seriously, Dad?"

"I think the Out-Monkeys got her. That's what happens, you know. Some of the pockets float up—not *up* exactly, but *ana*—"

"To the shape above Flatland," said Wendel.

"Right," said Dad. "We're in their Flatland, relatively speaking. And I want to get up there and find her."

"But you're just floating around in here. You're on the goddamn nod, Dad. You're not looking at all."

"Oh, yes, I am. I'm looking, goddammit. This happens to be just the right spot to stare down through the Alef and up along the Out-Monkeys' tunnel. Not their tunnel, exactly. The spot where they usually appear. Where their hull touches us. I'm waiting for them to show up."

"The Devil in his motorboat," said Wendel with a giggle. The bubble-rush was creeping back up on him. Dad laughed, too. They were thinking of the old joke about the guys in Hell, standing neck deep in liquid shit and drinking coffee, and one of them says, "Wal, this ain't so bad," and the other one says, "Yeah, but wait till—"

"Here it comes," said Dad, and it wasn't funny anymore, for the space up ahead of them had just opened up like a blooming squash-flower, becoming incalculably larger, all laws of perspective broken, and an all but endless vista spreading out, a giant space filled with moving shapes that darted and wheeled like migrating flocks of birds. It was hard to think straight, for the high of the bubble-space had just gotten much stronger.

"The mothership," said Threakman, who'd drifted down to join them. "Yaaar. Can you feel the rush off it? Ahr, but it's good. Hello to yer, there, Da . . ." He gave a deep, loose chuckle. Everything was glistening and wonderful, as perfect as the first instant of Creation; and, as with that moment, chaos waited on the event horizon: chaos and terror.

"Those shapes are the Out-Monkeys?" asked Wendel, his voice sounding high and slow in his ears. "They look like little people."

"Those little things *are* people," said Dad. "They're the pets."

"Livin' decals on the mothership's 'ull," said Threakman. "Live decorations fer the Out-Monkeys. An ant farm for their window box. Ah, yer'll know it when you really see an Out-Monkey, Wendel. When 'e reaches out through the hull . . ."

And then the space around them quivered like gelatin, and the cloud of moving people up ahead spiraled in around a shaky, black, living hole in space, a growing thing with fractal fringes, a three-dimensional Mandelbrot formation that, to Wendel, looked like a dancing, star-edged monkey made up of other monkeys, like the old Barrel of Monkeys toy he'd had, with all the little monkeys hooked together to make bigger monkeys that hooked together to make a gigantic monkey, coming on and on: A cross section of a higher-dimensional alien, partly shaped by the Rorschach filter of human perception.

Wendel thought: Out-Monkey? And the thing echoed psychically back at him—*Out-Monkey!*—with the alien thought coming at him like a voice in his head, mocking, drawling, sarcastic, and infinitely hip.

The Out-Monkey swelled, huge but with no real size to it in any human sense, and the fabric of space rippled with its motions—the Devil's motorboat indeed—and Wendel felt his whole body flexing and wobbling like an image in a funhouse mirror. Beneath the space waves, a sinister undertow began tugging at him. Wendel felt he would burst with the disorientation of it all.

"Dad—we've gotta go! Let's get back to the world! Tell, him, Jeremy!"

"No worries yet," said Threakman grinning and flaring his nostrils as if to inhale the wild, all-pervading rush. "Steady as she goes, mate. Your dad and me, we've 'ad some practice with the Out-Monkeys. We can 'ang 'ere a bit longer."

"Look at the faces, Wendel!" cried Dad. "Look for Jena!"

Around the Out-Monkey orbited the people imprisoned on its vast bubble. They seemed to rotate around the living hole in space, caught up in the fractals that crawled around its edges: faces that were both ecstatic and miserable; zoned-out and hysterical.

"There goes George Gravid," said Dad, pointing. "The original guy from DeGroot." Wendel stared, spotting a businessman in a black suit. And there, not too far from him were—Barley and Xiao-Xiao?

"Come on, come on, come on," Dad was chanting, and then he gave a wild laugh. "Yes! There she is! It's Jena!" His laughter was cracked and frantic. "It's Mom, Wendel! I knew I could find her!"

Wendel looked—and thought he saw her. Looking hard at her had a telescopic effect, like concentration itself was the optical instrument, and his vision zoomed in on her face—it was his mom, though her eyes were blotted with silver, like the faddish contacts people wore in the World. All those rotating around the Out-Monkey had silvered eyes, mirror-eyes endlessly looking into themselves.

Torn, Wendel hesitated—and then the fractal leviathan swept closer—he felt something like its shadow fall over him, though there was no one light source here to throw a shadow. It was as if the greater dimensional inclusiveness of its being overshadowed the other limited-dimensional beings here . . . and you could feel its "shadow" in your soul. . . .

"Dad!" Wendel shouted in panic, and his father yelled something back, but he couldn't make it out—there was a torrent of white-noise crackle upwelling all around him in the growing "shadow" of the Out-Monkey. *"Dad! We have to go!"* shrieked Wendel.

And then Dad plunged forward, arrowing in toward Mom, and Wendel felt himself on the point of a wild, uncontrolled tumble.

"Ol'roit, mate," said Threakman, grabbing Wendel's arm and pulling him up short. "Keep yer 'ead now. Ungodly strong rush, innit? It's 'ard not to go all the way in. But remember—if yer really want, yer *can* 'old back from its pullin' field. Let's ease in, nice and quiet-like, and try and snag your da."

Wendel and Threakman inched forward—Wendel feeling the pull of the Out-Monkey as strong as gravity. Yet, just as Threakman said, you didn't have to let it take you, didn't have to let it pull you down into that swarming blackness of the Out-Monkey's fractal membranes. Jeremy Threakman's grip on his arm was solid as the granite spine of the planet Earth. Wretched, stinking Jeremy Threakman knew his way around the Out-Monkeys. . . .

Wendel stared in at Mom and Dad: they were swirling around one another, orbiting a mutual center of emptiness, just as they and the others orbited the greater center of emptiness within the higher-dimensional being. It reminded Wendel of a particular carnival ride, where people whirled in place on a metal arm and their whirling cars were also whirled around a central axis.

"Dad!"

Dad looked at him—if it could be called looking. In the thrall of the Out-Monkey it was more like he was going through the motions of turning his attention to Wendel, and that attention was represented by the image of an attentive paternal face. "Wendel, I don't think I can get out! It's snagging my . . ." His voice was lost in a surging crackle, a wave of static. Then: ". . . purple, thinking purple . . ." Crackle. ". . . your mom! It wants us!"

Wendel's arm ached where Threakman clutched him. "We gotter go soon, mate!" said the scarred pocket-slug.

Mom turned her attention toward Wendel, too, now—she was reaching for him, weeping and laughing at once. He wasn't sure if it was psychic or vocal, but he heard her say: "We're pets, Wendel!" Static. "Waterstriders penned in a corner of the pond." His mother's face was lit with unholy bliss. "Live bumper stickers." A sick peal of laughter.

There was another ripple in the space around them, and all of a sudden Mom and Dad were only a few feet away. Close enough to touch. Wendel reached out to them.

"Come on, Mom! Take my hand! Jeremy and I—we *can* pull you out! You can leave if you want to!"

How Wendel knew this, he wasn't sure. But he knew it was true. He could feel it—could feel the relative energy loci, the possibility of pulling free, if you tried.

"We can go home, Dad! You and me and Mom!"

"Can't!" came his Dad's voice from a squirming gargoyle of his father with a fractal fringe, weeping and laughing.

"Dad don't *lie* to me! You can do it! Don't lie! You can come! . . ."

His arm ached so—but he waited for the answer.

Wordlessly, his father emanated regret. Remorse. Shame. "Yes," he admitted finally. "But I choose this. Mom and I . . . we want to stay here. Part of the gorgeous Out-Monkey. The eternal fractals." Static. ". . . can't help it. Go away, Wendel!"

"Have a life, Wendel!" Mom said. Several versions of her face said it, several different ways. "Don't come back. The nanomatrix—you can melt it. Acid!" Huge burst of static. "Hurry up now. It heard me!"

He felt it, too: the chilling black-light search-beam of the Out-Monkey's attention, spotlighting him like an escaped prisoner just outside the wall . . .

"No, Mom! Come back! Mom—"

Mom and Dad swirled away from him, their faces breaking up into laughing, jabbering fractals. The white noise grew intolerably loud.

"Gotter leave!" screamed Threakman in his ear. "Jump!"

With an impulse that was as much resentment of running away in fury as it was a conscious effort, he leapt with Threakman away from the hardening grip of the Out-Monkey, and felt himself spinning out through the dimensions and down the tunnels, he and Threakman in a whirling blur, one almost blending with the other . . . he thought he caught a glimpse of Threakman's memories, bleeding over in the strange ambient fields of the place from his companion's mind: a father with a leather strap, a woman giving him his first blow job in the back-room of a Sydney bar, his first paycheck, being mugged in London, a stout woman angrily leaving him . . . All this time Threakman was steering him through the bent spaces, helping him find his way back.

And then their minds were discrete again, and they were flying through a vortex of faces and pearly-gray glimmer, through a symmetrical lattice of copies of themselves, back out into the Big Bubble space he'd first entered. And just about then the bubble flattened down into normal space—and burst. He was back in the World.

Wendel knelt in the huge lab room, sobs of fury bubbling out of him, beside the floor mat of the little nanomatrix, slapping his palm flat on the floor, again and again, in his frustration and hurt. Especially, hurt. His dad and mom had chosen *that* over him. They hadn't really been inescapably caught—*it was a choice*. They'd chosen their master, the Out-Monkey; they'd gone into a spinning closed system of onanistic ecstasy; sequestered their hearts in another world, in the pursuit of pleasure and escape. They'd left him alone.

"Fuck *you*!" he screamed, pounding his fist on the nanomatrix. The magical bit of alien high-tech was a fuzzy gray rectangle, for all the world like a cheap plastic doormat. That's all the lab was, really. An empty room, some instruments, and a scrap of magic carpet on the floor.

"Roit," said Threakman hoarsely, slumping down wearily next to him. "My old man, 'e was the same way. But for 'im it was the bottle. The Out-Monkeys, they use the 'igh to pull their pets in. Something sweet 'n' sticky—like the bait for a roach motel. And, God 'elp me, I'm hooked. I won't make it back out next time. I need to . . . something else. Bloody hell—anything else."

"Mom and Dad coulda left! They weren't stuck at all!"

"Yeah. I reckon." Threakman was tired, shaky. Pale. "Lor' I feel bad, mate. I miss that rush like it was my only love. Whuh now?"

Wendel stared down at the nanomatrix. Tiny bubbles glinted in the hairs that covered it, endlessly oozing out from it. It was like a welcome mat that someone had sprinkled with beads of mercury. The little pockets winked up at him, as if to say, "*Wanna get high?*"

"The chemical factory," said Wendel. "Right next door. I know where there's a tank of nitric acid." He pulled at a corner of the nanomatrix. It was glued to the floor, but with Threakman working at his side, he was able to peel it free. He rolled up the grimy mat and tucked it under his arm, tiny bubbles scattering like dust.

The clock on the wall outside the lab said 12:03. All that crazy shit in the Big Bubble—it had lasted about a minute of real time. The next team wasn't scheduled till 2:00 A.M. The halls were empty.

Threakman shambled along at Wendel's side as Wendel led them out of the research building and across a filth-choked field to the chemical plant, staying in the shadows on one side. Wendel knew the plant well from all the hours he'd spent looking at it and thinking about modeling it. The guards wouldn't see them if they cut in over here. They skirted the high, silver cylinder of a cracking tower, alive with pipes, and climbed some mesh-metal stairs that led to a broad catwalk, ten feet across.

"The acid tank's that way," whispered Wendel. "I've seen the train cars filling it up." The rolled up nanomatrix twitched under his arm, as if trying to unroll itself.

"This'll be the 'ard bit," said Threakman, uneasily. "The Out-Monkeys can see down onto us, I'll warrant."

Wendel tightened his grip on the nanomatrix, holding it tight in both hands. It pushed and shifted, but for the moment, nothing more. They marched forward along the catwalk, their feet making soft clanging noises in the night.

"That great thumpin' yellow one with the writin' on it?" said Threakman, spotting the huge metal tank that held acid. Practically every square foot of the tank was stenciled with safety warnings. "Deadly deadly *deadly*," added Threakman with a chuckle. He ran ahead of Wendel to get a closer look, leaning eagerly forward off the edge of the catwalk. "Just my cuppa tea. Wait till I undog this 'atch. Let's get rid of the mat before I change my mind."

The nanomatrix was definitely alive, twisting in Wendel's hands like a huge, frantic fish. He stopped walking, concentrating on getting control of the thing, coiling it up tighter than before. "Hurry, Jeremy," he called. "Get the tank open, and I'll come throw this fucker in."

But now there was a subtle shudder of space, and Wendel heard a voice. "Not so fast, dear friends."

A businessman emerged out of thin air, first his legs, then his body, and then his head—as if he were being pasted down onto space. He stood there in his black, tailored suit, poised midway on the catwalk between Wendel and Threakman.

"George Gravid," said the businessman. His eyes were dark black mirrors and his suit, on closer inspection, was filthy and rumpled, as if he'd been wearing it for months—or years. "The nanomatrix is DeGroot property, Wendel. Not that I really give a shit. This tune's about played out. But I'm supposed to talk to you."

There was another shudder and a whispering of air, and now Barley and Xiao-Xiao were at Gravid's side, Barley sneering, and Xiao-Xiao's little face cold and hard. The plant lights sparkled on the three's reflective eyes, black and silver and lavender. Wendel took a step back.

"Run around 'em, Wendel," called Threakman. "I got the 'atch off. Dodge through!"

Wendel was fast and small. He had a chance, though the bucking of the nanomatrix was continuously distracting him. He faked to the left, ran to the right, then cut back to the left again.

Gravid, Barley, and Xiao-Xiao underwent a jerky stuttering motion—an instantaneous series of jumps—and ended up right in front of him. Barley gave Wendel a contemptuous little slap on the cheek.

"The Higher One picks us up and puts us down," said Xiao-Xiao. "You can't get past us. You have to listen."

"You're being moved around by an Out-Monkey?" said Wendel.

"That's a lame-ass term," said Barley. "They're *Higher Ones*. Why did you leave?"

"You're its pets," Wendel said, stomach lurching in revulsion. "Toys." The fumes from the nitric acid tank were sharp in the air.

"We're free agents," said Gravid. "But it's better in there than out here."

"The mothership's gonna leave soon," said Barley. "And we're goin' with it. Riding on the hull. Us and your parents. Don't be a dirt-world loser, Wendel. Come on back."

"The Higher One wants you, Wendel," said Gravid. "Wants to have another complete family. You know how collectors are."

The nanomatrix bucked wildly, and a fat silver pocket swelled out of its coiled-up end like a bubble from a bubble-pipe. The pocket settled down onto the catwalk, bulging and waiting. Wendel had a sudden deep memory of how good the rush had felt.

"Whatcher mean, the ship is leavin'?" asked Threakman, drawn over to stare at the bubble, half the height of a man now. It's broad navel swirled invitingly.

"They've seen enough of our space now," said Xiao-Xiao. "They're moving on. Come on now, Wendel and Jeremy. This is bigger than anything you'll ever do." She mimed a sarcastic little kiss, bent over, and squeezed herself into the pocket.

"Me come, too," said Barley, and followed her.

"Last call," said Gravid, going back into the bubble as well.

And now it was just Wendel and Threakman and the pocket, standing on the catwalk. The nanomatrix lay still in Wendel's hands.

"I don't know as I can live without it, yer know," said Threakman softly.

"But you said you want to change," said Wendel.

"Roit," said Threakman bleakly. "I did say."

Wendel skirted around the pocket and walked over to where the acid tank's open hatch gaped. The nanomatrix had stopped fighting him. He and his world were small; the Out-Monkeys had lost interest. It was a simple matter to throw the plastic mat into the tank . . . and he watched it fall, end over end.

Choking fumes wafted out, and Wendel crawled off low down on the catwalk toward the breathable air.

When he sat up, Threakman and the bubble were both gone. And somewhere deep in his guts, Wendel felt a shudder, as of giant engines moving off. The pockets were gone? Maybe. But there'd always be a high that wanted to eat you alive. Life was a long struggle.

He walked away from the research center, toward the train station, feeling empty, and hurt—and free.

There were some things at the apartment he could sell. It would be a start. He would do all right. He'd been taking care of himself for a long time. . . .

Catherine Asaro has a doctorate in chemical physics from Harvard and claims she is a walking definition of the word absent-minded, *managing to spill coffee in every room of her house.*

You wouldn't know it by her sharp, telling fiction. She's been nominated for the Hugo and Nebula Awards and has won a bunch of others, including the Analog Readers Poll and the National Readers Choice Award. Her most recent books were The Quantam Rose *and a near-future suspense novel,* The Phoenix Code.

For Redshift *she's written something that can only be described as, well, sharp and telling.*

Ave de Paso

CATHERINE ASARO

My cousin Manuel walked alone in the twilight, out of sight, while I sat in the back of the pickup truck. We each needed privacy for our grief. The hillside under our truck hunched out of the desert like the shoulder of a giant. Perhaps that shoulder belonged to one of the Four-Corner Gods who carried the cube of the world on his back. When too many of the Zinacantec Maya existed, the gods grew tired and shifted the weight of their burden, stirring an earthquake.

I slipped my hand into my pocket, where I had hidden my offerings: white candles, pine needles, rum. They weren't enough. I had no copal incense to burn, no resin balls and wood chips to appease the ancestral gods for the improper manner of my mother's burial.

Manuel and I were far now from Zinacant·n, our home in the highlands of Chiapas, Mexico. Years ago my mother had brought us here, to New Mexico. Later we had moved to Los Angeles, the city of fallen angels. But for this one night, Manuel and I had returned to New Mexico, a desert named after the country of our birth, yet not of that country.

An in-between place.

Dusk feathered across the land, brushing away a pepper-red sunset. Eventually I stirred myself enough to set out our sleeping bags in the bed of the truck. It wouldn't be as comfortable as if we slept on the ground, but we wouldn't wake up with bandolero scorpions or rattlesnakes in our bags either.

"Akushtina?" Manuel's voice drifted through the dry evening like a hawk.

I sat down against the wall of the pickup and pulled my denim jacket tight against the night's chill.

Manuel walked into view from around the front of the truck. "Tina, why didn't you answer?"

"It didn't feel right."

He climbed into the truck and dropped his Uzi at my feet. "You okay?"

I shuddered. "Take it away."

Sitting next to me, he folded his arms against the cold. "Take what away?"

I pushed the Uzi with my toe. "That."

"You see a rattler, you yell for me, what am I going to do? Spit at it?"

"You don't need a submachine gun to protect us from snakes."

He withdrew from me then, not with his body but with his spirit, into the shrouded places of his mind. I had hoped that coming here, away from the cold angles and broken lines of Los Angeles, would bring back the closeness we had shared as children. Though many people still considered us children.

"I don't want to fight," I said.

His look softened. "I know, *hija*."

"I miss her."

He put his arms around me and I leaned into him, this cousin of mine who at nineteen, three years older than me, was the only guardian I had now. Sliding my arms under his leather jacket, I laid my head against the rough cloth of his flannel shirt. And I cried, slight sounds that blended into the night. The crickets stopped chirping, filling the twilight with their silence.

Manuel murmured in Tzotzil Mayan, our first language, the only one he had ever felt was his, far more than the English we spoke now, or the Spanish we had learned as a second language. But he would never show his tears: not to me; not to the social workers in L.A. who had tried to reach him when he was younger and now feared they had failed; not to Los Halcones, the gang the Anglos called The Falcons, the barrio warriors Manuel considered the only family we had left.

Eventually I stopped crying. Crickets began to saw the night again, and an owl hooted, its call wavering like a ghost. Sounds came from the edge of the world: a truck growling on the horizon, the whispering rumble of pronghorn antelope as they loped across the land, the howl of a coyote. No city groans muddied the night.

I pulled away from Manuel, wiping my cheek with my hand. Then I got up and went to stand at the cab of the truck, leaning with my arms folded on its roof. We had parked on the top of a flat hill. The desert rolled out in all directions, from here to the horizon, an endless plain darkening with shadows beneath a forever sky. This land belonged less to humans than to the giant furry tarantulas that crept across the parched soil; or to the tarantula hawks, those huge wasps that dived out of the air to grab their eight-legged prey; or to the javelinas, the wild, grunting pigs.

We had come here from the Chiapas village called Naben Chauk, the Lake of the Lightning. My mother had been outcast there, an unmarried woman with a child and almost no clan. After the death of Manuel's parents, my aunt and uncle, she had no one. So eight years ago she brought Manuel and me here, to New Mexico, where a friend had a job for her. But she dreamed of the City of Angels, convinced it could give us a better life. So later we had moved to Los Angeles, a sprawling giant that could swallow this hill like a snake swallowing a mouse.

"The city killed her," I said. "If we had stayed in Naben Chauk she would still be alive."

Manuel's jeans rustled when he stood up. His boots thudded as he crossed the truck bed. He leaned on the cab next to me. "I wish it. You wish it. But Los Angeles didn't give her cancer. That sickness, it would have eaten her no matter where we went."

"The city sucked out pieces of her soul."

He drew me closer, until I was standing between him and the cab, my back against his front, his arms around me, his hands resting on the cab. "You got to let go, Tina. You got to say good-bye."

"I can't." It was like giving up, just like we had given up our home. I missed the limestone hills of the Chiapas highlands, where clouds hid the peaks and mist cloaked the sweet stands of pine. As a small girl, I had herded our sheep there, our only wealth, woolly animals we sheared with scissors bought in San Cristóbal de las Casas. Until an earthquake killed the flock.

As it had killed Manuel's parents.

I wished I could see my mother one last time, cooking over a fire at dawn, smoke rising around her, spiraling up and around until it escaped out the spaces where the roof met the walls. She would kneel in front of her *comal*, a round metal plate propped up on two pots and a rock, patting her maize dough back and forth, making tortillas.

"It's good we came here to tell her good-bye," I said. "It was wrong the way she died, in that hospital. In L.A."

"We did the best we could." Manuel kissed the top of my head. "She couldn't have gotten medicine in Naben Chauk, not what she needed."

"Her spirit won't rest now."

"Tina, you got to stop all this, about spirits and things." Manuel let go of me. I turned around in time to see him pick up the Uzi. He held it like a staff. "This is how you 'protect your spirit.' By making sure no one takes what's yours."

"How can you come to mourn her and bring *this*." I jerked the gun out of his hand and threw it over the side of the truck. "She would hate it. *Hate* it."

"Goddamn it, Tina." Holding the side of the pickup, he vaulted over it to the ground. He picked up the Uzi, his anger hanging around him like smoke. Had I been anyone else, grabbing his gun that way could have gotten me shot.

I climbed out of the truck and jumped down next to him. He towered over me, tall by any standard, huge for a man of the Zinacantec Maya, over six feet. His hook-nosed profile was silhouetted against the stars like an ancient Maya king, a warrior out of place and time, his face much like those carved into the *stellae*, the stones standing in the ruins of our ancestors. Proud. He was so proud. And in so much pain.

Faint music rippled out of the night, drifting on the air like a bird, strange and yet familiar, the sweet notes of a Chiapas guitar.

"Someone is here," I said.

Manuel lifted his gun as he scanned the area. "You see someone?"

"Hear someone." The music came closer now, stinging, bittersweet. "A guitar. On the other side of the hill."

He lowered the gun. "I don't hear squat."

"It's there." I hesitated. "Let's not stay here tonight. If we went back into town, they would probably let us stay at the house—"

"No! We didn't come all this way to stay where she was a *maid*." Manuel motioned at the desert. "This is what she loved. The land."

I knew he was right. But the night made me uneasy. "Something is wrong."

"Oh, hell, Tina." He took my arm. "I'll show you. No one is here."

I pulled away. "Don't go."

"Why not?" Manuel walked away, to the edge of the hilltop. He stood there, a tall figure in the ghosting moonlight. Then he disappeared, gone down the other side, vanished into the whispering night.

"Manuel, wait." I started after him.

The guitar kept playing, its notes wavering, receding, coming closer. Then it stopped, and the desert waited in silence. No music, no crickets, no coyotes.

Nothing.

"Manuel?" I called. "Did you find anyone?"

Gunshots cracked, splintering the night into pieces.

"No!" I broke into a run, sprinting to the edge where he had disappeared. Then I stopped. The slope fell away from my feet, mottled by mesquite and spidery ocotillo bushes, until it met the desert floor several hundred yards below.

"Manuel!" My shout winged over the desert.

No answer. I slid in a stumbling run down the hill, thorny mesquite grabbing at my jeans. About halfway down reason came back and I slowed down, moving with more caution.

I reached the bottom without seeing anyone. Yet a tendril of smoke wafted in the air. How? No fire burned anywhere.

Music started again, behind me. Turning, I faced the shadowed hill. My feet took me forward, toward the drifting notes, toward the hill, toward the music *in* the hill. Yet as long as I walked, as many steps as I took, I came no closer to that dusky slope. It stayed in front of me, humped in the moonlight.

With no warning, I was on the edge of a campfire. What I had thought was the hill, it was smoke, hanging in layers and curtains. I walked through the ashy mist, trying to reach the campfire that flickered red and orange, vague in the smoke-laden air.

Someone was sitting on the ground by the fire.

"Manuel?" I asked.

He didn't stir. I continued to walk, but came no closer to him.

It wasn't my cousin. The stranger gave no indication he knew I had come to his fire. He stared into the flames, a heavy man with rolls of flesh packed around his body. The ground began to move under my feet, bringing him toward me, while I walked in place.

Guitar notes drifted in the smoke, joined now by drums, a Chamula violin, and a reed pipe. They keened for my mother. The melody hit discords, as if offended that it had to play for itself when I should have brought the music in her honor. But where in Los Angeles could I have found Zinacantec instruments or musicians to play them?

I had so little of what I needed to give my mother a proper burial. She lay in an unmarked grave in California. But I would do my best in this in-between place. Manuel should have been the one to perform the ceremony, as head of the family, but I knew what he would say if I asked him. He trusted his Uzi far more than the ways of our lost home.

The ground continued to bring the stranger to me. He stopped only a few paces away. With a slow, sure motion, he turned his head and smiled, a dark smile, a possessive smile.

"Akushtina." He pressed his hands together and lifted his arms. When he opened his hands, a whippoorwill lay in the cup of his palms.

"No!" I stepped forward. "Let her go!"

He clapped his hands and the bird screamed, turning into smoke when his palms smacked together. "She's gone."

I knew then that he had trapped my mother's spirit when she died, catching it before she could return home to the mountains around the Lake of the Lightning. She hadn't been buried with the proper rituals, after a mourner's meal at dawn, her head toward the west. It had let this unnamed stranger steal her soul, just as he stole the spirit of the whippoorwill, her companion among the wild creatures that lived in the spirit world.

Wait.

The whippoorwill wasn't my mother's spirit companion. An ocelot walked with her. In her youth, she had met it in her dreams, as it prowled the dream corrals on the Senior Large Mountain. If the ancestral gods had been angry when she died, it was the ocelot they would have freed from its corral, leaving it to wander unprotected in the Chiapas highlands.

A whippoorwill made no sense. It came from this place, here, in the desert. During the year we lived in New Mexico, in the ranch house where my mother worked, she and I had often sat outside in the warm nights and listened to the eerie bird voices call though the dry air. So I thought of the whippoorwill when I thought of her. But if this stranger had truly captured her spirit companion, he would have shown me the ocelot.

Why a whippoorwill? I had no answer. All I could do was make the offerings I had brought. I pulled out the bag of pine needles and sprinkled them on the ground. The smoke around us smelled of copal incense, this stranger doing for himself what should have come from me. I fumbled in my pocket for the rum bottle. It wasn't true *posh*, a drink distilled from brown sugar and made in Chamula. This came from a store in L.A. But it was the best I could do.

The man snorted, giving his opinion of my offerings. He motioned at the rum. "You drink it."

Flushing, I tipped the bottle to my lips. The rum went down in a jolt and I coughed, spluttering drops everywhere. The rattle of the stranger's laugh made haze whirl around us, smoke curling and uncurling, hiding the desert, revealing it, hiding it again in veils of gray on gray.

Then I remembered the candles. Candles, tortillas for the gods. Taking them out of my pocket, I knelt down and set them in the dirt. They were ordinary, each made from white wax, with a white wick. When I lit them, they should have burned with a simple flame. Instead they sparked like tiny sky rockets straining to break free of the earth.

The man rose to his feet, ponderous and heavy. "This is all you have for me?"

I looked up, trying to understand what he wanted. A shape formed behind him, hazy in the smoke. It stepped closer and showed itself as a deer, a great stag with a king's rack of antlers. Two iguanas rode on its head, their bodies curving down to make blinders for its eyes, their tails curled tight around its antlers. They watched me with lizard gazes. The stranger had a whip in his hand now, not leather, but a living snake, its tongue flicking out from its mouth, its body supple and undulating, its tail stiffened into a handle.

I scrambled to my feet. "I know you," I rasped, my throat raw from the drifting smoke. "Yahval Balamil."

He stood before me and laughed, Yahval Balamil, the Earth Lord, the god of caves and water holes, he who could give riches or death, who could buy the pieces of your inner soul from a witch who took the shape of a goat, or trap your feet in iron sandals and make you work beneath the earth until the iron wore out.

Greed saturated his big-toothed smile. "You're mine now."

The smoke in the air curled thick around us. I tried to back away from him, but I was walking in place, my feet stepping and stepping, taking me nowhere.

"Mine," he said. "Both you and the boy."

"No! Leave us alone."

He cracked his whip, and it snapped around my body in coils, growing longer with each turn, pinning my arms. The head stopped inches from my face and the snake hissed, its tongue flicking out to touch my cheek. I tried to scream, but no sound came out.

"Mine," the Earth Lord whispered.

"Tina?" a voice asked behind me.

"Manuel!" I spun around. "Where have you been? Are you all right?"

"Yeah, I'm all right." He stood with the gun dangling at his side. "What's wrong?"

"Can't you *see* it?"

"See what?"

I glanced around. We were halfway up the hill, just the two of us. No snake, no spirits, no gods. The fire had vanished, and the smoke had solidified into the mountain.

Turning back to Manuel, I said, "He's gone."

"He?" My cousin scowled. "Why do you smell like liquor?"

"I drank some rum."

"When did you start messing with that shit?" He stepped closer. "I told you never to touch it. You know what happens when men see a pretty girl like you drunk? It makes them think to do what they shouldn't be doing."

"It was part of the ceremony."

"Ceremony?" He looked around, taking in the candle stubs and pine needles scattered on the ground. Then he sighed, the fist-tight knot of his anger easing. In a gentler voice he said, "There isn't no one here. I checked the whole area."

"Then why did you shoot?"

"It was a deer. I missed it."

I stared at him. "You shot at a deer with an Uzi?"

"It surprised me. I've never seen deer here before."

"What if it had been me who surprised you?"

He touched my cheek. "You know I would never hurt you."

"You didn't shoot at a deer. It was Yahval Balamil."

His smile flashed in the darkness. "Did I hit him?"

"Don't make fun of me."

"You're mine," the Earth Lord whispered.

With a cry, I jerked back and lost my balance. I fell to the ground and rolled down the hill like a log, with mesquite ripping at my clothes. When my head struck a rock, I jolted to a stop and my sight went black. A ringing note rose in the air like a bird taking flight, then faded into faint guitar music.

"Tina!" Manuel shouted, far away.

"Mine," the Earth Lord said. "Both of you." A snake hissed near my ear.

"Stop it!" I struck at the dark air.

"*Oiga!*" Now Manuel sounded as if he was right above me. "I won't hurt you."

My sight was coming back, enough so I could see my cousin's head silhouetted against the stars. He was kneeling over me, his legs on either side of my hips. "Are you okay?" he asked. "Why did you scream?"

"Mine," the Earth Lord murmured.

"*No!*" I said.

Manuel brushed a lock of hair off my face. "I didn't mean to scare you."

Smoke was forming behind him, tendrils coming together in the outline of a stag.

"Leave him alone!" I sat up, almost knocking Manuel over, and batted at the air, as if that could defeat the smoke and protect my cousin.

"What's wrong?" Manuel stayed where he was, his knees straddling my hips, his thighs pressing on mine. He grabbed my hands, pulling them against his chest. He held them in his large grip while he caught me around the waist with his other arm. "*Tu eres bueno, Tinita.* It's okay."

The smoke settled onto him, a dark cloud soaking into his body, smelling of incense. Curls of smoke brushed my hands where Manuel held them, my legs where his thighs pressed mine, my breasts where his chest touched mine. The invading darkness seeped into him.

Manuel jerked as if caught by the smoke. Then he pulled me hard against himself, his breath warm on my cheek, his body musky with the scent of his jacket, his shirt, his sweat. He murmured in Tzotzil, bending his head as if searching for something. I turned my face up—and he kissed me, pressing his lips hard against my mouth.

I twisted my head to the side. "No."

"Shhh . . .," he murmured. "It's all right." He lay me back down on the ground, his body heavy on mine, like the weight of the dead.

"Manuel, stop!" I tried to roll away, but he kept me in place.

"Mine," the Earth Lord said. "Both of you."

"*No.* Go away!" A breeze wafted across my face, bringing the smell of sagebrush—?

And candles?

Manuel kissed me again and pulled open my jacket with his free hand. "Akushtina," he whispered. "*Te amo, hija.*"

"Not like this." My voice shook as I struggled. "You don't mean it like this."

"Soon," the Earth Lord promised. The snake hissed again.

Panic fluttered across my thoughts. I still smelled candles. That scent, I knew it from when we had lived here. Luminarios. On Christmas Eve my mother had filled brown bags with dirt, enough in each to hold one candle. She lined the paths and walls of the front yard with the glowing beige lanterns. My mother's love in a paper bag, warming the darkness while distant whippoorwills whistled in the night.

"We can go together." Manuel moved his hand over my breast. "Together."

"Manuel, listen." I was talking too fast, but I couldn't slow down. "Do you remember the luminarios?"

His searching hand stopped as it reached my hip. "Why?"

"Remember what we swore when we were watching them? About family? How we would protect each other?"

He lifted his head to look at me, his memory of that time etched on his face. The smoke that had funneled into his body seeped out again. It swirled around him, as if trying to go inside and finding its way blocked by the power of a memory. Finally it drifted away, into the night. Somewhere an owl hooted.

Manuel made a noise, a strangled gasp he sucked into his throat. He jumped to his feet and backed up one step, still watching me. Then he spun around and strode away. Within seconds the shadows of the hill had taken him.

I got up to my knees and bent over, my arms folded across my stomach, my whole body shaking. A wave of nausea surged over me, then receded. What if he had gone through with what he started? It would have destroyed us both.

What had he meant by *We can go together*? Go where?

Then I knew. Under the earth. Forever.

I scrambled to my feet and ran up the hill. It wasn't until I came over the top that I saw him, a dark shadow by the truck. My hiking boots crunched on the rocks as I walked. I stopped in front of him and looked up at his face.

Once I had seen a vaquero forced to shoot his horse after a truck hit it on Interstate 10. The dying animal had lain on its side, dismay in its gaze until the cowboy ended its pain. Manuel had that same look now.

He gave me the keys to the truck. "Go back to town."

"Not unless you come."

He shifted the Uzi in his hands. "I'm staying here."

I struggled to stay calm. "When people hurt, sometimes they do things they shouldn't. But you stopped. You *stopped*." I pushed at the Uzi. "Manuel, put it away."

"You're all I got left." His voice cracked. "And now I made that dirty, too."

I thought of his words: *Te amo*. "You said you loved me."

"You don't know nothing about how I meant it."

"I'm not stupid. I know." I shook my head. "It was *him*, making you act that way."

He stared at me, his stark face hooded by shadows. "It was me. It's always been there."

"But you didn't do it." I tried to find the words to reach him. "Everyone has darkness inside of him. You turned away from yours. That says how strong you are."

He snorted. "You got this seeing problem, Tina, like you look at me with mirror shades. They reflect away the truth about me, so you see what you want, this good that isn't there."

"It's there." For all that Manuel denied it, the good lived in him. The changes we had weathered in our lives had worn him down, eroding him like the wind and thunderstorms on the desert, in part because he was older, more set in his life, and had lost both his parents as well as my mother. But also because his height, strength, deep voice, and brooding anger frightened people. He looked like the warrior he would have been in another time, and in his frustration with a world that had no place for him, he had begun to live out that expectation.

"It's still there," I repeated, as if saying it enough would make him believe it.

He just shook his head.

"Mine," the Earth Lord whispered. "Both of you."

This time I gave no hint I heard. I kept watching my cousin.

"Take the truck," Manuel said. "Go back to town. Back to L.A."

"Why?" Everything that mattered to me was slipping away. I knew what he would do if he stayed alone here in the desert. "So you can take away the only family I have left?"

"You'll do better without me."

"No!"

A shadow moved on the cab of the truck, a small one, barely bigger than my hand. Whippoorwill. With a soft flapping of wings, it rose into the air and circled above us, then flew away over the hill, into the endless open spaces of the night.

"*Mine,*" the Earth Lord rasped. His voice had an edge now, no longer gloating, more like a protest.

Then, finally, I understood. My mother's spirit had never been the one in danger. It was the two of us here, Manuel and me. We couldn't accept what we had lost, our home, our lives, our parents. That was why we had come to this in-between place. Our grief had made us vulnerable.

"I was wrong," I said. "The bird that Yahval Balamil was holding, it wasn't Mama. It was me."

Manuel clenched his fist around the Uzi. "What the hell are you talking about?"

"The Earth Lord," I told him. "He's come for us. He knows we're hurting now. It makes us easy prey. He's come to take the pieces of our souls."

"Stop it." Manuel's voice cracked. "We're the only ones here. Not dead people or fat gods. Just *us*. No one else. *No-fucking-one else.*" He flipped over the Uzi, holding it by the barrel, and swung it like a club, smashing it into the door of the truck, denting the weathered chrome. As I jumped back, he flipped the gun back over and aimed it at himself.

"Manuel, *no*!"

He didn't move, just stood like a statue, the Uzi pressed against his chest. I was afraid to breathe, to look away, even to blink.

Slowly, so slowly, he turned, and pointed the gun away from his heart, out over the desert—

And he fired.

Bullets punctured the night like rivets ramming metal. Shadow clouds of dirt flew into the air and rocks broke in explosions. He kept on firing, his long legs planted wide, his hands clenched on the gun, shattering the night, until I thought he would crack the land wide open and fall into the fissure.

After an eternity, the bullets stopped. Manuel sank to his knees and bowed his head, holding the gun like a pole in front of him. He made no sound. After a span of heartbeats I realized he was crying for the first time in years, in silence, even now unable to give voice to the grief that had torn apart his life, as he lost almost everything and everyone that had ever mattered to him.

I went to him and murmured in Tzotzil, nonsense words meant for comfort. He drew in a choked breath. Standing up, he wiped his face with the sleeve of his jacket. We stood with space between us, a space that would always be there now.

I gave him the keys. "Will you drive?"

He stood watching my face. Then, finally, he said, "We can stay in town tonight. Leave for L.A. in the morning."

"Okay." My voice caught. "That sounds good."

I knew that our surviving this one night wouldn't solve the problems we faced in L.A. It wouldn't take away the inner demons Manuel wrestled or bring back my mother. We still had a long way to go.

But it was a start.

We had finally begun to ride the healing path.

So we drove away, through a land haunted with moonlight, leaving behind the bone-desert of our grief.

Joe Haldeman and I share an abiding passion for telescopes and astronomical equipment—he's one of the few guys I know who I can talk to about Nagler eyepieces, splitting double stars, and Schmidt-Cassegrain versus Maksutov-Cassegrain. He also owns the same portable Tele Vue refractor as I do—only his is more fancy, and therefore enviable.

His fiction is pretty damned fancy, too—if, for instance, you haven't read Forever War *and* Forever Peace, *both of which won Hugo and Nebula Awards, it's time you bought a telescope and forget about reading—you're no good at it anyway!*

For Redshift *Joe has compressed an entire movie into a few pages—no mean feat.*

I'd much rather split double stars than live through this one.

Road Kill

JOE HALDEMAN

✳

Hunter is a serial murderer with an interesting specialty. He goes after solitary joggers and bicyclists on lonely country roads. He doesn't just run them down or shoot them from the car. He abducts them and slowly tortures them on videotape. Sometimes we see him at home, while he goes through his videotape collection and the rest of his rigid daily routine.

He's a big man, over three hundred pounds, most of it fat. His arms and hands are very strong, though; he works out with dumbbells and GripMasters. He lives on pizza and fried chicken and beer, and every day scarfs down three Big Macs, two large shakes, and a pint of Jim Beam, for lunch. On special days he likes to cook at home.

He lives in a single-wide trailer on an isolated lot in a pine forest in Georgia. His house creaks and sways when he walks through it. The power goes out all the time, but that's all right; he has a big Honda generator that switches on automatically. He needs it not just for his videotapes, but for the two big top-loading freezers full of his victims' remains, cut into steaks and chops and stew meat. The livers are carefully sliced, the slices separated with waxed paper. He doesn't like kidneys. The thymus glands, sweetbreads, are collected in a plastic bag until he has enough for a meal.

Sometimes he brings the victims home, but usually he videotapes them out in the woods, and when they are dead, or almost dead, he field-dresses them like deer. He prides himself on having provided the police with a useless clue; he's never actually been a hunter. He learned how to do it from a video.

* * *

Hunter is on the prowl. He parks his special van on a dirt road and labors a couple of hundred yards uphill to a place he's scouted out earlier: part of a jogging trail that offers him ample cover but also an adequate line of sight in both directions. He carefully sets up the monofilament line that he will use to trip his victim, and hides, waiting.

He's delusionary in a remarkably consistent and detailed way. He believes himself to be a S'kang, an alien soldier marooned on this miserable backward planet. Ugly and squat here, he is a model of male attractiveness on his high-gravity homeworld. But at least here he is immensely strong, and there are plenty of humans, who look and taste like the cattle back home. Here comes one now.

The attack is so swift and brutal that it lends some credence to the idea of his not being human. A teenage boy runs up and falls face-first on the paved path when Hunter yanks the line. He rises to his knees and Hunter swats him into unconsciousness with a casual backhand. He drags the boy down to a prepared tree beside his van, silences and secures him with duct tape. He hangs him upside down and slices off his running clothes with a razor-keen filleting knife. Then he sets up a camcorder and revives the boy with ammonia. He makes a few ornamental cuts, talking to the boy until he faints dead away. To his chagrin, the weakling can't be revived; he's had a heart attack. So he works for speed rather than esthetics, and a few minutes later sorts through the pile of organs and throws the edible parts along with the gutted corpse into the big cooler in the back of his van, and heads for home, two states east.

Spencer was badly wounded by a mine in the last minutes of Desert Storm, and spent more than a year recovering the use of his legs. He left the Army with a 75 percent VA disability, which, along with the GI Bill and a generous gift from his father, allowed him to finish pre-law and law school.

But when he joined his father's New York law firm as an intern, it was a disaster. Fifty percent of his disability was posttraumatic stress disorder, and the pressures of the city kept him jumpy all the time. He also didn't like the feeling that he got from the other members of the firm—that he wouldn't have a job if he weren't the boss's son. He suspected it was true and found a position as a junior partner in a small-town Florida law firm, and against his father's wishes, left the big city, and winter, with relief.

It went well for a year. He liked the little town of Flagler Beach. He was usually inside only half the day, helping prepare briefs; the rest of the time he was doing footwork, going out and interviewing respondents and occasionally doing repossessions, one of the firm's sidelines. Not just cars and boats, but sometimes children who legally belonged with the other parent. For this, the firm got him a private investigator license and a concealed-weapon permit. Half the men in Florida have guns, they told him; more than half of the ones who break the law do.

He tried to be good-natured about Spencer-for-hire jokes.

Carrying a gun again gave him mixed feelings. It was undeniably a comfort, but the associations with combat made him nervous. He was never called upon to use it, except on the first of every month, when he took it down to the target range and dutifully ran a couple of boxes of ammunition through it. It was a snub-nosed .357 Magnum, not very accurate beyond the length of a room. He also had an Army .45, like the one he had carried in Desert Storm, but that size cannon is hard to conceal in light summer clothes.

As his part of the story opens, after the horrific scene with Hunter, he has just married Arlene, the firm's beautiful secretary, and the boss is talking about promoting him to junior partner in a year or so. His mother gives him a hundred grand as a wedding gift. He can't believe his luck.

It was about to change.

The boss has sent him to the university at Gainesville for a few days of research, and when he comes back, the firm's office has a FOR LEASE sign on it. Stunned, he returns to his new house and finds that his new wife has left with the new car. There are annulment papers on the kitchen table. Their joint bank account is cleaned. All their credit cards have been maxed for cash. The mortgage payment is due, and he has less than a hundred dollars in his wallet.

The two disasters are not unrelated. She's gone to Mexico with his boss, and all the firm's assets.

He calls his parents, but their unlisted number has been changed. In the waiting mail, he finds a note from his mother saying that Dad was furious about the unauthorized $100,000 wedding gift. He'll get over it, though. Ron Spencer is not so sure.

He sells his old pickup truck to the guy who comes to repossess the furniture. He pawns his good bicycle and the .357, keeping his rusty beach bike and the .45. He has enough money to renew his P.I. license, so he rents a one-room office with a fold-out couch and an answering machine. He has some cards printed up and takes out an ad in the weekly advertiser.

He's been bicycling an hour or so a day, both as therapy for his legs and because it cuts down on his smoking. Now, with lots of time on his hands and no money for cigarettes, he starts bicycling constantly. Maybe he can break a bad habit, and a good thing will come out of this.

Every day he starts out at first light and makes a long loop down past Daytona Beach, coming back in the evening to check his silent answering machine. But staying on the bike does keep him from smoking, and the sixty- and seventy-mile rides tire him out so much he sleeps whenever he's not riding.

Daytona has a bad crime rate, and so Ron carries the .45—not in a conspicuous holster, but in an innocuous zipper bag in his front basket. The two big rear baskets, he fills up with aluminum cans that people have tossed from cars. It amuses him to help beautify the environment while making nearly enough to pay for the day's lunch break.

But it's the rusty bike full of aluminum cans, old clothes, and a couple of days' worth of bread that puts him on a path toward Hunter.

A Daytona cop busts him for vagrancy and finds the .45, and, of course, it was on a day when Ron had left his wallet home. No money and no permit. There's a reporter at the station when he tells his story, though, and after the police have verified that he is who he is, the reporter asks if he'd trade an interview for a steak. Ron figures a human interest story couldn't hurt business, so he goes along with it.

He doesn't think the story that appears on Sunday is very good; it makes him look kind of pathetic. But it does produce a client. A man makes a phone call, no details, and an hour later shows up at the little office in a new Jaguar convertible.

The man's in his sixties: lean, athletic, gruff. He gets right to the point:

Gerald Kellerman's son was a victim of Hunter. All they ever found were his entrails and genitals. And his bicycle. He had just started a coast-to-coast bicycle trek. It ended in a lonely swamp north of Tallahassee.

It's been two years, and the cops have gotten nowhere. Kellerman wants to hire Ron, who is about his son's age and build, to get on his bicycle and act as a decoy. And when the bastard shows up, use the .45 on him.

It doesn't sound too appealing. It's unlikely that Ron will run into the monster, since he's ranged all over the south—victims in Louisiana and Alabama, as well as Florida—and even if he did, Ron couldn't imagine a scenario where the man revealed that he was Hunter under circumstances where Ron could draw his weapon and plug him.

He explains this to Kellerman, who says yeah, he had that figured out already, but here's the deal: I'll give you a hundred grand to do it for one year. Ten percent up front as a retainer, plus a credit card to pick up all your road expenses. You pedal along like a camper, but take it easy; eat in restaurants, stay in motels. See the country, make a nest egg. Does it beat pickin' up cans alongside the road? If you do catch the bastard, dead or alive, it's another hundred grand.

Ron thinks the man is crazy, but then the government has certified *him* as 50 percent crazy, so he says okay, if you throw in an extra thousand for a new bike and supplies. The man takes out his wallet and counts out ten hundred-dollar bills. Get your bike, he says; my lawyer will come by tomorrow with a contract.

So the odyssey begins. Ron pedals cautiously through the rural South, with his New York accent and shiny new bike, finding a land that is about equal parts Southern charm and *Deliverance* menace. Meanwhile, the nameless killer cruises country roads in his panel van with the big cooler in back.

Hunter is returning to his trailer in the dead of night, complaining to himself about the heat on this accursed planet and panting in its thin oxygen as he drags the body to his kitchen worktable. The walls are covered with *Star Trek* and *Star Wars* posters; brick-and-board bookshelves are full of science fiction paperbacks and videotapes. So he's either an alien with a jones for sci-fi or a human geek with a really severe personality problem.

(He reads other things besides science fiction. In particular, he's made an extensive study of serial killers, so that he knows what the police and FBI will expect him to do. He's much more clever than they, of course.)

He strikes three times. The last one is particularly horrible, a trick he got from a book about the Inquisition. He's stopped a young female jogger, punched her senseless, and driven her deep into an abandoned turpentine forest. He ties her to a tree, naked, her wrists and crossed ankles duct-taped to tree limbs and trunk in a crucifixion pose, and when she wakes up he takes a scalpel and makes a small incision in her lower abdomen. He carefully slices through the layers of muscle and the tough peritoneum, and eases out a couple of inches of gut. Then he goes back to the van to fetch a cage that holds a whining, starving mongrel. He records her begging and hysteria for a while and then holds the cage up to her abdomen and opens it. The dog snatches its food and runs away, unraveling her.

He follows the dog to where it sits feasting and clubs it to death. Then he returns and videotapes the woman's face, staring at what has happened, until the life leaves her eyes.

For the first time, he leaves all the body there. The scene has a kind of perfect terrible beauty. His freezers are full anyhow, and he wants to see what the newspapers will say.

He always alternates boy, girl, boy, girl. Who will be the lucky boy?

Ron Spencer has fallen into a routine that is not unpleasant. He pedals thirty to fifty miles a day, stopping in motels when he can, campgrounds otherwise. He stays in touch with Kellerman by cellular phone, calling every day at five. He doesn't dare forget to call: if Kellerman hasn't heard from him by 5:30, he'll call the state and local police and FBI. There's a signal generator under his bicycle seat that will lead them straight to him, and presumably Hunter or some other foul player.

For the past several weeks, he hasn't been riding alone. He met an attractive woman a few years his senior who was also biking coast-to-coast, and they hit it off. When she asked whether they could ride together for a while, he considered refusing, or saying yes and pretending to be just another biker, but then after some awkwardness he explained to her the odd and probably dangerous quest he was on. He doesn't want to endanger her. She counters that she would be in a lot more danger alone.

In fact, she's the first sole female rider he's seen on the road, with all the media play about Hunter. At first, he even suspects her of being the killer.

Their relationship is friendly but platonic. Linda's not looking for a man, she says. That's okay with Ron, still hurting from his own betrayal. He doesn't need a relationship, though he wouldn't turn down some friendly sex; Linda implies that she's lesbian but deflects any direct queries.

Linda's a good bicyclist, but Ron is a lot better. He pokes along with her most of the time, but periodically says bye and sprints ahead for a mile or two, getting some real exercise. It also gives them each a few minutes of privacy for "using the bushes."

This afternoon, Hunter is using a ploy that has worked in the past, pretending to be fixing a tire. He's so huge and obviously helpless that people will stop and offer aid.

Ron is cranking along, sprinting about a mile ahead of Linda, and almost stops, but then decides to play it safe. He doesn't *really* want to confront Hunter, and this guy looks like one of the two suspects. (The FBI is looking for the Thin Man and the Fat Man, from two possible eyewitnesses.) As he passes, though, Hunter jams a tire iron into his front wheel spokes. Ron cartwheels and is knocked unconscious, his helmet shattered.

Hunter finds the gun and P.I. license and gets suspicious. Instead of killing him, he ties and gags him and throws him and his bike into the back of the van, and drives back to Georgia.

But Linda has come around a distant curve just in time to see the huge man tossing Ron's bike into the van. She's can't see the license number, but can tell from the peach color that it's from Georgia, and she can describe the van. She pedals like mad; it's at least an hour to the next small town.

Safe in his isolation, Hunter manacles Ron and tries to find out what's going on. He inspects the bicycle and finds the bug, which he triumphantly smashes in front of Ron.

In the process of wheedling and posturing and torturing, he reveals his True Identity. He shows Ron the freezers full of food and cooks him up a nice chop.

While all this is going on, Linda is trying to make some cracker police officer take her seriously. She tries to reach Kellerman, but he has an unlisted number. The FBI puts her on hold.

Of course once the tension is stretched to the breaking point, the cops come boiling out of the woods. Hunter is so huge he absorbs about twenty bullets before he falls down dead.

Epilogue

The coroner of Illsworth County, Georgia, has done hundreds of autopsies, but never one of such a huge person, and he's not looking forward to it. Mountains of messy fat to slice through before you get to the organs. But he prepares the body and makes his first incision. Then he staggers back, dropping the scalpel.

Inside, there's no fat, and not a single organ he can identify. Some of them are shiny metal.

Jack Dann has written or edited over fifty books, including the international bestseller The Memory Cathedral*. His Civil War novel* The Silent *has been compared to* Huckleberry Finn*. He's won the Nebula Award, the World Fantasy Award, and two Ditmar Awards, among others.*

He's also been a buddy of mine for twenty-five years, which had absolutely nothing to do with the story you're about to read.

For Redshift *he presents an absolute treat: an alternate history concerning Marilyn Monroe and James Dean.*

Ting-a-Ling

Jack Dann

✶

It was the same dream, the same ratcheting, shaking, steaming, choo-chooing dream of being back on the ghost train with his mother. She is imprisoned in a lead casket in the baggage car, and he *knows* that she is alive and suffocating. But he can't reach her, even as he runs from one car of the Silver Challenger Express to another. The cars are huge and hollow and endless, and he is exhausted; James Dean, forever the nine-year-old orphan, on his way again—and again and again—to bury his mother in Marion, Indiana.

Mercifully, the whistle of the train rings—a telephone jolting him awake.

"Hello, Jimmy?" The voice hesitant, whispery, far away.

"Marilyn? . . ."

"Well, who do you think it is, Pier Angeli?"

"You're a nasty bitch."

"And you're still in love with her, you poor dumb fuck, aren't you."

Fully awake now, he laughed mordantly. "Yeah, I guess I am."

"Jimmy? . . ."

"Yeah?"

"I'm sorry. I love you."

"I love you, too. Are you in Connecticut with the Schwartzes or whatever the fuck their name is?" Jimmy felt around for cigarettes and matches . . . without success. He slept on a mattress on the floor of the second-floor alcove. Shadows seemed to float around him in the darkness like clouds.

Marilyn giggled, as if swallowing laughter, and said, "Anti-Semite.

You mean the Greens, and I'm not staying with them anymore, except to visit and do business. I'm living in New York now—like you told me to, remember? I'm at the Waldorf Towers. Pretty flashy, huh? But that's not where I am this very minute."

"Marilyn . . ."

"I'm right here in L.A., and I've got news, and I want to see you." She sounded out of breath, but that was just another one of her signatures.

"I got a race in the morning," Jimmy said, feeling hampered by the length of the phone cord and the darkness as he felt through the litter around his mattress. "It's in Salinas, near Monterey. You want to come and watch?"

"Maybe I do . . . maybe I don't."

"Shit, Marilyn. What time is it? I've got to get up at seven o'clock in the morning. And I've got to be awake enough so as not to crash into a goddamn wall. And—"

The phone was suddenly dead.

Marilyn Monroe was gone.

Jimmy should have known better. But it was—he got up and flicked on the light switch—two o'clock in the morning. Not late for Jimmy when he wasn't racing; he'd often hang out with the ghoul Maila Nurmi and the ever-present Jack Simpson at Googie's or Schwab's on Sunset, which were the only places in L.A. open after midnight, or he'd drive . . . or talk through the night to Marilyn, who would call whenever she felt the need.

The lights hurt Jimmy's eyes, and although he hadn't been drinking or doing any drugs, he felt hung over; and as he looked around his rented house, forgetting for the instant that he needed a cigarette, he remembered his dream . . . running through the clattering passenger cars of the Silver Challenger. "Momma," he whispered, then jerked his head to the side, as if embarrassed.

But eventually the light burned away the dream. He found the cigarettes in his bed, the pack of Chesterfields crumpled, the matches tucked inside the cellophane wrapper; and he sat on the edge of the alcove, his legs dangling, and smoked in the bright yellowish light. Below him was a large living room with its huge seven-foot-tall stone fireplace. He had bought a white bearskin rug for the hearth, and on the wall was an eagle, talons extended, wings outstretched, a bronzed predator caught in midflight. It belonged to Jimmy's landlord Nicco Romanos. He could almost touch his pride-and-joy James B. Lansing loudspeakers that just about reached the ceiling. Below . . . below him was the mess of his life: his bongos, scattered records and album covers, dirty dishes, dirty clothes, cameras and camera equipment, crumpled paper and old newspapers and books . . . a library on the floor. The walls were covered with bullfighting posters and a few of his own paintings, but pride of place was given to a bloodstained bullfighting cape that was cut into spokelike shadows by the bright wheel lamp that hung between the beams of the ceiling. Jimmy gazed at the cape and remembered when the Brooklyn-born matador Sidney Franklin had given it to him as a souvenir. That was in Tijuana. Rogers Brackett had introduced Jimmy to the matador, who was a friend of Ernest Hemingway. Brackett introduced him to everyone. All he ever wanted in return was Jimmy's cock.

But Brackett knew *everyone*.

Jimmy could still feel the dark presence of his recurrent nightmare. It blew through him like hot, fetid air, the hurricane of a fucked-up past . . . of memory. He had named it, thus making it tangible, absolutely real.

Black Mariah. Black Mariah. Black Mariah . . .

Suddenly frightened, feeling small and vulnerable as his thoughts swam like neon fish in deep, dark water, he huddled close to himself on the landing. He wanted to cry.

Momma . . .

He flicked his half-finished cigarette in a high arc across the room and wondered if it would start a fire. If it did, he would sit right where he was like a fucking Buddha and die without moving a muscle.

If it didn't . . . he would race tomorrow.

The phone rang again. He picked up the receiver.

"Hi," Marilyn said. "You ready to go out with me?"

Jimmy laughed. "Why'd you hang up on me?"

"Because you were treating me bad. I've changed. The new me doesn't take shit from *anybody*, not even from the person I love more than—"

"More than who?"

"Anybody."

"More than Arthur Miller?" he teased.

She laughed. "Maybe a little, but you'd better see me now because who knows what could happen later."

"You're married, remember?" Jimmy said.

"But not for long, honey." There was a long pause, and then Marilyn said, "No, not for long." The sadness was palpable in her voice. "Well, you want me to hang up again or what? . . ."

"No."

"You going to see me then? . . . Please, Jimmy, I don't want to be alone right now. I'll come over to you." Then, changing mood, "And who knows, we might both get lucky. Anyway, I'll show you my new car. It's a gift. And it's fabjous."

"From who?"

"I got it for doing a show with Art Linkletter. It's a Caddy DeVille convertible, and it's pink as your cute little ass. I love it." She giggled and blew into the phone. "I'll give you a ride."

"You sure you didn't get it for riding that pink elephant in Madison Square Garden? That was a stunt-and-a-half."

"It was for a good cause. Now make up your mind, I'm hanging up . . . one . . . two . . ."

"Okay," Jimmy said. "I'm awake. But how the hell am I supposed to drive to Salinas tomorrow?"

"I'll bring you some pills."

"I can't drive stoned out. You want to kill me?"

"No, Jimmy."

He knew she was laughing at him.

"I'd show you the new Porsche, but it's at my mechanic's. I can pick you up with my station wagon. Where are you?"

"No, I want to drive," she said. "I'll be at your place in fifteen minutes. I've got something to tell you that you won't believe. You're still on Sunset Plaza, right?"

"No, Marilyn, I moved, remember? I'm in Sherman Oaks. 14611 Sutton Street. It's a log cabin, you have to—"

"I'll find it. Bye."

"I can't stay out long."

But Jimmy was speaking to dead air.

Although he couldn't be sure when—or if—Marilyn would arrive, Jimmy waited outside near the road for her. He wore jeans, a white T-shirt, scuffed black penny loafers, and the bright red jacket that Nick Ray had bought for him to wear in *Rebel without a Cause* after Jack Warner ordered the film to be re-shot in color. Eartha Kitt had told him to wear the jacket, that it would bring him luck. Something about its color.

Jimmy grinned as he thought about Eartha. He had once tried to seduce her, but she only laughed at him and curled up on his couch. "You shouldn't screw your friends . . . or your cat," she said. Jimmy could still hear the purr in her voice.

It was a cool night, with the promise that tomorrow would be a perfect day to drive his new flat-four 547 Porsche Spyder. He daydreamed about dancing with Eartha in Sylvia Forte's dance class in New York. He daydreamed about driving, dancing, driving; but there was nothing, nothing better than speed, the adrenaline surge that would open deep inside his chest, the pressure in his eyes as the liquid silver curve of the hood swallowed the road in one long drawn gulp, and the beautiful, perfect, third-eye sense that he was about to rise, to lift right off the pavement, to go so fast that the car would shudder like a plane as it became airborne; and he'd rip a hole right through the sky.

Marilyn drove into the gravel driveway. The top of the pink Cadillac was down, although she had neglected to snap on the decorative leather boot. She smiled at him, but she looked tentative, as if frightened that he wouldn't recognize her, or, worse yet that he *would* recognize her and turn away. She didn't look like Marilyn Monroe. That was the guise that she turned on and off like a lightbulb. Jimmy understood all about that. They'd even discussed it. They were both lightbulbs. Brother and sister lightbulbs. They were monsters that could turn into . . . themselves, that which was perfect and beautiful and completely cool-hep-can-do-no-wrong; and when they turned themselves on to each other, it was like . . . driving fast, except it was in the eyes *and* the crotch. She wore tan slacks, a man's sweater that was several sizes too large for her, and a black kerchief tied around her head. If it were daytime, she'd be wearing sunglasses—all part of the uniform of a private person. She wouldn't be wearing makeup either.

"Well, it's certainly . . . pink," Jimmy said as he moved toward the driver's side door. "You mind if I drive?"

"Yes, I do. I'm driving." Marilyn leaned toward him for a kiss.

"But I have something to show you," Jimmy said. "Give you a kick like nothing else."

"You drive like a maniac, Jimmy. You scare me."

"You drive any differently?"

"I may be as crazy as you, but this is *my* car. If anyone's going to mess it up, it's going to be me. Now get in."

Jimmy put on his pout face, jumped into the backseat—which was littered with slacks, dresses, girdles, shoes, empty bottles of soda pop, receipts, candy wrappers, coat hangers, magazines, blouses, and books—and then crawled into the passenger seat beside Marilyn. She laughed and hugged him.

"What's all that garbage in the backseat? You're going to lose half of it in the wind."

"I don't care," she said, clinging to him. "You're right, it's all garbage." She smelled strongly of perfume. *Joy*, her favorite.

"You smell like a French whore."

Marilyn didn't reply; she just burrowed against him like a frightened child.

"You want to come inside and see my house?" Jimmy asked.

"No, I want to drive," and with that she shifted the car into reverse and stomped on the accelerator. Tires spun in the gravel as the Caddy fishtailed backwards into the street. Jimmy was thrown against the dashboard. Marilyn changed gears and laid rubber as she accelerated down the hill.

"You're high as a goddamn kite," Jimmy said. "You didn't even look to see if anything was coming, and you almost put my head through the windshield."

Marilyn giggled as she crossed over the double yellow line. "I love these wind-y roads, except it's so easy to get lost."

"You're always getting lost."

"I found your house quick enough, didn't I?" She raced around and down the mountain until she reached Mulholland Drive; then she turned onto the wide, straight road and accelerated until the car began to shake. The pages of magazines in the backseat snapped in the wind, but miraculously the soiled dresses and blouses and slacks did not become airborne; it was as if they had all been carefully weighted down with heavier objects.

"Need to get your front-end fixed," Jimmy said.

Marilyn laughed and slowed down to eighty. There were few cars on the drive. She untied her kerchief, and her blond hair, stiff from too many bleachings, was swept back by the wind.

"So what's your news?" Jimmy asked. "I heard about your negotiations with Fox. Word is that you're going to get a hundred grand a picture."

"And I'm going to have director approval, too. John Huston, Billy Wilder, and Joshua Logan—they're already on the list. Fox isn't going to stick it to me again, I'll tell you that."

"We should be starting a company to make films. I'm going to be the best director you ever saw. Nick Ray thinks so, and he's the best director I know."

"You think the sun sets in his ass," Marilyn said.

"Well, he hasn't done bad for me. *Rebel without a Cause* is going to be a *big* hit."

"I hope so. I pray it'll be a smash."

"I should have insisted on doing my next picture with Nick," Jimmy said. "Man, I *hate* George Stevens. That bastard's got a God complex or something. He wouldn't even let me go to a race while I was working on his overblown abortion of a motion picture, and he wouldn't let me act either. All the good bits of *Giant* are on the floor. What an asshole. He couldn't wipe Nick's ass."

"So we're back to Nick's ass, huh?"

"Tell me if it's true about the money?"

She raised her head, exaggeratedly sniffing the air, and said, "My partner, Mr. Milton Green, thank you, is negotiating everything. We'll see what happens."

"It *is* true . . . you bitch." Jimmy laughed and moved closer to her; she put her arm around him.

"My *corporation* will be paid, but I might take just a teeny bit for myself."

They laughed hysterically.

"And your corporation should buy you all the pink Cadillacs you can drive."

"I'll have a different one every time I go out."

"Are you going out much?"

"Constantly, and I have to drive back and forth from New York to the Greens in Connecticut. Do you think I would condescend to drive the same car every time I go to Connecticut? That would be like wearing the same dress to every party. No, sir-ree, I'll buy myself a *fleet* of new Cadillacs."

Jimmy ran his finger over her sweater and played with her breasts. Marilyn didn't seem to notice, although her nipples became erect.

"I love these," Jimmy said.

"You could fool me. Your squeezing them like you're trying to make mud pies." Jimmy stopped touching her and stared ahead. His long brown hair, which was greasy and needed a wash, was tousled, and his eyes narrowed as they always did when he was concentrating. He pushed his thick-lensed glasses against the bridge of his nose; it was a nervous habit.

"Go ahead, you can make mud pies," Marilyn said.

"I never did that to Pier."

"You never squeezed her tits?"

"She didn't like it, maybe because they're tiny."

"So what did you do?"

"We just fucked."

"That's it?"

"Cuddled."

"You want to cuddle me?" Marilyn asked.

"Yeah, maybe, I don't know."

"I'll stop right here, we can do it right here. If we got caught, tell me *that* wouldn't make good copy."

"I want to talk for a little while," Jimmy said, sounding childlike. "And I want to drive."

"What do I get if I let you drive?"

"A cuddle and a ting-a-ling."

"A what?"

"You got to let me drive to find out."

"Okay . . . you drive." With that Marilyn slid onto Jimmy's lap and let go of the steering wheel. Jimmy grabbed it and pulled himself into the driver's seat.

"Jesus H. Christ!"

Marilyn giggled and let her hand rest on his crotch as he drove. She scolded him when he didn't get an erection.

"I can't do two things at once," he said.

"What if I do this?" and she slid across the leather seat so she could put her head on his lap. She bit him gently through the stiff denim of his jeans until he became hard. "Well, *that* seems to work," she said. She unzipped his fly, carefully worked his penis out of his shorts, and teased him with her tongue.

"You really do have a death wish, don't you," Jimmy said.

"If you say so. Do you want me to stop?"

"You probably should."

"Just think of it as a cuddle. My treat. I'm as good as any of those goddamn directors or producers you always used to complain about, aren't I?"

Jimmy laughed at that.

"Well? . . ." Marilyn asked.

"Yes," Jimmy said.

"And do you want me to stop now?"

"No." He gave in to warm wet bliss.

"Well, then you'd better say *please* or I'll stop."

"You're a bitch, Marilyn, do you know that?"

"Say *please*. I'm going to count to three. One . . . two . . ."

"Okay, *please*."

"Nope, too late," she said. She sat up and smiled at him.

"Too late is it?" Jimmy said, stepping hard on the accelerator. "I guess it's time to teach you a lesson."

Marilyn giggled. "Better put that thing back in your pants first."

Jimmy grinned at her, adjusted himself, zipped up his fly, and said, "This ain't finished yet."

"Well, I would hope not. I expect to get some satisfaction for my persistence, and just remember you said *please*."

Jimmy turned off the headlights. "It's going to be *you* saying *please* very soon now."

"Turn the lights on, Jimmy, what are you trying to prove?"

"See those taillights up ahead? Must be a big Buick or maybe a Caddy like this one. Well, this is going to be like one Caddy kissing another. We'll just give his bumper a little kiss, a sweet little kiss, maybe something like your kissing my dick."

"What are you talking about?" Marilyn asked. "You really are as crazy as everybody says." But rather than fear, there was an edge of excitement in her voice. "Now turn the lights back on and let up on the gas. I'm telling you right now, if you mess up this car, I'll take a tire iron to that new porch of yours."

Jimmy laughed. "It's a Porsche, and you'd have to find it first." After a beat, he said, "Okay, now let's see what this pig can do." He put the Caddy into overdrive, and the red taillights ahead seemed to be rushing toward them. "The dumb bastard doesn't even know we're driving right up his ass."

"Goddammit, Jimmy, slow down," Marilyn shouted, reaching for the steering wheel.

Jimmy knocked her hand away; his knuckles were white on the steering wheel. The speedometer read ninety. "You can scream, but don't touch."

Marilyn rolled up her window, as if that would protect her.

"No, roll it down," Jimmy said. "You got to be right there to hear it," The wind roared in his ears, a wonderful whistling whine, and Marilyn screamed as he drove Marilyn's Cadillac into the ghostly white Lincoln Continental ahead. But it was indeed just a kiss, as bumper clanged against bumper—one bell-like note and a glimpse of a terrified woman wearing a chic red hat—and then Jimmy was pulling ahead of the Lincoln as the horn of an oncoming car blared and headlights rushed toward them. Jimmy veered back into the right-hand lane just in time. Marilyn screamed.

"Did you hear it?" Jimmy asked "Ting-a-fucking-ling."

"Stop the car," Marilyn said.

"It didn't do no damage. It was just a kiss, sweet as a bell."

"Pull the car over right now, and put the lights on before somebody back-ends us or something."

"There's nobody else on the road."

"Jimmy!"

"Nobody else in the world." But he pulled over to the curb and turned off the engine. "Earth Angel" played softly on the radio, cicadas roared in the bushes, and the distant yet pervasive thrum of the road and city was felt rather than heard. The sky was black and smeary gray; here and there a star was visible through the clouds or smog.

"Did you hear the ting-a-ling?" Jimmy said. His voice was low, childlike.

"Yes."

"I told you it would be a kick. You want to check the bumper?"

"No." Then after a beat she said, "I'm still shaking."

"Yeah, so am I."

"You could have killed us."

"Yeah, that's the idea, isn't it?"

"You could have killed that poor woman in the other car. She doesn't deserve that."

"How do you know what she deserves? Or who she might have just screwed over? What happens happens. You can't change it."

"So you couldn't help but drive into her car, right?"

"Yeah, in a way, I guess," Jimmy said. "Just like you couldn't help calling me up in the middle of the night and coming over to my house."

"Jimmy, hold me. . . ."

Which he did, and they made love awkwardly and passionately and quickly on the front seat while the radio played "Maybellene" and "Ain't That a Shame." Marilyn began to cry when they were finished.

"That bad, huh?" Jimmy asked.

Marilyn smiled. "Yeah, Jimmy, you were terrible."

After a pause, Jimmy asked, "What's the matter then?"

"I don't know . . . oh, fuck it, yes, I do. It's Joe. He drives a Cadillac . . . a blue one."

"So? . . ."

"So . . . being here, doing this . . . made me think about him a little."

"Did you see him since you've been here?" Jimmy knew Marilyn's husband Joe DiMaggio and didn't like him. The most famous baseball player that ever lived was so overcome with jealousy that he followed Marilyn around like a store detective; and Jimmy thought that he looked like a skinny, upchuck store detective with his big, narrow nose, greasy hair, and ill-fitting though expensive suits.

"No, I was going to call him, but I called you instead."

"He's a prick, Marilyn. How many times has he kicked the shit out of you?"

"It wasn't so bad, Jimmy. Maybe a slap, that'd be it. Not what you think. He'd just get crazy, and then he'd be beside himself with guilt, and he'd be crying and begging me to forgive him, and buying me everygoddamthing he could think of. I could've opened up a flower shop every time we had a fight."

"That's not what you used to tell me."

"Well, I was upset. I needed somebody to talk to . . . someone I could talk to."

"So you were bullshitting me all the while, right?"

She sighed and twisted herself away from him. "No, Jimmy, I wasn't bullshitting you. You just don't understand."

"What don't I understand?"

"That Joe loves me."

"I love you."

She giggled, combed her fingers through her hair, and turned back toward Jimmy. "You love to make mud pies."

"No, I mean it."

"I know you do, Jimmy. But you know what I mean; it's different with Joe. He loves me before himself. You and me . . . I don't know. No matter what we do, it's different somehow. Joe loves me more than his career."

"That's why he wants you to give up *your* career."

"I'm divorcing him, isn't that enough? But I just can't be cruel to him. I can't do that. And no matter what, I'll always love him."

"Aren't you worried he'll get shitfaced again with his pal Frank Sinatra and break into your apartment like they tried to do last year? Christ, that was something. Did he go to court for that yet?"

"I don't know," Marilyn said.

"If you love Joe so much, what are you doing with Arthur Miller? Christ, he looks old enough to be your father."

"He's not old; he's only forty."

"I expect to be dead by then."

"You probably will be."

"So why are you getting rid of Joe, who loves you so much, and chasing this other guy?" Jimmy asked.

"What makes you think I'm chasing him?"

"You didn't tell me he loves you."

"Well, he does. He's crazy about me, and if he had his way, he'd have left his wife and kids for me, but I wouldn't let him do that. If you can believe it, I tried to talk him out of divorcing her. I don't want that on my conscience. But he says he can't live without me, and I love him."

"I can't believe that. But then I never understood your thing with Joe, either. Different strokes . . ."

"Joe and me tore each other apart. I couldn't be what he needs. But everything is different with Arthur. He's smart in a different way. He teaches me things I didn't even know I needed to know, and he's behind my career a hundred percent. With Joe, well, you know."

"Joe must know, the gossip's everywhere."

"I was going to tell him, so he wouldn't read it in the rags, but I just couldn't. I'm such a coward."

"You want to go back to my place?" Jimmy asked.

"Yes, but *I'll* drive." They switched places, and Marilyn turned the car around and sped back toward Beverly Glen.

"So what's your news that you wanted to tell me?"

Marilyn laughed. "You won't believe it, *I* can't believe it. It would certainly solve all my problems."

"Tell me."

"I was approached by a guy who publishes *Look* magazine. I met him last weekend at the Greens in Connecticut. He told me that he was approached by some big shot who works for Aristotle Onassis, who practically owns Greece. You know about him?

"Nope."

"And he owns half of Monte Carlo."

"How can you own half a goddamn country?"

"I don't know. It could all be bullshit, but that's what I heard. Anyway, this Gardner Cowles, the publisher, who's actually a sweet guy, he asks me if I'd be interested in marrying Prince Rainier, he's the prince of Monte Carlo. I was so shocked I laughed at him, but he was dead serious. He asked me if I thought the prince would want to marry me, and I told him to give me two days alone with the prince, and he'll want to marry me. I'd be a princess, all my troubles would be over."

"So what'd you say?" Jimmy asked.

"I told him to set it up. At least I'll get a trip to Monte Carlo and meet a prince."

"You're bullshitting again, aren't you, you bitch."

"No, Jimmy. I swear on everything holy, it's true."

"Why the hell would this prince want to marry you?"

"Thanks a lot."

"You know what I mean."

Marilyn turned onto Beverly Glen. It would be dawn soon, and she looked pale and worn and fragile in the dim, ambient streetlight. Her hair was frizzed by the wind. "It all has something to do with problems in Monte Carlo. The country is having a hard time, and Onassis figured that if the prince married someone glamorous, it would make the country more glamorous and bring in more money. Or something like that."

"So you think it's for real," Jimmy said.

"Yeah, I do."

Jimmy waited for her to laugh or joke about it, but she stared ahead and drove slowly up the winding road, as if she wanted the ride to last as long as possible.

"Did you have a fight with Miller, is that what this is all about?"

"No, it's about my life and not getting anything right."

"What would make it right?"

Marilyn laughed and said, "If I knew that I wouldn't be here. If the prince makes the effort, maybe he'll get me. Or maybe it will be Arthur. Or some secret somebody else you don't even know about."

"Why not me?"

"Because I'll always have you, Jimmy, just like you'll always have me."

Her timing was perfect. She drove into his driveway and kissed him good night.

"I thought you were coming in," Jimmy said.

"No, you go to your race."

"Where are you staying, I'll call you when I get back."

She gave him her generous lightbulb Marilyn smile and backed the car out of the driveway. "Maybe I'll call you from Monte Carlo."

Apparently, Catherine Wells decided that she wanted to be a writer when she was ten years old, and that was that. A novelist and librarian, she has only recently begun writing short fiction. Her novels include Beyond the Gates *and* Mother Grimm, *which was a finalist for the 1997 Philip K. Dick Award.*

If " 'Bassador" is any indication, she should definitely devote more of her time to the short stuff.

'Bassador

CATHERINE WELLS

*

We could hear the rumble of their hovercycles echoing through the concrete canyons long before they arrived. My mother seized my hand, terror in her eyes, and dragged me out of the street. "Trabina! Hssht! Come!" I resisted, dragging my feet, craning my neck toward the throaty sound of power.

A morbid thrill shot through me, a curiosity/dread, as the time I had seen the Pigatzo beat up a ganga outside my window. Only Powers rode hovercycles, sweeping down through the projects from the north, flaunting their wealth and their strength with their beautiful machines. I had seen three different Powers in my project: the Tunnel Runners, the Pigatzo, the Fetts. But rumors had been circulating all week that a new Power was coming, one that brought more trouble than all the others combined. I was seven years old; I wanted to see it.

My mother yanked at my arm, jerked it nearly from its socket, and hauled me up the steps of our building so that I fell and scraped my bare knees on the eroded cement. "Trabina! Come!" she snapped. "They almost here!" She caught me round the waist with one arm and ran for the door.

Suddenly the street was filled with the thunder of half a dozen hovercycles retroing to a stop in front of the building. My mother turned like a cornered animal, back braced against the door. From her protecting arms I saw them dismount, six helmeted figures in worn leather that winked with metal studs.

"Bookali," my mother whispered.

Four of them stood guard over the hovercycles, faced in four directions, rifles carried in the crooks of their arms. Another threw a disinterested glance toward my mother and me, then turned and nodded toward the empty building across the street. He and the sixth Bookali strode toward it, cleated boots ringing on the paving.

They tested the door, found it code locked. One produced a small box, long and flat, which he attached to the key panel. After a moment he removed it, touched the door handle, and the door sprang open. Powers, indeed, who could pick a code lock without triggering the building's defenses. Three ganga had tried to force that door once; two had died for their foolishness.

My mother keyed our own building now, quietly, carefully, not to attract any attention. The door gave a soft buzz and suddenly four rifles were trained on us. We froze, afraid even to breathe; then slowly, cautiously, Mother pushed the door open a crack and we melted inside. Even as the door shut off my view, the four rifles had not moved.

As soon as it was sealed, I wriggled from my mother's arms and ran for the landing, braced my arms on the windowsill and drew myself up to look out at the scene below. The four guards again faced four directions; their two comrades had gone inside. The hovercycles rested on their gravfoils, gleaming in the occasional ray of light that filtered through clouds and past concrete towers to play across the canyon floor. The bikes were black and silver, like their riders, and I thought they were the most beautiful things I had ever seen.

"Trabina!" my mother hissed. "Na! Come away!" But I would not, though I heard her clatter up behind me and knew my backside would pay the price for my disobedience. But I watched as the two Bookali came back out and sealed the building behind them. They were mounting their hovercycles as my mother seized me around my waist and hauled me away; but she, too, paused to look out as the six bikes coughed to life, hovering just off the ground. Then, almost as one, they engaged thrust and roared down the street, leaving only their echoes behind.

"Curse be," my mother muttered after them. "Stay away from my project." But it was not to be.

No one wanted the Bookali in their neighborhood, for it inevitably drew the attention of the other Powers. The Pigatzo were said to burn Bookali headquarters whenever they found them, and the Fetts to do worse. Anyone who associated with the Bookali could expect to come under scrutiny as well, and dire tales were told of innocent children who had been lured inside a Bookali headquarters somewhere.

My friend Shenka and I watched as the Bookali returned to our project with truckloads of boxes. Shenka was older than I by at least a year, and dark to my light. She was taller, as well, and stood on her tiptoes on the fifth-floor landing to see out the window and down to the street below. I, of course, braced my spindly arms on the sill to attain such height, strong from much practice of this particular exercise.

I looked at the featureless building below, its dull gray face blending with all the others in this concrete canyon. Awnings were long gone, painted signs obliterated, everything covered with the universal grime of the projects. I had seen that building every day of my life and thought nothing of it; now suddenly it was mysterious.

My mother passed by on her way to the laundry. "Outlaws," she muttered, pausing to peer over my shoulder. "Now be trouble." She yanked my twisting braid for no reason and continued on her way.

Outlaws. It was a strange condemnation. There was not much of law in the projects; Powers kept the law where Powers lived, and only came to the projects to visit retribution on those who dared to venture outside them. So what was this new Power doing here?

"What *are* Bookali?" I asked my friend as the dark-clad figures loaded the heavy boxes onto sleds. Sweat gleamed on their foreheads, and occasionally one would strip out of his leather jacket. Some of the Bookali were women, but most were men, and clearly accustomed to this hard labor.

"Trouble," Shenka replied, but I thought it was her mother's opinion. Shenka herself had little imagination.

"But Pigatzo make war on ganga, and Fetts chase Tunnel Runners—what Bookali do?" I persisted in the clipped speech of the projects.

"Keep secrets," Shenka replied with authority. "That what my uncle say."

The answer seemed silly to me. I did not know Shenka's uncle, and I was not prone to trust any man. When a boy turned ten, he went to the ganga; he was not given an option. Then he died, or became a Tunnel Runner, or simply disappeared. Few men stayed in the projects, and those who did tended to sleep by day and forage by night, so I did not see much of them. I had no reason for trust.

Below us, the power sleds loaded with boxes glided smoothly over the pocked paving and into the building across the street. Other things were carried in as well: gridwork, planking, unidentifiable jumbles of metal and plastic collapsed together. There was some furniture, all of it spartan; but mostly there were the boxes.

And through it all the four guards stayed at their posts, alert for any movement, any sign of trouble. They got none from us; the people of the project—even the ganga—stayed away. But I could not help but notice that the Bookali made no trouble, either: they searched no buildings, yelled no abuse to people inside, fired no weapons through open windows.

"Why Pigatzo hate them?" I wondered aloud, for they did none of the things the ganga did, that I could see.

"'Cause they tell secrets to people," Shenka replied. "My uncle say. Say they tell people things they shouldn't know, and it make them sick."

"But why Pigatzo hate them for that?" I asked, puzzled. "Pigatzo na care if people sick; then people na make trouble for Pigatzo."

Shenka shrugged. "Maybe they tell secrets about Pigatzo," she suggested. "Or maybe—" She strained with the effort of speculation. "Maybe the secrets make people crazy, as well as sick. Pigatzo na like people be crazy."

That was true. Tunnel Runners were all crazy, and Pigatzo would shoot them on sight. I wondered if the Bookali told secrets that turned people into Tunnel Runners. The thought made me shudder.

"Trabina, come from window," my mother admonished, on her way back upstairs again. Reluctantly we both turned away.

"Let's go my parmen," Shenka suggested. "Rikka's home."

Rikka was Shenka's older sister who had run with the ganga for a while. But when her ganga boyfriend went to the Tunnel Runners, Rikka had had enough; she came back home. Still, Rikka had seen and done things the rest of us could hardly imagine, so we liked to listen to her talk, even if she had the sharp edge of a ganga.

"Bookali, pah!" Rikka spat when we asked her about them. "Not so tough. See those big rifle they carry? Pff! Stun rifle only. Ganga is better armed, not to say Pigatzo. They na so tough, these Bookali."

"Then you go down there," Shenka challenged, unwilling to have this new terror diminished.

"Me? Na, I don't go. Who needs? Like a smashed head, I need Bookali. What they got?"

It was a question that still bothered me. "What *do* they got, Rikka?" I asked.

"Liiiieees," Rikka snarled, drawing the word out with her best ganga sneer. "They tell you they got something, something good, but they got nothing. Nothing but lies."

"They got secrets," Shenka piped up, and I looked for Rikka's reaction.

"Better they keep they secrets," Rikka retorted, but she did not deny the idea. "They secrets na good to me. Fill my belly? Na. Make me rich, ride a hovercycle like them? Na. Bring Pigatzo down on us? Yes, that they do. Let them keep they secrets, I had plenty Pigatzo beatings already my life."

"She's scared," I whispered, sure there was more to the Bookali than secrets.

But Shenka took this as an attack on Rikka and came suddenly to her sister's defense. "Rikka na scared!" she objected. "*You* scared, Trabina."

"You call me scared?" Rikka demanded, turning on me suddenly with a large wooden spoon in her hand. "You call me scared, little girl?" She was an imposing sight, taller than I would ever be, braids jutting out in all directions, and with a jagged scar under one eye.

"*You* scared," Shenka repeated, trying in time-honored fashion to refute the charge by reversing it.

"Am na!" I objected, being very much so.

"When you run with ganga, you na scared nothing," Rikka boasted, advancing on me with the wooden spoon. "I na scared some Bookali with stun gun. Pah! *You* little rat-rot *scared*."

"Am na!" I said again, edging my way toward the door.

"Are so!" Shenka taunted, trailing behind her sister.

"Na!" I insisted, wondering if I could bolt and run before that spoon whacked across my skull.

"So, so, so!"

"Na, na, na!"

Suddenly Rikka stopped and the sneer twisted back onto her lips. "You na scared, little rat-rot? Show us."

My heart stopped.

"Yeah, show us," Shenka echoed.

Rikka's sneer stretched her painted lips across her teeth and left traces of color there. "You go down to Bookali, little rat-rot, if you na scared."

"Yeah, *you* go down," Shenka chimed; then, "I *dare* you."

I hated Shenka for that. I could have run from Rikka, could have run back to my mother and avoided that spoon and that sneer, but not from Shenka. If I ran from Shenka, I might just as well keep running. There is no worse sin in the projects than to be scared in front of your friend. You can refuse a dare from your enemies, but you can never refuse one from your friend.

"All right," I blustered, fear twisting my insides. "All right. I *show* you then. I show you. I dare." Late, far too late, I turned and ran from the room.

Down the stairs I raced, toward my own destruction, for so I knew it was. Powers—Powers would beat or kill at the slightest provocation. Only at the front door did I stop, stop to catch my breath, stop to let reason strive with madness. Which did I fear more, the Bookali, or my friend's disdain?

There was no question; it has ever been so. I opened the door and slid out.

The near guard turned at the sound and zeroed her rifle in on my heart. I waited, eyes clenched shut, for the sound of the shot that would end my life; but I heard only a soft, "Huh," and the scrape of a cleated boot. I opened one eye to see the guard standing in her place, feet wide apart, rifle resting once more in the crook of her arm. "Jess," she called to one of her fellows. "We have a curious one."

The rhythm of her speech was of a kind I had never heard before. Another guard turned and looked me up and down, and a smile twisted up one half of his face. He was dark, like Shenka, and thick-limbed. "Curiouser and curiouser," he said obliquely.

"What you think, child?" the first one said to me, shifting to the lilt of the projects. Her skin was as pale as any I had ever seen, and in the shadow of her helmet shrewd eyes glittered.

My heart pounded, wondering if they were just toying with me the way Tunnel Runners would toy with children before they carried them off. At any rate, I knew I had to answer, for not to answer was to admit weakness, and to admit weakness in the projects was death. "Heavy boxes," was all I could think to say.

The woman laughed. "Heavy, yes. Reason for that. You think?"

"If you say," I replied cautiously. Two Bookali loading a sled had paused just briefly to glance in our direction. Their shirts were soaked with sweat and they were smiling, too, as though it were some great joke that the boxes were heavy. "What in them box?" I asked finally.

The woman looked furtively to left and right, then took half a step toward me. "Secrets," she said, and nodded knowingly.

Secrets, after all! Shenka's uncle was right. I remembered then that he also said these secrets made people sick. But the Bookali didn't look sick; they looked very fit and healthy, indeed, with biceps bulging as they stacked the heavy boxes one atop another. What kind of secrets could be held in boxes, anyway? And why should they be heavy?

Seeing that they were not going to blast me for being in the street, I edged down the steps, my back ever to the rail. I peered at the boxes from this distance, hoping for one that was torn or open so I could see what was inside. But they were well sealed, with numbers on the outside. I knew numbers because code locks had numbers, and one had to remember them to get back into the safety of a building.

"Those secrets coded?" I asked in a flash of insight.

The Bookali guard nodded wisely. "All coded. You know codes?"

"Just my codes," I answered, with visions of those boxes exploding if someone tried to use the wrong code to open them.

"You know numbers?" she asked.

"I know *my* numbers," I repeated.

"You know numbers, you can learn these codes," the guard said confidentially.

I stopped breathing. Was the Bookali offering me a chance to learn the codes for their secrets? I started to edge back up the steps. Maybe they were like the Tunnel Runners, who grabbed children that got too close and dragged them down into their lairs, there to do unspeakable things to them and make them crazy. Maybe these Bookali wanted to grab me and make me one of them.

Suddenly a shrill whistle pierced the air. "Fetts!" someone barked. In a flash the Bookali workers inside the truck slammed its gate shut. Another worker powered the half-loaded sled inside their headquarters, and the door sealed behind it. The truck roared off down the street. The guards covered this retreat, heading the while for their hovercycles, twitching nervously this way and that at any sound. When all the other Bookali had disappeared, the guards mounted their shining machines, keyed them to life, and flashed away around a corner. In less than a minute the street was deserted as if no Bookali had ever been there.

In the distance was the whine of other machines, of Fetts on hovercycles or in hovercars. My curiosity did not extend so far as to wait for their arrival, so I pelted back up the steps and into the building. Inside, eight steps passed in four bounds as I hurled myself to the landing and leaped up to brace my arms on the windowsill.

The hovercycles came first, streaking along the broken pavement, banking around corners, darting up and down streets and alleys. They found nothing, and soon were gone in their driving pursuit of a quarry too alert, too quick for capture.

Behind them came the cars, moving slowly, hovering near (but not too near) windows; stopping now and again as a uniformed Fett jumped out and tried a lock here, a lock there. Some buildings were open, their codes broken, but the Fetts didn't bother to check those. Who would stay in a building that could not be locked? For others, they slapped a small box over the key panel, waited a moment, then toed the door open cautiously.

Across the street several Bookali waited within their new headquarters. In my mind I saw them: rifles trained on the door, muscles taut, fingers sweating on triggers, afraid to breathe. But when the Fetts came to that building, they passed it by. I felt a sudden release of tension, a relief as though *I* had been inside, waiting in dread to be discovered. This puzzled me. Why should I care if the Bookali were found?

Suddenly I realized that I wanted to know what those secrets were. I wanted to go inside that building across the street and see what it was that made the Fetts and Pigatzo hate these Bookali so. Trembling at my own audacity, I crept up the rest of the steps to my apartment and crawled into my bed, hiding far beneath the covers.

The Bookali did not come back the next day, or the next. The Fetts came through again, and the Pigatzo; the Pigatzo beat up two or three ganga that were hanging around and took them away in a slow-moving cart that rumbled along the broken street on wheels. They promised to be back again soon; we believed them.

Other ganga slinked around the project, muttering about making an alliance with the Tunnel Runners, which we knew was only talk. Ganga sometimes became Tunnel Runners, like Rikka's boyfriend; and the Tunnel Runners would sometimes return a tormented victim; but no one just talked to them and came back all right. They came back dead, or crazy. So mostly the ganga melted away, waiting for things to cool down.

But the Bookali came back. Not in trucks this time, but on hovercycles, roaring up to their headquarters across the street. They hovered there a moment, engines throbbing; then the door opened and one by one, the hovercycles glided inside. They left one guard standing outside, rifle in hand.

I had to wait till my mother went out. She and Shenka's mother took bread crumbs and a big cloth bag and went to hunt pigeons on the roof. I was supposed to stay in the stairwell playing, but I glided quietly to the front door and slipped out.

The street was empty. Children had found another place to play. I crept down the steps, casting about for watching eyes. Then with a deep breath I screwed up my courage and crossed the street.

The Bookali guard saw me coming. He watched me calmly, never twitching a muscle, just letting me come closer and closer. I stopped square in front of him and looked up into his face.

How handsome he looked to me! His leathers were scarred and his helmet scratched, but his lean face was smooth and blue-shadowed from a beard that would be jet black if it grew. There was no smile on his lips, just a somber look in his clear blue eyes. We regarded each other wordlessly; then he reached back and keyed the door. With a gentle push he opened it for me. "Lee," he called softly to someone inside. "The ambassador is here."

His voice was so sober, so calm, that no dreadful visions came into my head of what might be done to me in this place. Instead I walked slowly through that open door, mouth gaping in wonder at the sights inside.

Books. I had heard of books on the vid, seen pictures of them with their strange markings, but there were none in the projects. Never had I imagined there were so many in the world. They were arranged on shelves throughout the room, in a riot of colors and sizes, row after row after row. I scarcely saw the young Bookali woman who approached me. "Hello, Ambassador," she greeted. "I thought it might be you."

I looked closely at her then and thought I detected in her pale face, her shrewd eyes, the Bookali who had spoken to me on the street days before. She had shed her leather jacket, so that a plain white T-shirt encased her upper torso, and without a helmet she sported a shock of curly yellow hair. But her voice had that same wise gravity as she spoke again. "Come to see those heavy secrets?" she asked.

"Na secret na more," I informed her haughtily. "Books."

She nodded. "Books."

But I could not keep my attention on her. Books towered to the ceiling: books on shelves, books on tables, books on carousels. There were a few chairs and some vid screens, no doubt, but all I saw were the books.

"So this Bookali headquarters," I said, trying to sound worldly and unimpressed when I was neither.

The woman Lee smiled. "So you call. We call it something else."

I approached the closest shelf, drawn as if by a magnet to those mysterious volumes. Dull blue, faded red, and a whole row with identical gold and black spines. I eyed them carefully, never thinking to reach out and touch one. Lee followed me at a respectful distance, waiting until I turned to her.

"What these book for?" I asked.

"Full of secrets," she replied.

"What secrets?"

"What book?"

Turning around, I pointed to a tall one, mustard yellow with faded green markings. "This one. What secret?"

She reached out, and with a practiced index finger extracted it from the shelf. "Ah, this one." She opened it and looked at the inside. "Stars," she replied. "This one has secrets about stars."

"Like what?"

She turned pages slowly. I kept waiting for an explosion because I hadn't seen her key the book, and she had told me before that they were coded. But page after page slid past her fingers and she remained whole. "It says," she said finally, "that the sun is really a star."

"Go na!" I scoffed. "Sun too big to be star."

"Stars are big," she replied. "Just far away. Sun is small star, just close—like building that's close look big, but far look small."

"You lie," I challenged, forgetting to whom I spoke.

"Na," she said gravely. "Book say." And she held the book so I could see the markings that were concealed inside. Her finger traced along a line of them: " 'The sun is a relatively small star.' "

"I na hear it say," I said suspiciously.

"In code," she replied. "Have to know code."

With sudden insight I realized that the markings in the books were somehow like numbers: when you grouped them together in the right sequence, they made things happen, like opening doors or firing defenses or spitting out food. But unlike number codes, these codes made words happen—words that you couldn't hear as on a vid, but heard inside your head like imagination. I jumped, startled at the revelation.

"You all right, Ambassador?" Lee asked.

"Trabina," I told her. "I na 'bassador. What that book say?" I pointed to a blue one.

Lee laid the first book aside and extracted the blue one. "This one is about gravity," she said. "That's what keeps us on the ground, instead of floating up into the air."

My brow creased and a tight little knot started in my stomach. Why *didn't* we float? It had never before occurred to me to wonder. What would it be like to float in the air? To fly up to the roof of my building, instead of climbing the stairs? "It say how bird fly?" I wanted to know.

"Not this book, I don't think," Lee said as she flipped through the pages. "But some book will. Shall I find you one?"

"You know all these book?" I demanded.

She laughed. "Not what in. Just how to find."

The little knot in my stomach had grown wriggly fingers, but I ignored it. "How you learn code all these book?"

"I was taught," she told me. "When I was your age." Then she squatted down and looked right into my eyes. "I can teach you, Ambassador."

"Trabina!" I said sharply, not liking the way my stomach was twisting. "I Trabina!"

"Ambassador Trabina," she agreed.

I thought of Crazy Rashalla and Ratface Tony, and I wondered what I was being called. "What a 'bassador?" I asked warily.

"Ambassador is first," Lee replied. "First to cross the street. First to come in. First to learn Bookali secrets."

"Learn secrets?" My stomach cramped sharply and I realized at last what I had done. "Na secrets. Na want to be sick. Na want to be crazy." I spun around and headed for the door.

"Na crazy," Lee called after me. "Only little secrets make crazy. Only half secrets. Books have 'most all secrets. Books tell you everything."

"Na, na!" I shouted, tugging at the door handle, terrified by a Power that knew everything. "Na want Bookali secrets! Na want to be crazy!"

But it was too late. Even the few secrets I had learned made me sick, left me cowering under the blankets in my room. I slept fitfully, seeing stars as big as suns, seeing a world gone black because the sun was only as big as a star. In my dreams I floated off the ground, up over the projects, leaving everything I knew behind. When I wouldn't get up for lunch, my mother fretted over me, asked what I ate, was I rat-bit. I couldn't tell her I ate a secret, and was bitten by a book.

And then the craziness came, the craziness Shenka had guessed at: I had to go back. It was the same kind of craziness that people got who tried to escape from the Tunnel Runners: they got sick, and then they had to go back, had to have what it was the Tunnel Runners gave them that made them sick in the first place.

Finally, late in the afternoon, I slipped out of my apartment and stole down the stairs.

Shenka was playing on the landing two floors down, the one from which we had watched the Bookali trucks. It seemed long ago. "Trabina, you still sick?" she asked as I approached.

"Na," I lied. The questions were eating at my insides; I could feel them. "Na sick na more." I started to go past her.

"Where you go?"

The idea and the act were one. I looked furtively to left and right, as Lee had done, then took half a step toward her. "Secret," I whispered confidentially.

Shenka's eyes got wide and her mouth dropped open. "Tell me?" she pleaded.

But I shook my head. "Na, can't. Secret." I went a few steps farther, then stopped, slyly. "But you can come."

I hated myself for saying it, hated myself for doing to Shenka what the Bookali had done to me. But that was how life was in the projects: getting your friend into the same trouble you were in, so you didn't have to be there alone. And Shenka, poor, unwitting Shenka, followed me out the door and across the street.

I heard her gasp when she saw where I was headed, but I grabbed her hand and held on tight, dragging her along. Committed now, I marched right up to the Bookali guard, bold as brass, and looked him square in the eye.

It was a different guard from before. "I 'Bassador Trabina," I told him with authority. "This my friend Shenka." He nodded courteously, and I could feel Shenka trembling at my side. Indeed, my own fear was not gone; but I was ruled now by a desire stronger than the desire to flee. I squeezed Shenka's hand and spoke again.

"We come to learn secrets."

What can I say about Larry Niven except, "Wow!" He's virtually defined much of science fiction, especially the hard kind, since his first appearances in the mid-sixties, and especially since the appearance of Ringworld *in 1970. He's got boxes of Hugos and Nebulas; it's the sheer inventiveness and technological brilliance of his stories, especially those of his future history sequence* Tales of Known Space, *that have solidified his place alongside such innovators as Heinlein and Asimov.*

He also owns a Questar telescope that I much envy.

For Redshift, *to my complete delight, he has produced a Draco Tavern story with empathic bite.*

Ssoroghod's People

LARRY NIVEN

✶

A week after the first chirpsithra liner arrived, a second ship winkled out of interstellar space. It paused to exchange courtesies with the ship now hovering alongside the moon, then pulled up next to it.

It was as big as the liner whose passengers had filled the Draco Tavern for seven nights now. We'd never had two of these in dock. The media were going nuts, of course. I worried about all these extra aliens. How was I going to fit them in?

The Draco Tavern's ceilings are high enough for bird analogues to fly. I could set some tables floating. . . .

When a handful of chirpsithra crew came in, I took the opportunity to ask, "How many more tables am I going to need?"

"One," said a ship's officer. "One occupant."

"How big?" the chirpsithra deal with entities bigger than a blue whale.

"Ssoroghod is one of us, a chirpsithra. Sss," as she touched the sparker with her fingertips. "She flies a long-term habitat and environment-shaping system. Much cargo space," she said.

Next day a ship's boat drifted down the magnetic lines to Mount Forel. Presently an inflated sphere rolled across the hard November tundra, attached itself to one of the tavern's airlocks, and deflated to let in a chirpsithra.

The newcomer made for the bar, passing six crew from the first ship. They all look alike, or pretty close, but I noticed differences. The newcomer's decorative crest (and news and entertainment set) was in a very different style. Her salmon armor differed just a bit, graying at the edges of the plates. She was old.

One spoke to her. She chose not to hear, walked regally past, and was at the bar. To me she said, "Dispenser, a sparker."

I had one ready. The chirps only have, or only show, this one sin.

She put her thumbs on the sparker and kept them there. I'd never seen a chirp do that. Her antennae were trembling. She was getting too much of a charge.

She let go. Her posture shifted, lolling. She said, "Dispenser, sparkers for my companions at table zith-mm. Tell them to remember—" She rattled off numbers in her own language.

I took sparkers to the chirps table. Props. They already had theirs. I said, "A gift from the citizen at the bar. She sent you a message." My translator also records. I ran it back to the right time and played it for them.

One said, "A location."

"That was *her* station," another said. "Whee-Nisht variants one through four. Ssoroghod had them in her charge. She sent us sparkers?"

"Memorial," said a third. "They must be extinct."

"She will not talk to us. Ssoroghod was always unsocial."

I asked, "Can you tell me what's wrong with her?"

They looked at each other. I thought they wouldn't answer, but one said, "She may choose suicide."

"How would I stop that?"

"Why would you?"

Death has happened in the Draco Tavern. Once it was a memorial service with the main guest alive until halfway through. Both times, the individuals kept it neat. I still don't like it.

One said, "She spoke to you, Rick Schumann, let her talk. She may persuade herself to live."

Humans use the bar chairs when they need to talk to the bartender. Most of the chirps' clients need a tailored environment; they go to the tables, which can be enclosed. The bar doesn't get much action from aliens. Chirps themselves can breathe Earth's air; it's the lighting that gets to them.

At the bar tonight there was only Ssoroghod, eleven feet tall though she weighed no more than I did, armored in red exoskeletal plates fading to gray at the edges, and some prosthetic gear. I told her, "The tables might have lighting more to your taste."

"I do not want the company of my kind. This bluer light, I endured it for—" She gave a number. My translator said, "—One million thirty thousand years."

Mistranslation? I said, "That's a long time."

Nothing.

"What were you doing?"

"Watching."

I guessed: "Watching the Whee-Nisht? Variants one through four?"

She said, "Variants two and three made pact, intermated, merged, crowded out the others. They were competing for too limited an environment. Variants one and four died out."

"Why were you watching them?"

For a minute I thought she wouldn't answer. Should I leave her alone, or risk driving her away? Then she said, "We found a species on the verge of sapience.

"The Whee-Nisht held a limited environment, a sandy coastline along the eastern shore of the megacontinent. Their metabolism was based on silicon dioxide. They adapted too well to the local diet, gravity, lighting, salinity of water, local symbiotes. They would never conquer any large part of their own world, let alone go among the stars. I could study them and still stay out of their way. This was the basis on which I was given permission to watch them evolve.

"I watched them grow along the Fertile Band. I was pleased when they tamed other life-forms and bred them for desired traits. Though sworn not to interfere with their development, I did divert a meteoroid impact that would have altered local coastlines. They might have gone extinct." She touched the sparker, just brushed it. "But they might have evolved flexibility. I cannot know. Mistake or no, I shifted the killer rock.

"Their numbers then grew overgreat. I wondered if I must act again, but they adapted, developed a yeast for contraception. It was their first clear act to change themselves."

"What went wrong?"

She focused on me. I had the impression that she was only now seeing me.

"Dispenser . . . Rick Schumann . . . Do you use something like sparkers? A jolt to change your viewpoint?"

I said my kind used alcohol. At her invitation I made myself an Irish coffee. I sipped meagerly. Being drunk might be bad.

She said, "Whee-Nisht have completed a cycle, a pattern. They are extinct. Does that always mean something has gone wrong?"

"It would to me," I said.

Her head nodded above me. Thumbs brushed the sparker. Then, "I saw no reason to interfere when they altered other life-forms. They made and shaped and reshaped foodstuffs, beasts of burden, guard beasts. Yeast analogues became flavoring for food, medicines, perception-altering substances. Plants were bred taller and stronger, to improve structure for their housing, then water-going vessels to explore beyond their domain. When they began using similar techniques to shape themselves, I saw startling implications.

"I acted at once," she said. "I set a terraforming project in motion on a large island just beyond their horizon. My intent was to build an environment the match for their own, without affecting theirs. Guiding weather patterns required exquisite care. When I finished, there was an island that might house the Whee-Nisht, and a sandy peninsula pointing straight at it.

"Now I—"

I asked, "Why?"

She focused on me. "They had shaped the contraceptive yeast. Now they began to breed their offspring and siblings and dependents to make patterns, to conserve wealth and power relations and to shape offspring more to their liking. Crimes were defined and criminals were subject to mental reshaping. How would they otherwise tamper with their selves?

"One mistake would drive them extinct. It has happened to other species, over and over. Dispenser, what is it your kind uses for reproductive code?"

"Deoxyribonucleic acid," I said.

"The Whee-Nisht used a different code, being silicon oxide based, but no matter. I was in a race for their lives. When they learned how to manipulate their own genetics, I was done. The ocean currents were bringing them bubble plants, telling them of a second habitat beyond the water. They built exploring vehicles, and they found it."

"Ships?"

"Great translucent tubes, grown as plants, that rolled along sand or waves. They reached my second land and named it Antihome. I watched them build a base and explore from there. I waited for them to enlarge it. My intent was that they would build a city. Nearby they could do their biological experiments, where any mistake could be confined."

She touched the sparkers again, held too long. I waited.

She asked, "Do you understand why this self-tampering kills so many species? It is so easy, so cheap. Knowledge of deoxyribonucleic acid is not needed. What you like, breeds. What you don't like is uprooted. Planned breeding may take generations, but not wealth. It is exploration that eats wealth. Your kind could tamper with yourselves for a million years for the cost of putting a city on your moon, using your own primitive techniques.

"But you, you have the option! Most species could not travel between worlds. It would kill them. The Whee-Nisht could barely cross a channel, half dead of motion sickness and running like thieves along their rolling ship, and reach an island prepared for them.

"And they threw it away.

"They explored, and came home, and stopped. They abandoned their bases, their tools, everything.

"Their laboratories shaped a cure for a genetic disorder out of a yeast variant. They did not guess that it would prevent the next generation from breeding. They did not guess that it would spread through their spiracle-analogues and infect all. I watched them grow old and die, and this time I did not interfere."

I asked, "Did you ask advice from other . . . xenoanthropologists? Others of your profession?" Amateur godlings? But a million years of practice does not leave an amateur.

"No."

Was she a jealous god? Or—"Ssoroghod, were you exiled?"

"No and yes. There was a professional quarrel, my view against the galaxy's. I could not return until I knew answers I could show. So, here I am returned, and the answer is that I was wrong. What else must you know, intrusive creature?"

As an invitation to go away, that was hardly subtle. I asked instead, "Why did you chirpsithra contact Earth?"

"I knew nothing of it. It was not my decision," Ssoroghod said.

"We'd gone to the moon, and come back, and stopped. We were fiddling with DNA, but we weren't doing it in any lunar dome. I was just old enough to see how stupid that was, and I couldn't do anything about it," I said. "You saved us. Why?"

"Merchants," said Ssoroghod. "They follow their own rules. You might have something of interest to entities with other forms of wealth to trade. So they interfere."

"I owe them," I said. I drank an unspoken toast to the Whee-Nisht.

"Dispenser, it may be you would have come to your senses. Experiments done in your own living space are lethal. You might have explored your moon under pressure of fear, built your domed city and your nearby protected laboratories, and saved yourselves. You can never know."

I knew.

"And the Whee-Nisht might have accepted my island despite the cost. I could not rob them of the chance! They chose convenience over adventure, short term over long. I gave them most of my life span, and they threw it away. I will beg a ride home and make another life for myself." She strode over to a tableful of chirpsithra crew and began to talk.

And I made myself another Irish coffee, but it was my own species I toasted.

Michael Marshall Smith lives in London with his wife and two cats; two of his novels, Spares *and* One of Us, *are under option in Hollywood, which means he's either doomed or saved. A three-time winner of the British Fantasy Award for his short stories, he recently produced a collection titled* What You Make It. *At the moment he's working as a screenwriter and completing his fourth novel,* The Straw Man.

His story for Redshift *was the fastest acceptance he's ever had, and the fastest I've ever made—when it arrived in my e-mail box, I was online, read it, and bought it immediately.*

Technology can't be all *bad, can it?*

Two Shot

MICHAEL MARSHALL SMITH

✳

The weird thing was that he didn't feel especially enthusiastic. Usually the prospect pepped him right up. He'd spend the last half hour pacing around the apartment, making sure everything was just so, building the scene. This afternoon he was a little excited, of course, but this was mingled with other emotions that made less sense. A feeling of distance, dislocation, and a kind of deep-down lethargy underneath it all—adding up to a kind of queasy anticipation that was unlike him. Probably it was at least partly due to the hangover. The memories of exactly how he'd come by it were vague, but it was sure as hell there. In force. He'd spent the morning drinking large quantities of expensive mineral water, in the hope this would mitigate it in some way. In fact it had just made him feel both hungover and full of water.

He rubbed his face hard with his hands and felt a little better. The clock panel on the wall of his living room told him there were still twenty-five minutes before she arrived. Plenty of time. He'd be fine. He knew the way she'd look when she turned up at the door. Nervous, a little flushed, feeling naughty as hell and not admitting to herself that she liked the sensation. Silly bitch.

He smiled suddenly, and all at once felt better still. The differential had kicked in. The differential between what they thought was going on and what was really happening. Between their assumption that they were caught up in a sexy, private little affair with someone who just couldn't keep their hands off them, and the way he really viewed the liaisons. The excitement he felt when they were in the apartment was nothing to what he knew when they were gone. That was the real business.

Feeling well-nigh pepped at last, he shoved himself up off the couch and quickly moved through the two stages of readying the apartment. The first didn't take a lot of doing. He lived tidily. Fan the magazines (carefully chosen to reinforce the impression that he was intelligent, sensitive, and yet sensuously physical—and why the hell not? He was, goddammit); plump the pillows on the couch (Lord, women did like fancy pillows); make sure there were too very clean wineglasses waiting ready on the counter, and that the bottle in the fridge was cool but not too cold. Anne liked a sip before they got to it, whether to relax herself, blur her conscience, or to gild the event with some half-assed romantic veneer, he neither knew nor cared.

The second half of the process took a little longer. There were eight digital camcorders in the apartment, over ten thousand dollars' worth of high-spec Japanese ingenuity. Two in the living room; four in the bedroom; two in the bathroom. He initially only put new tapes in six, almost electing not to bother with the ones in the bathroom. Never in the seven times he'd had sex with Anne had the action careered into that room. With some women it did, with others it didn't. With Anne it didn't. But sometimes it was worth watching for the expression on the women's faces as they had a pee afterwards, thinking they were in a backstage area and safe from view. Shame, smug glee, guilty and compromised tears: they all informed what had gone before. He put one tape in that room after all, in the camera which directly faced onto the lavatory. He could live without a two shot in here: her face was what really counted.

Each of the cameras was carefully hidden: in curtains, on bookshelves, in tidy piles of clothes. He'd experimented with pinhole cameras in the past, tiny devices not much bigger than the chip required to drive them and the miniature lens on top, but the quality just wasn't good enough, and they required stringing up to a recorder of some kind, which would be kind of a pain.

When he'd finished he went back into the living room. Ten minutes to go. He put a little music on, running it off a pre-chosen play list on the computer. He listened to all music this way now. Soon as he bought a CD, he used ripping software to store it on the hard disk as MP3 files. Each file was a mere couple of megabytes in size, and with the array of 100-gig racks he had built into the desk, there was room for thousands of tracks at resolutions none of his guests were likely to be able to tell from the real thing. Truth be told, he probably couldn't these days either. It had been a while since he'd even bought a CD. Couldn't remember the last time, in fact. Now he just culled the MP3 files direct from the Web. Some were legit, some rip-offs. It didn't matter. That was the great thing about the Web—the distance it put between you and the scene of the crime. No one was going to come and find him. Not down those countless little wires. They were too thin for culpability to seep through. You could spend your entire life on the Web without exposing yourself to anything more dangerous than spam or mail-bombing, both of which he was more than capable of dealing with.

The only people he had direct contact with, the only ones who ever learned his physical address and entered his corporeal world, were the women he met in the Web's virtual chat rooms. He'd cultivate them carefully, coming on like some newbie lurker: matching their own shy advances and only very gently nudging the conversation into the slow spiral that would end in them taking the exchange out of a public arena and into private e-mail. He only ever fished on boards that were loosely tied to his own geographical location. There was no point spending all that time and effort only to find that she lived on the other side of the world. Because eventually he would have convinced the woman—or, in her mind, they would have convinced each other—that it was time to take the relationship a little further. To take it backwards, out of these futuristic and nebulous lines of communication and back to the basic human levels that had worked since the dawn of time. It was never organized by phone. He had not once given his number out. Instead it would be a series of e-mails, a courtship of text: a careful progression for her, sentences fretted over, rewritten, revised or sometimes sent with a spastic click of a button before she had time to change her mind—but often the same old same old for him, as he'd found that he could cut and paste chunks out of previous campaigns and use them time and again.

And eventually the first visit would happen. A woman, slightly overdressed, eyes round with courage, would turn up at his door. The obvious would happen, and he was good. So it would happen again, and again. At intervals: when the woman could snatch the time; when the ennui she felt in her real life was so acute that it could only be assuaged by an action whose dishonesty jerked her out of her rut. Not all the women had been married, in fact probably not even the majority: but for the ones who weren't the very fact that they were prepared to enter into so one-track a relationship showed that none of them were worth taking seriously. It would carry on until something happened—a crisis of confidence, a tearful revelation to a husband, a prying boyfriend discovering an e-mail trail, which by now would be a lewd series of assignation-making—and it was over. He was never the one to make the move. He let them do it, because that way he knew they wouldn't be coming back and bugging him. They'd just be gone. To be immediately replaced by another one, whom he would have been cultivating in the meantime, keeping out there in the ether until the time was right.

The doorbell rang. He walked across the room toward the door, checking his hair in the mirror as he passed.

She was standing outside. Rather casually dressed, which annoyed him. He liked to see a bit of effort, not least because it proved that the affair was still at the hotter-than-hot stage. Though she did at least look a little flushed.

"Hi, David," she said, and he was pleased to notice a slight catch in her voice. "You're looking good."

Yes, he thought, I am. And later he found that what she was wearing underneath the blouse and pants wasn't casual *at all.*

Two and a half hours later he heard the door close behind her as she left the apartment. He'd been lying on the bed, faux dozing: he was prepared to do a lot of things to keep women convinced they were having one of the world's greatest affairs, but listening to them prattle after the event wasn't one of them. As soon as he was sure she'd gone, he was up and in the shower.

A good one, he thought, as he sluiced himself clean. And maybe the best-directed yet. He showered slowly, prolonging the moment.

When he was done, and comfortable in a fluffy white dressing gown that he liked because it never seemed to get dirty, he went through into the kitchen, fired up his other computer, and put a big pot of coffee on. He dropped the two wineglasses—hers empty, his still half-full—in the trash. He had plenty more. Then he went back through the apartment and collected up the tapes.

One from each of the living room cameras, which were triggered as soon as the door was opened and the woman came in. The four from the bedroom: two of these he had switched on as soon as they'd entered this room, via an extra spur off the bedside lamp; the others were on a trip delay to start recording fifty minutes later, to cover for the fact that one hour was the maximum tape length for the format he used. You could get longer, on different machines, but the quality was nowhere near as good.

Then the final one, from the bathroom—which he triggered by another switch once the sex was finished. It was this tape that he ripped to disk first, sitting at the desk with a steaming mug of very good coffee and a cigarette. It only took ten minutes to save it to an MPEG file, and then he set the others to rip in sequence in the background, porting the digital footage onto the array of hard disks, ready for a first quick edit.

After a slow first viewing.

This is what he did it for now. This was the moment he enjoyed. Not at first: three years ago, after his last genuine relationship had broken up, he'd just been looking for fun and companionship like everyone else. Maybe even someone to fall in love with. This hadn't happened with the first one, or the one after that. A pattern emerged. He didn't mind. Before, when he'd been taken, he'd envied his friends still out there in the market, the ones with the slew of drunken collisions in clubs and bars, with the long list of accidental one-night conquests. New breasts hefted, new buttocks splayed. David believed that men were collectors, taxonomists, seekers after and catalogers of variety—and he wanted some of it.

After a while the variety began to pall, however, and he felt less and less a part of what was going on. The women who turned up at his door started to seem too similar to each other. They might have different color hair, contrasting figures, and taste individual where it counted, but in the wriggles and grapples across couches and down corridors and round and round the bed they all ended up blending into one—not least because they shared a fundamental similarity. They weren't The One. He came to realize that it wasn't them who made him feel alive. What kept him going was himself, his own part in the proceedings. That, and the record.

It started more or less by accident. As accidentally, that is, as one can leave a camcorder running in a room where one is likely to be fucking a woman in the very near future. He'd bought the camera for the hell of it, mainly because a new computer had come with nonlinear video-editing software preinstalled. He ordered the camera over the Web, and it turned up at his door. Pretty soon he realized that he didn't have anything in his immediate environment worth recording, and no desire to be going out and shooting some shoddy masterpiece for Web distribution to net-heads with cable access and too much time on their hands. But then an idea struck him, one afternoon when a woman was coming round. Feeling suddenly excited, on the verge of something new, he found a place to wedge the camera in the bookcase, where it would capture whatever happened on the couch. What the hell, he thought: might be kind of interesting. When the doorbell rang he turned the camera on, carefully positioning books and a small ornamental box (a present from a past fuck) to hide the red light that indicated it was recording. The screwing moved into the bedroom after forty minutes, but when he watched the tape later that night it was still enough to make him lob his cock right out and achieve his third orgasm of the day: hunched over the desk, eyes wide and glued to the startling images on the screen. Afterwards, spent though he was, he watched the tape again and again, wiping it back and forward, reviewing the captured moments—acknowledging, as if for the first time, that the event really had happened. He really had screwed that woman: she had done *this* to him; he had done *that* to her. There it was. It was all recorded. He could see it. He could see it twice. He could see it whenever he wanted.

And she'd never know. It had passed out of the domain of her life, and into his alone. All she would have was vague memories, different occasions blending into one: he could have every event pinned to a board like a butterfly.

After that, he recorded the first hour as a matter of course, fixing a piece of tape over the red light to give more flexibility. It wasn't long before he wanted more. At first it was just a camera in *both* rooms. Then one in the bathroom, because a woman called Monica had got some obscure thrill from doing it in there. Then the extra one in the bedroom, and the second in the living room, because by that time he'd realized how much better it would be if he could get the raw material from two angles: partly just because you couldn't always position the woman to best effect without danger of it being obvious; mainly because it just seemed more real. The two-shot setup made all the difference. The cuts from angle to angle, from view to different view, showed just how true it was, filled it out into three dimensions. It was like a real movie. It was realer than real life.

Finally the extra pair in the bedroom, to make sure not a moment was lost.

He loved doing his films. He fucking loved it. It was partly to punish them for boring him. It was mainly because the films showed how much stronger his reality was than theirs, because whatever thoughts were fizzing around their desperate heads during the time they spent in his home, they had no idea what was really going on. That he was recording them, and later could edit the different shots together into any shape he liked. Picking the shots to show himself in control, to show them naked and exposed, leaving the soundtrack real to capture their gasps and squelches, their moans and pathetic avowals of love, of desire, of whatever it was they felt they had to say to make this seem okay to do. He had tapes of every session with every girl, all tidily filed in nested folders on his hard drives. He had "greatest hits" edits, too, each woman's best or most revealing moments. He had compilations, quick cuts of the same type of activity performed with a score of different women. He watched the digital films whenever he wanted, his breathing shallow but measured, face bathed in the monitor light, staring at himself, at his power. While the women were with him they had a kind of fake reality, shoved at him through their physical presence. When they were gone their true nature was revealed: as extras in his life, as vague presences at the end of an e-mail. He spent whole evenings reediting for the fun of it, and after a while his vision became more detailed, more refined. He culled through the bathroom tapes, catching the private moments and interspersing them with the other material: Marie looking smug afterwards, thinking she'd shown him the time of his life—when the next cut was that of David exaggeratedly yawning to camera while she enthusiastically sucked him half an hour before; Janine breathlessly declaring their sex as some kind of spiritual triumph, crapping on about how much she loved him—then later, sitting slumped on the can, sobbing in silent, racking waves and softly scraping the nails of both hands down her tear-tracked face.

Each time he made a tape he felt more himself, more vital. Sometimes he would start a film running on the computer and then switch the monitor off just before the current woman arrived. Though it could be neither seen nor heard, it was still playing, still being conjured up out of ones and zeros into image: footage of him plowing one woman while in real and current time he squeezed the tit of another; or of the same woman as she would be in the bathroom afterwards, the event contextualized before it had even finished.

The tapes had nearly done being digitized. It was time for another pot of coffee. David leaned against the counter as the water boiled, listening to the chirrup of the hard drive as the files of the raw material were written. He was noticing that he felt tired. Vestiges of the hangover, presumably, and Anne was a workout by anybody's standards. She'd seemed even more frenetic than usual that afternoon, as if testing him, or herself. Or maybe it was just too much coffee on an empty stomach, making him feel a little dizzy. Didn't matter. He was having more java anyway. It was traditional.

He took the new pot and a jug of cream over to the desk, so he wouldn't have to get up for a while. Then when the machine pinged to signify all the hard work was done, he reached out and clicked the first file. He always waited until they were all done. He liked it that way. Once he'd started watching, he needed to know he could jump to any part he wanted, immediately. It was part of the fun.

The bathroom tape started with ten minutes of nothing—Anne had lain beside him on the bed for a while after they'd finished. David sat and admired the fact that he'd remembered to refold the towels, to make them look just so. The women got good value out of him: the films were just a payment they didn't know they were making. Then there was the sound of the door being opened, and Anne's back swished into view with the sound of the door closing again. She stood in front of the mirror and ran the cold tap, nothing readable in the expression reflected back over her shoulder. She splashed some water over her face, and then sat down on the john. It was then, with her face much more directly visible by the camera, that David realized her facial expression wasn't actually unreadable after all. He watched for the few minutes she sat there, before flushing and leaving the room. Then he clicked back to an earlier frame in the MPEG. And watched it again.

It wasn't his imagination. He was sure of it. He'd seen "unreadable" before. Some women were like that. When not on stage, and making an effort to perform, the most vivacious of them could turn remarkably waxlike, as if they were nothing without an audience. This wasn't like that. There *was* something in her face. It was just something he'd ever seen before.

It was . . . what? Quietness? No. Dissatisfaction? Still no, but . . .

David frowned suddenly and put his cup down on the desk. He clicked the tape back again. His face felt a little hot.

She actually just looked a little bored.

He irritably lit a cigarette. That couldn't be right. Not after what they'd done. Not after the free-wheeling exhibition of technique he'd put on from the couch all the way through to their mutual and grunting climaxes. Perhaps she'd just had something else on her mind. Presumably things went on in her life. He never asked, but usually they'd say, filling him in regardless—wrongly assuming he'd care. Whatever. She hadn't been bored. It wasn't possible.

David shut the window on that tape and set another loading, wiping the back of one hand across his forehead as he waited. He still felt kind of hot. Embarrassment, maybe. At his initial thought that she might have regarded their coupling as less than earth-moving. Indignation was more appropriate. If she was frigid enough not to be jolted out of whatever little psychodrama from her outside life had been swirling around her head, then she was fucking on borrowed time. With him, anyway. Doubtless hubby would still limply put out, still engage her in the mildewy fumblings she'd come to David to escape. Assuming Anne had a husband. Right now he was so irritated he couldn't even remember.

The tape from the living room was better. A lot better. The fifteen minutes of chitchat and sipping, a spiral like the closing stages of the e-mail courtship—but one with a known destination. Then a frank movement from him: reaching out to stroke a breast through her blouse, then slipping his hand right up her skirt out of nowhere. He loved doing that. Making moves that assumed. Being in a position to demonstrate that this wasn't any coy long shot, but a fucking cert. It looked great on the video, too. Made the woman look just like what she was: a three-dimensional version of the pictures you could pick up on a zillion sites all over the Web. Just something within his field of vision. Something for him to play with. And they loved it. They really did. Loved being treated that way.

Soon they were both half-dressed. He turned her immaculately, cupping her breasts from behind, nuzzling her neck as she arched her head back, eyes closed—while he stared straight into the camera. There was a brief glitch in the digitizing and his hands frizzed for a moment, but otherwise it was a classic scene—with some superb cutaways possible to the other camera's point of view. Classic for the soft-core portion, anyhow: there would be meaner, better stuff later.

Then more of that, more of the usual. Building up. A button here, a strap there. Then a zipper. David could now judge how much time he had in the living room, how to steer things toward the corridor before there was any danger of the tapes running out. With three minutes to go, both still standing but with pants around their ankles, he touched her in a way that had her backing giggling out of the room, pulling him by something a man is bound to follow.

Just as they passed out of sight of the cameras, David noticed another little visual weirdness. He stopped the film, clicked back. Right at the end there was a two-second patch where there was a little streaming around the image of his head, tiny pixelated blocks of color. He flicked up the other camera's view of the same moment, and was relieved to see it looked fine. He'd just have to cut at that point. Something wrong with the tape, probably. Condensation. Or the recording head needed cleaning. He sorted through the cameras, found the offending tape, and put it to one side to check out later.

Then he kicked up the first of the bedroom films. He'd missed a little bit of action in the meantime, he knew. In the corridor Anne had bent to take him in her mouth for a couple of minutes. Not for the first time he mused it would be good to have a camera in there, too. Problem was, how to conceal it. Maybe he'd have to compromise, get a pinhole and hide it in a picture. Might even look good: a kind of voyeur, security camera–style section. Hmm. Think about that later: the bedroom tape showed events liquidly transforming into full flow.

He'd known at the time it was good. Not the sex, so much, as the way he'd controlled its movements, its ebb and flow. Her head there, in direct shot. His hand here, just where it could be seen. Seemingly spontaneous little rolls, taking the action from one view to another. Her moans and sighs, his encouraging grunts. Thrusts, acceptances, retractions and changes of position, all maximized for his eyes. Prime stuff, packaged and presented. A classic.

Except—shit.

He clicked back thirty seconds, not really knowing what he'd spotted. Watched the section again.

Straightforward shot, with them sideways across the bed, taken by the camera hidden up on the curtain rail. Him on top of her in missionary position, holding her shoulders down and grinding away. Her hands on his ass, pulling him in and out. Her hair spread over the sheets like a mermaid's floating in shallow water. Her legs raised up after a moment, clasping behind his. So much for the "boredom," he thought, with joyful spite—she was loving it. She moved her hands up along his back, nails out for a little playful scratching, and then slipped them both up and round to cup his face. Her eyes opened for a moment, looking up into his, searching for something. Maybe she found it. Maybe not.

Freeze. Click back two seconds. There. Her hands cupping his face.

He could see them.

The camera was high up and behind his back. He should be able to see the top and side of her face, and her hair. The tips of her fingers either side of his head. But for a couple of frames there, he could see her hands, too. Underneath his head. That shouldn't be possible.

He flipped back and forth a few times, bordering on very irritated. It was probable that the effect, a weird kind of transparency, had been caused by the filter set he automatically applied to the tape as it was being digitized. Preset algorithms adjusted contrast and light levels to maximum effect, seeking a medium range which made the edited result more consistent. The filters played with the image on the basis of numbers and theory, rather than reality. He was a lot more tan than Anne was, he realized: it hadn't been a problem before, but she hadn't been on vacation since he'd been screwing her. Perhaps the tones of his head had fallen foul of a glitch, blue-screening them into momentary translucence. It had fucking better be that. If not, then it was a tape problem again, and the Web merchant from whom he'd bought this batch would be hearing from the sharp side of his e-mail.

He clicked on and got back to watching the rest of the tape. It was fine. It was classic. But the fucking glitch kept coming up again. Never for very long. A second or two, here and there. It had to be the skin-tone thing. She was pale, he was golden. The filter range he'd set was too narrow to cope. And it kept getting worse. By the time he'd moved on to the second pair of tapes, the ones capturing the second hour in the bedroom—and the second, languid, fuck—the image was stuttering all over the place.

David grabbed the mouse and viciously stabbed the button, stopping the film. It didn't matter in the long run. He could rerip the tape without the filters, put up with the differences in lighting—or even manually tweak them himself. But the former would be disappointing, a drop in quality he didn't want, the latter several hours of hard slog. He didn't deserve this kind of hassle. He'd done a good job. Why the fuck couldn't it just work out the first time? Why didn't the silly bitch go to a tanning booth? He'd have to talk to her about it. He'd got her trained otherwise. This was good stuff. He wasn't losing it just because she was too fucking lazy to look after her appearance.

He slugged back another mouthful of coffee and stood up, feeling momentarily dizzy again. He wasn't going to be screwing around with manual filtering tonight, that was for sure. His eyes ached as it was. The mood lighting that remained from the setup for Anne was too dim for anything else, making the corners of the room hard to see.

He sorted through the cameras once more and found one of the second ones from the bedroom—just to confirm it wasn't the tape itself. He hesitated for a moment before plugging it in to the monitor. He was in a bad enough mood already. If he found it was a tape problem, then there was nothing he could do to save the film. Did he want news like that now, feeling as shit as he did?

Fuck it. He was going to find out sooner or later. He plugged in, waited while it rewound, pressed play.

The tape started just as they were building up to the second fuck. Anne lying on her back, groaning quietly as he sucked her nipples and coaxed between her legs. Then he gently pulled one of her hands across and placed it down there, while he straddled her chest, tugging at his cock, getting it to the point where he could commend it to her mouth for further encouragement. A section of this and then he withdrew, climbed off and turned her over, ready for—But it was wrong. It was all very wrong.

He wasn't there on the tape.

Anne did all the things he remembered. She moved in all the right ways. Her body showed the impressions of his hands. Her mouth opened, and her hands lifted up, as if controlling his thrusts. Then it shut, she looked up at nothing and turned over, the imprint of his fingers on her buttock. But she almost looked as if she were the only person on the bed.

David swore, yanked the tape out of the camera and threw it across the room. He grabbed another camera, plugged it in. Tape from the living room. He knew that worked. He'd already watched the MPEG. He rewound, watched it again.

Anne drank alone.

Anne's buttons undid themselves. Her zipper undid itself, and her pants dropped to the floor.

Anne backed out of the room, giggling, her hand held out as if pulling an invisible rope.

It was fucking horrible. The tape was so screwed up it made it look like he hadn't even been there. Of course he had been, there was no question of that: the evidence was actually still there in front of him. She hadn't undone her own buttons: her hands were nowhere near them at the time. He'd been there; he'd done that. But if he couldn't see it—how the fuck was it supposed to count?

He furiously lit another cigarette. Went and retrieved the thrown tape. He could hardly send it back as evidence of how faulty their merchandise was, but he could note the serial number. He'd need to quote it. Obviously a whole batch was screwed up. They'd probably already had complaints. They were sure as fuck going to get one more.

He sat down again. His heart was beating hard and ragged. His head felt terrible. The dislocation he'd felt before Anne arrived was back in force. For just a moment he wavered, doubted the point of his life, realizing that everything else he did had become superfluous, that the films were all he cared about, the only things that spoke directly to the man he knew himself to be. It only lasted a second, and then he was back again. Back, and angry. He needed grounding, that was all.

Hands moving like independent robots, one took the mouse and flash-navigated through the file structure on his computer, heading for one of the Greatest Hits compilations. The other tugging at the knot in the cord of his dressing gown, pulling it aside and finding what was inside. He double-clicked the file, already kneading in his lap. Okay, so one had got away. Technology had conspired against him. But there was so much already stored to enjoy.

The film, "Dogs I Have Known," flipped up onto the screen. He was proud of the title. A score of women in the doggie position, intercut with the little ladies gnawing on his bone. It was his finest hour, his finest hours, in fact: stripped of dead wood and cutting straight to chase after chase.

But he wasn't on it. Not in a single scene.

Feeling sick with confusion he raced back and forth through the tape, checking sections more than once. Monica, Claire, Janine. The women moved under his direction, but he wasn't there. Anne, Marie,

Helen, Liz. Parts of their bodies opened to accommodate him, but there was no him to be seen. Sue, Teresa, Rachel, Nikki, Maggie, Beth. And him fucking nowhere.

Closed out, checked another film. The same.

And another. And another. He staggered to his feet. He felt very strange now. Almost as if he were floating.

There was something wrong with his head.

Maybe it hadn't been alcohol that had done for him. Perhaps he'd been slipped a drug the night before, a delayed psychedelic, by some fucker at the club where he'd been. Wherever it was—he still couldn't properly remember. It couldn't all be gone. Not the things they'd done for him. The things he'd made them do.

No, it *was* a drug, because things off the screen were looking strange now, too. The table looked insubstantial. The little lamps, carefully placed around the room, these, too, seemed odd: as if flicking from one state to another outside his control. He pushed himself away from the desk, staggered back into the room. He felt sick, hollow, as if his grip on reality was fading.

Maybe not a drug, he thought suddenly. Not exactly. Not something slipped into a drink. Maybe one of the women had come back, or her man. Some kind of revenge: because now he thought about it, some of them did come back, for "just one more time" visits every now and then. Maybe one had left something in the room. Something that slowly leaked out, a gas, permeating the room and gradually fucking him up. Building up over days, weeks. His only respite the time he spent out of the apartment. Like when he . . .

He couldn't remember when he'd last left the apartment. He couldn't remember the night before. He couldn't remember where he'd been. Maybe he hadn't been anywhere, and it was only the gas that was making him think he had. Filling in the gaps, trying to explain the way he felt. He reeled across the room, heading for the corridor. Fresh air. He needed fresh air. He needed to get out and then find out which bitch had done this to him. And then he thought maybe he'd break his (virtual contact only) rule. Maybe he'd just find her and fuck her up bad.

As he careered across the room he seemed to move in a series of jump-cuts. When he passed the mirror he didn't even notice that he was not reflected in it.

He barreled into the corridor, doing his best to run but losing all speed to his thrashing. The drug was building up in his head. Maybe Anne had triggered it. He'd felt odd before she came, but nothing like this. She could have pushed him over the edge. As he hauled himself along the corridor, face pressed against the cool wall, he tried to imagine what he'd do to her next time she came. She didn't like rough stuff, he knew. He'd tried it, carefully choreographed for the cameras. Well, next time she was going to take it anyway.

He didn't feel sick anymore, just so light-headed he could barely think. Everything seemed too white. He couldn't even feel the wall now, but he could see the door. He reached for the handle, turned it, and yanked it open.

Outside there was nothing but a black void.

He turned, but his corridor wasn't there either now. It was just black all around, the last of the light fading out.

His last thought was this:

This isn't right. Don't you understand? This is *me*.

Anne checked her e-mail before she went to bed. The usual stuff: a few things from work, a couple of articles she'd sent her agent after, a newsy letter from her sister in New South Wales.

And one from private encounters.com. She opened it.

Dear Anne:

Grovel, grovel: what can I say! You were right—it wasn't your sensor pads at all. The site engineers have just found a deep code fault with the charactergen, and it looks like it's been accumulating for some time. As a result, the David Mate has been permanently withdrawn from service. Unfortunately this means that he will also have disappeared from the transcripts of previous SavedEncounters you have archived on our secure server—but rest assured he will be replaced within twenty-four hours, for your revisiting pleasure.

I do apologize for the inconvenience, and hope that a $30 rebate (against further purchase) and the promise of Generation IV EncounterMates just around the corner will encourage you to log in again very soon!

Yours sincerely,
Julie North, Customer Service

Anne nodded to herself, pleased to have been proved right. It just hadn't felt the same. And the prospect of revisiting old times, but with a different Mate, sounded really rather interesting.

She grinned greedily to herself as she shut down the computer. Whatever. She'd had enough.

For tonight, anyway.

Joe Lansdale, Hisownself here. Writing about Al Sarrantonio again. This is my second time to write a brief introduction to one of Al's stories. I also wrote an introduction to his wonderful short story collection, Toybox.

He could have written his own introduction, but modesty, damn near shyness, kept him from it, so he asked me. I'm honored.

This short tale, "Billy The Fetus," is undoubtedly one of the strangest, and in some ways bravest, stories he's written. It may seem like nothing more than a clever little tale at first, a cousin to one of Bradbury's more famous tales, "The Small Assassin," but this one is harder and truer and stranger and even more original than that of the master.

This story is so short, there's little that can be said about it that the tale can't say better itself, and this isn't because I fear I might give it away. You really can't give this one away. The title lets you know what it's about, but it's Al's magnificent prose that lets you feel what it's about.

—J. R. L. (Hisownself)

Billy the Fetus

AL SARRANTONIO

✶

Soon as I growed ears I heered things. My Mammy was a-singin' all the time, 'bout all kinds a-things—'bout the Moon, which was made a-cheese, 'bout flowers and bees and dogs that be a-barkin' in the dusty streets. She even sang 'bout the dusty streets themselves, what the clouds o' dust looked like when the stage rolled in or wagons pulled out from the genr'l store. I got me a fine picture o' the world from Mammy's singin'—a fuzzy place with a giant Moon made a-cheese hangin' overhead, which you could see sometimes through th' dust while the dogs a-barked.

She even sang about my Pappy:

Will Bonney's gone,
Gone to the devil,
The devil ain't happy,
And that's on the level.
Shot through the liver,
Then shot through the heart,
Will Bonney's gone,
'Fore Billy Bonney's start . . .

That Billy Bonney she be singin' 'bout, that'd be me, I figured.

I figured lots o' things, floatin' there in that watery sac in my Mammy, with the fuzziest sounds filtering through. Couldn't smell no dust, as I hadn't growed a nose yet, and I couldn't wait for seein' the dogs when I growed eyes. When Mammy really got to gigglin', she'd sing some o' the rest o' her song about my Pappy:

Will was a fighter,
He fought 'em with his gun,
They put him six feet under
'Fore it all was done.
Many a man went before him
Into a dusty grave,
For Will was fast—
Lord, fast with his hands!—
And nothin' if he wasn't brave.

I could just see my Pappy out there in the street, shootin' under the big ol' Moon a-cheese through the settling dust, mowin' them other fellers down with his six-gun. And he musta had a good reason, 'cause Mammy, when she got to tinklin' the glasses, sometimes sang the last part o' her song about m' Pappy:

Will Bonney had another gun, too,
And he used it just as fast,
And now little Billy's comin' along—
But Lord, that's just the past!
So if you meet Will Bonney in Hades,
Be sure to say hello,
From the gal and babe he left behind
While he dances down below . . .

There usually came gigglin' after that, and more glass tinklin', and then the bouncy ride, and then the pokin' thing, and loud noises, and Mammy yellin', and some feller-not-my-Pappy yellin', and then the really loud noise which I didn't understand but thought might be the Moon a-cheese fallin' out of the sky.

And that's the way I went along for a while, while my hands and feet growed a bit, looking like flippers, and my eyes growed too, and my brain I guess, and I floated and dreamed of the Moon a-cheese and wondered what the bouncy ride was, and the pokin' thing, and the feller-not-my-Pappy groanin' and yellin', every time a different feller, it seemed to me, and the loud noise like the Moon a-cheese fallin' from the sky—a noise as loud as my Pappy's six-gun.

And then one day while it was all happenin' again, the bouncy ride and such, and some feller-not-my-Pappy a-gruntin' and yellin', I suddenly figured it out!

As if my brain had growed just big enough to make me see, it became as clear as the Moon a-cheese in the sky!

That feller-not-my-Pappy was tryin' to kill me!

And he was hurtin' my Mammy!

Hurtin' her plenty, I'd say, she was a moaning and groanin' so, and now he was tryin' to kill me for sure, for here came the pokin' thing, a weapon if there ever was one—maybe even a six-gun!—jabbin' up from below and tryin' to bust my floatin' sac!

Well, no, sir, that wasn't gonna happen at all—nobody was a gonna hurt my Mammy—and nobody was gonna kill Billy Bonney like they killed my Pappy!

Nobody was gonna make me go below, down to the devil, and make me dance!

Not me, the son of Will Bonney!

I had to do something about it—

So I did.

"I'm a-comin', Mammy!" I hollered, though I didn't have much of a mouth yet, and the little noises came out like the bubble farts I made sometimes in the floatin' sac.

"I'm a-comin' t' save ya!"

By now she was well past the gigglin' and glass tinklin' and into the Mammy-yellin' stage—but she really started t' yell when I made my way out o' there. First I ripped off the cord 'tween Mammy and me—did a nice neat job o' pullin' it apart in the middle and tied it off on both the wriggly ends so's not to make a mess. That was a bit of a chore with my flipper hands and all, but I managed it. Then I began a' swimmin', paddlin' right for the hole where that pokin' weapon had been. Nothin' there now, and I saw the spot leadin' out and went for it. Dove right through with my hands out in front of me makin' a wedge, and closed my big eyes and *whoosh!* if that sack didn't break easy as I hoped, carrying me along for a ways before things began to dry out. Then I had to claw my way along. Not too far, which was good for me and Mammy, since she was a yellin' somethin' fierce by this time.

Things began to get lighter, and I waited for the fuzzy light to hit me, the color of the Moon a-cheese, but instead there was just a couple of flaps in front of me which I pushed apart and whoa!—there was no fuzzy light a'tall but somethin' that hurt my eyes fierce, like a burnin' itself!

I didn't let that stop me, though, or the little coughin' fit I had while my lungs filled up with what must have been air. The sounds were way clear now, with Mammy screamin' like the devil and the man I'd heard a-moanin'. I pulled my part of the cord out after me and kept on movin' while my eyes got used to the grand and glorious light o' the world, nothin' like the soft fuzzy light I'd expected but sharp as anything. And the colors! The reddest red you'd ever imagine, all around me and wet.

And there, suddenly, out the window of Mammy's room, floatin' in the black night that wasn't fuzzy a'tall, was the Moon a-cheese itself, which I got a good look at as my eyes began to focus sharp.

Then I dropped to Mammy's bed—

And there was a six-gun, laying right there beside me, and the man who'd hurt Mammy a-whimperin' and crouchin' in the corner, his pants around his ankles and his other-gun, like Mammy's talked about in the song, just as sad and droopy as could be.

So I worked up all my strength, and lifted Mammy's gun in my flipper hands, holding it on the bed and wrapping my flipper feet around it and aiming it real true, just like my Pappy would, and pulled the trigger twice, and I done shot that feller through the heart, then through the liver, and watched him drop dead t' the floor.

"I saved you, Mammy! I saved you!" I cried in little bubble farts.

And then I turned smiling with my tiny mouth and looked at my Mammy for the first time ever.

She was a-layin' there on the pillows of her bed pale as ghosts must be, pale as dust, her eyes big and drained. She lifted a weak finger, layin' there in a pool of blood around her middle like she was, where I'd come a-swimmin' out, and she pointed at me.

"Mammy!" I burbled happily.

I waited for her to smile, but instead her lips curled into a sneer and she screamed in a hateful way:

"You little *bastard*! I knowed you'd be a boy when you popped! Felt you like a *disease* inside o' me!"

She got real weak then, and her hand lowered to the bed—but then the rage crawled back up into her face and she hissed: "I would've killed you too when you came out natural! Just like I killed any man who ever come near me!"

"But Mammy—!" I said.

Her eyes got all big and wild then, and she pointed to her still-distended belly. "Just like I killed your pappy, that sonofabitch Will Bonney who did this to me!"

I looked down at my own other-gun, which was so itsy it didn't look like it could hurt nobody at no time.

"Mammy—!"

"I'll shoot you through the heart and liver yet! Just like I shot 'em all!"

She began to sing then, in a kind of gigglin', croaky voice, a song I'd never heard a'fore:

So if you're six feet under
And dancing down below,
Be sure to look up Billy Bonney,
Be sure to say hello!

She reached down for the six-gun, but before she could grab it she suddenly got to bein' real weak again.

She lay back on the bed and fainted.

And that was all the time I needed.

Didn't take me long to get fixed up again. The cord healed up pretty good, as I took my time getting the two ends to match up just right. I managed to get the hole I'd made closed, though I'll have to see how much good that does me, since the floatin' sac's gone. I figure the cord's the important thing, since the whiff I got of air while I was out didn't seem to hurt me none, and my lungs, small as they is, seem to be workin' okay.

Figure I can hole up in here as long as I need to.

Heck, who needs it out there anyway—I can wait to see flowers and bees and barkin' dogs, and that little peek I got o' the Moon convinced me it ain't made a-cheese, after all. Looked all wrinkly and dusty-cold to me.

She ain't gonna make *me* dance down below.

And o' course I got this here six-gun with four more bullets in it—and if she comes in after me I know how to use it.

This is true: Gene Wolfe, who grew up in Houston, Texas, attended Edgar Allan Poe Elementary School. Much later, he produced some of the most important science fiction of the last forty years, including The Book of the New Sun, The Urth of the New Sun, *and* The Book of the Long Sun. *He has won two Nebulas and three World Fantasy Awards, as well as the British Science Fiction Award and the British Fantasy Award.* The Urth of the New Sun *earned the Premio Italia.*

New short fiction from Gene Wolfe is always an event; stories besides this new wonder can be found in collections such as The Island of Doctor Death and Other Stories and Other Stories *(another wonderful title, as wonderful as that of the abovementioned Kit Reed collection) and the newest,* Strange Travelers.

Viewpoint

Gene Wolfe

✷

"I have one question and one only," Jay declared. "How do I know that I will be paid? Answer it to my satisfaction and give your orders."

The youngish man behind the desk opened a drawer and pulled out a packet of crisp bills. It was followed by another and another, and they by seven more. The youngish man had brown-blond hair and clear blue eyes that said he could be trusted absolutely with anything. Looking at them, Jay decided that each had cost more than he had ever had in his entire life to date.

"Here's the money," the youngish man told Jay softly. "These are hundreds, all of them. Each band holds one hundred, so each bundle is ten thousand. Ten bundles make a hundred thousand. It's really not all that much."

"Less than you make in a year."

"Less than I make in three months. I know it's a lot to you." The youngish man hesitated as though groping for a new topic. "You've got a dramatic face, you know. Those scars. That was your edge. Did you really fight a bobcat?"

Jay shrugged. "The bullet broke its back, and I thought it was dead. I got too close."

"I see." The youngish man pushed the packets of bills toward him. "Well, you don't have to worry about getting paid. That's the full sum, and you're getting it up front and in cash." He paused. "Maybe I shouldn't tell you this."

Jay was looking at the money. "If it's confidential, say so and I'll keep it that way."

"Will you?"

Jay nodded. "For a hundred thousand? Yes. For quite a bit less than that."

The youngish man sighed. "You probably know anyway, so why not? You can't just go out and stick it in a bank. You understand that?"

"They'll say it's drug money."

For a moment the youngish man looked as if he were about to sigh again, although he did not. "They'll say it's drug money, of course. They always do. But they really don't care. You have a lot of money, and if it gets into a bank Big Daddy will have it in a nanosecond. It'll take you years to get it back, and cost a lot more than a hundred thousand."

Though skeptical, Jay nodded. "Sure."

"Okay, I didn't want to give you this and have them grab it before five. They'll take a big cut of anything you spend it on anyway, but we've all got to live with that."

Jay did not, but he said nothing.

"Count it. Count it twice and look carefully. I don't want you thinking we cheated you for a lousy hundred thou."

Jay did, finding it impossible to think of what so much money could buy. He had needed money so badly that he could no longer calculate its value in terms of a new rifle or a canoe. It was money itself he hungered for now, and this was more than he had dared dream of.

"You want a bag? I can give you one, but that jacket's got plenty of pockets. It's for camping, right?"

"Hunting."

The youngish man smiled the smile of one who knows a secret. "Why don't you put it in there? Should be safer than a bag."

Jay had begun to fill them already—thirty thousand in the upper right inside pocket, twenty more in the upper left, behind his wallet. Twenty in the left pocket outside.

"You're BC, right?"

"Sure." Jay tapped the empty screen above his eyes.

"Okay." The youngish man opened another drawer. "As a bonus you get a double upgrade. Couple of dots. Sit still."

Jay did.

When the youngish man was back behind his desk, he said, "I bet you'd like to look at yourself. I ought to have a mirror, but I didn't think of it. You want to go to the men's? There's a lot of mirrors in there. Just come back whenever you've seen enough. I've got calls to make."

"Thanks," Jay said.

In the windowless office beyond the youngish man's, his secretary was chatting with a big security bot. Jay asked where the rest rooms were, and the bot offered to show him, gliding noiselessly down the faux-marble corridor.

"Tell me something," Jay said when the bot had come to a stop before the door. "Suppose that when I got through in there I went down to the lobby. Would there be anything to stop me from going out to the street?"

"No, sir."

"You're going to be standing out here waiting for me when I come out, right? I'd never make it to the elevators."

"Will you need a guide at that point, sir?"

The blank metal face had told Jay nothing, and the pleasant baritone had suggested polite inquiry, and nothing else. Jay said, "I can find my way back all right."

"In that case, I have other duties, sir."

"Like talking to that girl?"

"Say *woman*, sir. To that young woman. They prefer it, and Valerie is an excellent source of intelligence. One cultivates one's sources, sir, in police work."

Jay nodded, conceding the point. "Can you answer a couple more questions for me? If it's not too much trouble?"

"If I can, sir. Certainly."

"How many dots have I got?"

"Are you referring to IA stars, sir?"

Jay nodded.

"Two, sir. Are you testing my vision, sir?"

"Sure. One more, and I'll let you alone. What's the name of the man I've been talking to? There's no nameplate on his desk, and I never did catch it."

"Mr. Smith, sir."

"You're kidding me."

"No, sir."

"John Smith? I'll bet that's it."

"No, sir. Mr. James R. Smith, sir."

"Well, I'll be damned."

Scratching his chin, Jay went into the men's room. There were at least a dozen mirrors there, as the youngish man had said. The little augmentation screen set into his forehead, blank and black since he had received it between the fourth and the fifth grades, showed two glimmering stars now: five- or six-pointed, and scarlet or blue depending on the angle from which he viewed them.

For ten minutes or more he marveled at them. Then he relieved himself, washed his hands, and counted the money again. One hundred thousand in crisp, almost-new hundreds. Logically, it could be counterfeit. Logically, he should have shown one to the security bot and asked its opinion.

Had the bot noticed his bulging pockets? Security bots would undoubtedly be programmed to take note of such things, and might well be more observant than a human officer.

He took out a fresh bill and examined it, riffling it between his fingers and holding it up to the light, reading its serial number under his breath. Good.

If the bot had called it bad, it would have been because the bot had been instructed to do so, and that was all.

Furthermore, someone had been afraid he would assault the youngish man the bot called James R. Smith, presumably because metal detectors had picked up his hunting knife; but Smith had not asked him to remove it, or so much as mentioned it. Why?

Jay spent another fifteen or twenty seconds studying the stars in his IA screen and three full minutes concentrating before he left the rest room. There was no bot in the hall. A middle-aged man who looked important passed him without a glance and went in.

Jay walked to the elevators, waved a hand for the motion detector, and rode a somewhat crowded car to the lobby. So far as he could see, no one was paying the least attention to him. There was another security bot in the lobby (as there had been when he had come in), but it appeared to pay no particular attention to him either.

Revolving doors admitted him to Sixth Avenue. He elbowed his way for half a block along a sidewalk much too crowded, and returned to the Globnet Building.

The security bot was chatting with the young woman in her windowless room again. When she saw Jay she nodded and smiled, and the doors to Smith's office swung open.

Smith, who had said that he would be making calls, was standing at one of his floor-to-ceiling windows staring out at the gloomy December sky.

"I'm back," Jay said. "Sorry I took so long. I was trying to access the new chips you gave me."

"You can't." Smith turned around.

"That's what I found out."

Smith's chair rolled backwards, and he seated himself at his desk. "Aren't you going to ask me what they're for?"

Jay shook his head.

"Okay, that will save me a lot of talking. You've still got the hundred thousand?"

Jay nodded.

"All right. In about forty-seven minutes we're going to announce on all our channels that you've got it. We'll give your name, and show you leaving this building, but that's all. It will be repeated on every newscast tonight, name, more pictures, a hundred thou in cash. Every banger and grifter in the city will be after you, and if you hide it, there's a good chance they'll stick your feet in a fire."

Smith waited, but Jay said nothing.

"You've never asked me what we're paying you to do, but I'll tell you now. We're paying you to stay alive and get some good out of your money. That's all. If you want to stay here and tough it out, that's fine. If you want to run, that's fine, too. As far as we're concerned, you're free to do whatever you feel you have to do."

Smith paused, studying Jay's scarred face, then the empty, immaculate surface of his own desk. "You can't take those chips out. Did you know that?"

Jay shook his head.

"It's easy to put them in to upgrade, but damned near impossible to take them out without destroying the whole unit and killing its owner. They do that to make it hard to rob people of their upgrades. I can't stop you from trying, but it won't work and you might hurt yourself."

"I've got it." Jay counted the stars on Smith's screen. Four.

"The announcement will go out in forty-five minutes, and you have to leave the building before then so we can show you doing it."

The doors behind Jay swung open, and the security bot rolled in.

"Kaydee Nineteen will escort you." Smith sounded embarrassed. "It's just so we can get the pictures."

Jay rose.

"Is there anything you want to ask me before you go? We'll have to keep it brief, but I'll tell you all I can."

"No." Jay's shoulders twitched. "Keep the money and stay alive. I've got it."

As they went out, Smith called, "Kaydee Nineteen won't rob you. You don't have to worry about that."

Kaydee Nineteen chuckled when Smith's doors had closed behind them. "I bet you never even thought of that, sir."

"You're right," Jay told him.

"Are you going to ask where the holo cameras are, sir?"

"In the lobby and out in the street. They have to be."

"That's right, sir. Don't go looking around for them, though. It looks bad, and they'll have to edit it out."

"I'd like to see the announcement they're going to run," Jay said as they halted before an elevator. "Can you tell me where I might be able to do that?"

"Certainly, sir. A block north and turn right. They call it the Studio." The elevator doors slid back, moving less smoothly than Smith's; Kaydee Nineteen paused, perhaps to make certain the car was empty, then said. "Only you be careful, sir. Just one drink. That's plenty."

Jay stepped into the elevator.

"They've got a good holo setup, I'm told, sir. Our people go there all the time to watch the shows they've worked on."

When the elevator doors had closed, Jay said, "I don't suppose you could tell me where I could buy a gun?"

Kaydee Nineteen shook his head. "I ought to arrest you, sir, just for asking. Don't you know the police will take care of you? As long as we've police, everybody's safe."

The elevator started down.

"I just hoped you might know," Jay said apologetically.

"Maybe I do, sir. It doesn't mean I tell."

Slipping his hand into his side pocket, Jay broke the paper band on a sheaf of hundreds, separated two without taking the sheaf from his pocket, and held them up. "For the information. It can't be a crime to tell me."

"Wait a minute, sir." Kaydee Nineteen inserted the fourth finger of his left hand into the STOP button, turned it, and pushed. The elevator's smooth descent ended with shocking abruptness.

"Here, take it." Jay held out the bills.

Kaydee Nineteen motioned him to silence. A strip of paper was emerging from his mouth; he caught it before it fell. "Best dealer in the city, sir. I'm not saying she won't rip you off. She will. Only she won't rip you off as badly as the rest, and she sells quality. If she sells you home-workshop, she tells you home-workshop."

He handed the slip to Jay, accepted the hundreds, and dropped them into his utility pouch. "You call her up first, sir. There's an address on that paper, too, but don't go there until you call. You say Kincaid said to. If she asks his apartment number or anything like that, you have to say number nineteen. Do you understand me, sir?"

Jay nodded.

"It's all written out for you, and some good advice in case you forget. Only you chew that paper up and swallow it once you got your piece, sir. Are you going to do that?"

"Yes," Jay said. "You have my word."

"It better be good, sir, because if you get arrested, you're going to need friends. If they find that paper on you, you won't have any."

Jay walked through the lobby alone, careful not to look for the holo camera. Those outside would be in trucks or vanettes, presumably, but might conceivably be in the upper windows of buildings on the other side of Sixth. He turned north, as directed. Glancing to his right at the end of the next block, he saw the Studio's sign, over which virtual stage-hands moved virtual lights and props eternally; but he continued to walk north for two more blocks, then turned toward Fifth and followed the side street until he found a store in which he bought a slouch hat and an inexpensive black raincoat large enough to wear over his hunting coat.

Returning to the Studio, he approached it from both west and east, never coming closer than half a block, without spotting anyone watching the entrance. It was possible—just possible, he decided reluctantly—that Kaydee Nineteen had been as helpful as he seemed. Not likely, but possible.

In a changing booth in another clothing store, he read the slip of paper:

> Try Jane MacKann, Bldg. 18 Unit 8 in Greentree Gardens. 1028 7773-0320. Call her first and say Kincaid. Say mine if she asks about any number. She will not talk to anybody nobody sent, so you must say mine. She likes money, so say you want good quality and will pay for it. When you get there, offer half what she asks for and go from there. You should get ten, twenty percent off her price. Do not pay her asking price. Do not take a cab. Walk or ride the bus. Do not fail to phone first. Be careful.

It took him the better part of an hour to find a pay phone in the store that looked secure. He fed bills—the change from the purchase of his raincoat—into it and keyed the number on Kaydee Nineteen's paper slip.

Three rings, and the image of a heavyset frowning woman in a black plastic shirt and a dark skirt appeared above the phone; she had frizzy red hair and freckles, and looked as though she should be smiling. "Hello. I'm not here right now, but if you'll leave a message at the tone I'll call you back as soon as I can."

The tone sounded.

"My name's Skeeter." Jay spoke rapidly to hide his nervousness. "I'm a friend of Kinkaid's. He said to call you when I got into the city, but I'm calling from a booth, so you can't call me. I'll call again when I get settled."

None of the clerks looked intelligent. He circled the store slowly, pretending to look at cheap electric razors and souvenir shirts until he found a door at the back labeled DO NOT ENTER. He knocked and stepped inside.

The manager flicked off his PC, though not before Jay had seen naked women embracing reflected in the dark window behind him. "Yes, sir. What's the problem?"

"You don't have one," Jay told him, "but I do, and I'll pay a hundred"—he held up a bill—"to you to help me with it. I want to rent this office for one half hour so that I can use your phone. I won't touch your papers, and I won't steal anything. You go out in your store and take care of business. Or go out and get a drink or a sandwich, whatever you want. After half an hour you come back and I leave."

"If it's long distance . . ."

Jay shook his head. "Local calls, all of them."

"You promise that?" The manager looked dubious.

"Absolutely."

"All right. Give me the money."

Jay handed the bill over.

"Wait a minute." The manager switched on his computer, studied the screen, moved his mouse and clicked, studied the result, and clicked again. Jay was looking at the phone. As he had expected, its number was written on its base.

"All right," the manager repeated. "I've blocked this phone so it won't make long distance calls. To unblock it, you'd have to have my password."

"I didn't know you could do that," Jay said.

"Sure. You want out of the deal?"

Jay shook his head.

"Okay, you've got the place for half an hour. Longer if you need it, only not past three-thirty. Okay?"

"Okay."

The manager paused at the door. "There's a booth out here. You know about that?"

Jay nodded. "It won't accept incoming calls."

"You let them take calls and the dealers hang around and won't let anybody use it. You a dealer?"

Jay shook his head.

"I didn't think so." The manager shut the door.

One oh two eight. Seven seven seven three. Oh three two oh. Three rings as before, and the image of the heavyset redhead appeared. "Hello.

I'm not here right now, but if you'll leave a message at the tone I'll call you back as soon as I can."

The tone sounded.

"This is Skeeter again," Jay said. "I've got money, and Kincaid said you and I could do some business." He recited the number from the base of the manager's phone. "If you can give me what I want, this is going to be a nice profitable deal for you." Hoping that she would not, he added, "Ask Kincaid," and hung up.

He had slept in a bod mod at the Greyhound station, had left his scant luggage in a storage locker; that luggage was worth nothing, and seemed unlikely to furnish clues to his whereabouts when a criminal gang came looking for him and his hundred thousand.

The forty-five minutes Smith had mentioned had come and gone. His image had appeared in the Studio and millions of houses and apartments.

They might be looking for him already—at the bus station, at the Studio, at any other place they could think of. At the MacKann woman's.

The phone rang and he picked it up. "Skeeter."

"This's Jane, Skeeter." The loose shirt was the same; but the dark skirt had given way to Jeens, and her hair was pulled back by a clip. "Kincaid said to call me?"

"That's right," Jay told her. "He said we might be able to do business, and he gave me your number."

"He must be getting to be a big boy now, that Kincaid."

"He's bigger than I am," Jay said truthfully.

"How old is Kincaid these days anyway?"

"Nineteen."

"He gave you my address? Or was it just this number?"

"He gave me an address," Jay said carefully. "I can't say whether it's right or not. Have you moved recently?"

"What is it?"

Jay hesitated. "All right to read it over the phone?"

"I don't see why not."

The door opened, and the manager looked in. Jay waved him away.

"What address did he give you?"

Kaydee Nineteen's paper lay on the desk. Jay held it up so the small woman seated above the telephone could read it.

"The print's too small," she told him. "You'll have to say it."

"It doesn't bother you?"

"Why should it?"

Jay sighed. "I don't know. When I was in college, I used to play chess. Now I feel like I'm playing chess again and I've forgotten how."

He reversed the slip of paper. "Building Eighteen, Unit Eight in the Greentree Gardens?"

"That's it. When will you be here?"

The black raincoat had slits above its pockets that let Jay reach the pockets of the camouflage hunting coat under it. Extracting a bill, he held it up. "Can you read this?"

"Sure."

"I'll give it to you if you'll pick me up. You've seen me and how I'm dressed. I'll be in that little park at the corner of Sixth and Fortieth."

"No," she said.

"I'll be there, and I'll buy. I'll pay you this just for the ride." He hung up, rose, and left the store, waving to the manager.

There was a hotel down the street; he went in and stood at the front desk, a vast affair of bronze and marble. After five minutes a black woman in a transparent plastic blouse asked, "You checkin' in?"

"I'd like to." Jay laid two hundreds on the counter.

"We can't take those." She eyed them as though they were snakes. "Got a credit card?"

Jay shook his head.

"You got no bags either."

Jay did not deny it.

"You can't check in here."

He indicated the hundreds. "I'll pay in advance."

The black woman lowered her voice. "They don't let us take anybody like you, even if you got two dots."

In a department store a block away, Jay cornered a clerk. "I want a lightweight bag, about this long."

The clerk yawned. "Three feet, sir?"

"More than that." Jay separated his hands a bit.

The clerk (who probably called himself an associate) shook his head and turned away.

"Three and a half, anyway. Forty-two inches."

"Soft-sided?" The clerk clearly hoped Jay would say no.

"Sure," Jay said, and smiled.

"Wait right here." Briefly, the clerk's fingers drummed the top of a four-suiter. "I'll be gone a while, you know?"

Jay removed his slouch hat and wiped his forehead with his fingers. The hat had been a comfort in the chill air of the street, but the store was warm.

None of the milling shoppers nearby were giving him any attention, as far as he could judge; but, of course, they would not. If he was being watched, it would be by someone some distance away, or by an electronic device of some kind. Looking around for the device, he found three cameras, none obtrusive but none even cursorily concealed. City cops, store security, and somebody else—for a minute or two Jay tried to think who the third watchers might be, but no speculation seemed plausible.

Men's Wear was next to Luggage. He wandered over.

"What do you want?" The clerk was young and scrawny and looked angry.

With your build, you'd better be careful, Jay thought; but he kept the reflection to himself. Aloud he said, "I had to buy this raincoat in a hurry. I thought I might get a better one here."

"Black?"

Jay shook his head. "Another color. What've you got?"

"Blue and green, okay?"

"Green," Jay decided, "if it's not too light."

The clerk stamped over to a rack and held up a coat. "Lincoln green. Okay?"

"Okay," Jay said.

"Only if you turn it inside out, it's navy. See?"

Jay took the coat from him and examined it. "There are slits over the pockets. I like that."

"Same pockets for both colors," the clerk sounded as if he hoped that would kill the sale.

"I'll take it."

The clerk glanced at a tag. "Large-tall. Okay?"

"Okay," Jay said again.

"You want a bag?"

Jay nodded. A stout plastic bag might prove useful.

The clerk was getting one when the clerk from Luggage returned. He frowned until Jay hurried over.

"This's what we call a wheeled duffel," the luggage clerk explained. "You got a handle there. You can carry it, or you got this handle here that pops out, and wheels on the other end. Forty-four inches, the biggest we've got. You got a store card?"

"Cash," Jay told him.

"You want a card? Ten percent off if you take it."

Jay shook his head.

"Up to you. Hear about that guy with all the cash?"

Jay shook his head again. "What guy?"

"On holo. They gave him a wad so somebody'll rip him off. Only they see what he sees, so I don't think it's going to work. They'd have a description."

"They see what he sees?"

"Sure," the clerk said. "It's his augment, you know? Anytime he sees you they see you."

"Can they spy on people like that?"

"They don't give a rat's ass," the clerk said.

The angry Men's Wear clerk had vanished. Jay's new reversible raincoat lay on a counter in a plastic bag. He unzipped his new wheeled duffel and put the raincoat inside.

Outside it was growing dark; beggars wielding plastic broomhandles and pieces of conduit were working the shopping crowd, shouting threats at anyone who appeared vulnerable.

The little park was an oasis of peace by comparison. Jay sat down on a bench, the wheeled duffel between his knees, and waited. Traffic crawled past, largely invisible behind the hurrying, steam-breathing pedestrians. Some of the drivers looked as angry as the Men's Wear clerk; but most were empty-faced, resigned to driving their cubical vanettes and hulking CUVs at four miles per hour or less.

"Ain't you cold?" An old man with a runny nose had taken the other end of Jay's bench.

Jay shook his head.

"I am. I'm damned cold."

Jay said nothing.

"They got shelters down there," the old man pointed, "ta keep us off the streets. Only you get ripped off soon's you go to sleep. Right. An' they don't give you nothin' ta eat, either. So if you was ta give me somethin', I could get me somethin' an' go down there an' sleep without bein' hungry. Right."

"You could get a bottle of wine, too," Jay said.

"They won't sell it 'less you got the card." The old man was silent for a moment, sucking almost toothless gums. "Only you're c'rect, I'd like to."

"Sure," Jay said.

"I used ta get Social Security, only it don't come no more. There's some kind a problem with it."

"You could get yourself a sweater, too," Jay suggested. "Winter's just getting started."

"If there was enough I could," the old man agreed. "I could sleep in one a them boxes, too, 'stead a the shelter."

"A bod mod."

"Yeah, right."

"I slept in one last night." Jay considered. "I didn't like it, but they're probably better than the shelter."

"Right."

"You said you were cold. Would you like my coat?"

The old man appeared to hesitate. "You said you wasn't. You will be if you give it."

Jay stood up, pressing rubberoid buttons through plastic buttonholes. On Fortieth someone leaned down on the horn, a muted keening that suggested a dying whale.

"You're givin' it?"

"I am," Jay said. He held it out by the shoulders. "Put it on."

The old man pushed an arm into one of the capacious sleeves. "Lady over there wants you, is what I think."

"Those cars aren't moving anyhow." Jay waited until the old man's other arm was in the other sleeve, then fished a hundred out of his hunting coat. "If I give you this, are you going to tell those beggars with the sticks?"

"Hell, no," the old man said. "They'd take it."

"Right." Jay put the hundred in his hand and sprinted out of the park, thrust shoppers aside with the duffel, and strode out into the motionless traffic.

A red-haired woman in a dark gray vanette was waving urgently. He opened the right front door and tossed in the duffel, got in, and sat down, smelling dusty upholstery and stale perfume.

"Don't look at me," she said. "Look straight ahead."

Jay did.

"Anytime you're with me, you don't look at me. You got that? Never. No matter what I say, no matter what I do, don't look."

Assuming that she was looking at him, Jay nodded.

"That's the first thing. They've already seen me on the phone, but the less they see of me the better."

"Thank you for coming to get me," Jay said.

"I wasn't going to," the woman told him bitterly, "but you knew I would. You knew I'd have to."

Jay shook his head again, still without looking in her direction. "I hoped you would, that's all. You said you wouldn't, but after I'd hung up I decided that if I were you I'd have said the same thing, so they wouldn't be waiting for us if they were listening in."

"They were listening. They're listening now. They can hear everything you hear and see everything you see."

Mostly to himself, Jay nodded. "I should have known it would be something like that."

"They put our call on the news. That dump in Greentree? There's a mob there. I went there thinking I'd wait for you, and there must have been five hundred people, and more coming all the time."

"I'm sorry," Jay said, and meant it.

"I'll have to get a new dump, that's all." The woman fell silent; he sensed that her jaw was clenched. "Anyway, I came. I probably shouldn't have, but I did. Did you see my license plate?"

He searched his memory. "No."

"That's good. Don't look at it when you get out, okay?"

"Okay."

"Did you think Jane MacKann was my real name?"

"It isn't?" The thought had not occurred to him.

"Hell, no. This isn't even my car, but the guy I borrowed it from is kind of a friend, and he'd have to steal new plates. So all they know is a green car, and there are lots of them."

"My color vision's a little off," Jay told her.

"Yeah, sure. A lot of guys have that." The woman paused to blow the vanette's horn, futilely, at the semibus ahead of her. "Anyway, I came and got you. So you owe me."

Jay fished a hundred from a pocket and gave it to her.

"This isn't for your heat. This's just for the ride. You tell me where, and I'll take you there and drop you, okay? That's what you're paying me for now."

"If I tell you, I'll be telling them as well?"

"I guess so. I didn't watch it, but that's what the people I talked to said."

"Suppose I were to write it on a piece of paper without looking at the paper. Then I could pass it to you without looking at you, and you could look at it."

The woman considered. "That ought to work. I've got a pen in my purse, if you've got paper."

"I do." Jay hesitated. "You said heat. I want a gun."

"Sure. That's heat."

"Slang."

"No, it's just what everybody says. Or its tons if you got more than one. Like, I got fifteen tons stashed around now. So immediate delivery on them. What kind you want?"

Jay stroked his jaw, trying to reduce a hundred dreams to the pinpoint of a single gun small enough to fit into his wheeled duffel.

"Lemme explain my pricing structure to you while you're thinking it over," the woman said, sounding very professional indeed. "Top of the line, I got submachine guns and machine pistols. That's mostly nine millimeter, but there's some other stuff, too. Like right now, on hand, I've got this very cool little machine pistol that's seven sixty-five."

She had paused to see whether he was interested; he sensed her scrutiny.

"It's what we used to call a thirty-two, only this one's got seven point sixty-five on the slide."

He shook his head and said, "I understand."

"Okay, under that is your high-cap autos. Only they're not really full auto, they're semi. One I got's a nine that holds seventeen rounds. Honest to God. Twenty-five hundred for any of those."

Jay did not speak.

"Where you draw the line is eleven, okay? If it holds eleven or under, it's low cap. Twelve or better is high."

"These are handguns you're talking about."

"Yeah. Sure. Low cap is two thousand. Or eighteen hundred if it only holds eight. There's a lot of these single-stack forty-fives around, and eight is all they'll take. So eighteen hundred for one in good shape. Then if you want a real buy, you get a revolver. I've seen some that hold eight, but it's mostly six, and nine times out of ten six will do it if you're careful. Twelve, thirteen hundred and you can get two, so that gives you twelve rounds and you got two guns in case one breaks. It's a really good deal, because most people are too dumb to see that it is."

"I need a rifle," Jay told her. "Don't you have any rifles?"

"The feds melted them down, or most of them," the woman said dubiously.

"I know. But I hunt my food, for the most part." Jay cleared his throat. "I'm not from around here at all. I'm from Pennsylvania."

"So you don't really want to shoot anybody?"

"Deer," he told her. "Deer and black bear. Rabbits and so forth now and then. Birds. A shotgun would be better for those, but I can't carry both back with me, and if I had a rifle I could shoot birds sitting sometimes." Doubting her comprehension, he added, "Ducks on the water. That sort of thing."

"I don't have one in my stock. I don't have a shotgun, either, and the shells are really hard to get these days."

He nodded sadly. "I suspected that they would be."

"Listen, we're just sitting here in this traffic. Would it bother you too much if I banged on my laptop some? Maybe I can find something for you."

"No. Go ahead."

"Okay, turn around the other way. Not toward me, away from me. Push slow against the harness."

He did, and the vanette announced, "I am required by law to caution you that your chance of survival in a high-speed crash has been reduced by sixty-two percent."

The woman said, "We're not even crawling, you idiot."

"The vehicle that strikes me may be traveling at a high rate of speed, however," the vanette replied primly.

Jay had contrived to turn 180 degrees, so that he was kneeling in his seat and peering into the immensely cluttered rear of the vanette.

"Chinese red," the woman said.

He picked up the only red object he saw and held it up, careful not to look at her. "Is this it?"

"Sure."

Turning away from her again, he resumed a normal posture. "Would you like me to open it for you?"

"You can't. There's a thumbprint lock." She took it, and from the corner of his eye he saw her prop it against the wheel and plug a wire into the instrument panel. "You watch traffic, okay? If the car in front moves, tell me."

"All right," he said, and added, "Where are we going?"

"Nowhere." She sounded abstracted, and he heard the quick, hard tapping of her fingers on the keys. "We're going nowhere, Skeeter." More taps, and a little sound of disgust.

"They know that name already, huh? From when you phoned." The woman appeared to hesitate. "Yeah, I guess they have to. You can call me Mack."

"All right. Can't you find me a rifle, Mack?"

"Not so far. I got one more place I can try, though." She tapped keys again.

He said, "The car in front's moving."

"About time."

"Can I ask a question?"

"Sure. You can ask me a thousand, only I might not answer any."

"Who is *they*?"

He felt her incomprehension.

"You said they probably know my name. Did you mean the holovid people who gave me the upgrade?"

"Globnet."

"Yes, Globnet. Was that who you meant, Mack?"

"No. The feds. Big Daddy."

"So they can collect taxes on my money? I haven't refused to pay them. I haven't even been asked to pay."

Traffic had stopped again. Jay heard the rattle of its hard plastic case as the woman shifted her laptop back to the steering wheel. "They know you won't pay. Say, would you like a carbine? He's got a carbine."

Jay felt his heart sink. "Not as much as a rifle. Hasn't anybody got a rifle?"

"Not now. They might have something later, but maybe not. You never know."

Unwilling to surrender the new rifle he needed, Jay changed the subject. "How could the government possibly know I won't pay the tax?"

"How much did they give you? The holovid people?"

"That's my affair."

"Okay. Whatever it was? Have you still got it all?"

"No," Jay said. "I gave you a hundred."

"So you don't. So you wouldn't pay the whole tax because you couldn't."

He felt her hand on his arm.

"They want it all. The works. You'll find out. Not all you've got now, the most you ever had. Traffic like this—how many choppers do you think we ought to hear?"

He shook his head.

"About one every hour, maybe a little more. Three in an hour, tops. They been goin' over every three or four minutes lately. I just timed the last two on the dash clock. About three minutes."

From the corner of his eye he saw her hand reach out to rap the instrument panel. "Hey, you! Wake up there. I want you to open the sunroof."

The sunroof slid smoothly back, and the interior of the vanette was abruptly frigid. "Watch them awhile," the woman told Jay, "it'll keep you from looking at me."

He did, craning his neck to see the bleak winter sky where the towering office buildings had failed to obscure it. "Won't our open roof attract their attention?"

"I don't think so. There must be a couple of thousand people stuck in this mess who're wondering why they're flying over all the time."

"Black helicopters." Jay spoke half to himself. "Out where I live, way out in the country, people make jokes about black helicopters. Somebody in town did once, that's what I'm trying to say, one time when I came into town. He said the black helicopters would get me, and laughed, and I've remembered it for some reason."

"Sure."

"It's supposed to be like flying saucers, something crazy people see. But here in the city it's real. I caught sight of one a moment ago."

"Sure," the woman repeated. "They're looking for drugs out there is what we hear. Flying over the farmers' fields to see if they're growing pot in the middle of the cornfield. They're not really black, I guess. People who've seen them up close say they're UPS brown, really. But they sure look black, up there."

"They must have binoculars—no, something better than binoculars. Isn't there a chance they'll see me down here and recognize me?"

"Mmm," the woman said.

"If the government is really after me at all, I mean. The holovid people said it would be criminals." Jay paused, recalling his conversations with Smith. "Mostly criminals, unless I put the money in a bank."

"Okay, close it," the woman told the vanette, and the sunroof slid shut as smoothly as it had opened. "You're right about the binoculars," she told Jay. "They'll have something better, something they won't let us own. But I'm right about the feds being after you. Ten minutes after the broadcast, they'll have had a dozen people on it, and by this time there could be a couple of hundred. They'll be another news tonight at eleven, and we'd better watch it."

Jay nodded. "If we can."

"We can. The big question's how good a look they've had at you. Been looking in any mirrors lately?"

"Since I got the upgrade?" Certain already that he knew the answer, he squirmed in his seat. "Let me think. Yes, once. In a rest room in the Globnet Building. I was looking at the new stars in my screen, though. Not at my own face."

"You will have seen your face, though," the woman said thoughtfully. "I'd like to know if they broadcast that. In a toilet? Maybe not."

"I'd like to watch the news tonight. I know how silly this sounds, but I can't visualize it." Apologetically he added, "I haven't watched much holovid."

"I'd like to, too," the woman said, "because I haven't seen this either, just had people tell me. I'll fix it."

"Thanks."

"What about this carbine? Do you want it?"

"I don't know. Perhaps I'd better take it, if there's nothing else. No rifles."

"They're harder to hide, so the feds have about cleaned them out, and there's not much call for them. Later I might be able to find one for you."

"Later I won't be here. What caliber is it?"

"Forty. Same as a forty-caliber pistol is what he says, and uses the same magazine." She pressed more buttons. "It folds up, too."

"A folding stock?"

"Doesn't say. Just that it's thirty inches long to shoot and sixteen folded. What are you grinning about?"

Jay patted the duffel. "I was afraid this wouldn't be long enough to hold the rifle I was hoping to get."

She grunted. "Well, you could carry this under that coat. Put a loop of string over your shoulder and fold it over the string. It wouldn't be as handy as a pistol, but you could do it."

"I'd rather hang it by the butt, if it will stay folded." Jay was silent for a moment, thinking. "I'll have to see it first. I don't suppose that gadget gives an effective range?"

More buttons. "A hundred and fifty meters is what he says."

"Huh."

"Probably got a lot of barrel. Twelve, fourteen inches. Something like that, and even out of a pistol barrel a forty travels pretty fast."

"I imagine he's stretching it," Jay said slowly, "even so, most of the shots I get are under a hundred yards, and those that are longer aren't a lot longer."

"Going to take it?"

He nodded. "I've been using a bow. A bow I made myself and arrows I made myself, too. Did I tell you?"

"I don't think so. I thought maybe you had a shotgun already. You hunt a lot."

He nodded again. When ten minutes had passed, and they were crawling along steadily, he asked, "Where are we going?"

"Dump I got. You know that address? Greentree?"

"There were people there, you said."

"We're not going there. I just wanted to say I don't live there. It's a place I got where I make sales sometimes, that's all. Where we're going now's like that, only uptown."

The sunroof slid smoothly back, and a woman in an orange jumpsuit dropped into the rear seat. Jay released his seat harness to turn and look at her, and the vanette said, "I am required by law to caution you that your chance of survival in a high-speed crash has been reduced by seventy percent."

The woman who sold guns snapped, "Shut your sunroof!"

The woman in the orange jumpsuit had cleared a space for herself on the seat. She removed her helmet, shook out long, dark hair, and smiled at Jay. "I'm sure you know who I am."

He tried to return the smile. "I have no idea."

"Who I represent, I mean. My name is Hayfa, Hayfa Washington." She ran her finger down the front seam of her jumpsuit, reached inside, and produced a sparkling business card. "Look at this, please. Read it carefully."

Captain H. Washington
Fifth Airborne Brigade
Federal Revenue & Security Services
0067 5667-1339
www.hayfawings.gov

"You may keep the card, of course."

"I'd like to," Jay told her. "I've never seen such a beautiful one."

She smiled again. "You have a great deal of money belonging to our Federal Government. One hundred thousand, if not more."

The other woman said, "He thinks it belongs to him."

"I do," Jay said. "It was paid me by Globnet."

"Which didn't own it either," Hayfa Washington told him.

Jay said, "They ran advertisements, as I understand it, and included it in a lot of their news broadcasts. I was at a friend's house and saw one. My rifle's broken, and I need a new ax and—" For a moment, her expression silenced him. "And other things. You don't care about that, do you?"

"Not really."

"So I wrote a letter and my friend e-mailed it, with some pictures of me and my cabin. They said that if I'd come here and talk to them, they might give me the money."

"A hundred thousand."

"Yes, one hundred thousand. I borrowed money for bus fare, and I came. And they talked to me and gave it to me."

"No, they didn't." The woman in the orange jumpsuit looked sincere and somewhat troubled; she leaned toward Jay as she spoke. "They couldn't, you see. It didn't belong to them. All money belongs to the Federal Government, Jay. People—people who own small businesses, particularly—speak of making money. Quite often they use those exact words. But if you'll think about it, you'll see that they are not true. All money is made by Government, and so all money belongs to Government, which allows citizens like you and me to have some, sometimes, so we can buy the things we need. But Government keeps title to all of it, and by the very nature of things it can't lose title to any of it. I've most of last month's pay on me right now." She paused, extracting a hard plastic portemoney from an interior pocket of her jumpsuit.

"You're saying that what they paid isn't mine at all."

"Correct. Because no money really belongs to anyone except Government, which issued it." The woman in the orange jumpsuit opened her portemoney, took out bills, and fanned them. "Here's mine. You see? Eleven five-hundreds, three one-hundreds, and some twenties, tens, fives, and singles. This is what our Government lets me have, because my taxes were already deducted from my check."

The other woman said, "Except sales tax."

"Correct, although sales tax is actually paid by the seller. There's a pretense that the buyer pays, but we needn't get into that. The point is that I have this money, although it's not mine, and I'm showing it to you. This is what I've got, Jay. Now will you, in an act of good faith, show what you have to me?"

"No," Jay said.

"I'm sorry to hear that, very sorry." The woman in the orange jumpsuit paused as though expecting her expression of regret to change his answer. He said nothing more; neither did the other woman.

"There's an easy, painless way to handle this," the woman in the orange jumpsuit said. "You could turn the money over to me now. I'd count it and give you a receipt for it that would be backed by the full faith and credit of the Federal Government. When the Government had decided how much should be returned to you, it would be sent to you. I'm sure there would be enough for a new ax. Not for a rifle, though. The danger a rifle would pose to you and your family would far outweigh any possible benefit to you."

"They're against the law," the other woman remarked a little dryly.

"Yes, they are, for that very reason." The woman in the orange jumpsuit spoke to Jay again. "You wouldn't have to do prison time. I think I can promise you that. There probably wouldn't even be a trial. Won't you please hand that money—the Government's money—to me to count? Now?"

He shook his head.

"You want to think it over. I understand." The woman in the orange jumpsuit tapped the other woman's shoulder. "Where are we? Ninety-fifth? You can let me out now. Just stop anywhere."

The vanette stopped, causing several vehicles behind it to blow their horns, and the woman in the orange jumpsuit opened its sliding door and stepped out. "You've got my card, Jay. Call anytime."

He nodded and shut the door, the vanette lurched forward, and the woman driving it said, "Thank you for appearing on our show tonight."

Jay nodded, although he could not be sure she was looking at him. "That was for the holovid, wasn't it? She was so pretty."

"Prettier than me?" There was a half-humorous challenge in the question.

"I don't know," Jay told her. "You don't want me to look at you."

"Well, she was, and she wasn't just pretty, she was beautiful, the way the Government wants you to think all the feds look, beautiful women and good-looking men. She'll make the next news for sure. I wouldn't be surprised if they run everything she said. You still want to see it?"

"Yes," he said. "Certainly."

"Okay, we will. I've got a place a couple of blocks from here."

"What about my carbine? I'd like to buy it tonight."

"He's got to get it from wherever he's got it stashed. Ammo, too. I said fifty rounds."

"More," Jay told her. He considered. "Five hundred, if he has them."

"Okay, I'll tell him." The vanette pulled into an alley, and the laptop returned to the steering wheel. When the woman who sold guns had closed it again, she said, "Ten years ago I could have stood up to her. I was a knockout. You don't have to believe me, but I was."

He said he believed her.

"But I had two kids. I put on some weight then and I've never got it off, and I quit taking care of my complexion for a while. You haven't been looking at me."

"No," he said.

"That's good, but now don't look at anything else either, okay? I want you to shut your eyes and keep them shut. Just lean back and relax."

He nodded, closed his eyes, and leaned back as she had suggested, discovering that he was very tired.

As if it were in another room, her fingers tapped the instrument panel. Softly she said, "Hey, you. Open your sunroof."

Cold poured over him like water, and he shivered. She grunted, the vanette shook, and the seat he had shared with her sagged; after a little thought, he decided that she was standing on it with her head and shoulders thrust up through the open sunroof.

Sometime after that, the sunroof closed again and she left the vanette, got into the rear seat, and rummaged among her possessions there.

"Okay," she said. "Only don't open your eyes."

He said that he would not.

"I figured she might have planted some sort of bug, you know? Something to tell the feds where we went. Only it would have to be on the roof or in back, and I couldn't find it, so probably they figure you're all the bug they need. We're going to drive around some now, and I want you to keep your eyes shut the whole time. We'll be turning corners and doubling back and all that, but don't look."

They "drove around" for what seemed an hour; but though there were indeed a number of turns, Jay got the impression that the point at which they stopped was miles from the one at which he had closed his eyes.

"All right." She tapped the instrument panel. "No lights." The engine died; the soft *snick* he heard was presumably the ignition key backing out. It rattled against other keys as she removed it and dropped it into her purse. "You can look around. Just don't look at me."

He did. "It's dark."

"Yeah. Well, it gets dark early this time of year. But it's about eight o'clock. You don't have a watch."

"No," he said.

"Me neither. There's the dash clock if I'm driving, and the holovid will give it if I'm inside. Come on."

There was no doorman, but the lobby into which she led him was fairly clean. He said, "You don't really live here."

"Hell, no. But sometimes I sleep here, and I'm going to sleep here tonight. We both are."

He wondered whether she meant together. Aloud, he said, "You don't really live in Greentree Gardens, either. That's what you told me."

"Nope."

"I would think it would be horribly expensive to rent so many places."

The doors of an elevator shook and groaned, and at last rattled open. They stepped inside.

"It costs, but not nearly as much as you'd think. These old twentieth-century buildings are all rent controlled."

He said, "I didn't know that."

"So what it is, is the grease you've got to pay the agent to get in. That can be quite a chunk. You don't understand grease, do you?"

"No," he said.

"I could see you didn't. It's under-the-counter money, money the agent can put in his pocket and not pay taxes on. Money's like three, four times more without taxes."

The elevator ground to a halt, and they got out.

"So I pay that—I've got to—and the first month's rent. I buy used furniture, not very much, and move in. Then I don't pay anything else for as long as I can get by with it."

The keys were out again, jangling in her hand.

"That could be six months. It could be a year. When I get the feeling they're about ready to take me to court, I pay another month, maybe, or half a month. It's rent controlled, like I said, so it's not much."

She opened a door that had long ago been damaged by water. "My utility bills aren't much because I'm hardly ever here, and I don't complain or cause trouble. See? And they know if they go to court the judge will find out I just paid something and tell them to give me more time. So they don't. You want to turn that thing on? It's almost time for the nine o'clock."

He did, fumbling with the controls until he found the right control.

"It's an old one," she said apologetically.

A shimmering beach half filled the stale air of the dingy room; on it, young women with spectacular figures tossed a multicolored ball, at last throwing it into the ocean and swimming out to retrieve it.

"You were expecting voice control, right? I got it at the Salvation Army store. They fixed it up so it would work again."

He nodded. A brunette with flashing eyes had gotten the ball. She threw it to a blonde, tracing a high arc of red, green, and yellow against the clear blue sky.

"This's a commercial," the woman who sold guns told him, "See how their makeup stays on and their hair stays nice even in the water? That's what you're supposed to be looking at."

He nodded again.

An elderly sofa groaned as she sat down. "You want the sound? It's the next knob up, only they're going to be talking about hair spray and stuff."

He shook his head.

"Fine with me. Only we better turn it on when the news comes on."

He did, and by the time he had taken a seat next to her, a handsome black man and a beautiful Chinese woman faced them across a polished double desk. Both smiled in friendly fashion. "Thank you for inviting us into your living room," the black man said.

The Chinese woman added, "There's a lot of news tonight. What do you say we get to it, Phil?"

Phil nodded, abruptly serious. "There certainly is, Lee-Anne. Johns Hopkins has a new artificial heart so small you can have it implanted before your present heart gives out."

Lee-Anne said, "There's the cat in the mayor's Christmas tree, too. I like that story. The firemen way up on their little ladders look like ornaments."

Phil smiled. "You're right, they do. We've got a review of the new Edward Spake film, too. *The Trinidad Communiqué*. It got raves at Cannes."

"Aunt Betsy's going to show us how to make cranberry flan for the holidays."

"Almost live coverage of the big parade in Orlando."

"And a peek in on the Hundred Thousand Man. He's had a little visit from FR&SS."

"That's you," the woman who sold guns told Jay. "It's going to be a while before they get to you, though. You want something to eat?"

"Yes." He had not realized how hungry he was.

"I don't keep much besides beer in these places. Usually I just phone out. Pizza okay?"

He had not eaten pizza since college. He said it was.

"You've got to get out of here, 'cause I'll have to give the address. Why don't you go in the kitchen?"

A plastic model of a large artery enclosing a very small artificial heart stood in the middle of the room. He nodded and went into the kitchen.

"Bring me a beer, okay?"

The refrigerator was white, as his mother's had been; he knew vaguely that no one had white refrigerators now, though he did not know why. It held beer in squat plastic bulbs and a deli container of potato salad. He opened a bulb over the small and dirty sink, afraid that the foam might overflow the bulb. When he could no longer hear her voice, he called, "Can I come back in?"

"Sure."

He brought her the beer, and she said, "Pepperoni, hot peppers, and onions, okay? You can have a beer, too."

He shook his head. "Not until the food gets here."

"Don't you think it's coming?"

It had not even occurred to him. He said, "Of course it is," and returned to the kitchen to get a beer for himself.

"I need to make another call. I got to call my baby-sitter and tell her I won't be back tonight. But I'll wait till we see you."

He nodded, careful not to look at her. A towering Christmas tree, shrunken by distance, disappeared into the ceiling. Little firemen in yellow coveralls and Day-Glo red helmets clambered over it like elves.

"I turned off the sound so I could call. All right?"

"Sure," he said.

"Maybe you'd better turn it back on now."

He did, getting it too loud then scaling it back. Reduced to the size of a child's battery-powered CUV, an immense float trundled through the room, appearing at one wall and disappearing into the other while doll-size women feigned to conceal their nakedness with bouquets from which they tossed flowers to the onlookers. Lee-Anne's voice said, ". . . la tourista fiesta queen and her court, Phil. They say the fiesta is worth about three hundred million to the city of Orlando."

Phil's voice replied, "I don't doubt it. And speaking of money, Lee-Anne, here's a lady trying to collect some."

A good-looking woman in a skintight orange jumpsuit rappelled down a mountain of air, bouncing and swaying. Jay said, "I didn't see that."

"They were shooting from a helicopter, probably," the woman who sold guns told him.

It took about half a second for him to realize that by "shooting" she intended the taking of pictures; in that half second, the swaying woman on the rope became the helmetless woman he recalled, shaking out her hair in the rear seat of the vanette. "You have a great deal of money belonging to our Federal Government. One hundred thousand, if not more."

The other woman said, "He thinks it belongs to him." Then his own voice, just as he heard it when he spoke: "It was paid me by Globnet."

Their conversation continued, but he paid little attention to what they said. He watched Hayfa Washington's face, discovering that he had forgotten (or had never known) how beautiful she had been.

Too soon it was over, and a woman in a spotless gingham apron coalesced from light to talk about lemon custard. The woman who sold guns said, "You want to turn that off now?" and he did.

"I'm going to call my sitter, okay? You can stay, though. I won't tell her where I am."

"I'll go anyway," he said, and returned to the kitchen. Faintly, through the tiny dining nook and the door he had closed behind him, he heard her tell someone, "It's me, Val. How are the kids?"

The card was in his shirt pocket, under the hunting coat he had been careful not to remove. "Captain H. Washington, Fifth Airborne Brigade." He turned it over, and discovered that her picture was on the reverse, and that her soul was in her huge dark eyes.

"Hey!" the other woman called from the living room. "The pizza's here. Bring out a couple more bulbs."

He did, and opened hers for her while she opened the pizza box on the rickety coffee table, then returned to the kitchen for plastic knives and forks, and paper napkins.

"If we eat in there we'll have to sit facing," she said. "So I figured in here. We can sit side-by-each, like in the car. It'll be easier."

He said that was fine, and asked about her children.

"Oh, they're okay. My girlfriend is sitting them. She's going to take them over to her house till I get back. Ron's eight and Julie's seven. I had them right together, like. Then we broke up, and he didn't want any part of them. You know how that is."

"No," he said. "No, I don't."

"Haven't you ever been married? Or lived with a woman?"

He shook his head.

"Well, why not?"

"I've never been rich, handsome, or exciting, that's all." He paused, thinking. "All right, I'm rich now, or at least have something like riches. But I never did before."

"Neither was he, but he got me."

Jay shrugged.

"He was nice, and he was fun to be with, and he had a pretty good job. Only after the divorce his company sent him overseas and he stopped paying support."

"I've never had a job," Jay said.

"Really?"

"Really. My friends call me a slacker." He found that he was smiling. "Dad called me a woods bum. He's dead now."

"I'm sorry."

"So am I, in a way. We seldom got along, but well . . ." He shrugged and drank beer.

"I know."

"He sent me to college. I thought I was a pretty good baseball player in those days, and a pretty good football player, but I didn't make either team. I tried hard, but I didn't make the cut."

She spoke with her mouth full. "Tha's too bad."

"It was. If I had, it would have been different. I know it would. The way it was, I worked hard up until I was close to graduation." The pizza was half gone. He picked up a square center piece that looked good, bit into it, and chewed and swallowed, tasting only the bitterness of empty years.

"What happened then?" she asked.

"When I was a senior? Nothing, really. It was just that I realized I had been working like a dog to acquire knowledge that nobody wanted. Not even me. That if I did everything right and aced my exams and got my Master's I'd end up teaching in the high school in the little Pennsylvania town where we lived, or someplace like it. I'd teach math and chemistry, and maybe coach the baseball team, and it would be kids who were going to work on farms or get factory jobs when they got out of school. I said to hell with it."

"I don't blame you."

"I went back home and told my folks some story. They didn't believe it, and I don't even know what it was now. I got my camping stuff together and went out into the woods. I had a little tent, an air mattress, and a sleeping bag. The first winter was rough, so I built a cabin about as big as this room in a place where nobody would ever find it." He paused, recalling Hayfa Washington and the helicopter that had let her down on a rope and somehow made their sunroof open. "It's federal land, really. National Forest. I don't think about that much, but it is."

The woman shrugged. "If all the money's theirs, all the land is, too, I guess."

"I suppose you're right." He put his half-eaten piece of pizza back in the box.

"You just live out there? Like that?"

"It was always going to be for a little while."

"But you never came back in?"

"Oh, sometimes I do. For my father's funeral, and then for mom's. She died about a month after he did."

"I'm sorry."

"I was, too. But they left everything to me—I was the only kid. The house and so on. The car and a little money. I sold the house and the car, and I don't spend much. I hunt deer and snare small game, and that's what I eat, mostly. Wild plants in the summer." He smiled. "I use dead leaves for toilet paper."

"Do you want to know about me?"

"If you want to tell me."

"Well, I never got to go to college. I was a clerk in a store and a waitress. Then I got married and had the kids, and you know about that. You want to know how I got started selling guns? A friend wanted to know where she could buy one, so I asked this guy I knew, and he sent me to somebody else. And that guy said he'd sell to me only not to her, because the guy that sent me didn't know her. So I said, okay, sell it to me, and I paid him, and I told him I'd get my money back from her. And he said you ought to charge her about a hundred more, I would. So I charged her fifty over. And after a couple weeks, I guess it was, she sent somebody else to me, another woman in her building that was scared worse than she was. Now here I am."

Softly he said, "I steal from campers, sometimes. From hunters, too. That's how I got this coat. A hunter got hot, and hung it on a tree."

She nodded as though she had expected no less. "You want to get me another beer?"

The telephone buzzed as he rose; a thin-lipped man who wore a business suit as though it were a uniform said, "You still haven't called Captain Washington."

"No," Jay admitted. "No, I haven't."

"We don't like to arrest people over tax matters. You may have heard that."

Jay shook his head.

"We don't. Yet more than half the prison population is made up of tax offenders." The thin-lipped man vanished.

"They know where we are," Jay told the woman.

"Yeah. Get me that beer, will you?"

"Shouldn't we leave?"

She did not speak, and after half a minute or so he brought her another beer from the kitchen.

"Here's how I see it," she said when he (with face averted) held out the beer. "Let me go through it, and you tell me if you think I'm wrong.

"To start with, how do they know we're here? Answer—that FR&SS woman put a bug on our car, I just didn't find it. That means that if we take the car we might as well stay here. And if we don't take the car, we'll have to go on foot. They'll have people all around this building by now waiting to tail us, and with the streets pretty well empty it would be a cinch."

"Where would we go?" he asked.

"Damned if I know. We might end up walking all night. Next question. Are they about to break down the door and bust us? Answer—no, because they wouldn't have called first if they were. The FR&SS woman made the news, she was good-looking, it was dramatic, and blah blah. It was meant to. Now they'll be watching to see if that phone call makes it. I think what they'll do is get a little rougher every time, because every time they come around the chance that it'll make Globnet's news show gets slimmer. The woman was really pretty nice, on purpose. The guy on the phone wasn't so nice, and next time's going to be worse. Or that's how it looks to me."

"You're probably right. But you're leaving something out. They knew that we were in this apartment, and not in some other apartment in this building."

"Piece of cake. The guys staking it out talked to the pizza man. 'Who paid you?' 'Well, she was a middle-aged woman with red hair.' 'Anybody else in there?' 'Yeah, I could hear somebody moving around in back.' 'Okay, that's them.' They got a look at me when we talked on the phone, and the fed that got into our car probably described us."

Jay said, "You're not middle-aged."

She laughed. "When you've got two kids in school, you're middle-aged. How old are you?"

"Forty-one."

"See, you're middle-aged, too. You're older than I am." To his amazement, her hand had found his.

They kissed, he with his eyes shut; an hour later, turning off the lights in the musty little bedroom hid the stains on the wallpaper and let him look at her face.

Next morning she said, "I want to have breakfast with you. Isn't that funny?"

Not knowing what else to do, he nodded.

"I never used to have breakfast with Chuck. I'd have to get up early to see about the kids, and he'd sleep till ten or eleven. After he left me I'd have a boyfriend sometimes. Only we'd do it and he'd get up and go. Back to his wife, or where he lived. They weren't ever around for breakfast."

"All right," Jay said, "let's eat breakfast."

"We don't have to take the car. You don't mind walking three or four blocks?"

He smiled. "No."

"Okay. We've got a couple things to settle, and maybe the safest way is while we're walking. I don't know how serious they are, but if they're serious at all they'll have bugged this place while we slept. The café'd be better, but out on the street's probably as good as it gets. Keep your voice down, don't move your lips a lot when you talk, and if it's serious hold your hand in front of your face."

He nodded, and seeing blowing snow through a dirty windowpane, pulled the reversible coat he had bought the day before out of his wheeled duffel and put it on over the hunting coat that still (almost to his dismay) held his money.

Out in the cold and windy street she murmured, "They'll figure we're going back, so first thing is we won't. If they have a man watch it and maybe another guy watch the car, they could get a little short-handed. We can hope, anyway."

He nodded, although it seemed to him that if there were a homing device in the vanette it would not be necessary to have anyone watch it.

"When we go out of the café we'll split up, see? I'll give you the address—where to go and how to get there. Don't look to see if they're following you. If they're good you won't see them. Just lose them if you can."

"I hope I can," he said.

The little restaurant was small and crowded and noisy. They ate waffles in a tiny booth, he striving to keep his eyes on his plate.

"The way you lose a tail is you do something unexpected where the tail can't follow you," she said. "Say there's a cab, but just the one. You grab it and have him take you someplace fast, all right? Only not to the address I'm going to give you. Someplace else."

He nodded.

"I thought maybe you were going to say there's got to be a thousand cabbies, and they can't talk to them all. Only every cab's got a terminal in it, and it records when fares get picked up, and where they're going. Like if they know you caught the cab at eleven oh two, all they've got to do is check cabs that picked up somebody right about then. It's maybe a dozen cabs, then they can find out where you went."

"I understand," he said.

"Or maybe you go to the john. He's not going to come in the john with you because you'd get too good a look at him. He'll wait outside. Well, if it's got two doors you duck in one and out the other. Or climb out the window, if there's a window. It gets you ten or fifteen minutes to get away."

"Okay," he said.

She had taken a pen and a small notebook from her purse; she scribbled in it, tore out the page, and handed it to him. "Where we're going to meet," she said. "Don't look at it till you're almost there."

He was too stunned to say anything.

"You're finished."

He managed to say, "Yes, but you're not."

"I'm awfully nervous, and when I'm nervous I don't eat a lot. I look at you and see the two dots, and I know they're seeing what you do, your sausages or whatever. Let's go."

Out on the street again, in the cutting wind, she squeezed his hand. "See that subway entrance up ahead? Maybe you can see the escalator through the glass."

"Yes," he said.

"We're going to walk right toward it. When we get there, I'll go in and down. You keep walking."

He did, badly tempted to watch as the moving steps carried her away but staring resolutely ahead.

Soon traffic thinned, and the sidewalks grew dirtier. The vehicles filling every parking space were older and shabbier. He went into a corner store then and asked the middle-aged black man behind the counter for a package of gum. "This a bad neighborhood?"

The counterman did not smile. "It's not good."

"I heard it was really bad," Jay said. "This doesn't look so bad."

The counterman shrugged. "One and a quarter for that."

Jay gave him a hundred. "Where would it be worse?"

"Don't know." The counterman held Jay's hundred up to the light and fingered the paper. "You pushin' queer? I knows what you looks like now."

"Keep the change," Jay said.

The counterman stared.

"Where does it get really bad? Dangerous."

For a second or two, the counterman hesitated. Then he said, "Just keep on north, maybe six blocks?"

Jay nodded.

"Then you turns east. Three blocks. Or fo'. That's 'bout as bad as anythin' gits."

"Thanks." Jay opened the gum and offered a stick to the counterman.

The counterman shook his head. "Gits on my dentures. You goin' up there where I told you?"

He did, and once there he stopped and studied the shabby buildings as though searching for a street number. Two white men—the only other whites in sight—were following him, one behind him with a brown attaché case, the other on the opposite side of the street. Their hats and topcoats looked crisp and new, and they stood out in that neighborhood like two candy bars in a brushpile. He turned down an alley, ran, then halted abruptly where a rusted-out water heater leaned against a dozen rolls of discarded carpet.

Often he had waited immobile for an hour or more until a wary deer ventured within range of his bow. He waited so now, motionless in the wind and the blowing snow, half concealed by the hot-water tank and a roll of carpet, a sleeve breaking the outline of his face; and the men he had seen in the street passed him without a glance, walking purposefully up the alley. Where it met the next street they stopped and talked for a moment or two; then the attaché case was opened, and they appeared to consult an instrument of some kind. They reentered the alley.

He rose and ran—down that alley, across the street and into the next, down another street, a narrow and dirty street on which half or more of the parked cars had been stripped. When he stopped at last, sweating despite the cold, he got out Hayfa Washington's card and tore it in two.

Threadlike wires and their parent microchips bound the halves together still.

He dropped both halves down a sewer grating, pulled off his reversible coat, turned it green-side-out and put it back on, then unbuttoned his hunting coat as well and transferred the hunting knife his father had given him one Christmas to a pocket of the now-green raincoat, sheath and all.

An hour later—long after he had lost count of alleys and wretched streets—he heard running feet behind him, whirled, and met his attacker with the best flying tackle he could muster. He had not fought another human being since boyhood; he fought now as the bobcat had fought him, with the furious strength of desperation, gouging and biting and twice pounding the other's head against the dirty concrete. He heard the bottle that had been the other's weapon break, and felt the heat of the blood streaming from his ear and scalp, and by an immense effort of will stopped the point of the old hunting knife short of the other's right eye.

The other's struggled ended. "Don' do that, man! You don' want to make me blind."

"Give up?"

"Yeah, man. I give up." The jagged weapon the bottle had become clinked on the pavement.

"How much did you think I'd have on me?"

"Man, that don't matter!"

"Yes, it does. How much?"

"Forty. Fifty. Maybe credit cards, man, you know."

"All right." The point of the knife moved a centimeter closer. "I want you to do something for me. I want you to work. If you'll do it, I'll pay you a hundred and send you away. If you won't, you'll never get up. Which is it?"

"I'll do it, man." The other at least sounded sincere. "I'll do whatever you says."

"Good." Jay rose and dropped the knife back into his pocket. "Maybe you can pull me down. I don't know, but maybe you can. Whenever you want to try . . ." He shrugged.

"You bleedin', man."

"I know. It will stop, or I think it will." Jay got out a hundred. "You see this? It'll be all yours." He tore it in two and gave half to the other. "You get the other half when you've done what I'm hiring you to do."

"Okay if I gets up, man?"

Jay nodded, and the other got slowly to his feet. His Jeens and plastic jacket were old and cracked, his Capribuk athletic shoes nearly new.

"Listen carefully. If you don't do exactly what I tell you, our deal is off. I'm going to give you a piece of paper with an address on it."

The other gave no indication that he had heard.

"I want you to read that address, but I don't want you to tell me what it is. Don't say it, and don't let me see the paper."

"What is this shit, man?"

"Do you watch the news?"

"I got no time for that shit, man. I listens to music."

For two or three seconds Jay stared at the blank screen on the other's forehead, recalling that his own was—or had been—equally blank. "There's no point in explaining. Do you understand what you've got to do?"

"Look at the address. Not tell you. Not let you look, even. You want me to tear it up?"

Jay shook his head. "I want you to keep it, and I want you to take me there. If we have to spend money to get there, I'll pay."

Reluctantly, the other nodded.

"When we get there, you give me the paper so I can see you took me to the right place. When you do, I'll give you the other half of that hundred and you can go."

He had expected the subway, but they took a bus; the ride lasted over an hour. " 'Bout two blocks now," the other said when they left it at last. "You wants to walk?"

Jay nodded.

"You going to turn me in, man?"

"No," Jay said. They were walking side by side. "I'm going to give you the other half of that hundred, and shake hands if you're willing to shake hands, and say good-bye."

"You a pretty fair scrapper, you know? Only you catches me by surprise. I wasn't expectin' you to turn 'round like what you done."

"Wasn't that what you were trying to do to me? Take me by surprise?"

"Sho'!" The other laughed.

"So that's all right. Except that right and wrong really don't count in things like this. I hunt a lot. I hunt animals to eat."

"Do tell?"

"And for hide and bone to make things out of. Generally I try to give the animals a fighting chance."

"Uh-huh."

"But when I'm hungry, really up against it, I don't. I kill any way I can."

"We here." The other waved at one of several squat concrete buildings. "Got a number on it 'n' everythin'. You don' want to look at that?"

"I don't think it matters now," Jay said, and looked.

"Number eighteen." The other fished in his pockets and pulled out the page of notebook paper, now much folded, that the woman who sold guns had given Jay in the café. "All right. It says here Greentree Gardens. An' it says buildin' eighteen. Then it says number eight. Have a look."

Jay did.

"Now this here's Greentree Gardens, all right? You look right over there 'n' there's a sign on top of that buildin'. What do it say?"

"Greentree Gardens."

"Right on, man. Right over there's buildin' number eighteen, like you sees. Number eight will be ground flo', mos' like, or maybe next up. Places like this ain't bad as some other places, you know? Only they ain't real safe neither. You wants me to go in there with you? Be glad to if you wants it."

Jay shook his head, took out the remaining half of the torn hundred, and handed it to the other. Then he offered his hand, which the other accepted after putting the torn half bill into one of his pockets.

Abruptly his grip tightened. Jay tried to jerk away, but the other's fist caught him under the cheekbone.

He went down, rolling and trying to cover his head with his arms. A kick dizzied him, its shock worse than its pain. Another missed, and another must have struck his forearm, because his arm felt as though it had been clubbed.

Somehow he got to his feet, charged the other and grappled him. *I killed that buck like this*, he thought; the buck had an arrow in its gut, but that had hardly seemed to matter. His knife was in his hand. He stabbed and felt it strike bone.

Then it was gone.

At once the other had it, and there was freezing cold where his shirt pocket should have been, cold followed by burning heat, and he was holding the other's wrist with both hands, and the blade was wet and red. The other's fist pounded his nose and mouth. He did not hear the shot, but he felt the other stiffen and shudder.

He pushed the other's body from him, insanely certain that it was only a trick, only a temporary respite granted so that he might be taken by surprise again in a moment or two. Rising, he kicked something.

It was the knife, and it went clattering over the sidewalk. He pulled it out of some snow, wiped the blade with his handkerchief, returned it to its sheath and the sheath to his pocket.

Then the woman who sold guns was tugging at his sleeve. In her other hand she held a short and slender rifle with a long box magazine. "Come on! We've got to get out of here."

He followed her docilely between the hulking building that was eighteen Greentree Gardens, and a similar building that was probably sixteen or twenty. Two floors down in a dark underground garage, she unlocked a blue CUV. As he climbed in he said, "Borrowed from another friend?"

"This's mine, and if I didn't sell what I do I couldn't afford it."

It reeked of cigar smoke; he said, "In that case, I'd think they'd know about it—the plate number and so forth."

She shook her head. "It's registered under a fake name, and these aren't my plates."

He considered that while she drove eight or ten blocks fast, then up a winding ramp and onto the Interstate.

When they were in the leftmost lane, he said, "Why are we running away?"

She turned her head to look at him. "Are you crazy? Because I killed that guy."

"He was going to kill me." He looked down at his wound, and was mildly surprised to find that it was still bleeding, his blood soaking the two-sided raincoat and, presumably, the hunting coat under it.

"So what? Look, I can't even defend myself, according to the law. Say you were going to rape me and kill me."

"I wouldn't do that."

"Just suppose. I couldn't shoot you or stab you or even hit you, and if I did you could sue me afterward."

"Could I win?"

"Sure. What's more, I'd be defending your suit from a cell. And if I hurt you worse'n you hurt me, you'd be out."

Jay shook his head. "That doesn't make sense."

"Not for us it doesn't." The Interstate sloped sharply down here, but she kept pedal to the floor; for a moment the CUV shook wildly. "For them it does—for the feds. If we got used to the idea of going after somebody who went after us, we'd go after them. *Capisce?*"

"We should."

"Sure. Only for me it's a lot worse. For you, too. I killed that guy. Don't say maybe he's not dead. I saw him when I hit him, and I saw him afterward. He's gone."

"How did you know we were out there?"

"Saw you out the window, that's all. It'd been a while, so I kept looking outside, hoping you were just looking for the right number. I'd stopped off and picked up your gun on the way home, and I was afraid you'd come and gone before I got there. You want to see it? It's on the backseat. Only be careful, it's loaded. I think I put the safety on."

Jay took off his seat belt and picked up the carbine, careful not to touch its trigger.

"Keep it down so the other drivers can't see it."

He did. "This car doesn't talk to us."

"I killed that bastard as soon as I got it. It's pretty easy."

Sensing that she was about to cry, Jay did not speak; he would have tried to hold her hand, perhaps, but both her hands were on the wheel.

"And now I've killed the bastard that was trying to kill you. There's tissues in back somewhere."

He got them, heard her blow her nose.

"I told you how bad that is. It's murder one. He was trying to kill you, but that doesn't make a damned bit of difference. I should have called the cops and showed them your body when they got there. That would have been when? Two or three o'clock. My God, it's lunchtime."

He looked at the clock on the instrument panel. It was nearly one.

"You hungry?"

"No," he said.

"Me neither. Let's skip lunch. We'll stop somewhere for dinner tonight."

He agreed, and asked where they were going.

"Damned if I know."

"Then I'd like you to take Eighty."

"We need to get off the Interstate before too much longer," she said.

He nodded. "We will."

"Listen, I'm sorry I got you into this."

"I feel the same way," he said. "You saved my life."

"Who was he, anyway?"

"The man I'd gotten to read your note. You didn't want Globnet to get it on the air before we'd left, so I had to have somebody who would look at it for me and take me there. I tried to find somebody who wouldn't call the police as soon as we separated. Clearly that was a bad idea." Jay paused. "How did you think I'd handle it?"

"That you'd guess. That you'd go there and look at my note and see that you were right when you got there."

"No more crying?"

"Nope. That's over. You know what made me cry?"

"What?"

"You didn't understand. You can't kill people, not even if they're killing other people, and I did it with a gun. If they get me I'll get life, and you didn't understand that."

"Who'd take care of your kids?" He let his voice tell her what he felt he knew about those kids.

She drove. He glanced over at her, and she was staring straight ahead, both hands on the wheel.

"I'm going back into the woods. Maybe they'll get me in there, but it won't be easy. If the holovid company can't help you, maybe you'd like to come with me."

"You had it all doped out." She sounded bitter.

He shook his head. "I don't think I understand it all even now, and there's a lot of it that I just figured out a minute ago. How much were you supposed to get for this?"

"A couple thousand."

He thought about that. "You're not an employee. Or at least, you don't work for Globnet full-time."

"No." She sniffled. "They did a documentary on the gun trade last year, and I was one of the people they found—the only woman. So I was on holo with this really cool mask over my face, and I thought that was the end of it. Then about a month ago they lined me up to do this."

He nodded.

"They figured you'd want women or drugs, mostly, and they had people set for those. I was kind of an afterthought, okay? Stand by for a couple hundred, or a couple thousand if you called. Another thousand if I sold you a gun. I did, but I'll never collect any of it."

"The bot must have called you after he gave me your number."

"Kaydee Nineteen? Sure. That's how you knew, huh? Because you got it from him."

Jay shook his head. "That was how I should have known, but I didn't. It was mostly the phone call you made last night to somebody who was supposed to be sitting your kids. Real mothers talk about their kids a lot, but you didn't. And just now it hit me that you'd called your friend Val, and James R. Smith's secretary was Valerie. Then I thought about the bot. He took his security work very seriously, or at least it seemed like he did. But he had given me the number of a gun dealer as soon as I asked, and he had been friendly with Valerie."

"So I was lying to you all the time."

He shrugged.

"Don't do that! You're going to get that thing bleeding worse. What happened to your ear?"

He told her, and she pointed. "There's a truck stop. They'll have aid kits for sale." Cutting across five lanes of traffic, they raced down an exit ramp.

That night, in an independent motel very far from Interstate 80, he took off his reversible raincoat and his hunting coat, and his shirt and undershirt as well, and sat with clenched teeth while she did what she could with disinfectant and bandages.

When she had finished, he asked whether she had been able to buy much ammunition.

"Eight boxes. That's four hundred rounds. They come fifty in a box."

He nodded.

"Only we don't have it. It's back in that place in Greentree Gardens."

He swore.

"Listen, you've got money and I've got connections. We can buy more as soon as things quiet down."

"A lot of the money's ruined. It has blood on it."

She shook her head. "It'll wash up. You'll see. Warm water and a little mild detergent, don't treat it rough and let it dry flat. You can always clean up money."

"I thought maybe I could just give it to them," he said. "Show them it wasn't any good anymore."

She kissed him, calling him Skeeter; and he shut his eyes so that Globnet and its audience would not see her kiss.

He had been after deer since before the first gray of dawn; but he had never gotten a shot, perhaps because of the helicopters. Helicopters had been flying over all morning, sweeping up and down this valley and a lot of other valleys. He thought about Arizona or New Mexico, as he sometimes did, but concluded (as he generally had to) that they would be too open, too exposed. Colorado, maybe, or Canada.

The soldiers the helicopters had brought were spread out now, working their way slowly up the valley. Too few, he decided. There weren't enough soldiers and they were spread too thin. They expected him to run, as perhaps he would. He tried to gauge the distance to the nearest.

Two hundred yards. A long two hundred yards that could be as much as two hundred and fifty.

But coming closer, closer all the time, a tall, dark-faced woman in a mottled green, brown, and sand-colored uniform that had been designed for someplace warmer than these snowy Pennsylvania woods. Her height made her an easy target—far easier than even the biggest doe—and she held a dead-black assault rifle slantwise across her chest. That rifle would offer full or semiautomatic operation, with a switch to take it from one to the other.

Less than two hundred yards. Very slowly Jay crouched in the place he had chosen, pulled his cap down to hide the stars of his upgrade, and then raised his head enough to verify that he could keep the woman with the assault rifle in view. His wound felt as hot as his cheeks, and there was blood seeping through the bandage; he was conscious of that, and conscious, too, that it was harder to breathe than it should have been.

A hundred and fifty yards. Surely it was not more than a hundred and fifty, and it might easily be less. He was aware of his breathing, of the pounding of his heart—the old thrill.

Thirty rounds in that black rifle's magazine, possibly. Possibly more, possibly as many as fifty. There would be an ammunition belt, too, if he had time to take it. Another two or three hundred rounds, slender, pointed bullets made to fly flatter than a stretched string and tumble in flesh.

For an instant that was less than a moment, less even than the blink of an eye, a phantom passed between him and the woman with the black assault rifle—a lean man in soiled buckskins who held a slender, graceful gun that must have been almost as long as he was tall.

A hallucination.

Jay smiled to himself. Had they seen that, back at Globnet? They must have, if they still saw everything he did. Would they put it on the news?

A scant hundred yards now. The little carbine seemed to bring itself to his shoulder.

Seventy yards, if that.

Jay took a deep breath, let it half out, and began to squeeze the trigger.

I was working at Doubleday when Ardath Mayhar began her career in the early 1980s—since then, she has published forty novels in various fields besides sf, including Young Adult and Westerns. I can't believe that was twenty years ago, and I can't believe that Ardath is seventy years old!

She describes herself as a "tough old lady," but if that's so, then tough old ladies must have sharp senses of humor, as the following story proves.

Fungi

ARDATH MAYHAR

*

Jonathan drew a deep breath, tainted, as usual, by the smell of recycled air. His space suit was awkward and it still rubbed his left knee, though the techs had worked on it again. He hated the suit, the domed station, and the world on which it sat. Almost airless, barren, holding only fungi and rock, the place was a disaster from the viewpoint of an ecologist.

He was thinking about that when the purple fungus spoke to him.

Damn! Contaminants in the air supply again, he thought, heading back for the airlock. He'd always had a sensitivity; the mold spores that often invaded the interiors of the breather units gave him hallucinations.

"You! Silver fungus! Have you no manners? I spoke to you!"

It wasn't a voice in his ear, but one inside his head. He'd never had anything quite like that before. Jonathan stopped and popped the top of his helmet with his gloved fist. Sometimes that put things back into place.

Not this time. A stream of images entered his mind, along with words. Real human words, not spoken but *thought* with great vigor. He stopped in his tracks and turned slowly, staring back at the clump of purple fuzz on top of a grim gray stone.

He increased magnification in his eye-plate, staring closely at the fungus. Each of the filaments that formed it was tipped with a speck of black so shiny it glittered in the unfiltered sunlight. As he stared, the entire group curved with synchronized choreography to point straight toward him . . . and stared back.

Eyes?

"Was that you?" he asked aloud, though he knew the helmet swallowed sound almost entirely.

There was no audible reply, but he knew the answer anyway. *"Of course. I have been perceiving you and the other silver fungi for several black-times now. I have learned how you communicate, though the vibrations you make are painful. Where did your spores originate? You appeared so quickly—no other intruder fungus has ever grown so large in such a short span."*

Jonathan backed up a step and found himself against another stony shelf, this one almost as high as his shoulders. Another silent voice said, *"Watch it! Do you want to crush me?"*

When he turned to look, a gray-green clump was staring back at him. He felt the hairs rise on his neck beneath the helmet, and sweat popped out on his chest inside the air-conditioned suit.

"You must understand," the purple fungus continued, *"that this world does not contain sustenance for more life-forms than it now contains. No stone here can support more than a single organism, and all are occupied. You will have to encapsulate and send your spores elsewhere."*

"But . . . but we are not fungi. We travel in other ways, and we don't live on rocks. I assure you . . ." He caught himself and stopped in mid-sentence. Apologize and explain to a clump of fuzz? Ridiculous!

Something very like a sigh, though soundless, wisped through his head. *"Very large specimens always feel they are above the laws of survival. We have noted that in the past, on other worlds. We have, however, invented techniques with which to defend our habitats, over the millennia of our travels between worlds. Be warned, silver fungus. Leave our planet or suffer the consequences."*

Jonathan opened his mouth, but he could find no words. He knew he had gone mad. He had to get inside the dome, clear himself of the mold spores, and get the medication Dr. Tait kept for such situations.

He hated to think what Commander Robb was going to say when he made his report. Robb was a military man of the old school. His reply to any challenge to human authority was a blast of laser fire, and he had no use for "slackers," as he called those who developed psychological problems on alien worlds.

Although Jonathan was a civilian, Robb had a way of making him feel lower than the fungi back there among the rocks. Flinching at the thought, the ecologist made his way cautiously toward the dome, avoiding the boulders with great care as he went. Only when the lock cycled shut behind him did he relax.

At last he stepped out into the dome, finding himself face-to-face with the commander. "Eckles! What are you doing back so quickly? You were to examine Sector Sixteen of the north quadrant. Surely you cannot be done with that already!"

"Medication," Jonathan gasped. "Spores in breather . . . hallucinations."

Robb frowned ferociously, but he stepped aside. "When you finish with Dr. Tait," he said in a warning tone, "come directly to my quarters. I want a complete report from you, Eckles. I will not tolerate slackers!"

The doctor was interested in Jonathan's description of his aberration while outside the dome. "Not your usual reaction," he mused as he shot the medication into Jonathan's skin. "I would like to examine your breathing equipment before the techs clean it up. Have them bring it to my laboratory, with your recording computer."

On his way to Robb's quarters, Jonathan left word for that to be done, but he was so worried about the coming interview that he didn't think much about it. His push on the commander's may-I-enter button was timid, but the port popped open at once.

Robb sat at his desk, looking stern. "Sit down," he snapped. "Now give me a complete report of your very *brief* activities while outside the dome."

Feeling both foolish and terrified, Jonathan obeyed. When he was done, Robb's coarse white eyebrows were meeting above his craggy nose, and his thin lips had disappeared into a straight line.

"You expect me to believe that a *fungus* spoke to you?" His tone was dangerous.

"No, no. Not at all. That is only what *seemed* to happen. I am sensitive to the mold that sometimes grows in the breathers. The stuff makes me hallucinate. This was simply the strangest hallucination I have ever had. Dr. Tait is examining the equipment now to find what sort of mold it might be."

The commander pressed his com button. "Tait! Have you completed your examination of Eckles's equipment?"

"Yes, sir," came the smooth reply.

"Report to my quarters at once. I want this cleared up without delay." He glared at Jonathan as they waited for the doctor.

When Tait arrived, he was not nervous, not breathless, not terrified. Jonathan envied him his lack of fear around the commander. No, Tait seemed amused, if anything. He trundled behind him a wheeled table on which lay the breather and Jonathan's recording computer.

Robb stared at the table, then at Dr. Tait. "What's all this?" he asked.

"Proof," said Tait, his tone crisp. "You will find the result of my scan on the mini-comp."

Robb took the memo pad in hand and said, "Report on Eckles's breathing equipment."

The sexy voice, that of every computer sent into space, said, "No trace of mold spores was found in either oxygen tank or breather. No trace of hallucinogen of any kind, either on interior or exterior surfaces."

"Aha!" Robb stared at Jonathan. "So what do you have to say for yourself?"

Jonathan found no words, but Tait interrupted smoothly, "You need to hear the report on the material contained in the recording equipment. Before you make accusations, Commander, I recommend that you listen to the next report."

"Report on Eckles's record of mission begun at 21:35:10 this date." He sounded dubious, Jonathan thought.

"Overhead screen on, link to office com complete," the mini-com began. "If you will watch the progress of subject, you will see that he was on course and taking notes to point A-6." The overhead showed the boring terrain through which Jonathan was moving, and an overlay showed the mapped grid of his assigned sector.

"At that point, subject's verbal report is interrupted. Unusual auditory effects are recorded." A buzz, almost subsonic, sounded as the com replayed the record. "Subject turns, surveys terrain, focuses on fungus located on boulder. Note magnification." There the picture enlarged as Jonathan magnified his eye-plate, and the clump of purple fuzz came into sharp focus.

"Note behavior of fungus. Entire clump swings toward subject as if examining him visually."

Now the com replayed both visual and auditory recordings, only Jonathan's side of the conversation being comprehensible. As the report proceeded, Robb became very still, and his face reddened.

When the com clicked off, the commander turned to Jonathan. "This . . . this *thing* dared to threaten us? A *fungus* wants us to leave this world we are assigned to survey and has the gall to suggest we might suffer *consequences*?" He looked as if he might explode at the slightest provocation.

He rose, and the other two jumped to their feet. "We will go back out there now. I want to . . . talk to this upstart mushroom. Prepare for external mission."

It was with considerable trepidation that Jonathan followed the commander out of the airlock. Dr. Tait seemed excited, but he hadn't communicated with the fungus directly. There was something terribly self-assured about that clump of fuzz, and references to millennia of travel between worlds hinted at knowledge that even a fungus might have acquired.

They reached the area more quickly than before. After all, he had been making verbal notes into his computer, pausing to examine anything the least bit unusual. Now they stood before the big gray rock, looking at the purple fuzz, which seemed to be dozing in the sunlight.

Even as he watched, Jonathan saw the fuzzy tendrils stiffen, curve toward the three men, those shiny black eyes focusing upon them. He felt a shiver down his back, and he hoped the commander did, too.

"*You return? After our warning? Silver fungi, you have no manners!*"

The commander clapped both hands to his helmet, and Dr. Tait shook his head as if trying to locate the source of the communication.

Jonathan said, "No, it's not a voice you hear, but it gets inside your head anyway. Listen to what it says. I think maybe we should consider . . ."

"You cowardly slacker! Be silent!"

Jonathan could see the fungus quiver as the commander's roar penetrated the helmet. It focused upon him, now, and Jonathan could not hear what it said, but whatever it was, the commander was clearly becoming more and more agitated. Hopping mad, he would have put it, concerning anyone else.

Then Jonathan remembered that other one, the gray-green clump behind them. He turned cautiously to see what it was doing, and he found it, too, directing its attention toward Commander Robb. Something about the glint of those distant beads of black made him feel suddenly cold.

He backed away. Dr. Tait came into view, also backing away. By unspoken consent, they took shelter behind a slab of rock atop which a pinkish fuzz was also turned toward their commanding officer. Jonathan didn't know what to expect, but whatever it was he wanted to be out of the way when it happened.

"I believe Robb has met his match," the doctor whispered over the suit-to-suit radio. "Look at him!"

Now Robb was quivering with rage, his feet leaving the ground as he literally bounced up and down. Something very tense and powerful filled the air, felt even through the protection of Jonathan's suit.

He was about to ask Tait if he felt it when Robb's suit popped open and expelled the commander upward. If there had been more air or more gravity he might have fallen to the ground again. As it was, he zoomed up under what was obviously great pressure and disappeared into the glare of the sun. The remnants of his suit lay crumpled beside the rock where the purple fuzz was now relaxing.

Jonathan turned to stare at Dr. Tait. Through the face-plate, the doctor looked greenish-pale, the way he felt, himself.

Then, using courage he did not know he had, Jonathan rose and moved toward the purple fungus. "What did you do to him?" he asked. "Did you intend to kill him?"

The fuzz stirred lazily. *"Of course not. Life is rare and valuable. We have learned to concentrate our energies and force alien fungi to expel their spores prematurely, sending them on toward other worlds. In this way, they pose no threat to us while continuing their life cycles."*

Jonathan almost explained what had really happened to Robb, but he realized that this thing would never understand. Spores and fungi were all it knew, and it dealt with its problems on those terms.

Tait touched his shoulder with a bulky glove. "Let's go," he said. "I'll list this as a world containing toxic materials that are too dangerous to deal with. I think that will be accurate, don't you agree? Those bits of fluff could have exploded the dome, I suspect, as they did the commander's suit."

Jonathan nodded, and the two turned toward the distant dome. They would be ready to leave in three days, he knew from old experience. In the meanwhile, no one else would leave the shelter until it was time to take the shuttle up to the orbiting ship.

He hoped the purple fuzz and its companions never met another human being. The doctor's report, he was sure, would make certain of that.

I first met Neal Barrett, Jr., face-to-face in the fall of 2000. This is incredible because (a) I feel like I've known him forever and (b) I was *Neal Barrett, Jr., for a short period of time in 1995.*

Here's what happened: in the autumn of '95, when I was starting to look forward to Thanksgiving, Neal's agent called and asked if I'd be interested in taking a project over for him—seems he was just too *popular and was overbooked (that's a pun) with work. The project in question was a* Babylon 5 *novelization titled* The Touch of Your Shadow, The Whisper of Your Name, *and all that existed for it was a ten-page outline that Neal had written. Another problem was that the book had to be turned in around Thanksgiving. And yet* another *problem was that the publisher had already printed up the cover with Neal's name on it—which meant that I had to* become Neal Barrett*! Horrors!*

Suffice it to say, Neal got his revenge for what I've just written—by producing an absolutely drop-dead great story to end this book.

In actuality: if only the rest of you could be Neal Barrett, Jr., for a while, what an honor that would be. I commend to your astonishment, besides "Rhido Wars," the following: The Hereafter Gang, Pink Vodka Blues, Through Darkest America, *and the remarkable story collection* Perpetuity Blues.

Rhido Wars

Neal Barrett, Jr.

*

What I do I hear this fart an a squirt an a squirt after that an then splat. Dont hardly have to wake up Im seein this big red ass with a bright blue ring round the hole where the shits comin out. He squattin maybe thirty hands off an it isnt even Light an I know its Sal Capone. You dont gotta see a face, you can see that ass, isnt any two alike. Drills are like Persons. Persons dont look or smell the same. Ever things different from ever thing else.

Sal, he knowin I there, an when he all done he turn an blink his baby crap eyes. The stripes on his face is black stead of blue cause theres hardly any Light.

Sal, he not wearin nothin, not wearin anything at all. Ever thin showin, hangin, stuff stickin out. A Drill dont care bout that. Only thing he care bout, he gotta have a hat.

"You are not being sleep," Sal says. "Dark is for the sleep. Persons must sleep in the Dark and working in the Light."

I was sleepin good, Im thinkin, *then you com an shit in my yard. Im not sleepin real good after that. . . .*

"The rain fell much in the forest last Dark," Sal says, the way they all do, like they got a sack of gravel in their craw. "The ground is being wet. Seven baskets for each of your Persons, seven by the time the sun is high. *Nine* for you, Ratch, for you are ever insolent to me. I am angered and sad that you show me disrespect, this is great sorrow and a bad thing to do.

"Be telling your Persons, a basket will not be padded with little leaves and shoots to seem full when it is not. There will be sufficient beetles and snails. Snails will be about on a wetting day as this. There will also be the grubs, Ratch, grubs of most sufficient fat.

"I should like to see voles. Not voles that are deceased, eaten by the ant. Voles are not difficult to catch. Young Lily is quick. Tell her to catch me many voles, I shall bring her honey on a stick. How is the Lily, Ratch? She is well, I am hope. And little Macky and Dit? And the one who is bit by a snik?"

"He fine too. Hows Florence an Sil? How Miz Pain?"

"You will see that there are voles, Ratch. Voles are expected. Grasses are not."

Sal was all done. A Drill say what he got to say, thats it, he done. While they talkin an scratchin an pluckin some crawly out their fur, you maybe okay. A Drill just lookin, lookin right at you with baby crap eyes, he got some ugly in mind.

A Drills flat ugly outside, but insides ugliern that. You dont know bout ugly till you know whats in a Drills head. . . .

Its so phuckin hot you are drownin in sweat you are poundin in the head. Ever skeeto ever nat for a thousan miles aroun is crawlin in your eyes is crawlin up your ass. The sun is up but the trees has smothered all the Light. Its Light somewhere but it isnt down here. You haven ever crawl through creepers an tanglers wrappin roun a tree, you dont know what I talkin bout here. Im talkin trees you cant even see roun, trees got snicks an stingers so big you dont want to think what maybe lookin at you there.

Im crawlin onna ground, Im turnin over rocks, I cant see dick for a phuckin foot ahead. I got a couple snails, I got a buncha grubs. Down here theres ever kinda of bug there is. Down here you a bug or a leaf. Maybe you a root. Ever thing down here squishy, ever thing wet, ever thing tangled in ever thing else. Ever thing fat bout to busting down here, an ever thing one phuckin color, ever thing *green*.

I hear Lily she off somewhere, Lily chasin voles. Dont hear Macky, an you hardly never do. Macky, he gonna spook you sometime, Macky dont make a sound at all.

Cant say that bout Dit. Know where Dit goin to be bout a hour fore he is.

A whole lotta green start shakin an here come Dit. Dit grinnin like a fool an he got a bunch of orchits in his hair. Some of em pink and some of em white, some of em colors hasnt got a name at all.

"I was you," I says, "I wouldnt let Darc Anthony see me lookin like that. Darc he likely to haul you off inna bush somewhere."

"Darc cant see no further than he nose," Dit says. "Darc isnt goin to see me."

Darc cant see real good, but Darc can smell nats phuckin half a mile away. Isnt no use telling Dit, Dit dont listen to anyone at all.

"I got some real fine grubs," Dit says, "they sweet as they can be. Been down in the dirt, hasnt ever seen the Light."

He doin that mouth-smackin shit, he holdin a grub, it squirmin an twitchin like it know what Dit goin to do. Dit hold it up bout a inch from his lips an his cheeks get holler an he suck it right in. Dit says this is a trick. What it is is somethin anyone could do, but Dit think he made it up his self.

He gets me a grub an another for his self an I dont say a thing bout this. His baskets are full, an even Sal Capone wont know if theres any gone or what.

"You see Macky," I tell him, "say he got enough snails hes to go help Lily, see if he can help her catch voles. Sals set up bout somethin, I dont know what. I dont want no trouble, so get him lots a voles."

"Set up bout what, Sal is?"

"If I know, then thats what I be sayin, now wouldnt I, Dit?"

"I guess."

"Guess I would. Listen to me good, all right? When I be talkin, listen to what I got to say."

I eat another grub, an put a couple more in my cheek for later on.

"Dont eat no more," I tell Dit. "Dont think bout grubs, go think about snails. Get some more snails."

"Dont like them snails. Dont like em at all."

"Now you got it, Dit, get you ass movin, find a buncha snails. . . ."

Lily bout where I figured she be. Theres a place where chokegrass growin so high you cant see over it at all. Crawl on in theres a hollow where Light sneaks down an make goldy spots on the ground. You look at them spots an they shiver an blur an you look real long, you off somewhere, not where you think you be.

Thats where Lily is, sittin in greeny moss, sittin by the creek. She lookin awful pretty, lookin awful good. I feelin somethin funny, cause she not wearin nothin which she never do at home.

The goldys is dancing in her hair, dancing off her legs which she dippin in the creek, dancing of her little buds which is poppin out fine.

Shes found her some cappers, holdin the stems in her fingers an chewin off the tops, eatin real slow. Lily dont eat like other folks, Lily eats nice. Takin little bites like you see a critter do. I can see Mama doin that, cept Lily wouldn't know, she wouldnt member that.

I sit there watchin, which I hadnt ought to do. Its hard not to, cause a sister dont look no different than someone you isnt kin to. If you didnt know you was, youd be thinking what I was thinking too.

"You goin to sit there, Ratch, you going to take root an turn into a tree . . ."

I glad she isnt lookin, if she was shed of seen me turnin a couple shades of red.

"Didnt want to scare you or nothin," I tell her, "just jumpin out a bush. Wouldnt want to do that."

Lily laugh an she do turn then, givin me a smile an her sparkle-dark eyes.

"What you talkin bout, Ratch? You couldnt scare me if you tried."

"I could, I bet. I could if I tried."

"Huh-uh, you couldn't scare me. I doubt you could even scare Macky. You might scare Dit."

"Anyone could scare Dit. A leaf could scare Dit. I bet a—a *rock* could scare ol Dit."

Lily laugh at that. She pats a place beside her an splashes her feet in the water, an I dippin mine in too. Mine are all big an crookity lookin an hers are real small. Mens an wimins are different. An it isnt just feet I talkin bout.

I try not to look at those buds. A little bit of fuzz is growin round her cut an I try not to look at that too. Even though I wearin a clothes, I fraid she might see what I tryin not to do.

"I sent Macky over, I bet he didnt come," I tell her. "I said, Dit, you tell Macky go on over an help Lily catch a buncha voles. What I bet, he didnt show at all."

"Course he didnt. You think he would?"

"I dont guess. I always thinkin, I thinkin, Ratch, why you go an open your mouth, why you say somethin it dont do any good?"

"You tryin is why," Lily says. "That's just the way you do. The way you always been."

She lookin at me then an I got to look away, got to look at somethin else. Lacers and brighters are buzzin in a beam a goldy Light. A dragunwings dippin down quick, kissin the water an flyin on away.

"I got to be like I am, Lily. Im oldest. Its what I got to do."

"I know you do, Ratch. . . ."

"You an older, you lookin after Famly, thats what you got to do. I gotta watch Macky, I gotta watch Dit, he dont do somethin dumb. Spose he get in his head he gonna eat all his grubs? What I gonna tell Sal, Dits maybe doin that?"

"I dont think he will."

"You dont but I do. Thats what I gotta be thinkin alla time. An Macky, hes spose to help you findin voles. Whats Macky doin, what he doin now? What if you not findin voles, what Sal goin to say bout that?"

"Ratch . . ."

"What?"

"I got Sals ol voles, all right?"

She turn an look at me then, look at me real soft like.

"You worry bout me, Ratch, an I dont want you doing that."

"Course I do, Lily. Nothin wrong with that."

"There isnt, not if you worry the ordnary way. Not if you worryin right . . ."

I see right off what she talkin bout now. She look away quick an I look away too, cause I know she scared she thinkin just the way I thinking too.

I tell her I got to find Macky, I tell her I got to find Dit. See if Niks swellin has gone down where he got bit.

Im out through the chokegrass, outta there quick. Lily dont watch an Im not lookin back. I forget to give her the grub I savin in my cheek. I go head an chew it, an swallow it myself. It dont taste good like the other one did. . . .

Stay down low, not movin at all. Darc Anthony cant see shit, Dits right bout that. But there isnt nothing wrong with the ol bastards ears, he can phuckin *hear*, isnt no doubt a that.

Isnt no tellin how ol Darc is. Even if you know em, you cant never tell. Ever Drill got baby crap eyes an that ugly red muzzle pokin out. Ever one got cheeks like puckerin scars—like someone cut em, then go an paint em blue. Sometime a cheek bein purple stead of blue. Sometime they ruffs bein yellow, sometime they dirty white.

Darc I figure is oldern Sal. He isnt too ol cause he sniffin round Florence of Arabia when Sal not around. Sal likely kill him if he know bout that.

Darc, he squat there ever single day, squattin on his big black rock. Squats an shits and scratches, squats an shits again. Picks little chitters off his fur an cracks em in his teeth. Sometime he play with that big pink knobber stickin tween his legs. You see a Drill got nothin else to do, he likely doin that. Likely doin that, or lookin for a hat.

What you dont know, is while he doin that, Darc Anthony knowin where every picker is in the tangle, in the hot, in the strangle down below. What they doin down there, what they pickin, if they workin or they takin a nap. An when the days done, ol Darc tellin Sal what he seen, tellin Sal what he know.

Tellin, or keepin somethin to his self. Waitin till he got somethin good he can use on someone hadnt got sense. Someone like Dit. Then Dit got to do what Darc want him to, an wonder how he got into somethin like that.

How he did, is he dont ever listen to Ratch. Ratch spend ever minute helpin Famly, keepin ever body right. I do the best I can. Someone dont listen, what am I sposed to do? . . .

Niks a lot worse. He burnin with fever he all swole up. A green snik got him, an theres nothing worsen that. He not goin to make it through the night. Lily know that, but she wont give up. She keepin him cool, wipin him off, drippin water on his mouth. His lips is dry as dirt. His eyes is open, but Nik not lookin at any thing at all.

"Hes little, Ratch. He isnt hardly six. He hadnt ought to leave, you little like that."

"Little dont matter to a snik," I tell her. "A snik dont care if you six. Dont care if you seven, dont care if you ten."

"You shouldnt oughta, though. Not if you six."

"Thats what happen, Lily. You go whenever you go."

"I guess . . ."

I had a fire goin, nothin real big, moss an dry sticks. You not spose to, you spose to be sleepin if its Dark. Phuck it if a Drill dont like it, Little Nik goin to have a fire tonight.

Macky an Dit is sleepin in the corner of the hooch. Both of em oldern Nik, an Lily short of me. A couple of years, they start thinkin important stuff too. They will, if they dont do somethin real dumb or get bit. Lilys already smart as she can be. Wimin get smarter fastern mens. Dont know why they just do.

"Im awful sleepy," Lily says. "I dont know I can stay awake, Ratch."

"You dont have to," I tell her, "I can do that, I can watch Nik."

"You go to sleep is what you gonna do."

"I wont neither. I be watchin little Nik."

"You vow that you will?"

"I vow, now get to sleep, here?"

So she did. I did too, bout a minute after that. Didnt matter if we didnt or we did. Not to Little Nik. I waked up once an we were touchin one another, sleepin real close. Didnt do nothin, but I know she was wake a while too.

Somewhere close to Light, when the grays comin in, Lily she sit up straight, sit up shakin, making funny little sounds. I sittin up cause I hear it too, comin in soft, comin on the wind. Snortin an gruntin, shufflin about. Bumpin and pushin, stompin on the ground. Movin like they real uneasy, like somethin stir em up. Closer, too, closern they been for a spell.

"Down in the draw," I say, "down past the trees."

Dont hardly whisper, but ever body hear. No one got to tell Lily, or Macky or Dit. Ever Person, ever Famly, awake right now. Isnt no one sleepin with Rhido out there. . . .

I reach out and take Lilys hand. Its freezin cold, like water from a spring, from way down deep somewhere.

"What they doin, Ratch, what they doin here?"

"I dont know that, Lily. Might be somebody tell us come Light. Might be we know then."

"Im kinda scared. You scared too?"

"Nothin to be scared of, far as I can see. You try an sleep now. You boys too."

Macky and Dit turn over, they eyes real bright in the last of the fire. Lily look at me, like she want me to talk for a while. I make like I sleepin. Dont wont to tell her I dont know nothin more to say. . . .

Isnt no sleepin after that, dont anybody try. Little Niks gone. Lily get him clean an I take him outside. Macky got the fire back up, Dit got us fruit an some grubs he hid from Sal.

Nobody talkin bout Rhidos or Nik or bout anything else. Talkin dont do no good. Ever day I tell Dit an Macky that. Somethin is or somethin not. Lily dont ask me nothin, even if she wantin to.

After I eat I go out an have a look. Sackers there cross the way, standin by his Famlys hooch too. I dont like him an he dont like me. Still, he know somethin goin on, same as I do.

I hear gruntin and fartin an such, an fat Mama Gass come lopin down the draw, bouncin an swayin, fatter she was the week before. Florence of Arabias right on her tail, dirty brown hair standin up on her back, muddy little eyes shiftin this way an that. Both of em wearin floppy hats with flowers stickin out.

Florence dont like me too much. She wrinkle up her muzzle, givin me a growl. I dont pay her no mind. Go back in, toss a stick on the fire, do somethin busy, walk out again. Watch the sun swellin through the trees. Macky an Dit wander out back to pee.

I know Lily, know what she thinkin in there. Long as she dont come see Little Niks not there, in her head he maybe is.

Wimin dont think the same as mens. Ever ones different from ever one else. . . .

* * *

If I hadnt shit already bet I likely would. Sal keep us waitin a hour in the sun, an that mean somethins not good. Cant be nothin youd ever want to know. Not after what we hearin, out there in the Dark.

An when I see Sal lopin up the draw, I know its goin to be awful, know its worsen that. The parts I not tellin Lily are bustin in my head, an my mouth tastin bad. I look at Sacker, an Sacker look sickern me.

Sals got a good stout pole, sharpened on the end. Got slabs of scrapwood strapped to his forelegs, strapped to his shoulders, strapped to his chest. Ever piece he wearin got circles and jaggeds painted yeller an red. Got somethin on his head. Looks like a turtul with the innards scooped out. Looks like that, cause thats what it is.

"Persons is listening good," Sal Capone says, "persons is very much hearing what I be saying now. Anyone is not listen good, is in extreme trouble and this is not good."

With this, he pounds that stick on the ground, looks at ever hooch, looks at Sacker, Mockit, an Brig, looks right at me.

"There will be no picking of foods this day. No one shall gather the kindles, no one is lifting the rocks or the stones. All Persons shall be leaving this place in orderly manners when the sun is going down. You will gather your stuffs and leave nothing behind. You will do as you are told. You will be starting this now."

Sals got nothing more to say. He turns an totters back down the draw, back to the shade. The turtul hat bounces on his head. Two hunks of wood are strapped to fit his humpy back. The wood is painted in loopy swirls of white. His asshole is ugly, purple, blue, and red.

I talk to Mockit after Sals gone. Mockits Famly is two hooches down, an he bout as old as me. Mockit wants Lily, an wants to give me Dandra Bee. Mockit dont know it, but nothins ever goin to come of that.

"I heared em," Mockit tells me, "ever one did. Bicky an Dandra is real upset. The little uns is climbin up the walls. I sorry bout Nik. Pock, he lost a gurl to a big sinnerpede."

"Didnt know that."

"That was bout a week. No, it was some moren that."

Mockit looks past me to see if anyones there.

"Pock, he takes stuff down the hill. Goes right in the fort, he got a pretty a Drill might give him somethin for. He comin back late, he seen em down there."

"Seen what you an me talkin bout here."

"Rhidos. Real close by."

"Shit, I know that."

"He say a thousan, maybe a milyun, hard to see em in the Dark. Pock say they smellin, say they smellin real bad."

"Dont want to smell em. Smelled em onct before."

Mockit shakes his head. "That isnt what Pock sayin. Not that kinda smell. Pock says mad. Pock say they smellin red, like they got some kinda crazy in they heads."

"I never heard bout smellin crazy, nothin like that."

"I just sayin what he says. What you think, Ratch? What they goin to do?"

"Rhidos here, Drills wearin shit like that? What you think it goin to be?"

Mockit looks away. "Ratch, I dont want it bein that."

"Good. Then maybe it be somethin different. You dont want it to, it likely be somethin else."

I go on back, leave Mockit standin there. No use talkin, cause Mockit think like a chile sometime. A chile dont like to member nothin less its somethin good.

I member an so does he. I wasnt biggern Nik, but its clear as yesterday. Somethin like that, its not about to go away. . . .

It dont take long to "gather our stuffs" like Sal Capone say. Drills, they gotta lot of stuff. Persons dont hardly have any stuff at all. What Persons do is carry stuff a Drill dont like to be haulin round they selves. Which is ever thing but they dicks an they hats.

First night out, it isnt too bad. We walkin in the Dark, an we fresh, cause we dont have to work till we startin on the trail. We walk through the forest till it start thinnin out, an the land rise up to grassy hills. I been this far onct before. Haulin rock back fore they got me pickin bugs. Lily an the boys hasnt seen a lotta open, an they actin kinda scared.

"Its all right," I tell em, "it just like anyplace else."

"No it isnt, Ratch," Macky says. "Why you sayin it is when its not?"

"Dont talk back to me," I tell him, "you know better, boy."

What else I goin to say? What else I goin to tell him cept he right about that?

Isnt just Macky an Lily and Dit. Lots of the younguns is whinin, an some of the older Persons too. Drills start lopin down the line, snappin they teeth, telling us we better keep em quiet, or you know what they goin to do.

I know what botherin the Drills, what make em shaky too. We cant see no Rhidos, but we surely know they there. You can hear em clear, an they not far away.

An that be somethin I member in my head. Rhidos dont like Persons. Dont like the way we smell, any moren we like the stink of them.

We only stoppin onct in the Dark. We thirsty, dont got nothin to eat. What a Person do, you eat what you got, find somethin else next Light. Only we not home now, we somewhere else. Nobody think bout carryin water or somethin to eat. Isnt what we do, so nobody did.

Mockits grumblin, sayin how we oughta tell the Drills give us somethin to eat. They got plenty, they can give us some of theirs.

"Drop it," I tell him, "hush up. Get us all in plenty phuckin trouble, you start talkin like that."

Mockit mutterin some, but he keep his complainin to his self. You gotta think fore you talk. Im always tellin Dit and Macky that.

The good part is, we can rest for a while. Ever body needin that. Up in the hills theres a cool wind blows in the Dark. It dont in the Light, but its nice in the Dark.

The boys is sleepin, an me an Lily is lookin at the brights. The brights an the moon is the biggest wonders ever is. The moon an the brights an specially the sun.

You can hear the Rhidos, shiftin and gruntin, some of em squealin sometimes. Moren onct, I seen a Drill go careful down there, not makin any sound at all. I seen em comin back an talkin with the rest. They not real happy, whatever they doin down there.

"We goin back, you think," Lily says, lookin up in the Dark, lookin at the brights. "I dont like it, Ratch. I like it home, dont like it out here."

Im glad its Dark, so Lily cant see me too good. Been thinkin what to say, what to tell her and Macky and Dit. Dont like em think I dont know ever thing, the Famly they countin on me.

Only, I dont know a lot moren them. Me and Mockit an the olders, wasnt much bigger than the younguns is now.

It happened.

It wasnt good, an it was somethin like this.

Somethin like this, and there wasn't any Mamas, wasnt hardly anyone bigger after that.

"Dont want you thinkin bout goin back, Lily, least not yet. I think they keep on goin for a while."

"Why, Ratch? Why they want to do that? Where they want to be?"

Even in Dark, I can see a little scared in her eyes, in the way she move her mouth.

Somethin happen, Lily. Somethin fore you, somethin barely after me, an you dont want to hear bout that. . . .

Lily does a little sniff. "You mad with me, Ratch? I dont want you doin that."

"Im not mad at you, Lily."

"Good. I dont want you to."

"There isnt no way I ever could. You gotta know that, least I hope you do."

"I do, Ratch. I surely do. . . ."

Near Light, a lot of the younguns is whinin again an we try an keep em still. Sal Capone come by with Persons from another hooch, luggin pots of water to drink. It isnt much, an he dont bring any thing to eat.

Lights when it gets real bad.

I never seen any thing like that. Its Dark one minute, then the sun come blazin up hot. The sky dont have any color, its awful searin white. When you down in the tangle, in the wet and the rot, you steamin an sweatin an the bugs is bitin an crawlin up your nose. A Person, he gettin used to that. Your head start bustin you can dunk it inna creek. You can eat a grub, an you can get a drink.

Out heres nothin, out here its bare an flat. Ever tree ever bush is brittle as a bone, the juice sucked out an all the green gone. Ever things dry an ever things dead.

Theres nowhere to go, isnt nowhere to hide. Drills, they got mats whats made outa straw. Mats on sticks thats keepin off the sun. Persons dont got any mats, we walkin in the heat. Who you think made them phuckin straw mats? Persons, thats who.

Not far off, the land drop a little, makin a gully to the right. We been stayin real close ever since we hit the flats. Cant see Rhidos, all you can see is the dust they kickin up, but thats where they at. Mockit says you walk over, you can see em clear. Dont, I tell him, an keep your mouth shut. We dont need folks thinkin bout that.

The suns straight high when they tell us all to sit. Why, Im thinkin, they want to stop here. Isnt nothing but dirt an a bunch of dead trees. Not enough shade for a vole or a snik. I dont know, an I not bout to ask.

We get a little water but we dont get enough. What we got we givin to the younguns, some of em lookin real bad.

Macky come over an say one of Pocks whos eight is maybe dead.

"Well he phuckin dead or not?" I ask him, "make up your mind, boy."

"I can go see," Macky says, an look at somethin else.

"Don't do nothin, just stay right here."

"Whatd I do, why you mad at me?"

"He isnt mad," Lily tells him, "go sit over there with Dit."

"Sorry," I tell her. "I cant help it, Im worried bout this."

"Macky know that."

"I dont know he does or not."

"Dits bad off. I thought he was better but he gettin awful hot."

"Ill try an get water. They got to give us water an somethin to eat, they goin to have to carry this shit by they selves."

"You goin to tell em that?"

"No, Im not goin to tell em that."

"What, then?"

"I dont know yet."

"You come up with somethin. I know you always do."

And what, I thinkin, *you rekon thatll be*?

Sal Capone come round with Persons bringing water, an a pot of grub soup. Just like last time, isnt near enough. I tell ever one I can dont drink all you got, an save a little soup.

Course nobody doin that.

Wasnt long after we seen dust comin off the flats. When they gets closer we seen they more Drills. Only we never seen em before, this bunch is strangers, they come from far away. I seen traders, outsiders before, these Drills is nothin like that. These phuckers has clearly come to fight.

Soon as they comin in sight, a fearsome sound sweep through the Persons, ever Famly there. Ever body squeezin close, ever body moanin, shakin, holdin one another, coverin they faces, coverin they heads.

Dont blame em any one, its a dreadful thing to see. Even Sal Capone dont look too happy, an Sals not scared of any one.

A Drill, he walkin on his hands an he feet, dont hardly come up to your hip. Dont weigh much as a Person an a females smallern that. Weight an high, though, isnt what you want to think, you thinkin bout Drills. What you want to think bouts *mean*. What you want to think bouts strong, they strongern shit. What you want to think too, you want to think bout teeth.

Whatever you magine that phuckers thinkin, that likely isnt it. Isnt nothin inside that head cept hate an blood an killin boilin up, just waitin to bust on through. I tell a youngun that, sure as shit some Drill hops by an give him honey on a stick.

Teachin folks stuff, whats the use of that?

* * *

I listen real good, they think I doin somethin else. Pickin up stuff, puttin stuff down, listenin good. The big one with the little red eyes got teeth painted black. His armor isnt plain like Sals. Its real fine wood, got a lot of shiny stones, gotta lot of pretty shells. Got feathers offa birds, skins offa lizerts an sniks. An ever inch of that armor, on his arms on his shoulders, on his knees on his chest, ever phuckin inch is covered with spines, thorns, stickers of ever sort. You get even close to this Drill he gonna punch you fulla holes.

Sides all that, he got a turtul hat an he got a wood shiel, an the shiel an the hat they fulla thorns too. He got a big spear, which is longern Sals, longern any I think I ever saw.

Theres two stays close to the big un with the thorns, an they got fine armor too. One of ems Mormon Nailer. The other ones Orangey Harding, and the main asshole, the one with the thorns, is Gandolph Scott. He tells ems all what to do, an they tell ever one else. Includin Sal Capone, who dont much care for doin that.

A couple Drills from their bunch an ours go down where the Rhidos are. They gone a long time. We listen, but we dont hear anything at all.

"What they doin, you think," Mockit wants to know, "I wouldnt get close to those things you give me all the wimins there is."

Pock an me we laughin bout that. Pocks hooch right next to Mockits, an he know what goin on there.

"You dont gotta worry," Pock says, "no one goin to do that, long as them wimins can run."

Mockit dont say nothin to Pock. Pocks bout as big as me.

"They not doin nothin," Pock says. "All they doin is they goin down an look."

"Why they do that?" Mockit want to know. "You seen a Rhido, why you want to see it again?"

"Just do is all."

"Why you just do? You just sayin, you not sayin what."

"A Drill do somethin cause he want to do it," Pock say, getting tired of this, "thats why. He dont have to ask you."

"What they doin they listenin. Thats what the Drills is doin down there. . . ."

For a minute Im thinkin isnt anyone there, then Froom, he edgin by the fire. Isnt anyone expectin that, cause Froom dont like no one an nobody like him.

"What you talkin bout," Mockit says, "listenin to *what*?"

"Rhidos," Froom says, "listenin to them."

Mockit laughs, but dont anyone else.

"Theres nothin to listen to," I tell him. "Nothin a Rhido goin to do but grunt."

"Grunt an fart some," Pock puts in. "I wouldnt listen to that."

"Its not that kinda listenin. Didnt say that."

"What kinda listenin there is?"

Froom look like he want outta there, like he wish he never come.

"I ast you somethin," says Pock.

Froom dont answer, an bout then the Drills come back. None of em talkin, just all walkin back. None of em lookin real happy at all.

"Thats Orangey Harding," Pock says, pointin to the shortest one of all. "Got a brother come to the fort one time. Got a knobber long as your arm."

"Who tol you that?"

"I seen him he was here. Brother looks just like him."

"I guess its so, Pock say it is," Mockit says.

Pock dont say nothin. In a minute Mockits gone.

The worst part is, we dont stay put till Dark. Ever one gotta get up, lift your shit an go. Darc Anthony an Sal, them an Doc Cabbage, they dont like it, but they wont cross the other Drills.

Theres five, maybe six hours Light, the longest Light I ever seen. The heat come down, then it rise up again, burnin your eyes and blisterin your feet. The grounds like walkin on fire. You look anywhere an ever things wavy, ever thing poundin in your head.

The younguns is already beat, an pretty soon they droppin on the trail. A Famly try to carry em on, some of em cant hardly carry theyselves. We bout lose Dit, but Im not leavin him behind. Lily cant help. She an Macky are keepin one another from fallin to the ground.

Isnt real long theres younguns by the way, covered up with dust, lookin like Persons made of clay. You walkin, you dont see bugs, dont see em anywhere. Soon as a youngun hits the ground, they swarmin ever where. Shiny black waddlers, clickin they pinchers, ants, nats an fat green flies. How they knowin, I wonder? What they eatin when we isnt there?

Florence of Arabia an fat Mamma Gass, them an little Silly Marlene, they got their hands full, lopin up an down, draggin folks off fore the bugs clean em out. Silly Marlene, she all swole up. I figure Darc, he the cause of that.

I said its the most awful Light I ever seen. You figure Dark would help, but Dark is worsen that. . . .

* * *

Near as I can tell, theres leven, maybe ten went down, might be moren that. Most of em younguns, some of em not. Sackers one, an hes old as me, close on to sixteen. Strong as he could be. Whats his Famly goin to do now?

Drills gettin all worked up just fore the sun goes down. We hadnt seen nothin in the Light. Just a buncha zeebos that run fore we even got near.

What the Drills seein now is a Leon way off neath a sticker tree. Isnt nothin get a Drill goin like a Leon will. They lopin up an down, hoppin an screamin an beatin on they chests. Some of em throwin they sticks, make em feel like they doin somethin good. Females, they havent got sticks, so they throwing lotta shit.

Drills got reason for not likin Leons much. Ever now an then, a Leon trot down to the fort, waitin for a Drill to come by. Ever now an then, a Drill not comin home at Dark.

It start gettin cool an we huddle in a little stand of rock. Sal come round with water, moren we ever got before. We can smell cookfires burnin, but all we gets fruit that the Drills wont eat no more.

Theres Persons out there, come with the other Drills. We can hear em cryin close by. I dont think they got water. I dont think they got anything to eat.

Drills got a lotta mean in they heads. Drills dont see stuff the way a Person do. They did, theyd try an keep ever one alive to do shit they dont want to. A Drill, though, he dont think bout that.

Dit, he hot an he cold, he got the fever bad. Macky give him bout all of his water an I stop him doin that. I tell him its a fine thing to do, an how he gotta quit.

Lily hear me say it. She knows its what I gotta do. All the water in the world, Dit wont make it to the Light.

"I know what happenin, Ratch," Dit tells me, the words stickin scratchy in his craw. "You dont be worry bout me."

"I always worry bout you," I tell him. "You a lot of trouble, Dit. You fillin six baskets a grubs, you bringin home two. What you figure happen to them other four?"

Dit cant hardly make a grin, but he give it a try.

"Sometime I eat moren that. You just didnt ever see."

"You know what? I did the same thing, Dit. An nobody ever catch me cause Im as sly as you."

Dit too weak to answer that. I dont know if he hearin me at all.

Me an Pock talk some, an Brig is there too. Mockit, he not comin round since he aggravatom Pock. Booker an Tyro stoppin for a while.

Tyro lost two younguns on the march. Booker got a girl sick as Dit, an figure she likely goin too.

They all leavin, its only Pock an me. Macky sleepin, Lilys watchin Dit.

Pock says, "Ratch, its somethin bad, I got a feelin inside. Dont know what, but its bad, an likely worsen that."

"You tol me that bout a hunert times," I tell him. "Dont need to hear it again."

"Im just sayin."

"Thats it, you sayin. Dont be sayin anymore."

"Wont, then."

"Dont."

Pock, he squattin on his heels, got him a stick, makin circles on the ground.

"It shouldnt oughta be, you know it? Shouldnt be the way it is. You think bout it, same as I do, same as ever one, dont say you never doin that. I member stuff, Ratch. Just dont like to say I do."

"Good. Then dont."

"Whats the good of not talkin, you member too, you thinkin same as me."

"Maybe I thinkin some once. Im not thinkin now."

"Might say you don't. Doesnt mean you not. . . ."

Thats when I push him down flat. Pock look surprised, me doin that.

"Im sayin this. Whatevers in your head, keep it to yourself. Dont want to hear what you thinkin or anyone else. Go do somethin. Dont be sittin round here."

Pock, he dont say a thing. He put down his stick, he get up an go, I sittin by my self.

The fire bout gone. I stick a little dead grass on, it dont do any good.

I can hear whinin where the other Persons are, I can hear Rhidos shufflin in the Dark. Some of the Drills is movin about. A Drill dont ever keep still, you can count on that.

Lilys asleep, Im glad she doin that. Theres nothin she can do bout Dit. Dits goin, if he isnt gone now. Im lookin at the sky, lookin at the brights. Theres clouds goin by real fast. Im thinkin way Pock acting, I got to watch him now. He talkin to me like that, he talkin to somebody else. Some people not thinkin, some people hasnt got a bit of sense—

I stand up quick cause I know hes right there. I see him, now, a shadow gainst the Dark. Then I see the other one, over by his self.

"I am ever having to admonish you, Ratch," Sal tells me. "There is no cause to having a fire. It is not be cooling, there is plenty of warming in the air."

Isnt a fire no more, its phuckin gone out.

"This time I am forgetting what I see. I am closing my eyes to your actions, I am seeing nothing of this. Ratch, you will have Lily rise from her sleeping. You will bring her here."

"What? What for?"

Sal dont like me sayin that. He lopes up closer an kicks my water pot. It breaks an clatters on the rocks. The ground sucks it up an thats all I got.

"Bring her, Ratch. Bring Lily here."

Somebody grunt an somebody shits, an now I can see whos up there with Sal. Somebody with a dead turtle hat, somebody with dirty little eyes. Somebody with a lotta thorns an stickers on pokin out. . . .

Im not thinkin bout Lily at all. Lily pops in I get her out quick. The more I do that, the more she poppin in again. I oughta not get ina bother but I do. No ones taken Lily off before. What I thinkin, they wouldnt for nother year or so.

Only this isnt home no more. These Drills is not the same as Sal Capone or Darc, or Lon Peron.

"I think Dit maybe goin," Macky says. "He lyin awful still."

I go look an he cold as the ground, and I say, "Macky, Im afraid he is."

Florence an the others wont be checking till Light. Dont want Dit where the bugsll get him, so I cover him with dust an leave him where he is.

"You done a good job watchin," I tell Macky. "Good as anyone could."

"Not as good as Lily."

"Just bout as good. I bet she tell you herself when she gettin back here."

Macky wants to ask, wants me to tell him, but he keep it all in. He growin up good, but I wouldnt tell him that.

Long before Light sets in, Drills is up gruntin an lopin about, yellin an barkin, do this an do that. Mockits Persons an Pocks is gettin up slow. All of ems hungry, thirsty an sick.

Sal come over an tell Macky come along with him. Sal don't even look at me. Macky comes back, bringin water an grubs. Macky looks scared, an he goes off again. This time he got Lily too.

I dont hardly know its her. I look at her I wanta be sick. Her skins all dirty, caked in dust, flakin like the ground when the sun dry ever thing up. She shakin awful bad. Her eyes is open an I have to shade her cause she starin at the sun.

I can see her fuzz I can kinda see her cut, but she all scratched up on her belly down there. Theres blood an dust an I cant clean her up, theres not enough water to spare.

"Here," I tell her, "you drink some of this. You feel real better soon."

I take some water in my mouth an open her lips an let the water seep in. She chokin some, then she swallow an I know its goin in. I give her another an she try an say somethin but nothin comin out.

"She be all right, Ratch? She dont look too good."

I turn up an theres Mockit an he starin at Lily, his eyes getting bigger all the time.

"You seen enough," I tell him, "now be outa here fore I standin up."

I know what he doin an he know it too. He look off quick an go back where he come.

Im thinkin, they coulda give her a clothes, they coulda give em back. A Drill, though, they dont think bout that. Dont matter to them they got a knobber or a cut they got buds hangin out. Clothes is somethin Persons do.

I lay a little stitch I took off Dit an put it cross her parts. Wasnt anything to hide her buds, they just be pokin out. An Mockit, he can find somewhere else to look.

Me seein her now isnt like I seen her at the creek. Dont have the feelin I had bout her then. She back bein a sister an I feel good bout that.

If the heat was bad before, its worsen that now. Worsen I ever magined it could be. Ever one startin off sick, ever one hungry, beat an dried up from the awful Light before.

The shit we sposed to be haulin, me an Lily, Macky an Dit, is bundles of sticks so the Drills can have a fire. Where wes at, there isnt any sticks, isnt anything at all. Only now Dits gone, an Lily she barely on her feet. Im haulin three loads an Macky haulin one.

Same things happenin with all the others too. The younguns cryin an rollin all aroun. Ever Person can is haulin they load, but the heat is meltin us down. Isnt half a mile fore folks start droppin what they got, and fallin to the ground.

The Drills, they real upset bout that. Sal Capone an Sherbert Hoover come lopin down the line, growlin an snappin they teeth at ever one in sight. Sherb Hoover got a stick an starts hittin Persons on the back. Ever ones squealin, ever ones scared. You cant ever tell what Sherbs bout to do.

Sal tells him stop, he done enough of that. Sal gets me an Mockit and Pock an the rest of the olders an make us pick everbody up.

"It is shameful to me you are not being proper in your work," Sal says. "We have many fars to go. You must not be falling down. You must not be dropping your burdens to the ground. I am greatly disappointed. You will not be doing this again."

Sal scratches on his knobber, and turns and lopes away. Sherbert Hoover shakes his stick at me, an follows Sal down the trail. Two of the new Drills is watchin all this. Both of ems got hats. Both of ems got mats on a pole to keep the sun out. One of em is Orangey Harding. The other ones Gandolph Scott, who taken Lily off. He dont even look at us, an Im glad when they both gone away.

Isnt even high noon, an Macky says bout six has dropped away, but I countin moren that. I know for certain Lily cant last. She hasnt hardly spoke since Macky brung her back.

"I can pick you up," I tell her, "you dont have to walk. I know you feelin bad."

"You got plenty to carry, Ratch. You dont need to be haulin me too."

"This stuff isnt heavy. I could do it all day. Bet I could do it longern that."

"I can take some," Macky says, "I'm big enough to."

"You bout as big as a vole," I tell him. "Shit, you no biggern a ant, thats you."

"I can do it. I can do it same as you."

"You cant neither. Dont be askin me again."

I see right off the hurt in Mackys eyes. Lily lookin off, but I catch her sad too.

I wish I hadnt yell at Macky but I did. It isnt him, its ever thing else. Ever thing wrong, ever thing bad bout what we doin out here. Walkin in the sun, hungry an nothin to drink. Whats the good of that?

Somethin is happenin up front. Somethin goin on, somethin givin Drills a fit. We all lookin at ever one else, wonderin what it all about. Then Darc Anthony trottin on back, barkin up a storm. Ever body gotta stop, he tell us, ever body put his stuff down, we better be still, better not make a fuss.

I look at Mockit, he lookin back. He can smell em same as me fore they even in sight. They stink blowin straight up the draw, a dry an chokin smell strong enough to gag a stone.

Its shit an dust an the smell of they parts hangin down tween they legs. Isnt nothing bad as that, isnt nothin foul an nasty as a Rhido is. You maybe not member you Mama, you may not member nothin else, you goin to member how a Rhido smell. You five maybe ten, you wakin an smell em you hear em out there, you edgin in close to you kin.

"Im scared, Ratch," Macky says, huggin the dirt next to me. "Im scared real bad. I dont wanta see em, dont want em seein me."

"They not after you, boy. They dont care bout you."

"I think I gotta pee."

"You do, better not be on me."

"You be smellin em before," Lily says, talkin best she can. "You member I tell you, that song we used to sing? You member that, Im certain that you do."

Macky too scared, dont even know his name. Theres other younguns close by hasnt ever smelled Rhido fearsome an awful as this. They howlin an whinin, the olders tryin to still em fore the Drills comin back.

"Stay down," Mockit says, an Pock tells his Persons too. "Stay down low, dont even try an look."

Im holdin Macky, he rollin his eyes, he shakin like a vole hear a snik close by. Lily too sick to hardly try.

I seein em now, keepin down an eatin dirt just raisin up my eyes. They heavin, rumblin, snortin and fartin, gruntin and poundin the ground. Isnt nothing bigger, isnt nothin ugly as a Rhido swingin his big head about, thrashin his terrible horns, thisaway and that. Phuckin horns is pointy, phuckin horns sharp, longern a chile, near longern a man.

I want to shut my eyes tight, want to be cryin like a chile. They comin so close I can see they little mouth, I can see they tiny eyes.

Theys worse, too, worsen even that. The Drills has painted white circles round the Rhidos eyes. Painted jaggy lightnin on they great saggin hides, painted moons, painted suns, all kinds a scary sights. Somes got yeller on they horns, some got stripes goin all down they sides, blackern blood, near blackern Dark. . . .

Then ever Person there they screamin and moanin, ever one tryin to dig they selves a hole. Some of em lets they bowels go, which dont help at all.

Someone cryin, someone tearin at the ground. I look round, isnt anyone but me. I shakin real bad, I tryin to breathe. What I seeins not real cause now I seein Drills too, screechin an barkin, snappin they muzzles, barin they teeth. . . .

Gotta not be, gotta be somethin in my head. They ridin, what they doin, perched right up on the Rhidos theyselves, right on the Rhidos phuckin backs!

I think my heart goin to stop right there. Mockits eyes is rollin, Macky is throwin up spit. I never even thought about, never even magined nothing awful as this. . . .

When its over you can hear the awful quiet, so heavy it pressin on the ground. The Rhidos is gone, leavin dust an a fearful smell behind.

You listen real close, you can hear em still, hear em like far off thunder, rollin off the edge of the world.

Im standin real slow. Some of the others is gettin up too. Nobody talkin, no one makin a sound. Nobody cept Mockit, Mockit cant keep from talkin too long.

"What you think they doin, Ratch? Where they goin to go?"

"Why you askin me, what the phuck I know?"

Mockits face covered up with dust. Cant see nothin but his eyes. Looks like somethin hangin from a tree, somethin livin in the Dark.

"They doin that dream," he sayin. "Whatever they done before. They doin it again."

"Wasnt any dream, Mockit. That look like a dream to you?"

Mockit dont answer. He scared an I scared too, but I wont let it show. I look out over the far. I mightve seen Rhidos, I mightve seen hot stuff risin off the flats.

One of the wimins starts wailin somewhere, then another after that. I waitin, watchin the path goes up the little draw. Waitin for a Drill maybe tell us what to do. Nobody there, nobody comin down.

What I better do, I thinkin, I better squat an wait. Squat down boilin in the sun like ever body else. Squat down waitin, ever body sick, ever body dyin, waitin for a drink.

That's what I oughta do. I oughta but I dont. Somethin happen inside me, somethin in my head. Im not squattin no more, I standin up walkin, walkin up the draw. Mockit say somethin behind me, Pock, he sayin somethin too. I keep goin, I not lookin no where.

At the top of the draw, I stop an look down. I lookin where the Drills is campin. They stuff is scattered all bout, they cookfires burnin behind a stand of rock.

Shit, I sayin to myself, isnt nobody there. Nothin but females under a little straw tent. Mama Gass an Silly Marlene, Florence of Arabia too. Dim Bassinger and little Semi More. Pain Fonda got a youngun suckin on her buds.

I turn round an start back the other way. Florence start screechin, showin her gums, gnashin her teeth. She get the others goin too.

Mockit and Pock is waitin, Pock lookin at me like I crawl out of a hole.

"What they doin," Pock say, "what they up to down there? What we spose to do now?"

"Not doin nothin, isnt nobody there."

"How we goin to get water, then, how we goin to do that?"

Him an Mockit is yappin, I walkin away. Persons is moanin, Persons is rollin on the ground.

Macky, he sittin over Lily, shakin this way an that.

"Lily she gone, Ratch. Not even breathin no more."

I gettin down to look, put a hand on her face. Her skin is burnin, her lips is swole dry.

"She sleepin, Macky. She isnt gone yet."

"She goin to be, though?"

"Try an shade her. Be doin what you can."

"We goin to get some water, Ratch? They havent brought us water in a real long time."

"Boy, you got any sense? Got any sense at all?" I standin, lookin at Macky, lookin at Lily, thinkin bout her in the mossy place, in the pretty goldy light.

"Isnt no water. Isnt goin to *be* none, either. Lily goin to die like Dit an Little Nik. I spect you an me, we goin to die too."

I turnin an I gone, Macky cryin an theres nothin I can do. Cant do nothin for Lily, cant do nothin for me. Pock say somethin I dont hardly hear. Whatever that somethin doin in my head, it doin it again. . . .

The sun, he boilin in a white an empty sky. My skin be fryin, sweat burnin in my eyes. Dont figure goin far, just far nough to see. Dont know why, just know it gotta be.

Theres a little place I can hunker down some, look past the draw an down on the flats, stretchin out below. I inchin up an look, inchin up slow. My heart near stoppin, they right there close. I could throw a rock an hit Sal an phuckin Knob Dole. I could hit Gandolph Scott, sittin on a stripy Rhido.

Isnt no use tryin to count. Theres Rhidos far as I can see, black old hides covered in the dust they feet stirrin up. Dust an shit an bout a zillion flies. Switchin they tails, shakin they pointy horns bout. Snortin, snuffin, pawin at the ground, Drills perchin on they backs.

Ratch, Im thinkin, what the phuck you doin here, get up get outta here fast. This is what part of me thinkin. Other parts thinkin what Froom is sayin, how Drills they *hearin* Rhidos, only that kinda hearins not the same. . . .

"Ratch, you outta you head? What you doin up here?"

"Shit, Mockit, don't be doin that!"

Mockit, he come up behind me, I bout jump outta my skin.

"Get on back," I tell him, "you dont belong up here."

"Whats the matter with you? Dont no one belong up here."

"Maybe I do."

"Do what?"

"I here, you seein that plain. Maybe thats where I spose to be."

"You talkin funny now. Dont be doin that, Ratch. You kinda scarin me."

I lookin up, lookin Mockit in the eye. "You the one said it. They doin that dream out there. They done it before, they doin it again."

"Huh-uh," Mockit shakin his head. "I never said a thing like that. Even if I did, I dont know what I talkin bout, you know that."

"Mockit . . ."

Mockit, he stop. He hearin it too. So do the Rhidos, so do the Drills. Theres thunder way off, thunder an a awful cloud of dust. Whatever it is, its just cross the flats, comin up behind a little rise. The ground begin to tremble, like the world be comin apart. I can feel it in my belly, I can feel it in my parts. Lookin down theres little grains of sand, dancing on the dirt.

Thunder dyin, the ground not shakin, ground keepin still. Hot wind blowin cross the flats, hot wind burnin, chokin ever breath. Hot wind scorchin, scarin off the dust, showin whats hidin up there. . . .

Mockit, he seein it first, eyes comin outta his head. Then I seein it too, seein what he see, seein what a chile be seein, wakin up cryin, wakin from a dream.

My gut wanta be throwin up, but they nothin in there, nothin it can do.

What waitin, what sittin up there is Rhidos, Rhidos standin with they heads down low, Rhidos still as they can be. Rhidos that got no color at all, Rhidos white as the moon, Rhidos pale as dead bone! . . .

"Phuck phuck phuck," Mockits moanin, shakin his head, sweat drippin off his nose. Somethin wet, somethin runnin down his leg.

"Stop doin that," I tell him, "ever thing stinkin enough round here."

"Cant help it, Ratch. I likely doin somethin else too."

"Mockit, that be the last thing you do, I tellin you that."

If me an Mockit havin a dream, it getting more scary all the time. Hunkered on them Rhidos is Drills, an they isnt like Drills I ever seen. They fur is dull as dirt, they baby shit brown. They whiskers an they ruff is kinda white. They all got long pointy sticks, an the sticks got raggedy skins hangin off the end. Some got skins, an some got strings of yeller bones. Even far off, you can hear bones rattlin in the wind.

Our Drills wearin armor made of wood, stickers an dead turtul hats. These Drills isnt wearin anything at all. Nothin but snik an lizert skins wrapped about they heads.

"Isnt many of em," Mockit sayin real low, "we got moren that."

"I can see, you dont have to tell me that."

"What you gettin on me bout, Ratch? Havent done nothin to you—"

Mockit, he stop, cause somethin happenin cross the flats. One of the Rhidos movin outta line, clompin up ahead of the rest. The Drill on his back, he got his head covered with a scary lookin mask. Mask got big white teeth, got shiny red eyes, got a muzzle painted black.

The Drill standin up, start hoppin, screechin an shakin his pole at the Drills over here. The rest of his bunch, they start jumpin round too.

I leanin up an lookin down. Gandolph Scott, he be bout to have a fit. He howlin, barin his teeth. Wavin *his* pole, screamin at the Drill across the flats. He turn round, an bark at Sal Capone. Whatever he sayin, Sal sayin no. He yellin at Gandolph, Gandolph yellin back.

Then, fore you can blink, Gandolph swingin his pole, slammin Sal hard across the head. The blow lift Sal off his Rhido an knock him to the ground.

Doc Cabbage and Darc and Lon Peron is comin at Gandolph, they eyes blazin red. Gandolphs Drills is ready for that. They pokin they spears, drivin the other Drills back. Darc keeps comin, hoppin over one Rhido an then the next. Orangey Harding just waitin, then he run Darc right through, his spear comin out the other side.

Sals Drills is howlin, snappin they muzzles, but theres nothin they can do. Gandolph Scott dont bother to look. He give a loud yell, raise his pole, pointin at the sky. The Rhido he ridin shake his big head, give a rumble an a snort, give a tremble an a fart. Then he start walkin, then he start to *move*. . . .

Rhido startin real slow, trottin, clompin on his big stubby feet. Gandolph clutchin the Rhido, holdin on tight, purple ass slappin up an down.

"Phuck," Mockit sayin, diggin a hand in my back, "oh phuck, Ratch," same thing he sayin before.

Ever Rhido in the bunch, they headin after Gandolph Scott. All of em racin toward a thicket of spears, waitin just across the flat.

"Gotta get outta here, Ratch. Gotta get outta here *now*."

"You wanta go, get."

"What? You outta you head? It happenin. The dream be happenin now. Doin it, right out there!"

"I know what they doin."

"We not spose to be here. Shouldnt be seein all this."

Ratch, things you dont member good, thats what a dreams all about. . . .

Where that come from, what it doin in my head?

"Get back an see what you can do, Mockit. See bout your folks, an see bout Macky too. See if Lily dead. See you can get any body walkin, gettin outta here. Dont know if it do any good, but wont hurt nothin to try. . . ."

Mockit dont answer. I turn round an Mockit isnt there.

Sun fryin my back, bugs itchin ever where. Throat closin up I cant even spit.

Ever thing fast out there, ever thing blurrin, ever thing makin me dizzy in the head.

Rhidos from here is poundin cross the plain, raisin clouds of dust, getting closer all the time. Somethin on the other side, somethin not right. White Rhidos not movin, just standin there, silent an still. Like nothin wrong, nothin be goin on at all.

Gandolph seein this too, an he shakin his stick, movin his Rhidos faster still. . . .

I wipin off sweat, slappin at a bug. When I lookin up, seein again, somethin cold, somethin scary, climbin up my neck. Wasnt but a blink be passin but ever thing different, nothin look the same. The whites, they shiftin, movin, turnin round fast, some of em left an some of em right. Baby shit Drills they hangin on tight.

Gandolph, he keep comin, eatin up dust, ridin straight in where the other Rhidos been. Gandolph see it, smell it in the air. Know somethin comin, know somethin bad, cant figure what it is. Know, in a blink, they nothing he can do. Rhidos snortin, diggin up ground, goin so fast cant nothin stop em now. . . .

First ones to know is Rhidos headin the pack, Rhidos bigger, faster than the rest. Rhidos heavy with muscle an bone, Rhidos with awful killin horns. Best Rhidos got the meanest, ugliest phuckers on they backs, Drills with armor, stickers an barbs. Drills with big turtul hats: Gandolph Scott and Orangey Harding. Spank Sinatra, Hairyass Truman. Mormon Nailer an Phony Curtis too.

They all famous bout a second, second an a half. It happen that quick, happen in a blink. One blink they somethin, next they phuckin meat. Yellin, screechin, twitchin on the ground, bones be snappin, guts squishin out.

Hardly a one of em see what get em, most of em dead fore that. I see em though, seen they awful heads when they comin up the rise, seen they big tuskers, they little black eyes, seen they awful noses, hangin like snakes, sweepin on the ground.

Cant believe the awful things I seein, not anybody could. They biggern anything, anything they is. Coming right at you, not ever slowin down. Seen one steppin on Mormon Nailers head, smushin it flat, all the juices spurtin out. Seen one pick up Orangey Harding with his nose, lift him up an toss him flat. Orangey screamin an thrashin about.

Rhidos fightin, doin what they could. Slammin they horns at a mountain of hide. Mountain, he screechin, givin a terrible cry. Shakin, swayin, slashin his tuskers, sendin that Rhido screamin to the ground.

Rhidos turnin now, shovin one another, crazy in they heads. Ever one wantin outta there.

Drills runnin too, but there nowhere to go. Rhidos, they don't stomp em, somethin else will. Ever one of them phuckers got a bunch of baby shit Drills, hoppin on they backs, barkin, howlin, tossin them bony rattle spears.

No one, nothin, got a chance of getting outta that. Isnt nothing to do out there, nothing to do but die. . . .

Im not dead, I stayin alive. Maybe I figure what for. Got down diggin like a vole, got a half ass hole, curlin up cryin while the monsters stompin by.

Not comin out till the sun bout down. Ever thing dead now, ever thing gone. Out on the flats theres Rhidos an Drills, bodies ever where. Ever thing flat, ever thing stinkin out there. Even one of them nightmars, lyin on its back, big ol legs stickin up in the air.

Birds an jakuls they havin a feast. Some of ems eatin out the belly, some of em chewin on the nose.

First thing I dos get me a couple pointy sticks. Next thing I find me some full water pots. Lots of em broke but plenty of ems not. Ever body gone, we got lots of water now. Even got some fruits thats nearly fit to eat.

Awful thing is, you cant even tell who anybody is. Persons an Drills they all cut up, an them thats not is flat. Cant find Macky or Lily. I hope Lily dead fore any thing got back here.

I found Sal Capone. Wasnt much left but a head an a buncha broken bones.

"I require help," Sal says. "You are bringing water, Ratch, and I am needing shade."

"You be fine," I tell him, "bout a blink an a half."

How they do it, Im thinkin, them Rhidos the color of bone, them baby shit Drills? What kinda creatures was that, where they comin from? I know the dream, an it never had that. Any of the younguns they gettin outta this, some of ems Mamas some day an they gotta have a new dream, they gotta member this. . . .

I walkin past the camp where the females been, Florence an Silly an the rest. Isnt nothin there to see. Ever thing flat cept off behind the rocks, where they got the cookfires. Big phuckers didnt get that. Some of the spits still standin from supper the night before.

Im walkin on, down to the draw. Isnt somethin you want to bother bout. Mightve been kin, or someone you know, an no sense thinkin on that.

What I be thinkin is what Pock said. Somethin most ever body thinkin now an then. How its not right. What we gotta do, way we gotta be. Itd be different there wasn't so many. If we was moren them. Seems to me thats the cause right there. Seems like thats how it is. . . .